"Ms. York makes you think more than twice about turning out the lights and closing your eyes..."
—*Romantic Times*

"...the extremely talented Rebecca York... sweeps you into a wonderful world of romance and mystery that only she can create."
—*Romantic Times*

REBECCA YORK

is the pseudonym of Ruth Glick and Eileen Buckholtz, who started Harlequin Intrigue's popular 43 LIGHT STREET series together. Recently, Ruth has been writing the series on her own as Rebecca York. Her book *Shattered Vows* was honored as Intrigue's 500th book. Eileen Buckholtz is a master computer scientist and Internet consultant. Taking a break from writing fiction, she fulfilled a lifelong dream to work on Capitol Hill, published a bestselling business e-book and developed several popular worldwide community service Web sites.

Relive the romance

by Request ®

Three complete novels
by one of your favorite authors

Dear Reader,

Romantic suspense is my passion. I love writing stories about a man and a woman falling in love against a background of heart-stopping danger. There's no better place to combine my two loves than Harlequin Intrigue, where I've been writing the 43 LIGHT STREET series since 1990.

In this By Request™ volume, you'll find three early LIGHT STREET books: *Whispers in the Night, Only Skin Deep* and *Trial By Fire*.

These stories all have some of my favorite elements: a tortured hero, an emotional love story and lots of surprising twists and turns in the plot. And two of them include the paranormal elements that often provide the icing on the cake for me.

If you're enjoying the 43 LIGHT STREET series now, you'll recognize some familiar faces. One wonderful thing about writing a long-running series is that I never have to say goodbye to my heroes and heroines. After starring in their own stories, they take important secondary roles in later books.

So you may have met Dan Cassidy, the hero of *Trial By Fire* in my recent Intrigue novel, *From the Shadows*. If I need a lawyer in a current story, I often call on Laura Roswell, the heroine of *Whispers in the Night*. And Dr. Katie Martin, the heroine of *Only Skin Deep*, is on duty when I need a physician. So if you've met Dan, Katie and Laura in later books and want to read their stories, you'll find them here.

Ruth Glick, writing as Rebecca York

REBECCA YORK

Dark Secrets

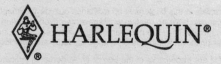

HARLEQUIN®

TORONTO • NEW YORK • LONDON
AMSTERDAM • PARIS • SYDNEY • HAMBURG
STOCKHOLM • ATHENS • TOKYO • MILAN • MADRID
PRAGUE • WARSAW • BUDAPEST • AUCKLAND

HARLEQUIN BOOKS

by Request—DARK SECRETS

Copyright © 2002 by Harlequin Books S.A.

ISBN 0-373-18511-1

The publisher acknowledges the copyright holder
of the individual works as follows:
WHISPERS IN THE NIGHT
Copyright © 1991 by Ruth Glick and Eileen Buckholtz
ONLY SKIN DEEP
Copyright © 1992 by Ruth Glick and Eileen Buckholtz
TRIAL BY FIRE
Copyright © 1992 by Ruth Glick and Eileen Buckholtz

This edition published by arrangement with Harlequin Books S.A.

Visit us at www.eHarlequin.com

Printed in U.S.A.

CONTENTS

WHISPERS IN THE NIGHT

Prologue

Twenty years in the past

Falling sleet bit into Dorian's skin like shards from a broken whiskey glass. Gusts of wind buffeted him toward a stand of tall pines. The first storm of the season. Why did it have to be tonight of all stinking nights?

His arms ached from the hundred pounds of dead weight he was carrying. When he tried to pull his coat tighter, he almost dropped the bundle he'd hastily wrapped in one of the damask tablecloths. Cursing, he staggered forward.

In the moonlight, bare branches rose up in his path like the outstretched arms of bogey men. Stopping, he listened for footsteps above the howling wind. All he heard were the faint strains of a Beatles tune drifting out into the darkness. "Nowhere Man." He shivered.

Somehow out here in the cold, he'd forgotten about the others in the house. What if one of them came out? They could circle around. Grab him. Drag him back. Terrifying images slithered through his head—a man with a net leaping out from behind a tree. The net disappeared. The man's arms stretched impossibly long as bony fingers curved toward Dorian. Claws at the end tore into his face.

Shrieking, Dorian staggered back, clutching the table-cloth-wrapped bulk like a shield. Sweat poured off his skin and froze into droplets of rancid ice.

He filled his lungs with a deep gust of the cold mountain air, but wicked visions still flickered on the backs of his closed lids. Slowly, slowly, reason penetrated his fear. He was safe. Nobody had followed him out here. The guests inside were havin' a good time. Plenty of bunnies. Plenty of juice. Plenty of hash.

Special party. Special for the nosey blonde who had thought she was so smart. But he'd tumbled to her game.

Just a little farther from the house. The old quarry. Nobody's been there in years.

In the moonlight, he almost missed the rim. Only the branch of a tree kept him from pitching off the edge of the cliff into oblivion. Staggering back, he flung the bundle onto the ground.

As the cloth gaped open, a slender arm flopped out and lay across the rocky ground like a white exclamation point. Panting, he stared at it.

Some unnamed compulsion forced him to stoop and pull the material farther back. Sucking in a jagged breath, he peered down at the girl. A strand of long, corn-silk hair lay across her pale face. Once her expression had been mobile. Now it was rigid.

She'd been witty. Manipulative. Devious. At the end, she'd been afraid. The look of fear was still there—erasing everything else. Something deep inside him had responded to that fear. He'd liked it. Her defenselessness had been exciting. His mastery had been a power trip. Once he'd gotten started, he hadn't been able to stop.

Now the sightless eyes accused him. With a shudder, he reached out and closed them. That was better. He'd never have to look at her again.

Too bad he'd had to kill her. She was such a pretty chick. And sexy. Damn sexy. But it was her own fault she was dead.

A gust of wind picked up the edges of the tablecloth—whipping up the fabric like a ghost trying to claw its way out of the ground. Dorian moaned and would have run, except that he wasn't finished.

With stiff fingers he started to wrap the girl once more in the makeshift winding sheet. Then he stopped. No. He'd almost made a big mistake. If anyone found her down in the ravine, they might think she'd stumbled and fallen over the edge. But not if she was all wrapped up. He pulled the cloth away before dragging her to the edge of the cliff.

He didn't see the cross-shaped crystal slip from her grasp and bounce down into the gully; he only saw the girl as he sent her plummeting into space. Like a soul taking flight from its body.

Frozen moments later, she disappeared into the gaping chasm.

Chapter One

Sights and sounds were muffled by the cloth wrapped around her face, but Laura Roswell knew where she was. She'd been trapped in this nightmare landscape before. Chill air stung her skin. The wind moaned around her like a chorus of lost souls. A man's rough hands crushed her body, shifted her limp weight over his shoulder as if she were a sack of oranges—not a person.

No, not a man. It was death that held her in his icy grip.

She tried to scream. The terror clogged her throat, clamoring for release, but no sound escaped from her numbed lips. She had to get away or die, but her muscles had stopped obeying her urgent commands.

God, no. Oh, please. No.

The words were frozen in her soul along with the horror.

She was helpless. At his terrible mercy. He could do anything he wanted with her, and no one could save her. No one would even know where he'd taken her.

Then, in an instant, everything changed. She was falling, plummeting into space, spiraling down, down, down into a midnight chasm.

In that moment, she knew she had a choice. She could either wrench herself from the dream or crash against the rocky ground below. The immobilized scream tore from her throat. Even as she catapulted from sleep, Laura realized it had been her own voice crying out in the shadowy bedroom.

She struggled to a sitting position, half expecting chilly air to sting her lungs as she gasped in a ragged breath. Ordering her body to relax, she unclenched her death grip on the covers. Her death grip on reality. Yet her fingers still trembled as she smoothed them across the crisp flowered sheets and soft wool blanket.

Darting a hand out from under the covers, she snapped on the light beside the bed. The yellow glow from under the fringed shade warmed the room she'd redecorated in Victorian splendor after her husband had moved out. She looked around at the polished mahogany dresser, the fainting couch piled with its lace pillows. The dried flowers. The cluster of framed photographs on the marble washstand. Bill would have hated it. That as much as anything had made her fall in love with the style.

Just as she'd clutched the covers, she clutched the familiar surroundings. This was her world, the cozy nest she'd made for herself, where she felt warm and comforted and in control of her life.

As she plumped the pillows behind her head, the last wisps of the dream dissipated like the scent of wildflowers drifting away on the breeze. The flowers were so out of kilter with the rest of the half-remembered images. Yet their perfume tantalized her. Dreams didn't leave an aroma. Maybe she was smelling the perfumed soap she hadn't been able to resist at Sabrina's lobby shop yesterday.

But an unidentified scent was the least of her worries. For months, she'd been congratulating herself on how well she'd gotten back on track after the separation and the divorce. Then the nightmares had come creeping up on her like evil spirits lurking in the dark corners of her mind.

Laura shuddered. No, not just ordinary nightmares, she corrected herself; the same dream, over and over. Even if she couldn't quite remember what it was, she was sure of that much. And sure of the terrible feeling of defenselessness that always left her sick and trembling when she awoke. Maybe her good friend Dr. Abby Franklin would tell her she really didn't have it all together. Or maybe she'd just been working too hard. But it was getting more and more difficult to deny that something was seriously wrong.

She wanted to sink back into the warmth of the bed covers and catch up on some of the sleep she'd been missing, but it took only a few minutes to acknowledge that she wasn't going to turn her brain off. On a sigh, Laura swung her legs over the side of the bed and stretched. She'd brought home several folders of work last night and only gotten to two of them. The extra time this morning would give her a chance to go over the Rutledge custody case before she got to the office.

Two hours later Laura arrived at 43 Light Street, the turn-of-the-century building where she worked. The offices were large and the rent was cheap for downtown Baltimore, but there were inconveniences, she mused as she waited to see whether the ornate brass elevator was working. As it arrived, Jo O'Malley joined her. Not only was the small but successful private investigation firm of O'Malley and O'Malley housed in this building, but its owner was one of Laura's closest friends.

"How are you doing?" Jo asked.

"Fine," Laura answered automatically, smoothing her shoulder-length blond hair and casting the woman a side-wise glance. Talking about personal problems, even to her friends, was never easy for Laura. And it was particularly difficult with someone like Jo, who was newly married and bathed in the warm glow of happiness.

"How's Cam?" Laura asked.

Jo launched into an enthusiastic account of her husband's latest electronic gadget, and Laura murmured quiet responses, wishing she could change the subject.

Unlucky in love, lucky in law, Laura characterized her own situation as she headed down the hall toward her third-floor office. In the year and a half since Dr. William Avery had left, her legal practice had really taken off. Probably because she now had the time and the need to pour herself into it. When she'd married in her second year of law school, she'd been naive enough to think she could have it all.

Having it all had lasted five years.

"And good morning to you, too," a familiar voice intoned.

"Oh, sorry." Laura realized that while she'd been deep in thought, she'd opened the door and come to a halt in front of her paralegal's desk.

"Sara Spencer canceled her appointment for this afternoon," Noel Emery said. She'd come to work as Laura's secretary but had upgraded her skills in night school. Now she handled much of the routine work in the office.

"Darn! This is the second time. She's afraid her husband is going to beat her up again if she goes ahead with the divorce. Or take it out on their daughter."

Noel nodded.

"Okay. I'll have another go at seeing if social services can get her and Emily into a group home. Or if they can't do it, we'll hit one of the private shelters. When I've found a place where she can stay, I'll call her back."

Laura was heading for her office door when Noel called

her back. "Wait. You've got a special-delivery letter."
The petite brunette handed a thick envelope across the
desk. "And the Jacobson petition is ready for your signature."

"Thanks." Laura slit the seal on the envelope with her
fingernail.

"What is it?"

"A letter from a land development company called
ASDC. They want to buy my property in western Maryland. Only I don't have any."

Then the context clicked into place. Years ago, her father had been conned into investing in a limited partnership in the middle of nowhere. Because the location made
the property unsalable, it was about the only thing he'd
left her when he'd died. But she'd been surprised that
she'd been mentioned in his will at all. He'd walked out
on the family twenty years ago and hadn't called, written
or visited.

The letter from ASDC was like a hand reaching out
from the past to grab her by the back of the neck. That
was why she suddenly felt cold and clammy, she told herself. She wanted to simply toss the communication into the
trash, but she was too disciplined to let her emotions overcome logic.

"Did a ghost walk over your grave?" Noel asked.

Laura realized her assistant had seen her reaction. She
laughed. "Kind of. My father always did clomp through
people's lives with combat boots." She bent her head back
to the correspondence. "After thirty years, it looks like his
mountain is finally worth something. The company that
wants to develop it is dying to wine and dine the investors
at a mansion house in Garrett County. A place called Ravenwood."

Laura wondered why the name sent another shiver up her spine. She'd never heard of the place.

"Sounds good to me," Noel observed.

"I think I'll pass. Write them a letter and ask for more information about their proposal." She tossed the correspondence into Noel's in basket and went into her own office.

SIX-FOOT-TWO, two-hundred-pound Jake Wallace usually stood out in most crowds. It wasn't just his size that made both men and women give him a second look. It was the easy way he moved, the ready-for-anything expression on his square-cut face and his animal energy. Until you engaged him in conversation, you didn't encounter the offbeat sense of humor that made his sports column in the *Baltimore Sun* so popular. If you looked deeper, you realized something had given him a deep understanding of human nature. You didn't perceive the pain. He kept that too well hidden.

Wednesday morning, however, only a couple of staffers glanced up when Jake sauntered into the news room at twelve fifteen. The rest of the crew was used to his irregular hours—and too aware of their own deadlines.

Sports reporting was a bit like being on the swing shift. When you covered night games and had to turn your copy in for the morning edition, you weren't expected back at your desk before lunch.

The previous evening Jake had filled in at a Capitols-Fliers game. He'd composed the story in his head on the hour drive back to Baltimore, banged it out on his laptop while waiting for a Hungry Man dinner to heat in the microwave and filed the copy via modem.

Jake had just settled into his chair when Brenda Montell,

the intern from Essex Community College, sidled up. "How was the game last night?" she asked.

He gave the girl what he hoped was an avuncular smile. The kid was centerfold material, and she had a crush on him. For about ten seconds, he'd considered inviting her to O'Grady's for a private little party after work. Then he'd given himself a silent lecture on robbing the cradle mixed with a strong reminder that trolling for dates at the office was asking for trouble.

When she came on to him with one of her sports questions, he always answered as if he were shooting the breeze with one of the guys. "Sobolov, the Caps' new goalie made three incredible saves that kept us in the game. Lucky for us we finally scored in the last thirty seconds."

"That must have been really exciting."

"Yeah, but I have to work on my high school football forecast." Brenda left, and Jake began pawing through the press releases and wire-service reports on his desk, looking for his notes on the area's best young players. Four years off the field, and something inside his chest still went tight when he realized another season was starting and he was on the sidelines. But he'd had a good career while it had lasted.

Jake flexed his bum knee. He would have had surgery and tried for another couple seasons—if Holly hadn't needed him. Staying with her at the end had been more important than his career. Except that he hadn't exactly been there at the end.

As always when that terrible memory surfaced, he felt as if he'd been tackled by a two-hundred-and-fifty-pound linebacker. But just like on the field when you were the bottom man under a pile of heavy bodies, you learn to pick yourself up and go on.

Actually, he was surviving a lot better than most former

players. Thank God he'd had the sense to major in journalism and that he had some small talent for putting words together.

He located the football material and started going over the players' stats when a messenger from the mail room showed up.

"Special delivery."

Jake examined the envelope. "This looks like it was meant for the real-estate section."

"It's addressed to you."

The messenger left, and Jake inspected the letterhead. ASDC? He'd never heard of the outfit. However, by the second sentence, he felt excitement expanding in his chest. It was a development company offering to buy the land his uncle had left him, the tract in western Maryland that he'd always assumed was worthless. He sure as hell could use the money. Maybe he'd finally be able to pay off Holly's medical bills. And if he was really lucky, there'd be some change left over so he could take a leave of absence and finish the research for his book.

Except there was probably a catch somewhere. There usually was.

Jake looked over at his calendar. No harm in taking a little trip up to Garrett County. If he didn't like the setup, he could always get a head start on the article he was planning on the western Maryland ski resorts.

BECAUSE SHE WANTED to finish the notes on an abandonment case before going home, Laura didn't get out of the office until almost seven, long after she'd sent Noel home. Thinking about how much her life had changed, she made a quick stop at the gourmet section of the grocery store on her way home and picked up some of her favorites—marinated vegetables, curried chicken and tabouli.

Twenty minutes later as she sipped a glass of wine and savored the goodies, she read a chapter of the historical romance she'd started the day before. Reading was a lot more relaxing than listening to a running report on the tremendous profit margin on lab tests. Of course, there was no one to hear about her day, either—not that Bill had really given a damn. And she did get stuck with all the chores, she admitted, as she transferred the morning's load of laundry from the washer to the dryer. At least, she didn't have to drop a bundle of shirts at the cleaners on the way to work.

Laura's energy reserves gave out while she was folding towels. Leaving them in the basket in the guest room, she flopped into bed and turned on the TV hidden in the antique armoire.

Her eyelids drooped in the middle of a miniseries. Flipping the button on the remote control and settling down under the covers, she was asleep in less than five minutes.

It took a bit longer for the dream to snare her. At first it was as refreshing as a windswept meadow. She was standing in the wilderness in her nightgown. Tiny flowers as delicate as baby's tears glistened in the moonlight. Her bare feet crushed them as she walked and the fragrance wafted upward like a cloud of incense. Music floated toward her on the wind.

It was coming from a mansion house. Ravenwood. That was the name. Ravenwood. She'd been here before, long ago. As Laura approached, she could see the lights, hear the laughter. A party, and she'd been invited. The letter had come this morning.

Suddenly she longed to join in the merriment. But someone barred her way. She couldn't see him in the darkness. Yet he was there. And he was coming to get her. Coming to kill her. No, not just kill her. Worse than that.

Please, somebody help me. The mute plea died before she could give it voice. If she called out, she would only give herself away. On silent feet, she turned and fled into the dark woods, blond hair streaming out behind her. In the blink of an eye, midsummer warmth changed to bone-numbing cold. The white flowers were snow, biting into her bare feet. She slipped, fell, picked herself up with desperation born of panic. Horror closed the gap behind her—puffing and crashing through the underbrush.

Closer. Closer. Until merciless fingers dug into her shoulder. He stopped her in her tracks and whirled her toward him. They were face-to-face. No! He had no face. Only red, glowing eyes that burned into her, windows into the depths of hell.

White-hot terror zinged through every cell of her body. *Run. Save yourself.*

But flight was impossible now. The hand on her shoulder pressed. Under his touch, her flesh grew cold and numb. Like evil magic, the paralysis spread until her whole body went limp as a dead flower stalk. Gagging and choking with revulsion, she sagged against him. She was helpless. Trapped. At his mercy. Night after night he had come for her. Now he had her again, and she knew exactly what he was going to do to her.

Chapter Two

Somehow, from some reservoir of strength deep within her, a scream welled up and tore from her lips. A scream that released her from the paralysis and the bondage of the dream. Once more Laura had wrenched herself from the clutches of evil forces.

Again she sat up in bed and wrapped her arms around her knees. Her skin was clammy. Her heart threatened to pound through the wall of her chest. Her breath came in labored gasps. But this time she wasn't simply overcome by mindless panic. This time the dream memories were more distinct.

With a determined effort, she brought her terror under control as her mind scrambled to make sense of the midnight phantom. Taking slow, calming breaths, she grasped at the only explanation available. The faceless man chasing her in the nightmare was Bill. She'd felt so helpless in the dream. Just the way she'd felt helpless as she tried to keep their marriage from falling apart.

Bill Avery had hurt her more than she'd ever believed she could be hurt. He was the one who'd wanted out of their marriage, and she'd had sense enough to acknowledge that there was no way to heal the breach. But much as she longed to put the past behind her, she was still preoccupied with what had gone wrong.

As the idea caught hold, she began to fit facts to the dream's symbolism. It was convoluted, but maybe subconsciously she was letting the aftershocks of rejection bar her path to what could very well be an entertaining weekend in the country. Then, for good measure, she turned Bill into a murderer pursuing her through the frozen wasteland of her imagination. *Shades of Little Eva,* she thought with a wry laugh.

Well, she tried to keep her clients from playing the victim role—and she'd worked hard to keep from playing it herself. She wasn't going to give her ex-husband any power over her now. Bill was probably planning a great time for himself, starting with a T.G.I.F. party Friday night. She could darn well do something similar. Tomorrow she'd call ASDC and tell them she accepted their kind invitation.

THE MOUNTAIN AIR WAS CLEAN and crisp. The fall leaves were bright enough to have been cut from red, yellow and orange crepe paper. Along with the impossible china blue of the sky, they foretold a glorious fall weekend.

She should be feeling marvelous, Laura thought as she unconsciously tightened her hold on the steering wheel of her new Dodge Shadow. Yet somehow, the farther she got from Baltimore, the more unsettled she became. Probably bad memories were taking the edge off her anticipation. The last time she'd driven to western Maryland, she and Bill had been on a skiing weekend. After the first morning, he'd been in a snit because she had no difficulty with the expert trails while he'd been more comfortable on the intermediate runs. She'd forgotten about the episode until today.

The exit ramp dumped her onto a two-lane road that wound through picture-postcard mountain scenery.

"No wonder you sunk some money into the area, Dad," she muttered as she rounded yet another curve and gazed out across another jewellike valley. "You always had a weakness for beauty."

There was little sign of human habitation, only an occasional house or trailer set well back into the trees. Laura could understand why development had taken so long to catch up to Ravenwood. Probably you had to drive for forty-five minutes to buy a quart of milk.

She had started wondering if the directions ASDC had provided were correct when she finally spotted the town of Hazard. Luckily, she didn't blink on the way through or she might have missed it.

A couple of rustic motels. A grocery. Three gas stations, two of them with convenience stores attached. Thankful for the chance to fill up her tank and stretch her legs, she turned in at the station that took her credit card.

A sleepy-looking beagle eyed her car as she pulled alongside the one unleaded pump, but the mechanic leaning into the jaws of a Jeep's hood didn't emerge. Self-service apparently wasn't an option, and Laura was wondering how to get some attention when another man came sauntering out of the office. Fishing-rod thin, he had a face remarkably similar to the beagle's.

"Help you, ma'am?" he asked as he wiped blackened hands on a pair of green overalls. The name embroidered on the breast pocket was "Cully."

"Could you fill my tank and check the oil and water? And I'd like the key to your ladies' room."

"Ain't locked."

Laura got out of the car and stretched. Following the sign around the side of the building, she found a stoop-shouldered old woman with her hair pulled into a wispy bun mopping out the little room.

"Be out of your way in two shakes of a lamb's tail, honey."

"That's all right. Take your time."

Two minutes later the washroom was spotless.

"What a wonderful job you've done," Laura said to her.

"Why, thank you kindly." The woman smiled, displaying uneven yellow teeth that sported several gaps.

Maybe she should tip her, Laura thought as she closed the door, but when she emerged several minutes later, the attendant had vanished.

"Right pretty day you've got," Cully observed as he ran Laura's gas-company card through the machine. "Your first visit up here?"

"I've been to Western Maryland before. But not around here." Laura opened the door and pulled out the directions. "Is this the road to Ravenwood?"

Cully had been about to give her the credit slip. Now his hand hung suspended about six inches from his body. At the corner of her vision, Laura caught a sudden movement and turned slightly. The mechanic who hadn't budged from under the Jeep's hood the whole time she'd been at the gas station straightened up and stared at her.

The friendly smile had evaporated from Cully's face. Laura saw his eyes narrow as he gave her a ruminating look. "Ravenwood. Didn't know the place was back in business."

Uncertainly, she took a step back. "I'm—uh—spending the weekend there."

"Ain't got no directions to that place."

"Well, uh, thanks anyway." Laura opened the car door. Cully had already turned his back, but the mechanic was still watching her with hard eyes.

Suddenly anxious to depart, Laura inserted the ignition key. She was just about to turn it when a bony hand clamped itself over hers.

Laura gasped and tried to jerk away.

"Wait."

The fragile-looking blue-veined hand held her with surprising strength. In the next moment, the old woman who'd mopped the restroom was leaning in the window of the car, her wrinkled face only inches from Laura's.

"A sweet girl like you shouldn't be goin' to Ravenwood."

"Why not?"

"Bad doin's up there. Bad doin's. I should know."

"Leave her be, Ida." Cully had come back and was tugging gently on the stooping shoulder.

"She's a nice girl." The old woman was still leaning in the window, but she'd let go of Laura. She seemed to be fumbling in her pocket. "You take this, child." Her hand was trembling slightly as she held out an ivory-colored crystal shot through with gold streaks. About an inch and a half long, it was shaped like a cross.

"It's a good-luck piece, a fairy cross," Ida answered Laura's unspoken question. "Go on, now. Take it. Maybe it'll keep you out of trouble."

Wanting to get away from this bizarre scene and not sure what else to do, Laura plucked the crystal out of the old woman's grasp. It felt warm and smooth in her fingers.

Ida straightened. "You take care."

Laura nodded uncertainly. In the next moment, she dumped the fairy cross onto the passenger seat, turned the key in the ignition and pressed her foot to the accelerator. With a screech of gravel and a jerk, the car shot out of the gas station. She didn't understand what had just happened, but it seemed important to put as much distance as possible between herself and the station.

It was strange. At first, the people had been friendly. Then everything had changed—when she'd mentioned Ravenwood.

A creepy feeling washed over her, the same creepy feeling that had been haunting her all the way from Baltimore. Her foot eased up on the accelerator, and she pulled over to the shoulder of the road, strangely uncertain about continuing the trip. Slumping forward, she wrapped her arms around the wheel. What was she getting herself into? Was something funny going on at the estate where she was supposed to spend the weekend?

Perhaps she should listen to the old woman's warning, turn around and go back where she belonged. Just then, a flash of light caught the corner of her eye, and she turned her head. The crystal. What had Ida called it? A fairy cross?

The gold vein running down the center had captured the sunlight like a stained glass ornament hanging in a window. Feeling a strange compulsion, Laura stroked a tentative finger across the smooth surface. The stone had felt warm before. Now it was hot, probably from the sun. Picking up the talisman, she turned it back and forth, watching the gold vein shimmer in the light. The crystal was shaped like a perfect little cross, with the four arms of equal length. It was intriguing and beautiful. Was it also valuable? Maybe she should return it to the old woman. But she didn't want to go back to the gas station. And she couldn't bear the idea of giving up the charm.

Laura continued to rotate the crystal, almost mesmerized by the light dancing and quivering in the depth of the strange trinket. It seemed to tug at her in some curious, unexplained way. At the same time, it had a calming effect on her frazzled nerves.

On Monday, she'd have to show the charm to Sabrina and see if she'd ever heard of a fairy cross. Sabrina Barkley had opened a herb-and-dried-flower shop off the lobby of 43 Light Street. Laura had stopped in a number of times to buy pomander balls and fresh basil, and she and Sabrina had gotten into some fascinating conversations about the uses and history of herbs. Sabrina also seemed to know a lot about new-age stuff, too. Maybe she could explain something about the powers of crystals.

Smiling, Laura closed her fingers around the cross, imagining for a moment that it pulsed in her hand. It did seem to have some sort of power—at least, to make her feel more confident. Or perhaps that was simply the strength of the old woman's suggestion. She'd sounded so earnest when she'd said it would bring good luck. After slipping the little talisman into the zipper compartment of her purse, Laura pulled back onto the road.

About five miles farther on, she spotted a newly painted green-and-white sign incongruously attached to a faded white gatepost. The elegant gold letters said Ravenwood.

Laura peered up the drive but could see nothing except trees. After checking her odometer, she started up the track. Someone had spread a layer of new gravel over old ruts. But the cosmetic application didn't do much for the uphill ride. After she'd jounced along for almost two miles, she still didn't see any signs of habitation. In fact, the lane was losing a battle to the underbrush encroaching from either side.

There was no place to turn around, and the prospect of backing down the mountain was daunting. Rounding a sharp curve, Laura was rewarded with her first sight of the house.

It was a massive stone structure, built on the lines of a baronial castle with diamond-panel windows, turrets, balconies and steep gables decorated with Gothic bargeboards cut in incongruously lacy patterns.

Stopping the car, Laura sat for several minutes, fascinated by the romantic style and the way the disparate combination of elements produced an intriguing harmony. Yet for all its charm, there was something forbidding about the sprawling mansion. Perhaps it was the sheer massiveness of the stone walls that looked as if they might have been built to hide dreadful secrets. No, that was just a silly fancy.

As she cleared the woods, Laura noticed a rectangular area where several cars were already parked. An Eldorado, a Mercedes, a faded Chevette, and an old but well cared for 280Z. The guest list encompassed a considerable economic range, she surmised as she pulled in between two of the cars. It would be fun to match the people with their vehicles.

She was getting her overnight bag out of the trunk when the arched front door opened and a man came down the stairs, smiling hospitably. Dressed in a three-piece suit with a paisley handkerchief that matched his tie, he managed to cover the distance between them quickly without looking as if he was exerting himself.

"You must be Laura Roswell. I'm Andy Stapleton." His handshake was straight out of an executive salesmanship course—firm but friendly. Unfortunately his diamond ring pinched her hand when he squeezed.

"Nice to meet you," Laura responded automatically, allowing him to take her overnight bag and close the trunk.

"I hope you didn't have any trouble finding us. We're a little off the beaten track."

He swept Laura toward the house as if he were afraid

she might change her mind. In truth, she did hang back slightly when she stepped across the threshold and took in the contrast between the bright sunlight outside and the gloomy interior. The effect was heightened by the decor, which carried through with the Gothic theme. The dark woodwork and tiny panes of glass were more oppressive than charming.

"Why does the house have a bad reputation in town?" she asked. Springing a question out of the blue was one of her proven courtroom techniques. It often elicited a revealing answer. This afternoon she felt as if the entrance hall had swallowed up her voice.

"The house was leased by a Baltimore industrialist who had extensive renovations done. When he went bankrupt, he had a lot of outstanding bills with local merchants and contractors."

The explanation was plausible, but the pat delivery made Laura wonder if Stapleton had had the answer ready all along, just in case one of the investors asked.

Further speculation was cut off by an emphatic male voice that boomed out from a doorway just ahead of them along the hall.

"Never give advice. Sell it. That's what I always say."

Looking inside, Laura saw that the speaker was a short, rotund man with a florid face who appeared to be in his midsixties. His hair was wavy, thinning and a vivid shade of red that had to have come out of a bottle.

He was standing under a brass chandelier and addressing a tiny, gray-haired woman seated on a wine red velvet couch. But when he sensed the movement in the doorway, he turned.

"Laura!" he greeted her like a long-lost daughter. Crossing the room, he squeezed her in a bear hug and then stood back to give her a closer inspection. "Darlin', I'd recognize that blond hair and those blue eyes anywhere. You're the spittin' image of your old dad.''

She stared at him, feeling as if she were acting in a movie for which she didn't know the script.

''It's Uncle Tim. Or at least that's what you used to call me when you were a wee mite and I bounced you on my knee. I'm Timothy O'Donnell.'' He turned to include the woman on the couch. ''And this is Martha Swayzee, another of the old gang.''

Laura crossed the room and shook the old woman's hand. It was dry as a starched doily and about as resilient.

''We were so sorry to hear about your father, dear. It's so tragic to die alone, cut off from your friends and family,'' Martha murmured. ''Too bad your mother wouldn't have him back when he tried to reconcile with her.''

Before Laura could dredge up a response, the old woman was rattling on. ''How is your mother, anyway?''

''She died several years ago.''

''I'm sorry to hear it. Such a long-suffering woman. We'll get a chance to talk later, dear, and you can fill me in on all the details of your divorce.''

''Umm,'' Laura responded noncommittally, unconsciously backing away.

Andy touched her shoulder. ''Why don't I show you your room so you can freshen up.''

Laura followed him gratefully down the hall. When they were out of earshot, he leaned closer. ''Martha is quite an old busybody. Don't say anything to her you wouldn't want to see on the front page of the *Baltimore Sun*.''

''Don't worry, I won't.'' The confident promise belied the agitation churning in Laura's chest. She hadn't thought about the other investors when she'd decided to come. Now she realized that at least some of them had been close friends of her father's.

Laura had always told herself she wasn't the least bit interested in what Rex Roswell had done after deserting his family. But her mother's accounts of his defection had never included a chapter on attempted reconciliation. Was she going to hear the other side of the story, Laura wondered as she climbed the circular stairs that wound through one of the turrets.

Stapleton ushered her past a door at the top and down another long hall. They took another turn before he stopped in front of a door, inserted a key in the lock, and stepped aside so she could enter the room beyond.

Inside, the furniture was antique, but the moss-green-and-peach carpet, upholstery and wallpaper were new. The wall opposite the bed was covered with elaborately carved paneling.

"The ladies have private baths," Andy said as he set her suitcase on the stand under the window. "The gents are going to have to share."

"I'm sure I'll be very comfortable."

"Remember, we'll be serving high tea in about twenty minutes."

Alone at last, Laura sat on the bed for a moment, but got up again quickly. The room was pretty enough and should have made her feel welcome. Instead, she was edgy. Probably because she was wondering if Martha was going to be the only unpleasant surprise, she told herself as she hung her dresses in the closet. Yet she knew that wasn't all of it. Something about the chamber filled her with a sense of anticipation and dread—the way she felt in the seconds before a judge rendered his decision.

The bureau drawers were a bit musty, so after hanging her dresses in the closet, she left the rest of her things in the overnight bag. But she had too much energy to rest. Instead, she wandered around the room, picking up knickknacks and putting them down again in different places, as if the new arrangement were somehow more suitable. She didn't touch the fruit basket ASDC had left. But she moved the statue of Psyche and Cupid from the dresser to the nightstand and the ceramic flowers from the nightstand to the shelf along the paneled wall where she paused to trace the garland pattern carved into the wood. It was delicate and beautiful, the craftsmanship of a bygone era.

She had started to move the overstuffed chair away from the window when she stopped herself in midpush, wondering what had gotten into her. She wasn't the kind of person who rearranged other people's belongings.

Shaking her head, she went to wash up. The renovation hadn't extended to the bathroom. The black-and-white tiles were cracked in several places and the faucets moaned when she turned them on.

After changing into her raspberry knit dress, Laura freshened her makeup. Locking the door behind her, she stepped into the hallway again. In the waning late-afternoon light, the long corridor was dark and gloomy, and her imagination conjured up the image of a woman holding a candle. Either Stapleton *should* have given out candles to the guests, or he could have put in higher wattage bulbs, she thought as she made her way down the hall. Everything was ghostly quiet, except for the creaking of the floorboards. It was just her own feet making them squeak, Laura assured herself. Yet the farther she got from her room, the less able she was to shake the eerie feeling that someone was following her—almost breathing down her neck, in fact. When she spun around to look, no one was there, although she did see a flicker of light, as if a door had silently opened and closed.

All at once, Laura couldn't keep herself from quickening her steps. However, when she came to the turn she and

Stapleton had taken, she hesitated. She'd never had a great sense of direction and she wasn't sure where to find the stairs. Although both ends of the hall looked identical, instinct urged her toward the right. As she hurried along the passage, she strained her ears, trying to catch some hint of conversation from below. But the mansion was so large, she might as well have been alone. She was almost running by the time she reached what she hoped was the entrance to the stairs.

When she grasped the knob and pulled, the door creaked open on rusty hinges. At the same time, she was almost physically assaulted by an unpleasant odor that seemed to be composed of charred wood, mold and something indistinguishable but repugnant.

Realizing she'd made a mistake, Laura was about to draw back and slam the door. Some impulse she couldn't identify compelled her to take a tentative step and then another into the dark interior. A cold wind blew from somewhere in the darkness, making her shiver, and she thought she caught a faint whistling sound that set her teeth on edge. As she put one foot before the other, she was seized with a sense of unreality. It was almost as if some unnamed force were drawing her forward against her will.

Reality slammed back into her as a Hulk Hogan-sized hand clamped down on her shoulder. Laura's heart stopped, and the breath froze in her lungs.

"I'd stay out of there if I were you," a whiskey-smooth voice advised.

For a moment, she was paralyzed. Then she whirled around to find herself confronting the owner of the outsized hand. He was blocking what little light came down the hall and she couldn't see him well. She sensed, however, that the body was as large and sturdy as the hand.

Although she wasn't a short woman, this man towered

over her. When she didn't move or speak, he pulled her back with surprising gentleness for someone so large. Then he reached to close the door. As his body brushed by hers, Laura caught a quick impression of powerful thighs and well-honed muscles under his jeans and nubby sports jacket. His after-shave was a no-nonsense masculine scent.

"Whoever forgot to block this entrance off is two bricks short of a load," he said as he pushed the door firmly shut. "I stumbled in there, too, thinkin' it was another way out."

She couldn't quite picture him stumbling. "I was looking for the stairs."

"You'll have more luck at the other end of the hall."

When he stepped back and gestured, Laura got a better view. His face wasn't pretty—but it was rugged and square and certain of its basic values. She imagined a lot of women would find the combination appealing. But she wasn't going to acknowledge the interested look in his dark eyes, not when she was feeling foolish at having the wits scared out of her. Besides, she was no longer attracted to male self-confidence. And whatever else you could say about him, this guy was very confident and all male—from the natural waves of his chestnut hair to the tips of his size-fourteen Reeboks.

"Thanks for your help." Breezing past him, she started for the other end of the hall at a rapid clip.

He followed. With his long strides, he didn't have any problem keeping up.

"You can't be one of the original investors because you're under sixty-five," he observed in a conversational tone.

"I inherited a share from my father," she tossed over her shoulder.

"Then we've got something in common. I inherited mine, too."

"Umm."

She effectively squelched further conversation until they reached the ground floor, where Andy Stapleton emerged from the drawing room.

"Ms. Roswell. Mr. Wallace. I was just about to send a search party."

"Ah, the two eagerly awaited ingredients." The observation came from a wiry man who'd followed Stapleton into the hall. At first, Laura would have guessed that he was in his late forties or early fifties. As she drew closer, she decided that he was probably older—but very well preserved.

"Sam Pendergrast." He held out his hand.

Laura shook it. So did the Wallace character. Pendergrast's arm was hard and muscular, as if he worked out regularly. From the way he looked her over, Laura also got the distinct impression that one of the ways he stayed young was by keeping company with women half his age. However, in this case, she had the feeling that the man couldn't decide which of the newcomers he wanted to talk to more.

She was both a bit relieved and a bit irritated when he turned to the giant who stood beside her.

"Jake Wallace. Ohio State. The Buckeyes. Your team won the Rose Bowl, didn't they? And then you made All-American and went on to the Broncos."

"It's nice to be remembered," Wallace returned modestly.

"A lot of football players wait too long to retire. You opted out a little too soon."

"I—uh—decided the odds weren't too good on knee surgery."

"Damn shame. But football's loss is journalism's gain."

"Thank you."

Laura had been following the conversation. She'd never heard of Jake Wallace, but she gathered he was an ex-football player of some notoriety. Now he was some sort of journalist, although she was pretty sure she'd never read him.

Pendergrast led the famous Jake Wallace into the parlor, where Tim O'Donnell joined the admiring circle of men around him. They began quizzing him about the Redskins' chances for the play-offs.

Laura had no interest in joining the Jake Wallace fan club. She was left with the choice of looking as if she were sulking in the corner or approaching Martha Swayzee, who was sipping a cup of tea beside a table on which a maid was setting out little sandwiches and scones.

At least it wasn't going to be a one-on-one gossip session. Martha was talking to another woman of about the same vintage.

It was interesting to see the way different people aged, Laura thought. Martha had dried up like a milkweed pod, while her friend was fighting a rear-guard action. Like Tim O'Donnell, she dyed her hair. It was too dark to be flattering to the deep lines grooved in her face, although she'd tried to compensate with a liberal application of makeup. The pink cheeks, blue eyelids and red lips were garish rather than youthful. Her dress, too, was flamboyant. And the whole effect was emphasized by a pair of gold party slippers.

"Laura," Martha called out. "Come over and meet Emma."

Something about the tone of voice put Laura on the alert. The watchful look in Emma's eyes was another indication that the two other women knew something she didn't.

"I'm Laura Roswell," she murmured, wondering what had possessed her to drive up here from Baltimore. The weekend certainly wasn't turning out the way she'd anticipated.

"Emma Litchfield."

"Doesn't she look just like Rex?" Martha asked.

"There is a resemblance."

"The eyes. The hair color. The shape of her face," Martha continued. "Of course, you can see some of her mother, too."

"Really, you don't have to prattle on." Emma's voice was quiet, but her words put an abrupt stop to the other woman's critique.

"I take it most of the investors knew each other," Laura said as she poured herself a cup of tea.

"Oh, yes. We were such good friends," Martha answered. "But you know how it is. People go their separate ways. And at our age, they're more likely to be written up in the obituary column than in the gossip column. It's a shame Rex and Arthur couldn't be here. Then we'd have a real reunion. Arthur was Jake's uncle. But then, it is nice to meet you two young people."

The men had drifted toward the tea and food and had begun helping themselves with more enthusiasm than the ladies. But they were less adept than the women at balancing both cups and plates of little sandwiches and miniature pastries.

"Well, let's all pull up seats and get comfortable," Andy suggested, bringing up side chairs and arranging them around the oriental rug.

He escorted Emma toward a settee that had been pulled

up under the brass chandelier, but she shook her head. "A straight chair is better for my back, young man."

Sam took the settee. Laura found herself not so subtly maneuvered into sitting next to Jake on the couch. How sweet, she thought. Everybody probably thinks I'm just dying to hear about his exploits with the NFL.

When the guests were settled, Andy cleared his throat. "I thought I might start outlining the opportunity that's become available to the Ravenwood investors. After twenty years of tax write-offs, you finally have a chance to make a tidy profit on land that hasn't appreciated in ten years."

"Why the sudden change in the picture?" Jake asked, leaning back and stretching out his left leg.

"The shortage of recreational land closer to the city. Progress is finally moving out this way."

"Then why wouldn't it be better for us to hold on to the property and develop it ourselves?" Tim asked.

"It might be, if you had the monetary resources and the expertise to—" Andy never got to present the rest of his argument.

Laura was aware of a loud rattle overhead, followed by a blurred motion.

The brass chandelier had broken loose and was plummeting from the ceiling.

Chapter Three

A tenth of a second later, the chandelier crashed onto the settee. Tipping and swaying, the heavy light fixture balanced for a moment on the cushion, inches from where Sam had been sitting, and then toppled off onto the floor with an ominous thud.

But Laura caught only a brief impression of what was happening. Before the chandelier had stopped swaying, two hundred and twenty pounds of weight forced her back into the pillows of the couch. Jake had twisted around, folded her into his arms and interposed his solid body between her and the falling light fixture. She felt safe there. If you needed a man's protection, Jake Wallace was definitely the one to pick. Then, to her chagrin, she realized she was clinging to the front of his shirt. Unclenching her fingers, she tried to push herself away.

He didn't relax his hold.

"Give it a few seconds, honey. Let's see if anything else besides plaster dust falls out of the ceiling."

For a moment she relaxed against him. When she realized she was enjoying the intimate contact, she twisted around to see what was happening in the rest of the room. Sam had leaped from his seat like a sprinter at the starter's gun. Now he stood shaking and white faced beside the settee. "Jumping Moses!"

Andy rushed to his side, his features an almost comic mixture of incredulity and horror. "Are you all right?"

"Yeah. But I hope you got a guarantee from the people who did your renovation."

"Mercy me!" Martha's brittle exclamation was followed by a squeak. "I believe Emma's fainted."

"I know first aid. I'd better see what I can do," Laura offered.

After another cautious look at the ceiling, Jake released her. Swiftly, she crossed the room to the woman who had slumped forward. With her body bent, the pale skin of her scalp showed through the too-dark hair, making her head look like a large egg covered by a thin bird's nest.

"What—" Emma pushed herself to a sitting position, knocking off one of her gold slippers. When she saw Laura bending over her, fear flickered in her eyes and she cringed.

"It's all right. I only want to help you," Laura murmured.

The older woman blinked.

"Just relax," Laura soothed as she lifted Emma's delicate wrist and took her pulse. Peripherally, she was aware that the attention of everybody in the room was now focused on the two of them. Trying to shut out any distractions, she concentrated on counting pulse beats. But another part of her mind was silently observing the woman she was attending, trying to figure out why Emma had reacted to her so oddly.

Tim started to cough, and Laura's attention, as well as everyone else's, was distracted. Red-faced, he took a gulp from his cup of cold tea. "That's better. Just my corksacking emphysema kicking up."

"It looks like you should have had a doctor on call for this little get-together," Jake said to Andy.

"Folks, I'm so sorry this happened. Believe me, if there are any medical bills associated with this unfortunate incident, ASDC will be glad to cover them." Andy checked his watch. "Let's postpone dinner until seven. That will give us a chance to clean up and you a chance to unwind. You might want to take a walk around the grounds, they're lovely this time of year." Then his placid expression became troubled, as if he wished he hadn't made the suggestion. "Just don't wander too far afield. I wouldn't want anyone tumbling into the old ravine."

"I wouldn't think of it." The acerbic remark came from Emma, who had just pushed herself shakily to her feet. Sam took her arm to steady her.

"You all right?" he asked.

"As well as can be expected." She turned to Laura. "Thank you, my dear."

"I didn't do much."

"It's the thought that counts."

Members of the group were still talking about how lucky they'd been that no one was hurt as they filed out of the room. Jake, who had unfinished business in the drawing room, hung back until the room emptied. Most of the other guests opted for a rest.

Laura decided to take Andy up on the suggestion of a walk, particularly since the fresh air might help her think about Emma. In her work, she enjoyed putting bits and pieces of information and testimony together to come up with a complete picture. She was pretty sure she'd never met Emma before. But she had the unshakable feeling there was something about the woman she should know.

The sun had started its descent toward the west, and the air was a bit nippy. Laura walked briskly to keep warm, deep in thought as she followed a path away that led into the woods.

"Hey, I wouldn't go that way if I were you."

She turned to find Jake rapidly closing the distance between them. His walk had looked agile. When he put on a bit of speed, she could tell that his left knee didn't function quite properly. He'd said something about surgery. Maybe he hadn't gotten it, after all. Or it hadn't worked.

For an unguarded instant, she was glad he'd sought her out. Then she was annoyed with her response to him. "What's wrong with this path?" she challenged.

"It leads straight to the ravine Andy was warning everyone about."

"How do you know?"

"I checked out the grounds."

"You seem to have done a lot of exploring." Laura continued in the direction she'd been walking—wishing she weren't so conscious of the man beside her. But why shouldn't she be conscious of him? He took up more than half the path.

"I like to get the lay of the land when I'm in a new situation. That way there are fewer surprises," Jake said, answering her spoken question.

His tone of voice made Laura cock her head to one side as if she'd just come up with an entirely new thread of logic in the middle of a cross-examination. But she didn't say anything.

He slanted her an appraising look. "Something funny is going on around here."

"Oh?"

"I had a look at the chandelier cord. It was cut."

Laura stopped dead in her tracks. "You must be mistaken."

"No mistake. I had a look at it after everybody left the

room. Too bad the bulbs weren't lit when we first arrived, then I'd have some idea when it was done.''

"It's an old house. It could have happened anytime. Maybe some kids did it for a prank last Halloween," Laura suggested.

"Or someone could have wanted it to fall in the middle of that meeting."

"What are you implying?" Laura asked carefully. Talk about letting your imagination run away with you. Maybe the Gothic mansion looming behind them was having the same effect on him that it was on her.

"I'm not implying anything. I'm just stating facts."

"Suppositions."

"Sam Pendergrast almost got hit," he continued.

"*Almost* is the operative word."

"You sound like a lawyer."

"I *am* a lawyer."

"I won't hold that against you."

"Thanks," Laura returned dryly. "Have you discussed any of your suspicions with Mr. Stapleton?"

"He could have been the one who cut the wire. He was leading Emma to the settee before she said she wanted a straight chair."

"Are you making accusations now?"

"Nope. I'm just being cautious."

"So why have you spilled the beans to me? Maybe I snuck up here yesterday and did it," Laura suggested, wondering if he could fit that into his little scenario.

To her surprise, Jake threw back his head and laughed. "Now you're tryin' to do me one better." Then his expression sobered. "But it's not a joke. I'm serious enough to keep my eyes open and watch my back while I'm up here at this little get-together. I suggest you do the same thing. And since other people could be looking out the window, I also suggest we amble on back to the house as if we've just been getting to know each other better—not discussing attempted murder.''

"Murder?'' The man must be paranoid. Or trying to scare her.

But what if, somehow, he were right? The chandelier was pretty heavy. What if it had fallen on Sam or Emma? Or someone else? Would the victim have survived.

Victim. Murder. Laura shivered and peered into the gathering gloom that suddenly seemed to press in around her. It wasn't hard to imagine shadowy forms slipping through the trees. No, it was just a trick of the fading light. While they'd been talking, the sun had been setting, and if you let your imagination run wild, you might be able to convince yourself of all sorts of frightening things.

As if sensing her uneasiness, Jake moved in closer and slung his arm over her shoulder. In her present condition, it was tempting to burrow into his warmth, to let him protect her the way he had when the chandelier had fallen.

Yet a more rational part of her mind knew he was the one who had helped maneuver her into her present state. Besides, she didn't like the way he kept offering protection and she kept accepting. It was dangerous to depend on anybody except herself. If she'd learned anything in life, she'd learned that.

Turning her head slightly, she gave him a considering look. His speculations had made her uneasy, all right. But suppose he'd had some ulterior motive? He could even have made the whole thing up to give himself another chance to get close. She had the feeling the man wasn't above taking advantage of a favorable situation when it came to male-female relations.

He saw her watching him and gave her a lazy smile, as if they really had just come out here to get to know each other better. When a tiny answering smile flickered on her lips, he gave her arm a little squeeze.

Aghast that she'd encouraged him, she hastened to set things straight. "Don't get any ideas, Mr. Wallace."

"What ideas did you have in mind?" he asked innocently. Before Laura could answer—or pull away—they almost bumped into Andy Stapleton, who had rounded the curve in front of them at something between a walk and a trot.

Jake dropped his hand a proprietary couple of inches lower on Laura's shoulder. "Nice evenin'."

Andy took several panting breaths before answering. "I saw you two wander off down this way a while ago and started to get worried."

"We're fine," Jake replied easily. "Just headin' home to get ready for dinner."

Andy turned and accompanied, or rather, shepherded them back to the house. Laura would have broken away from Jake, but he held her clamped against his side.

"Any ideas on what happened to the chandelier?" he asked in a conversational tone.

"Why—uh—no."

Jake shot Laura a look that said, "He's not being straight with us."

She nodded imperceptibly.

The real-estate promoter didn't follow them up the circular stairs to the second level. Laura was preparing to make a quick getaway to her room when Jake put a restraining hand on her shoulder.

"I think you can drop the act now," she said, in his ear.

"Act? Oh, I think we're being honest with each other. I'm attracted to you. You're attracted to me. Let's see what develops."

"Nothing's going to develop."

"If you say so, honey. But play it cool. I think someone is peeking at us from one of the rooms down the hall."

Laura swung partially around. Following the direction of Jake's gaze, she saw a door ease shut. It was probably Martha, getting a jump start on the Ravenwood gossip. But there was no way to be sure right now. And the best course of action was to make sure there was nothing for her to gossip about. With a curt goodbye, Laura took her leave of Jake Wallace.

A half hour later, Laura stood at the window, looking out as the last pink tinge of the sunset faded from view. Nightfall had intensified her feeling of uneasiness. And in spite of her best efforts, she couldn't get Jake out of her mind. It wasn't just the sexual undercurrent flowing between them—she was perfectly competent to deal with that, she assured herself. It was his attempted murder theory that kept pushing its way back into her mind. Besides, more than just Jake's suggestions had her spooked. There was a brooding atmosphere around this place that gave her the creeps. She had half a mind to sweep her clothes back into her suitcase and head for home. Except that it would be a long, dark ride. And the first part would be down the overgrown, twisting road that led up the mountain. It wouldn't be much fun to negotiate now.

Unwilling to let herself feel trapped, she drew the curtains. There was probably a logical explanation for what had happened to the chandelier. Maybe Andy Stapleton was simply being evasive because he was trying to smooth over the mess. After all, he'd gone to a lot of trouble to arrange the weekend, and things weren't going the way he'd hoped.

LAURA GAVE Jake a cautious look when he took the seat next to her at the oval dining table. He responded with one of his lazy smiles and then began to chat amiably with Martha, who was sitting across the table.

As Laura unfolded her napkin, she watched her dinner partner out of the corner of her eye. His easy conversation almost convinced her that she'd imagined their talk on the path to the ravine. Except that she remembered very distinctly that they'd been discussing murder. Now a person wouldn't know Jake Wallace had a concern in the world, except a good dinner and a little light flirtation. *The man must be an expert at concealing tension when he wanted you to think he was relaxed,* she thought.

Her attention was distracted as Tim, who was now a bit unsteady on his feet, dropped into the vacant seat to her left. After a whiff of his breath as he leaned over to grab the basket of rolls, Laura was certain he'd spent the early evening drinking.

To the discomfort of the group, he began to make a concerted effort to liven up the proceedings with a string of not very funny jokes. At the lukewarm response, he upped the ante. Sober, he'd been almost charming; in his cups, he wasn't very appealing.

"Give a husband enough rope and he'll skip," he quipped in response to a comment about a Maryland politician who'd recently left his wife.

There was silence around the table. Martha shot a knowing look at Emma, who lifted her chin defiantly.

"Don't get your feathers ruffled, Emmie," Sam muttered.

What were they really talking about? Parts of the weekend conversation were so confusing that Laura felt as if she'd come into a play after intermission—and only the senior citizens had been there for the first act.

"Or give him enough rope and he'll say he's tied up at the office," Tim said, trying another variation.

"The office. Yes, tell us what it's like to work at the *Baltimore Sun*," Sam asked Jake in a pointed attempt to change the subject. Jake obliged with a tale about how the automated interoffice communications system was driving him crazy.

Laura felt some of the tension ease out of her shoulders as she listened. Jake was a good storyteller. And in a few minutes, he had everybody chuckling at his battle with the new five-hundred-page instruction book.

Laura was just taking a sip of wine when she felt a hand brush her left knee. When she glanced up at Tim, the expression in his bloodshot eyes didn't change. Maybe the familiar touch had simply been an accident. But five minutes later, the caress was repeated.

It would serve the drunk old geezer right if she slapped his hand under the table, Laura thought. But she didn't really want to make a scene. Instead, she turned her back and slid her chair closer to Jake, hoping to convey to Tim that if he was going to keep bothering her, he'd have to deal with the ex-football player.

Jake gave her a warm look. To her disquiet, she felt answering warmth suffuse her nerve endings. Jake Wallace had a way of making her feel more like a woman than she had in a long time. But he probably had the knack for making a woman feel special. That didn't mean getting involved with him was smart. Not when the thought of letting her vulnerabilities show was still so scary.

Still, they continued to stare at each other. To her chagrin, she realized the conversation around the table had stopped and everyone was taking in the exchange.

Then Sam came to her rescue. "So, Jake, what do you think about women reporters in the men's locker room?"

Jake reluctantly pulled his gaze away from Laura.

"Women have a right to interview the players. Just so they don't beat me out of a scoop," he quipped.

"Well, I think it's an invasion of privacy," Tim chimed in loudly. "How would you have liked to have to look over your shoulder every time you dropped your towel?"

"It wouldn't be a problem if you set up a special interview room—and make the male and female reporters use it. That would give everyone the same advantage." Jake went on to give a thoughtful analysis of reporter rights versus player privacy.

Laura found herself listening with interest. It would have been easier if she could have dismissed him as a dork-brained former jock who'd weaseled his way into a reporting job. But he was actually quite sharp, with an analytical mind. She found that as appealing as the rugged planes of his face and the way his long lashes framed his dark eyes.

Why was she letting herself think of him this way? She was struggling to change gears mentally when Andy broke into the conversation.

"Well, this is all very interesting," he said, "but shall we have our coffee in the library while we get ready for the presentation?"

"Only if there's no chandelier," Sam remarked soberly.

The developer shot him a quelling look. "I've done a thorough safety check of the room," Andy assured them as he pushed back his chair. The others followed him down the hall and into the book-lined chamber.

Andy had set up a screen and slide projector. After dimming the lights, he went into his act. His voice was smooth. Only the way he rotated his diamond ring with his thumb betrayed any nervousness.

First, there were pictures of the Ravenwood mansion and the surrounding real estate, accompanied by a spiel extolling the virtues of the tract for recreational and vacation-home development. Next came estimates of costs, in stages—starting with zoning approval and perc tests and ending with roads and possible municipal water service.

In a dark corner of the room, Tim was slumped back in his chair, snoring gently.

But Laura found herself listening with heightened attention. Was she understanding Andy correctly, she wondered. She'd thought he wanted to buy the shares in Ravenwood, but that wasn't exactly what he seemed to be saying now.

Around her, she could sense a certain restlessness in the audience. Apparently she wasn't the only one getting the mixed message.

"Would you mind turning on the lights so we could talk," Sam's voice finally cut through the thickening atmosphere like a blunt knife parting soft cheese.

"If you'll bear with me, I'm almost through with the slides," Andy said.

"I'd rather have some straight talk," Sam persisted. Then in a huffy voice he said, "And for God's sake, turn on the lights so I can see what the hell I'm doing."

At his tone, Laura turned to look at the man. Did Sam suffer from night blindness, she wondered. A man like him, who was so obviously into physical fitness, would probably consider the infirmity a sign of advancing age. And that might make him grouchy.

But he wasn't the only one of the old crowd who was out of sorts. Other voices were raised. Sighing, Andy crossed the room and switched on the lights. For a moment, everybody blinked in the unaccustomed brightness.

"Young man, are you asking each of us to risk additional money in the hopes that this tract of land can be developed?'' Emma asked the question that had leaped into Laura's mind.

''I thought you—'' Andy looked at her in confusion before abruptly changing tack. ''That's a rather blunt way to put it.''

''Is it a fair description of the situation?'' Emma persisted.

Andy cleared his throat. ''In the very early stages of a major project, there are certain minimal costs—''

''Cut the phoney-baloney,'' Tim advised, as if he'd been paying strict attention to the presentation instead of snoozing. Apparently he'd awakened in time to catch the drift of the protests. Or maybe he was making a lucky guess. ''Did you ask us up here to convince us to pour more of our hard-earned money down a rat hole?''

''It's not a rat hole. In today's market, it's a very sound investment decision.''

Martha stood up. ''If you'll excuse me, I believe I've heard enough.''

''Where are you going?'' Andy asked the gray-haired woman.

''Up to my room.''

Others were standing now. Andy moved rapidly around the room, talking to the investors, but it was clear that he'd lost their confidence. In exasperation, he turned back to Emma, who shrugged. What was going on between them, Laura wondered.

When Jake stood with his hands in his pockets, Laura could see that they were balled into fists. He hadn't joined the protest, but apparently he was angry about having been dragged up here under false pretenses. Had he been counting on making some money from the deal, she wondered.

As the developer approached them, Jake gave him a cold

stare and Laura shook her head. Instead of attempting any more argument, he turned away.

Jake muttered something under his breath that Laura was glad she couldn't hear. "I could use a drink," he added. "Our host left a gift-wrapped bottle of bourbon in my room."

"Bourbon. The women got fruit baskets. At least, I did."

"Sometimes there's an advantage in being one of the guys. Care to come up and drown your sorrows?"

"No thanks."

He gave her a boyish smile that she was sure most women would have found irresistible. "Oh, come on. We might as well salvage something from the weekend."

For just a moment, she was tempted to accept the invitation. He was right. They were attracted to each other. Yet she was afraid to take a chance on him. If she ever let another man get close to her, it would be one cautious step at a time. But if she went up to Jake's room, he'd assume she was agreeing to a lot more than a drink.

"I think I'll follow Martha's example and salvage a good night's sleep."

"You sure do blow hot one minute and cold the next."

"I'm sorry," she said before turning away and heading rapidly toward the steps.

She would go to bed early, Laura told herself as she reached her door. That way it wouldn't be hard to get up at the crack of dawn and leave before anything else happened. The locals back at the gas station had been right about her trip to Ravenwood, even if they hadn't known any of the reasons. She should have turned around and gone home as soon as she'd left the pump.

For the past few hours, Laura had erased the disturbing

incident from her mind. But now, recalling Ida's word made her remember the fairy cross.

It was for protection, she'd said. How silly. Laura didn't believe in good-luck pieces.

Nevertheless, before she could examine her motives, she hurried to the dresser where she'd left her purse and fumbled inside. She couldn't even remember which compartment she'd shoved the cross into, and several moments passed before she located it. A sense of profound relief washed over her as her fingers closed around the hard, bevelled stone. It was the same way she felt when she thought she'd lost her keys or her wallet and then found where it had dropped. For some unexplained reason, she'd half expected that the little charm would turn up missing. Drawing it out, she held it up to the light the way she'd done in the car, twisting it so that the gold vein winked and twinkled. Then, feeling a bit foolish, she transferred the crystal from her purse to her overnight bag.

Next, she locked her door, listening with satisfaction as the latch clicked. There were worse ways to spend an evening than in her own company.

In the bathroom she began to draw a tub full of water, profoundly grateful that she didn't have to go down the hall to use the facilities. That was one advantage the ladies had over the gentlemen—even if they hadn't been gifted with a bottle of bourbon to compensate for the disappointing anticlimax of Andy Stapleton's presentation.

The hot bath did wonders for Laura's frayed nerves. Somewhere between the lavender bath oil and scented soap she'd brought, she decided that Jake Wallace was the kind of man who could take care of himself. She also began to construct a philosophical view of the land developer's ploy.

So she wasn't going to make a million dollars on her

father's western Maryland investment. Well, she hadn't known until a few years ago that she even had a share in the property, and she certainly didn't need the money. There was no reason not to just sit tight and wait until a better offer came along.

Relaxed, Laura climbed out of the tub, dried off with a fluffy white towel and slipped into her silk pajamas. She may have been having trouble sleeping lately, but it wasn't going to be a problem tonight, she decided after nestling under the wool blanket and soft sheet. She was even too tired to read the book she'd brought along. Ten minutes after she'd turned off the light, she was asleep, unaware of the phantoms hovering in the darkness, ready to seize her when she gave up conscious control of her mind.

JAKE HAD NEVER BEEN the kind of guy who liked to drink alone. Nevertheless, as his solitary evening wore on, he kept glancing up from his Tom Clancy novel and looking at the bottle of bourbon on the dresser.

It was no wonder he couldn't concentrate on Clancy's high-tech toys. The whole trip had been a real fiasco. Because he'd wanted to get his hands on some cash, he'd been dumb enough to get his hopes up about Ravenwood. Then, after the chandelier business, he'd started wondering if the whole weekend was some sort of bizarre setup. Maybe part of a ploy to get a few of the investors to drop out so the rest could strike a new deal and split the increased profits. Or was someone really trying to kill off members of the group? He'd made the suggestion to Laura to see how she'd react, but he wasn't sure things had really gone that far. Or who would be doing it. On the other hand, he did know something for sure: the ASDC land-development deal had gone sour. That had been a major disappointment.

And then there was his near miss with the beautiful lawyer. At dinner, he'd gotten the distinct impression that he and Ms. Roswell were going to get to know each other a lot better after Stapleton's presentation.

Okay, so that hadn't worked out, either. So what? One woman was as good as another. If he was looking for company, there were half a dozen numbers in his black book he could call.

Of course, that argument was a damn lie, he admitted as his large fist clamped around the paperback novel, twisting it permanently out of shape. Unfortunately, one woman wasn't as good as another. For a moment Jake squeezed his eyes shut and pressed his fist against his forehead. His wife's sweet, heart-shaped face shimmered in his inner vision—the way she'd looked on their wedding day. Sometimes, it was hard to remember how pretty she'd been before she'd gotten so sick. Sometimes, all he could recall was the gaunt, haunted face of the last few weeks when it had torn him apart to think about what she was going through.

He'd loved Holly so much. They'd been a matched pair. But he was never going to risk that kind of pain or terror or guilt again. He'd been a basket case after she'd died. And it had taken him a long time to get back to any kind of normal life. Once he had, he'd kept things simple. He liked women. He knew how to show them a good time. The trick was making sure that the emotions never cut too deep. Because he wasn't willing to risk getting blown away by grief again.

So why was he lying here regretting the near miss with Laura? She was just a pretty blonde who'd crossed his path this weekend. He wanted to believe that. Which meant he'd better not examine his feelings too closely.

What he needed was a good night's sleep before he

headed back to Baltimore in the morning. And Andy Stapleton had thoughtfully provided an effective sedative. Getting off the bed, he picked up the bottle of bourbon. He wished he had some ice. Cold water from the bathroom down the hall would have to do.

He'd just climbed back into his jeans and opened his door a crack when he realized someone else was in the hallway. In the dim light, he saw her coming toward him.

It was Laura Roswell. Her long blond hair billowed out behind her as she walked rapidly in his direction. Silky pajamas hugged her shape from the curve of her shoulders down to her gorgeous legs.

Her steps were light, as if her slippered feet were barely touching the floor. As she advanced toward him, he was struck by the odd expression on her pale face. It was intense. Urgent. Obsessed. Not at all the countenance of a woman on her way to a romantic meeting.

"Laura?" he whispered.

He caught the tantalizing scent of lavender as she drew abreast of him. She didn't seem to realize he was there, although that was unlikely, since he'd put down the bottle of bourbon, stepped out in the hall, and was standing almost in her path.

"Laura?" he questioned again.

Again she didn't answer. Now he could see her eyes. They were glazed, flat, unseeing. Yet she moved with unfaltering steps, as if some invisible force were drawing her forward.

Jake felt the hair on his scalp prickle. "What the hell is going on?" he growled.

Laura marched past him in a cloud of silk and lavender. She didn't stop until she was standing in front of the door where he'd found her earlier. When she opened it, the familiar repelling odor wafted out.

The dark cavern beyond was lit only by a few shafts of moonlight from the window at the end of the hall, but Laura's gait didn't falter. Jake's first impulse was to pull her back the way he'd done this afternoon. But he'd had a look around in there after Stapleton had showed him to his room. The floor was safe—at least for fifty feet or so down the hall.

If he stopped her, he wasn't going to find out what she was up to. Instead of interfering, he followed her, repressing a cough as the dead air assaulted his lungs. Laura's steps were purposeful—the steps of a woman who knew exactly where she was going. She halted at the second door on the right, turned the handle and pushed it open. For a second or two, Jake lost her. Speeding up, he gained the doorway and saw her walking across an empty room. When she reached the far wall, she stooped and began prying at one of the floorboards. It came up with a little squeal of protest. Reaching inside, she extracted what looked like a box about the size of a brick. Then she carefully replaced the board, apparently still unaware that Jake was lurking in the shadows.

He took a step forward and the floor groaned under the extra weight of his football player's body.

"Laura, watch out."

It was as if the stuffing had suddenly whooshed out of a giant rag doll. Laura's knees buckled, all the strength deserted her body and she pitched forward, collapsing against him. As he pulled her toward the door, he snatched the box out of her trembling fingers.

Chapter Four

Laura's mind snapped back to some sort of awareness as arms like tree trunks clamped her to an unyielding male body. Shocked, terrified, disoriented, she began to struggle, whipping her head from side to side, balling her hands into fists and raining desperate blows against a broad chest.

Naked arms. A naked chest.

She was trapped in the bedroom. Just like in the dream. Her pursuer had her again. He was going to kill her. She knew that at some gut-wrenching level below conscious thought. Yet even as she opened her mouth to scream, some tiny compartment of her fear-crazed mind realized the cues were all wrong. His body. The wrong size, the wrong shape. His touch. Comforting not rough. It wasn't *him.*

Still, panic bubbled up when a large palm choked off any hope of sound.

"Take it easy, honey. Laura, take it easy. You don't want to bring them all running in here."

The reassuring voice and the hands stroking across her back penetrated the fog in her brain and the hysteria clawing its way up her throat.

"Laura. It's Jake." He trailed a finger against her cheek before lifting his hand away.

"Jake?" His name was a gasp on her lips. "What's happened?" she asked as she looked up at his face. "What are you doing in my room? Where's your shirt?"

She heard a deep, masculine chuckle. "The last thing you need to worry about is my shirt."

He had unclenched his restraining grip on her shoulders, but he still kept her firmly erect with the pressure of his solid arms around her slender body. It was a good thing. Somehow, she seemed to have lost control of her muscles. They were trembling, and her knees felt too weak to support her weight.

"You're not in your room. You're in the damaged part of the mansion."

"How did I get here?"

"You walked down the hall and opened the door."

"That's impossible."

"You think your room smells like a burned-out mushroom farm?"

She took a breath of the rank air and gagged.

He waited until the spasm passed. "All right?"

"Yes."

"Let's get the heck out of here."

Grasping Laura's ice-cold hand, Jake backed cautiously out of the room, bringing her along with him. At each step, the boards under their feet groaned ominously.

The floor stopped quivering when they reached the relative stability of the hall. At the end of the corridor, Laura could see light shining like a ray of hope from heaven. Jake didn't have to urge her to hurry after him now. When they stepped out into the carpeted corridor, she breathed in a lungful of fresh air. Jake closed the door. Then, before Laura could voice a protest, he opened another door and pulled her inside.

"This is your room!" she exclaimed.

"Right. Yours is at the other end of the house. Do you want to be seen in the hall with me—dressed like that?"

Laura crossed her arms and grasped her pajama-clad sleeves. At the same time, her gaze riveted to the broad expanse of Jake's naked chest. It was covered with a thick pelt a bit darker than the hair on his head. "No one has to see *us*." She turned and reached for the door handle.

Jake wasn't making any concessions to Miss Manners. He pulled Laura's hand away from the door, dragged her farther into the room and pushed her to a seated position on the bed.

"You're not going anywhere until we have a little talk."

"About what?" She couldn't quite manage to keep her voice steady.

Instead of answering, Jake turned to the double-hung window. Laura followed his gaze to the inky blackness beyond the dimly lit little room. All at once, it was impossible not to feel isolated and vulnerable. Almost as vulnerable as she'd been in the dreams.

As Jake drew the drapes shut with a decisive snap, Laura folded her arms across her chest. When he turned back and began to advance on her, she flattened her shoulders against the headboard. The scream that had come so often to her lips in recent nights hovered in her throat again.

Then with an effort of will, she shook herself out of the fantasy. He wasn't coming for her. He was holding up the box as if it were exhibit A in a courtroom.

As much to avoid his gaze as anything else, Laura carefully examined the exterior. Dull, blackened metal reinforced with brass strips at the corners. A hasp but no lock.

Jake set the chest on the bedside table. When she stroked her finger across the top, she drew a line in soot. This thing had been through the fire.

"Let's see what's inside." Jake pried up the lid using

the end of a key as a lever. The top gave a groan of protest but finally yielded.

They were both silent for several seconds as they looked into the interior. As far as Laura could see, there was nothing here but a pile of charred papers. Jake cursed. "Not your typical buried treasure." He switched his attention back to Laura. "Want to tell me what you were doing sleepwalking in the burned-out part of the house? Or why you knew exactly where this box of trash was hidden under the floorboards." He tapped exhibit A for her inspection.

"I wasn't sleepwalking!"

"What would you call it?"

"I—" Laura's objection had been the automatic denial of a woman who'd never before strayed unaware from her bed in the middle of the night. But it was a fair question and one she couldn't answer. Straining her memory, she cast about for some clue to what had happened. It was no good. The last thing she recalled before regaining consciousness in Jake's arms was snuggling under the bed covers in her room at the other end of the hall.

Blind terror had engulfed her in the moments before she'd realized where she was and who was holding her. And she'd been having trouble holding herself together ever since. Without warning, the terror swept her into its cold embrace once more.

The whole thing was too much. Too much to take. Too much to try to explain, even to herself. Especially to herself.

Laura's muscles began to spasm again, and her teeth started to chatter as if someone had pressed a bowl of ice cubes to the base of her spine.

Just as he'd done when the chandelier had fallen, Jake pulled her close, taking her with him as he leaned back against the headboard. This time, she had no strength to fight him. This time, she knew in some deep, instinctive way that giving solace came naturally to this man.

She might have reached out and anchored herself to the safe harbor of his arms if her muscles had cooperated. Instead of clinging, she melted against him, burying her face in the comforting warmth of his neck.

Her eyelids fluttered closed, and her hands hung limply at her sides.

"It's all right, honey," he crooned over and over, rocking her tenderly in his arms. Once more, she was struck by how gently someone so big could handle a woman's body. Slowly, the words and the solid reassurance he offered brought her some measure of calm.

"Better?" he asked, sensing the change.

"Some."

Jake gave her a few more minutes. It was strangely tempting to stay in his embrace again. Perhaps that was why she pushed herself away.

He gazed at her consideringly. "You still look like you bumped into Lucifer out there in the corridor. I think you're going to take me up on that drink I offered you earlier this evening."

Before she could object, he swung his legs off the bed, crossed to the dresser and began to open the bottle of bourbon. Laura watched him pour a little of the amber liquid into two water glasses.

"I don't drink that stuff straight."

"Think of it as medicine—for your nerves." He wrapped her fingers around one of the glasses.

She didn't take medicine for her nerves. Yet as she watched him drink, she followed suit—although quite a bit more cautiously. The bourbon burned her mouth and throat, and she didn't much like the taste.

Setting his glass on the night stand, Jake leaned back

comfortably against the pillows and put his long legs up on the spread. He took up more than his share of the double bed. He also seemed perfectly content with the situation.

Laura was still too unsure of her legs to get up. Wishing Jake would put on a shirt, wishing he'd opted to sit in the chair, she lifted up her side of the bedspread and slipped underneath as much from wanting to shield herself from Jake as from the chill. Then she found a tiny corner of the headboard to lean against.

When the man beside her didn't speak, she nervously took several more sips of the bourbon.

Jake drained his drink and began to toy with the glass. She knew he was watching her out of the corner of his eye. "Do you know what happened to you back there?" he finally asked.

She'd been thinking about it. Not just the strange circumstances of waking up and not knowing the wheres and whys. Even more unsettling was the way she'd felt. Afraid. No, terrified with the certain knowledge that some man was going to kill her. Somehow, she knew Jake hadn't triggered the runaway emotion. She also knew she wasn't willing to share the fear with him.

Laura shrugged. "I don't know why I wandered into that part of the house." When Jake continued to stare at her, she swallowed. "Uh—after my father bought into the Ravenwood deal, he used to talk a lot about the place. He'd been up here—to a couple of parties or something. Maybe he told me about the box. Maybe I just don't have any conscious memory of the conversation."

"Maybe." Jake's voice mirrored her own inner doubts.

"How else would I have known where to find it?" she asked.

"Inside information."

Laura sat up straighter, her eyes boring into those of the man on the other side of the bed. "You mean like somebody gave me a tip or something?"

He shrugged.

"Who? Why?"

"I couldn't say."

She gave him a direct look. "All right, maybe there's something we missed in the box."

"Good luck."

Gingerly, she removed the tightly wound bundle of charred newsprint.

"Burned offerings," Jake muttered.

"Baked, actually."

The papers were as brittle and insubstantial as the wasps' nest she'd knocked out from under the eaves last fall.

Hoping some trace of print remained, she held pieces of it up to the light. The words were unreadable, and charred flecks of paper dropped onto the bedspread.

"Well, I'll be damned."

Laura swiveled toward Jake. He wasn't looking at the flaking paper; he was staring into the bed of ash at the bottom of the container.

Following his gaze, Laura saw a glint of buried metal. Jake poked into the ashes and the elongated shape of an ornately carved handle emerged. It stood out clearly against the gray debris.

"What have we here?"

"A knife!" Laura exclaimed as Jake extracted a small, sharp dagger and held it flat across the palm of his hand so they could both get a good look. As Jake turned the weapon, she could see that the hilt was of some red metal, the blade a dull silver. It looked old and valuable—an artifact from another age. Perhaps from some ritual or arcane ceremony.

Laura reached for the dagger, taking it in her own hand and feeling the weight and balance. With the index finger of her other hand, she traced the raised design of vines and leaves that snaked up the grip. Then she looked at the pattern more closely. No, not leaves. Tiny red drops of blood. She shuddered and drew her hand back.

Jake's gaze swung to Laura. His question echoed the ones in her own mind. Only he expected her to have some answers. "What can you tell me about that thing?"

She put the knife back into the box. "I can't tell you anything about it. I—I—never saw it before in my life."

"You're sure?" He studied her white face and drawn features.

"Of course, I'm sure! I'm just spooked. Anybody would be, finding a wicked looking thing like this."

"Yeah."

Silence filled the room again. As much to distract herself from the evil-looking instrument as for any other reason, she picked up the wad of ruined papers and turned it in her hands. More pieces flaked off.

"Wait a minute," she exclaimed.

"What?"

"I think there's something here in the center." Carefully she began to peel away the damaged exterior and was rewarded when she came to a sheet of paper that was only scorched, not burned beyond legibility.

"Articles from the local newspapers," Jake observed.

Laura handed him some of the sheets. Very delicately, they unfolded the brittle pages and spread them across the bed. Actually, they were from two sources. Besides the county papers, there was also a front page of the *Baltimore Sun*.

The article in the worst shape was a story from the *Garrett County Times Union* about the sale of Ravenwood to a group of investors.

Laura went very still when she realized Jake wasn't looking at the article. He had taken her hand and turned it over.

"Your fingers."

She glanced down and saw that the skin on her fingertips was abraded. It must have happened when she'd pried up the floorboard. But until this moment, they'd both been too preoccupied to notice.

"Do they hurt?"

"No…well, yes. A little."

His fingers delicately stroked her injured flesh as if he could draw away the pain.

She looked up and their eyes met and held.

"You should put some antiseptic on that."

"There's some in my room. I'll take care of it later." Her voice had turned a bit husky. Probably from the bourbon, she told herself.

Somehow, there was more intimacy between them now than when he'd been holding her in his arms. Laura clung to her explanation. She didn't want to consider the possibility that some subtle sexual dynamic had shifted. Yet, now she was very sure the awareness she'd felt when they'd been sipping their drinks hadn't been her imagination.

Well, why not, she asked herself. A man and woman alone in a bedroom in the middle of the night. There were too many cultural signals switched on by the situation— and their clothing—or lack of it.

Sucking in a draft of air, Laura turned back to the article, but she could still feel Jake's eyes on her. To shift the focus away from the two of them, she pointed to a paragraph near the end of the readable portion. "Look here. It talks about my father."

"Yeah." He read the few lines. "And Sam and Emma. But what about Tim and Martha? They were in on the original deal, too."

"Maybe they were mentioned in the burned part."

They both read the rest of the article, but there wasn't much they didn't already know. Laura moved the page aside and turned to an editorial from the same paper. It was a diatribe condemning a series of wild parties at the mansion.

"Looks as if a bunch of carpetbaggers from the city were coming up here and corrupting the morals of the rural area," Jake commented dryly. "I see we've got disorderly conduct, drug-related arrests and a woman from town who was hired as a maid and got beaten up by one of the guests."

"I guess people in Hazard have long memories," Laura murmured.

"What are you talking about?"

"When I stopped for gas back in town, everybody was friendly until I mentioned I was going to Ravenwood." She gave him a brief summary of what had happened—except for the part about the fairy cross.

"Maybe they thought you were some kind of party girl."

Laura scowled in distaste at the idea.

"You get any names?"

"The guy pumping gas was called Cully. I think the old woman was Ida. Why?"

"They might talk to a reporter."

"You?"

"Yeah."

"I thought you wrote for the sports section."

"Maybe the gas jockey is a football fan." Jake gave her his most engaging grin.

"Right." Laura turned her attention back to the contents of the box. "Too bad so much is burned. We might have a better idea of why someone was saving this stuff."

"And whether it's related to anything else that's been going on here today."

"These articles are over twenty years old. You think that's possible?"

"This whole setup has been weird. Anything's possible. I don't know how many of the current guests have been up here before. Maybe one of them knows about the box."

"I hadn't thought of that."

"There's still the front page from the *Baltimore Sun*."

"Does it have a story about Ravenwood?"

It took several moments before Jake answered. When he did, his voice had turned rough and hard as a piece of corrugated steel. "No. Not a thing about Ravenwood."

Laura glanced up quickly to catch the expression on Jake's face. She couldn't see it because his head was bent toward the paper, but the rigid set of his shoulders matched the voice. Trying to figure out what had caused his sudden change of mood, Laura scanned the headlines. There were articles about a Mafia boss being assassinated, the president's drive against drug addiction and the inadequacy of the state's education budget. At the bottom of the page was the first in a series of articles on environmental-health issues. Across from it was a story on capital punishment. Rounding out the day's top stories were reports about a bomb attack on a Quebec restaurant and a mass murder in Florida.

"Have I missed something?"

He shrugged.

"Something in one of these articles?"

"Nothing that's relevant." He sighed. "Listen, I'm sorry. It's kind of late. I guess I'm getting tired of poring over this stuff and trying to come up with any conclusions."

"I think we're both tired." Laura began to gather up the papers, folding them carefully so as not to inflict any more damage. Setting them back on top of the dagger in the box, she closed the lid.

"What are you doing?"

"As you pointed out, I'm the one who found this stuff. I'm taking it back to my room." She arched an eyebrow, waiting for him to object.

His Adam's apple bobbed, and she wondered if he'd been planning on looking at the papers when she'd left. However, he didn't protest as she tucked the box under her arm.

"Uh, I guess it would be best not to discuss this with anyone else," she ventured.

"Umm-hmm."

She didn't tell him her motive was as much personal as anything else. If she hadn't been able to explain to him how she'd found the box, she doubted she'd do better with anyone else at Ravenwood.

"Thanks for for helping me out."

"Take care of yourself."

Did he think they were going to talk about this again tomorrow? Or was he planning to conduct his own investigation? And was it going to have something to do with one of the front-page articles? She didn't ask and he didn't volunteer.

Getting off the bed, he accompanied her to the door.

She'd just put a foot into the hall when another door opened. Sam Pendergrast looked directly at them, his gaze wide with surprise in the dim light. Instinctively Laura slipped the hand with the box against her thigh.

Jake's instincts were much more dynamic. For a heartbeat, his dark eyes burned a silent message into Laura's blue ones. Then he swept her into his arms and lowered his mouth to hers like a hungry lover who'd just come to the conclusion that he hadn't slaked his desire.

Dumbfounded, Laura went limp. In the next second, she began to struggle but Jake's muscular arms didn't give her much room to maneuver.

"Don't." The command vibrated against her lips. "Make this convincing." Before he finished the sentence, one hand began to tangle greedily in the silky strands of her long hair and the other caressed its way across her back. Earlier, his touch had been meant to comfort. Now it conveyed blatant male sensuality.

Jake Wallace was one hell of an actor. Or maybe he was simply one hell of a lover. It was hard to believe he was only pretending passion as his lips began to move over hers.

She hardly knew this man, yet she'd sensed the sexual pull between them tightening and twanging all evening, like guitar strings being stretched taut. She'd kept the feelings under control. Until now.

Taken by surprise, taken in his arms, taken by his mouth, she felt her lips open under his, and she gave in to his kiss.

As he sensed her acquiescence, his strong arms enveloped her body, gathering her close. With the kiss she tasted a hint of bourbon. It was far less potent than the essence of the man himself.

Joining the deception, her free hand traveled possessively across his broad shoulders and then up the back of his neck, stroking over the stubble from a recent haircut.

One silk-clad leg whispered against rough denim of his jeans.

He was growling deep in his throat when he pulled her back into his room and shut the door. Caught between his hard body and the even harder wall, she arched against him, echoing his response with a little cry of her own. It took several hot, breathless moments before Laura realized no one could see them anymore. She had crossed the line between acting and passion—if there ever had been a line.

He sensed the change in her even as she felt her muscles stiffen. Raising his head, he looked down into the confusion shimmering in her eyes.

"Was that necessary?" she managed.

He chose to answer the more obvious part of the question. "Did you want Sam to know what we've really been doing this evening—what *you've* really been doing?"

She swallowed slowly. "No."

Backing away, he ran unsteady fingers through his hair. At least she had the satisfaction of knowing he'd been as caught up in the dramatization as she.

"I have to leave."

"Not yet. He might be watching."

She stood with her back pressed to the door, staring at Jake, trying to comprehend what had flared so white-hot and so quickly between them. Not just desire. Emotion. She couldn't have responded like that unless she'd felt something for the man. But she didn't want it. Couldn't handle it.

"No."

She didn't care if Sam was still watching. She didn't care if everyone at Ravenwood was watching. All she knew was that the little room had suddenly become too hot and cramped for the two of them. Turning, she threw open the door and fled down the hall to her own room.

Sometimes when her emotions were in turmoil, Laura could make her mind a blank. Tonight, she didn't want to think about any of the things that had happened this evening. She only wanted to escape into the oblivion of sleep. Setting the box on the dresser, she slid into bed and pulled the covers up to her chin. Only a few minutes after she'd rolled onto her side and pulled her knees up against her chest she was asleep.

Angels, or maybe it was ghosts, might have hovered around her in the darkness, offering their protection. At any rate, she slept peacefully through the night, more peacefully than she'd slept in weeks.

"Laura... Laura... Wake up, Laura...."

She wasn't sure what roused her in the misty light of morning. A noise? A shout? One moment she was lost in slumber. The next moment she was sitting up in bed and looking around in alarm.

"Who's there?"

No one answered.

Laura's eyes focused on the paneled wall at the other end of the room. The noise seemed to have come from behind it. No, that was just her sleep-drugged mind playing tricks.

For several heartbeats she was enveloped in the early-morning silence. Then she heard a shout, high and thin and frightened. This time she knew it wasn't in her room. It seemed to be floating up from downstairs.

The hair on Laura's scalp prickled as she reached for her robe and swung her legs out of bed.

"Help... Please help me." The plea was followed by a thump from the floor below.

Opening the door, Laura peered into the corridor and saw no one. Thinking she heard scurrying noises somewhere below, she ran down the dimly lit corridor and took the steps two at a time.

"Is anybody there?" she called out. "Is somebody hurt?"

No one answered. In fact, the house seemed deathly quiet. Perhaps it had all been another one of her dreams. She wanted to believe that—except she couldn't.

Her breath rapid and shallow, she tiptoed toward the parlor. As she stepped through the doorway, she saw a figure huddled in the middle of the rug. It was a woman who wore a dressing gown of bright red and orange flowers—and gold slippers. Her too-dark hair was plastered over a white scalp.

"Emma!"

The woman didn't stir, didn't breathe.

"Emma?" Pulse racing, Laura knelt beside her, reached for one of her narrow shoulders and turned her over. For a moment Laura couldn't believe what she was seeing. The flowers of the dressing gown were darkened with blood. And they made an intricate new pattern with the knife she'd found last night. But how could that be? She'd left the weapon in the box in her room under the burned papers. Now it was buried to the hilt in the middle of Emma Litchfield's chest.

Chapter Five

Reflexively, Laura's fingers closed around the handle of the knife. Then she drew her hand back as she realized there was no use pulling it out. That wasn't going to help Emma. The woman was dead.

"Oh God—Oh God!"

Her anguished exclamation echoed in the empty room. Then people were running along the upstairs hall. When she'd needed help, the large house had seemed deserted; now, a crowd pelted down the stairs. Moments later, they clustered in the sitting room.

Andy. Sam. Jake. Tim. And finally, Martha. Most looked as if they'd been wrenched from sleep, the way Laura had been a few minutes earlier. The majority were still wearing night clothes. Only Andy and Jake had pulled on trousers.

Shock, horror, incredulity registered on the faces around her.

"Emma—Emma—called for help," Laura stammered. "That's why I came down here. Didn't anyone else hear her?" The explanations tumbled out. Laura knew her own voice was rising on a tide of panic as she began to realize just how this must look.

"We heard *you*," Tim said.

Others nodded in agreement.

Andy squatted beside the body and touched Emma's cheek. "She's already cold. She couldn't have called for help. Not in the last few minutes. How long have you been here?"

"I just found her." Laura looked around for support. "I tell you, I heard somebody calling me. I came down to the sitting room and found her like this."

Laura searched the faces of the crowd gathered around her. Some of the Ravenwood guests were giving her speculative glances. Others looked accusing.

No one moved.

Laura's eyes sought Jake's. He was staring at the dagger—the one she'd found last night, the one she'd insisted on taking to her room. Now it was sticking out of Emma's body. Laura held her breath, waiting to see if he was going to blurt out something about the night before. He didn't. In fact, to her profound relief and gratitude, he knelt and put his arm around her shoulder.

"It must have scared you out of your mind—finding her like this," he said.

She nodded wordlessly. The simple statement and the encouraging tone of his voice were like a balm. The others might be staring at her as if she'd jumped out from behind the curtains and assaulted Emma, but Jake was on her side.

Ignoring the knot of spectators, Jake helped Laura to her feet. As she stood, her knees threatened to give way, and he slipped his arm around her waist, supporting her weight against the side of his body.

"You're doin' fine. But let's get out of this room—so you don't have to stare at the body," he suggested. As they moved toward the door, the crowd parted for them.

When they'd turned the corner into the hall, he bent his head toward her ear and spoke rapidly. "We've only got a few minutes to talk. You're a lawyer. You know what you should and shouldn't say.''

If she could make her mind function.

He glanced back over his shoulder to make sure no one had followed them. ''We'd better not tell anyone about your finding the knife last night. It could make things worse for you.''

Laura felt her chest tighten. A phrase she'd once heard from a police detective had come bouncing into her head. *The person who discovers the body is the chief suspect.* She hated to lie. But she hadn't had a chance to think this through. ''Yes,'' she agreed again in an unsteady voice.

''Was your door locked?''

''I think so.''

''It looks as if someone set you up.''

''My God, Jake, who?''

''I don't know, but we'd better call the police. The sooner this is cleared up, the better for you....'' He hesitated. ''Last night, I would have bet I was the only other person who knew the knife was in your room.''

Her head whipped up.

''You would have thought of that sooner or later.'' His gaze didn't waver from hers. ''You don't have any reason to trust me. But I hope you do.''

Laura nodded uncertainly. She was confused and frightened and unable to give him an answer.

They were walking down the hall toward the room where Andy had made the presentation. Laura stopped abruptly. ''If I'm going to talk to the police, I think I'd like to get dressed before the interview.''

''Good idea.''

They both turned and headed for the stairs.

The first thing Laura did when she reached her room was check the dresser. The box was missing. Not just the knife—the whole box. A sick feeling rose in her throat. Jake was right. It looked as if she'd been a very convenient scapegoat for someone who wanted to kill Emma. But who? And how had the person known about the box? Sam leaped to mind. He'd seen them last night. But she had no way of knowing if he'd spotted the box. And what would he have had against Emma?

Laura felt as if she'd been thrust into the middle of one of those mystery weekends in which everyone goes off to a country house with a bunch of interesting characters, witnesses a pretend murder and then tries to figure out who did it. Only this wasn't an elaborately staged scenario with actors and actresses playing amusing or sinister roles. Emma's lifeless body was lying on the sitting room carpet.

Shuddering, Laura battled the impulse to crawl back into bed and pull the covers over her head like a little kid afraid of the dark. Instead, she began to wash and dress. She knew she should hurry, but speed seemed impossible. She felt as if she were walking around under water, with each movement of her arms and legs held back by the liquid's resistance. By the time she'd slipped into yesterday's knit outfit and put on a little makeup, Andy was rapping at the door to inform her that the chief of police wanted to talk to her.

Laura came back downstairs reluctantly, wondering what to expect. As she stood in the hall, she saw Sam Pendergrast come out of the room in which the real-estate developer had made the presentation the evening before. She tried to catch Sam's eye, but he brushed by her without a word, his muscular shoulders tense, as if he wished he'd left the scene before she arrived. A bad sign, she decided.

However, Sam was swept from her mind as soon as she met Police Chief Hiram Pickett. He was a tall, balding man with sleepy eyes and stooped shoulders. Perhaps to compensate for the thinning hair on the top of his head, he had cultivated a flowing mustache that made him look a little like Wyatt Earp. It appeared to be his only vanity. He wore his uniform as if it had been issued by Goodwill Industries. No tie. Nonstandard shirt so limp, the collar spread wide across the shoulders.

Scuffed hunting boots poked out from under his slate blue pants. On the other hand, a shiny star-shaped badge was pinned to his shirt pocket. And a holstered gun rode prominently on his right hip.

He was standing stiffly with his arms folded across his chest, looking around the room. Laura had the distinct impression that he was holding his emotions as tightly as his body—as if he found being at Ravenwood distasteful and wanted to get things over with as soon as possible. That might work to her advantage, and it might not.

"I hear you found Ms. Litchfield," he began after inviting Laura to take a seat on the couch. The way he sat opposite her, with as little of his body as possible touching the upholstery, confirmed her impression that he wasn't very comfortable here.

His initial questions were about what had happened the first thing in the morning. Why had she come downstairs so early? Why did she think she was the only one who heard the call for help? What did she do when she found Emma? Had she touched the knife?

To her surprise, Laura discovered she honestly didn't know the answer to that question. She'd been so upset that she couldn't remember.

After taking Laura back through her morning, he began to ask about the events of the day before.

Maybe she was going to have to get herself a lawyer—someone who was a lot more savvy than she in criminal law, she thought. No, she'd rather handle this by herself. Besides, even if she was the one who'd found the body, she certainly didn't have a motive.

As she and the police chief talked, Laura tried to gauge his attitude toward her. He wasn't acting friendly, but he was being very polite. Almost too polite, as though the rituals of courtesy and deference put a barrier between them. Was she at the top of his suspect list? There was no way of telling. But he ended the interview with a request that she not return to Baltimore that day.

Tim, apparently the next up to be interviewed, was hanging around the door to the sitting room when she came out. He was clasping and unclasping his hands, and his broad face was pale under the florid complexion. Standing up, he came over to her. Again, his breath was tinged with alcohol. Did he drink all the time? Or was it his way of dealing with tension?

"Laura," he said in a slightly slurred voice, "I'm sorry this happened."

"So am I," she agreed, taking a step back.

"I guess it looks pretty grim for you, darlin', what with the bad feelings between you and Emmie."

"What? What are you talking about?"

"Are you still pretending you don't know she's the one who took your father from your mother?"

Laura's mouth dropped open.

Tim didn't seem to notice her dumbfounded reaction. "Everybody knew about it. We were all wondering if there were going to be fireworks when you two met up."

The fireworks were exploding in Laura's head as she stared at him.

"I just couldn't resist needlin' her at dinner." Tim laughed. "But you were a real good sport about it. Until..." His voice trailed off.

Jake, who had just come into the room must have seen the expression on her face.

"What's wrong?"

"Tim says—I—"

He led her rapidly into the hall and turned her toward him, his large hands gripping her shoulders. "What is it?"

Her answer came in a frightened rush. "Why didn't I figure it out for myself? All that innuendo I didn't understand. Martha watching to see how I'd react when she introduced me to Emma. Emma looking frightened when I tried to help her after the chandelier. And then those jokes at dinner. Tim just told me Emma was the woman who took my father away from my mother. Now Pickett's going to think I was out for revenge."

The hands on her shoulders became gentle. "Not after all these years. Why wait until now? Why not do it when you had a lot less chance of getting caught? Killing her this weekend wouldn't make sense."

"A smart prosecutor would have no trouble coming up with a convincing motive. He'd say I'd been brooding about my father all these years and seeing Emma face-to-face drove me over the edge."

"No. You're too controlled for that."

He'd read her pretty accurately. Somehow that was the last straw. "Jake, I need to be alone. To think this through." When he didn't loosen his grasp, she wrenched herself away. She was heading for the stairs when a brusque voice stopped her.

"Just a minute, Ms. Roswell."

Laura looked up to confront a member of Pickett's staff. While the police chief was questioning the guests, other members of the department must have been photographing the crime scene and collecting physical evidence. Maybe they'd find something that would clear her of suspicion.

Her mind glommed on to the possibility even as she knew she was grasping at straws.

"We'd like to get your fingerprints."

Laura nodded tightly. As she allowed her thumb to be squished against the ink pad, she wondered again if she'd touched the knife that morning. But what did it matter? She'd handled the dagger last night. So had Jake. So had someone else. Unless Jake had stolen the knife after she'd gone to sleep. With a gulp, she admitted she couldn't discount that possibility. He could have taken it and the whole box back to his room. Except that she hadn't heard him unlock her door. She hadn't heard anyone unlock the door.

Finally, Laura was able to escape to her room. But she was too restless to stay in any one place for more than a minute or two. Downstairs, Pickett was interviewing people, gathering information, trying to make a case against her. Probably Sam had already told Pickett about her father and Emma before he'd interviewed her. Tim was probably adding more facts to the story. And Martha.

The realization made her feel trapped. Now, she cursed herself for not having jumped into her car and left when she'd thought about it last night. Even before she'd arrived, she'd had bad feelings about this place. She should have trusted her instincts. As she paced to the window, she pictured herself making a ladder out of her bed linens, sliding down to the ground and speeding off in her car. But then what? Running away clearly wouldn't solve her problem. It would only make her look guilty.

Laura brought her thoughts back to more constructive channels. What she had to do was think logically about the whole thing. There was no doubt that Emma's relationship with her father put her in an awkward position. It would be even more awkward if Pickett found out about what she'd been doing last night. But how could he, unless

Jake told him? And they'd both agreed not to talk about that. Suddenly she couldn't help wondering if he'd stick to the bargain. She knew so little about the man, and now her fate seemed inexorably wound up with him. It had been stupid not to talk to him again when he'd given her the chance. She needed to know what had gone on in his interview with Pickett and what he intended to do.

Laura was just heading for the door when someone knocked.

"Who is it?" she called out.

"Jake."

Speak of the devil. When she opened the door, she found him standing in the hall with a tray. It had two cups, a coffeepot and a plate of sandwiches.

"You skipped breakfast and lunch. You need to eat, Laura."

Was it that late already? She stepped aside and let him in, suddenly very glad to see him. And in truth, the smell of coffee and food made her stomach rumble. It was amazing that she could think about eating, she mused as she poured herself a cup of coffee and added milk.

Jake joined her. This time he sat in the easy chair. She perched on the side of the bed. As she watched him take a swallow of coffee, she couldn't help remembering the way the evening before had ended. She wasn't about to bring it up, yet the kiss that had gotten out of control couldn't exactly be ignored, she admitted silently, whether either one of them said anything or not.

He looked around the room. "Are the papers gone too, or just the knife?"

"The whole kit and caboodle."

"I didn't say anything about the box to Pickett."

"Thanks. I guess."

"It's better this way."

"I don't like to lie."

He reached out and pressed his fingers over hers. "Laura, I'm sorry this is happening to you."

"I keep wishing I'd never come up here."

"I can imagine."

She sat stiffly, not responding to the hand over hers. After several heartbeats, he removed it.

Laura took a sip of hot coffee. "I'd be tempted to think I made up the whole thing about the knife and the box—except that you remember it too, don't you?"

"Yes."

"Who do you think could have taken them out of my room?" Laura watched Jake's face carefully as she asked the question.

"I don't have a clue." He seemed genuinely perplexed.

"What else did Pickett ask you?" As she listened to his answer, she was thinking about how much she wanted his help and support. But she had to know if she could trust him. When he was finished speaking, she unclenched the fingers that gripped her coffee cup. "Jake, I hardly know anything about you—I mean, how do I really know—" She spread her hand in a helpless gesture.

"I could give you some character references. Guys from the Broncos. My editor down at the *Sun*. My mother."

Laura couldn't help smiling. "I'm sure your mother would be very laudatory."

"She was real strict about the things that counted when I was growing up. Homework first, play later. But she never could get me to keep my room straight. When she visits my apartment, she cleans out the pantry."

"Why aren't you married?" Yesterday, she wouldn't have asked such a personal question. But that could be an important clue to his personality. Why was an attractive, eligible man in his early thirties still unattached? Had the football star dumped his high school sweetheart?

"My wife died."

There was no way to miss the pain that accompanied the simple statement. "I'm sorry."

"Why aren't you married?" he countered.

Her chin lifted. "My husband moved on to greener pastures."

"He must have been stupid—or crazy."

"I'm doing fine on my own. At least I thought I was until I came here."

"I get the feeling he destroyed your faith in the male sex."

"I wouldn't go quite that far." Laura took a bite of ham sandwich and swallowed.

Jake concentrated on his own sandwich for a moment. "Had you met any of the other Ravenwood investors before you came here this weekend?"

"Tim O'Donnell claims he knew me when I was a little girl. I don't remember him."

"And you never met Emma?"

"I don't think so. And I didn't know about her and my father. My mother never talked about the woman who broke up their marriage."

"I believe you."

The simple words meant a lot.

They would have continued with the quick exchange of information, each judging reactions as much as listening to answers, except that the conversation was interrupted by another knock at the door.

"It's Chief Pickett, ma'am."

Laura glanced at Jake. Then, with a hand that wasn't quite steady, she opened the door.

"Laura Roswell, I'm arrestin' you for the murder of Emma Litchfield."

LAURA HEARD A ROARING IN her ears, and the world seemed to contract until all she saw was Pickett's mustache-draped face. She must have heard him wrong. No, he was reading her her rights.

Laura took half a step back and thudded against Jake, who had sprung out of the chair and come up behind her. His arms cradled her shivering body.

"Is this what you do up in Garrett County, railroad innocent bystanders into jail?" Jake bit out.

"In Garrett County, we don't like city slickers comin' up here and tryin' to pull the wool over the eyes of the country bumpkins. We may not be a big-city police department, but we know how to enforce the law."

Pickett's rejoinder was delivered in a level tone. However, they could both hear the dangerous edge in his reply. Antagonizing the man was probably a bad idea.

"Do you mind telling us on what grounds you're arresting Ms. Roswell," Jake asked in a cooler voice.

Pickett stepped into the room. "I don't mind answering a civil question when I'm asked." His voice and manner of speaking became more formal, almost as though he were testifying in court. "Just like the law-enforcement agencies in the big city, out here we look at motive, opportunity, evidence and malice. First, there's Ms. Roswell's cockamamie story about hearing someone shout for help this morning. Three people have rooms closer to the stairs than she did, and no one heard any distress call."

Laura opened her mouth to protest and then closed it again. She couldn't prove she'd heard anything. It was her word against three other people. She was beginning to feel as if she were sinking into quicksand.

"Then there's motive," the police chief continued, giving Laura a direct look. "I got an earful about the bad blood between you and the victim."

"Bad blood! I never met the woman until yesterday."

"Well, she told Sam Pendergrast last week that she was afraid to come up here because of you. He had to persuade her to change her mind."

Laura sucked in a deep breath, as if it were the last one she was going to get before the quicksand swallowed her up. There had to be more. Pickett couldn't arrest her on what he'd just said.

"And finally, we have the knife." He paused for emphasis. "It has Ms. Roswell's fingerprints on the handle—and only Ms. Roswell's."

"That's impossible!"

The exclamation came from Jake. Laura whirled around to face him and their eyes locked. They'd both touched the knife. But she had to think through the implications before she admitted anything about last night. Now she shook her head almost imperceptibly.

"How's that?" Pickett asked. "You got some information you've been holding back, Mr. Wallace?"

Jake swallowed. "I mean, that's impossible because she couldn't have done it."

"Well, she'll have her opportunity to try and prove that in court. But right now, I'm going to book her and take her before Judge Ketchum."

"It's going to be all right," Jake whispered, giving Laura's arms a squeeze. "Do you want me to call someone for you?"

"My friend Josephine O'Malley. She's a private detective in Baltimore." Quickly, she gave Jake Jo's home number.

"They have to let you out on bail. You'll be home tonight or tomorrow morning," he reassured her.

"Yes," Laura answered automatically, wondering if they were both mouthing lies.

If the hours since she'd discovered Emma's body had been a bad dream, the remainder of the day degenerated into the surreal landscape of waking nightmare.

It seemed as if everyone at Ravenwood was in the front hall to see her led away in handcuffs, just as they'd all come running to find her kneeling over the body. Laura pressed her lips together and held her head high as Pickett escorted her past eyes that ranged from curious to accusing.

In the back of the police car, she fought to hold on to self-control the way a naked disaster victim clutches a blanket. It only got worse. She'd been in lockups and courthouses before, but never as a prisoner. When she arrived at the jail, her pocketbook and other personal belongings were taken away. She was booked, photographed, searched and left in a cold, damp holding cell until deputies came to bring her before Judge Warren Ketchum.

Well, this was her chance, she told herself, squaring her shoulders and marching out to the courtroom to meet the judge. She'd find out what bail he'd set and make arrangements to be released so she and Jo could start collecting evidence in her defense.

Her first view of Ketchum was daunting. He was a short, barrel-chested man with iron gray hair and colorless eyes that were magnified by rimless glasses. They inspected her from head to toe before spearing her with a look that ripped a hole in her resolve. Still she went ahead with the formalities.

She hadn't reckoned on the judge's attitude toward what he obviously thought of as a criminal onslaught from the city. Apparently his perspective was remarkably similar to that of Police Chief Pickett.

"We will not tolerate being invaded by outsiders who think they can ride roughshod over the residents of our rural area," he began his justification for setting bail. "This is a law-abiding community, not a prime site for felonies."

A prime site for felonies? Did that mean other serious crimes had been committed by visitors to the county? Or more specifically, visitors to Ravenwood. She'd have to check that out.

But all thought of past indiscretions at Ravenwood fled from her mind when she heard the judge's next words.

"In view of the seriousness of the crime and the uncertainty that the defendant will return to the county for trial, bail is set at one million dollars."

Laura's mouth fell open. A million dollars. It might as well have been the interest on the U.S. national debt for all the chance she had of raising that kind of money.

Chapter Six

Jake Wallace sat cooling his heels outside Hiram Pickett's office the next afternoon. He'd tried to see the man after Laura had been taken away. He'd also tried to see Laura. Both attempts had been no go.

Last night, he'd talked to a number of people in town—including Cully, the gas station attendant, who'd clammed up on Laura. Unfortunately, the old woman named Ida was nowhere to be found. Still, it hadn't been difficult to get the locals talking. Although he knew a great deal more about the history of Ravenwood, he hadn't discovered anything that had any bearing on Laura's immediate problem.

Jake looked at his watch again. One-thirty. He'd been here since eight in the morning and had, thus far, been ignored.

He wasn't a man who went around popping off for no good reason. Except in a few dire circumstances his approach to life had been pretty laid back. In the past few hours he'd become intimately acquainted with the meaning of the phrase "makes your blood boil."

Laura's friend Jo O'Malley hadn't returned any of the messages he'd left on her home or office answering machines—which must mean she was out of town. Either that or she didn't give a damn about what happened to Laura. That, he simply couldn't believe.

Every time he thought about Laura, he remembered the way she'd looked when Pickett had carted her off to jail. Her hands had been cuffed, but she'd held her head up and walked right by the crowd in the hall as if she were on her way to a meeting with a client. You only saw the vulnerability when you realized how tightly she was clutching her arms against her middle. Had she cracked when she'd found out about the bail? He was willing to bet she hadn't given Judge Warren Ketchum the satisfaction.

Getting up, Jake strode back to the secretary's desk again. Over the course of the past few hours, he'd turned his considerable charm on her. She'd responded with a sort of nervous hesitancy. But she hadn't been willing to go out on a limb by ushering him in to see Pickett.

"I'd sure appreciate it if the chief could fit me into his busy schedule," he tried once more.

"I'm sorry." The woman looked both genuinely perplexed and genuinely regretful. "There's no use buzzing him again. He knows you're out here."

Jake paced to the water cooler, filled a paper cup and swallowed the lukewarm liquid as he glanced once more at the police chief's closed door. A half dozen people had bustled in and out—including the doctor who'd done the autopsy last night. He'd stayed the longest. Almost forty-five minutes. Four or five times during the day, Jake had been on the verge of bursting in and demanding that Pickett give him five minutes of his valuable time, but he knew that was the wrong way to handle things if he wanted to help Laura.

Of course, that didn't make it any easier to explain to himself why he was sitting out here prepared to swear to a lie to save a woman he hardly knew. Not when he'd be a heck of a lot better off heading back to Baltimore. She was in a heap of trouble. And either she wasn't rowing with both oars in the water or she was holding information back.

Jake sighed. He'd tried telling himself he was responding to the appalling predicament in which Laura found herself—and to the strange way the Ravenwood conundrum was tied to his own very personal interests. He knew that was simply too easy an explanation.

This time, he'd decided he wasn't going to run out on a woman who needed his help. At least until he saw her past the crisis point.

Almost as if the police chief had heard Jake's thoughts, Pickett finally opened his door and stepped out into the hall. When his eyes lit on Jake, his jaw muscles tightened.

"What can I do for you, Wallace?"

"I have information that might be important in the Laura Roswell case—something that didn't seem relevant until you arrested her."

"Then I guess you'd better come on in."

Jake kept himself from asking why he was finally being given an audience. Instead, he followed the police chief into his office and dropped into the offered seat. Without appearing to make an inspection, he sized up the opposition. Pickett was wearing the same clothes he'd had on yesterday, which probably meant he hadn't gone to bed. What had kept the man so busy? And why was he looking a bit green around the gills? Just lack of sleep? Or was he worried about the trumped up case he'd tried to build against Laura?

"You say you got important information," the police chief prompted. Last night, he'd been annoyingly polite when he'd interviewed the Ravenwood guests. Now, he'd dropped that pose.

Jake pretended a reluctance to begin. "I'd like to talk to you man to man."

The police chief leaned back in his swivel chair. "Go ahead."

"I can provide Ms. Roswell with an alibi. She couldn't have killed Emma Litchfield last night because she was in my bed."

Pickett fixed Jake with a piercing look. "Why'd you hold that piece of information back when I questioned you yesterday? For that matter, why didn't Ms. Roswell say anything?"

"It was a private matter between the two of us. I was protecting her reputation, and she probably thought our being together didn't have any bearing on the investigation."

Pickett snorted. "Actually, Pendergrast saw the two of you smooching—but I didn't think it proved nothin' since he pegged the time at around midnight."

Jake felt his chest tighten as he watched the play of emotions on the police chief's face. Something was going on here. Something. But what?

Finally, the man sighed. "You just came here to brag about a sordid little affair."

"Now wait a minute—"

"And I was hopin' you were going to give me some evidence that would help me hold on to her," he added with remarkable candor.

"I'm not going to sit here and listen to you insult the lady."

"I figure any woman who shows up for a party at Ravenwood ain't no lady."

Jake's hands grabbed the arms of the chair to keep him from lunging across the desk at the man.

Pickett eyed him coolly. "You want to be arrested for assaulting a police officer?"

"No," Jake ground out.

"Good. Because just remember—in this office, I handle things any damn way I please."

For a full minute, the two men stared at each other. Then, apparently satisfied that he'd made his point, Pickett leaned back in his chair again. "As a matter of fact, I'm a big enough man to admit when I'm wrong."

Jake hoped he didn't look as if he were gaping.

"I thought I had an open-and-shut case against Roswell, until I talked to the medical examiner this morning. It looks like Litchfield died hours before she was found in the sitting room."

"Thank God."

"But the real killer, so to speak, is that the victim didn't die from the knife wound in her chest—so it don't matter whose fingerprints are on the weapon.

Jake rose half out of his chair. "What?"

"There was a head wound and other contusions. Doc Lawrence thinks she was pushed down the stairs. That's what he's going to put in his autopsy report."

"So if you'd just waited for the report, you wouldn't have arrested Ms. Roswell in the first place."

Pickett glared at Jake. "Yesterday, I didn't think I had to wait for an autopsy report. This morning, it looks like somebody went to a considerable amount of trouble to frame your girlfriend."

"We finally agree on something."

"Yeah. But it's not just her. That same somebody was out to make a fool of me." Pickett's gritty gaze didn't waver from Jake, as if he were evaluating his candidacy for the position of chief suspect in the sting operation.

"Why are you telling me all this?"

"Not because I want to be your best buddy. I've gotten a bunch of reports on you. You've been poking around all over town, stirrin' things up. I'm saving you the bother of stirrin' up any more old dirt. But let me give you a real heartfelt piece of advice, boy." Pickett leaned over his desk toward Jake. "You and Ms. Roswell run on back to Baltimore—before you get in real trouble."

LAURA GLANCED covertly up at Jake as he led the way to the parking lot. When he'd met her at the lockup entrance, he'd wrapped his muscular arms around her and hugged her to him like a man greeting an airplane-crash survivor.

She'd clung to Jake with equal fervor. But the reaction was pretty natural under the circumstances, she told herself. She'd just been through a hellish ordeal—one that she could hardly believe was over. And his was the first friendly face she'd seen since she'd been arrested.

"I'll drive you back to your car," Jake offered.

"Thanks." Laura swallowed. She still felt completely off balance—with Jake and with herself. It was difficult to believe that she was no longer a murder suspect. Except that after the lecture Pickett had delivered before releasing her, she had the feeling that she'd better not show her face in Garrett County again. The police chief had as much as threatened that he'd find a reason to bring her in if she crossed his path a second time.

"How do you feel?" Jake asked as they stepped out of the shade of the building and into warm sunshine.

"Exhausted. Grubby. Relieved. Confused." The last was added in an almost inaudible whisper. She didn't want to think about her feelings. And she didn't want to talk about details like the metal jail bunk with the springs that had dug into her back or the vile graffiti scratched into the wall or the way she'd felt when the bars had clanked shut behind her. Instead, she folded her arms across her middle, the way she'd done when the police chief had taken her away.

Jake didn't press her for the particulars. Perhaps that was why she volunteered a quiet observation. "I didn't like being led off in handcuffs."

"I would have hated it. But the important thing is that you're free now." Jake bent to unlock the door of his 280Z. The low-slung car was a leftover souvenir from his NFL glory days. Only Jake and his mechanic knew how much he'd had to spend to keep it running smoothly.

"I tried last night and this morning to call your friend, Jo O'Malley. I guess she's out of town."

"Really, I don't know how to thank you. You didn't have to stick around like this."

"I wanted to."

Laura glanced over her shoulder at the police building and then waited until they'd closed the car's doors before saying anything else. "I feel so paranoid. You don't think Pickett had your car bugged, do you?"

Jake shrugged. "Not legally."

"I know *that*. I'm just wondering what lengths the man would go to make a real case against me."

"Against *us*, maybe. Let's get the hell out of here and we'll worry about the details later." The car's engine roared to life. Apparently, Jake thought better of tempting the law by speeding down the main street. He tooled out of town at a sedate twenty-five miles per hour and only stepped on the gas when they reached the open road.

Laura was too preoccupied to notice where they were going and wasn't paying attention when Jake turned off onto a gravel road leading into the mountains. But as he pulled off at an overlook that provided a spectacular view of a gold-and-orange valley below, she came out of her reverie.

"What are we doing?" she asked.

"We have to get our stories straight in case Pickett, or someone else, gets back to us."

Laura raised questioning eyebrows.

Before he went on, he rolled down his window. A pine-scented breeze ruffled his hair and played across Laura's face.

"There's no easy way to say this," Jake began. "I guess Pickett did a number on me this morning. I was so damn focused on giving you an alibi that I didn't pick up the right signals from him. He let me give my story and then told me the coroner's report knocked his case against you into a cocked hat."

Laura hadn't failed to catch the chagrin in his voice. "What exactly *was* your story?"

"I told him we spent the night together."

"But we didn't! I don't spend the night with men I've just met."

"I know."

"Then—"

"It was a calculated risk. I figured I'd only end up an accessory after the fact if Pendergrast opened his door again while you were marching down the hall."

Laura's muttered response was far from ladylike.

"I couldn't turn my back and leave you in jail!"

"Why not?"

"I—I guess I decided I cared about what happened to you."

She sat with her arms drawn in to her sides and her knuckles pressed against her lips.

Jake reached out with one of his hands to cover her shoulder. "Is that so hard to take?"

"Yes."

"Why?"

"Because the only person I want to rely on is me," she answered in as steady a voice as she could manage.

"Sometimes you have to open up to other people. If you don't, you lose an important part of yourself."

Laura rolled down her own window and stared out at the fall splendor, but the valley spread out below them was just a place to focus her eyes. The autumn foliage had lost its appeal some time ago.

"Nothing worth anything is easy," Jake persisted.

Before she could answer, he leaned across the console, took her chin in his hand and turned her face back toward him. Too stunned to move, Laura gazed into his dark eyes. She saw questions there. And also answers.

A little anticipatory shiver zinged through her body. At the last moment, just before his mouth claimed hers, her eyelids fluttered closed.

"Laura, let it happen. Whatever it is."

She wasn't sure if he'd spoken the words or if the advice came from her own head, but she was sure about the kiss. She sensed reassurance. She sensed a challenge. She sensed reined passion as Jake's lips moved over hers.

She didn't want to respond to any of it. Somehow she found herself opening to all of the nuances—to the blend of what he was offering and what he was asking.

Unable to resist the pull, she let her lips part so she could taste him. Then her hands crept up and anchored themselves to his broad shoulders.

As he gathered her closer, her heart began to pound, heat danced over her skin and a sense of rightness unfurled deep in her being.

His lips savored hers. His hands clasped her with tender possessiveness. But he didn't push it any further. Instead, he lifted his head and looked down at her again. This time, there was something warm and confident in his gaze. "I had to know."

"Know what?"

"If last night was only pretend. It wasn't."

"Jake, a kiss doesn't prove anything. Especially not with a woman who feels as if she's about to shatter into a million pieces." She couldn't believe she'd admitted that much.

"I understand."

"No, you don't."

"Better than you know." He swallowed. "I'm scared, too, if you want to know the truth. So I'm not going to push you into anything."

She lifted her eyes and searched his. "You? Scared?"

"When I know you better, maybe I'll explain it to you."

They were both silent for several moments. Part of her wanted to ask what he meant. The part that didn't won.

"There's one more important thing we have to talk about," Jake finally said as he leaned back in his seat again.

"What?"

"The person who murdered Emma. Either he or she intended to frame you, or you were just a convenient scapegoat...." Jake ended the sentence with a little rising inflection, making it more of a question than a statement.

"Why would anyone want to frame me?"

"I don't know."

"Neither do I." Laura tried to swallow and found her mouth was too dry. "Maybe Pickett will figure out what's going on."

"Maybe he needs some help."

"Not from me. At least, not right now. Jake, I just want to go home and stand under a hot shower and scrub off the jailhouse smell."

"I understand."

He reached for the ignition key. "I'll drive you back to Ravenwood so you can get your car."

HE DIDN'T HUG HER GOODBYE. He didn't even tell her he'd be in touch. He didn't have to. She knew he was going to call her soon. But at least she was pretty sure she'd have a few days to marshal her defenses. She was grateful for that because she didn't want to get involved with him, no matter what he thought he was offering right now. She had enough to cope with without the added complication of a man in hot pursuit.

On the way home, Laura turned the radio up loud and listened to rock music. That was better than dwelling on any of her recent experiences.

She had already called Noel Emery from Ravenwood to tell her she was all right. But after she'd dropped her overnight bag in the front hall, she discovered that there were three messages from Jo on her answering machine. They ranged from alarmed to frantic.

"Laura, thank God," Jo answered her office phone on the first ring. "Cam and I were in New York on this spur-of-the-moment trip. A guy named Jake Wallace must have called half a dozen times. He said you were in jail—for murder. Is that true?"

"Not anymore. It's a long story."

"I've got all afternoon."

As briefly and dispassionately as possible, Laura recounted the pertinent details of the weekend.

"Sheez! I've heard about those deals where they give

you a set of free knives for listening to a real-estate pitch. But this!''

Taken by surprise, Laura laughed.

''Are you sure Pickett's not going to come up with something else against you?''

''I hope not.''

''I guess I'd take his advice and stay away from Raven-wood from now on.''

''Exactly what I was thinking,'' Laura agreed. Just the name of the place gave her a sick feeling in the pit of her stomach.

Changing the subject abruptly, Jo said, ''So, what about this Jake Wallace guy? He isn't the one who writes the sports column in the *Morning Sun,* is he?''

''You know him?''

''I read him. He's good in print. Funny. Thoughtful. What's he like in person?''

''He's an ex-football player. Not my type at all.''

''He sounded pretty upset about your being in jail.''

''Umm,'' Laura responded noncommittally.

''I guess I'll debrief you when you're in a better mood.''

''I'm sorry.''

''You've had a pretty rough experience. Why don't you come over for dinner this evening?''

''Jo, I think I'd rather be alone.''

''If that's what you want. But just remember, Cam and I are here if you need anything.''

''Thanks. I know.''

Her shoulders sagging, Laura headed up the stairs to her bedroom. Stripping off the burgundy dress she'd worn since yesterday, she dropped it in a heap on the floor. It had come from an expensive shop at Owings Mills, but she'd never wear it again. Picking up the damaged goods between thumb and forefinger, she dropped the dress into the trash. She suspected that ridding herself of other after-effects of her ordeal wouldn't be as easy.

The assumption that she wasn't going to be allowed to forget the weekend was confirmed a half hour later. As she stood in front of the bathroom mirror vigorously towel drying her hair, the phone rang. It was Andy Stapleton.

"I just wanted to make sure you were all right." Now that she was no longer the chief suspect, he sounded both solicitous and apologetic.

"I'm fine, Mr. Stapleton."

"If there's anything I can do, let me know."

When hell freezes over, Laura thought, but she was too polite to voice the sentiment.

"I'll be getting back to you soon with a revised Ravenwood proposal," he continued.

Laura stared at the phone. Emma Litchfield had been murdered. Laura had been falsely accused. And Andy Stapleton was still trying to put together a land deal. With very little pretense to politeness, she broke off the conversation.

She wasn't hungry, but she made herself eat a little bit of leftover Tarragon Chicken before crawling into bed. There'd been no hope of sleeping last night in her jail cell. Not when a guard had come by for an hourly check. Not when every nerve in her body had been quivering with tension. Now, she found herself burrowing down into the comfort of her own scented sheets. Gratefully, she slipped into slumber almost as soon as her head touched the pillow.

For a few hours, she was at peace, until another dark, disturbing dream grabbed her by the throat and almost choked off her breath.

This time, a terrified voice called to her from the darkness. *Help me. Please help me.*

"Emma? Is that you, Emma."

Julie...Julie...my name is Julie.

"Julie?"

Help me. Please. Help me.

The dream. Laura strained her eyes, focusing on a white-robed figure flickering in the blackness. It was a woman with her arms outstretched, as if urging Laura forward. The scent of wildflowers hovered around her.

In the grip of an overwhelming compulsion, Laura began to walk toward the woman. But all at once the image was gone and she was terribly alone in the cold, dark hall at Ravenwood. Frightened, she turned to run. But there was no escape. The man who had pursued her night after night was behind her again. Behind Laura. Behind Julie. Somehow, Laura had become Julie, too.

Again, she ran. She could hear her pursuer's breath rasping in her ears like the scrape of a metal file against sand. Fear almost choked off her breath. Almost stole the strength from her legs, but somehow, she found the power to keep running. She dared not look over her shoulder. But a horrible truth dripped like acid into her brain.

There wasn't just one man after her. There were two. The one who was going to murder her. And the other, a shadow lurking in the background.

One of them caught her, whirled her to face him and fixed her with the blazing red stare of his terrible eyes. Suddenly, they were in a bedroom. In the next moment, he threw her onto a bed. Then his weight came crashing down on top of her, and she knew she was fighting for her life.

For long moments, terror clogged her throat. Then it found release in a scream that filled the darkness of the bedroom.

Laura sat up in bed, her heart threatening to hammer its

way through her chest. This time she remembered more of the details than she had before.

The murder. Not Emma's murder. *Her* murder. The way she kept dreaming it over and over. No, *Julie's* murder. A woman named Julie. That was the way it had happened. They'd clamped a hand over her mouth so she couldn't scream, couldn't send them away.

Laura pressed her palms against her eyes, trying to rub away the confusion. The first part was so much like what had really happened at Ravenwood Saturday night. She'd heard a voice call to her in the darkness—just like when she'd gone downstairs and found Emma's body. Maybe she'd transferred it to the dream. That was why it seemed so real. But the rest had been just as vivid. The man who had pursued her night after night had grabbed her and thrown her onto a bed. And now there was a shadowy figure behind him.

Snapping on the bedside light, Laura huddled in the pool of illumination, her arms clasped tightly around her knees. Her eyes searched the framed pictures on the marble washstand as if they held the answers to her questions. They told her nothing. She couldn't shake the nightmare's stranglehold. As her conscious mind replayed the dream scene, she felt her scalp prickle as if ghostly fingers were combing through her hair. She shuddered. It was all so palpable. There was even a strange, lingering smell of perfume hovering around her like the cloying scent of flowers at a funeral.

But that wasn't the most disturbing part. It was the room in which the dream murder had taken place. The bedspread was different and so was the wallpaper. But she recognized ornaments on the dresser and the table, the chair in the corner, the distinctive carving of the paneled wall. It was the room in which she'd slept at Ravenwood.

Was the dream a prediction? Was she going back to Ravenwood? Would somebody murder her?

No. The nightmare was about someone else. A woman named Julie who'd been murdered. Laura was sure of that. As sure as she was of her own name.

For a few moments, Laura was absolutely convinced. Then she clenched her fists in denial. The dream wasn't a glimpse into the past. She was so stressed out from what had happened over the weekend that her mind was playing terrible, unhealthy tricks. No wonder she'd glommed on to that room as the scene of a murder. She'd just slept in it.

That was the logical explanation. Except that the dream was so convincing. As if another woman was reaching out across the years and pleading for her help.

Fiction or reality?

No, just more craziness, Laura told herself.

Chapter Seven

Somehow Laura managed to get back to sleep, probably because her body was simply too exhausted for her to sit up all night clutching her knees. She wasn't sure whether the dream came again. At least she didn't remember it, although she awoke with a vague uneasy feeling that seemed to hang around her in a stale cloud like the perfume from the previous installment.

Determined to put the incident behind her, she climbed out of bed and started to unpack the overnight bag she'd left on the floor the night before. In the bottom of the side pocket, she found the fairy cross, which she'd forgotten all about.

Even stashed away out of the sunlight, it still felt a bit warm, as if the little gold vein running through the center were an electric heating coil. Somehow, the minute Laura's fingers closed around the charm, she felt better. More peaceful. Safer. Maybe the old woman was right. Maybe it did have some sort of protective power.

On her way in to the office, Laura stopped to see Sabrina Berkley, the woman who'd opened a shop off the building's lobby. It sold herbs and condiments as well as a charming assortment of whatever had taken Sabrina's fancy. In fact that's what the shop was called: Sabrina's Fancy.

This morning the proprietor had pulled her untamed red hair back and fastened it at the nape of her neck with a gold filigreed barrette. The sleeves of her cowl-neck dress were pushed back to the elbows. Bent over an antique East Indian table, she was grinding some fragrant combination of leaves and seeds with a marble mortar and pestle.

"Wouldn't it be easier to throw that stuff into a food processor?" Laura quipped.

Sabrina looked up in horror, as if Laura had suggested throwing her cat in. "No. The potency of the mixture comes as much from adhering to ancient ways as from the ingredients."

"You sound like a white witch."

A whimsical smile flickered on Sabrina's lips. "Sometimes I wonder—" She switched gears in midsentence. "Did you want some more of that scented soap? Or the May Wind tea?"

"No. I wanted some advice about magic amulets." Laura held out the gold-veined charm.

"A fairy cross."

Laura slid it into Sabrina's hand.

"It's beautiful. I guess you must have been up in Appalachian country."

"How do you know?"

"That's where they come from. People find them in certain rock formations. Did you buy this one at a country shop?"

"It was a present." Laura made the explanation as neutral as possible. "I was told it's a good-luck charm."

"I've heard that. You know, crystals can be in tune with a person's natural harmony. Believers say they benefit everything from your digestion to your love life." Sabrina caught Laura's skeptical look. "But if you don't buy any of that, you can just wear it. This one is perfect for your coloring. I think I've got just the right chain." She got up and began poking through one of the drawers in back of her counter. A few moments later she brought out a beautifully worked length of gold links.

Laura hadn't realized she could make the cross into a piece of jewelry. As soon as she heard the suggestion, it sounded exactly right. In fact, the idea took on a certain urgency. She found she was longing to slip the crystal over her head and feel its weight against her chest. "I'd like that," she murmured.

"Leave it with me, and I'll make you a fastening. You can pick it up this afternoon."

"How much is the chain?"

Sabrina named what sounded like a surprisingly modest price.

"That's all?"

"I've had it for a couple of years. I think it was just waiting for the right person."

Sabrina was like that, Laura mused as she headed for the elevator. When she wanted someone to have a particular thing from her shop, she practically gave it away. They'd engaged in a bit of reverse bargaining over the chain. In the end, Laura extracted a promise that Sabrina would make up the difference by asking for legal advice if she needed it.

Upstairs in her office, Laura tried to concentrate on an upcoming child-support hearing. Finally she gave up the effort and snapped the folder closed. Leaning back in her chair, she closed her eyes.

Yesterday she'd told Jake she wasn't interested in helping Police Chief Pickett. All she'd wanted to do was run from the horror and the fear. Now, the reprieved convict in her desperately wanted to go on with her life as if nothing had happened. But the lawyer couldn't be content to count her blessings. Someone had killed a human being. And that same person had tried to pin the murder on her. She wouldn't be serving herself—or justice—if she didn't see this through.

But there was something else going on, too. Something to do with nightmares. And an old murder. Something frightening because it was so outside of normal experience. Ravenwood had affected her in some strange way that she didn't understand. Maybe the effect had started even before she'd gotten there, although she couldn't begin to understand how. But she was afraid to poke into the twisted pathways of her own psyche.

With a shake of her head, Laura turned her attention back to the more concrete problem. She wasn't a criminal lawyer, but she'd studied the basics. Reaching for a pad of paper and a pencil, she wrote down a list of names and tried to fill in some blanks.

Andy Stapleton. He was hiding something about the ASDC deal. Had Emma found out? Would he have murdered her to keep her quiet?

Sam Pendergrast. Maybe he'd lost Emma to her father and taken an opportunity for revenge?

Ditto for Timothy O'Donnell. Or was he working some kind of scam that Emma had uncovered? Laura didn't know much about him, yet he seemed like the kind of man who might have all sorts of shady deals going.

Martha. What if she'd wanted Rex for herself? What if she'd been jealous all these years? But would she have been strong enough to push Emma down the stairs? Perhaps she was less fragile than she looked.

Finally, reluctantly, Laura came to Jake Wallace. He didn't seem to have a motive. But he was the only one who'd seen the knife. Or was he? Maybe Sam had spotted the box she'd been trying to hide. Maybe one of the other guests had known where it was and had planned to pick it up that weekend. Anyone could have seen her walking down the hall and into the burned part of the house. Which would mean they'd seen Jake, too.

Jake. Now that her mind was on him, it wasn't eager to change subjects. He had lied to Pickett to try and get her off. Surely he wouldn't have done that if he'd wanted to frame her. Laura leaned her elbows on the deck and cupped her chin in her hands. Thinking about Jake brought a whole wealth of feelings that she really didn't want to examine.

Just the facts, ma'am, she told herself sternly as she picked up the phone to call Jo O'Malley.

"You aren't free for lunch by any chance?" she asked her friend.

"Actually, I am."

"I'd like to talk to you some more about what happened at Ravenwood."

"I was hoping you'd open up with me."

Over soup and salad at Phillips Harborplace, Laura went into more detail about the weekend.

"I want to figure out what's going on, but I don't want to go back to Garrett County," she concluded.

"Yeah, Pickett and Ketchum both have a real law-and-order reputation." For a moment, Jo looked a little uncomfortable.

Laura raised inquiring eyes to the detective. Then she nodded slowly. "That's right. I forgot. You're from Garrett County."

"Yeah. So both those guys are part of the context of my life. You know," she mused, "you recognize people in a specific role and it's hard seeing them a different way.

Pickett was the police officer who came to school and gave
the kids safety lectures. And Ketchum—well—most people appreciate his tough approach.''

Laura nodded.

"The trouble is, you're one of my best friends and they
were both pretty rotten to you. Not only that, I feel bad
that I wasn't here for you over the weekend."

"Nobody could anticipate what was going to happen."

Jo ran her fingers up the side of her water glass. "I've
got some slack time this week. Why don't I see what I can
dig up about the land deal. I won't be an outsider poking
into things."

Laura took a slow sip of her tea. For a moment, she
considered telling Jo about the nightmares. Yet how could
nightmares have any bearing on the investigation? "I'd
really appreciate it. But could you also maybe check out
Tim O'Donnell? I'll be glad to pay you for the time."

"Don't be ridiculous," Jo shot back.

"At least let me take care of the expenses." Laura swallowed, feeling foolish but determined to examine one more
possibility. "Uh—do you think you could also find out
where Bill Avery was this weekend?"

"Bill? You don't think he had anything to do with this,
do you?"

Laura shrugged. "I'm not on his list of hundred favorite
people."

"I hope I can put your mind to rest on that one."

"Jo, I don't know how to thank you. Meanwhile, I'll
see what I can find out about Emma and my dad."

Laura spent that evening and the next going through the
things of her mother's that she'd stored in the basement.
She stayed late at the task, deliberately tiring herself out,
hoping she'd sleep at least until dawn. Monday it worked.
But not Tuesday. She woke in a cold sweat, haunted by

dream images, dream warnings, even that distinctive dream fragrance. Instead of staying in bed, she got up and went back to the boxes in the basement.

In one of the cartons she opened, she found a box that had once held Russell Stover Candy. Now it was full of letters that her parents had exchanged when her father had been in Korea.

Her fingers unconsciously played with the fairy cross and the gold chain as she read the correspondence. It was obvious that her parents had loved and missed each other. At first, reading the letters gave her a warm feeling about the two people who had brought her into the world. Then her cynicism kicked in. Her father had been far from home, afraid and lonely. No wonder he'd clung to her mother's letters and written to her with such ardor. But he hadn't loved his wife or his daughter enough for the long haul. That was the way it often went with men and women.

When Laura had finished sifting through the letters and other papers in the basement, she tried staying late at the office, doggedly working until she was almost ready to drop. On Thursday, as she was entering some notes on a child-custody case into her computer, she heard Noel talking animatedly to someone. Laura was tempted to get up and join the conversation. Then the talking stopped and the door closed. Laura returned to her work. After a few minutes, she began to feel uneasy.She knew she was alone in the office, but she didn't feel as if she was really alone.

Finally, it was impossible to ignore the prickling sensations that danced across her skin. Sliding out of her chair, she tiptoed to the door and peeked out.

A large male body was planted in the easy chair by the window. At first, Laura didn't register who it was. Jumping back, she gasped.

"Sorry." Jake rose out of the chair. "I didn't think I

looked quite so threatening. I had a nice chat with your paralegal, Noel. She said it would be all right to wait for you.''

"You're not threatening! I just didn't think Noel would close up shop with someone in the office. Why didn't you let me know you were sitting there?''

He put down the copy of the *New Yorker* he'd been perusing and flexed his left leg. ''Noel said you had some stuff to finish up, so I was giving you a few more minutes.''

Laura's initial reaction gave way to a quick rush of feeling she didn't want to label. How could she admit that she was soaking up his presence the way a wilted flower soaks up water? Jake looked good even in worn jeans, scuffed Adidas and a baggy crew neck sweater. Apparently, they didn't stand on ceremony down at the *Sun* papers, she decided, trying to bring her feelings back into perspective. She wasn't so much reacting to him as a man, she told herself. She was recalling how he'd been the only one who had stood by her after the murder.

''Aren't you going to ask me why I'm here?''

''I expect you have some information about Raven-wood.''

Standing up, he hooked his thumbs through the belt loops of his jeans and rocked back on his heels. ''How do you know?''

''I think you'd make sure you had a good reason for getting in touch with me—so I couldn't accuse you of simply making a social call. What do you have to tell me?''

He laughed. ''You seem to be feeling a good bit better than the last time we saw each other, counselor.''

Actually, she was suddenly feeling better than she had in days. ''Well, I'm back on my own turf. And no one is trying to frame me for a murder I didn't commit." She didn't realize that her fingers had gone to the fairy cross hanging around her neck. As always the familiar warmth was comforting. Somehow the thing had turned into a kind of security blanket. She'd worn it every day since Sabrina had attached it to the gold chain.

Jake's eyes followed her hand. "What's that?"

"Just some new jewelry."

"It's pretty. Have I seen it before?"

"I don't think so."

When he came toward her, she realized she wasn't feeling quite so confident. Had the size of her waiting room shrunk, or was he just displacing too many of the air molecules for her to draw a deep breath?

His gaze rose from the cross to her face. "I do have some things to discuss with you."

"What?"

"I'd rather talk over dinner."

That sounded like a better idea than continuing the dialogue in such cramped quarters. "All right. Do you have someplace in mind?"

"Yes. My apartment."

"Jake—"

"Think about it. Where else can we have a really private conversation?"

Laura tried to remember all the reasons why she should say no. Instead she found herself asking, "Did you cook dinner?"

"I picked up carry-out from the Greek place around the corner. They've got great food."

Laura realized he was holding his breath, waiting for her decision.

"I suppose there's no point in wasting great food."

She saw him expel the captive air.

"Why don't I drive," he suggested. "You can pick up your car later."

"Okay. I was planning to come back here and get a little work done afterward."

"Don't you ever quit?"

"I'm taking time off for dinner and a discussion, aren't I?"

"I guess I'd better not push my luck."

It was only a short drive to Jake's apartment, which was in a former men's clothing factory off Paca Street, one of the older industrial buildings in the city that had been converted to residential use. As they rode up to the sixth floor in the elevator, she wondered what Jake's apartment was like.

"Come on in and make yourself at home while I check on dinner," he said as he turned the key in the lock. "Everything except the salad is in the oven."

Jake disappeared into the kitchen, and Laura looked around. Basically, the apartment was one huge room, with areas defined by various groupings of modern furniture. The effect would have been streamlined, except for the piles of books and papers on almost every surface.

Sports magazines and computer reference manuals were stacked on the square table beside the U-shaped sectional sofa and next to the pine shelves crammed with entertainment components and books. The overflow even extended to the stair risers leading to the loft—which must be where Jake slept, unless the sectional opened into a bed. Given the state of his housekeeping, Laura doubted it. Making his bed in the morning didn't appear to be Jake Wallace's style.

Laura drifted over to the outside wall. The warm red brick was set off by a fan-shaped window that looked out over the city.

Jake came up behind her. "What do you think?"

"I love your view."

"I spent a couple of hours straightening up the place."

"What did it look like before?"

"Don't ask."

He was standing so close behind her that she could feel his breath stirring her hair. The sensation sent a little tingle up the back of her neck. If she wanted to, she knew she could let it build into something more sensual. She deliberately pulled her attention back to business.

"What did you want to discuss?"

"Don't you want to eat first?"

"We can talk while we eat."

"Okay."

Jake had set several aluminum-foil pans on hot pads on the dark walnut table. Laura helped herself to *moussaka* and a couple of *spanakopitta*—flaky triangles filled with cheese and spinach—and some Greek salad.

"You're right. This is excellent," she acknowledged after a few bites.

"I may not be much of a cook, but I know how to order out."

Laura could see that he'd piled his plate with a generous helping of everything. "What did you want to tell me?" she prompted.

"I used some contacts down at the *Sun* to get a line on the original Ravenwood deal."

"There was a government restriction on developing the land. That's why the tract wasn't sold years ago and why the original investors were stuck with a dead turkey," Laura filled in before he could continue.

"How do you know that?"

"I asked a detective friend to check into it. She didn't find out much more than that. Except that Andy Stapleton came in like the Wizard of Oz and got the restriction lifted.''

Jake took a swallow of the inexpensive white wine he'd poured into both their glasses. "The restriction dates back to the early forties. Andy Stapleton wasn't exactly being straight with us when he made his little presentation."

"Maybe whatever he did to get the land status changed was illegal," Laura suggested. "Maybe he paid someone off and Emma found out about it."

"My speculations were running along those lines, too. Andy could have killed her to shut her up—and decided to pin it on you."

"But the knife, the box—"

"He could have planted them. And taken the knife from your room later. I assume he had a key."

"But how did I know where to look for the stuff in the first place?" That was the question Laura had been subconsciously avoiding while she'd pursued other lines of inquiry. Now it had leaped to her lips.

Jake shrugged. "I don't know. Maybe if you tell me some more details about what happened to you that weekend, we can figure it out." He was staring at her chest. "Like, for example, is that the good-luck charm Ida gave you?"

The unexpected shift of subject and the challenging tone of his voice made her jump. "What?"

"Ida. You know, the old lady who was cleaning the rest room at the gas station."

"How—how do you know about her?"

"When I couldn't get Pickett to talk to me after he'd locked you up, I did some nosing around town. Cully, the guy who pumped your gas, told me about it. Said it's called a fairy cross."

"Why didn't you ask about it back in my office when you were admiring it?"

"I was waiting to see if you'd tell me." He reached for her hand across the table.

She snatched it away. "Why?"

"Because ever since we've started talking that first night at Ravenwood, I've had the feeling you were holding something back. I was hoping you'd decided to trust me enough to come clean with me."

Laura pushed her chair away from the table and stood up. Perhaps because she hadn't satisfied her own doubts about her strange midnight walk, she lashed out at Jake. "You think someone told me where to find that box."

His own chair scraped back and he faced her across the table. "I didn't say that. We were talking about the fairy cross, not the box."

"The fairy cross. Right. What else have you been digging up about me?"

A guilty look swept across his broad face like a cold front moving over a TV weather map. "I was checking up on your ex-husband."

Laura had thought of the same thing, yet she didn't like finding out that Jake's mind was working along the same lines and that he'd gone ahead and started poking into her private life.

"Somebody killed Emma and framed you," he continued in answer to her scowl. "I want to find out why."

"It isn't your problem and I don't need your help." Laura started for the door.

Jake caught her and spun her around before she had taken two steps. "I think you do. You're going to start by telling me what has you so frightened that you won't even talk about it. Is somebody blackmailing you? Are you getting threatening letters? What?"

"Blackmail. My God. What do you think I've done?"

He took her by the shoulders. "I don't know what to think. Tell me, dammit!"

The air had solidified in her lungs. It was a surprise to discover that she could speak. "Nightmares, Jake. Just nightmares." Laura's voice rose half an octave. Now that she'd started, it was almost a relief to spit it all out. "The kind that make me wake up screaming. I keep seeing this woman who looks a lot like me. Her name is Julie and she's at Ravenwood. She calls out to me, begging me to help her. She's sleeping in the same room where I was sleeping and a man comes in and attacks her. No. Maybe it's two men. One of them kills her. Then he wraps her body in a tablecloth and dumps her into the ravine. You know, the ravine where Andy warned us not to go."

Laura stopped and sucked in a shuddering breath. She hadn't realized she knew so many coherent details. They'd come tumbling out of her mouth as she'd told the story to Jake.

"Laura. Good God."

"That's it. That's all. My deep dark secret." She swallowed. "I guess you think I'm cracking up."

"No."

She knew he'd answered automatically.

"Laura. I'm sorry. I don't know what to say."

Was he responding to her words or the hurt in her eyes?

"Jake, you don't have to say anything. I don't want to talk about it anymore. I'd just like to go back to my office and go to work now. If you don't want to drive me, I'll get a cab."

"I'll drive you."

They didn't talk on the way to 43 Light Street. When

Jake pulled up at the front door, he turned to her. "I don't like leaving you like this. I don't like leaving *us* like this."

"Jake, just forget about *us*."

Before he could say anything else, she slid out of the car, shut the door and hurried toward the building.

Chapter Eight

Laura strode briskly across the parking lot, pulled open the glass door and walked into the Monday-morning hush of Macy's. It would have been an ideal time for a leisurely shopping expedition, but she hadn't come out to the department store at Owings Mills to buy anything. Yesterday, she'd gotten a surprise call from Martha Swayzee, the busybody who'd had so much to say about everybody at Ravenwood. They were meeting in the coffee shop adjoining the store's gourmet grocery.

The very idea of seeing Martha again had brought back the murder weekend in all its terrible detail. But Martha was an expert at preventing people from hanging up on her. She'd kept Laura on the phone by claiming to have some important information about the Ravenwood events. Laura was pretty sure Martha's real purpose was to pump her for juicy tidbits about her stay in jail. But she hadn't been able to turn down the opportunity to learn something about the estate and the original investors.

After taking the escalator to the upper level, Laura followed the smell of cinnamon to the small café. There were no other patrons except Martha, who sat at one of the round tables sipping a cup of tea and eating a bun. She was just as Laura remembered her. Gray hair, appraising eyes, brittle smile.

Martha gave her a head-to-toe inspection. "You're looking so well after your untimely incarceration, dear."

"Thank you," Laura answered tightly.

"Did that obnoxious sheriff treat you decently?"

"He wasn't a sheriff, and I'd rather put all that behind me, if you don't mind."

"Of course you would."

"If we're just going to talk about my stay in jail, I might as well say goodbye now."

"I was just offering my condolences before I told you a bit about your mother and father."

Maybe this *was* going to be interesting, Laura reminded herself, if she could sort fact from fiction. But she needed some fortification. "Let me get a cup of coffee first."

"And treat yourself to a cinnamon bun. They're so good here."

Laura was pretty sure she couldn't manage to choke down more than the coffee. When she came back to the table, Martha's dry-as-dust hands were delicately pulling apart the oversized bun and popping little pieces into her mouth.

"So what did you want to tell me about my parents?" Laura prompted.

"Your parents and Emmie."

"I already know Emma was the one who took Dad away from Mom."

"That's only the bare outline of the story. It made me feel so disloyal to say anything while Emmie was alive— or Rex, either."

Disloyal? Laura thought as she took a small sip of coffee. *What a joke.* "And now?"

"Emma was a strange woman. Sometimes she was utterly charming, sometimes ruthlessly calculating." Martha paused for effect. "I think she had some kind of hold over Rex. Something she knew he'd done that he didn't want anyone to find out about. She used whatever it was to get her hooks into him."

"How do you know?"

"She had this way of gloating about her conquests—of giving you little hints of a story and letting you speculate about the rest."

Laura wondered how much credulity she could give to the information source, yet she couldn't stop herself from asking the next question. "What did my father do that was so terrible?"

"I don't know, except that I think it was something to do with Ravenwood."

"Ravenwood!" Laura shivered, and Martha smiled smugly at the reaction.

"Maybe you just want to leave the past buried. I only thought you should know that Rex really did love your mother and that he was devastated when she wouldn't take him back. Although I can see her side of the story, too."

Laura stared unseeing at a display of gourmet jelly jars stacked on shelves in back of Martha.

"Sometimes the wrong relationship can be disastrous," the old woman went on. "I noticed that you and that Jake Wallace were getting kind of cozy."

At the mention of Jake, Laura's attention focused back on her companion.

"That man is bad news, dear. Maybe even dangerous."

Laura had just taken a sip of coffee. The hot liquid went down the wrong way and she started to cough.

"Are you all right?" Martha asked solicitously, reaching out to pat Laura vigorously on the back.

"Yes," Laura managed to say. "What do you mean, 'dangerous'?"

"There's talk that he killed his wife."

Laura's shock came out as denial. "I don't believe it!"

Martha shrugged delicately. "I'm afraid I don't know any of the details. But I've heard that she was dragging him down just at the peak of his career and he wanted to get rid of her. At any rate, she's dead."

As she stared at the old woman, Laura felt something inside her twist painfully, like a length of barbed wire unrolling. But she was absolutely determined not to give Martha the satisfaction of letting her strong reaction show. Probably, the woman was also counting on the shock value of her words to cut off further questions. Well, Laura wasn't going to oblige in that respect, either. "I've never put much faith in gossip," she said in a steady voice. "How did Jake's wife die?"

She had the satisfaction of seeing Martha's cheeks redden. "You don't have to get so huffy. I was just trying to help you, dear. I believe Holly Wallace died of an overdose of sleeping pills."

"And you're assuming Jake gave them to her? Why not assume she was depressed?"

"I understand she had inoperable cancer," Martha said carefully.

"Then how is Jake to blame for her death?"

"They do say he was the one who filled the prescription."

"Are you trying to suggest that he went a step farther?" Laura said carefully.

"Nobody knows what actually happened. I just thought you should have the information so you could make an informed decision about him."

"Well, thank you so much for taking the time to get in

touch with me," Laura said coolly as she pushed back her chair.

Martha's expression was uncertain.

"I really do have to be getting back to work," Laura continued as she stood and gathered up her purse.

"We'll have to get together for another chat very soon."

"Mmm."

Laura made a graceful exit. The composed look on her face didn't slip until she was at the door of the coffee shop. But the barbed wire was ripping her insides to shreds.

At the same time, she was mounting a campaign of denial. In court, Martha's testimony would have been slashed to bits. She hadn't come up with a single concrete fact. Just hearsay and speculation.

But cool logic couldn't choke off Laura's pain. Her father being blackmailed? Jake giving his wife an overdose of sleeping pills? Oh, God, poor Jake. What had he been through when his wife was dying? What if she'd begged him to help her escape the torment? What would he have done? Stood by and watched her suffer, or let her persuade him to help her end the ordeal? Laura's chest squeezed painfully as she thought about the horrible choice.

And why had Martha told her about it, she wondered, steering her thoughts back to the old woman. Did Martha want Laura to be afraid of Jake? Morally outraged? Shocked? And why? So she'd stay away from him? That would make sense if Martha was worried that Laura and Jake could find something out about Ravenwood by working together.

Laura almost bumped into a stock boy who'd pushed a cart of fancy canned vegetables across the aisle.

"Are you all right, lady?"

Laura nodded automatically. It took several moments for the cart to be moved out of the way. When she realized her path was no longer blocked, she strode off again, running from her own emotional turmoil as much as from the evil accusations of the old woman back in the coffee shop.

Hardly conscious of where she was going, Laura stepped onto the down escalator. It took her to a different side of the store from the one she'd entered. Momentarily confused, she looked around for the shortest route back to the parking lot. It was over toward the left on the other side of the jewelry and belts. However, as she started into the scarf department, the suggestion of an aroma made her hesitate and then come to a dead stop like a sail boat caught in a sudden calm. Only she was feeling anything but calm as the memory of wildflowers washed over her.

All at once her original intention of leaving was forgotten. As if her feet had developed a will of their own, Laura turned and started moving in the other direction, weaving among displays of gloves and handbags, following the beckoning scent of the flowers. Their fragrance was mixed with other bouquets, yet she was pulled forward by the one haunting scent. Where had she encountered it before?

Her mind had blocked the memory, yet the sweetness of the aroma stood out among the rest like a searchlight on a moonless night. Taken by itself, the fragrance wasn't all that distinctive—sweet and delicate, as much as anything else. Yet it conjured up a whole wealth of lingering associations.

Beauty. Calm. Peace. Mind-numbing fear.

Laura stopped again, her whole body rigid with tension. The dreams. She'd wakened in the middle of the night with this fragrance lingering around her bed like shrouds of mist.

On legs that swayed unsteadily, she wobbled over to

one of the perfume counters and leaned against the glass case for support.

"Can I help you?" a chicly dressed young woman asked.

"What is the name of that perfume I smell?"

"Which one?"

"The wildflowers."

"We have several that fit the description. Rambling Rose, Wild Clematis, Spring Meadow—let's see...and Queen Anne's Lace."

Laura had never heard any of the names before, but one pulled some inner cord. "The Spring Meadow."

"It's an older scent, but it's making a comeback. We have it available as cologne, perfume, body lotion and bath beads."

Laura watched in growing agitation as the woman worked the stopper from a small crystal bottle.

When she reached for Laura's wrist, she jumped back as if the sales lady had pulled out a hot poker to brand her flesh. "No! I don't want that on me," she gasped out.

Although the stopper hadn't touched Laura's skin, the scent from the uncapped bottle enveloped her like a cloud of poison gas. In the next instant, the sights, sounds and smells of the department store seemed to shimmer and fade into a white cloud of swirling snow.

She was cold. Icy. Terrified.

Laura clutched at the edge of the counter. Somehow, she kept herself from slipping to the marble floor.

"Miss, are you all right? Miss?" the clerk asked urgently as she recapped the flask.

It was as if an evil genie had been sucked back into a bottle. The world swam into partial focus, real and yet not real. When Laura blinked and tried to draw in a shaky breath, the essence of Spring Meadow seared her lungs.

"I'm sorry." Laura pressed frigid fingers to a brow that was beaded with icy perspiration. "I guess I'm not feeling too well."

"You must be allergic to the perfume. Sometimes that happens," the sales clerk said, but her voice sounded doubtful as she gave Laura an uncertain look.

"Yes. I guess that must be it." Laura was incapable of explaining further, even to herself.

"Do you want me to call a doctor?"

"Oh, no. Please don't go to any bother. I'm fine, really." Laura wanted to turn and bolt from the store, but it took a few moments before she was sure her legs would function properly. Then she began to edge her way out of the perfume department. Wisps of Spring Meadow followed her, almost like fingers clutching at her flesh, trying to pull her back. The light-headedness didn't dissipate until she had stepped out into the October sunshine again. Gratefully, she dragged in a deep lungful of the cold, crisp, uncontaminated air.

Spring Meadow. She could put a name to the scent from her frightening dreams. Up until now, the fragrance was the only pleasant thing she remembered from her nighttime journeys into terror. It wasn't pleasant any longer. Just a whiff had sent her spinning into the twilight zone like a drug addict having a flashback.

Opening the door of her car, Laura slid behind the wheel and sat with her head thrown back against the seat, fighting the sick terror rising in her throat. She'd always thought of herself as the kind of person whose feet were firmly planted on solid ground. And she'd never put much stock in first-person stories of experiences with the occult or extrasensory perception. Even when she'd blurted out the account of her dreams to Jake, she hadn't given her fear a label. But how else could she explain what was happening to her? It was as if some presence—call it a ghost—was hovering around Ravenwood. Somehow, the ghost was invading her dreams, forcing her thoughts into unfamiliar channels, tearing her life into shreds.

She knew that the idea had been creeping up on her slowly, like a prowler tiptoeing stealthily through the dark corridors of her psyche, waiting for the right moment to spring. Now it had thrown open some previously bolted door and leaped into the bright sunlight of the Owings Mills parking lot.

"No. I won't let it happen. It isn't true."

Laura shook her head vehemently, mentally slamming the door shut. She wasn't going to give in to that analysis. She'd been more upset than she'd realized by her discussion with Martha. She'd been susceptible to suggestion when she'd smelled the perfume. She was perfectly all right now.

Starting her car, she pulled out of her parking space and headed for the exit. She'd already taken too much time away from work this morning.

"Right now, you're not going to worry about Ravenwood or Jake or your father or Martha or ghosts," she told herself as she headed downtown. "You're going to attend to some of the clients who are paying you good money to handle their legal business." But the lecture couldn't stop the censured topics from chasing each other around in her mind like buzzards circling Emma Litchfield's dead body.

As she waited for a light to turn green, Laura tapped her foot lightly but impatiently against the accelerator. Briefs, case summaries and appeals were piling up on her desk. But when the signal changed, she turned left instead of continuing toward 43 Light Street. In a few minutes, she had reached the main branch of the Enoch Pratt Free Library.

The knife she'd found in the box had been buried under a pile of newspaper articles. Although they'd disappeared from her room along with the weapon, they were a matter of public record. She didn't have to figure out who had stolen them to read the news stories. All she had to do was get a duplicate.

Once inside the library, she located a public phone. First, she had to check in with Noel.

"Has anything come up this morning that I need to handle personally?" she asked when her paralegal's upbeat voice answered.

"You're in the clear," Noel said. "Until that custody hearing at two."

"Then I'll be at the library doing some research. Don't expect me back until after I finish at the courthouse."

"Okay. But you'd better leave me the number at the library, just in case something comes up."

Laura complied. After hanging up, she stood looking at the receiver. She'd been trying to deny her feelings, but the need to call Jake was like pressure building up inside so that her skin felt tight all over. Suddenly, it was desperately important to hear his voice and get his side of the story Martha had told her.

"Jake?" she asked eagerly when he answered the phone.

However, it was only a recording saying he'd be back later. Before the beep, she hung up. If she tried to leave a message, he'd know by her voice that she was upset. And there was no way she could go into any kind of explanation with a machine.

But she was feeling depressed and cheated as she headed slowly toward the library's reference section, as if she had to resolve everything this morning before it was too late.

She tried to shake off the melodramatic reaction. There was going to be time for the two of them to talk. Maybe not this minute. But later. This evening or tomorrow. Right now, she was playing hooky from work, and she'd better justify her unexcused absence.

At the reference desk, Laura put in a request for the issue of the *Morning Sun* whose front page she and Jake had discovered in the box. Ten minutes later, she received a roll of microfilm that she took to one of the viewer-printers. After locating the issue, she scanned the front-page articles, trying to fit each one into what she already knew. The Mafia boss who'd been assassinated. Did he have something to do with Ravenwood? What about the mass murderer in Florida? Either of them could have used the remote estate for a hideout if they'd had the right connections to the investor-owner.

Drug addiction. That could be related to the wild parties given at the house.

The state education budget. A connection was unlikely. But had that been the article that triggered Jake's obvious interest?

Finally she reached the story in the series on environmental-health issues. Again, that didn't seem like a hot topic with regard to Ravenwood. The estate wasn't near any factories or sources of pollution as far as she knew.

She also dismissed the articles on capital punishment and the Quebec restaurant bombing.

Laura was disappointed. But she wasn't going to give up. What about the material she and Jake hadn't been able to read? The stories that were burned to a crisp. They probably came from the same time period. Still not sure what she was looking for, Laura kept advancing the reel and scanning the headlines.

Whoever invented microfilm must not have been fazed

by eye strain. Half an hour later, Laura's head was throbbing, and she was having trouble focusing. She'd leave as soon as she finished this section of the paper, she told herself, as she began to turn the wheel faster.

Just before she reached the end of the tape, half-inch-high letters on one of the inside pages stopped her hand in midspin.

WOMAN DIES AT GARRETT COUNTY ESTATE

The partially clad body of a young woman was discovered in the ravine at Ravenwood, a Garrett County estate, yesterday. Identified as Julie Sutton, the woman was a feature reporter for the *Baltimore News American* who had been vacationing in the area. She had been officially missing since the week before when she failed to return to work.

According to the county medical examiner, Miss Sutton, 29, died as the result of a fall, possibly while walking along the ravine.

The body was found by the members of Baltimore Boy Scout Troop 10594 who had taken advantage of several days of good weather to hike in the area.

Ida Licotta, a maid employed at the estate, confirmed that Miss Sutton had been a guest at a party there the weekend before and had disappeared under suspicious circumstances. "I cleaned her room Saturday. I weren't mistaken about which one it was 'cause she had that fancy paneling. When I went in there on Sunday, all her things was gone. But we had a devil of a snowstorm that night, and there weren't no car tracks in the driveway. I couldn't figure how she'd left," Mrs. Licotta said.

Rex Roswell, one of the other weekend guests, remembered that Miss Sutton had gone to bed early Saturday evening and had not appeared for breakfast on Sunday. However, a number of other guests also missed the early meal and he simply assumed they were all sleeping late.

Miss Sutton was described as slender, about five foot four, with blue eyes and wavy blond hair. Local authorities are asking area residents for any information.

Police are also in the process of contacting guests who attended the affair.

In the past few years, the Ravenwood estate has acquired a questionable reputation in the community due to a number of incidents related to boisterous parties. Ravenwood owners have also filed a trespassing complaint against the Boy Scout troop members who found Miss Sutton's body.

Laura's skin seemed to have taken on a coat of ice as she read the article. Gasping for air, she tried to push herself away from the microfilm viewer-printer and found her body was shaking too violently.

All this time she'd been terrified that she was going crazy. Now here was evidence in black-and-white that her dreams had at least some basis in reality. She hadn't read this article before. But it confirmed important details from the horrible nightmares that had been plaguing her sleep for months. A woman named Julie—Julie Sutton—had died at Ravenwood and been found in the ravine. She'd been blond and blue eyed. And she'd stayed in the same room that Laura had occupied on her own visit. Laura was willing to bet the woman hadn't died as the result of an accidental fall.

There was always a man in the dream. A man and another shadowy figure with him. The man had killed Julie and carried her to the ravine. That part was so vivid. But there wasn't a hint about it in the article.

Laura's father, Rex, had been at Ravenwood that weekend. Was he the man she kept dreaming about? The murderer? Or his accomplice, the figure in the background? The very thought made her stomach clench. No. Not her father. Not the man who had written those warm, loving letters. Or had he totally changed? Had Emma somehow coerced him into a terrible immoral role? Laura forced her mind to consider other details. What about Ida? It wasn't all that common a name. Was she the old woman from the gas station? Thinking back to their brief talk, it had sounded as if she'd had firsthand knowledge.

How was it all tied together? Did Emma's murder have anything to do with Julie's?

Julie was a reporter. Had she been digging into a story at Ravenwood? Was that why she'd been at the party? Had the Mafia boss been one of the guests?

With a shudder, Laura's mind went back to the dreams. It was as if Julie had been calling out to her across the years—begging her to set things right. Of course, that didn't make a lot of sense. Unless you believed in ghosts. Unless you believed that Julie's tortured soul was still at Ravenwood—longing for justice, longing to be set free.

Laura printed a copy of the article before returning to the reference desk and requesting microfilm from the next few months. This time, she scanned the headlines, looking for additional articles on Julie.

The follow-up story she found in an issue from about a month later made her draw in a sharp breath, although she'd been half expecting something like it. According to Deputy Chief of Police Hiram Pickett, there were no leads in the case. All the guests at Ravenwood had water-tight alibis, and no one else had ventured onto the premises because of the storm. The deputy police chief had come to the conclusion that the death was an accident. There had been a considerable amount of alcohol in Julie's bloodstream. Maybe she'd simply wandered out into the storm and lost her way and no one had missed her until it was too late. With the goings on at the estate, he wouldn't be surprised.

So, their buddy Pickett had been the investigating officer. Was he covering up a murder? Or had someone pulled the wool over his eyes? Who? Laura's father? One of the other guests? Maybe Martha had been at that party, too. Maybe even Emma.

Laura made several more trips to the reference desk. Next, she requested microfilm from the *Baltimore News American,* from six months before the fatal party. The paper had gone out of business in the late seventies, but the back issues were still on file.

She found a whole slew of material written by Julie Sutton, all from the feature section. Stories about summer fun at Ocean City, Babe Ruth's house, the art show at Druid Hill Park. It didn't look as if Julie had been an investigative reporter. The only thing that seemed remotely pertinent was a piece about vacation property in Garrett County. Maybe she'd been at Ravenwood doing a follow-up on that. Or maybe she'd just been there having a good time with people she'd met on her previous trip and had stumbled into something dangerous.

Deep into the investigation now, Laura would have stayed at the library all day doing more research, except for her custody hearing at two. She left with printed copies of both *Sun* articles and a stack of material Julie had written.

To her relief, the custody hearing went well. Because

the husband had been abusive, Laura and her client walked out with sole custody of the woman's daughters and a restraining order against harassment by the father. When her client gave Laura a grateful hug, she felt guilty. Her full attention hadn't been on the proceedings. Luckily, she'd already prepared the groundwork weeks ago.

Back in her office, she inspected the mountain of work that needed her attention. But instead of tackling it, she started in again on the Ravenwood material. First, she read some of the articles by Julie Sutton. They were well researched and often funny and charming. The woman had talent. What a shame she had never been allowed to develop to her full potential. It was hard to tear herself away from Julie's writing, but Laura finally acknowledged that the articles weren't going to shine any light on the Ravenwood murders. She was going to have to take a more direct approach.

At five-thirty, Noel stuck her head in the door.

"Do you need me for anything else?"

"No. And you should have left already. I'll see you in the morning."

"You're sure?"

"You've put in a full day. Go on home before I chase you out. I'm just fooling around with personal stuff."

She couldn't ask for a more loyal assistant than Noel, Laura mused as she turned on her computer and modem. She started by querying data bases, requesting correlations between key words in the *Sun* articles she'd found and Ravenwood or Garrett County. A half hour later, the system had provided bibliographic references to a dozen articles. She looked over the summaries and requested the full text of four. Only one was downloaded, the rest would be sent by fax.

The lone article was about a company named Fairbolt

sponsoring an educational program on ecology in the Garrett County schools. Laura scanned the story but couldn't see anything significant tying it into Ravenwood.

While she was waiting for the service to send her the faxes of the off-line articles, Laura realized she hadn't eaten anything since breakfast. Her first thought was to pick up some dinner at the deli next door, until she remembered that it closed at two. She'd have to walk down to one of the food stands at Harborplace.

It was light when she left her office, and a number of suites in her hallway were still occupied. When she returned half an hour later with her hard-shell crab sandwich, the marble lobby was dark and quiet, with only one brass-shaded lamp providing any illumination. The other bulbs must be burned out. Or maybe the cost-conscious owners were cutting corners again. Shadows and silence had never bothered Laura until the past few weeks—until the nightmares had started. Unable to stop herself, she turned and pressed her shoulders against the wall while she waited for the elevator to wheeze down from one of the top floors. She just hoped nobody came out and saw her cowering there like a fool or a criminal.

The hard marble was cold but reassuring against her back. Just to fill the silence, she began to hum "You've Got a Friend" under her breath.

It was such a long wait that she almost decided to take her sandwich home and forget about finishing up the on-line search until the morning. But that would mean leaving her computer on overnight. And also that she wouldn't have any additional material to study until tomorrow morning. Instead, she hummed all the way up in the elevator and all the way down the hall to her office.

Unlocking the door, Laura stepped into the waiting

room, the key still dangling from her fingers. "You've Got a Friend" died on her lips.

Something wasn't right.

She'd been nervous all the way up here. Now she remembered the way she'd reacted last week when Jake had been sitting in the chair by the window and she'd been at her computer. Somehow she'd known she wasn't alone. She felt the same way now. Only this time, she was in the waiting room and someone was hiding in her office. Again, the hair on the back of her neck stirred.

No, she was letting her imagination play nasty tricks. Everything was just the way she'd left it. The desk light and the computer were on; the door was slightly ajar.

Still, she couldn't shake the fear that she wasn't alone. "Jake?" she called, feeling irrational even as she said his name. Had she been sending him extrasensory messages. Had he somehow known how much she wanted to talk to him and come over after work? But how would he have gotten in? And would he want to talk to her after the way she'd left things between them.

Laura reached for the light switch beside the door. Illumination flooded the waiting room, making her instantly more secure. However, in the next moment as she blinked in the light, she caught a blur of motion at the office door.

Gasping, she took a step back. It was too late. A hand thrust through the door. A hand holding a gun.

Laura saw the flash from the muzzle and heard the report reverberate in the small room. A millisecond later, she was knocked backward. Pain exploded in her chest. Doubling over, she sagged to the floor.

Chapter Nine

The story of another death was spread across the bottom of Tuesday *Evening Sun*'s "Maryland" section front page. It was accompanied by a photograph.

LOCAL ATTORNEY KILLED
IN ARMED ROBBERY

A Baltimore attorney, was killed yesterday during a robbery attempt at her office. Laura Roswell, 31, who specialized in women's and children's issues, was working late and apparently surprised an armed intruder when she came back to her office with a carry-out dinner. She was shot once in the chest.

Dr. Kathryn Martin, a tenant in the building at 43 Light Street where Ms. Roswell maintained her law practice, discovered the body in the morning on the way to her own office. Noticing that the door to the third-floor suite was ajar, she stopped to investigate and discovered Ms. Roswell sprawled on the floor.

Building superintendent Lou Rossini speculated that the attacker came in during normal business hours and waited to burglarize one of the offices.

In a bizarre twist, Ms. Roswell herself had been

arrested recently in connection with the murder of a houseguest at a Garrett County mansion. Charges were later dropped. Police are investigating to determine if the two incidents are related. According to Detective Evan Hamill, there are no suspects in the robbery-murder.

Other tenants at 43 Light Street expressed shock when they learned of Ms. Roswell's death. "Laura was a wonderful person," said private detective Jo O'Malley. "I don't know who would want to do this to her. She was well liked by everyone in the building." Noel Emery, Ms. Roswell's assistant, expressed similar views. "She was a great person to work for. I keep thinking that if I hadn't let her talk me into going home while she was still working, maybe she'd be alive now."

HEART PUMPING against his ribs like a steam piston, Jake tried to hold the newspaper steady. His hands were shaking too much. With a curse he spread the front page across his computer keyboard. Last night at the Caps game, he'd had to stop himself from finding a pay phone and calling Laura. The conviction that she'd needed him had been so strong.

He'd still been thinking about her the whole time he'd been getting dressed and driving to the office. And now—

Fighting the sick feeling churning in his stomach, Jake scanned the first paragraph again, hoping against hope that his mind was playing terrible tricks, hoping it was all a mistake. But nothing had changed. The harsh black newsprint that swam before his eyes said the same thing.

Laura was dead. Laura Roswell. Not some other attorney with the same name. The woman he'd pulled into his arms that night at Ravenwood thinking they were participating in an Oscar-winning performance. Then he'd found out how wrong he was. And the kiss had only been the beginning.

Now there was an ending. She'd been shot in the office where he'd waited for her last week. His mind still couldn't make any sense of it.

Eyes closed, Jake fought to draw oxygen into his lungs. But his chest felt as if a three-hundred-pound linebacker were stomping on him—with cleated shoes.

Laura. No, not Laura.

He'd been taken by surprise when she'd told him about the nightmares. It had been the last thing he'd expected her to say, and his response hadn't exactly been supportive. But once he'd started thinking about the whole thing, it had fit.

Like the way she'd kept going back to the burned-out part of the house. Or the way she'd looked as if she was in a trance when he'd followed her that night. And then there was her reaction afterward. Her fear. Her reluctance to tell him what she thought was happening. Finally, the pressure of what she'd been going through had been too much and she'd finally spilled it all out. But he hadn't been any help. He'd only acted as if she was a nut case.

Jake leaned his elbows on the desk top and cupped his forehead in his hands, unable to hold back the tears that brimmed in his eyes and began to spill down his face. He could picture Laura lying on the office floor—cold and pale—because he was intimately acquainted with death.

It was still too much to absorb. He needed to hear what had happened—more than just the impersonal newspaper account. Scrabbling through the pieces of paper in his wallet, he found Jo O'Malley's number. She was the friend Laura had asked him to call before Pickett had marched her away, and was quoted in the article. With quick, jabbing motions, he punched her number.

"Jo O'Malley speaking."

"This is Jake Wallace.

"Yes, Jake." Her voice was soft. "I was wondering if you'd call. I'm sorry I was out of town when you tried to reach me from Garrett County."

"Yeah, well, Laura wanted me to get in touch with you when she was in jail. A lot of good that does her now."

"Jake, I know you're shocked. This is pretty bad for me, too. For everybody down at 43 Light Street."

"Do you know any more than they're sayin' in the papers?"

"Not really." She cleared her throat. "Laura told me about meeting you at Ravenwood."

"She talked about me?"

"Yes."

"What did she say?"

"She liked you, Jake. But—she'd been hurt by Bill, her ex-husband. And she was afraid to trust her feelings."

He swallowed around the baseball-sized lump in his throat. "I know."

"I'm sorry the two of you didn't have a chance to work things out," she added.

"Do you think we could have?"

"Yes. I think you were good for her."

It was cold comfort, but he clutched it to his breast. "I—Jo—thanks."

"I'll call you when we know about the funeral."

"I'd appreciate that."

He hung up quickly before his voice got any thicker. Then he sat hunched in his chair with his eyes squeezed shut and his fists clenched against his chin.

A messenger came into the tiny cubicle, left a stack of

photo copies Jake had ordered from the library last night and backed away. Jake didn't acknowledge the intrusion.

"Laura, I'm sorry," he whispered when he was alone again.

He'd failed her. Just the way he'd failed Holly. No, this was different. Holly's haunted gaze had followed him around the room until he could hardly bear to make eye contact. Laura had been in one hell of a mess. But she hadn't asked for anything until the last time he'd seen her. And then he'd blown it. He'd let her down. The way her father had. And her husband.

Now he felt a strange mixture of self-disgust and grief. It had almost happened again. He'd almost let himself care too much. Only this time, fate had stepped in a little more quickly. But somehow, that didn't make it hurt any less.

"I'M SORRY, JAKE," LAURA murmured as she stared unseeing out the bedroom window at Kathryn Martin's Ellicott City garden. She'd gone to sleep thinking about Jake, and he'd been the first thing on her mind when she woke up. She knew how much this charade would hurt him. But the police hadn't given her any other choice.

Everyone who'd been at Ravenwood during the investors' weekend was a murder suspect—and not just in the Emma Litchfield case. Now they were conducting the Laura Roswell attempted-murder investigation, as well.

With tentative fingers, Laura touched the center of her chest. It still felt as though she'd been sandblasted. The only reason she wasn't in the hospital for observation after her close brush with death was that Dr. Martin had volunteered to keep an eye on her.

"Laura, are you awake?" The low-voiced question was followed by a light knock at the door.

It was five in the afternoon. Laura hadn't gotten to bed

until eight that morning because there'd been so many details to take care of once she'd realized that playing dead was the best way to stay alive.

"Come on in."

A couple of years older than Laura, with sparkling blue eyes and wavy brown hair, Katie was subletting Abby Franklin's office while the psychologist was on a six-month tour of India with her husband. Now she stepped into the bedroom carrying a tray with a cup of coffee and an English muffin. She also had a stethoscope hanging around her neck and a medical bag tucked under her arm. They were a bit incongruous with her faded jeans and plaid flannel shirt.

"How's our patient doing?"

"You didn't have to bring me breakfast—dinner—whatever it is—in bed."

"You're supposed to be taking it easy. And while I'm here, let me listen to your heart and lungs again." The physician made quick work of the examination and then changed Laura's bandages. "You're doing fine."

"And damn lucky to be alive." Once more Laura gingerly moved her fingers against her chest, still half expecting to find a hole gushing blood. The police were amazed that the crystal cross she'd worn around her neck had stopped the bullet. So was Laura. Was it possible the talisman had supernatural powers? What else could explain it? She had debated whether to share her speculations with the police, then decided to keep her mouth shut and let them simply think she'd been lucky. Maybe she had. Her worst complaint was that brittle shards of crystal had shredded the fabric of her blouse and left needle-sharp slivers in her flesh. None of the wounds was too deep, so Katie had simply removed the fragments and bandaged the wounds.

But that was just the beginning of an incredible twenty-two hours.

Katie hadn't discovered Laura in the morning as the newspaper article had reported. That was part of the fabrication they'd worked out. Lou Rossini, the building's superintendent—who'd been making his evening rounds—had heard the shot and rushed into the office to investigate. He'd known Katie was still upstairs working and had called her when he'd found Laura sprawled on the floor.

Things had really gotten interesting when the police arrived twenty minutes later. The detective who had walked in the door was Evan Hamill, the same man who'd helped the task force when Jo O'Malley had been abducted by a psychopathic killer the year before. Laura, Lou and the black detective had gotten to know each other during the search for Jo.

"Can you identify the man who shot you?" Hamill had asked.

"I'm afraid I only saw an arm and hand with a gun and then his legs when I was lying on the floor."

"Did he take anything?"

Laura began to open file and desk drawers. "I don't think so. No—wait. The newspaper articles I got from the library this afternoon are gone." She pressed some buttons on her keyboard. "And the computer queries I was making are wiped out."

"What's important about the articles and the computer stuff?" Hamill demanded.

Swallowing her reluctance, Laura told him and Katie about Ravenwood, Emma's death and the murder charge against her. She also speculated about the Julie Sutton connection. "But why didn't they leave the newspaper articles?" she asked the detective. "As soon as I saw they were missing, I started thinking that the break-in must be connected."

"You weren't going to see they were missing. You were going to be dead," the detective replied evenly. "And no one else would have known you had the material."

The unimpeachable logic made Laura's scalp crawl.

"Maybe when you beat the murder rap up in Garrett County, whoever killed Emma decided to follow you to Baltimore and finish the job. Too bad he can't go on thinkin' he did."

"But why can't he?" Laura asked in a quiet voice. "The guy shot me from ten feet away and didn't stay around to take my pulse. As far as he's concerned, I'm history."

Hamill pursed his lips. "If he doesn't find out otherwise, that would sure be the safest thing for you."

"But wouldn't he check the TV and newspaper to make certain he really put you away?" Katie asked.

"Yeah. He'd have to be certain it was true, all right. And I'm not sure the department would go along with pulling a fast one like that. They're not exactly *Miami Vice*," Hamill added. Yet there was a gleam in his eye that told Laura his agile mind had begun to turn over the idea.

"I was just thinking out loud," Laura interjected before they all got too carried away. "Actually, I'm not sure I could go for it, either. What happens to my clients if they think I'm dead?"

"What happens to them if the guy who shot you comes back to finish the job?" Katie asked.

"You've got a point."

"Let's talk about it," Hamill suggested.

As they hashed over the idea, studying the pros and cons and enumerating what needed to be done, the impossible scheme began to look as if it could work. With the help of the police department and Jo O'Malley, and with the okay of the District Attorney's Office, Operation Opossum went into effect.

Now sitting in Katie's bedroom, Laura clasped her hands together and pressed them against her lips.

It wasn't just Jake who'd be hurt by her deception. She'd gotten so involved in some of her clients' lives. Now she felt conscience-stricken about running out on them, even after Jo had promised to arrange for another attorney to take over the most pressing cases.

Laura might have been worried about her clients, but her mind kept coming back to Jake. What if her premonition at the library had been right? If she hadn't been wearing the fairy cross, there never would have been a second chance to talk to Jake. But what if there never was going to be a second chance? What if he felt so hurt and betrayed once the truth could be told that he could never trust her again? Guilt and loss gnawed at her. She drove the hurt away the only way she could—with another question. Had Jake really been honest with her?

"You look pale. Do you want to go back to sleep?" Katie asked.

"No, I want to get up and get dressed."

"If you take it real easy."

Laura climbed out of bed and stood holding on to her friend for a moment.

"How do you feel?"

"A little shaky. But a shower would feel great."

"Make it a bath. And don't get your chest wet."

"Okay," Laura agreed.

"Leave the door ajar—in case you need help."

Laura sat down on the edge of the tub while she opened the taps. As far as Hamill was concerned, the plan was for her to stay in hiding at Katie's while the police tracked down the killer. She hadn't told anyone that staying in seclusion was impossible. She was involved in this mess the way no one else was. At first she'd been afraid that her dreams were a symptom of mental illness, but the newspaper articles about Julie Sutton had changed everything.

Perhaps the police would dig something up. But they didn't have the advantage—or maybe it was a curse—that she'd been given.

Every time she put the theory into words, it still sounded like the ravings of a lunatic. Julie Sutton's spirit—or ghost or whatever it was—had reached out to her across the years and provided her with special information. She didn't understand why she'd been picked. Maybe it had something to do with looking like Julie. Or maybe it was because of her father. What if she were being called upon to atone for his past mistakes?

She could wait for another one of the dreams she dreaded. Or she could go back to Ravenwood where the vibrations—or whatever they were—were strongest. While she was there, she'd do some exploring. She didn't consciously admit that somewhere along the line, the need to return to the Garrett County estate had turned into a compulsion that she couldn't fight.

The next morning, when Katie went out to get some groceries, Laura put on the disguise Jo had provided in case she had to go down to police headquarters and wrote Katie a note explaining she'd gone to Ravenwood and would call that evening. She also apologized for taking Katie's car, even though the physician had another.

As Laura drove toward western Maryland, she slipped a finger under the edge of her brunette wig and scratched her temple. The damn thing itched. Or maybe the problem was having to jam it down on top of her pinned up blond hair.

Glancing in the rearview mirror, she was amazed at the transformation in her appearance. It was weird how big a difference could be made by darkening eyebrows and using different makeup. Of course, Katie's jeans and flannel shirt didn't hurt. They were the right size, but they definitely weren't Laura's normal style or color. And neither were the huge sunglasses she'd purchased at the drug store. She'd wear them if she got out of the car.

Her altered appearance gave Laura some sense of security, although she certainly didn't plan on buying any gas from Cully. Still, she'd have to be crazy not to be anxious about what she was doing. The chief of police had as much as promised he'd arrest her if he saw her in the area.

Laura was suddenly unable to hold back a wild little laugh. There was one gigantic factor that kept slipping her mind because it was such a bizarre concept. No one would be looking for her. No one would be expecting her at Ravenwood or anywhere else in Garrett County. No one would be giving a thought to Laura Roswell because she was supposed to be dead. There were newspaper articles and TV reports to prove it.

Still, the closer she got to her destination, the tighter her hands gripped the wheel. Dead or not, she hadn't lost her reflexes.

It was early in the afternoon when Laura turned in at the Ravenwood gateposts. This time, she was grateful for the underbrush pressing in on either side of the rutted drive because she knew it would hide her car. Instead of following the winding tract all the way to the house, she turned onto an almost invisible side road she hadn't even noticed on her first visit. It was about an eighth of a mile away from the house, but somehow, it seemed prudent to walk the rest of the way. Climbing out of the car, she reached for the knapsack that she'd brought along and hoisted it over one shoulder.

At the edge of the woods, Laura stood still and regarded the looming mansion. It was just what she remembered, a gigantic fortress of gray stone. Except that now it looked abandoned. There were no lights in the windows and no cars in the parking area. Over the past two weeks, dry leaves had blown across the front lawn and drifted against the foundations. Nothing moved but the wind, gently stirring the leaves and swaying the branches of the trees. Up here, the wind was cold, and Laura was glad she'd borrowed Katie's woodsman jacket.

For several minutes, Laura cowered in the shadows of the oaks and maples, eyes and ears straining as she focused on the house. She knew she was marshaling her courage to approach it. Maybe no Garrett County residents were on the property. But Julie Sutton was in there somewhere. Not her body. Her restless spirit.

The sun was hidden behind a cloud as Laura made her way toward the mansion. Pulling up the collar of the borrowed coat, she hunched her shoulders against the wind and shoved her hands into her pockets.

As she walked across the parking area, her sneaker-clad feet crunching on the fallen leaves, she wondered how she was going to get into the house. She'd brought a screwdriver, a rope and a hammer in her pack, but she wasn't sure what she was going to do with them. She might have been accused of murder, but she had never been on the wrong side of a breaking-and-entering charge.

Deciding on a less invasive option, she tried the front door. It was locked. But the window next to it was unlatched. It yielded when she gave the sash a hard upward push.

Until now, she still hadn't broken any laws, except maybe trespassing—like those Boy Scouts in the ravine. As she hoisted herself up and climbed through the window, she was conscious of taking a step into unknown territory.

When Laura's feet hit the floor, her first thought was that it felt good to get in out of the wind and chill. Her second was that it was eerie to be in this place where she told herself she'd never return. She wanted to flip on a light to dispel the shadows lurking in the corners, but that wouldn't be a good idea. Instead, she pulled out the flashlight she'd stuck in her backpack and trained it on the stairs.

On the drive up, she'd planned her course of action. Eventually, she'd have to explore the burned-out portion of the house. But she also needed to search the room in which she'd slept. Someone had taken the box from the night table and then awakened her when everyone else was asleep. Either the intruder had had a key or there was some way to get into the room besides the door. At the very least, she needed to see if there was a ledge outside the window. And she also wanted to look for evidence. Maybe the intruder had left something behind.

An almost palpable silence followed her up the stairs and down the long hall. As she tiptoed down the corridor, she couldn't shake the conviction that she was being watched, even though all the doors were closed.

"Julie?" she whispered, feeling a little frisson of fear skitter up her spine. It was one thing to acknowledge the existence of a Ravenwood ghost when you were in the parking lot of Owings Mills Mall. It was quite another to contemplate the prospect from this close a vantage point.

A patch of light knifed across the hall in front of her.

It was coming from her room, she realized. The only one to which the door stood ajar. Why?

As she tiptoed up to it, Laura could feel her heart start to gallop. Inching the door open, she peered inside. To her profound relief, the room was empty. Yet the tension didn't lessen.

"Julie?" she questioned again. There was still no response.

The bed had been stripped, and the mattress was covered with clear plastic, but the knickknacks she remembered were still on the tables and the shelf along the paneled wall.

First she checked the window. It was at the back of the house and three stories above the ground with no balconies or ledges. No one had climbed up there unless he'd had an extension ladder.

Next she searched the closet. There were no telltale pieces of physical evidence. And the walls seemed to be solid. Laura was disappointed. She'd been so sure she would find something.

"Now what, Julie?" she whispered.

You haven't finished with the room. The answer echoed in her head. But it could just as well have come from her own mind as from the supernatural. Once you started expecting ghostly communications, you were more likely to receive them, Laura thought wryly.

Still, it was startling to turn back to the bedroom and find that the light had changed completely, as though someone had flipped the switch. But the illumination wasn't coming from inside. The sun was no longer blocked by a cloud, and warm rays streamed through the window, shining directly on the paneled wall.

The illumination brought out the rich color of the wood and highlighted the carved design—particularly a row of circular flowers about five feet from the floor. The center of each one was deeply indented—but two right in the middle caught the light in a different way from the others. With an odd, shivery feeling, Laura crossed the room and poked one of the dissimilar flowers with her finger. When the finger went right through the wall, she gasped and pulled her hand back.

A mixture of trepidation and excitement churning in her chest, Laura began to tap lightly on the paneling. It was solid, except for a three-foot section in the middle. Just the right size for a hidden door. In fact, now that she knew what to look for, she could see the seam. But how did it open? And did it lead to secret storage or a secret passage?

Laura had read about this sort of thing in books on old houses. Hidden passages had a number of purposes. Sometimes, the owner of the property had wanted to spy on his guests. Sometimes, he'd been preparing for midnight assignations—or to make a quick getaway from the law. Sometimes he'd simply been eccentric.

Laura began to run her fingers along the wall, checking for pressure points or concealed latches that might spring the mechanism open. Finally, when her fingers hit one of the flowers on the left side of the wall, it slid up, revealing a circle with a button in the center. It looked like an old-fashioned buzzer.

For a moment Laura hesitated. Maybe this thing was a booby trap and the light fixture or something worse would come crashing down on her head. Or maybe it was an alarm. With her teeth clenched, she pressed the button. For a moment, she thought that nothing had happened. There was no sound of wheels moving or gears grinding. As if the tracks had been oiled that morning, the panel slid to the side and she was staring into a dark, musty tunnel wreathed with spider webs.

She'd found a secret passage, all right. And in the room where she'd slept. But where was the other end of the tunnel, she wondered as she peered inside. It looked about as inviting as the burned part of the house, but she was going to have to investigate.

She had just taken a tentative step inside when she stopped dead in her tracks. The house had been blanketed in brooding silence. Now she could hear something.

Footsteps. Coming toward her from the lightless, gaping hole into which she'd stepped.

Heavy footsteps. Unmistakably moving in her direction. Around a bend, she saw the beam of a flashlight.

Laura ducked back into the room, knocking off her wig as it brushed the opening. She didn't even notice as she jabbed at the button that controlled the panel. It didn't respond. Could she outrun whoever was about to turn the corner? Probably not. And he had a big advantage. In a moment, he'd be able to spot her standing there in the room, and she wouldn't be able to see him in the dark passage.

Jumping to the side, she looked wildly around for a weapon and grabbed for the statue of Cupid and Psyche. It wasn't much, but it was all she had.

Laura's blood roared in her ears. Her whole body tensed. Then a large man ducked his head to step through the opening, and she brought the statue down in a sweeping arc.

Chapter Ten

Laura gasped as a man in a navy windbreaker and faded jeans crumpled to the bedroom floor. It was Jake.

"Jake! Oh, my God, Jake." The heavy ornament she'd used as a club slipped from her fingers and smashed against the floorboards, landing beside the wig. She didn't spare either one a glance. Dropping to her knees beside Jake, she gently felt for the place where she'd hit him on the head. There was a lump, but the skin wasn't broken. At the last moment, when she'd recognized who he was, she'd pulled back on her swing, striking him with less force than she'd originally intended. Still, the blow had been hard enough to knock him unconscious.

Cradling his head in her lap, she smoothed her fingers across his brow. His eyes were still closed, but his breath accelerated in response to her touch.

"Don't—don't go. Don't leave me." His voice was slurred but urgent.

"Jake. I'm here. It's all right. I'm sorry."

He didn't seem to be paying attention because he kept muttering over her words of reassurance. "Need you."

Jake's cheek moved against her lap, and he groaned in pain. As one of his large hands flailed up to touch the back of his head, it hit her in the ribs. She grabbed his hand and knit her fingers with his, trying to keep him still.

"I'm right here."

"Holly. Oh, God, Holly. Don't..."

"Jake, please. It's Laura. I'm sorry. I didn't know it was you."

"Laura's dead, too." His lids were squeezed shut now as if he were fighting his return to reality.

"No, I'm not."

All at once, Jake was staring up at her like a diver coming up from the dark depths of a turbulent ocean. As if he didn't trust his own senses, he extended a shaky arm and lightly touched his fingers to her face. They began to move over her eyebrows and cheeks. When they reached her mouth, Laura pressed a tiny kiss to his fingertips.

"It's me," she whispered.

"Lord God almighty. You really are alive!" As he uttered the exclamation, he was dragging her down to the floor, wrapping his corded arms around her and clasping her body against his as though he thought she would vanish if he let her go. His lips moved over her face, just as his fingers had done earlier. Laura clung to him with the same intensity, until she felt him begin to shake.

"You'd better take it easy."

"I'm okay."

But he wasn't. Holding himself very still, he closed his eyes again. Sweat had broken out on his brow, and Laura knew he was fighting against shock—both physical and mental.

Half sprawled on top of his large body, she stroked her cheek against his. "Please forgive me, Jake."

It was several moments before he answered. "My God, Laura, what happened?"

"I hit you with the statue. I'm so sorry. I didn't know it was you coming up the tunnel."

"I mean, what happened to you? The paper—the story said you'd been shot by a burglar. It was on the news, too."

"Someone was hiding in my office and tried to kill me. We decided it would be safer for me if he thought he'd succeeded."

Jake pulled them to a sitting position. The effort left him breathing raggedly. Leaning his head carefully against the wall, he stared at Laura. "You should have told me. I saw that story and just about went crazy. Does your friend Jo think you're dead, too? Or is she one hell of an actress?"

"She knows."

"But you couldn't tell me." His hand had been gripping her shoulder. Now it dropped to his side.

"Jake, Detective Hamill said the fewer people who knew, the better." The excuse stuck in her throat.

"You mean after I lied to Pickett because I thought it would get you out of jail, you still didn't trust me?"

"Trust you! My father did a whole bunch of things that made me trust *him*. And what did it get me?" The words exploded from her lips. "He told me I was his best girl. He took me out to the park or a museum or a movie every Saturday. He used to read me stories at night in bed to help me fall asleep. Then one day while I was at school, he packed up his clothes and left. He didn't even say good-bye to me." Realizing how much she'd just revealed about her own insecurities, Laura stopped short. At the moment, she couldn't face Jake. Standing up, she walked toward the knapsack lying on the floor. "I brought aspirin. Do you want some?" she asked with her face slightly averted.

"Yeah. That would be good."

"I—uh—hope I didn't give you a concussion."

"Every football player knows the symptoms. I'll tell you if I start seeing double."

Laura fished out the small first-aid kid she'd brought, handed over two tablets and went to get a glass of water from the bathroom. Letting the cold water run, she looked back to where Jake was slumped against the wall. He was sitting quietly, and his eyes were closed. She thought of how he'd hugged and kissed her so fiercely when he'd first found out she wasn't dead.

It was so hard to say anything personal now—after her little outburst about her father. But she had to give him something to try and make up for her gigantic lie of omission.

Kneeling, she handed him the glass of water and the analgesic, watching his Adam's apple bob as he swallowed.

"I guess I was afraid to trust you," she said in a low voice. "I trust you now."

He nodded tightly and she knew he was still smarting. Not just from the bump on his head. For several moments, he seemed to be brooding.

Then he sat up straighter. "So, if you're supposed to be running a scam on the guy who shot you, what the hell are you doing here instead of laying low and letting the police handle things?"

"That's what I was supposed to do. But I couldn't, not when the answer's in this house."

"To Julie Sutton's murder?"

Her mouth dropped open.

"I guess we've been doubling up on our research again. When I haven't been scraping through my assignments, I've been buried in the morgue at the *Sun*. It didn't take a genius to find out what happened at Ravenwood twenty years ago.''

''And I've been haunting the library.'' She stopped abruptly. ''Jake—''

Maybe it was the tone of her voice that made his eyes lock with hers. ''What?''

''Remember when we found the box with the articles. Something on that front page upset you. But you wouldn't talk about it. Will you tell me now?''

He ran shaky fingers through his hair, encountered the bump on the back of his head and winced. ''It was the story on environmental toxins.''

''What does that have to do with Ravenwood?''

The lines around his mouth tightened. When he spoke, his voice was raw. ''I don't know. But I'd been thinkin' for a long time that it had something to do with Holly's death.''

''Your wife?''

He swallowed painfully. ''It's not easy for me to talk about this. For a year, I couldn't deal with it at all.''

Laura knelt beside him and slipped her arm around him, silently lending him her support. For long moments, he leaned against her. ''Holly was only twenty-eight when she died,'' he finally said. ''She had a kind of cancer that has a very low statistical occurrence in women her age. But in Danville, Ohio, where she was raised, there's been a hell of a lot of cases. Like her cousin, for example. And two other women on her street. Pretty suspicious, don't you think?''

Laura turned so she could press her cheek against his shoulder. His arms came up to stroke across her back as if he needed the contact.

''Are you talking about something like Love Canal?'' she asked.

"Not that blatant, unless the EPA is keeping it under wraps. I had to dig like a mole to get anything at all. But I've found out that the army had a secret chemical-weapons plant outside of her town during World War II. I've been trying to find out what they were producing and if anyone's done any environmental toxicity studies. I'm going to write a book about it. An exposé. At least then maybe her death will mean something."

Laura nodded. "Jake, I'm so sorry about Holly."

"Yeah, it's tough when someone you love gets ground up in the gears of government bureaucracy."

Her arms went around him, cradling his large body as best she could. He seemed to be drawing strength from her, and the knowledge made her heart swell. Yet his next words made her realize that he still didn't want to share all of the pain that he'd sealed inside himself.

"Too bad I couldn't give you a lead on the Ravenwood problem."

The easy thing would be to let him withdraw. She was past being able to take the easy way. "Martha asked me to meet her for breakfast yesterday. She acted like she wanted to be helpful."

"I get the feeling Martha enjoys stirring up trouble. Do you put much stock in what she says?"

"I don't know. After she got through with my father and Emma, she warned me to stay away from you." Laura felt his body tense.

"What does she have on me?"

"She told me you killed your wife."

Jake swore. "Funny how nasty rumors make the rounds."

"Tell me what happened."

He swallowed convulsively. "It's not a very nice story."

Her own tension matched his. "I want to hear it."

His voice was harsh and self-accusing. "Okay. The big football-star husband had enough pull to get his wife in at the top clinics in the country. But there was nothing the specialists could do for her. Laura, she was in a lot of pain, and we both knew it was only going to get worse. At home, she had a bottle of sleeping pills in the drawer beside her bed. I could have hidden them. I didn't. And I let her talk me into going down to Annapolis for the Army-Navy Game because I needed to get away from the pressure of watching her suffer." He stopped and gulped in air. "I didn't know that she told her nurse not to come in that weekend because I was going to be home. When I got back Sunday night, it was all over."

Imagining all those heartbreaking months and then the terrible ending, Laura ached for him. No wonder his emotions were still raw. Her marriage had ended in disillusionment. His had ended in tragedy. And she knew that what he'd suffered had been far worse than her own loss. She turned and wrapped her arms around him again, feeling his body shake as the memories assaulted him.

"You didn't know what she was going to do. It sounds as if she thought it out pretty well."

"Yeah. Sometimes I can convince myself it was better the way it happened. Other times I can't live with the knowledge that I wasn't there when she needed me. Or that she died alone, with no one to hold her."

"Jake, her illness—her death—they were both terrible things to have to cope with. You did the best you could."

"I wish I could be sure of that."

Laura continued to hold him, continued to offer comfort with the gentle stroking of her hands across his back and shoulders. "You wouldn't feel so guilty if you didn't have a strong sense of morality. That's getting rarer and rarer these days.''

''A lot of good that does me.''

''It counts for a lot with me.''

Jake raised his head and his eyes searched her. ''Why?''

''In my practice, I meet too many men who leave wives and children destitute and don't have a milligram of remorse.''

''The way your husband left you?''

''Sort of.'' Laura broke the eye contact. Even after what he'd told her, it was still so hard to talk about herself. ''Except that I wasn't destitute. I had an established law practice and no one else to support....'' She stopped short. She was so used to letting people see only what she wanted them to see that it had become an automatic response. She wasn't going to do that to Jake now. But how could she tell him that when Bill had left, it had made her question herself as a woman? How could she talk about the way she'd lain awake at night wondering what deficiencies of hers had sent her husband into the arms of someone else? She'd told herself she didn't need another man. Perhaps the truth was that she was afraid to take the risk again.

''Maybe I drove Bill away,'' she said in a barely audible voice.

''Maybe he was an insensitive clod.''

She laughed. ''I've heard that from some of my clients, too.'' Thinking about her practice made a shadow cross her face.

''What?''

''You aren't the only one who thinks I'm dead. There are women who need my help, and I can't give it to them until we get to the bottom of all this.''

''Then let's get on with it.'' Jake pushed himself up and

stood with his back against the wall, breathing in deep lungfuls of air.

"What do you think you're doing?"

"I'm going to go exploring—like I planned when I came up here."

"You can't—you've got a lump on your head."

"I've had worse and carried a ball for a forty-yard touchdown. Come on."

"Wait. We don't want anyone to know we were in the house. See if you can make the secret panel close. The button's right here." She showed him the mechanism hidden in the carved design.

While he fiddled with the wall, Laura began gathering the pieces of the broken statue into a pile. Mixed with the debris was a small metal disk slashed with a lightning-bolt symbol. Apparently, it had been embedded in the bottom of the ornament, because there was a corresponding indentation in the broken ceramic.

"Got it. The mechanism must have been stuck."

Laura glanced up to see that the wall had silently slid closed again. Jake was staring at the metal disk in her hand, his brow furrowed.

"Where did you get that?"

"It was in the base of the statue—like a nameplate. Only it's just got this symbol."

"I've seen—" He stopped and shook his head.

"You've seen it before?"

He shrugged and rubbed the back of his head. "Can't remember. Maybe it will come to me."

Laura wrapped up the pieces of the statue in a T-shirt she'd brought along and stuffed them into her knapsack along with Katie's jacket and the wig.

When she finished, she found that Jake was looking at

her expectantly. "Where to?" Reaching out, he helped her to her feet.

"I'm not sure."

He didn't let go of her hand. "That first night we were here, you sniffed out that box under the floorboards like a bird dog makin' a beeline for a pheasant."

Laura nodded. "I think I was in some kind of trance. I went to sleep, and the next thing I remember, we were in that room. I don't recall getting out of bed or walking down the hall." She watched Jake, trying to sense his reaction to the admission.

"I want to try and understand what happened."

"At least you've got an open mind."

"I did some reading on ghosts and extrasensory perception. Stuff like that. You took me by surprise when you sprang that dream stuff on me. I didn't know what to think at first."

Laura smiled at him shyly, touched that he'd taken the trouble. "I guess I took myself by surprise. I'm a very logical, down-to-earth person. Having my sleep invaded by something I didn't understand was disturbing. I didn't want to talk about it with anyone—and then it just sort of came out when you started asking me questions." She laughed. "And it sounded just as bizarre as I thought it would."

Jake's grip tightened on her hand. "You're not crazy."

"That means a lot coming from a man I assaulted with a deadly weapon."

He grinned. "So now that we've gotten that out of the way, have you picked up any strange vibrations since you've been back in the house?"

"The whole place makes me feel strange."

"Yeah."

"I keep turning around expecting to see someone looking over my shoulder. And before you came up the tunnel, I had this fantasy that Julie was trying to tell me something. But I'm pretty sure it was just my overactive imagination.''

''So you don't have any, uh, extrasensory idea where we ought to look?''

''I don't know. Give me a minute,'' Laura answered slowly. She closed her eyes, hoping some special inspiration would waft into her brain. It didn't. ''Maybe there's nothing else left to find at Ravenwood,'' she mused. ''Except, if that's true, why are the dreams still getting worse? Why did I feel compelled to come back?''

''Maybe the ghost can only speak to you at night or when you're asleep. Do you ever remember it happening while you were awake?''

''No.'' Laura wrapped her arms around her shoulders. ''I didn't think of that. But I'm not sure I'm up to spending the night here.''

''Who would be, after what's happened? I guess I'd feel like I was in the middle of a haunted house story. The kind kids tell to spook each other around the campfire.''

Laura laughed uneasily. They both glanced toward the window. There were still a few hours of daylight left, but not many.

''Okay, if you don't have any better ideas, let's go back to the part of the house where you found the box,'' Jake suggested.

''Sounds logical. You first.''

It wasn't the need to have Jake run interference that made Laura ask him to go first. As they made their way out of the room and down the hall, she watched him carefully. He seemed to be steady on his feet, but he wasn't moving anywhere near fast enough to run for a forty-yard touchdown.

This time the door to the unused wing of the house was locked, and they had to pause while Jake pulled a set of compact tools out of one of the pockets in his windbreaker.

"You came equipped to burgle the place," Laura accused.

"I just came prepared—for whatever I was going to find."

"Did you bring a gun?" she asked, half jokingly.

Jake reached into the waistband at the side of his slacks and brought out a snub-nosed .32.

Laura stared at the weapon, which had been hidden by his windbreaker.

"My dad started taking me to the practice range when I was ten. I know how to use a gun. I know gun safety. And I assume that whoever thought he'd killed you shot first and didn't stick around to ask questions. I also assume it's not a ghost."

"Yes," Laura agreed on a breathy sigh.

"Do you know how to use this thing?"

"My husband dragged me to a firing range a couple of times—when he was on a home-safety kick."

"Home safety! Do you know how many home-safety nuts end up shooting members of their own family by mistake?"

"I'm not sure I could shoot anything besides a paper target."

"I hope you don't have to."

Laura swallowed. Jake worked on the lock. After a few moments, it clicked. The familiar musty, charred odor assaulted them as he opened the door. They both switched on their flashlights and trained the twin beams down the hall.

"Stay close to me," Jake warned.

"Don't worry. I'm glad I'm not trying this alone."

He reached back to squeeze her arm. "Me, too."

They moved cautiously down the hall, listening to the creak of the old wooden boards. When they reached the room in which Laura had found the box, Jake hesitated. "I'm not sure I'd advise going in there again. The floor wasn't too stable. Let's see what's in the next room."

"Okay."

Jake took several more steps. Laura hung back and glanced nervously over her shoulder. The same strange feeling that had hovered around her earlier had started to coalesce in the dank atmosphere of the passage. All at once, it was hard to breathe and hard to put one foot in front of the other.

"Jake, wait!"

"What's wrong?"

"I'm not sure."

In the next second, they both found out. With a sickening groan, the burned boards under Jake's feet gave way, and he plunged through the floor.

Chapter Eleven

It seemed to happen in slow motion. Laura watched in horror as first Jake's legs, then his hips and finally his chest disappeared into the chasm that had opened in the hallway. Debris rained on the ground below. Sooty dust rose in a fine black cloud, choking Laura and obscuring her vision.

"Jake. Oh, Lord, Jake."

A millennium passed before the surface stopped creaking and splintering.

"Jake?"

"It's okay." He coughed several times. "I'm still hangin' in."

The observation was literally true. To her relief, Laura could see the upper part of his body a few yards in front of her. He looked like a man hanging through a hole in the ice of a frozen pond. Only the margin of the opening was black and charred.

"Thank God," she breathed. Now they just had to get him back on solid ground. Instinctively, she started to move forward.

"No. Stay back," he choked out. "The damn floor's not stable."

Before he finished issuing the warning, the surface was tipping like the deck of a ship caught in an ocean storm.

Laura shrieked as she found herself rolling downhill toward the hole. If she crashed into Jake, they were both going to go through.

She bent and twisted her body, desperately trying to stop her forward motion. Then her shoulder brushed the door of the room Jake had just passed, and she grabbed for the frame. For a terrifying moment, her fingers slipped. Finally, they held. Panting, Laura clung to the swaying door. When her body had stopped shaking, she gritted her teeth and began to pull herself slowly back to safety.

"The whole thing's likely to go," Jake warned. "You get the hell out of here."

"I will not."

They were both breathing hard. And Laura's chest, where it had scraped along the floor, felt as if it had been dragged across the Sahara.

Feeling helpless, she watched as Jake tried to heave himself up. His face turned red with the effort, but he didn't move more than a few inches. "I can't get enough leverage."

The floor creaked and shifted again from his efforts. Was he right? Was the whole hallway going to collapse, Laura wondered. Then she remembered the rope she'd stuffed into her pack.

Jake's grim expression brightened when he saw her pull the coiled hemp from her knapsack.

Casting around for an anchor, Laura gave a tug on the doorknob. It seemed solid.

After securing one end of the lifeline to the knob, she tossed the other end toward Jake. It wasn't quite long enough. Her exclamation of dismay would have been right at home in a marine barracks.

"It's okay," Jake said in a voice that hovered between

reassurance and frustration. ''We just need to make it longer.''

Laura looked frantically around for something she could use. There was nothing suitable—except the clothes on her back. Unbuttoning the flannel shirt, Laura slipped out of the garment. She was shivering in the cold, damp air as she tied one sleeve to the end of the rope and tested the knot. It was only after she'd tossed the lengthened rope back to Jake that she realized how she must appear conducting a rescue operation in her bra—with bandages across her chest.

Jake shot her a turbulent look but didn't waste any breath on a comment. Wrapping his powerful hands around the fabric of the shirt, he began to pull himself out of the hole. As Laura's gaze fixed on the place where the shirt and rope were connected, she prayed the knot would hold. Grabbing her end of the rope, she began to tug. He was heavy, and the strain of pulling made her shoulders ache.

''Come on, Jake. You can do it.''

He grunted and speeded up his hand-over-hand progress. When a section of the hallway under him gave way, she gasped. He had slipped back several inches. She tugged harder.

Precious seconds stretched into minutes, but finally, he was flopping onto the relatively solid section of the floor where she'd made her stand.

''Move,'' he barked. They could both feel the boards vibrating ominously under them.

Laura snagged her knapsack and scrambled back toward the door through which they'd entered. Jake followed.

Not until they had reached the corridor in the renovated section of the house did they sink to the floor, both breathing heavily.

"Are you okay?" Jake asked.

"Yes."

He peered at her critically. "You look like you've been through a black-and-white snowstorm."

"What do you think you look like, Wallace?"

"Damn glad to be on solid ground. Damn glad you are, too."

"Jake, I was so scared. I thought you were going to get killed."

When he pulled her into his arms, she clung. His broad hands swept across her bare back and shoulders, rubbing the goose bumps from her chilled skin, warming her from the inside as well as the outside.

When she tipped her face up, he pinned her with a fierce, dark look that stole the breath from her lungs.

"That was too blasted close."

No, this is. She was too close to him, too sensitive to what he'd suffered, too glad that he was safe and sound and in her arms.

She stopped trying to make sense of her emotions when his mouth came down hard against hers. The kiss was hot and possessive, the kiss of a man telling a woman exactly where things stood between them.

The woman responded. Opening to him, welcoming him.

He sensed the answer to his unspoken question. His lips were no less greedy as they slanted over hers. But they were gentle now, seductive instead of insistent.

She made a low sound in her throat as her body shifted, fitting itself more intimately to his.

He murmured her name as his hands lifted her hair and kneaded the muscles of her shoulders. His lips trained kisses down her neck. When he reached the bandage on her chest, he stopped. "God almighty—what am I thinkin' about? You're hurt. Are you all right?"

Laura's eyes snapped back into focus. Her mind followed several seconds later, and she nodded. "The bullet shattered the fairy cross. It saved my life, but there were a few pieces of crystal in my skin."

"And you've been running around like a deck hand on the *Titanic.*"

"You haven't been doing too badly yourself."

He pulled Laura to her feet. "We have to get out of here. I don't suppose you have another shirt in your bag of tricks."

"My friend's jacket." She extracted it from the knapsack and was stuffing her arms into the sleeves when there was a loud crash behind them.

Jake took her hand and tugged her toward the door. "Let's go."

"I guess the whole wing of the house must have been weakened by the fire," she said as she followed him down the hall.

"Not just the fire. While I was hanging in that hole, I had an up-close-and-personal look at the floor. It didn't break at random. Parts were cut."

"Cut?"

"As in booby-trapped. You know like the chandelier cord."

"My God, Jake you've been right all along."

"And whoever set the trap may be on his way here to see what he's caught."

Bypassing the front of the house, they climbed out the back window through which Jake had entered. As they made their way along the edge of the woods, Laura could see that Jake's teeth were clenched and that he was limping.

"You hurt your leg when you fell."

"I've got a bum knee from my football days. I gave it a good whack when I went through the floor."

Laura slowed her pace.

"We gotta put some distance between us and that house. I'll be okay."

The reassurance didn't match the expression on his face as they hurried away from the house.

"Where's your car?" Laura asked.

"At the tourist cabins about three miles down the highway. I hiked up through the woods."

"Lucky I didn't think of anything so tricky. My friend's Chrysler is just down the drive, hidden on a side road. Let's hope it makes out better than her shirt."

Before getting into the car, Laura tried to brush some of the soot and plaster off her pants and out of her hair. Then she slid behind the wheel. Jake climbed in the passenger door. Moving the bucket seat back as far as it would go, he leaned against the head rest and winced as he stretched out his leg.

"What's the name of the place we're going?" she asked as she cautiously backed up to the main drive.

"Slumbering Pines."

Nosing the car down the drive as fast as she dared, Laura gripped the wheel with white knuckles, half-expecting to round a curve and come face-to-face with another car roaring toward her. The most persistent image she had was of a police cruiser driven by her good friend Hiram Pickett. But she and Jake seemed to be alone on the Ravenwood property.

When they came to the highway, she let out the uneasy breath she'd been holding.

"Turn left," Jake directed, wearily settling back into the seat. "Look for a dented green sign with gold lettering."

If he'd glanced behind them, he might have seen a car pull out of the side road just beyond Ravenwood and trail them down the highway at a discreet distance. Unfortunately, Laura wasn't thinking about being followed, either. She was still too off balance from their narrow escape.

When she slowed to pull in at the tourist court, Jake leaned forward and pointed toward the left.

"My cabin's up that way. It's got two double beds— and a shower."

Laura contemplated her options. She couldn't exactly walk into the office and register, and it was safer being with Jake if someone came after them, anyway. On the other hand, there was nothing about his kiss that had made her feel safe. But there was another factor she had to consider. She'd thumped him pretty hard over the head. Even if he was too macho to admit he needed watching, he probably shouldn't be alone.

"Which one?"

"Number 11. It's around back and up the hill."

Instead of Jake's 280Z, a beige Ford Tempo was parked in front.

"Where's your car?"

"I rented something that wouldn't stick out up here."

After pulling up beside the Ford, Laura reached into the back seat and grabbed her overnight bag.

The sun was disappearing behind the mountains, streaking the sky with soft orange and pink as Jake unlocked the door. The light helped soften the cabin's rather stark effect.

It was nothing fancy. The promised two beds both had metal frames. The pine dresser was scarred with rings from a legion of cold soda bottles. And the upholstery on the one chair had faded to bilious yellow.

Jake noted her reaction. "I was lookin' for close, not fancy."

"I'm not complaining. Just give me first dibs on the shower." Laura shouldered her bag, disappeared into the bathroom and locked the door.

She hadn't taken anything but a cautious bath since the shooting. And Katie had told her not to get the bandages wet. Stripping them off, she gave her wounds a critical inspection in the mirror. They seemed to be healing all right. Maybe she could just skip the dressing.

Ten minutes under a hot, needle-sharp spray restored her sense of well-being. Until she heard Jake pacing around the bedroom on the other side of the locked door. After dressing quickly, she slipped back into the bedroom and busied herself with towel drying her hair while Jake took his shower.

He emerged wearing a clean pair of jeans and a dark-green-and-white rugby pullover that made him look as buttoned up as a preacher. Except that few preachers had the physical presence of six-foot-two, two-hundred-pound Jake Wallace. Few were as ruggedly masculine. And none of them made her pulse start to pound with a mere look. Laura wiped her damp palms on the legs of her jeans as she eyed him uncertainly.

Since she'd hit him over the head with the statue, they'd been coping with one crisis after another. Now, they were in the eye of the storm, and the undisturbed tranquility wasn't having a soothing effect.

Laura expelled a tattered wisp of air from her lungs. Alone in a tourist cabin, she and Jake were perfectly capable of creating their own tension. Sexual tension. And something else, as well. A new intimacy. A new awareness of each other.

Trying to find neutral territory for her gaze, Laura found herself focusing on Jake's shirt. In response, he brushed a nonexistent speck of lint off the cuff.

So Jake was nervous, too. That was a totally new phenomenon.

"I—uh—brought some food so I wouldn't have to go out for dinner. We could have an indoor picnic."

"Yes. Right. I am hungry."

They'd found a safe subject for the moment. Safer than talking about the way they were feeling. "It's just sandwiches and beer." He swung a cooler out of the closet and hoisted it onto one of the beds. Sitting down, he began to take out several wrapped packages. "Roast beef on whole wheat, turkey and ham on rye, bologna on white."

"This is dinner for one?" she teased.

"And maybe breakfast."

"You eat cold-cut sandwiches for breakfast?" Laura inquired.

"When there isn't any leftover pizza."

"Maybe there's a muffin shop in town."

There were several moments of silence. Apparently, they had run out of scintillating conversation. Jake unwrapped one of the sandwiches and began to eat. When Laura realized she was watching him again, she quickly reached for her own dinner. But as she eyed the sandwich in her hand, she licked her suddenly dry lips. There was no hope of washing down bread and roast beef without a drink.

"I guess I'll get myself a Coke."

"Planning on makin' an appearance as the second ghost in the area?"

Laura didn't miss a beat when she answered. "I brought a disguise." She retrieved her dark wig from the knapsack, shoved her hair underneath and turned back to Jake.

"What do you think?"

"I think blondes have more fun."

"I didn't come up here for fun."

"Too bad," Jake commented as he tried to move his leg into a more comfortable position.

Laura didn't miss the grimace on his features. "Will an ice pack help?"

"For my head or my leg?"

She smiled. "Your choice."

"I'm willing to give it a try."

"I'll be back in a few minutes." Making a quick exit, Laura closed the door. As she drew in a deep lungful of the cold mountain air, she tried to reach for some inner reserve of composure. She'd gotten to know Jake pretty well by now. Nothing was going to happen between them tonight that she didn't invite. The problem was, now that they were alone together, she wasn't sure what she wanted. Not with all her insecurities about men and women churning in her chest. Not when she was so conscious that the first step toward intimacy could be the first step toward disaster.

When she saw the telephone next to the Coke machine, she remembered Katie.

Fishing out more change, she called Ellicott City.

The phone was answered on the first ring.

"Sorry I forgot about you," Laura apologized.

"Forgot!"

"I've been kind of busy. And I, uh, lost one of your shirts." Laura sketched an account of her adventures.

"Don't worry about the shirt. Are you sure you're going to be all right?" the physician asked.

"I'm with Jake."

"Well, that answers the question."

"I'll be at your place late tomorrow. Or I'll call again."

Before coming back to the cabin, Laura also filled a bucket with ice. When she returned, Jake was sitting on one of the beds, propped against the headboard. But his body was far from relaxed, and the sandwich in his hand was barely eaten.

"I was just getting ready to send out a search party."

"I forgot I'd promised my friend Katie I'd call."

As Laura finished the sentence, she tugged off the itchy wig. Turning toward the mirror, she began to run her fingers through her hair and fluff out the curls. The absence of motion on the bed behind her drew her attention. Jake had put down the sandwich and was watching her. His eyes had changed from brown to ebony. The way they followed the motions of her hands made her stomach flutter. She hadn't intended to be provocative. Now, her hands dropped away from her hair.

She scooped some of the ice into a plastic bag and wrapped the bag in a towel.

"Which will it be your knee or your head?"

He laughed. "My head's not too bad. I can never be sure about the knee."

"This should cool you off." The observation was barely audible, but she was pretty sure he'd heard. He closed his eyes for a moment as she adjusted the makeshift ice pack.

"How's that?"

"It feels good."

Laura took in the smouldering look in Jake's eyes and the husky tone of his voice and knew she had to put some distance between them. She picked up her soda and settled herself on the other bed.

"I was thinking about the implications of what happened this afternoon."

"Oh yeah?"

"I mean, the floor was probably cut by whoever stole the box from my room," she clarified. "Saturday night, he must have come in through the tunnel behind the panel. Where does it lead?"

"There's a door behind the drapes in the sitting room—where the body was found."

"I'll bet that as soon as I left my room to run to Emma's rescue, whoever was on the other side of the wall stepped through and exited that way. Then he could have woken everyone up with a shout in the hall and come downstairs with the rest of the crowd."

"That's probably the way it happened. I wish I could remember whose voice woke me up. But I vote for Andy. He's the one who tried to seat Emma under the chandelier."

"That's just circumstantial evidence."

"You don't have to be a stickler for legal technicalities."

As she finished the sentence, Jake had put his finger to his lips. He had turned to stare at the closed curtains. Laura followed his gaze, eyes and ears straining. She couldn't see anything through the curtains. But after a moment, she picked up a faint crunch of gravel outside. Someone or something was right on the other side of the window trying to be quiet. She was willing to bet it wasn't a mountain lion.

"It's been a long day," Jake said loudly. Easing off the bed, he walked around the cabin, turning off lamps until the room was illuminated only by a shaft of light from the bathroom.

Laura watched him reach into his overnight bag. When he took out the gun, she sucked in a sharp breath. Flipping off the safety, he laid the weapon on the bed beside her. "Sit tight," he whispered.

She was afraid to answer as he glided toward the door. In the next moment, he threw it open and disappeared into the night. Laura sat perfectly still on the bed, her pulse pounding, her eyes flicking from the gun to the door.

There were no shouts, no verbal challenges in the darkness. But the gravel outside the window seemed to boil up as if it had been hit by a tornado. Then the sounds of two sets of running feet tore off across the parking lot and faded into the distance.

Laura hardly dared to breathe as she waited in the darkened room. Jake should have taken the gun. But he had left it to protect her.

It was only a few minutes later when one set of footsteps returned. Laura's heart skipped a beat, but she reached out a surprisingly steady hand toward the pistol. Her fingers had closed around the cold metal of the grip when she heard the hobbling step.

"Jake?"

"I couldn't keep up with the sonofagun."

"Your knee…"

He responded with a string of curses. "I'm a pretty sorry bodyguard."

Matter-of-factly, she set the weapon on the bedside table and slid the safety into place. Then she crossed the space between the two beds, picked up the ice pack and put it back on Jake's leg. "I didn't hire a bodyguard. I came up here with some half-baked idea of communicating with the ghost and spying around Ravenwood, and I'm pretty sure I would have gotten into a lot more trouble without you."

"Yeah, well, you would have had better luck chasing that guy than I did."

"But what would I have done when I caught up with him?"

Jake couldn't stifle a wry laugh. "There's that."

"Who was it?"

"Couldn't tell in the dark. He had a wool cap pulled down low and some kind of funny-looking goggles that hid the rest of his face. And he's got great reflexes. He ran like the devil was after him as soon as he saw me hit the door.'' Jake sighed and began to smack his fist against his palm. ''I made a bad judgment call on that one. I thought I could move fast enough to tackle whoever was out there listenin'. I didn't think it was going to turn into a hundred-yard dash.''

''Didn't your knee hurt when you got up?''

''I've learned to ignore pain when I have to.''

The bleak statement made her chin lift. She suspected he wanted to look away. Her gaze didn't give him permission. ''You did the best you could under the circumstances.''

''Sometimes that's not good enough, is it?''

Laura understood the hidden meaning in that remark. ''Don't. Jake, you did the best you could for Holly.''

''Don't make assumptions about the way I feel.''

''Then tell me.''

He swallowed hard but didn't turn away from her. ''After Holly died, I couldn't do much more than sit and stare out the window for six months. When I finally got my head screwed on halfway straight, I promised myself I was going to nail the SOBs who were responsible—expose them so the whole world would know. It gave me a reason to get up every morning. It's still important. It just doesn't rule my life anymore.''

''Jake—''

''Let me finish. I may not be saying this in a very direct way, but I'm getting to it. Once something like that happens to you, you never go back to the way you were. Holly and I were pretty damn close. But for the past three years, I've stayed away from any kind of relationship with women that wasn't based on the mutual pursuit of fun and games. That's what I was looking for with you at first. A quick fling. Then these warm, kind of protective feelings ambushed me. I wasn't sure how to cope with them. When I opened the newspaper and read that you were dead, I thought I wasn't going to get the chance to try.''

Laura didn't know that her eyes had filled with tears until they spilled over and trickled down her cheeks.

"I told the *Sun* there'd been a death in my family and that I needed to take some time off. Then I came up here to snoop around. It was as good a place as any to start looking for the animal who shot you. When I found him, I was going to beat the bejesus out of him. Then I was going to turn him over to the police.''

"Oh, Jake.'' She took his face between her hands and kissed him very gently on the lips. Words she had been afraid to say suddenly spilled out. "I don't think I can give you what you want. I don't think I can give it to anybody. Once I was naive enough to assume that if you loved someone, he'd love you back, and the two of you would live happily ever after. I found out how stupid that was.''

An unprotected expression flashed across Jake's face before he got control of his features. Then he reached up to gently stroke a finger across her trembling lips. "I wish I could spin you stories about happily ever after. But I'm as confused as you are. I still don't know what kind of relationship I can handle. I just know what I need tonight.''

Perhaps his total honesty was her undoing. She didn't have to worry about a string of broken promises because he wasn't making any. No. She forced herself to be honest. There was a lot more to the way she was feeling than that. All evening she'd been afraid of the emotions tugging her toward him. She'd been worrying about herself. Worrying about what she had to lose if she let herself open up to intimacy. Now she knew Jake needed her. And suddenly, it seemed more important to give than to receive.

He sat as still as the dark shapes of the mountains looming behind the cabin. A moment ago, his breath had been warm against her face. Now she didn't feel it and knew that the air had stopped moving in and out of his lungs while he waited for her reply.

Jake didn't realize he was holding his breath until Laura's lips moved against his. At first the kiss was as soft as a drop of dew sliding down the velvet petal of a flower. It deepened by slow degrees.

Her lips parted on a sigh. When his tongue made an expedition into the inviting warmth of her mouth, he tasted the sweetness of nectar. And then her tongue was moving caressingly against his, sending his senses spinning.

The kiss went from sweetness to blatant hunger in the space of a heartbeat, a man and a woman communicating with each other on a primitive level.

Remembering her bandages, he had gathered up handfuls of the chenille bedspread to keep from dragging her against him. Now the need to touch her made his whole body shake.

"Your cuts. I don't want to hurt you," he whispered hoarsely.

"It's all right." She lifted his hands and cupped them over her breasts. He sucked in a shuddering breath. Her nipples were like hard, plump berries against his palms— and there was nothing between his hands and her flesh except a thin layer of flannel. "You're not wearing a bra."

Her body swayed. Murmurs of pleasure welled up from deep in her throat. "It's—hanging—up—to—dry—" She managed the explanation between nibbled attacks on his lips.

She had finally let down the barriers and opened herself to the joy of being with Jake.

Hard, frantic kisses punctuated his shaky movements as

he slid open the buttons of her shirt and pushed it off her shoulders.

When he'd bared the upper part of her body, he gently touched the healing skin in the center of her chest.

"I'm all right."

Reassured by her words, he bent so his mouth could find her nipples. The pleasure of it ignited the pool of heat that had coalesced in her center. Suddenly, it wasn't enough to have his hot, arousing hands and mouth sliding over her skin. Urgently, she tugged at the hem of his shirt. He tore it over his head and tossed it onto the floor.

With a glad little exclamation, she burrowed her face into the crinkly hair that fanned across his chest, drinking in the warm male scent of his skin.

She liked the way he felt. Liked the rumble of excitement deep in his chest when she caressed him.

She'd thought she might be shy the first time after so long. But she was too eager to be in Jake's arms, kissing and being kissed. Touching him. Feeling his touch. Feeling his naked body pressed to hers.

His needs were the same as hers. He murmured fierce, sexy words as his hands and lips learned all her womanly secrets.

When she felt him hesitate, she lifted her head. "What is it?"

"Just a little problem with my knee."

"Not to worry."

Laura found there was something very sexy about getting to be in charge. With a seductive, feminine smile, she moved on top of him, straddling his body, bringing him inside her. Then she began to move, and nothing existed in the world besides the two of them delighting in the discovery of each other.

It was hot. Perfect.

Beyond the fantasies he had conjured up.

Beyond what experience had taught her a woman could expect.

As she moved in sensual rhythm, his strong hands stoked her passion with sweet, languid caresses. The heat built, consumed her, fed their mutual ecstasy until she tightened around him, gasping his name as they both exploded in shimmering, incandescent release.

Chapter Twelve

Bright morning light danced at the edge of the curtains as Jake eased down onto the edge of the bed. Laura shifted in her sleep and smiled.

He was glad she was smiling now. Near dawn, she'd gone into one of her nightmares. But he'd woken her up as soon as he'd felt her thrashing around next to him. Then he'd held her and stroked her until she told him she was all right again. Somehow, comforting her in bed in the darkness of the night had brought him a profound sense of peace.

Probably because tenderness had been missing from his life for such a long time. So had caring, for that matter. He'd convinced himself he was getting along fine without them. He'd been wrong about that—and a lot of other stuff.

Unfortunately that didn't make things simple when it came to him and Laura. She'd said she didn't know whether she could trust any man enough to give him her love. Well, he still didn't know whether he could give her what she needed, either.

With any other woman, he could take it one step at a time. See how the relationship developed. But Laura was different. If things went too far, he could end up hurting her terribly. And that was the last thing in the world he wanted to do.

The part of him that was still afraid said that backing off was the easy way out. Then neither one of them would be at risk. But he couldn't just do that, either, because he wasn't going to make the same mistake he'd made with Holly. If he understood anything at all, he understood that Laura needed his strength and his protection right now. And if he didn't have the guts to see her through this ordeal, he wouldn't be able to look himself in the eye.

Suddenly needing to touch her, he brushed a lock of tangled hair from her forehead.

"Jake?"

"I don't want you to wake up and wonder where I am. I'm gonna look for those muffins you wanted. And some coffee. You want cream and sugar?"

"Mm-hmm. How's your leg?" she murmured.

"A little stiff. But I'm not complaining."

She reached for his hand and the covers slid away from her bare shoulders, making her shiver in the cold mountain air.

He squeezed her fingers and pulled up the blanket again. "How are you?"

"Fine."

"The nightmares—are they like that every night?"

"Just about. Thank you for waking me up before it got bad."

He answered with a soft kiss on her cheek. "I'll turn on the heat and it'll be nice and toasty in here by the time I get back. You catch a couple more minutes of sleep."

"Mmm." She was already snuggling back under the covers.

It only took twenty minutes to get the muffins and the

coffee because he was lucky enough to find a convenience store at the next crossroads.

The moment Jake pushed open the door of the cabin again, he knew something was terribly wrong. Choking fumes made him start to cough. Gas. The whole room was full of gas. Eyes watering, he dropped the bag of food and dashed toward the bed.

"Laura!"

She was lying on her stomach, her blond head barely visible at the top of the covers. She didn't move. If she was breathing, he couldn't tell.

"Laura!"

He had to get her out of there. Fast.

Still coughing, he scooped her limp body up in the bedclothes and tore outside. Slamming the door with his foot, he laid her on the porch and peeled back the covers.

The heater. He'd turned it on before he left. Had it been pouring gas into the small room the whole time?

He'd taken a couple of first-aid courses in Boy Scouts and later when he'd been a camp counselor. His mind scrambled for the facts he knew about asphyxiation. Once the victim was unconscious and in respiratory failure, the heart kept beating for a few minutes.

He found a weak pulse at her neck. How long had Laura been unconscious? Knowing that every precious second counted, he tilted her head back to clear the airway, inhaled a deep gulp of air and started mouth-to-mouth resuscitation.

His own pulse was ragged and his lungs ached as he tried to force life-saving oxygen into her system. In between breaths, he checked to see if she was breathing on her own.

Not yet. He refused to stop believing he could bring her around.

Time narrowed to the mechanics of inhaling and exhaling—his life force desperately trying to reawaken hers. Somewhere deep in his mind, a scream of anguish welled up. He was going to lose her again. And this time, it was for real. He couldn't afford to give the terror voice. Not when Laura's life depended on staying calm and steady.

Finally, she started to cough. Then she was gasping in cold mountain air.

"Laura. Thank God!"

Her eyes fluttered. "Jake?" Another coughing spasm took her and her eyes watered. "What happened?"

"The heater. It was pouring gas into the cabin." He threw a glance back at the closed door. "I guess it still is."

She began to shiver and he tucked the covers more closely around her. "I think you're going to be okay. But I want to take you to a hospital."

"No!"

"Laura—"

"You can't. They're going to want identification—and information on insurance coverage. And I'm supposed to be dead, remember?"

"The hell with that." But even as he denied her protest, he was evaluating the risks. Maybe no one had turned on the heater since last season. Maybe the damn thing had simply malfunctioned. But that would sure be a hell of a coincidence. He'd put his bet on sabotage—carried out by the creep who'd been sneaking around the cabin last night. Had the intruder known Laura was there? Or had he been the target?

He lifted his head and looked around at the stand of trees screening the cabin from the others in the tourist court, trying to pierce the shadows. Someone could be watching to see how things turned out. Or maybe the assailant had done his dirty work in the middle of the night and decided it was too dangerous to stick around.

If nobody had spotted Laura, then she was right. She was a lot safer playing dead. But in any case, the sooner they got out of there, the better.

"Okay," Jake finally said. "I'll take you back to your friend Katie. You said she's a doctor, didn't you?"

Laura nodded.

"I've got to go in and get our stuff."

"Jake—don't." Her fingers clamped around his hand with surprising strength as her gaze shot to the closed door.

He stroked his thumb across her palm. "Not to worry. I'll be careful." Taking a deep breath, he opened the door just wide enough to enter. First he shut off the heater and pushed open the window, then he grabbed their overnight bags and Laura's knapsack. It took two more very brief trips to clear everything out.

Laura had pushed herself erect and sat with her back against the cabin wall.

Jake eyed her critically. "How do you feel now?"

"Okay." She shook her head, remembering the experience. "It's strange. The gas made me feel kind of peaceful. I could have just drifted off to sleep and never woken up."

He sat beside her and slung an arm around her shoulder, holding her against his side, but keeping his eyes on the woods. "Oxygen deprivation does funny things to your brain."

"I guess so." She watched Jake eye the two vehicles in front of the porch.

"You'll be more comfortable lying down in the back of your friend's car."

"What about the Ford?"

"I can tell the rental company the keys got locked inside and they're gonna have to pick it up."

"But they're not."

"They will be. As soon as you make sure Katie's are in your purse."

Laura fumbled around for the keys, surprised at how groggy she still felt and hoping Jake didn't notice. After unlocking the car, he tossed most of their stuff into the trunk.

"Am I going to ride back to Ellicott City in my nightgown?"

"You're not going into that cabin. Can you change in the back seat?"

"More or less."

He reached for her hand, helped her up and swung her into his arms. For a long moment, he simply held her, nuzzling his lips in her hair.

"Jake, I think I forgot to say thanks for getting me out of there."

"No charge."

After carrying her to the car and settling her in the back seat, he waited with his hips propped against the car door, his gaze sweeping the vicinity, as she slipped into last night's jeans and shirt.

"I'd feel better if you lie down in the back under the blanket while I stop at the office."

"Okay."

He drove to the manager's cabin and parked out front. "Back as soon as I can."

"I'll be right here."

Still not entirely happy with the arrangement, Jake turned so that he could watch the Chrysler out of the corner of his eye while he told the manager of the cabins about the heater and the car. The manager was so upset that he wouldn't accept any payment.

"Nothing like this has ever happened to me," he kept repeating as he walked Jake to the car.

"Did you have the heater checked at the beginning of the season?"

The man flushed. "I do that every other year. That's been good enough until now."

Jake wasn't going to take the time to give the man a lecture, not when his primary mission was getting Laura back to her doctor friend. But he did ask one more question. "Did you see anyone suspicious around here last night?"

"Suspicious?"

"A guy with a hat pulled down over his face and goggles. He was outside our cabin earlier in the evening."

"Didn't see nobody like that."

"Well, get the heater checked out before you rent the room to anyone else." Turning, he headed back toward the car.

"Are you still feeling okay?" he asked Laura again after he pulled out onto the highway.

"Can I sit up?"

"Wait till we get out of town."

Jake kept glancing in the rearview mirror as they made their way toward the interstate. No one seemed to be following. But he waited until he'd put twenty-five miles between them and the tourist court before stopping at a gas station so Laura could wash up. When she came out, she insisted on sitting in the front seat—with the back reclined. Twenty minutes later, her eyes drifted closed. Ten minutes after that, she began to thrash around and moan.

Was she having a convulsion? An after-effect of the gas?

"Laura?"

"Don't hurt me. Please, I won't tell anyone—" She gasped and cringed back into her seat.

It was one of the nightmares. And this time it was happening in broad daylight. Jake's knuckles whitened as he clenched the wheel. Was a dream going to ambush her every time she fell asleep now? He reached out to shake her awake, then he pulled his hand back. They were coming up to a rest area; it was safer to wait until he could stop the car. Watching her grimace and shiver made his stomach churn. But if she woke up now, she might flail out at him. Somehow, he brought the vehicle to a slow, smooth stop, under some trees at the edge of the parking lot.

"Please—oh, God—no—I won't tell—" Laura gasped, her eyes still tightly shut. She folded her arms protectively across her chest. Beads of sweat glistened on her forehead.

Jake was reaching out to gently stroke her cheek. Before his fingers contacted her flesh, he resisted. If the terrible nightmares were really a pipeline to the truth, maybe he'd be doing both of them a favor by letting her ride this one through a little longer.

To keep from touching Laura, he clenched his fists at his sides. "What is it?" he whispered. "What's happening to you?"

"One of them has a mask!" The exclamation was a strangled sob. "They—they're going to—rape me."

His whole body tensed. "Rape you? Who?"

"Dorian," she sobbed out.

Now every protective instinct screamed at him to wake her up and end the torture. But he had to try for more information. "Dorian who?"

"Dorian. Just Dorian." A whimper of pain followed the words and Jake couldn't take it any more. Grasping Laura by the shoulders, he shook her. For a few seconds, the dream held her in its thrall, and she thrashed frantically against him as if her life depended on escape from her attacker.

"Laura, it's Jake," he repeated over and over. "I'm not going to hurt you."

Laura's eyes snapped open. They were dull with terror as she cringed away from the large male form leaning over her.

"It's all right, honey. It's me. You're safe with me."

She sucked in a trembling breath. "Jake. Oh, God, Jake. It was so horrible."

Her teeth began to chatter and he held her close. "It's okay. It was just a nightmare."

"No. It happened. To Julie." She pushed her hands against his chest so she could find his eyes with hers. "It's too real to be just a nightmare. They raped her. Both of them. While everybody was out of control at the party."

"Are you sure?"

"Things got pretty wild and Julie was frightened by the way people were acting. So she went upstairs and locked herself in her room. But they didn't need a key. They knew about the secret passage. That's how they got in." She stared wide-eyed at Jake. "The two men. They came up the passage, found her and raped her." Laura's hands dug into Jake's shoulders. Her mouth quivered, making her voice rise and fall. "It was horrible. She was so frightened and they—they—"

"It's a dream." Jake stopped her. "You don't know—"

"It's not just a dream." Laura's voice thinned as she struggled to get the terrible words out. "They gagged her. Then they took turns holding her down on the bed."

"Who? Do you know who it was?"

"One of them had a mask. That's why I could never see his face.

"Dorian?"

Her whole body convulsed as if she'd touched a live wire. "Dorian!"

"Who is he?"

Laura closed her eyes for a moment, concentrating. "That's what they called him. That's all I know."

"Someone who isn't on the suspect list?"

"I guess so. But the other one looked familiar."

"One of the guests at Ravenwood?"

"I don't think so. But the murder was years ago. He must be older now."

"What else do you know about Dorian?"

She shuddered. "He waited until his friend left. Then he—he—killed Julie."

Jake's fingers knit with hers. "With the dagger?"

"No. He wanted it to look like an accident, so he hit her on the head with—" she moaned "—with the same—statue..." Her voice trailed off.

Jake pulled her against the protective wall of his chest, feeling the frantic pounding of her heart. He rocked her in his arms, willing the fear away. "Jake, that was the worst dream yet." Her voice cracked. "It isn't even safe to fall asleep in the car."

He offered what comfort he could. "Maybe it had something to do with the gas from the heater."

But her face turned chalky. "Or maybe I'm never going to be able to sleep without waking up in a cold sweat."

"Yes, you will. We're going to figure out what Julie was investigating. Then the nightmares will stop."

"God, I hope so!"

The tension was slowly seeping out of her body when she went rigid again.

"What is it, honey?"

She gulped. "The one in the mask. The one in charge. You don't think it was my father, do you?"

"No." The reassurance was automatic. Jake had no way of proving things either way, or of even knowing the dream was the truth. Yet her terror and anguish were terribly real. "Do you really think your father was capable of something like that?"

"How much can a child tell? I loved him. I think we had a good relationship until he left. But I was only eight. My mother was so bitter, she made him sound like a monster. After a while, I got so confused, I didn't know what to think."

"Don't jump to conclusions about your father. We don't know about my uncle, either."

"Your uncle! I forgot he left you his shares." Laura looked relieved and then guilty. "I feel terrible hoping it's him."

"That's all right. I hardly knew the man, but I'm sure gonna start checking up on him. I should have done it before now."

"There may have been other investors we don't even know about. But I bet Andy Stapleton does. I guess you're right. Even if he's not the one who killed Emma, paying him a visit is next on our agenda when we get home." Laura raised her head and looked around, aware of her surroundings for the first time. "Where are we anyway?"

"West of Cumberland."

"It'll be so good to get back to Katie's."

He reached for the ignition key and then hesitated.

"What is it?"

"I hate bringing any of the nightmare back again, but while it's fresh in your mind I have to ask you one more question. There's something you said while you were still dreaming. That you wouldn't tell—some secret, I guess. Do you remember what it was?''

Laura's brow wrinkled. ''A secret...Jake, I'm sorry, I just don't know.''

''Keep it in the back of your mind. Maybe something will come to you.''

After Jake pulled out of the parking area, Laura closed her eyes and leaned back against the seat. He knew she wasn't sleeping—that she wouldn't dare sleep in the car now. But he sensed that she wanted to be alone with her thoughts, so he didn't ask any more questions.

Two and a half hours later, they arrived at Katie's.

After quickly introducing himself, Jake got right to business. ''I want you to check Laura over.''

''What happened to her?'' the physician demanded, sweeping a worried gaze toward her friend.

''When I came back with breakfast, I found her unconscious in our cabin, with gas pouring out of the heater. She didn't want to go to a hospital, so I compromised on coming straight here. On the way back, she had another nightmare. A bad one.''

Katie took her houseguest to the bedroom, and Jake sat in the living room, trying to concentrate on a copy of *The New England Journal of Medicine*. When Katie came back without Laura, he threw down the periodical and stood up.

''How is she?''

''In amazingly good shape for what she's been through.''

''That's the best news I've heard since I found out she wasn't dead.'' There was a hollow ring to the quip.

Katie took a seat on the couch and leaned forward, her fingers clasped together in her lap. ''Jake, Laura felt terrible about leaving her clients in the lurch. But not being able to let you know what was going on was the worst part of that whole performance for her.''

Jake swallowed. ''It looks like they're still trying to kill her. Or maybe they were just after me and she got in the way.''

Katie glanced at the window. ''Is this place still safe?''

''I don't think we were followed, if that's what you mean.''

''Do you need a place to stay, too?'' Katie asked.

''To tell you the truth, I'd feel better not letting Laura out of my sight.''

As if on cue, he looked up to see her standing in the doorway. Fresh from the shower, she was wearing a terry robe, her hair wrapped in a towel.

Jake gave her a quick inspection. The color had returned to her face, and she seemed both more animated and more composed. She also looked a bit unsure as her eyes flicked to him. He wanted to cross the room and put his arm around her shoulder. Instead, he wrapped his hands around his knee.

Katie looked toward her friend. ''I've only heard the high points of your adventures. I was about to ask for a full account. But maybe I should feed you first. Have you eaten?''

''No. I wanted to get Laura back to you as soon as I could,'' Jake answered.

Katie nodded at Laura. ''You finished getting dressed, and Jake and I will get lunch on the table. When I'm nervous, I cook. And I've been nervous since I got home yesterday and found you'd flown the coop.''

''Sorry.''

''You did what you had to. Now, you have a choice between Chicken Cacciatore, Beef Bourguignon and homemade cheese ravioli. Unless you want meat ravioli.''

Jake laughed. "Quite a lineup. But don't you have any dessert?"

"Scones, apple pie, Black Forest cake."

When Laura returned, the table was loaded with half a dozen different dishes and Jake was already filling his plate.

Katie had a little of the beef. Laura nibbled on the ravioli. To Katie's delight, Jake took man-sized helpings of everything and was lavish in his praise of her culinary accomplishments.

While they ate, Jake and Laura recounted the events of the past thirty hours. The narrative was liberally punctuated by questions and exclamations from their hostess.

"If that's a sample of life in the fast lane, I think I'll stick to my quiet little genetic studies," Katie murmured as she twirled a slender finger around one of her dark ringlets.

"I'll pass next time around, too," Laura assured her, getting up to clear the table.

Katie also stood and began reaching for serving dishes. "Let me do it. You can go get that broken ornament. I want to have a look at it."

A few minutes later, Laura set the knapsack on the living room table and pulled out the T-shirt-wrapped chunks. "If my dream was right, then we've got the weapon he used to murder Julie," she said in a low voice. "Although I'm not sure what good it's going to do us in pieces like this."

Katie knelt beside the table and examined the fragments. "I'm afraid there's not much we can tell from these now."

Laura threw Jake a guilty glance. "I wish I hadn't hit you over the head with it."

"It's my fault. I should have been whistling the Buckeye fight song on my way up the tunnel."

Katie picked up the metal disk and fingered the lightning-bolt symbol. Then she fitted the disk into the matching depression in the base. "What does this thing have to do with Fairbolt?"

"I don't know," Jake said.

"The lightning bolt is their corporate logo."

"Fairbolt—never heard of it," Laura mused. "No, wait a minute. I remember it from one of my data searches when I was trying to find out which of the newspaper articles had anything to do with Ravenwood. Fairbolt funded some school co-op projects in Garrett County. Maybe they were giving the statues away, too."

"I don't know about statues," Katie said, "but they're big into working with schools. That's why I know them. When I was in college, they had an arrangement to supply the chemistry department with reagents at cost."

"They're a chemical company?" Jake asked.

"That and a bunch of other stuff. Like everybody else, I guess they've diversified over the past few years."

Jake stroked his chin. "I've never heard the name, but there's something about the symbol that rings a bell. I just can't make the connection."

"Maybe you saw an ad somewhere."

He shrugged, but while the conversation continued, he sat with his chin propped on his hands.

"Jake?" Laura finally asked.

"Sorry." He ran his fingers through his hair. "Listen, I don't like leavin' you, but I have to go home and check my notes. That symbol has something to do with the research I did on Holly's death. I want to know the connection."

Fear flashed in Laura's eyes. "Jake, if you were the

target of the heater gas leak, it could be dangerous for you to go home. Someone could be waiting for you to show up.''

''I know. But I need to get a look at those notes.''

''Jake—''

''Don't worry, honey. I'll be real careful.''

''How long are you going to be?'' She struggled to keep the panic out of her voice. It only made things worse for him.

''Two or three hours.''

''Call me when you get to your apartment, so I know everything's all right.''

''I don't think I should. What if someone's bugged my phone?''

''I didn't think of that.'' Would the man who'd been lurking under the cabin window go to such elaborate lengths? Laura didn't know. Jake was right. Why take a chance? Jake pulled her into his arms and for just a few seconds, she felt warm and safe the way she always did when he held her. However, the embrace was over before she could bind him to her.

He was halfway out the door before he turned and gave the women a sheepish look. ''I don't have a car.''

''Take the Chrysler,'' Katie offered.

When he'd left, Laura stood in the middle of the rug, biting her lip, wanting to call him back, yet knowing he needed to go—for his own peace of mind, if nothing else.

Chapter Thirteen

Laura stood at the window until the car disappeared around a bend in the street.

Katie came over and laid a hand on her sagging shoulder. "You look tired. Why don't you get some sleep while he's gone?"

"No!" Laura answered before she had a chance to consider how the exclamation must have sounded.

"You're afraid of the dreams."

"I can't help it."

"I could give you a strong sedative."

"Maybe tonight." Laura stared out the window in the direction in which the car had gone. "I want to be awake when Jake comes back."

"I think you need to take your mind off your problems." Katie's voice was warm and encouraging. "Let's go out in the garden."

"I probably shouldn't be outside."

"The backyard is very well screened, and you can't see it from the street. Come on, it's nice and warm out there in the afternoon."

Katie led her to a sunny patio protected by the back of the house, the garage wall and a stand of miniature hollies. Laura stretched out on one of the comfortable chaises.

"I'll be right back. Do you want tea or something cold?"

"Tea is fine."

Laura looked around at the herbs and fall mums planted in U-shaped beds at the edge of the open space. What a nice place to relax. If she could relax.

Closing her eyes, she listened to the soothing gurgle of the little shell-shaped fountain. Ever since she'd been arrested by Hiram Pickett, she'd felt as if she were bouncing from one tense, perilous moment to the next. In between were periods of strained waiting. She wasn't sure which was worse. Now her stomach was in knots because Jake was putting himself in danger again. It was hard to keep herself from calling to make sure he'd gotten to his apartment and everything was all right. She knew that could cause trouble for both of them.

The depth of her anxiety was surprising—and alarming. It seemed as if Jake Wallace had become important to her very quickly. But there was no way to rely on what she was feeling. Or what he was.

Obviously, he was still emotionally tangled up in his memories of Holly and still driven by his need to avenge her death. Or why else would he have rushed off like that to go over his notes? Laura told herself she understood. Even as she tried to convince herself it wasn't true, her stomach clenched again. This time she knew it was from jealousy. Jake had turned to her last night. Yet she didn't have any claims on him. So why was she so upset that he was still in love with another woman? Because irrational as it was, despite all her fears about involvement, she had started imagining what a future with Jake might be like.

Footsteps on the patio made Laura's eyes open.

Katie was holding two mugs of tea.

Laura sat up straighter, grateful for the interruption.

Looking around the garden, she tried to dredge up some sort of normal conversation. "This is so pretty. Maybe I'll put in something like it in the spring."

"You can have a garden just like it, if you want. Sabrina did the planting. She even keeps it weeded and pruned for me. All I have to do is enjoy it."

"I didn't know she did landscaping."

"Mostly herb gardens. But I don't really think you want to talk about gardens."

Did she want to talk about Jake? No. That was too dangerous. "I've been wondering about my father," Laura said instead.

"You've been letting yourself worry about whether your father was a rapist and a murderer."

Laura nodded tightly and set down her mug.

"What was your father's name?"

"Rex Roswell."

"Not Dorian."

"That could have been a code name the conspirators were using. Or a nickname."

"Have you ever heard anyone refer to your father as Dorian? What about your mother when she was angry with him?"

"I guess not."

"What about that investors' weekend at Ravenwood? Did anybody talk about him?" Katie persisted.

"Yes."

"What did they call him?"

"Rex."

Katie's next question seemed to come out of the blue. "What conspirators?"

Laura looked puzzled.

"You used the word just now. Do you think there's some kind of conspiracy involving Ravenwood?"

Laura hadn't put her thoughts into exactly those words until she'd made the offhand statement. Now she hesitated for a moment before answering. "Yes. And even if my father wasn't the man who murdered Julie, he could still be in on it. He and Emma."

Katie looked at her friend's drawn features. "I was trying to make you feel better—not worse."

"I know."

The two women sat in the sun, drinking their tea in silence. But as the afternoon lengthened, the air began to cool, and they decided they'd be more comfortable in the house.

Katie went into the kitchen and began browning bony pieces of meat in a large kettle. "For Ox-tail soup," she explained to Laura.

"We've already got enough food for an army!"

"Jake can put some in his freezer. You start chopping the onions and the leeks. And when you finish with them, do the carrots, celery and parsnips." She got out a recipe book, opened it to a page near the middle and set the book on the counter.

There *was* something sort of soothing about cooking, Laura decided as the cutting board filled up with vegetable slivers. And it kept her from glancing at the clock. Jake had said he'd be back in two or three hours. It was past the deadline now.

Katie was just dumping the onions into the pot with the oxtails when the doorbell rang. Laura's knife clattered to the cutting board. "I'll get it."

"Look out the window before you open the door."

Jake was standing on the porch, a thick expanding file holder under his arm.

Relief flooded through Laura. He was back—safe and sound. Throwing open the door, she launched herself at him. He caught her and held her tightly for long moments, as if he'd been worried about her as she had about him.

"I'm glad you're back," she murmured.

"So am I. And wait till you see what I found."

"Something important?" she asked, making an effort to match his mood.

"Yeah. But I'm not sure what it all means." He strode inside, set the expanding file on the coffee table and extracted a spiral-bound notebook. "These are my original interviews from residents who lived in Danville, Ohio."

Katie had come in from the kitchen wiping her hands on her apron.

As they watched, Jake flipped through the book and folded open one of the pages. "Look at this." It was a crude sketch of a lightning bolt inscribed in a circle.

Laura pulled the disk out of her knapsack and laid it on the paper. They were a good match if you allowed for the artist's inexpert rendering.

"Where did the drawing come from?" she asked.

"A farmer. He said it was painted on the side of some trucks coming to the weapon's plant. We both assumed it was the emblem of an army division. But when I tried to trace it through army records, I didn't find anything that matched."

He slapped his hand against the page. "Now it looks like Fairbolt was involved in the army project."

"That opens up a whole new line of investigation," Laura murmured.

"Yes. But what does it have to do with Ravenwood?" Katie asked.

Neither Jake nor Laura could answer.

"Well, what exactly was Fairbolt supposed to be doing in Garrett County?" Katie said attacking the question from another angle.

"An environmental educational project." Laura struggled to remember the details of the article she'd skimmed. "I think it included free health screenings."

"Nice of them to go to so much expense—unless they had their own agenda." Katie thought for a moment. "For example, health screenings are a good way to collect data."

"What kind of data?"

"Perhaps to assess long-term health risks and epidemiological factors. Sometimes, rural populations are used as control groups."

Jake raised questioning eyebrows.

"Like the Framingham, Massachusetts study where healthy men are being followed for several decades to see how their life styles affect their incidence of heart disease. There are lots of others. Some are concerned with very narrow risk factors, like the relationship of sun exposure to skin cancer or the correlation of coffee drinking to heart disease. Others are very broad."

"Are they ever done by private companies?"

"Sure. Cigarette manufacturers used to run them all the time. They're still claiming that the link between smoking and lung cancer hasn't been proven."

"I still don't see why Fairbolt would want to test a large population of kids in Garrett County. Could they have been doing something else in the area, too?" Jake wondered aloud.

"That's just speculation," Laura countered. "The trouble is, we still don't know what we're looking for."

"How about a chemical-weapons plant? Apparently they had one in Danville, Ohio," Jake suggested in a strangely quiet voice. "One that released all sorts of toxic chemicals into the environment."

The hair on the back of Laura's neck stood on end.

"Maybe that's what Julie was investigating!"

"I think one quick way to get some information is to sneak a look at Andy Stapelton's files," Jake went on. "If he got the government restriction on the sale of the land lifted, he probably had some idea why it was issued in the first place."

"Sneak a look at his files—as in breaking and entering?" Laura asked.

"Let me worry about that."

"If you're going, so am I."

"You had a rather bad experience this morning."

"And I'm fine now." For the past few moments, they'd been ignoring Katie. Now Laura glanced at her for confirmation. "Ask my doctor."

"Your doctor thinks you're both crazy," Katie shot back, but she couldn't change Jake's mind—or Laura's. The best she could do was point out that they'd be better off waiting until dark.

At eight o'clock, they started for the office park near Baltimore-Washington International Airport where the ASDC offices were located. First, they checked out the building. It was three stories of red brick and glass with a guard desk in the lobby to control evening and weekend access. After circling the structure, Jake suggested a plan for getting in.

Laura, who had donned her disguise again, would go in and say her car wouldn't start. When the guard came out to have a look, Jake would slip into the lobby. Then he'd hide in the rear of the building and open the back door for Laura.

"What am I supposed to claim is wrong with the car when it starts right up?"

"That you've been having carburetor trouble and it must

have flooded. Be sweet and thank him for taking the trouble to help you. Men always go for that.''

''I haven't had much experience in playing games with men.'' She gave Jake a direct look. When he didn't comment, she added, ''But I'll give it a try.''

Laura left the car in the parking lot around the corner and headed up the sidewalk to the front entrance. Jake stayed in the shadows until the guard had been lured away from his post. Then he crept inside with as much invisibility as a man his size could manage.

By the time Laura had driven out of sight and circled back to the other side of the building, he was waiting by the exit.

''I already checked. ASDC is on the second floor,'' he whispered.

Laura was feeling strangely calm. This was her second breaking and entering in two days. Maybe once you got into a life of crime, it became second nature. ''I hope we didn't set off an alarm,'' she murmured.

''I don't think there is one.''

''What about the guard?''

''Either we're out of here before he makes his rounds again or we hide behind the desk.''

The second-floor corridor was dark and quiet with only a few hall lights glowing dimly. Jake had brought along his burglar tools again, but not his gun. If they got caught, they didn't want to get pinned with armed robbery. But they weren't going to get caught, she reminded herself. And she wasn't going to make the same mistake she'd made with the knife at Ravenwood. This time they were both wearing gloves.

The outer door of the ASDC offices yielded with the same facility as the lock at Ravenwood. After they stepped into the waiting room, Jake quietly closed the door. Laura stuffed her wig back into her pocketbook, and they got out their flashlights.

Everything was sleek, tasteful and expensive.

"It looks like this ASDC operation is either making big money or they're putting up a good front," Jake muttered.

He stopped at the secretary's file cabinet. It wasn't locked.

"The good stuff is probably in there." Laura jerked her arm toward a glass door with Andy Stapleton's name on it.

"Yeah, but you take a quick look in these files anyway. Maybe he uses the hide-in-plain-sight system. I'll start on his personal stuff."

Laura was just about to pull a file drawer open when she heard a muffled exclamation from the inner office.

"Jake? What is it?" Somewhere along the line, her calm had begun to unravel. With her pulse pounding in her ears, she hurried toward Andy Stapleton's office. The moment her feet crossed the threshold, she knew something was terribly wrong.

A slash of light from the parking lot illuminated a limp male form slumped over the wide rosewood desk. The hand with the diamond ring Laura remembered was clamped around the handle of an ugly little revolver. Andy Stapleton! A dark stain spread across the blotter under his head. It wasn't ink.

Laura felt an icy chill sweep over her skin. "My God."

Jake drew her close. This time, his warmth couldn't stop the shivers racing up and down her arms.

"Another death." Her voice quavered as she said the words.

"Yeah."

"Jake, when is it going to end?"

"When we figure out what's really going on." His voice was hard.

Somehow, his harsh response helped her mind start functioning again. Sucking in a steadying breath, Laura looked around the office, glad they were both wearing gloves.

"We've got to get out of here." She tried to tug Jake toward the door.

"Not yet."

"Jake, we can't let anyone find us!"

Ignoring her words, Jake took a quick look out the window and then crossed to the files.

Laura glanced back toward the door. Somewhere down the hall, she thought she heard a noise. "Jake, we've got to get out of here."

"Not until we've gotten what we came for."

"Jake!"

"Give me just a minute."

Opening a file drawer, he began riffling through folders. There was one on Ravenwood. It was empty. Jake cursed and began looking through other folders.

She could either stand with her back to the wall, or join the search, Laura decided. Maybe if she found something, she could pry Jake loose.

Gloved hands pressed to her hips, she edged closer to the body. As she rounded the corner of the desk, she spotted a piece of paper half off the edge. It looked as if it had whooshed out of place when Andy had fallen forward.

"I've found a suicide note," she whispered as she scanned the words. "He says he killed Emma and can't live with himself."

"That nails it down pretty tight," Jake muttered, but the didn't slow his search of the filing cabinet.

Just then, the door of a nearby office opened, and

Laura's body went rigid. She realized she'd heard the same sound before—only farther down the hall.

"The guard's making his rounds!"

"Yeah. I heard him."

He'd known and he'd coolly kept searching!

Laura glanced back toward the silent outer office. Did the guard just check out front or did he come into the back? They'd talked about hiding behind the desk. They couldn't take the chance now. "He can't catch us here!"

Jake crossed to the casement window and began rapidly turning the crank. "There's a roof on the next level. It's only a one-story drop. I think we can make it out that way."

"Sounds better than the alternative."

When the window was open, he helped Laura onto the sill. Then he leaned over and lowered her as far as their outreached arms could stretch. Bracing for the impact, she let go.

Laura hit the gravel roof, lost her balance and fell to her seat. However, only her dignity seemed to be injured. Brushing off loose bits of gravel, she stood and looked up, expecting to see Jake's legs dangling from the window-frame. Instead, he had disappeared from view.

"Jake!" she called.

There was no answer.

Chapter Fourteen

Laura's heart stopped and then threatened to thump its way through the wall of her chest.

"Jake!" she tried again in a hoarse whisper. Nobody answered.

Frantically, she looked up at the long expanse of wall above her. There were no projections suitable for climbing. The window through which she'd escaped might as well have been at the top of the Washington Monument for all the chance she had of getting back in again.

What was happening in the office? Had Jake deliberately lowered her to safety to get her out of danger while he kept searching? Or had the guard come in and discovered what looked like a murder-robbery in progress? Was he holding Jake at gunpoint while he called the police? Laura couldn't stop her imagination from running wild.

Seconds ticked by. Or was it centuries?

Finally, a muscular arm reached out the window. "Here, catch."

"Jake. Thank God."

Like a perfect touchdown pass, a bulky manila envelope sailed through the air. Laura snagged it with considerably less style. It was sealed like a Christmas present with several silvery lengths of duct tape crisscrossing at right angles.

Jake's arm withdrew and Laura suffered another panic attack. In the next moment, she realized he was only trying to figure out how to wiggle through the opening. As he twisted and turned, maneuvering first one shoulder and then the other out the window, she unconsciously imitated his gyrations—while clutching the envelope to her chest.

When he dropped to the gravel beside her, she wanted to throw her arms around him with relief. He didn't give her a chance. Grabbing her shoulder, he urged her toward the roof's edge. "I'm tired of feelin' like a fish in a barrel."

"I guess the guard didn't see you."

"No. He only stuck his head in the front door. He must just do a spot check on a couple of offices each time he makes his rounds. Maybe he won't investigate Stapleton's inner sanctum tonight."

"Where did you find the envelope?"

"Stuck to the bottom of the center desk drawer. My guess is it's a duplicate Ravenwood file."

When they reached the edge of the roof, Jake repeated the process of lowering Laura to the ground before joining her.

"You're limping again," she said between puffs of air as they trotted to the car.

"So what's new?"

The words were clipped. From pain or tension, Laura wondered. She wasn't sure what response he wanted from her. So she held her tongue until they were back on Route 195, heading toward Katie's house. Then her anxiety came bursting out. "Jake, that was a pretty stupid stunt."

"Which? Breaking into Stapleton's office or staying behind to look for evidence?"

"Both."

"You came along for the break-in."

"I wasn't going to let you do it alone. But I didn't know Andy was going to be slumped over his desk—dead."

"Sometimes when you make an end run, you don't have any idea how it's going to come out."

The tone of his voice made her head jerk up. "What do you mean?"

"This Ravenwood deal is tied to Fairbolt, which is tied to Holly's death. I'm going to find out how."

"Is it worth getting charged with murder?"

"He killed himself. He had the gun in his hand. You found the note."

"I'm starting to wonder if it's a little bit too convenient. Besides, however it went down, if the police find any evidence that we were in that office, we're in big trouble."

"Come on, Laura, we can't have it both ways. It was either murder or suicide."

Laura didn't see any point in continuing the argument. Tension seemed to fill the car like humid air, making it hard to draw in a satisfying breath. It wasn't all generated by their narrow escape. She kept throwing Jake covert glances, although she couldn't see his face in the darkness. But as she imagined his grim features, her fingers curled over the edge of the seat.

Why were they so on edge with each other? From the scene in Andy's office? Or was Jake sorry about last night? Was he wishing he'd never gotten so deeply involved with her?

It was a relief to get back to Katie's, to another person who could act as a buffer between them.

"Why haven't I heard anything from the police? They're supposed to keep you informed of developments," was the physician's first question after they'd told her about Stapleton.

"We didn't call them." Laura's voice was carefully neutral.

"They're going to find out about it soon enough," Jake added. "When ASDC opens for business tomorrow morning."

"But—"

"I've been trained to respect the law," Laura said, cutting her friend off. "Keeping quiet about a dead body makes me feel as if I'm teetering at the edge of a cliff. But it would be pretty risky to have to explain what we were doing breaking into Stapleton's office tonight. Besides, now that I'm thinking a little more clearly, I realize we could make a mess of things for Detective Hamill. He laid his job on the line setting it up so I could go underground. If his superiors find out that I haven't been hiding out like I'm supposed to, he'll be in big trouble."

"I didn't think about him," Jake admitted.

"That's because you haven't met him. But I owe him a lot. And I hope I haven't let him down."

The conversation had been taking place with the three of them huddled just inside the door. Now, Jake shifted his weight and Laura saw a grimace flash across his features.

"Maybe we ought to sit down," she said.

"What am I thinking about, keeping you standing here in the dark?" Katie reached for the light switch.

"Better close the curtains first," Jake warned. "Just in case we have another busybody outside." He was already easing onto the sofa.

Both women looked at him critically. "What's wrong with your leg?" Katie asked.

"An old football injury."

"Aggravated by jumping down from two roofs," Laura added.

"Want me to have a look at it?"

"No, I just need some ice."

"And a painkiller," Katie added.

"I won't argue with that. I guess it's convenient to be hiding out with a doctor."

As their hostess began bustling around dispensing the medication and the ice, Laura was struck with a new pang of guilt. "We're getting you into a lot more than you bargained for," she murmured.

Katie paused and looked at Laura. "I signed on for the duration. I'm not going to quit when the going gets rough."

Laura nodded and ducked her head. If the going got much rougher, she'd figure out a way to get her friend off the hook. But she wasn't about to start a debate about it in the middle of the night. Especially when Jake needed to take care of his leg.

"Can I get anyone a drink?" Katie asked.

Jake eyed the brandy on the sideboard. "I suppose that stuff doesn't go too well with whatever you just gave me."

"Sorry. That's a combination I wouldn't recommend."

"Then how about coffee. I have the feeling we're going to be up pretty late." He was already pulling the papers from the envelope as Katie went to get the coffee.

Dropping down beside him on the couch, Laura tried to read along with him. She was so wired that the script on the ancient deed of sale wasn't making any sense.

Without thinking about it, she let her head drop to Jake's shoulder.

He touched her hand lightly. "I guess I was kind of sharp with you back in the car." His voice was gruff. "You doin' okay now?"

"No."

He turned, giving her his full attention.

She sat up straight again. "I'm no worse off than you are, I guess."

Just then, Katie stepped into the room with a tray of mugs and a coffeepot. For a few minutes, they were all busy pouring and stirring coffee.

Then they began to read the deed. Apparently, the Ravenwood tract of land had been purchased from the state of Maryland by a Colonel Miles Ravener in 1849 for what sounded like a ridiculously small amount of money.

"Looks like it wasn't worth much back then, either." Jake punctuated the remark with a long pull on the coffee mug.

Under the deed was an annotated list of Ravener's descendents.

Laura studied it thoughtfully. "I think it was typed on an old electric machine," she observed.

"Why?" Katie asked.

"The print's pretty even. But the typeface reminds me of my dad's old Remington portable."

"But it's not the same machine," Jake clarified.

"His was manual. When anybody typed on it, the q's and z's were always faint."

They went back to the list. Ravener had had two sons, one of whom had been killed in the Civil War. A daughter had died in her early twenties without having any children. Her husband had remarried soon after and had made no subsequent claim on the property.

The remaining son had moved to Baltimore and had never married. Ravenwood had been inherited from him by a cousin named Stewart Middleton, an Illinois resident.

"This information wasn't all in one place. Somebody went to a lot of trouble to dig it up and put it together."

Laura set down her coffee mug and ran her finger along the page.

"They must have had a pretty strong interest in the property."

"Or maybe they were looking for land that met certain requirements, and this happened to be one of the candidates," Katie suggested.

Below the list was a letter written in 1950 to Stewart Middleton on official stationery from the Defense Department. It began with a patriotic appeal, a reminder of every citizen's duty to support the country's fight against Communist aggression in any way possible. It ended with a request to buy eight hundred thirty-two acres of Garrett County, Maryland, property owned by Middleton. Located as it was in the Allegheny foothills, the land had little commercial value. But its isolation would make it perfect for the training of U.S. troops being sent on sensitive missions.

"Troop training?" Katie wondered aloud.

"Nobody in Hazard mentioned anything like that when I was asking questions," Jake told her. "In a small town, you'd think a concentration of troops would have been a big deal."

"If it was supposed to be a secret training camp, maybe they didn't know about it," Laura suggested.

"Or maybe the request was deliberately misleading. The Defense Department had to give Middleton some reason why they wanted the land," Laura offered.

Apparently, the owner's patriotic spirit had been stirred by the appeal. Or perhaps he'd seen the request as a way to unload seemingly worthless land on which he was paying property taxes year after year. At any rate, a copy of the new deed of sale was attached to the letter.

"I don't know a lot about land prices back then. But I think the army got Ravenwood dirt cheap," Jake observed.

Laura wasn't listening. Instead, she was staring at the deed, her face bloodless.

Jake sensed the sudden stillness of her body. "What is it?"

"Look at the signature of the clerk who recorded the sale."

Everyone's eyes went to the bottom of the yellowed paper. Written in precise black script was the name Warren Ketchum.

"Warren Ketchum. Judge Ketchum," Laura breathed. "The last time we met was in his courtroom when I was arraigned for Emma's murder. He's the man who set my bail at a million dollars because he couldn't be sure that I'd return to the county for trial if he let me out of his sight."

"I thought he was doing a law-and-order number. Now you have to wonder how he really fits into all this."

"I'd like to know exactly what he's been up to."

Jake began to shuffle rapidly through the rest of the papers. "Here he is again in 1951, authorizing the building of a county road to the property. And what do you know. He graduated from clerk to head of the planning commission."

"Wasn't he awfully young for a position like that?" Katie interjected.

"Yeah. And why wasn't he off in the army himself?"

"Either he was 4F or he had some kind of special status."

"Is there anything personal on him?"

"Give me a minute." Jake shuffled through more papers. "There doesn't seem to be any private stuff. All the material in the envelope is related to the history of Ravenwood.''

Laura gave a disappointed sigh.

"But here's a new deed for the property in 1960, selling the tract to the Ravenwood Limited Partnership," Jake continued. "That must be the group of investors that included Martha and Sam."

"And my father and your uncle."

"And Warren Ketchum."

"What?"

"We wanted to know who else had invested. Well, his name is here on a list along with the rest of them."

"Warren Ketchum is one of the investors?" Laura clarified.

"Yes."

"But nobody ever mentioned him. Not Andy Stapleton. Not the other partners."

"Maybe only a few of them knew—and they were keeping quiet about it. This isn't his signature. It's just a typed list. Maybe it was a payoff for services rendered. Or maybe he was some kind of silent partner."

Laura took the stack of papers off the coffee table and shuffled back to the first typed sheet they'd found, the one with the names of the Ravener descendents. "It's the same typewriter," she said.

"Let me see." Jake held the two pages side by side, comparing individual letters. If it wasn't the identical machine, it was a twin.

"Of course, none of this proves Judge Ketchum did anything illegal. There's nothing criminal about recording a land sale. Or authorizing a county road project. Or joining a group of investors. Or typing a list of names."

"No," Laura said slowly, her eyes unfocused as she stared across the room in the direction of a Renoir print that hung over the fireplace. But the lush flower garden in the picture was just a blur before her eyes. Her inner vision was focused on a far less peaceful scene. "I'd like to see a picture of the judge when he was younger," she said slowly.

Jake looked at her inquiringly.

She fought to keep her voice steady. "Do you remember when I had that dream in the car—the one where the two men raped Julie Sutton?"

"Yeah."

"I told you I thought one of them looked familiar, but I wasn't sure where I'd seen him."

"Was it Ketchum?"

"Now that I think about his face, it could have been him. But the man I saw was thinner, and there wasn't any gray in his hair."

"You mean you wouldn't want to swear to it in a court of law."

"I'm afraid it's the kind of evidence that would be laughed out of court."

"Yeah." Jake thumped his fist against his palm. "But if we're sure it's him, we can go after better evidence. Ketchum's a public figure. I'll bet his picture has been in at least a couple of newspaper articles."

Laura nodded hesitantly. She'd thought they knew what they were looking for. Now a new piece had been thrown down on the table with the rest of the puzzle and she couldn't quite fit it in.

Katie, who had hardly joined the conversation over the past forty-five minutes, sat up straighter and stretched. "I vote we get a good night's sleep and start again in the morning."

Laura hadn't realized how wiped out she was until her

friend spoke. Now, her body sagged back against the cushions.

Jake's gaze took in her whipped appearence. "Sorry. I got so caught up in this that I just wasn't thinkin'," he muttered. "You started off the day in a gas-filled room."

"It seems so long ago."

They all stood up a bit uncertainly.

"As I said before, you're welcome to stay here," Katie told Jake.

"Thanks. When I went home to go through my notes, I stashed some clean clothes in my duffel bag. It's still in the car."

Laura cast a quick glance up at him and then dropped her gaze. They'd made love last night—and slept in the same bed. What happened now?

It was Katie who made the decision for her. "I think the couch is long enough for you," she told Jake. "And I'll get you a blanket and a pillow."

"Appreciate it."

When their hostess had departed, Jake and Laura stood awkwardly in the center of the rug.

Jake cleared his throat. "Laura…I thought I could handle this by not saying anything—by putting the personal stuff on hold until this crisis was over. I guess that's not going to work."

She nodded tightly.

"But I can't lie to you, either."

"My God, Jake. I don't want lies. That's the last thing I want."

"I know that, honey. And I care about you a lot. More than I ever thought I'd care again. But I lost so much the last time." His eyes were very bright, and he had to stop speaking for a moment. When he started again, his voice was thick. "I want you. I want to take the risk of loving you. But there's this part inside of me. This tight, closed part that's afraid to open up. Do you understand what I'm trying to tell you?''

"Yes. And I appreciate the honesty. More than you know." She gave him a quick, hard kiss on the lips, a kiss that was over almost before it had started. Then she was running down the hall to her room before he could see the tears in her eyes. She knew how he felt because she'd felt that way herself. After what Bill had done to her, she'd been afraid to love again. She'd told herself she wasn't going to let anyone hurt her like that again. Only she didn't have the iron control of Jake Wallace. She simply hadn't been able to help herself. She loved him and there wasn't a damn thing she could do about it.

Chapter Fifteen

The morning after they'd made love, Laura had awakened to the feel of Jake's fingers stroking back her hair. She awoke that way now. For a moment she thought she was simply dreaming about wanting him to be there. Then she looked up and saw him gazing down at her with a tenderness that made her breath stop. If he could look at her like that... No, she wouldn't try to convince herself it meant any more than what he'd told her last night. He cared about her. But he didn't know if it could go any further than that.

"Honey, I'm sorry I have to get you up." There were dark circles under his lower lashes, and his face was haggard.

"Didn't you get to bed last night?"

"I had stuff to do."

"What?"

"I'll tell you about it in a minute. But there are some things you need to know. Your friend Hamill called this morning to fill you in on the Stapleton development."

Laura felt tension bloom in her chest. "What did you say?"

"Katie answered the phone, so she didn't have to pretend she hadn't been there and seen the body for herself."

Laura winced. "Do the police think it's murder or suicide?"

"You know how it is. They don't broadcast information until they have a suspect nailed down." He hesitated for a moment. "But she could read between the lines. Hamill was worried about you. So she put me on the line and I had to tell him about our trip to Ravenwood—and the heater."

"Jake, why?" The question was a protest against the way events were overtaking her. She'd gone into hiding to avoid being staked. Now everything was closing in on her again.

"If whoever killed Stapleton has figured out you're alive, then you're in danger. He thought he got you once. Next time he's going to make sure."

Laura swallowed past the grit clogging her throat.

Jake slipped his arms around her and pulled her against the shelter of his body. As always, she felt as if she'd found a haven. "I'm not going to let anything happen."

"You're a good man to have in my corner."

"Yeah." She felt him swallow. "And I brought some pictures for you to look at."

"Okay." Laura stayed with him for just a moment longer. Then she sat up in bed and plumped the pillows behind her. Jake took a manila folder off the bedside table and laid it across her lap. Inside, there were several newspaper photographs and some black-and-white glossies.

"Where are these from?"

"The morgue at the *Sun*. After I finished going through the Ravenwood file, I couldn't sleep, so I figured I might as well drive back downtown."

Laura hefted the pile. "You must have spent half the night in the file room."

Jake shrugged. "Once I got into searching, I just kept

going." He gestured toward the pictures. "These aren't all of the same man. I thought it would be a good idea to give you some choices."

"Kind of like a police lineup."

"Right."

Laura studied the first photograph. Jake had started with faces from the investors' weekend. On the top of the stack was what looked like a twenty-five-year-old picture of Sam Pendergrast taken at a black-tie dinner.

"From that celebrity photo section the paper runs on Sundays," Jake told her. "Everybody gets his fifteen minutes of fame."

Her laugh was brittle as she began to spread out the rest of the pictures.

Under the photo of Sam was one of a much younger Tim O'Donnell, caught tossing a ball at what appeared to be a bush-league baseball game. He'd been quite a handsome man in his early years, Laura decided. And a lot healthier looking, too.

The next photo made her hands tingle. "My father."

"Uh-huh."

"I guess this was taken a couple of years after he moved out."

"But you don't get any kind of vibrations from the picture?"

"Nothing to do with the dream. It just makes me remember him not being at home with us." Laura was anxious to go to the next exhibit. When she did, the tingling feeling danced all the way up her arm and triggered an erratic pounding of her heart. The photograph showed a dark-haired man dressed in a conservative business suit. He was smiling as he handed a check to a solid-looking matron.

"Ketchum," she breathed. "Years ago."

All at once, the atmosphere in the room was like the last moments before a thunderstorm breaks.

"It was him." The sentence came out as a little gasp.

"Take your time and be sure," Jake whispered.

"I don't need to take any more time. He's the man in the dream. I told you. That's why I thought he looked familiar." She closed her eyes for a moment. "I mean, he's one of the men who raped Julie Sutton. The one whose face I could see."

"Not the one who killed her? Not Dorian?"

"Not Dorian."

"Even if he didn't kill her, he's guilty of rape!"

Laura shook her head. "No jury is going to convict him on evidence from a murder suspect's dream."

"Former murder suspect," Jake corrected.

"And no one is going to accept the secondhand testimony of a ghost," she continued, sitting up straighter. "Besides, we don't really know anything for sure." She sensed that Jake was going to speak, and she shook her head. "Let's be logical for a moment. I've been caught in the grip of a terrible, overwhelming feeling that my nightmares are somehow being broadcast to me by a woman who was raped and murdered twenty years ago because she was investigating a conspiracy. It's flattering that you believe me."

He covered her hand where it still gripped the edge of the photograph. "I'm with you all the way."

"But it's not very realistic that anyone else will be." She swallowed. "And I *could* be dreadfully wrong, you know."

"Okay, so forget about the dreams if you want. There's all the evidence we found in Stapleton's file."

"Evidence we illegally obtained by breaking and entering—at the scene of a suicide or murder. No good, Jake."

"But there's no reason I can't duplicate at least some of the stuff with material from the newspapers. I can even go up to Garrett County and get a copy of the deed at the county courthouse. And Ketchum's on record as the head of the planning commission, too."

"Which doesn't prove any wrongdoing," Laura pointed out. "So what if his name keeps coming up in connection with Ravenwood? It's all got perfectly logical explanations. Anyway, his being involved in the land deal could be a coincidence."

"Why are you playing devil's advocate like this?"

"It's the way I was trained. You always try to come up with the objections the other side is going to make. But in the final analysis, it doesn't matter what we think," Laura added. "Evidence obtained without proper search warrant isn't admissible in court."

"Couldn't you plant it somewhere and let an—uh—third party discover it?" a voice asked from the doorway. It was Katie.

Laura and Jake laughed, glad the tension had been broken for a moment.

"I think you've been watching too much TV," Laura observed.

"Okay, so that won't work. But we're going to figure out what will. And we've got a lot of extra brain power." At Laura's puzzled look, Katie explained. "I remembered Jo was from Garrett County, told her about what we'd discovered last night and asked if she could come over. Not only is she here but she brought Cam."

"Yes, it's good to have a genius inventor on our side," Laura murmured.

Katie and Jake went to join the others while Laura quickly got dressed. When she stepped into the living room, the first thing she saw was the strained look on her friend Jo's face.

"What did I miss?" Laura asked.

"Nothing. I've just been hearing how Judge Ketchum is mixed up in all this. It's sort of a shock for me," Jo said.

"That's right. You know him, don't you?"

"Actually, my aunt has been cleaning his house since before I was born. I can't say I knew him well, but sometimes, Aunt Pauline would have me come up to his place to pick up stuff he was getting rid of—clothes my brothers could wear or furniture he didn't want. Things like that. And while I was there, the judge would ask me to do a small job for him—like weed his flower garden—and then pay more than the chore was worth." She cleared her throat. "You've got to understand how it is in a small community. People live in each other's pockets. Everybody knew that my family was dirt poor after my father died and that we needed help."

"Jo—" Cam said softly, reaching for his wife's hand.

"It's okay. Being poor is something we couldn't help. I'm just trying to make a point. Everybody in town admires Warren Ketchum. It's a folk legend how he went off to college when he was fifteen and how he suddenly had a lot of money. People used to wonder about where it came from."

The implications of what Jo was saying began to sink in.

"Everybody wondered but nobody did anything?" Jake asked.

"What should they have done? Launched an investigation? He was a respected member of the community. A lawyer and a judge. Besides that, he contributed a lot to charity, so his wealth benefited people who were less well off. Another thing, he was a strong moral influence in the county, and a local celebrity. People talked about the way he dressed, the food he bought, the addition to his house, his Christmas parties for poor kids." She looked at Laura. "I'm sorry. When you told me he was the judge at your arraignment, I just thought 'Well, that's the kind of thing you'd expect with Judge Ketchum.' But I should have started making other connections."

"Jo, you had no reason to make any other connections," Laura said softly. "Anyway, I wasn't telling you the whole story when I asked you to do some investigating for me. I still couldn't talk to you about the dreams I was having. Even if I had told you about them, I hadn't dreamed about Ketchum yet."

"The important thing is to go on from here and find out what we've got," Jake cut in. "So now we have more of a circumstantial case against the judge. He's been getting large sums of money from somewhere. Maybe they were payoffs from Fairbolt."

"We could ask for an audit," Jo mused. "But they might have found a way to hide the transactions. Maybe there's no way to make the links we need. Or even if we could, it might take months. Laura doesn't have that kind of time."

"What if you can get the judge to confess? That would solve a whole lot of problems." The suggestion was tossed off by Cam.

"Sure." Katie couldn't keep the sarcasm out of her voice.

"No. I guess I sounded flip, but I really mean it," Cam insisted. "Guilt makes people do strange things. Maybe he's been contributing to charity all these years because he's been feeling as if he needed to atone for his sins."

Laura looked doubtful. "He was pretty self-righteous when he set bail."

Jo's face had taken on a flush of excitement. "Wait. Don't make assumptions the way I did. Suppose coming down hard on other people is one of the ways he copes with his guilt?"

"Where does that get us?" Jake asked.

"Keep an open mind," Laura said catching Cam's enthusiasm, too. She turned to Jo. "Okay, what else can you tell us about the judge? Personal stuff. Something he wouldn't want people to know. Something we could use against him."

"I don't know what you can use against him. Unless you want to spill the beans about his collection of lucky charms."

"Don't tell me he wears a fairy cross around his neck!" Laura exclaimed.

"If he wears one, it's under his shirt. But he's got some in a case in his living room. He's also got rabbit's feet. Four-leaf clovers encased in lucite. Hex signs. He's got stuff like that all over his house. When I was a kid, I used to love looking at all of it."

As her friend spoke, Laura felt her excitement mount. "So we know the judge is superstitious. How do you think Judge Ketchum feels about ghosts—or evil spirits?"

"You mean, does he believe in them?"

"That. And is he afraid of them?"

"If you'd seen all the stuff in his collection, you'd make that assumption. It's a pretty odd hobby."

"Where is all this getting us?" Jake asked.

Laura had unconsciously flattened her hand against her chest where the fairy cross had shattered. Now she turned excited eyes to Jake. "I've got an idea. Maybe it's too dangerous. And I'm not even sure if it will work." She glanced over at Cam. "But I'm going to need your help if there's a chance of pulling it off."

"Of course."

"Let's hear about the dangerous part," Jake said.

"I'm going to need you, too. If you don't mind," she told him in a low voice.

"Honey, you've got everything I have to give."

Everything, Laura asked herself. Or everything short of the one thing she wanted? For a moment she closed her eyes as if she were gathering her thoughts. Then she began to tell the group about her plan.

TUESDAY AFTERNOON, JAKE pushed himself back from one of the computer terminals Cam had provided, rubbed his bloodshot eyes and shook his head. Over the past two days, he and Laura had been correlating material from sources as disparate as the EPA, the Defense Department, the Maryland Extension Service, the *New York Times* Data Base, the National Cancer Institute and the Center for Disease Control.

"It's amazing what you can deduce when you can put together enough facts. The trouble is, this stuff is so convoluted, I'm not sure we'd be able to prove it to anyone else."

Laura laced her hands behind her neck and stretched tired muscles. Standing up, she went over to Jake and began to knead his shoulders. He leaned into her hands. "That feels great."

She wanted to brush her lips against his hair. But she didn't. In a few days, he might disappear from her life, and she didn't want him to think she was trying to hold him. Yet, while they were together, she wasn't going to deny herself everything. Not the pleasure of touching him, for example.

And there was something she could give him. Information. Falling back on the pattern that had served them so well when things got too personal, she began to talk about the work they'd been doing.

"I've just come up with another site and put the data on one of those worksheets we designed. Spruce Valley, Tennessee. It's set up like Ravenwood, purchased through the army but really under the complete control of Fairbolt. I've used the Center for Disease Control data to correlate with clusters of cancer deaths and miscarriages."

"You've come up with more places than I have."

"My analytical mind, I guess."

"Well, with your stuff and mine, we've got correlations for plants and chemical dumping sites around the country. Pine Grove, Georgia. Centerville, Illinois. Layton, Nebraska. Hazard, Maryland. And none of the communities knew."

"They will now. Like for example, Fairbolt was dumping every thing from trichloroethylene to ethylene oxide and dioxin in the Ravenwood ravine. No wonder they were studying schoolchildren to find out if there were long-term effects."

Jake stood up and paced to the window. "You know how it is when the line of a song keeps running through your head?"

"Yes."

"I keep thinkin' about the phrase 'heartland of America.' You know an idyllic little town where all the kids are cute, none of the dogs bite and you can leave your door unlocked."

"The great American myth."

"Yeah. Except that was the kind of place where Holly grew up. A picture-postcard community. She had a great childhood. Teachers who cared. Ice-cream socials. Summers at the swimming hole. And all the time, the sod on the playground was laid over a chemical field. And the cows in the nearby meadows were munching on the stuff. And it had leached into the water supply."

Laura could feel her eyes sting. "I know. It's such a damn cheat. But your book is going to blow the lid off the whole thing. Not just in Danville and Hazard."

"Finally Holly's death is going to make a difference. And I don't think I could have put the research together without you. I guess I haven't said thanks yet."

"You could have done it yourself. It just might have taken longer."

"But your help means a lot to me."

Laura pressed her lips together and nodded. She'd wanted—needed—to help. But had she been hoping all along that nailing the company whose chemicals had killed Holly would free Jake from the bonds of the past? She was too tired and confused to be sure of her own motivation anymore.

Jake broke into her thoughts. "The question is, if Ketchum knew about the dumping, why did he stay in Hazard?"

"I checked that out with Jo. His house was way out on the east edge of town. That's not exactly in the danger zone. And thank God she was in a pretty safe place too.

"Yeah." Jake nodded. Then his mind returned to the Ravenwood puzzle. "I keep wondering if anybody else was being paid to keep their mouths shut? Any one of the other investors could be involved. Did Tim look like he was in the money? Or Martha? What about your father?"

"Tim was trying to look prosperous. He had a rented Cadillac El Dorado for the weekend. But Sam Pendergrast is the one who's pretty well off."

"Yes. But I checked his financial rating. His car dealerships are doing just fine."

"What about Emma?"

"Either she was in on the cover-up from the beginning or she stumbled on to something. Or maybe she just found out how Andy Stapleton got the development restrictions lifted."

Their speculations were broken off by the ringing of the telephone. It was Cam, who'd finished testing the equipment they'd ordered.

"Everything's ready," he announced over the speaker phone. "So anytime you want to leave for Ravenwood, I'll bring the van and we can go over the instructions."

"Are we ready?" Jake asked Laura.

There were still pieces they hadn't fitted into the picture. But she was pretty sure they had enough information to convince Ketchum that they knew what had been going on all these years. "The sooner we get it over with, the better," she said in a voice that projected more confidence than she felt.

The moment they hung up, Laura got out the draft of the note she and Jake had been working on and filled in a meeting time. Then she read the whole thing over once more.

Dear Judge Ketchum,

You picked the wrong person to humiliate. Probably you thought my death eliminated me as a problem. I'm glad to inform you that I'm very much alive and well and have been digging into your relationship with the Ravenwood property over the years. I have information related to the toxic-waste dump site at the ravine. If you want me to keep the secret buried, bring your checkbook to the Ravenwood mansion at three p.m. Wednesday.

Laura deliberately omitted a signature. If her quarry wanted to think the note was from Julie Sutton, so much the better. Let him start to worry about what he was up against.

For the past two nights as she'd lain in bed, she'd pictured Ketchum's smug face as he gazed down at her from the bench. That had made her anticipate how good it was going to feel to make the judge sweat. Up till now she'd been the one trying to scramble out of the hole someone else had dug for her. Now she was going to push someone else over the edge.

Chapter Sixteen

Laura and Jake left for Garrett County at midnight so they could stop at Judge Ketchum's house and leave the note before driving to Ravenwood under cover of darkness—using the special infrared headlights Cam had provided. There was a three-car garage at the back of the house where they could park the van. But to keep from being spotted, they'd have to wait until daylight to set up the equipment Cam had put together.

Everything went according to schedule. Jake locked the garage doors behind them at four-thirty in the morning and then climbed into the back of the van, where Laura was sleeping on the mattress they'd sandwiched between the boxes of equipment.

She'd asked him to wake her when they arrived, but he knew she'd hardly slept during the past days of frantic activity. Now he decided she could use a few more hours of rest before the rough stuff began. Besides, the chance to lie down beside her was just too tempting to pass up.

When he eased onto the mattress, she snuggled against him. An automatic response to his body heat? Or did she know it was him? Closing his eyes, he inhaled her unique scent and pressed his chin tenderly against the top of her head. She felt so damn good, he thought as he lightly stroked her hair. He had to fight the desire to tip her head up, find her lips and kiss her awake. But this wasn't the time or place to start anything.

Besides, he was exhausted, too. And a little sleep wouldn't do him any harm, either.

It was still well before sunrise when Jake's eyes snapped open again. There was a fleeting moment of disorientation. Then he realized that Laura was moaning in her sleep. In the darkness, her small fists began to drum against his chest, as if she were trying to fight him off. Another dream. The first in days. Perhaps because she was back at Ravenwood again.

"Laura."

She didn't respond to him. But her head swung from side to side in panic. He knew whom she was fighting off.

Once, he'd let her suffer so he could get more information. This time, he couldn't allow the torture to go on.

Gently, he grasped her shoulders. "Laura, it's Jake."

"Please—no—"

"It's Jake. Wake up, honey."

Her face was pressed against the fabric of his shirt, but he sensed the change from sleep to waking. He wanted it to be a metamorphosis from panic to calm, but he could still feel the pounding of her heart.

"You're safe," he murmured, his lips skimming the top of her head, his hands enveloping her shoulders.

"The snow. The cold. Just like I always dream it." She forced herself to hold on to the images. "But this time was—I don't know—Julie was talking to me again. Warning me."

"About what?"

"Today. She was there in the swirling snow. And she was terrified, Jake."

"Didn't Dorian carry her out into the snow?" he asked softly.

"Yes. But that wasn't it. She was frightened for me. She wants us to leave before something terrible happens."

A chill that had nothing to do with the cold morning air had settled over his skin. "We can still call it off. The police can meet Ketchum."

All at once, their roles were reversed. Laura reared back and looked down at him. "It won't work. They won't get a thing out of him. We have to stay."

"But—"

"I'm okay now. I was just spooked. Dreams don't foretell the future."

"Laura—"

She forced an exaggerated smile onto her lips. "Don't tell me a big strong football player is panicked by a ghost."

"Don't get smart with me."

"I guess I'm way past getting smart." Before he could ask her what she meant, her arms captured his shoulders, and her warm lips touched his. Neither one of them was prepared for the power of the kiss. It drove away ghosts, drove away reason, drove away the fear they hadn't been able to talk about.

"You want me," she breathed.

"God, yes."

Now it was Jake who took control of the kiss. And Laura gloried in her surrender. They shifted on the narrow mattress, clinging to each other.

She and Jake were here together, mouth to mouth, breast to chest, hip to hip. And nothing mattered except the need to get closer to him still—as close as a woman could get to a man. Because if he walked away from her tomorrow, at least she'd have this one last time to remember.

THEY DIDN'T TALK about what had happened in the van. In fact, they didn't talk much at all except about where to string wires and set up hidden projectors and video cameras.

But by one o'clock they had everything working, including the link to the remote-reception station. Sighing, Laura brushed back the lock of hair that kept drooping across her eyes and looked out the window. She had expected to see the sun still shining brightly. Now she drew in a sharp gust of air as she realized that the sky had darkened to navy blue.

Jake turned, his face watchful. "What?"

"Look out there." She pointed to the window. "What do you think is going on?"

"I'll check."

A few minutes later, the word came back from their remote station that a freak snowstorm was hovering over the mountains.

So it was going to happen the way Julie had warned her. Icy fingers danced down Laura's spine. She knew the biting cold of a winter squall up here—from her dreams.

Jake must have seen the dead white of her face before she quickly turned away. "Honey, we're not going to get trapped. A storm can't dump that much snow in a couple of hours," he said soothingly. But she was tuned enough to him now to pick up his own uncertainties.

"Here comes the judge!" The warning crackled from a speaker hidden behind the drapes.

"He's over an hour early," Jake snapped.

"I guess he decided to get the drop on whoever showed up for the meeting."

They made a frantic last-minute check of the equipment before Ketchum's BMW pulled up in front of the house.

The final thing Jake did before withdrawing into the

secret passage where they were going to hide was spray a cloud of Julie Sutton's Spring Meadow perfume into the air.

The scent made Laura feel as if she were choking. She hoped it had the same effect on the judge.

"You all right?"

"Yes," Laura lied.

Jake closed the panel and set up the protective barrier Cam had provided. "Show time, honey," he said as he pushed a button and a monitor gave them a picture of the front hall. Moments later, the front door opened and Warren Ketchum stepped into the mansion. They hadn't turned on any lights. The hall was as dark and shadowy as a haunted house on Halloween.

The setting was a perfect match for the judge's countenance. Even on a small black-and-white screen, he looked frightened—a far cry from the stern, imposing figure who had glared down on Laura from the bench. There, he'd appeared robust and vigorous. Now old age had bowed his shoulders and bent his body. Or perhaps it was fear that had doubled him over.

Pushing his glasses higher on his nose, he stood with his back to the door, apparently trying to quiet the shaking of his body. His left hand clutched and stroked a small bit of fur.

A rabbit's foot? Had he really stooped to that? But Jo had told them about his superstitions.

"He looks scared spitless," Jake whispered.

"Good."

The low-voiced exchange was cut off abruptly.

"Is anyone there?" Judge Ketchum bellowed with surprising force. When he stood up straighter, Laura caught a glint of gold around his neck. A fairy cross. Like the one that had saved her life. She hoped it didn't hold any special powers for him.

Laura swallowed around what felt like cotton batting in her throat and reached for a microphone. Jake stayed her hand. "Let him stew for a minute."

They watched as he took several cautious steps down the hall. "We don't want him to go the wrong way," Laura warned. But she still hesitated for several seconds. Would their elaborate scam really work? She was the star of the performance, and if she failed, the whole thing would blow up in their faces.

Jake sensed Laura's nervousness and moved closer to her, slipping an arm around her waist. "You're going to do just fine."

"I hope so." Laura cleared her throat and pressed the button that activated the mike in her hand. "In here…" she called in a soft voice. "I'm waiting for you in here."

On the monitor, Ketchum swung sharply around like a weather vane that had reversed direction in a windstorm. "Who is that?" he challenged. "Come out and show yourself, you coward."

Laura ignored both the question and the order. "Come in here…" she repeated in a slightly louder voice. There was a great deal of satisfaction in using the same technique that the killer had employed to lure her into the drawing room.

Another hidden camera followed their quarry down the hall. Before he reached the drawing room door, he slid his hand into his breast pocket and put away the rabbit's foot. Seconds later, he pulled out an automatic pistol.

Laura stifled a startled exclamation. He might be superstitious, but he wasn't going to trust magic to save himself.

Jake turned off the mike. "So much for Jo's intelligence. I thought she said he wasn't supposed to have a gun.''

A firearm in the hand had done wonders for Ketchum's confidence level. Stiff-armed, he jumped through the drawing room doorway like a narcotics agent on a drug bust. ''Freeze!''

''Lethal Weapon One and a Half,'' Jake muttered. The words died in his throat as the gun swung directly toward the draperies behind which they were hiding.

Laura was pretty sure she could do something about that. Quickly, she slammed against one of the control buttons in front of them. Behind Ketchum, the doors banged shut and the lock clicked into place with the finality of a prison door clanking shut.

Again, the judge whirled. With a squeal of mingled anguish and rage, he fired a burst of shots into the doors, splintering the wood.

''He's out of control,'' Jake whispered. ''It's happening too fast.''

''Then let's get him to start talking.'' Laura clicked on the microphone again. ''Bullets can't kill a ghost,'' she taunted. As she spoke, Jake activated a holographic projector. In the next second, the translucent image of a woman seemed to float eerily out of the door that Ketchum had just shot.

The apparition wore a white robe. Blond hair wafted out behind her and her arms were flung wide, as if to beckon the judge into her cold embrace. It was a recorded image of Laura. But with the right makeup, she looked a lot like the young Julie Sutton.

''Go back. No. Go back,'' the judge screamed, his fingers gripping the fairy cross around his neck. Gibbering in terror and confusion, he stumbled away from the apparition, firing another barrage as he went.

The bullets went right through the flickering image that kept advancing toward him, until, at the last second, it winked out of existence.

Ketchum sagged against the back of the sofa, panting and clawing the velvet fabric for support. His face had turned the color of cobwebs. Sweat stood out like blisters on his clammy skin. "Where are you? I smell your perfume. Where are you?"

Laura kept silent.

"Go away, do you hear? I didn't do it. I didn't kill you," he screamed.

"But you know who did! You know. You know. You know." The accusation came from every corner of the room, echoing from half a dozen speakers.

"Let me out of here. Leave me alone." He ducked down, holding up his fairy cross as if it were a shield.

Jake activated another projector. This time, the Julie Sutton image came sailing at Ketchum from another angle.

The victim ducked, dropped the talisman, covered his head with his hands and began to moan.

"Tell me about the murder," Laura intoned as Jake turned up the lights so that the judge was spotlighted like the lead singer in a rock group. And he was going to sing, all right. "Tell me! It's the only way to save yourself from my revenge."

"You know it wasn't me. Dorian did it. I didn't even know he was going to."

"What did you think was going to happen?"

"I thought you'd be too frightened and humiliated to talk."

They had him babbling now. And it was all being recorded on videotape.

"Talk about what?"

"Fairbolt. Their army contract. You tricked us. You pretended you were coming up here for fun and games. But you were snooping around—digging up secrets. You found out about the toxic-waste dump. You were going to ruin everything.''

Ketchum had slid down to a heap of quivering flesh on the couch.

''And what about you? You found out about Fairbolt's business up here when you transferred the deed.''

''No. Dorian asked me to set it up for him. He needed me. I was proud of that.''

Laura kept the verbal pounding coming hard and fast, not giving her victim time to think. Ketchum must have been storing this stuff up for years like the poison chemicals in the ravine. ''Who? Who are you talking about?

''Dorian,'' he choked.

''That's not his real name.''

''But it's what we all called him. All the fraternity brothers. We used to ask him if he had a picture hidden in the attic—a picture that got nasty looking while he stayed the same.''

''Like a picture of Dorian Gray.''

''Yes! He was so rich. We kidded him that he could buy anything—do anything. We acted like it was a joke, but we whispered about it in secret because we were all afraid of him, too,'' the judge gibbered on. ''He's capable of anything. We used to think he got us drugs and girls because he wanted to be everybody's best friend. But it wasn't like that. When you accept something from him, it gives him power over you.''

''Who is he?''

''Please. I can't tell. I can't tell. He'll kill me. Or worse.'' Ketchum was sobbing now.

''Where did he get his money?''

"His family. They were some of the original investors in Fairbolt."

Laura and Jake exchanged glances. He was answering all their questions but the most important one. "It's ironic that you're protecting Dorian. He's tricked you again. Why do you think you're here?" she jeered. Recorded laughter filled the drawing room. Ketchum clamped his hands over his ears and curled into a tight ball.

"Did he kill Emma Litchfield?"

"Yes."

"Did he kill Andy Stapleton?"

"Shut up, you fool!" The roar of protest didn't come from the man huddled on the couch. Laura and Jake had been focused on the judge. Now they watched in horror as the door Ketchum had shot at shattered and splintered under the impact of a heavy boot propelled by powerful leg muscles. The knob and lock came flying across the room and landed on the rug several feet from the judge.

"You're not going to ruin everything now, you miserable coward. Not when we're finally going to get out from under this mess." The promise was spoken by Sam Pendergrast, who stepped into the room and stood looking around intently.

"Sam!" Laura's exclamation carried across the open mike and was broadcast to the room.

"That's right. And Laura and Jake. The two investors who couldn't leave well enough alone." His piercing gaze seemed to pick out each of the projectors and microphones they had carefully hidden.

He was holding a dagger in his hand. The same dagger Laura had found in the box. No, that was impossible. Police Chief Hiram Pickett had the knife with the murder evidence. Unless he'd given it back to the rightful owner. Or had Sam stolen it back?

With the speed of a man half his age, Sam Pendergrast advanced on the quivering judge. Somehow, Ketchum found the will to resist. He raised the gun, but before he could fire, Pendergrast knocked the weapon out of his hand.

"You swore to live by the sacred dagger. Now die by it!" Then he was slashing down with the knife. With a grunt of fear, Ketchum ducked to the side. The two men went at each other, and Ketchum's glasses went flying across the room. The fight couldn't last for long, not when Sam was in so much better shape.

Jake snatched the microphone away from Laura and threw a toggled switch on the console in front of them.

"Cam? Come in Cam. As they had since the beginning of the show, the words should be going out to the remote station Cam and Evan Hamill had set up down the road at the Slumbering Pines. But there was no answer. Not even static.

"Cam, are you picking us up?" Jake tried adjusting several dials. Still no answer.

He swore. "I can't raise him. I think that bastard Pendergrast damaged the transmitter." He grabbed Laura's arm. "Time to bail out."

Laura cast one last look at the monitor.

Pendergrast had raised the knife again, and Ketchum was trying desperately to keep it from plunging into his neck.

They couldn't save the judge. Could they save themselves?

"Come on!" Jake stood up too fast, whacking his knee against the control console. He grimaced in pain.

"You're hurt."

"I'm all right. Let's get out of here." He gave Laura a

little push toward the other end of the passage, and she started moving, listening to make sure he was following.

When she reached the exit, she stopped short. "I don't know how to open the door from this side!"

"I hope I do."

Jake squeezed past her and felt for the mechanism. The door slid back on the noiseless tracks.

Laura's mind was racing. If Sam had cut off their transmission, then he'd probably also disabled the van. But they could hike to the motel through the woods, the way Jake had come up last week. That was their best bet. Or had Cam, Hamill and the police team already started on their way when they'd lost communication? There was no way to know. And no way to warn them about what they'd find.

Laura glanced at the window, and an exclamation of dismay tore from her throat. The only thing she could see was a solid wall of swirling white. The blizzard Julie had warned her about had moved in with supernatural swiftness.

Nobody was coming to help them now. And there was no way they were going to make it through the woods to safety because they wouldn't be able to see more than two feet in front of their faces.

They were trapped!

Chapter Seventeen

Jake followed Laura's frozen gaze, silent as he contemplated the enveloping whiteness and the roar of the wind tearing at the roof and windows. Then he squeezed her arm. "We'll be okay. There must be tons of places in the house to hide. Other secret passages. Stuff like that. And Cam's got four-wheel drive. He and Hamill are probably already on their way up here."

"Right." There was no use dwelling on the obvious flaws in Jake's reasoning. Any hiding places in the mansion were probably already well-known to Sam Pendergrast. And if the reinforcements arrived, they'd have no idea where to look for anybody. Laura pressed her lips together. She'd put a lot of energy into convincing her friends and Hamill that this crazy scheme would work. Now it looked as if she was going to be hoist on her own petard.

"I don't know how much time we have before Sam opens the panel down there," Jake said. "Or how fast he can get around the electronics equipment and the bulletproof shield. So you get out of here. Find Hamill. I'll hold the bastard off."

A bolt of emotion shot through Laura as the impact of his words hit her. It was almost like being hit by lightning and miraculously surviving. A few days ago Jake had told her he didn't know how much he could care. Now he was saying he'd risk his own life to save hers.

"Jake, we're in this together."

His voice was low and urgent. "Laura, I'll only slow you down. This damn knee of mine has been bad news every step of the way."

The words only strengthened her resolve—and the feeling of elation coursing through her. Despite the terrible danger, she'd just learned something precious. "I'm not going anywhere without you. If you want to make a stand in here, we'll both stay."

Jake muttered a few choice expletives.

"But I vote we go," Laura continued. "And we're wasting time arguing."

"Yeah." They turned and started rapidly down the hall.

When Laura didn't hear footsteps directly behind her, she risked a glance over her shoulder. Sweat had broken out on Jake's forehead, and he was limping badly. His left knee looked as if it wasn't going to support his weight much longer.

"Go on—"

She dropped back and shoved her shoulder under his arm. There was no way she was going to leave him to the killer pursuing them.

"You go ahead," he insisted. "I want you to."

"No."

He didn't spare any more breath. Together, they stumbled down the hall. When they reached the turn, Laura hesitated. Earlier in the day, they'd locked the doors to the main stairs to keep Ketchum where they wanted him. The keys were still in the control room.

"Either we climb out a bedroom window and take our

chances in the storm or we squeeze past the hole in the burned part of the house," Jake said.

Laura wondered if Jake could make the climb and what their chances were outside. But the other alternative wasn't very attractive, either. "We can't get by that hole."

"I'm pretty sure there's enough room. I remember thinking that the floor wasn't cut all the way to the edge. If we watch what we're doin' and keep our backs to the wall, we'll be okay."

Somewhere in the distance, above the moaning of the wind, they heard a crash. The electronics equipment falling to Sam's angry onslaught? If so, he'd be on the second floor pretty soon.

Jake gritted his teeth and picked up speed as they moved down the hall. But when they reached the end of the corridor, the door was nailed shut.

"Damn!" Jake glanced over his shoulder as if calculating their chances of going back the other way. They were both flushed and gasping for breath. At this point, neither one of them could win a forty-yard dash.

"I should've been prepared for that." Without further consideration, he rammed the barrier with his shoulder. When the door didn't give, he muttered a curse and redoubled his efforts. On the second try, the door groaned, gave and sent him tumbling forward into the corridor.

"Close it," Jake gasped as he pushed himself to a sitting position. "Maybe he won't figure out what happened."

Laura eased the damaged door shut and leaned against it, sucking in lungfuls of the dank, stale air and fervently wishing she were somewhere else.

Since the first time she'd bumbled in here, she'd been wary of the place. Now she felt as if she'd deliberately walked into a death trap. With the door shut and the storm outside, there was very little illumination. And the light that reached the hallway was eerie—a continually shifting aura of swirling snow making odd patterns on the floor and walls. Above them, the wind tore at the burned shingles like a howling lion, sending in gusts of frigid air and snow.

However, the gaping chasm in the floor was more compelling than the roof. But at least Jake had remembered correctly; it didn't cover the whole surface. There was a narrow ledge of flooring along the right wall.

"Maybe whoever started the fire was trying to get warm," Jake quipped.

"Uh-huh." She reached for his hand to help him up and heard him stifle a grunt of pain as he came to his feet. She didn't ask him if he could make it to the other side of the abyss. They both knew he had to. Moving cautiously forward, they kept to the side of the flooring, feeling an all-too-familiar creaking and shifting under their feet as they reached the margin of the crater. But there were no further earthquakes.

Jake gestured Laura forward. "You're lighter."

By now she knew how his mind was working. "So maybe I'll get across—even if you don't?"

His harsh features softened for a moment. "We both will. Quit stalling. Or are you chicken?"

"Of course not! But I'm not a tight-rope artist. You're going to have to help me keep my balance." She reached for his hand and felt a surge of warmth as their fingers knit together. Let him think she needed his help, if he wanted.

As they began to inch toward the other side of the chasm, the wind shook the fire-damaged rafters above them and tore off more shingles. If they didn't fall into the hole on their own, maybe they'd be blown in.

How many minutes had ticked by? How much time did they have left? Maybe they really had fooled Sam about which way they'd gone. But what would he do when he didn't find them at the other end of the hall?

Laura's hands were icy, her pulse was pounding in her ears, and she was breathing in shallow gasps as they neared the three-quarters mark. *Please, we've made it this far. Let us make it all the way,* she prayed silently. *Both of us.*

Still, Laura could hardly believe it when she reached the firm ground on the other side. Jake was only a few steps behind her when the door through which they'd entered blew open as if a hurricane had swooped through the hall. But the door hadn't been seized by the wind. Laura watched as a grim-looking Sam Pendergrast stepped into the dank, dark hallway. He was holding the judge's gun.

"End of the line," he grated.

Jake turned so that his body was shielding Laura. For just a fraction of a second, he risked a look back at her. "Get ready to run," he whispered. Then he raised his head and looked Sam in the eye. "You're right. This is the end of the line. You've lost."

"No, I haven't."

"It's all on tape." Jake's words were bold, but Laura could feel the tension in his body. She knew what he was doing. Playing for time. And if that didn't work—if the cavalry didn't arrive—Sam's attention would be focused on Jake, so she'd have a chance to get away.

Her mind scrambled for alternatives and drew a blank.

"I'll take care of the videotape after I take care of you," Sam shot back.

"It was transmitted directly to the police. All they have to do is start interviewing Ketchum's fraternity brothers. You couldn't have bought them all off. Someone will tell the police which of the guys was called Dorian."

"Not the ones who count. Not the ones in my secret society will talk! Anyway I'll be out of the country before any of them cracks."

"The judge cracked!"

"Because you tricked him with your stupid haunted house show. The fool believed in ghosts. That's why he hadn't been up here since the night of that party."

Was there a note of desperation in Sam's voice, Laura wondered. Was he close to the edge? Could they get him to make a mistake? She racked her brain. Was there any detail—some tiny thing—that would make a difference? She thought back rapidly over what she knew about Sam Pendergrast, hoping for a flash of inspiration, like the kind that often came in the middle of a tense courtroom battle.

The tension worked now. A concept seemed to leap out at her. Night blindness! During Andy Stapleton's presentation, Sam had complained about not being able to see well in the dark. And it was getting darker by the minute in here.

Hope bloomed and withered in almost the same moment. Logically, Sam must have been the man Jake had chased that night at the motel. How come he'd been able to run away so rapidly without crashing into a tree or something? Because he'd been wearing special goggles. They weren't just a disguise. They had allowed him to see. And he didn't have them on now because he hadn't expected it to be dark at three in the afternoon. Maybe he couldn't see well enough to shoot accurately.

The reasoning had taken only seconds. Inching toward

the far end of the corridor, Laura gave a slight tug on Jake's hand. If Sam noticed, he didn't react. Maybe they had a chance.

She was so preoccupied, that she barely heard the elements tearing and clawing at the damaged roof above them.

"Did Andy Stapleton double-cross you?" Jake continued the dialogue.

"I don't have to tell you a thing."

"I'll bet you didn't know that Julie Sutton left a box of incriminating papers. That must have been as shocking as realizing she was getting ready to blow the whistle on to the whole Fairbolt toxic-waste deal."

"Shut up." Sam raised the gun.

They had inched farther away—almost to a doorway right in back of them. Did they have a hope of throwing themselves into the room beyond, Laura wondered. It was a risk. But one worth taking, if she'd guessed correctly about Sam. She squeezed Jake's hand, hoping he understood it was almost time to make their move. He squeezed back, his eyes flicking to the doorway. He understood!

Every muscle in Laura's body coiled in readiness. But before they could leap, there was a rush of movement near the ceiling, just as when Jake had worked the projectors. Now it was accompanied by a rending, tearing sound. Or was it a shriek?

A stream of icy, swirling white swooped into the passage, arrowing straight toward the man with the gun. It was a column of snow driven by the wind. But it looked incredibly like a woman with a long white dress trailing out behind her, her arms outstretched—ready to pull Sam Pendergrast into her cold embrace.

Screaming, Sam held up his arm to shield his face and bolted forward. Either he didn't see the pit, or panic had made him stop thinking clearly. He screamed again when he sailed into space. And again when the gun in his hand went off with a muffled crack.

Then there was only the dull thud of a body hitting the floor below.

"My God—what just happened?" Jake croaked.

"The roof. A piece of the roof ripped off. And the snow came pouring in on Sam."

"Snow. That was all you saw? Snow?"

"No. I felt like Julie was there, too. As if she came back to save us."

It was hard to believe the terror was really over. Laura didn't quite take it in until Jake had folded her into his arms. The tender gesture released the mix of emotions brimming inside her.

"You damn fool," she muttered. "Don't you know what it would have done to me if you'd gotten killed trying to save my life?"

He took her chin between thumb and forefinger and tipped her face up toward his. "I didn't have a choice. Standing in the hallway, knowing Sam was probably on his way up the stairs with the gun, I realized that if he killed you, I couldn't go on."

"That's how I felt about you."

"A man likes to hear that from his woman." Jake's voice was husky. "But it's not true. You're a survivor. You've already proved that."

"Sure. I've been surviving. But meeting you made me realize I wanted a lot more."

He held her tighter. "Oh, God, Laura. I realized today that that's the way I've been feeling for weeks."

"Why didn't you tell me?"

"I guess I was a coward. Loving you was too scary. It

wasn't just that I couldn't risk the pain I'd been through before. I couldn't risk your rejection.''

"*My* rejection!"

"Yeah. You'd been hurt, too. Suppose I admitted I love you, and you just thought I was saying what you wanted to hear. Or that it couldn't last. Like with your ex-husband. Or like your father.''

There were three important words Laura picked out from his sentences. "You love me?"

"Yeah." His voice was raw. "I love you, all right. I didn't plan it. I just couldn't help it.''

"Oh, Jake. I love you so much. The night we climbed out of Stapleton's office, I realized I couldn't help myself, either.''

"Oh, honey.''

"Jake—'' The next part was hard to say. But he had to understand. "When I started falling in love with you, I couldn't help being jealous of Holly. Of the way you loved her so much. Then, when I thought about it, I realized that if you ever loved anybody again, you'd make the same commitment. Because you're that kind of man.''

She could feel him swallow convulsively. "Making a commitment. For life. That's why it was so hard. That's why I'm glad I finally could.'' All at once, he laughed. "I feel—I don't know—brand-new. Reborn.''

They held each other as if they never planned to let go.

"I can't believe we're saying these things," Laura whispered, her face pressed against Jake's chest.

"Nothing like a brush with death to bring your life into focus.''

"All this time, I thought the most important thing for you was revenge.''

"For a long time, I thought so, too. I was wrong.''

WHEN THEY GOT BACK TO THE front hall, Cameron Randolph and Evan Hamill were waiting, obviously relieved to see the pair.

"Ketchum was still alive when we got there," Cam said. "I think he was hanging on because he needed to set the record straight before he died."

"Did he say anything about my father?" Laura asked the question that had been hanging over her.

"He thought you'd want to know that he wasn't involved."

Laura closed her eyes for a moment. "That means a lot to me."

"Jake's uncle wasn't in on it, either. It was really just Pendergrast. And what Ketchum told me matches with what Jo picked up in town. Once she asked the right questions, it was easier to get answers. Up until twenty years ago, Ketchum had a much worse reputation. Then he seemed to undergo a change for the better."

"I guess it was the shock of knowing Sam had killed Julie," Laura said.

"According to the judge, Pendergrast's family money bankrolled Fairbolt," Hamill continued. "And he knew about the wide-open spaces up here through his good friend and fraternity brother Warren Ketchum. I think we can assume he organized the original investment deal to cover up the toxic-waste dump and keep the land out of circulation. That gave him a long-term tax shelter along with the possibility of making money on the eventual development of the property. But he didn't see anything wrong with making short trips up to Ravenwood to let his hair down. It was the perfect setting for the wild parties he'd acquired a taste for in college."

Jake nodded. "He sounds totally ruthless. The kind of man who used anyone and everyone for his own purposes. I guess he talked up the land deal as a great investment—neglecting to tell the other stockbrokers they were in for the long haul.''

''But Emma must have found out.'' Jake glanced at Laura. ''I've been thinkin' about her and your father. For a while, I was worried because I figured she'd been the mistress of whoever masterminded the Ravenwood deal. Now I guess it's pretty clear your father wasn't her only conquest. She had Sam hooked, too.''

''Two ruthless people. You couldn't ask for a nicer couple.''

''And I have the feeling Martha was green with envy. That's why she was stirring up trouble.''

''Your analysis sounds pretty good,'' Hamill said, breaking in to the conversation. ''The department got a search warrant for Emma Litchfield's safe-deposit box. She kept a coded notebook in it. The woman didn't trust anybody. But we knew she was getting regular payments from someone over the years. We just couldn't figure out who.'' Hamill looked at Laura.

''When Sam Pendergrast came in the door wielding that knife, everything fell into place,'' Cam said, picking up the narrative. ''The trouble was, we knew we had to get up here fast—in the middle of a snowstorm.''

''Was Andy Stapleton in on it?'' Laura asked.

''Believe me, we've investigated Stapleton back to kindergarten. There's no evidence that he even met Pendergrast before he got interested in Ravenwood. It looks like he was the wild card—a sharp operator looking for resort land in the path of development.''

''And Sam had to go along with Stapleton's proposal just like everyone else until he could figure out what was going on,'' Laura speculated. ''Maybe Emma was threatening to spill the beans to Andy unless she got more money from Sam. I guess his first plan was to kill her with the chandelier. Then when she didn't want to sit where he'd suggested Andy put her, he took that place himself to allay suspicions later. When his first attempt failed, he must have decided the so-called bad blood between me and Emma gave him the perfect opportunity to kill two birds with one stone. But I guess he was shook up when he saw us with the box. He had to get it away from me in case it had any incriminating evidence." She paused for a moment.

"What about Pickett?" Jake asked.

"Nothing's been pinned on him yet. Arresting you so fast could just be a case of misguided zeal, although that doesn't rule out the possibility of his getting some kind of payoff in the Julie Sutton case. But you can be sure everything that went on up here will be under investigation now."

"He didn't give Sam back the dagger?" Jake asked.

"No," Hamill told them. "It's a twin to the one from the box. According to the judge, they were both part of a set that was used in some kind of secret rituals a group of the fraternity brothers initiated. Swearing an oath of allegiance in blood, I think. Sam had the new one specially made."

Laura shuddered. "Fraternity rituals! That's hard to believe."

"It wasn't all of the boys. Just the ones who wanted to suck up to Pendergrast," Cam clarified.

"So how much did you get on tape?" Jake asked.

Cam looked pleased. "Everything. Including Pendergrast's attack on the judge."

"But I thought we'd lost you," Jake said.

"You couldn't raise us, but I had a fail-safe backup system for your transmission. I left Jo back at the motel, monitoring the broadcast. She's probably mad as hell about missing the action.''

''No. She's decided she's content with a ringside seat.'' The voice of Jo O'Malley boomed over the speaker in the hall.

Cam laughed. ''That's my wife. How did you get back on the air, sweetheart?''

''Hooked the walkie-talkie into the main unit in the van down here. I'm learning.''

Jake looked meaningfully at Laura. ''Wife. How does that sound to you?''

''Awfully good.''

The speaker crackled. ''Katie and I were taking bets on how long you were going to last.''

''Me or him?'' Laura asked.

''Both of you.''

''Whatever.'' Jake looked at Cam and spoke in a whisper. ''Can you turn your darn surveillance system off, and give us a little bit of privacy?'' Without waiting for answer, he turned his back on the rest of the group and pulled Laura into his arms.

The door closed behind Hamill and Cam, but the man and woman on the couch didn't even notice.

After a long, passionate kiss, Jake nuzzled Laura's neck. ''Marriage goes with commitment, you know. And if you accept the proposal, it's going to be for keeps.''

''Oh, Jake. Yes.'' She reached for his hand.

''I'm glad. Because you don't have a ghost of a chance of getting away.''

One of the lights beside the couch flickered out. Laura smiled. ''Julie's leaving us alone, too.''

''Yeah. Have you noticed the house feels different?'' Jake asked. ''Since she swooped in to save us, I mean.''

''You really think it was her?''

"I don't know. It sure was perfect timing."

"Yes. And whatever happened back there, I think the ghost of Ravenwood is finally at peace," Laura murmured, before snuggling into Jake's arms again.

ONLY SKIN DEEP

Chapter One

Kathryn Martin stared into the eyes of madness. Once the wide-set orbs had sparkled with mischief. Now, below the blue of the irises, dark currents of lunacy stirred like vipers slithering into the sunlight.

Katie reached across the leather sofa cushion and laid a gentle hand over her sister's. "Val, are you feeling all right?" she asked softly.

"Don't start that doctor stuff with me. I'm fine. Just fine." Beautifully manicured hands snatched up a copy of *Vogue* from the chrome-and-glass coffee table. With jerky movements she began to fan through the pages.

Katie ran her finger down a sofa seam. She'd been so busy with her research grant and the group of friends she'd made down at 43 Light Street that she'd accepted Val's excuses for not getting together more often. Now she wished she'd brought her medical bag up from the car.

With a little snort Val shoved the magazine at Katie. "Look at this model. Her body's okay, but you can see the lines around her eyes. That's not happening to me, sweetie."

"No, your skin is flawless," Katie agreed.

Val raised her head, a brilliant smile on her lips. All at once there was nothing more sinister in her blue eyes than the familiar self-satisfied flush that compliments had always brought.

It's my imagination, Katie thought as she leaned back into the plump cushions and tried to look relaxed. *I've just forgotten what a couple of hours with Val is like—especially when she's worried about something.* Except that this afternoon was worse. One moment Val was like a porcelain doll that had shattered into a million pieces. The next, she'd glued herself back together.

"No one would guess I'm ten years older than you," Val murmured.

Twelve, Katie silently corrected.

"We could almost be twins—if you'd do something about your hair and your makeup."

Twins.

The observation sent Katie's mind off on its own track. They'd both inherited their blue eyes and fresh-faced looks from their mother. But any similarities ended there. Val had always been the life of the party. Katie had been the shy mouse in the corner until her academic achievements had won her the recognition she deserved.

"You're not listening to me. You never listen!"

"Yes, I am. What should I do about my hair?"

"Why don't you let me fit you into my schedule down at Genesis? It's good enough for half the Washington in crowd. It ought to be good enough for you. I know it's expensive, but I could write up the ticket on my employee discount." Val giggled. "My hair used to be as dark as yours. You need some highlights. And a makeup lesson. Fifteen minutes in the morning with the right foundation and accent colors would do wonders."

Katie couldn't imagine spending that much time on makeup—or anything else so self-indulgent. As an intern, she'd learned how to shower, pull on her clothes and get out the door in ten minutes. Since she'd left hospital practice to work on a genetic study, her routine was no longer frantic, but she'd never gotten into the habit of pampering herself. Maybe it was a holdover from all the years their mother had counted pennies just to keep food on the table. On the other hand, being poor appeared to have worked just the opposite with her half sister. Val seemed determined to gather up every luxury she'd missed as a kid.

"It was sweet of you to come take me to lunch on my birthday, but I've got to chase you out. Tom and I have big plans this evening, and I need to get ready." Val got to her feet.

Katie sucked in a deep breath. She could do things the easy way—the safe way—or she could make a stand. Not wanting to be at a disadvantage now, she got up, too. "Val, I know something's bothering you."

"What do you mean?"

"You've been on edge all day. Maybe I can help. Why don't we talk about it?"

For a fraction of a second, Val seemed to waver. Then her face contorted to the old, familiar look of wrath that Katie remembered so well from her childhood. "Sure. Talk. Spill my guts. So you can lord it over me how much better you've done for yourself with your fancy medical degree and how they've got your name in reference books and all. Well, Miss Who's Who and What's What, you may have gotten hotshot grades in school, but you don't know squat about men. Or anything else really important."

"Val, please don't throw up a smoke screen," Katie protested gently. "If you're sick—or in some kind of trouble—I want to be here for you."

"No you don't. Go back to Baltimore where you belong. And don't come back." She gave Katie a shove toward the door that almost made her lose her footing.

Katie steadied herself with a flattened palm against the wall. When she moved her hand away, she could see a sweaty mark on the dove-white paint. No one knew better than she how dangerous Val could be when provoked. She simply couldn't handle this by herself. At least not right now.

"I'll call you later. We'll talk then."

"Don't do me any favors."

Val turned her back, walked to the sliding glass door and stood looking out as if there were no one else in the room.

Katie stared at her sister's rigid neck. "If you need anything, just let me know. I mean that." As she backed toward the door, she felt consumed by a sudden, overwhelming emptiness.

AS SOON AS SHE GOT RID of meddling little Katie, Val fixed herself a very dry martini. *The nerve. Trying to pump me for information.*

She took a gulp of the potent drink. It didn't help her head or the clawing fear in her chest. For weeks she'd felt like the guy in that sci-fi movie—what was it? She shook her head. The name wasn't important. It was that guy. The one who looks perfectly normal until he collapses at dinner and starts to scream. Then this horrible little monster digs its way out of his chest.

Val shuddered and clamped her lips together, afraid she was going to start screaming like the man in the movie. And once she started, she was never going to stop. There was a monster inside her, too. Maybe not something with teeth and claws and a body, but something trying to scratch and gnaw its way to the surface where everyone could see it. Not in her chest, in her head. It was in there, buzzing and snarling. Making it hard to think.

When Katie had made that big sob-sister play, she'd almost started babbling to her. But she'd held herself together. The way she always had when things got tough. She couldn't share the fear. Especially not with self-righteous little Katie.

With jerky, automatic motions she pulled off her clothes and lurched into the bathroom. After filling the tub, she sank into the warm, scented water. As she leaned back against her inflated rubber pillow, she tried to make her mind blank. After a while, the pain in her head began to diffuse.

Wondering why she'd been so upset a few minutes ago, she began to hum a pop tune. By the time she pulled the plug and stood up, she felt one hundred percent better. Her only problem was that she'd been staying out too late with Tom. Sixty-three and he wanted to dance all night.

Val executed a little two-step as she rubbed a towel across her shoulders. Not just dance. The old mule thought he was a stallion in bed. But she liked him more for what was in his pants pockets than what was in his pants. If she wanted fireworks between the sheets, she called Greg, the great-looking stud she'd met at the gym a couple of months ago.

Smiling saucily at her high-breasted figure in the mirror, Val reached for a little dab of Flawless Skin Restorer. She'd tried all the Genesis products and treatments, and this almond-scented cream was the best. It went for a hundred dollars an ounce, and only Genesis's most valued customers could purchase the limited supply. But she'd watched Ming open the cabinet enough times to write down the combination. The trouble was, Ming counted everything, so she couldn't snitch a whole jar. She could only take a smidgen out of the top of the new ones. But even a little bit was enough to make a big difference in the way her skin looked, she thought with satisfaction as she examined her face in the magnifying mirror beside the sink.

THE RUSH-HOUR TRAFFIC crawled up Connecticut Avenue toward Chevy Chase Circle with the speed of a disabled caterpillar. Katie had been waiting for a string of motorists to turn left when a horn in back of her blared. With a start she realized that while she'd been worrying about Val, the line of cars had moved.

She wasn't her sister's keeper, she told herself firmly as she stamped on the accelerator and plowed through the intersection just before the light turned red. When Val was on a rampage, the best thing to do was to clear out of the way and wait for the dust to settle.

But as she eased the car into the stream of traffic rounding the circle, she couldn't keep a particular legal phrase from flowing through her mind. *A danger to herself or others… A danger to herself or others.* That was just about the only criterion left for forcing an unwilling patient to have a psychiatric evaluation. But had the situation with her sister really come to that? Reluctantly Katie tried to supply an answer.

She'd seen Val angry. She'd seen Val spiteful. She'd seen Val hostile. But never quite like this.

What would her older sister have done to her if she hadn't left? Was Val a danger to herself? How did the law work in D.C.? And what about that man she had a date with? Did he know what he was walking into this evening?

Purely on automatic pilot, Katie continued toward the Beltway. But as she approached the turnoff, her foot faltered on the accelerator. Pulling onto a side street lined with solid-looking brick houses, she cut the engine and sat for a moment hunched over the steering wheel.

"Stop being a coward, Kathryn Martin," she whispered.

Still it was several moments before she eased the gear lever into reverse, backed up, and started retracing her route into Washington. If she didn't find out what was making Val so edgy, she was never going to forgive herself.

AFTER FINISHING her makeup, Val ambled into the bedroom and threw open the door of her walk-in closet. It took forty minutes and three complete changes to settle on a slinky red velvet dress. She was just stepping into snappy slingbacks when the door chimes sounded.

Early again. Damn him.

She didn't dare let her annoyance show as she answered the door. Tom Houston's gray hair was carefully parted on the wrong side, and his square jaw sported a couple of shaving nicks. Tacky. But his first words made up for the deficiencies.

"You look beautiful, honey."

Val accepted the compliment with a glittering smile and a little tingle of anticipation as she thought about the expensive birthday present she'd hinted she wanted. Tom could afford it. That Medizone Lab of his was a gold mine. At least if he'd stop sharing so much of the profits with Mac McQuade. She'd tried to say something about that and had gotten a lecture on the great stuff Mac was doing. You'd think the guy walked on water.

When she and Tom were settled on the couch, he pulled a small box from his pocket. "Happy birthday, honey."

"Oooo. You shouldn't have," she cooed as she tore into the wrapping. However, when she lifted the lid on the suede box, her face fell. Nestled inside was a dinky opal pendant on a silver chain.

Tom watched expectantly. When her lips drew into a

pout, he frowned. "Wasn't that what you said you wanted?"

"No." Val leaped off the couch, walked to the sliding glass door, and stepped onto the balcony. The temperature had dropped since she and Katie had come home, and the cold air made her shiver. If she'd been alone, she would have gone back inside. Instead she wrapped her arms around her shoulders to ward off the wind and drew in a deep breath. It brought the pain back to her head. This time it felt as though a steel needle stabbed her brain. "Don't you know anything?" she snapped, without looking at Tom. "Springs don't wear silver. They wear gold."

"Springs? What do you mean?"

"My season. My colors. Don't you know anything?" she repeated.

Shaking his head, Tom came out to the balcony. After hesitating a moment, he tried to draw her back against his chest. "Sorry. I guess I got mixed up again. I don't know." He shook his head. "It's been happening a lot lately. But it doesn't matter. We can go down to the jewelry store tomorrow, and you can show me what you want."

Val barely heard the words. All at once, the touch of his square hands was revolting. Trying to get away, she leaned forward, her body slanting over the wrought iron railing.

"Val, that's dangerous. Come on back inside, hon."

Wrenching out of his grasp, she whirled. "I'll come in when I damn please. How dare you give me something so cheap!"

"Cheap? That bauble set me back two hundred bucks." His eyes were cold. "I'm starting to think Mac was right all along. You've been using me, baby, and I'm not going to eat dirt anymore."

"Mac. That jerk who works for you. You care more about him than you do about me." Anger exploded in her head like a heat-seeking missile. She lunged forward, her daggerlike nails striking at his eyes.

Tom's hands came up to protect his eyes as he dodged backward and to the side, so that the nails only scraped down one cheek.

With his bulk removed from her path, Val was thrown off balance. Restricted by the tight red dress, she couldn't check her forward momentum.

"Help me!"

Tom dropped his hands from his eyes just as Val grabbed for the railing. She clawed desperately at empty air, but couldn't stop herself from pitching forward. Even though Tom made a frantic grab for her, there was no way he could reach her in time. A scream of mingled surprise and terror tore from her lips as she took flight. It followed her down to the pavement ten stories below.

ON A RAINY DAY in April eight years ago, everything had changed for Mac McQuade. The dark hair and lean body were about the same—except for one small detail. But something in the gray eyes had altered like smoke shifting unexpectedly in a strong wind. Once he'd been an optimist. Now he was a realist. Once he'd chased the American dream—comfort, money, prestige, love. Now he went after less conventional rewards. If his goals took him to the jungles of Borneo or the bottom of the Pacific Ocean— away from other people—so much the better.

Skin like fine leather crinkled at the corners of his eyes. The trouble was, when the trip was over, you had to write a report, and Mac considered report writing in the same league with walking barefoot over hot coals. Which was why he was here at his desk after everyone else had gone home—planning to work straight through until he got the damn thing done.

Hearing a door slam somewhere in the distance, he looked up, annoyed. Then footsteps pounded down the hall of the lab building, and Mac's personal warning system went from irritation to full alert. Pushing his six-foot frame out of the comfortably padded chair, he turned to face the door. Ever since he'd come back from Central America, he'd felt something malevolent hovering just at the edge of his perception like a predator waiting to strike. The worst part was that there'd been no way to head it off.

Remorse billowed up inside his chest when he saw Tom Houston hurtle into the room. Mac knew he should have done something before this. But how? What?

The man's eyes were dazed. Streaks of blood had dried on his face. "Thank God you're here. I need you…I need you to make it come out right."

"Tom, what happened?"

Tom's shoulders hunched as he sank into the desk chair.

"Were you mugged? In an accident?" *Did you kill someone?* Mac's last question went unasked. It was a measure of how bad the situation had gotten that he hadn't been able to censor the thought.

The older man began to tremble.

Struggling for outward calm, Mac grabbed a sterile cloth and distilled water from the supply cabinet. When he reached toward the scratches on his friend's paper-white cheek, Tom jerked away. "Don't!"

"These cuts need attention."

"Just leave them alone."

Mac let the sterile pad and the subject drop. "Does anything else hurt?" The most likely explanation was a mugging, he decided as he gently probed for broken bones. He used his good right hand. With his left hand—the one made out of stainless steel—he loosened the older man's tie, the delicate operations of the metallic fingers almost second nature now.

The metal hand was a very fine precision instrument. But then, he'd had considerable input into the microchip-controlled prototype. And the rehab department had made some refinements since he'd begun field-testing it. Probably when they brought it to market, they'd go for flesh tones. Right now, it was performance he wanted, not looks. If the new batteries just held up under jungle conditions, he'd use the thing when he went back to Honduras for some more snake venom.

"You've got to help me," Tom pleaded.

"I will." *Why didn't you come to me as soon as I got back?* he wanted to shout. Instead he kept his voice steady. "Whatever it takes."

Until a couple of months ago, Tom Houston had been the most intelligent, forceful and stubborn man he'd ever met. About the only thing still intact was the stubbornness—along with a new defensiveness and secretiveness that had made it impossible to reach him.

What did you do when the man who'd been like a second father to you went off the deep end? Hope he'd snap out of it? Drag him bodily to the hospital for a mental and physical exam? For the first time in years Mac McQuade had been paralyzed into inaction.

"She's dead. Her sister."

Mac's head snapped around. "Whose sister? What are you talking about?"

"Damn. I never told you that part. I was gonna. Honest. And now it's all a mess." Tom started to sob. It took a long time to calm him down and get the disjointed story out of him. Even then Mac could hardly believe what he was hearing.

"Val was angry with you. She tried to claw your eyes and went off the balcony," he clarified, his voice measured.

"Yes. I tried to grab her. But I couldn't—I couldn't get to her in time."

It was strange to hope he was simply listening to a sick man's ravings. Still, that was all he could cling to now. "What's her number?"

"Seventy-three—" Tom stopped and shook his head. "Or thirty-seven. Can't remember."

Mac looked away so that he wouldn't have to meet the sudden confusion in Tom's eyes. He'd been calling Val's apartment for months. Now he couldn't remember the number. Picking up the receiver, Mac got it from information.

"May I please speak to Ms. Caldwell?" he asked when a man answered Val's phone.

"Who's calling?"

"Who is this?" Mac countered.

"Fred Richmond, the building manager."

"I'd like to speak to Ms. Caldwell," he repeated.

"I'm afraid there's been a serious accident."

"What happened?"

"Ms. Caldwell is, uh, deceased. Wait a minute. There's a police officer here who wants to speak to you."

Mac's eyes swung toward Tom as he cupped his palm over the mouthpiece. "The police are at her apartment."

The older man's hand whipped out like a spring-loaded dart, snatched the receiver from Mac's grasp and slammed it back onto the cradle.

"Tom!" Mac stopped abruptly and made an effort to curb his own frustration. "Why don't we go down there together, and you can tell them what happened."

"No!" The syllable was as full of fear as anguish.

"It's all right. I'll be with you. We're a good team, aren't we?"

The older man wasn't listening. Scrambling up, he backed away, his eyes focused on some unseen terror. When his shoulders hit the wall, he moaned and looked around as if searching for an escape route.

"Tom, take it easy."

"Not the police. Don't you understand? They want to pin this on me. They'll find out I was paying the rent on her apartment, and my fingerprints are all over the place. They'll want to put me away for murder."

"But if it was an accident, you don't have anything to worry about."

"No! If you tell them I had anything to do with Val's death, I'll kill myself."

"Tom, please." Mac pushed back his own chair and took a cautious step toward his friend.

"Stay away from me. I'll do it. I swear." He snatched up a letter opener from the desk and held it like a dagger.

"I won't come any closer." Mac stopped in midstep and stared at the man who had picked him up when he'd hit rock bottom and convinced him he had a choice about the way he was going to spend the rest of his life. He hadn't figured out how to cope with the way the strong bonds of their relationship were dissolving as if they'd been eaten away by acid. But he did know one thing for sure. He owed Tom Houston everything. His self-respect. His sanity. Maybe even his life.

"You've got to find out if—if—they suspect anything, and take my stuff out of there," Tom pleaded.

"What stuff?"

Tom dropped the letter opener and cradled his head in his hands. "Underwear. Monogrammed shirts, maybe. And, oh God, those pictures we took in the Bahamas."

There was probably more, Mac thought, and it was highly unlikely that he could accomplish the kind of clean sweep that Tom wanted with the police crawling all over the place. The feeling of helplessness that had been building over the past few weeks twisted in Mac's gut again. What did he do now? Risk Tom's life by calling the authorities and laying it all on the line? Risk leaving him alone? Unfortunately he believed what Tom was saying. "Do you trust me?" he asked.

"I trust you."

"I trust you, too," he murmured, hating the way the lie swelled and expanded in his throat. "If I go back to Val's, and see what I can find out, will you promise you'll let me take you to a doctor tomorrow morning?"

Tom twisted his big hands. "I—okay. But you gotta get my stuff. I want it back here."

Mac sighed. Partial victory. And while he was downtown, he could take care of his own agenda. "You've got to promise not to get into any trouble while I'm gone," he admonished Tom, aware now that he was speaking the way he would to a child.

"I promise. I won't get in any trouble. Mac, I won't forget this."

"You're going to lie down on the couch in your office and wait for me."

"Yes. Anything you say."

"I'll give you something to help you relax while I'm away."

He ushered Tom down the hall to the medical dispensary, unlocked the door and found a sedative. Then he handed his friend one of the capsules and a glass of water.

Tom threw his head back with an exaggerated flourish as he swallowed. Then his gaze skittered away from Mac's.

"I assume you've got a key to the apartment."

"Um." Tom felt in his pocket and handed over a leather case.

"Which one?"

It took several moments of fumbling before the older man detached a brass-colored key.

"You'll wait right here for me," Mac reiterated.

Silently Tom lay down on the couch, pressed his arms against his sides and squeezed his eyes closed. As soon as the door shut behind Mac, they snapped open again—glittering and feverish in the dim light. With a grimace he spit out the medication he'd pretended to swallow and sat up.

Chapter Two

She'd been here only a few hours before. Now a strip of yellow tape barred the entrance to apartment 1015. It read: Police Barrier. Do Not Cross.

Katie's heart began to thump against her ribs. "Val? Val?" she called.

The door was thrust open by a tall, broad-shouldered black man in a rumpled sport coat. His hair was military short, and his voice held the note of a drill instructor addressing impossibly incompetent recruits. "I told you people, this isn't a circus. Now clear out." Dismissively he turned away.

"My sister. Val. What's happened to my sister?" Although Katie stood her ground, the question came out high and strangled.

The borderline hysteria apparently caught the man's attention. Pivoting back toward the door, he peered into Katie's bloodless face, and his own expression softened. "There's been an accident. I think you'd better come in and sit down."

She looked up pleadingly into his brown eyes, sensing compassion but also reserve, as if he were withholding judgment about her until he found out more.

"I'm Detective Perkins. D.C. police," he said as he led

her into the living room where several other men moved about taking pictures and dusting black powder onto the credenza.

"My sister," Katie repeated. "Valerie Caldwell."

"I'm sorry. There's no easy way to tell you this. She jumped off the balcony."

"Is she…"

Perkins nodded. "I'm sorry, ma'am."

She'd known something terrible was going to happen. Somehow she'd known. Now, as her worst fears were confirmed, Katie's knees buckled, and she dropped to the couch. The same couch where she and Val had been talking only hours before. "But we just had lunch," she protested weakly.

Perkins's expression sharpened. "You were with her this afternoon?"

"A couple of hours ago."

"Then you may be the last person to have seen her alive."

Katie's throat felt raw. The last person. No. Unless Val had canceled her plans. "What about her date? She asked—asked—me to leave," Katie stammered, "because she needed to get ready." It wasn't a complete account of the way they'd parted but it would do for now. "I thought about going home. But I decided I'd better drive back to my office because I had a lot of work to do," she added, unable to keep random facts from tumbling out under the spotlight of Perkins's scrutiny.

The detective had taken out a notebook. "I didn't catch your name."

"Kathryn Martin."

"Your office is downtown?"

"No, I live in Ellicott City and work in Baltimore."

"And your sister had a date with whom?"

Katie racked her brain. It was simpler to try and answer the man's questions than deal with her own shock. Val had mentioned a couple of guys when they'd talked on the phone to set up the luncheon date. Greg. No, he was the one from the health club. The one she was seeing this evening was Ted. No, Tom.

"Tom," she murmured.

"His last name?"

Katie shrugged. "I'm sorry. That was all she told me."

"You said you were on your way back to Baltimore. Why did you return to Ms. Caldwell's apartment just now?"

"I was worried about her."

"In what way?"

"She was nervous—on edge about something. But she didn't want to talk about it." Katie gulped. "I guess that was one of the reasons she asked me to leave."

"Was someone threatening her? Tom? Was she apprehensive about the date?"

"Not the date," Katie said slowly, her numbed brain coming to grips with the direction of Perkins's thoughts. Funny how differently a policeman and a physician approached the same set of facts. It hadn't even occurred to her that someone might have really been threatening Val.

Perkins's dark eyes focused on Katie's face as if he suspected she might be withholding important information.

She bowed her head. Her own theories were hard to talk about, yet what was the point in being evasive now? Drawing in a steadying breath, she met his probing gaze. "I'm a physician. I was worried about my sister's mental health."

Perkins wasn't able to hide his surprise. "You're a doctor?"

"Georgetown Medical School. You want a summary of my vita?"

"No. Sorry, Dr. Martin." He cleared his throat. "Do you think Ms. Caldwell was depressed?"

She tried to answer in the same professional tone with which the question had been asked. "No. Not in the clinical sense. Frightened is a better description. Agitated. Paranoid."

"Did she have a history of mental illness?"

"Well, she was troubled. And unstable. She was married and divorced three times. But she never shared the details of her medical history."

"Umm."

Katie laced her fingers together in her lap and squeezed until the knuckles were bloodless. She could feel Perkins watching her again. If she didn't explain, he wasn't going to appreciate how it had been between her and Val. Suddenly she wanted him to understand why she'd run away this afternoon—and why she'd come back. Still, when she began to speak, her voice was barely above a whisper. "Val is—was—twelve years older than I am. We're half sisters, actually. After Mom divorced Val's father, she married mine. He died when I was only two." She swallowed painfully. "Val was the star of the family. She was pretty and popular. A cheerleader. The homecoming queen. When I was little, she treated me like a kind of pet—styling my hair and painting my nails. Then when I went to school and my teachers started talking about how smart I was, she became resentful." Katie stopped and closed her eyes for a moment as if that could shut out the hurtful memories. "First she teased me. Then she escalated to mean tricks—like getting me to chew on a hot pepper—or spilling nail-polish remover on my homework papers."

Perkins seesawed his pen between large fingers. "Sounds like a serious case of sibling rivalry."

"After I went to college, we didn't even see each other." Katie plowed on, talking quickly now so she could get the telling over with. "But about four years ago, when my mother died, we sort of mended our fences. I—I guess I wanted to keep seeing her, so I let her set the rules for the friendship. It was important for her to feel superior to me. I think that's why she didn't want me to know there was something wrong with her. I didn't press her this afternoon, and now it's too late," she finished bitterly.

Perkins laid a broad hand on her shoulder. "Don't blame yourself, Dr. Martin. A person who's disturbed and wants to commit suicide, they'll find a way to do it."

"She didn't leave a note, did she?"

"Not that I can find. But before you arrived, a couple of old ladies who live on her floor were eager to tell me that your sister had been acting weird lately. However, I'm still going to keep investigating—follow up some other leads. See if I can locate this Tom person. Find out if he was here this evening. Make sure I can rule out foul play."

Katie and the detective regarded each other for several moments. Then Perkins cleared his throat. "There's one more thing I'm afraid I'm going to have to ask you to do for us."

"I was Val's only relative. I guess you want me to identify the body."

"If you would. I can have one of my men drive you down to the morgue."

IT WAS DARK by the time Mac reached Val Caldwell's apartment building. After finding a parking space in the next block, he sat in the plush front seat of his silver Jaguar looking at the way the light from an overhead street lamp reflected on his high-tech hand. Reaching up, he used the mechanical fingers to adjust the rearview mirror so he could see the sidewalk in back of the car.

In a lot of respects, the precision-made digits were better than the real thing once you got the knack of making them work. They were stronger. Almost as dexterous. Impervious to pain. And designed to carry out a number of specialized operations. However, he wasn't ready to recommend that the rest of humanity line up for a similar set.

Metal fingers had no sensitivity. And wearing an artificial body part was a pretty good test of peoples' values and prejudices. The two responses he hated most were being pitied or being dismissed as less than competent because he didn't have two flesh-and-blood hands. However, it was damn useful to know where you stood with someone right from the first. That was one reason he never dodged the issue by hiding the prosthesis. The other was that he'd made some promises to himself when he'd agreed to work for Tom. He was never going to pretend he was something he wasn't. If you didn't like Mac McQuade the way he was, too bad. What you saw was what you got.

This evening, however, he couldn't keep a hypothetical scenario out of his mind. *Police officer: "Did the man skulking around Ms. Caldwell's apartment have any distinguishing physical characteristics?"*

Witness: "Nothing special. Just a stainless steel fist."

If he was going to do some checking up on Val, it was essential that no one connect him with Tom. So before getting out of the car, he thrust his left hand into the pocket of his trench coat. He also turned up the collar around his face, as if he were seeking protection from the biting wind. The tactic hid not only his features but also his grim expression as he hurried along the sidewalk.

All the way into the city, he'd been wrestling with unpleasant thoughts. Given the time to reflect, he couldn't help being angry with Tom for putting him in the position of having to choose between personal loyalty and the law. He'd been in enough primitive environments to know that society's rules were part of the glue that held a civilization together. And he appreciated being able to return to a world where you didn't have to watch your back every moment.

Realizing he was marching through the gathering gloom with his teeth clenched, he made an effort to look like a more normal part of the city scene.

Deliberately he turned his mind back to Val Caldwell. Tom had bragged about some of his expensive presents to her. Now he'd let it slip that he'd been paying her rent, too. Had the woman been milking him for thousands every month? Had money problems been part of Tom's recent anxiety? And what other mess had Val gotten him into? At first he'd wondered if Tom had Alzheimer's disease or something. But maybe his girlfriend had introduced him to drugs. That would certainly explain his personality changes and erratic behavior.

Mac grimaced. He and Ms. Caldwell had never met, but there wasn't much he'd heard about the sexy little beautician that he'd liked. She'd been demanding, unstable and manipulative. Now she was dead, and before her relatives started dismantling her apartment he was going to have a crack at finding out exactly what kind of trouble she'd gotten Tom into. Then once he had his friend safely under a doctor's care, he'd tell the police what he'd found out.

A patrol car was still sitting at the curb when Mac rounded the corner. Instead of entering the apartment building, he detoured to the little restaurant across the street. After buying a *Washington Post,* he found a booth in the back and ordered a cup of coffee and a hamburger.

While he waited for the food and pretended to read the sports section, he listened to the talk around him.

"Did you see her lyin' there on the sidewalk? They picked her up and the whole right side of her face was crushed."

Unbidden, Mac's mind flashed back to the evening when he'd lain on a cold, cracked sidewalk with a crowd of curious spectators gathering. He'd fallen on his left, not his right. And he'd instinctively put up his hand to soften the impact. That had been a mistake.... Underneath the table, he pressed his metal fist against his middle and brought his mind back to the present.

"She was a real hot number..."

"Yeah, she came on to me once like gangbusters..."

"But she had a temper..."

"I'm not surprised she jumped..."

The excited chatter continued. But how much of it could you believe, now that Ms. Caldwell wasn't here to set the record straight? Mac wondered.

After twenty minutes, he noticed the police car had left. Still, he dawdled over the newspaper and a second cup of coffee. He knew he was stalling, but while he'd been sitting here, he'd been having serious second thoughts about what Tom had asked him to do.

WITH EXAGGERATED CARE, Jade Nishizaka set down her cup of tea on the marble-topped table beside her contour recliner.

"I'm not sure I understood. Please repeat that information."

The young manservant she'd hired as much for his looks as his martial-arts skills and a number of other useful talents bowed slightly and flattened his palms against his sides. His name was Koji, and she'd brought him over from Japan on one of her trips to the laboratory complex that developed Genesis's expensive cosmetics for her.

"We have a report from the police that one of your employees is dead," he enunciated carefully.

"Who?"

"Valerie Caldwell."

There was a slight elevation of Jade's classically arched brows. Otherwise the expression on her youthful face didn't change. In fact, nothing much about her ever seemed to change—unless one observed her quite carefully. She was almost sixty, but she was a faithful user of her own products—and the well-equipped gym she'd installed in her luxury condo. With her trim figure and flawless complexion she might have passed for a woman in her mid-thirties. "Do they know what happened?"

"The officer in charge has turned in a preliminary report. The most likely explanation is suicide."

Only a small exhalation of breath betrayed Jade's tension. "How horrible. I must send my condolences to the family. Check our personnel records and get me the address."

"*Hai,* mistress."

"You will have that information on my breakfast tray in the morning. For now, I wish to be alone with my sadness. But I will require your services later—for a massage." Her eyes met his, and a small smile played at the corners of her beautiful lips.

"*Hai,* mistress." Koji's eyes flickered for a moment as he bowed again and backed out of the room.

Yes, he was the perfect servant for her needs. But not until later. Not until she had thought through this crisis.

Alone once more, she sat with her eyes closed for several moments, trying to calm the storm that swept through her spirit. She knew herself well. If there was any fault in her personality, it was the inability to find the peaceful center of her being.

But she had reason to be troubled. So much was at stake. She'd worked for years to achieve her goals. Tomorrow the wife of the deputy secretary of commerce was coming to Genesis for the first time. Talk of Val's death in the salon would hardly make a good impression on a new customer. She would have to remind the staff about the penalties for spreading gossip.

Jade swung her lithe body from the recliner and crossed to the porcelain vase of cherry-blossom boughs decorating a black lacquered table. Her vision blurred as she stared at the fragile pink flowers, inviting their velvet petals to take away her tension. She knew now that she should have done something about Valerie Caldwell long before this. But there was no point in regretting errors in judgment.

Val had been good at her job—one of the few beauticians whose skills met Genesis's exacting standards. Which was why she'd been hired. After she'd begun working on the salon's exclusive clientele, she'd built up a steady base of repeat business. But lately, the woman had started showing symptoms of instability. Jade's first impulse had been to fire her. Then she'd decided it was dangerous to turn her loose. Better to keep her close at hand where she could be watched. Just in case.

Had the judgment been wrong? Jade went to the Louis XIV desk under the window. There was no hesitancy as she looked up a number in her private directory and placed a call. It might be after hours, but she was paying for special services—it was better to be safe than sorry now. She wanted someone to have a look around Val Caldwell's apartment. And she wanted it done tonight. Then she'd have to make some other calls.

IT WAS ALMOST NINE by the time Katie and her police escort got back to Val's apartment building. "Are you sure you're going to be all right?" Officer Bryant asked.

"Yes." Katie's muffled assurance was automatic. For hours she'd felt as if she were walking around at the bottom of the sea. The weight of the water made even the smallest motion almost too much effort. And when she'd stood in front of her sister's pale, lifeless body, the pressure against her chest had been suffocating.

"Where did you leave your car?" Bryant asked.

"Around the corner. But, uh, I'd like to go back inside for a few minutes."

"I guess that would be all right."

Katie opened the door and felt a cold blast of air knife through the light coat that had been fine for the middle of the afternoon. Suddenly the evening chill seemed to penetrate all the way to the bone. She knew she wasn't just reacting to the cold. It was Val, too. The way she'd looked laid out under a white sheet—one side of her face looking perfectly normal, the other ruined.

In the impersonal little viewing room, self-preservation had demanded that Katie keep a tight hold on her emotions. Now tears gathered in her eyes, and she blinked.

"You're sure you're gonna be okay?" the young officer repeated. "Anyone you want to call?"

Katie shook her head and pushed the door wider, determined not to break down in front of this stranger. Quickly she stepped out to the sidewalk.

"Thanks."

His unintelligible reply followed her as she fled into the apartment lobby and tried to warm her icy hands in front of the radiator. Really there was no need to go upstairs now. There was no hurry about sorting through Val's things. Yet she wanted to wipe out the terrible image of her sister lying there broken and vulnerable and so silent. She wanted something else to remember tonight. Some tangible token of Val's life, of the things that had made her happy. Turning away from the radiator, she strode to the elevator and pressed the button.

Was it all right to take a few mementos from the apartment? she wondered as she made her way down the hall. Perhaps she should call Detective Perkins tomorrow and tell him what she'd done, she decided as she entered Val's apartment.

After the earlier bustle of police activity, it was dark and silent as a tomb. She noticed a plastic garbage bag beside the door. Had the police set aside some evidence that they intended to pick up later? Or was one of the officers still on the premises?

"Is anyone here?"

No answer.

"Officer Perkins?"

From somewhere back in the unseen rooms, Katie thought she detected a muffled noise. Standing very still, she waited to find out if it was repeated. She heard nothing, except the beating of her own heart.

Katie shivered, unable to shake the fancy that she wasn't alone in the apartment. Was Val's ghost returning for one last visit? *Oh, come on,* she rebuked herself. *You're just hearing the people in the next unit.*

She was reaching for the light switch when she let her arm drop against her side. Leaning her head back, she stood with her body pressed against the door, needing the support to keep herself on her feet. As if drawn by a flashing red beacon, her eyes swung to the sliding glass doors and the balcony beyond. Only a few hours ago she'd watched Val standing at the floor-to-ceiling window looking out. Had she already been thinking about jumping? Or had she stood there with her back to her sister unable to ask for help?

"Oh, Val, why didn't you trust me?" Katie whispered into the darkness.

An answer reverberated in her mind. *I wanted you to look up to me the way you did when I was little. I wanted you to think I was perfect.*

"Nobody's perfect," Katie choked out. "Not you. Not me. Especially not me. There were times I needed you, too. And I couldn't ask. Oh, Val, why couldn't we help each other?"

The tears she had been struggling to hold back began to flow. Wrapping her arms around her shoulders, she stood in the foyer weeping silently.

She wasn't sure how long the emotional storm lasted. Finally she fumbled in her purse. With a crumpled tissue, she wiped her eyes and blew her nose.

She should go home, get some sleep, and come back in the morning. But she didn't want to do that now. What she wanted—needed—was a token of the time when everything had been all right between her and Val. That had been years ago. She'd been in nursery school, and whenever she'd come into her big sister's room, she'd been drawn to the fuzzy green-and-yellow *W* with the little gold megaphone pinned to the front. The letter had been one of Val's prized possessions, an emblem of her glory days at Woodrow Wilson High School, and she'd never discarded it. In fact, Katie had seen it in a box of memorabilia right after Val had moved in here. Now she felt a compulsive need to find it.

Val had probably put the box in her closet. It would be easy enough to grab it and take the whole thing home.

Yet as she started down the shadowy hall, Katie was unable to shake the eerie feeling that she was being pursued by ghosts. Her footsteps rang hollowly on the wooden floor as she bolted into the bedroom. There was no light switch by the door, so she rushed to the bedside table and turned on the lamp. The puddle of illumination made her feel a little more steady. Still, she stood staring at the walk-in closet for several moments and dragging in lungfuls of air.

She realized she was straining her ears the way she had when she'd first come into the apartment. Did she hear a furtive rustle among the dresses? Not very likely.

Here in the bedroom she could smell Val's perfume. It was almost as if her sister had just stepped out for a moment and was coming right back. But she could also smell something else. Someone else? The scent teased at her memory, but she couldn't give it form. Well, Perkins and Bryant and a bunch of other guys had been here for hours. Maybe she was smelling their after-shave. Or maybe it had nothing to do with the police. Val had been getting ready to see a man named Tom. Had they been in here together?

Katie glanced toward the bed. The spread was smooth and unwrinkled, and she felt suddenly like a voyeur. It wasn't any of her business what Val had been doing with Tom—unless it had some bearing on her death.

With a little shake of her head, she turned again to the closet. The door was open, and the interior was as dark as midnight. But there was probably an overhead light, maybe with a pull chain.

Stepping into the unlighted chamber, she began to wave her arm around, feeling for the cord. Her fingers grazed a row of dresses before hitting something more solid.

Air drained from her lungs as the solid object moved. In the next moment, she felt the cold steel of a knife blade against her throat.

Chapter Three

A scream tried to tear itself from Katie's throat. It was cut off as hard fingers clamped over her mouth. Stark, elemental terror lanced through her, giving her an urgent strength she hadn't known she possessed.

Perkins had been right, and she had been wrong. Someone had been after Val. Now they'd come back to get her.

The unseen attacker grunted as he tried to hold her fast, the hard fingers of one hand digging painfully into her side. They seemed to clutch at her with inhuman strength. Struggling backward, she was thrown off balance as her shoulders sank into the folds of a fur coat.

Regaining her footing, she tried to pound her fist against his broad chest. He didn't go after her with the knife again. Had he dropped it in the struggle? A tiny corner of her mind thanked God for small favors, even as one of her wildly flailing arms hit the pull chain for the light.

As if it were a lifeline, she clutched and yanked at the slender cord.

In the instant the bare bulb flashed on, blinding her with the sudden brightness, she realized she'd made a mistake. Her assailant would know exactly where to aim now. Blinking, she cringed away from the blow she knew was coming.

However, nothing was—nothing could be—what she had expected. Ever again. Awareness was a rocket bursting in her brain. Or perhaps it was more like the world heaving and buckling as if a fault in the earth's crust had suddenly opened up beneath her feet, leaving her dangling helplessly over a gaping pit.

Katie heard a strangled cry that was part shock, part astonishment. She couldn't say whether the sound had come from her own lips or the man who held her in his grasp. There was simply no place left in her mind for rational thought. She was standing in a closet crammed with fur and silk and velvet and other expensive apparel. None of it registered. The universe had shrunk to much more circumscribed dimensions.

Mac McQuade. A ghost from her past. A man she had known she would never see again.

Dizzy, disoriented, her breath frozen in her throat, she stared up helplessly into smoky gray eyes. The only way to save herself from falling into the abyss was to anchor her hands on the broad shoulders in front of her.

Moments ago they'd been antagonists in the dark. Now his arms came up—holding her as a lover might, pressing her against the tensile strength of his lean body. Her face lifted toward him. His head lowered.

"Mac." The name was a shuddering cry. It had been such a long, lonely time since he'd held her like this.

The sound of his name—or perhaps the emotion behind the strangled syllable—broke the spell. She felt his body stiffen. Then his head lifted as if he had finally realized where they were—and when.

"Mac, please."

A stiff arm thrust against her shoulder. "No."

Reality was like a bucket of frigid water sloshing over her. She took a step back and became enmeshed in folds of silk. The fabric had no more relevance to her reality than imaginary cobwebs. Nothing had changed. Eight years ago she'd tossed away her pride and begged him not to shut her out of his life. And he'd dismissed her with a coldness that had frozen her heart.

The memory and the way he had thrust her away again now gave her the strength to look him in the eye and demand some answers. "What in the name of God are you doing skulking in my sister's closet?"

She had the satisfaction of seeing the shock register on his face. "Val Caldwell was *your* sister?"

"Yes. And what are *you* doing here?" she repeated.

He sighed. "It's a long story." The weariness in his voice was reflected in his countenance. She'd been seeing memory as much as present reality. At that moment she became aware of how much he'd changed. The dozens of lines etched into the tanned flesh around his eyes were startling. But it wasn't simply that his skin was weathered. The Mac McQuade she'd known had been equal parts boyish devil, dreamer and serious student. All the boyishness had been scoured away along with the dreams. He'd matured, but the process had not been gentle. My God, what had happened to him?

"Did you go back and finish medical school the way you told me you would?" she asked.

His stony gaze held hers. Instead of answering, he raised his left arm and held it a foot from her face.

Her gasp of surprise as she focused on the metal replacement brought a cynical look to his eyes. "It works pretty well, but it's not the hand of a surgeon."

For several seconds, she couldn't find her voice as she remembered the knife against her throat and the rigid fingers digging into her ribs. Now she understood what she had been feeling.

"You probably know, Dr. Martin—" He stopped abruptly. "It is Dr. Martin, isn't it?"

She nodded.

"You probably know that in the field of medicine, first opinions aren't always correct."

"But you said you were going to be all right," she insisted like a school child who'd memorized a set of facts without really understanding them. "That you didn't need me."

"That's right. I didn't. I don't." He pushed past her out of the closet and left her standing amid Val's fancy clothes trying to cope with her surprise and hurt—and new insights.

He'd lost his hand. Seeing the metal one had been like a rabbit punch. But her reaction had been from shock and surprise, not revulsion—although she suspected he wouldn't believe her if she tried to tell him. When Mac McQuade was sure he was right, he was too stubborn to listen to another opinion. Had he known he was facing amputation when he'd made it clear that he never wanted to see her again? Or had the doctors already done it? That would explain a lot. Or it might explain nothing at all.

She watched his rigid posture as he disappeared down the hall. Eight years ago he'd hurt her so deeply that it had taken every drop of strength she possessed to reclaim her self-respect. Afterward she'd told herself she didn't give a damn about Mr. McQuade. That was before he'd taken her in his arms a few minutes ago. For that brief space of time, the past had been wiped away. She'd thought she had both feet firmly planted in the present. Suddenly she knew that she'd been fooling herself for a long time. She wasn't over Mac McQuade.

However, there was more than an old wound or her own confused feelings to deal with now. Her sister was dead, and Mac was snooping around in her closet. Had he been involved with her? Or was it worse than that? Did he know something about Val's death? Had he come here to remove incriminating evidence?

Her suspicions were confirmed as she saw him pick up the plastic garbage bag beside the front door.

"Wait a minute! You can't just walk away."

"Why not? It'll be better for both of us if you pretend you never saw me."

Sure, she thought. Take the easy way out again. "How did you know Val? Were you dating her?"

He laughed. "I wasn't that crazy."

The words and the harsh tone of his voice sent a stab of pain driving into her chest. "You're talking about my sister. My sister who went over the balcony tonight. My sister who's dead." The protest came out high and fragile.

Mac paused, his good hand resting on the doorknob. His gaze flicked to Katie's face as if he were finally taking in her red eyes and pale skin. His own features softened. "I'm sorry."

She squeezed her eyes shut, wishing he'd look away as she struggled to keep the tears from spilling onto her cheeks again.

After long moments, he stared down at the plastic bag on the floor. When he spoke again, his voice was almost gentle. "This can't be easy for you. I guess you have a right to know why I'm here. Tom Houston is a friend of mine."

The mysterious Tom? "The man Val was supposed to be meeting tonight? What happened?" Katie watched Mac closely. He didn't shift his position. But his Adam's apple bobbed. "Officer Perkins thought Val was being threatened," she prodded. "Was it Tom? Did he kill her and send you to cover up for him?"

"Don't jump to crazy conclusions."

"What am I supposed to think? Stop playing games with me and spell it out."

Mac crossed the room, maneuvered Katie onto the couch and sat down beside her. "Tom was wild about Val. For months she was all he could talk about. He bought her anything she wanted—this apartment included. I can't believe he would hurt her—if he'd been in his right mind."

"In his right mind? What are you talking about?"

He wiped his hand across his forehead. "I wish I knew what the hell happened this evening."

"Then he was here! When she died?"

"Maybe. Or maybe he came over after it happened and saw her. He was too incoherent for me to tell for certain. But I was sure of a couple of things—Val was dead, and he was going to commit suicide if I didn't bring back the personal effects he'd left in the apartment."

It took several moments for Katie to digest the new information. "Who exactly is this Tom Houston?" she finally asked.

"My partner."

"In what?"

"Medizone Labs."

"*You're* a partner in Medizone Labs?"

"Tom's the president and founder of the company. He gave me a job about seven years ago. Since then, I've worked my way up."

Katie suspected that the simple statement wasn't the whole story. Anyone who kept up with the biotech industry knew that in the past half-dozen years or so Medizone had rocketed from a small research lab to one of the country's most innovative developers of pharmaceuticals and treatment modalities. A promising therapy for rheumatoid arthritis. A vaccine for encephalitis. A combination of drugs effective against ovarian cancer.

"How did Tom hook up with Val?"

"Would you believe he picked her up in a bar?"

Perhaps casual contacts weren't Tom's style. But Katie silently acknowledged that even in an age of sexual caution, Val had been reckless about her personal life.

"Is he married?"

"Of course not! His wife died a couple of years ago."

Katie sighed. "Trading veiled accusations isn't going to get us anywhere."

"You haven't lost your piercing insights, Dr. Martin."

"I said—"

"You're right. This isn't getting us anywhere. I'm angry with myself as much as anything else. I shouldn't have agreed to come here. Probably I just should have called the police and forced Tom to face reality. But I owe him one. More than one."

She heard the self-accusation in his voice. Whatever else was true, Mac cared about Tom Houston, and he'd wanted to protect him. "Sometimes it's hard to know what's the right thing to do," Katie said softly.

He nodded almost imperceptibly.

"Has Tom been acting...out of character lately?"

"Yes." His brows arched. "Why do you ask?"

"You implied he wasn't in his right mind."

"Yeah. Right."

"What are his symptoms?"

"Paranoid. Secretive. Forgetful. Wild mood swings."

The description sent a tremor racing up Katie's spine. "My God. That's exactly what I've been going through with Val. The worst part was that she wouldn't let me help her."

"Tom, too." Mac leaned forward, his eyes intense.

"But was there anything physically wrong with her? As far as you could tell, I mean."

"Physically, she seemed better than ever."

They stared at each other, both wondering why two previously healthy adults would exhibit the same set of symptoms.

"Maybe they were hooked on the same drug. What was Val into?" he asked sharply.

"She wasn't into anything that I know of before she met your friend Tom. What wonder drugs has he been cooking up in the lab lately?"

"Nothing illegal. That's not Tom's style."

"Maybe Medizone has a secret operation you don't have a clue about."

"Tom wouldn't do that!"

Katie stood up. "I vote we try to find some evidence one way or the other."

"As a matter of fact, I already started searching the apartment," Mac admitted grudgingly.

"And?"

"Your sister's clothes closet's clean. So is the kitchen. I was just about to tackle the bathroom."

"All right. I'll look in here," Katie volunteered, getting up off the sofa.

They might not want to work together, but for now it was the most efficient way to get the job done.

ARNIE BEALE'S stringy hand froze as he reached for the doorknob.

Blessed Mary! There was someone in the apartment. More than one someone. Ready to spring back if anyone inside made for the door, he pressed his ear against the cold metal. It was a man and a woman. And they weren't exactly having a friendly discussion.

Of all the rotten luck. He'd wanted to make sure the police were gone before he came over. Which was why he'd figured it was okay to stop at Flanigan's for a couple of quick ones.

Bad move, Arnie. Somebody beat you to the goodies. But who?

The man and woman inside had stopped talking, but they were still in there. Because he knew there wasn't another way out of the apartment. Unless they were planning to take a flying leap off the balcony like the previous occupant.

Damn. Now how was he supposed to do the job? Should he risk a quick look-see? No. That was too dangerous. What if one of them was still in the living room? Lifting his hand to his mouth, he began to gnaw on his left thumbnail—which was already bitten almost to the quick.

Whoever was in the apartment couldn't stay all night. He'd just have to wait until they'd left. Looking around, he spotted the stairway, a dozen yards away.

With a sigh, he plopped down on the stairs, inspected his nails for a suitable candidate, and began to chew at the tip of his middle finger. This was supposed to be an easy job. It wasn't his fault someone had gotten there first, and he sure as hell wasn't going to tell anyone about it when he made his report.

The bravado lasted a couple of seconds, until an involuntary shiver danced across his skin. Suppose he made up a story and the people he was working for found out he was lying? They'd hang him out to dry.

MAC DISAPPEARED down the hall. Remembering some of the details she'd read in newspaper articles about the places people hid drugs, Katie began searching under fur-

niture and cushions and lamp bases. Should she unscrew
the grilles on the heating ducts? she wondered.

"Got something interesting! Come look at this," Mac
called out, a note of accusation in his voice.

Katie's heart began to thump as she hurried down the
hall. She found Mac gesturing toward the linen closet.
He'd folded back a stack of towels to reveal two small
opaque jars. Her hands were trembling as she drew one
out and unscrewed the top. Inside was about a tablespoon
of a milky-white, faintly glossy cream. It looked like moisturizer. When she lowered her nose to the jar and sniffed,
she caught the trademark scent of almonds. A Genesis
product. Scooping up a dab, Katie smoothed a little bit
between her fingers. It felt lush and silky—almost like a
fairy godmother's touch. She could picture her cells soaking up the rich concoction.

"What is it?" Mac leaned over and sniffed the almond
scent.

"Moisturizing cream. From Genesis."

"Genesis. Yeah. There was some expensive-looking
makeup in the medicine cabinet with that name. What is
it, an exclusive brand?"

"That's right. You can only get it at the salon where
Val worked. I've never been there, but Val's told me it's
kind of an Elizabeth Arden-type place, where they'll do
just about anything you want, even collagen injections and
body wrapping. Or you can spend a half hour vegging out
in their special environmental room."

Mac grabbed the other jar, unscrewed the top, peered in
and sniffed. It had the same almond scent and the same
glossy appearance. "More moisturizing cream. But if it's
from Genesis, why isn't it in one of their fancy jars? And
why is it buried in the middle of a stack of towels? You'd
think she'd stolen it or something."

"Don't *you* jump to crazy conclusions. Val was doing all kinds of strange things. Probably there's money hidden in the flour canister.''

''I didn't find anything.'' He sighed and slipped the small jar into his pocket before turning abruptly back to the bedroom. Still clutching the other jar, Katie followed him, determined that she was going to be in on any more discoveries. But as he began to open drawers and boxes, she realized that her body felt leaden. She'd been through so much today, and now her energy reserves were zero. After hesitating for a moment, she sank into the boudoir chair by the window. If she'd been alone, her eyelids might have fluttered closed. Instead she found she couldn't take her eyes off Mac as he made a quick but thorough search of the room.

He didn't ask for her help, and it was clear he didn't need it. He was fast and efficient. But she wasn't really surprised. The confident, lithe way he moved was one of the things that had made her notice him in the first place back in medical school.

Against her will, she found the old memories flooding her mind. Back in medical school, even though she'd wanted to get to know the very appealing Mac McQuade, she hadn't made the first approach because she hadn't had a clue about how to interest popular guys. On the other hand, she was one of the best students in their class. That's what had made him notice *her,* she supposed. He was on a scholarship, too, she'd discovered when he'd invited her for coffee in one of the little cafés near the campus. It turned out that talking to him was easy. They'd gone from discussing test results to studying together, from sharing supper to spending the night in each other's apartments when they were studying late. Maybe if she hadn't been so focused on seeing that both of them passed their senior midterm exams, they would have been making love, too. They'd come pretty close. They'd both wanted to. At least that's what she'd told herself later. Although maybe that part had simply been her fantasy.

Resting her chin on her knees, Katie clasped her arms around her legs as if the protective posture could give her some comfort. Over the years, she'd spent a lot of time wondering about how things might have turned out if Mac McQuade hadn't left right after exams to fulfill a previous commitment to work for a couple of weeks in a free clinic in Morgantown, West Virginia.

She'd known he was going to be terribly busy, and she hadn't expected to hear from him right away. But after a week she'd gotten worried and called the clinic. Mac had never gotten there because his motorcycle had been struck by a pickup just inside the Morgantown city limits.

Frantic, her fingers stiff with dread, she'd dialed the hospital where they'd told her he'd been taken. To her enormous relief, Mac had been well enough to talk to her on the phone, although he'd insisted she not come down. Three days later, she disobeyed instructions. When she'd tried to find his room, she'd learned to her shock that he'd flown home to his family's Montana ranch without telling her he was leaving.

They'd only talked once after that, and he'd assured her that he was mending nicely—including his badly injured hand. But he was going to take some time off from school to get his head together. They'd been so close to each other that at first she couldn't believe he was coldly saying goodbye. But he'd made it very clear that any plans for the future didn't include her.

Katie winced with remembered pain. His rejection had been like a deep incision cutting away an important part of herself, and the only way to cope with the hurt was to go back to school and pretend that studying was the biggest thing in her life.

Realizing she had a death grip on the arms of the chair, Katie unlocked her fingers and glanced up quickly. Thank God Mac wasn't paying any attention to her, because she could picture the wounded look that had settled over her features. She wasn't going to make a fool of herself over something that had died and been put to rest years ago. Except that when he'd held her, for just a moment she'd thought that he...

As if her disturbing memories had drawn his interest, he stopped and turned. Color flooded her face, and she blurted the first thing that came to mind. "You can do an awful lot with that hand."

"Yeah. It's almost as good as the real one."

"I mean—" the heat in her cheeks grew more vivid "—I haven't seen anything that sophisticated before. Did you design it?"

"Not my specialty. But I had some input."

"What is your specialty?"

"Exotic toxins—and antitoxins."

"Oh."

"Look, we're both tired. I don't think we're going to find anything else here tonight."

Katie nodded.

"The best thing for you would be to go home and get some sleep."

She sat up straighter and pressed her heels against the carpet. "The best thing for me would be to talk to Tom Houston."

"No."

"What do you mean, no?"

"Just what I said. Tom was in pretty bad shape when I left him. And he's going to have to face the police in the morning. I don't think talking to you is in his best interests.''

She'd been grieving, hurt, shocked and numb by turns this evening. Now she was angry. "Since when do you make my decisions for me? What if I call the police tonight and tell them he was with Val when she died? What if I tell them I met you over here removing evidence?''

She saw the fingers of his right hand clench, but his face remained impassive.

"That's up to you, of course. But I'm not going to make it easy for you.''

Before she could continue the argument, he turned abruptly and stalked out of the room. A few moments later she heard the front door open and close.

Katie glanced at the closet. She'd come here to get her sister's school letter. That would have to wait now. Pushing herself to her feet, she headed for the living room and snatched up her purse.

The door to the stairs whooshed shut as she stepped into the hall, and for a moment she thought Mac had gone that way. Then she saw him standing by the elevator at the end of the hall. He must have heard her coming, but he didn't look up, and he didn't hold the car for her.

However, the next one came almost at once. Out on the street, she spotted his familiar stride as he rounded the corner.

Score one for her. Apparently the thought of being pursued by docile little Katie Martin didn't even enter his head. A few minutes later he got into a low-slung sports car and pulled out into traffic. Luckily her car was around the corner. She caught up with Mac at Connecticut Avenue and followed him out of the city. Keeping her quarry in sight wasn't difficult because the traffic had thinned in the late-evening hours. Where was he heading? she wondered. To his apartment? Tom's house? The lab?

Flipping on the radio to keep herself company, Katie tried not to think about the strange twists her life had taken since this afternoon. The confrontation with Val. Her death. The awful trip to the morgue. And then a surprise encounter with the man who had been haunting her dreams for eight years—transformed into flesh-and-blood reality in her sister's closet. Her hands locked around the steering wheel as she followed the sports car onto the Beltway. Maybe Mac was right, and she should let the police take care of things in the morning. Still, she didn't give up the pursuit. Ten minutes later she realized that their route was taking them into the outskirts of Columbia, a planned community just south of Ellicott City where she lived. The thought that Mac had been working, or living, so close without her knowing it brought a lump to her throat.

They had turned off the main highway and onto the curving roads of a quiet industrial park full of research-and-development companies that had been attracted to the high-tech atmosphere of the new town. At this time of night, the park was almost deserted, and Katie dropped back several hundred yards, afraid that Mac would realize he was being followed. Up ahead he swung into a parking lot. She drove past, her headlights illuminating a Medizone company sign. At the next driveway she made a U-turn.

The lot in front of the one-story brick building was empty, but she found Mac's sports car around back beside a rear entrance.

Katie turned off the engine and sat twisting the keys between her suddenly cold fingers as she battled with more second thoughts. Was she doing something stupid—barging in there to confront Val's lover? Mac had been adamant about her not seeing Tom tonight. Yet what if Mac couldn't persuade him to turn himself in? What if Tom Houston was so scared that he went into hiding or fled the country? Then she might never know what had really happened in Val's apartment earlier in the evening. Taking a deep breath, she climbed out of her car and marched toward the building.

The door closest to Mac's vehicle was unlocked. Fate was making things easy for her. But she was still torn by doubts as she pulled the door open.

It shut decisively behind her, and Katie found herself in a dimly lighted back hall without a clue about where to look for Tom Houston. However, in the next moment, a muffled exclamation sent her sprinting toward the left.

As she came abreast of heavy double doors, she heard Mac curse. Pushing the doors open, she stepped into a well-equipped lab—as it might have been set up by a horror-movie director with a weird sense of humor.

Glassware littered lab tables. A printer spewed out paper. Equipment hummed ominously. And an uncaged white rat scurried across the tiled floor.

Mac had just turned back toward the entrance. His face went from dismay to shock as he spotted Katie.

"Get down," he shouted as his body shoved hers back out into the hall. Seconds later an earsplitting explosion rocked the room.

Chapter Four

Flying glass shot past Katie's head like shrapnel from a bomb and pierced the wall behind her. The breath was knocked from her lungs as she landed with a thud on the hard tile floor. Mac had flung himself between her and the source of the danger as he shoved her down.

For several seconds there was eerie silence. Then a second explosion shattered the air. Mac's large body covered Katie's, and his arms came up to shield her head. More glass rained down, striking the floor around them like hail hitting a tin roof.

Katie pressed her face tightly to Mac's chest, feeling the staccato beating of her own heart. She knew it would be perilous to look up or open her eyes with the glass showering around them. Just above her ear, a shard pinged against metal, and she guessed that Mac was using his steel hand as a deflector. Then she heard him wince sharply and knew the flying glass had connected with his flesh as well.

"Mac, what happened? Are you hurt?" she whispered urgently, struggling to see the damage.

He pulled her face closer to his chest and tunneled his fingers through her hair, the pressure against her scalp holding her still. "Don't move yet."

"You've been hit."

"I'm okay. My coat's taking the worst of it."

For endless seconds she clung to him. Shifting, he cradled her slender form against his sturdier one, enfolding her protectively. If she hadn't known better, she might have said the gesture was fiercely possessive. Except that he was just giving her the aid and comfort he'd give any other woman in similar circumstances.

Her mind worked out the logic. Her body knew that she was in Mac's arms again for the second time in as many hours. She could feel her breasts pressed against his chest, her thighs glued to his, all her soft contours molded to his harder ones. Despite the peril, she couldn't stop herself from reacting in the old familiar way. Fear had made her pulse race. It raced faster now. The reality of Mac Mc-Quade was too much for her to handle. Or did the fantasies she'd spun over the years give him this power over her?

Katie breathed in and out with shallow regularity and tried not to move again, tried not to do anything that would make her more aware of him. But her nerves felt raw as she strained her ears for a change in the barrage. A second before she realized she was listening to silence once more, Mac was shifting his weight off her. Apparently he was as anxious to break the intimate contact as she. Shrugging out of his overcoat, he spread it on the floor over the glass and eased into a sitting position. Yet his eyes searched hers, and his fingers slid over her face. "Did I hurt you when I threw you down?" he asked, his voice concerned as he dropped his arm.

"You saved me from a face full of glass, I think." Katie smoothed her fingers over her cheeks, aware that he was following the motion with his smoky gaze. Her hand fell to her side. Then she flexed her arms and legs. "I'm okay."

Standing up, he pulled her to her feet and watched her

take a couple of tentative steps, her shoes crunching on the broken glass.

When he saw she was all right, his voice took on a different tone. "You followed me back here."

"Yes."

"You shouldn't have."

"It was my decision."

"Well, it's too dangerous in here for you to stay." He turned her around in the direction of the door to the parking lot.

Katie had started for the exit when she realized Mac wasn't behind her. She whirled and saw him reentering the lab, grinding glass under his heels with every footfall.

"Mac! No!" As he disappeared through the doors, fear leaped in her throat, blocking her windpipe. If it wasn't safe for her, it wasn't safe for him, either.

Acrid smoke was billowing into the hall now. Something in there was burning. But surely the building had an automatic sprinkler system. Why wasn't it pouring water onto the flames?

Casting around for the fire alarm, Katie located the panel several feet down the hall. As she pulled the handle, she braced for the loud clanging of the warning bell. It didn't sound. *My God, none of the safety systems is working.*

But at least there was a good old-fashioned fire extinguisher near the alarm panel. Without stopping to think about her own welfare, Katie wrested it from its bracket. Unhooking the nozzle, she bolted into the lab after Mac.

Immediately her eyes began to burn from the smoke as she looked frantically around for him.

"Mac!"

He was bent over a computer terminal cursing under his breath as he worked the keyboard with a right-handed typing system and thumped down on the shift with his metal fist.

His head jerked up when he spotted her. ''Get out of here before something else happens.''

''Not without you.''

''The damn automated system's got to be shut down before it does any more damage. Get out before the whole place goes up in smoke,'' he repeated.

As if to punctuate his words, a pile of steel-wool pads in back of Katie began to flame and spark. Turning, she coated them with foam. When the papers from the printer blazed up, too, she doused them as well.

Tears streamed down her face, and she began to cough. Across the room, Mac was choking, too. How long would either one of them be able to stay here? The speculation was cut off as her attention swung to a third small fire, which had taken hold on the seat of a lab stool, sending choking fumes into the air. As she saturated the fabric, she watched Mac out of the corner of her eye. He had moved away from the computer and was yanking open windows. Then he grabbed the fire extinguisher he'd been using earlier and began to soak a trash can that had turned into a bonfire. There were no more flames in the room, but thick smoke still hung around them like poison mist.

Between gasps for breath, Mac turned back toward her. ''The air's too bad. Get back in the hall.''

''You?''

''One more thing I've got to take care of. I'll be out in a minute.''

She was about to protest, until another spasm doubled her over. If she didn't get out of here soon, she was going to faint—and then she'd be more hindrance than help. Chest aching and eyes watering, she staggered into the hall and sucked in several grateful drafts. She wanted to go back into the lab, but her lungs vetoed the plan, and she was forced to wait in white-knuckled silence. Finally Mac reappeared, and she threw her arms around him and clung.

He held her just as fiercely, his heart thumping against her breasts and his hand stroking over her back and shoulders. "You don't take orders very well," he growled.

"I didn't like the ones you were giving."

He reached up and began silently picking glass out of her hair. As she watched the unguarded look of tenderness in his eyes, her chest tightened.

"Mac." Spontaneously, her face lifted to his just as it had a few hours ago. His head lowered. This time their lips met. She'd thought she'd figured everything out. But nothing was as simple as it seemed. Not when he was holding her in his arms again. Not when his mouth moved over hers. Urgent. Claiming. Making demands he had no right to make. She yielded freely. For long moments they were both lost. Then he broke the contact. As though nothing earthshaking had happened, he took a step back and inspected her hair.

"That's the worst of it." He looked over his shoulder toward the disaster area. "I'm sorry. I'm not thinking very clearly."

What exactly was he apologizing for? she wondered.

"I finally remembered that every lab has an emergency exhaust system. I turned it on manually. The smoke'll be gone in a while."

She could be just as cool about the kiss as he. "Shouldn't we call the fire department—just in case?"

He nodded. "But I've got to check on Tom first. I left him sleeping in my office. Thank God it's at the other end of the building. We can call from there."

Before she could ask what had triggered the explosion

and why none of the safety systems had kicked in, Mac was striding down the hall.

Katie ran to catch up. "Tom slept through *this?*"

"I gave him a pretty strong sedative before I went back into the city."

Despite the explanation, Mac's voice betrayed his concern. Katie couldn't match his rapid gait as he hurried into the executive wing of the building. She got a quick impression of walls and furnishings in a pleasing combination of mauve and gray, and thick carpet muffled their footsteps. They passed an L-shaped seating area, a secretary's desk and an oak door with Mac's name and the words Vice President on a polished brass plate. An identical door led to Tom's office. Except that his title was President.

Inside, the furnishings were rosewood and leather. But Katie's eyes honed in on the shelves behind the desk where a picture of Mac and a forceful-looking older man was prominently displayed. Mac was dressed in a safari outfit. His smiling companion, who wore a conservative business suit, was clasping him on the back. The vice president and president of Medizone.

Mac made a rapid check of the office, his manner more frantic than she'd ever seen it. "Where the hell is he? I watched him take the medication. It should have put him out," he muttered.

"Is this it?" Katie held out her hand. A small red capsule like a poison berry lay in the middle of her palm.

He snatched the medication out of her hand. "Where did you get that?"

"It was on the rug beside the sofa."

"Oh, Lord. He only pretended to take it." Cursing under his breath, Mac thumped the metal fist against the desk in a gesture of defeat and frustration. "I didn't want to believe it. But I guess he's the one who set up that Rube

Goldberg experiment down the hall. Whatever it was supposed to be.''

"We didn't see him in the lab," Katie soothed.

"But I've got to go back there and check. He could be under a table. Or behind a storage cabinet." The last words were tossed over his shoulder as he sprinted back down the hall once more.

Katie trotted after him.

The smoke had cleared, and the small fires that might have enveloped the room were cold and dead. Katie and Mac both glanced around for signs of structural damage. Although the place looked like a war zone, there didn't seem to be any twisted posts or blasted-out walls. Encouraged on that point, Katie helped Mac search behind the tables and under the desks. They found no one.

"Thank God for small favors. At least he's not in the lab." Mac led the way into the hall again. "Maybe he left. No. His car was still in the parking lot when I arrived."

"He could have walked out of the building. Or called a cab."

"I didn't think about that." Mac brushed back his hair with his fingers. "What the hell did he think he was doing? And why was he sterilizing all that equipment?"

Katie shook her head slowly. As she'd helped search, she'd realized what had caused the explosions. Two autoclaves—the machines that sterilized glassware and instruments with steam pressure—had exploded, shattering their contents and spraying deadly missiles all over the room. Superheated glass had started the fires.

She gestured back toward the mess. "I can't believe you didn't have automatic cutoffs. Or did someone disable every safety device in the building?"

Mac sighed. "We've been trying to go on-line with a computer-controlled total operating system for each lab. It runs the machinery, the ventilators, the sprinkler systems. Everything. It's going to be wonderful when it's working right. But all the bugs aren't out of it yet, and it's only supposed to be activated for carefully monitored tests. Anyone who wants to access the program has to know the password. And any time it's turned on, a whole series of warnings flash across the screen. You'd have to be suicidal or crazy to ignore them.''

Katie saw the impact of the last sentence hit Mac like an avalanche hurtling down a mountain. Yet all he said was, ''Tom has a hell of a lot of explaining to do.''

''But where is he?''

''I guess he's hiding, since he knows I'm going to be damn angry with him.''

Katie had a hard time imagining the forceful-looking man in the photograph cowering in a broom closet or some other dark corner. But most of the things that had happened this evening had been hard to imagine.

''We can cover more territory if we split up. Do you mind?'' Mac asked.

For the first time this evening, he was actually asking for her help, and she felt her heart squeeze. But there was no time to let herself examine that emotion. ''Of course I don't mind,'' she said softly.

It was Katie who found Tom—in the anteroom to the hematology lab. Wearing a grease-streaked white shirt and gray slacks, he was sprawled on the floor. His sightless eyes were focused on the open refrigerator door, and his fingers were curved as if they had been clutching something. But his hand was empty. Beside him were instruments and glassware that looked as if they'd been swept off the lab table when he'd fallen.

Another death. Although she'd never met this man, his lifeless body brought a stab of pain. Yet she forced herself to do the things that were necessary. Kneeling, she checked for a pulse in his neck. As she touched his flesh, she felt as if a river of sadness were flowing through her. This man had cared for Val. Now they were both gone. The only thing she could still do for him was try to catalog details that might be important later. His skin was still warm, and his limbs were still flexible—which meant that he'd only been deceased for a few hours.

Mac came in as she was gently closing Tom's eyes. She heard the breath whoosh out of his lungs as he focused on his friend's face. Like Katie, he had no trouble recognizing death. Yet he knelt beside Tom and grasped his shoulders urgently, raising him up slightly as both the good hand and the metal one dug into the fabric of his dress shirt.

"Oh, Lord. What was I thinking about? I never should have left him alone."

"Mac, you did what you thought you had to."

"No, I had a pretty good idea of the kind of shape he was in. He was distraught. He told me what he was going to do. I should have stayed with him!" Anguish seeped out of him with every word.

Katie felt tears gather in her own eyes as he laid Tom carefully back on the floor.

"He asked you to go down to Val's apartment. He said he'd feel better once you brought his belongings back."

Mac didn't seem to hear her. When she reached for his hand, he stood up before she could make contact and exited into the hematology lab where he stood with his back to her. He was a man who knew how to control his reactions. At least on the surface. Now he looked as if he were staring intently out the window into the night. As far as Katie could tell, there was nothing to see but the parking lot.

Her own emotions in turmoil, she got up and closed the

refrigerator just to give herself something to do. Then she tiptoed to the doorway. The tension gathering in Mac's broad shoulders was like a physical force. His back was rigid as a stockade fence—with a No Trespassing sign slapped in the middle.

Katie gripped the door frame with stiff fingers, knowing he wanted her to turn around and leave so she wouldn't see any more of his pain. But she'd already stopped taking orders from him—both spoken and unspoken—once and for all tonight. Before she lost her nerve she crossed the room, slipped in front of Mac and slid her arms around his middle to hug him close.

His arms hung at his sides.

"Please. We've each lost someone tonight. Someone we cared a lot about. Please, hold me."

She knew some iron band inside of him had snapped when he whispered her name. His voice came close to breaking as he folded her into his embrace. For long moments they simply held each other, each drawing strength from the human contact—from each other.

"I was a fool tonight, charging off to your sister's apartment to play cops and robbers when I should have been taking care of my friend. Now Tom's dead because of me," he finally said.

"You weren't playing cops and robbers. You were trying to reassure Tom. If he was acting like Val, I'll bet he made it pretty hard for you to say no."

Mac didn't answer, but she felt the truth of her guess in the way a little of the tension eased from his shoulders. "You were looking for evidence," she continued. "Well, it didn't come out the way you expected. Now you feel the same way I do about Val. Guilty." She gulped. "I shouldn't have left her alone this afternoon, either. But I did."

His hand soothed over her back. "Maybe we both did the best we could."

"God, I hope so."

He held her for a few minutes longer. Then she felt him begin to ease away and knew that they couldn't stand there forever. They were going to have to call the police. Mac would have to face the same ordeal she'd been through. But he wouldn't be alone. Whether he wanted her support or not, she was going to give it to him.

She looked around the room, her eyes following the trail of broken glass and scattered instruments on the floor back to the lab table. The polished surface was a disordered mess, although not quite as bad as the scene down the hall after the explosion. Maybe Tom had forgotten he was sterilizing equipment. Or maybe he'd abandoned his lab experiment and come back here to take care of something more important. But what?

Katie's scalp tightened when she spotted something she hadn't noticed in the middle of the debris on the table. An empty hypodermic. No, not empty, she noted as she glided closer. There was a bit of pink liquid in the bottom.

Had Tom given himself an injection? Medication? Had he taken an accidental overdose? Or was this some designer drug? Was that the cause of his death?

Her gaze swept the cluttered countertop. A few yards away from the syringe was a small bottle with what looked like the dregs of the same stuff. Snatching it up, Katie read the label. It consisted of a series of meaningless letters and numbers and told her nothing.

HI 320 DQ

"Was Tom taking any medication that had to be injected?"

"Not that I know of."

"Then what's this stuff?" Katie held out the bottle and the hypodermic on her flattened palm.

Mac turned, focused on the syringe, and closed the distance between them in a few giant steps. Lifting the bottle from her hand with cold metal fingers, he inspected the contents and the label.

"It looks like it's from one of our experimental batches."

"Batches of what?" She couldn't keep the accusation out of her voice.

"I told you before, we don't make illegal drugs at Medizone."

The sharp denial meant that his mind had at least been skirmishing with the same thoughts as hers.

He sighed. "I do most of my work in the field. Tom is in charge of development. But he's a stickler for careful documentation. Everything we produce is logged in and updated on a regular basis."

"Then let's see what your records say about HI 320 DQ."

The challenge in her voice made his eyes narrow, but his voice was deadly calm. "If you insist, Dr. Martin."

Folding the bottle into the prison of his steel fingers, Mac ushered Katie out of the room by a different door so that they avoided the body in the anteroom. Earlier his strides had been decisive, now he walked more slowly.

Second thoughts? Katie wondered.

She had her answer after he sat down at a computer terminal and typed in a hidden password. "These files contain proprietary information."

"I'm not going to reveal your company secrets."

Mac nodded and entered the code number from the bottle. A moment later, the screen brought up a lab status report for HI 320 DQ.

Katie leaned over Mac's shoulder, scanning the test. According to the background summary, Mac had brought back the basic compound being used from an expedition to Nepal. It was a plant resin that was native to the central highlands of that country, but Medizone had succeeded in establishing several specimens at their Beltsville greenhouses. Next was documentation on concentration and purification.

"Yeah, now I remember this stuff," Mac muttered. "Tom was talking about it a couple of months ago. He was excited about the preliminary results. Let's see what came of it."

"This is all very interesting, but what are you using it for?" Katie asked.

Mac scrolled down to the next page of the text and moved the cursor to one of the paragraphs.

Katie read rapidly through the information and then read it again. Puzzled, she turned back to Mac. "Do I have this right? You're using this compound against HIV?"

"Correct. In early laboratory trials, it was shown to slow down the growth of the AIDS virus."

He brought the next several paragraphs into view on the screen. "The problem is, it turned out to have highly toxic side effects."

"But the bottle. The hypodermic. Why would he inject himself with that?" Katie asked.

"I don't know." Mac scanned the figures on the screen. "But if HI 320 DQ was really in the bottle, it was enough to kill a grizzly bear."

Chapter Five

Mac looked up from the computer screen, rubbing the side of his hand down his jaw. It scraped against the evening stubble of his beard, and for a moment Katie found herself focusing on the barely audible rasp. It was a very male sound and a very familiar one that reminded her of long nights studying together in her tiny student apartment. Now they were together again in the middle of the night. With another problem to solve, she reminded herself. One that was a whole lot more immediate than the study of diseases in textbooks.

"This isn't getting us anywhere. And the longer I wait to call the police, the worse it's going to be." Mac paused and gave Katie a direct look. "Maybe you don't want to be here when they arrive."

Katie met his level gaze. "I'll stay."

"And tell them what? That you followed me here because your sister killed herself this evening and you thought Tom Houston might be able to tell you something about it?"

She sucked in a sharp breath. "I didn't know Tom's name. But Perkins, the detective who interviewed me, wanted to talk to him."

"He can't do that now."

She was so tired, it was hard to think. "It's not right for me to leave. I was here. I found him. Couldn't we just tell the police what happened after we arrived at Medizone?"

His gaze swept her disheveled appearance and focused on her face, making her vividly aware of how she must look.

"It's three in the morning, and you've had a hell of a day. Do you really think you're up to sorting through questions and deciding which ones to answer honestly?"

"I—"

"Do you want to go through the story of Val's suicide again?"

Katie shook her head wearily. He was right; she didn't know if she could face that again.

"It's better if we keep things separate—Tom and Val. Until we know what's going on."

Katie still didn't like the idea. But as she considered the evening's events, she realized that if she stayed, she might have to explain how she'd met Mac down at her sister's apartment—where he'd gone to remove evidence. That wasn't going to look very good for Mac now that Tom was dead. "Will you call me when it's over?" she asked.

"No. It's already late."

"Then we'll talk tomorrow."

He nodded tightly. "Go on. Get out of here so I can make the call."

WHEN CORNELL PERKINS came in at eight-thirty Wednesday morning, there was a blue memo sheet in the middle of his blotter. It read: "See me ASAP." There was no signature, but he knew the handwriting. The message had come from Captain Gantry.

Now what? Perkins checked to see that he wasn't wearing scrambled egg on his tie.

He'd never seen himself as Eddie Murphy in *Beverly Hills Cop,* he reflected as he started down the hall. He was just a homeboy who had made it in the big city by doing his job. But after forty years in the department, the strain was starting to wear him down. And all he was going to get for his efforts was a D.C. pension if the city government didn't run out of money.

Gantry's secretary ushered him through to the inner sanctum after barely a five-minute wait. Something was definitely up.

"Close the door and have a seat."

Perkins complied. As he dropped into one of the imitation leather chairs across from the chief's desk, he felt his mouth go dry.

"I've got some good news," Gantry murmured but didn't immediately elaborate.

"Oh?"

"The task force on drug abuse has gotten funding for a departmental liaison to check out how the problem is being handled in various other locations around the country. Honolulu. New Orleans. San Juan. It's a four-week tour. And there's per diem on top of the base salary."

"Yeah? Which lucky son of a bitch has the job?"

"You do."

Perkins's jaw dropped open. "You've got to be kidding."

"No joke."

The detective stared across the desk. "How long do I get to make up my mind?"

"They want to know right away." Gantry hesitated, then continued in a lower voice. "Somebody's either rewarding you for a whopping big favor I don't know about—or they want you out of the way for a while. If it's the latter, you'd better accept. Otherwise, they might come up with some other bright idea that isn't quite as pleasant.''

Perkins sat back in his chair. In a few moments, he looked up at Gantry. ''When do I pack?''

''After you report to the District Building this morning.''

''What about the cases I'm working on?''

''I've had your folders pulled. Everything's being reassigned.''

Perkins had always gone with his hunches. Now his spider senses told him someone was pulling him off the Caldwell case. And it looked like he'd better go along with it.

Gantry waited until Perkins had closed the office door behind him. Then he reached for the phone and dialed a Chevy Chase exchange.

''Hello.''

''Blackbird has flown west,'' he said in a stiff voice and hung up. If the police commissioner got wind of this, his thirty-year career was down the tubes. But like he'd told Perkins, when the right people called in a favor, you either played ball or applied for disability retirement.

THE MOMENT Katie opened her eyes, everything came back. Val. Mac. Tom. For silent moments she stared at the clock. Ten a.m. Mac hadn't called. Did that mean everything had gone all right with the police last night? Or had it gone badly? When she sat up and reached to find a phone book in the stand beside the bed, she winced. Her body felt as if she'd gone fifteen rounds with Mike Tyson.

More cautiously, she stood up and tentatively flexed her arms and legs. Being slammed against the floor during the explosion hadn't done her body any permanent harm, nothing a hot shower wouldn't relieve. But how much was it going to do for the ache in her heart? The ache had a cable link to the emotional elevator she'd been riding since the previous afternoon. Most of the trip had been straight to the subbasement. But when Mac had kissed her, she'd gone all the way through the roof. That had made the subsequent plunge all the more sickening.

The best thing for her would be if she never saw Mac McQuade again. Last night he'd made it very clear that he didn't want anything from her. Not her help. Not her support. Not her comfort. And certainly not a resumption of their relationship after all these years. But that didn't stop her from worrying about him and wondering how he'd gotten through the police interview.

After finding Medizone in the phone book, she dialed the number. When she asked to speak to Mac, she was put through to his secretary.

"Who's calling, please?" a motherly-sounding voice asked.

"Dr. Martin. A friend of Mr. McQuade. Is he available?"

"I'm afraid not. Our company president died suddenly last night, and Mr. McQuade has a lot of things to deal with."

Katie caught the protective note in the secretary's voice. The woman obviously cared about Mac.

"Is Mr. McQuade all right?" she asked.

"Yes. If you want to leave a message, I'm sure he'll get back to you when things calm down around here."

Katie left her name and number. She could imagine Mac had an awful lot to cope with today. Maybe even the police. At least he could call his family if he needed someone. No, he wouldn't do that. She remembered he'd never asked them for help when he'd been in school. Probably he'd hated having to go back to the ranch after he'd lost his hand. How long had he stayed? What had he done before he'd joined up with Tom? Katie brought herself up short. She had her own problems to worry about today. Like her sister's funeral.

After turning the shower taps to full blast, she adjusted the temperature and stepped under a hot spray. While she washed her hair, she made mental notes about what she needed to do.

As she was drying herself off, she spotted the little jar of face cream she'd taken from Val's last night—and remembered the lecture her sister had delivered on morning beauty care. Well, she certainly wasn't in the mood for makeup, but maybe the expensive moisturizer would help soothe her skin. Scooping up a dab, she smoothed the cream over her cheeks and around her eyes. It felt marvelous. She rubbed a little on the sore spots over her ribs where Mac's metal fingers had bruised her flesh. Probably it wouldn't help. But it wouldn't hurt, either.

Although her body was feeling less creaky by the time she'd gotten dressed, she wished she didn't have to go down to the office. But since she didn't have a secretary to rearrange her appointments, that was the only way she was going to clear her calendar.

When she'd begun her genetic study on Huntington's disease, she'd planned on working at home—partly because she'd been through a rather bad experience in her last job. She'd been on the staff at a private hospital called the Sterling Clinic, which had been rocked by a series of unsavory revelations. Katie hadn't been involved, but the clinic had finally been forced to close, and the negative publicity had made it difficult for her to get another hospital job.

So she'd designed a research study and applied for a grant. Then her friend Abby Franklin had mentioned she was looking for someone to sublet her office at 43 Light Street in downtown Baltimore while she and her husband Steve were on an extended trip to India. The timing and the location were perfect, since Katie had found her home wasn't really a very good setting for the interview phase of the project. Now she was hoping to lease her own office at 43 Light Street.

She'd come to love the charming old building. And Abby had introduced her to a whole group of supportive women who worked there. They shared not only their good times but also their problems. The feeling of having someone to turn to when you needed her was one of the best things she'd gotten from the experience.

However, this morning when Katie walked into the black-and-white marble lobby, she felt more withdrawn than she had in months. Which was probably what set off Sabrina Barkley's radar. Before Katie could press the elevator button, the vivacious redhead waved from the engagingly cluttered shop—called Sabrina's Fancy—where she sold herbs and other merchandise.

Stepping through the door, she gave Katie a critical inspection. "You look like you need a cup of mulled cider."

"Sabrina, I—I have some stuff to take care of."

"Come on in and tell me about it."

It was hard to refuse her friend's warmth and encouraging smile. Over a mug of spiced cider, Katie found herself talking about the evening before—leaving out the intimate details of her encounter with Mac.

"I'm so sorry about your sister," Sabrina murmured. "What can I do to help?"

"Thanks for asking. But there's nothing I need right now. I think I'm just going to have a simple graveside service. No open casket, not when Val cared so much about how she looked."

"Oh, honey. It must have been terrible for you having to go down to the morgue all alone. Why didn't you call one of us?"

"It's a long drive to D.C." Katie's voice choked up, and she stopped abruptly.

They were both quiet for several moments while Sabrina straightened up a shelf of herb-vinegar bottles and Katie collected her scattered control.

"I'd better go make those calls," she murmured. "Before my interviewees start showing up."

"Yes."

As she stood up, Sabrina patted her arm. "By the way, do you want me to put a hex on that guy who popped out of the closet? Warts on his face. A rash on his bottom. A flat tire on his fancy car."

The images coaxed a little smile to Katie's lips. "Don't tell me you've added a new service."

"No. But it's fun to read about the old superstitions. When you're up to it, you can come over to dinner and I'll show you some of my books."

"Maybe after I get through the next couple of weeks."

Sabrina walked Katie to the elevator. "Remember, call me if you need anything."

"Yes. Thanks."

Katie unlocked the door to her fifth-floor office and flipped on the lights. Sinking down in the leather desk chair, she spared a quick glance at the answering machine. No calls, she observed with a little sigh of relief. At least she wouldn't have to spend time returning them.

It took longer than she expected to cancel her appointments because word quickly spread around the building about Val's death. During the morning there was a steady stream of people in and out of the office all wanting to offer comfort and support.

By lunchtime she'd rescheduled all her interviews for later in the month and turned to the task she dreaded: Val's burial arrangements. First she dialed Craigstone's, the funeral home she'd used four years ago when her mother had died. They'd helped her and Val through a number of difficult decisions at a time when she'd felt least capable of making them. Now as she went through a similar set of questions, a wave of unreality swept over her. No viewing. A graveside service. Hillside Cemetery. Yellow roses. Val had always loved roses. Even to Katie's own ears, her responses sounded like tinny echoes through a cheap microphone.

"I think we can take care of everything from here. All we need to know is when the body will be released," the funeral director said.

"I'm not sure," Katie replied. "But I'll call the morgue and let you know as soon as I find out."

Noel Emery, Laura Roswell's paralegal assistant, stopped by with a crab-cake platter for lunch. Ordinarily Katie would have considered the seafood a treat. Today she could hardly force herself to take a few bites. Finally she stuffed the plate into the office refrigerator and called information for the number of the D.C. medical examiner.

What should have been a simple task turned into another ordeal that ate up much of the afternoon.

"I'm sorry, Ms. Martin, an autopsy is required whenever the deceased was not under the care of a physician," a clerk explained. "According to my files, the police department hasn't signed off on the procedure."

"Dr. Martin," she corrected.

"I'm sorry, *Dr.* Martin. We can't release your sister's body yet."

"Does that mean the autopsy showed something abnormal?" Katie asked.

"We only received the remains last night, so it may not have even been done yet. Besides, I'm not allowed to give out pathology information without specific authorization."

Katie silently fought her exasperation. As next of kin, surely she was entitled to the results. But that really wasn't the important issue, anyway.

She took a calming breath. "All right. I understand you have your rules. But I need to make funeral arrangements."

"You might try talking to someone at district police headquarters."

Katie hung up and went in search of her purse, where she'd put Detective Perkins's number. As she removed the business card, she also took out two aspirins. Her ear ached from the pressure of the receiver, and the knot of tension at the base of her neck was growing tighter by the moment.

Perkins had seemed curt with her at first, but after he'd heard her story, he'd been more sympathetic. Maybe he could tell her what was going on. Picking up the phone again, she tried his number. It rang five times before the call was transferred to another extension.

"Sergeant Nathans speaking. Detective Perkins is out of town on police business, could someone else help you?"

Out of town on police business? He hadn't mentioned that when he'd given her his card and told her to call him if she had any more questions. "Is someone else working on the Val Caldwell case? I'm her sister."

"I'll check." She was put on hold for a few minutes.

"Sorry to keep you waiting," Nathans said when he returned. "I don't seem to have any record of a Caldwell case. Are you sure it was assigned to this office?"

Katie stared at the phone. All she wanted was to schedule her sister's funeral. "I'm sure about which detective interviewed me for hours last night," she said, enunciating every word carefully. "Don't you people have logs? Can't you get in touch with Detective Perkins and find out what he did with the file?"

"Calm down, ma'am. I'm sure the report is here somewhere. Leave me a number and I'll get back to you."

Katie left her number with Nathans, wondering if she'd hear from him again. Lacing her hands together, she massaged her white knuckles with the fingers of the opposite hands. But it was impossible not to keep imagining Val's body lying in some storage freezer while the police hunted for a misplaced file and made up their minds about the autopsy report.

Maybe that was S.O.P. in an overworked big-city police department. Maybe she was so stressed out that her expectations were unreasonable, Katie told herself. Or maybe there was another explanation, she thought with a sudden chill.

Last night she'd gone from thinking Val was paranoid to wondering whether her sister and Tom were on the same drug, to coming up against the brick wall of Tom's suicide. But what if this wasn't just some personal tragedy that had destroyed two lives? What if she'd walked into the middle of some sort of cover-up? What if Val and Tom had been into something illegal that the D.C. police department wasn't prepared to talk about yet?

Once the idea surfaced, Katie found it was hard to keep her imagination from going wild. Had Tom really died from an injection of HI 320 DQ? Or had someone wanted it to look that way? And what if the experimental drug was in his bloodstream? Had he injected himself? Or had someone else done it for him?

Maybe she and Mac should put the Howard County Police into the picture. Except that Mac had wanted her out of the way when he talked to them, and she still had no idea what kind of story he'd come up with.

Her chest began to tighten as she thought about the way he'd rushed her out of the Medizone building last night. And, as she considered a number of other incidents from their evening together, it became hard to breathe. My God, look at the way they'd met! In her sister's clothes closet.

He'd given her a plausible explanation for what he was doing there—and his insistence that she leave Medizone before the law arrived. But what if she'd been too off balance to see the real truth? Her feelings about him were colored by the warm glow of good memories. But it was obvious that he'd changed. How much? What was he really like now?

Blood pounded in her ears, and it was several moments before she could get her mind to function effectively again. Yet there was a very disturbing possibility she had to consider. What if Tom and Mac were involved in something illegal, and he was trying to cover it up? She closed her eyes, as if that would shut out the terrible thought. But it hung there behind closed lids. Scrabbling for a replacement, she came up with something that wasn't quite as damning. What if he'd uncovered something very damaging about his friend Tom—something that he was determined nobody else was going to dig up? What lengths would he go to in order to cover it up? All at once, she knew she had to find out.

BY NOON, Mac had accomplished a day full of essential tasks. He'd gotten a confirmation from the fire marshal that the Medizone building was safe for occupancy. He'd brought in a cleaning crew. He'd called a meeting of all his employees to break the news of Tom's death and to assure them that the tragedy would not have an adverse effect on their jobs. And he'd also talked to several reporters who'd been camping on the front walk when he'd returned to the office at seven-thirty. Then he'd canceled his return trip to Latin America. He'd have to be stateside for the next few weeks.

Thank God that over the past few months he'd assigned a number of Tom's administrative duties to Marlin Stoner. The man was up to speed on company projects and policy and would be able to run the day-to-day operations while he took care of funeral arrangements and other unexpected details.

After talking to Tom's lawyer, he put down the phone and tried to roll the tension out of his shoulders. Walking to the window, he stood and stared at the traffic going by on Green Branch Road.

Marcia, his and Tom's secretary, stuck her head in the door to find out if she could get him some lunch. She'd come to work for Medizone six years ago after her kids had graduated from college, and would have mothered the management team if they'd wanted that kind of relationship. But he'd never acquired the habit of letting women smother him with concern. Today she looked shocked and weary, and he suspected she was having almost as bad a day as he was.

"What did *you* have?" he asked.

"Just coffee."

"I'll take some, too."

Marcia didn't bother arguing that he needed to eat. Eventually his body would force him to do that. Right now, the idea made his throat clog.

"Mac, I can call Phil and tell him I'll be staying late."

"Thanks for the offer, but not tonight. The next few weeks are going to be tough on all of us. I don't want you burning out on the first day."

"If you need me, all you have to do is ask."

"I know."

After Marcia went back to her desk, his fingers tightened on the white crockery mug she'd brought. It had his name on the side in gold lettering. Tom's was sitting on the shelf over the coffee machine. Could you give away a monogrammed mug to Goodwill or some other charitable organization? Or should he keep it?

Taking a too-quick gulp of the hot brew, he grimaced as it burned his throat. He was doing everything at a frantic pace, which was a deliberate ploy to keep him from thinking too deeply. Now that he had a moment alone with his thoughts, there was nowhere else to hide.

Eight years ago he'd given up on himself. You couldn't sink much lower than sleeping under the Whitehurst Freeway and scratching out a living by volunteering to be a guinea pig in experimental drug-testing programs. Tom had turned him down flat for a Medizone protocol. But he must have seen some spark of talent in the grubby, one-handed former medical student sitting on the other side of the desk—because he'd gotten him to talk about his lab skills and then he'd offered him a job. Not something easy. A research project the company had already given up on. At first he'd been angry. Then he'd been curious. Finally he'd been challenged. And by the time he was halfway through, he knew that Tom Houston had suckered him into caring again.

Oh, Tom, what am I going to do now, he wondered silently. *I'm a good researcher. You proved that. But can I really take on this whole company?*

He didn't want to think about that now, and that left his mind open for another topic he'd rather skip. Katie.

He sighed. She ought to be the least of his worries, the

one factor he could control; yet every time her image stole into his mind, he had to struggle to banish it.

Suddenly there was nowhere else to hide from old pain and fresh new wounds. He'd told himself he'd gotten over Katie Martin. Except that seeing her again had been like tumbling into a jungle pit full of sharpened stakes. The physical impact of realizing how much he wanted her had been both astonishing and agonizing.

Part of the shock had been the way he'd reacted to the new Katie Martin. The last time he'd seen her she'd been a girl, dewy with promise. Now she was a mature woman. But maturity had only made her more beautiful and more desirable. And another dimension had been added. Eight years ago, when he'd coldly explained that he wanted her out of his life, she had meekly acquiesced. Last night when he'd warned her to keep her nose out of Tom's business, she'd followed him back to Medizone. The pointed questions she'd asked had made him angry. He suspected that the only reason she'd agreed to go home before the police arrived last night was because she thought that saying too much would get *him* in trouble. He didn't want to think about that. Besides, all the reasons why he'd severed the relationship still stood.

He pressed metal fingers against the side of his leg, focusing for a moment on the small stabs of pain as if that could drive away the memories. It didn't work. Eight years ago when he'd lain in that hospital bed contemplating his altered future, he'd known that when Katie saw his hand, shock would come first—and then pity. He hadn't wanted her pity then. And he didn't want it now. Not hers or anyone else's. Back then, he'd told himself he didn't want her to spend her life picking up the pieces of his broken dreams. He hadn't been able to admit how much his own pain and pride had influenced his decision. He and Katie had both been at the top of their class, and friendly competition had added a spark to their relationship. More than that, they'd been convinced that life was going to be a succession of happy choices and easy triumphs. Then, suddenly he'd been forced to drop out of the race—and out of the winner's circle. But Katie had still been there—and on the brink of the career that had been denied him. It was hard enough adjusting to a new physical image of himself. Having her around as a daily reminder of his deeper loss would have been unbearable. It still was.

Standing up, he set the half-full mug of coffee down with a thunk and strode across his office. Maybe Tom's computer files would take his mind off Katie.

Tom had an encrypted directory that Mac had never accessed, but he knew the password. With the touch of a few keys he was staring at Tom's most private files. Several were obviously intended to be read by him. One labeled MAC1 was date-stamped three years in the past—when Tom had made him vice president. It contained a very detailed message reiterating their partnership agreement and giving instructions for the continuation of Medizone if anything should happen to the senior partner.

Mac had to stop reading for a moment when he realized he was trying to see through a film of blurry moisture. Here it was—proof if he'd ever needed it of how much faith Tom had in him. It was a hell of a lot to live up to. Frightening. Or a challenge—depending on the way you looked at it.

"Sorry pal," the message concluded. "I know you're good at field work. And I know why getting off by yourself has been important to you. But I've watched you grow and mature over the past couple of years. The company's going to need you at headquarters, and I hope you'll accept my judgment that you're going to have to stay put for a while.''

Mac felt his eyes smart again as he read words written by the old, logical, prepared-for-any-contingency Tom. The man knew him pretty well. He knew his vice president would do what needed to be done.

Another file was labeled MAC2 and was date-stamped several months ago. Right before Tom had gotten sick. Mac's fingers tingled as he keyed in the password. His whole body started to tingle when he saw the first words.

''I'm just making a couple of notes here in case I don't get to finish this project. Buddy, if you're reading this, you're probably going to be angry with me for messing in your affairs. But I've decided that it's time for a little fatherly counseling. Since Brenda died, I've been doing a lot of thinking about what I've had and you've missed. Every man needs a personal life—a chance at happiness. And if you didn't want me to try and do something about the way you're killing part of yourself, you should never have told me about that woman in medical school—Katie Martin.''

It was a while before Mac could keep reading. The note went on to talk about some private research Tom had been doing. Research that had started with Val Caldwell. Tom had met her at a singles bar she frequented. But it hadn't been an accidental encounter. Tom had gone looking for Val because he'd tracked down Katie Martin's sister. His original plan had been to ask for her help in staging a reunion between Mac and Katie.

But things hadn't turned out the way he'd anticipated. Val didn't seem close to her sister, and he'd decided it might take time to get around to the subject. Meanwhile, he'd soon realized how thrilled he was to be dating someone as pretty and sexy as Val. Probably when he'd gotten sick, he'd almost forgotten about the original scheme.

"Oh, Lord," Mac muttered. "That's how he got hooked up with her. Some crazy plan to save me from myself." For the past twelve hours he'd been cursing fate that the woman who had walked into that closet was Katie Martin. It wasn't fate. It was poor old fatherly Tom's plan. And the irony was that he'd accomplished his purpose at the cost of his life.

Mac was cursing as he signed off the computer. He wasn't emotionally prepared to deal with any more of Tom's private files right now. Instead he stalked down the hall to the ruined lab, hoping he could find out what his friend had considered so important last night.

Inside, he began poking through the equipment and papers littering the tables. Even with his heavy load of administrative duties, Tom had usually kept his hand in a few experiments. He'd always taken careful notes, but as far as Mac could see, the documentation on this project was about as decipherable as hoofprints on a rocky trail. Still, he kept pawing through the paper, hoping to find some clue.

Outside, he could hear people walking around, and realized with a start that it must be near quitting time. It was almost twenty-four hours since this whole nightmare had begun. When he'd gotten home last night, he'd hardly closed his eyes. But there was no point in leaving again now. Better to stay here and keep busy.

A slight movement to his right brought his eyes up from the notebook he was thumbing. The woman he'd been trying not to think about stood in the doorway.

KATIE'S EYES swept over Mac, noting the pallor below his tan, the circles under his eyes, the lines of strain across his forehead. His day had probably been as bad as hers. Worse, since a prominent biomedical company had suddenly become his sole responsibility. And even worse yet if he was in the middle of some kind of cover-up.

It looked as if she was the last person on earth he wanted to see. His greeting did nothing to dispel the impression. "What are you doing here?" he demanded.

"You said we'd talk. I want to know what you said to the police," she came back at him in the same tone of voice.

"I've been busy. And I wasn't planning on your coming out here."

Katie's chin lifted. "As far as you and I are concerned personally—I agree. But there are other issues involved."

He didn't bother to dispute the assertion, but he didn't jump in to advance the conversation, either.

"Did you do a chemical analysis of the liquid in the bottle?" she asked.

"That isn't any of your concern."

"Let's pretend it is."

He sighed. "I had one of my technicians take care of that. It was what it said it was. HI 320 DQ. I guess the medical examiner will let me know if a lethal dose was in his bloodstream."

"You told the police about his taking the injection?"

"Of course!"

Well, that would be a matter of record, if she wanted to question the police report later.

"What else happened after I left last night?"

"I talked to an Officer Butterfield. I told him about the explosion. And about finding Tom—leaving you out of the story."

"Why did you say you came back here?" As she asked the question, she watched his face carefully.

"I was worried about Tom. He'd shown some signs of instability over the past few weeks, and I knew he was here late."

She could see the tension around his mouth and eyes. Maybe he was telling the truth, but not the whole truth. "You didn't mention anything about Val?"

"No. Did you give Perkins Tom's last name?" he shot back.

"No. Actually, I couldn't. He's made a sudden trip out of town. The records on the case are missing from his precinct. And the medical examiner's office won't tell me if they've done an autopsy on Val. What do you think about all that?"

He looked surprised. "That sounds like a couple of interesting coincidences."

"You have any hypotheses?"

"Like what?"

"You're keeping something from me," she challenged.

"Nothing relevant," he snapped back. "Just the messages Tom left me about how to run the company if he was out of the picture. Forgive me if I'm a bit brusque, but reading your best friend's last instructions to you is a little hard on the emotional equilibrium."

Katie pressed her hands against her sides, holding back the impulse to open her arms to him. Obviously he didn't want her help dealing with any of this. And she couldn't let her feelings distract her from her purpose. There were ways to find out if he intended to be honest with her. "Let's try another approach," she suggested in a businesslike voice. "Does HI 320 DQ require refrigeration?"

Mac seemed relieved at the abrupt change of subject. "No. Why?"

"The refrigerator door was open when I came into the hematology lab."

"I didn't notice."

"At the time, it just seemed like part of the general disarray in the room so I closed it. But, I've been thinking about the way Tom was lying on the floor. He was staring at the refrigerator. I don't suppose you checked to see what was in there."

"No."

"Why don't we?" Without waiting for his permission, she turned and started down the hall. Mac caught up with her after a few steps. From the corner of her eye, she saw he was about to say something. Then he abruptly closed his mouth. When they arrived in the hematology lab, she noted that the room had been cleaned and tidied.

Before she could cross the room, Mac yanked open the refrigerator and began shuffling through the contents. As expected, there were several racks with vials of blood. But she heard Mac suck in his breath as he pulled one of the tubes out and held it up.

The label was barely legible. But she could make out an initial and a last name. T. Houston.

"Tom's blood," Mac muttered.

"Was he planning to test it for something?"

"The whole time I worked at Medizone I knew exactly what he was thinking. But the past few months, I gave up trying to figure out what was in his mind."

"What did you do before you came to Medizone?" The question was out of Katie's mouth before she had time to censor it.

"Nothing constructive."

"What?"

His gaze turned inward as he remembered his earlier thoughts. It was almost as if she'd gone in and plucked them from his brain. "I was hanging around D.C. picking up a few bucks here and there volunteering for medical protocols. I was one of the first group that tested an experimental malaria vaccine. I did a new cold-remedy trial, a test of saturated fat on cholesterol levels in healthy males in their 20s.''

''Oh, Mac, you didn't. That stuff can be dangerous.''

''Somebody has to do it.''

''Not somebody like you, somebody with a future.''

''That's what Tom said. I met him when Medizone advertised for volunteers to try an antidepressant drug.''

''Mac!''

''Tom read my questionnaire and told me I wasn't suitable for the study. I was getting up to leave when he surprised the hell out of me and offered me a job with the company.'' Mac's voice clogged and he stopped speaking.

''He saw the potential in you when you'd given up on yourself,'' Katie whispered.

''Yes. Now do you understand what I owe him?''

She nodded. Mac had just revealed an awful lot—about himself and why he felt so strongly about Tom Houston. But he didn't give her a chance to dwell on the information.

''So let's find out what the hell he was trying to accomplish last night.'' Mac grabbed a glass slide, spread it with a drop of the blood, and set it under one of the microscopes on the counter against the wall. Adjusting the focus, he stared into the eyepiece.

''I don't see anything unusual.'' He sighed. ''I guess we could try some standard drug tests.''

''We could. Or we could have a look at a blood sample using an electron microscope.''

Mac was silent for several seconds. Then he gave her a direct look. ''Okay, last night we were talking about AIDS. You think that's what Tom really had? You think he infected your sister? You think that's what made them both flaky? That quickly? Without any of the more obvious symptoms?'' The questions came out low and gritty.

'`I don't know. But AIDS is a sexually transmitted disease.'' She swallowed and looked away from Mac. "And I assume they were lovers.''

"Yes, I think that's a pretty valid assumption.''

"Whether Tom had AIDS or not, that appears to be what he was thinking about.''

"Okay. We'll look at the blood under the electron microscope and see if we can find any virions,'' Mac clipped out.

"Yes. Good.'' She felt something unfurl inside her chest. He wasn't happy about agreeing. But he wasn't trying to block their mutual investigation, either.

It had been eight years since Katie and Mac had worked together on any kind of project. Now they fell back into their old rhythm as if there had never been an interruption in the partnership. That at least hadn't changed. For a moment Katie felt a surge of pleasure—until she reminded herself what they were doing and why.

Once the specimen was ready, Mac sat down at the keyboard of the scanning electron microscope and began to adjust the resolution and the magnification. As Katie stared at the CRT screen she realized that Medizone had one of the most sophisticated instruments available. The resolution was the best she'd ever seen.

She drew in a sharp breath as she realized what she was seeing.

Beside her, Mac muttered a low exclamation. "It's loaded with virus particles. But what the hell are they?''

Katie stared at the screen, her mind trying and failing to fit the images into a familiar pattern. "I don't know. But it's nothing we studied in school, and nothing I've ever seen before.''

Chapter Six

"Not very pretty, are they?" Mac muttered, stealing the words from her.

"No." Katie slid a sidewise glance at him. Obviously he was as perplexed as she.

Viruses were tiny. A thousandth of a thousandth of a millimeter. Even with an electron microscope, their image was apt to be indistinct—perhaps a fuzzy-looking sphere or a blurry filament. But with Medizone's state-of-the-art equipment, Katie had a better view of this one than she'd ever had before. It reminded her of an octopus, and she shuddered as she watched the limp, dead arms. She could imagine them when they'd been moving—scrabbling at Tom's tissues, getting a grip, choking off his life.

Mac pressed a button that activated the camera in the microscope's lens. Thirty seconds later they had a Polaroid of the picture on the CRT screen.

Katie stared at the photograph, the researcher in her challenged by the medical mystery. Hundreds or perhaps thousands of viruses could cause illness in humans—ranging from acute respiratory infections to chronic hepatitis and AIDS. But the form of a virus could change as it mutated or recombined with DNA borrowed from its host. Take the flu, for example. One form could make you achy and congested for a couple of days. The next mutation might be deadly—like the flu virus that had killed twenty million people in 1918-19. Often these seemingly new variations of an old virus came from tropical areas where they had already infected local populations—or been transmitted from animal reservoirs. And sometimes medical science was called on to do battle with something that seemed to be entirely new—like the HIV virus.

"Has Tom been in any exotic locations?"

"No."

"What about animal imports?"

"The only animals we have here are homegrown white lab rats."

"The first place they found Seoul virus was in Baltimore alley rats."

Mac pointed to the screen. "But that isn't Seoul virus." He got up from the console and walked over to the table against the wall where he stood shifting a pen back and forth between his good hand and the metal one. "Tom hasn't been on any trips out of the country in the past six months, but I have," he said, enunciating the words carefully. "Honduras. Borneo."

As she took in the deadly implications of Mac's words, Katie felt an arctic wind sweep over her body. It penetrated her flesh, all the way to the marrow of her bones. "Mac, no! You don't have any of the symptoms." She wouldn't allow it to be true.

"Not yet."

"Let's be logical. If *you* brought it back from the jungle then you should have run into trouble before Tom."

"Okay. You're right. Maybe I'm not at risk. Maybe I'm just a carrier."

"No." She wouldn't accept that conclusion, either.

"I hope to hell it isn't true. But we've got to find out."

He went dead still. "When Tom came back to the lab last night he wouldn't let me clean up the scratches on his face. He must have suspected his blood was contaminated."

Struggling for an outward calm that masked her internal trembling, Katie nodded.

"I guess we can start by looking at some of my blood," Mac said.

How could he be so cool about this? Katie wondered as she followed him back to the hematology lab. Her own heart was thumping like the bass line in a rock number as she assembled a tray with a syringe, glass tubes and the other supplies she'd need.

Mac sat down in one of the lab chairs and began to fumble with his right shirtsleeve. As she watched a metal finger stab through the fabric, she knew he wasn't as cool as he wanted her to believe. She longed to roll back the sleeve for him. She knew he wouldn't accept the help. Turning away again, she pretended she wasn't quite finished with the tray.

"Put on rubber gloves," he growled as she prepared to take the seat opposite him.

"It's a little late for that."

"We don't know exactly how this virus is transmitted."

Their gazes caught and held. Last night he'd kissed her very thoroughly. Now a flush blossomed on her skin as she recalled every nuance, every subtle pressure of his lips moving over hers. His smoky eyes shifted to her mouth, and she knew he was remembering the same things she was.

For a long moment, neither one of them seemed capable of moving. Then Mac stretched out his arm along the chair armrest, and the spell was broken.

"Let's get this over with."

She nodded and sat down opposite him, pulling her stool

closer to make it easier to work. She'd taken blood enough times so that the procedure should be easy. Yet this was different. As she tied the rubber tourniquet around Mac's upper arm, her nerve endings noted every touch of her fingers against his warm flesh. The disquieting sensation was even more acute as she investigated the inside of his elbow looking for a good vein.

"I never like having blood taken." His voice was gruff.

"Me neither. I'll try to be quick—and accurate."

He didn't wince when she inserted the needle. He didn't move while she drew two tubes of blood. But when she turned back to him with a small adhesive bandage for the needle mark, he took it out of her hand, and she knew he was worried about her coming into contact with his blood.

Her fists clenched as she kept her face averted. *Talk to me, Mac. Tell me how you're feeling. Let me share it.* The plea remained locked in her throat as he silently picked up the tubes of blood.

They looked at the sample with the electron microscope. Katie felt a surge of elation when they didn't find the nasty-looking virus particles.

"Not conclusive," Mac muttered.

Katie wished she could protest the summary judgment. Instead she nodded tightly. Mac could be in a different stage of the infection. The only way to be sure he didn't have the virus would be to grow more of the organisms from Tom's blood, inject them into an animal to obtain antibodies, and check for those antibodies in Mac's blood. Their absence would be the definitive proof.

"I wish it didn't take twenty-four hours to get enough of the virus," Katie murmured.

"It may not. Medizone's been experimenting with accelerated techniques."

"I'll help you set up."

She'd half expected him to insist that he didn't need her help to continue the work. Except that they'd be using "hot lab" procedures where hazardous material was handled in an isolated environment to prevent the spread of dangerous microorganisms. You had to reach inside the sealed hood with rubber gloves permanently affixed to access ports. If metal fingers could tear through shirt fabric, they could just as easily tear through the glove while he was working. That was one of the realities he lived with, and his accommodations had become automatic.

IT HAD BEEN a long, tense day, and the raw edges of Jade Nishizaka's nerves were frayed as if she'd been lashed repeatedly with a bullwhip. Still, a warm smile was fixed on her face as she glided across the Italian tile floor to one of the hairstyling stations. Like the rest of the Genesis salon, it was decorated with white wicker furniture, beveled mirrors and dozens of hanging plants.

"Mrs. Castleton, stardust blonde looks wonderful on you," she murmured.

"I just love it." Donna Castleton patted her elaborately coiffed hair. "The other wives at the country club will be green with envy."

"Be sure to tell them where you had your hair done. And before you go, you might want to stop by the cosmetic counter. Ming will be glad to show you our line of cosmetics including our exclusive cell-building moisturizer. It can take years off your skin with nightly applications. I've been using it myself since our exclusive lab began experimental trials."

"But you're so young!"

Jade gave her a mysterious smile. "No, I'm fifty-nine."

The blonde's eyes widened incredulously. "No one

would ever guess. And you're right, I definitely must have that moisturizer.''

The patronizing expression fell away from Jade's lips as she closed the door to her office. Sinking into her cushioned leather chair, she sat with her head bowed and her eyes closed, trying to steady herself.

With trembling fingers she unlocked the traveling campaign chest beside her chair and took out the ivory inlaid box. Inside was a worn picture album.

Slowly she began to turn the pages, studying the old black-and-white photos with their agonized faces and twisted bodies. She'd longed to bring them beauty. But it had been too late. Now the beauty belonged to her. And the women with the money to pay for Genesis's expensive treatment.

As always, the pictures tempered the iron of her resolve. Closing the book reverently, she slipped it back in its special place. Then she opened the personnel file on her desk. Val Caldwell. Age: forty-five. Marital status: divorced. Parents: deceased.

Was the information true? Or was it all a pack of lies? There'd been no evidence in her apartment to mark her as a spy. But perhaps she'd had a cover tight enough to breach the Genesis security check.

Jade's eyes scanned down the form. There was no one to notify in case of emergency. Had the omission been careless or was there really no one who'd be interested in Val's death? During the day, Jade had talked to her staff individually, telling them of Val's demise, reminding them not to discuss the tragedy with customers and tactfully pumping them for information about the dead woman's personal life. But her efforts had yielded very little. Val seemed to be a shallow woman interested in little else but herself, her sexual conquests and impressing her customers with her skill. Had that all been some kind of act to throw them off guard? Several of the other staff members had been told she was seeing an exercise instructor at a health club and a man who bought her expensive jewelry. Were they the same person? And what about the half sister she met for lunch occasionally? Truth or lies?

Jade was about to phone the detective agency she'd often employed, when she was interrupted by a knock on the door. "Who is it?"

"Ming."

"Come in."

A diminutive brunette carrying a cardboard box that had once contained bottles of Genesis setting lotion pushed open the door. "Here are the things from Val's station and her locker."

"You can put them on the table."

Ming followed her employer's instruction and waited to be dismissed.

"Before you go, I have a few questions. Is it possible that Val might have helped herself to our exclusive treatments?"

"No, madam. I inventoried the supplies just this morning, and everything seems to be accounted for. Besides, only the two of us know the combination." Ming's voice hesitated on the last word.

"What?" Jade snapped.

"I remember now. She was hovering in the background several times when I was opening the cabinet."

Jade's agile mind followed the train of her assistant's thought. "Go check again. And this time weigh each container on the milligram scale."

MAC HAD LEFT the lab while Katie prepared the tissue culture. When she finished, she found him waiting in the lounge next door. On a square table was a makeshift dinner. He'd brought her coffee, a sandwich and a chocolate bar. For himself there was only a cup of the dark brew.

After stuffing her lab coat into the hamper, Katie sank into the chair opposite Mac and took a long swallow of the coffee. It was just the way she liked it, with sugar and extra cream. Her sandwich was tuna, what she probably would have asked for if given a choice. For dessert she had a Mounds candy bar. As she looked at the meal laid out on a paper-napkin place mat, she was swept with a warm rush of feeling. After all these years, Mac had remembered her favorites.

"Not exactly up to your gourmet standards." It seemed he also remembered that she liked to work off her tension after a trying day by preparing elaborate dishes.

"This is great. Thanks." Hunger had finally caught up with her, and she tore into the food with enthusiasm.

When she realized he was watching her eat, she set down her sandwich. "Sorry, I must look like a pig at the trough."

"You look like you're starving. When was the last time you had a meal?"

"Lunch with Val yesterday, I guess." She gestured toward the other half of her sandwich. "I'll bet it's been about that long for you, too."

"I'll have something later." Once more he rubbed the side of his hand against his jaw, and she heard the scratching sound of his beard. This time it seemed to rasp against her nerve endings.

Katie busied herself blotting her lips, but her eyes searched Mac's face. He looked tired—and tense. But basically healthy. Of course, appearance could be deceptive. "I wouldn't like having to wait for the antibody tests, either,'' she murmured, hoping she could get him to open up with her.

"Maybe this will be an incentive for Medizone to develop some superacceleration techniques."

"Uh-huh."

She finished her sandwich and unwrapped the candy bar. "How did you remember I like Mounds bars?" she asked.

"Are you kidding? I used to call them your K rations. There was always one in your purse and a couple in your locker."

"So you're trying to see if I still have the addiction."

"You couldn't or you'd weigh three hundred pounds by now."

"Thanks."

He laughed, and all at once she knew that since he'd come back into her life, some deeply buried part of her had been waiting to hear that glad sound. The transformation was startling. The harsh lines in his face softened. The flatness went out of his gray eyes, and they took on depth, as though she were standing on a high mountain and looking down through layers of cloud to the ground far below. For just a moment, he was once again the engaging companion she remembered.

"I've missed you." As soon as the words had tumbled out, she wished she hadn't revealed so much.

"You miss that time in your life when everything was spread out in front of you like a Sunday brunch waiting for you to dig in."

"Yes, I miss that. I missed you, too."

"I'm not the same man you remember."

She'd thought that, too. Yet the old Mac McQuade had peeked out from behind his granite facade long enough for her to know that he was still there. She knew he'd only dispute her if she commented. Instead she shredded the bread crusts on the table in front of her. There was a question she was afraid to ask him. Yet what else did she have to lose? "When you said goodbye eight years ago, did you already know you were going to lose your hand?"

He crushed the coffee cup between a metal thumb and finger.

"So what if I did?"

He hadn't exactly answered the question. Except that he had.

"It's late, we're both tired," he continued. "And it won't do any good to sit in the lab staring at the petri dishes." Pushing back his chair, he stood up and began to clear the table. Watching him, Katie was struck with a sudden piercing insight. Eight years ago, when Mac had known he was facing amputation, he'd sent her away because he hadn't wanted to rely on anyone else for strength and comfort. Now he was waiting to find out if he had the same virus that had killed his friend. But he wasn't going to let her help him cope with the terrible uncertainty. She was just here as a lab assistant.

His back was to her, so she could watch him carefully as she tested the theory. "Yes. I think I'll go home and get some sleep."

Tension seemed to ooze out of his shoulders like water seeping from a broken main.

As quietly as possible, she pushed back her chair and stood up. When he turned from getting rid of the trash, she was standing a foot behind him. "But I'm not quite ready to leave yet," she murmured, her voice husky with both determination and trepidation.

For a breathless moment, she preserved the slight distance between them. Then she stepped forward and circled his body with her arms.

He tried to move out of her grasp but wasn't quick

enough to prevent her from locking her hands together behind his back. She heard him suck in a sharp breath as she rested her cheek against his chest and closed her eyes, absorbing the warmth of his body, giving him back as much of her own warmth as he would let himself take.

"Katie, you don't know what you're doing."

"You're wrong, I know exactly what I'm doing."

"The virus. You're taking a stupid chance getting this close to me." She could feel him swallow. "Tom gave it to your sister."

"You don't know that."

"Come on. They had the same symptoms. Those nasty little things we saw under the microscope turned Tom's brain to mashed potatoes. From what you said about Val, she was the same way."

"And you're not."

"Katie—"

"You don't have it!" she insisted fiercely.

"Until we know for sure, we have to assume I do."

She could feel him try to ease away. She didn't loosen her grip. "You know, really dangerous viruses aren't highly contagious."

"Oh yeah? What makes you think so?"

"The fact that the human race has survived all this time."

"Humph."

"Besides, that's a direct paraphrase of Joshua Lederberg," she added, referring to the Nobel Prize-winning geneticist who had recently turned his professional attention to emerging viruses.

"You always were a smartass." Grudging admiration mingled with a chuckle in his voice.

"Only some of the time."

"What about the rest of the time?"

She didn't answer. Instead she tipped her head up and stared at him. Neither one of them stirred, except that his eyes shifted so that he focused on her lips, the way they had earlier in the evening in the hematology lab.

"Would you mind telling me what kind of a game you're playing?" he grated.

"It's not a game, Mac."

He stared into her upturned face. It had always been pretty and intelligent. Maturity had added depth and beauty. The old Katie had haunted him through so many sleepless nights. This new woman he didn't understand— who wouldn't defer to him anymore—had taken her place. She certainly wasn't a match for his superior physical strength. It should have been easy to slip out of her grasp. Yet tonight he'd stopped trying to break free of her embrace. He couldn't.

Once before, he'd told her he didn't need her. He'd delivered the message over the phone, because he'd known what would happen if she took him into her arms and offered him the things he'd been afraid to ask for. Now he was caught in precisely the trap he'd feared.

Only it didn't feel exactly like a trap. It felt like warmth and sharing and all the other tender emotions he'd denied himself all these years because he hadn't been willing to let down his guard.

He'd never thought of Katie as provocative. Now as she reached out to stroke the stubble on his cheek, her fingers brushed erotically against the bristly hairs, sending little tremors deep into his body. She saw he was looking at her mouth, and her tongue flicked out to delicately touch her top lip. The back of his throat burned as he remembered the taste and texture of her. At that moment, he would have sold his soul for the chance to drink in those pleasures again. His soul. Not her life.

He wasn't going to take the chance. He couldn't. Yet he was powerless to break away, powerless to stop his arms from coming up to cradle her back.

A tiny shudder racked her body. It fired an answering charge in every one of his nerve endings. Life force seemed to surge through him. Life. The denial of death.

"Katie, this is crazy." The words were little more than a hoarse whisper.

As if in a trance, she shook her head in denial.

He had to stop. Now. Before things got completely out of control. But he couldn't stop. Not yet.

Her lips were parted. Her skin was flushed. Never taking his eyes from her face, he brushed his body against hers, watching the blue of her eyes darken and the red of her cheeks deepen.

The hard little buttons of her nipples against his chest made his own body tighten to a level that approached pain. The knowledge that she was as aroused as he almost sent him over the edge.

With the back of his left hand, he pressed her hips more tightly to his. But there was no need to hold her captive. Her body moved against his now of its own accord. His left arm moved, tipping her upper body back. Still watching her face, he cupped one soft, rounded breast in his palm.

For just a moment her eyes fluttered closed. Then they snapped open again—and locked with his.

He ordered himself to stop touching her. His fingers didn't follow the instructions. She was too alluring, too perfect, too responsive. And he needed her too much. Her little gasp was transformed into a moan of pleasure as his fingers played across her knit top and teased her nipple. The bulky fabric was a frustrating barrier. Slipping his hand underneath, he claimed her through the silky fabric of her bra, his hand moving greedily from one breast to the other.

Her breath came in a series of little gasps now.

His own breath was no more than a ragged counterpoint to the frantic pounding in his blood. She was in his arms again—offering him all the sweet passion he'd craved through all the lonely years.

His head lowered. Her lips parted, trembled.

They were a whisper away from contact when he realized what he was doing.

"No. God, no."

He took a step back, saw her sway and put a hand out to steady her. Her expression was dazed as she stared up at him.

"Katie, we both know how Tom gave the virus to Val. Through intimate contact."

"You don't know that for sure. We don't even know Tom was the source of the infection. And you don't have it."

"I hope to hell you're right. But if you're not, you may have to finish the investigation by yourself."

"Mac." Her face went white as driftwood in the moonlight, and he thought she might go to pieces. Then she seemed to visibly pull herself together.

"You need to go home and get some sleep." He resisted the impulse to tell her she wasn't thinking very clearly.

"All right. But I'll be back in the morning."

The look on her face told him there was no point in arguing.

Chapter Seven

Katie lay rigid in bed, her mind refusing to shut off and let her succumb to fatigue. Mac was right. There was a chance he could be infected. But she wouldn't allow him to be right. And like an earthquake victim clinging by her fingernails to an ever-widening chasm, she clung to the desperate belief that he had escaped the virus.

Sometime during the darkest hours of the night she finally fell into a restless sleep. And sometime in the expectant time just after the sun had crested the eastern horizon, she awoke with a fine sheen of perspiration on her skin and her heart pounding with fear.

"Mac." His name was a breathy sigh on her lips. "You're going to be all right," she whispered. "You have to be."

She might have sat up and turned on the light, or gotten up and drawn herself a drink of water. Instead she burrowed deeper under the covers, away from the pale light seeping around the curtains, and tried to stop her mind from churning. But the effort was wasted. Mac was in her life again—and the worst part was that there was no control over this time, either.

Her mind fled from the present and found the past just as painful. During the first three and a half years of medical school, she'd decided exactly what she wanted in a mate. The man she married would have to be her intellectual match. He had to be curious. He had to love solving problems. He had to be willing to take risks, to stand up for his convictions, to buck the system if that's what it took to accomplish his goals. He had to be able to make her laugh. He had to make her feel wild, singing passion when he took her in his arms.

Later, after she'd graduated, she'd admitted to herself that she was describing Mac McQuade. Perhaps, even though she'd gone on with her life, she'd never given anyone else a chance to show her he could step into the matrimonial profile. Years ago she'd decided if she couldn't have what she really wanted in a husband, there wasn't any point in settling for second best. So the only course for her had been to make the most of other things.

She'd been very successful, except for one stunning disaster in her professional career—the episode at the Sterling Clinic. Now that she'd put it behind her, her work was challenging and satisfying. She had a great group of friends. She loved her house and her garden. She loved to cook. She'd taken some memorable vacations.

She'd convinced herself that was enough. After a while it had been. Until Mac McQuade had come barreling back into her life, and she'd suddenly realized that all her rational thinking was as substantial as dandelion fuzz floating in the wind.

"Mac." She whispered his name, and this time she wasn't sure whether it was a curse or a benediction.

It hadn't been a one-sided exchange last night. She might be inexperienced with men, but she'd known he wanted her. Not just wanted. Needed. Enough to almost shatter his iron control.

However, *almost* was the operative word. At the last

moment, he'd wrenched himself back from lowering his mouth to hers, from taking what she was so obviously offering. Which didn't make things any easier now. Because she knew that he'd been thinking of her safety, not his own desires.

Pushing things that far had been her fault. No, she was being too hard on herself. She and Mac had both been caught up in the terrible uncertainty of the moment.

There wasn't any point in trying to go back to sleep. Swinging her legs out of bed, she headed across the carpet to the bathroom.

Under a mild pounding from the shower massage, she struggled to bring her fragmented thoughts to some sort of resolution. Mac couldn't be harboring the virus. And once they were perfectly sure that he was all right, it would be better for her emotional stability if she simply went about her own business. However, she couldn't leave this investigation to him. He needed her help to track down the infection to its source. Which meant she was going to have to walk into the lab this morning and act as if nothing out of the ordinary had happened between them. Logic told her he'd act that way, too, because the situation couldn't be much easier for him than it was for her. Yet she was going to be the one who got hurt if they couldn't pull it off.

MAYBE MAC hadn't expected her to come back, after all. When Katie arrived at the entrance to the hot lab at eight the next morning, he was giving directions to one of the technicians. Before she could stop herself, Katie searched his eyes again for signs of the illness that had ravaged Tom and Val. His countenance was haggard—but essentially unchanged. He didn't have it, she told herself again.

She was willing to bet that he hadn't gotten to bed at

all. However, either he'd gone home to shower and change into the fresh blue shirt and dark slacks he was wearing under his lab coat, or he kept a change of clothing in the building.

She saw him go very still when he glanced up and found her standing in the doorway. He didn't look her directly in the face, but he didn't need to, to make her heart start pounding as if it might batter its way through the wall of her chest.

The attack of nerves diffused as he introduced her to the woman who was taking in their silent exchange with apparent interest.

"Dr. Martin, Ms. Prager."

"Hello," they both said in unison.

"Ms. Prager was in early today to check on some cultures in the research department. I asked if she'd mind giving me a hand." Mac pointed to the isolation hood where they'd been growing the cultures. "There was enough of the virus to go on to the next step this morning."

Katie favored the technician with a smile she hoped was warm and reassuring as she took a clean lab coat from the drawer. "Thanks for filling in, but I think I can take over now."

The woman looked from Katie to Mac, seeking clarification of contradictory instructions.

Mac slipped his hand into his coat pocket. "I wasn't sure Dr. Martin would be back so early. Thank you, Ms. Prager. I'll call you if we need any further assistance."

There was another awkward moment after the technician had left, and Katie wondered if she should have been so quick to dismiss her. In a way, it made things easier to have a buffer between them.

"What did you tell her you were doing?"

"She can see what we're doing. An antibody test." He paused for several seconds. "I was getting ready to bring the serum from the refrigerator."

Katie tried to swallow past the sandpaper coating her throat. She hadn't realized he was almost ready for the crucial step.

It was hard to control the telltale shaking of her hands as she slipped them into the rubber gloves fixed to the side of the isolation chamber. The trembling was only slightly less apparent as she selected the necessary equipment inside the chamber and lighted the Bunsen burner. At least while she was setting things up, she had her back turned to Mac. It gave her the time to compose her face when she turned to take the serum from him. He was holding it in his metal hand—to make the contact as impersonal as possible, she supposed.

Neither one of them spoke as she operated the air lock. Nor could they think of any conversational gambits as she heated the serum.

Mac watched as she added the antibodies that had been produced overnight. If he had the same virus, they'd see antibodies clumping under an ordinary light microscope.

After preparing a slide using negative staining techniques, Katie turned to the microscope built into the wall of the chamber. When she'd set the slide on the platform, she felt Mac's hand on her shoulder, his touch a light caress that delayed the moment of truth. Then his fingers squeezed more tightly.

"Let me look."

Not trusting her voice, she nodded and stepped aside so he could stand in front of the microscope.

Her gaze was glued to his face as he bent to the eyepiece. His expression was absolutely neutral while he adjusted the focus.

For heart-stopping moments, Mac studied the slide. Finally she couldn't hold back the anxious question blocking her windpipe.

"Mac, what do you see?"

"Nothing."

"You mean I didn't prepare it correctly?"

"Your technique was faultless. I don't see any reaction."

"Thank God. Oh, Mac, thank God." The release of tension was like a tidal wave sweeping across a coastal plain, uprooting trees, tumbling boulders in its wake.

"You'd better take a look, too. Just in case I'm fooling myself."

He stepped aside and stood stiffly a few feet away. Pulse pounding, Katie lowered her face to the eyepiece and repeated the visual inspection. "You don't have any antibodies," she whispered.

Behind her he let out a deep, thankful breath. "I was afraid I was seeing what I wanted to see."

"You're clear," she repeated. "You don't have the virus."

The look of relief on his face made her ache to take him in her arms and hug him fiercely to her breast. For one unguarded moment he stood staring at her as if he wanted the same thing. Then he turned away and started stripping off his lab coat. After stuffing it into the hamper, he rolled his shoulders.

"Tired?" she asked softly.

"Yeah. But at least the waiting's over."

"How long have you been here?" she asked.

"It seems like forever." He pressed his hand against his forehead. "Since yesterday morning."

"Then you need a change of scene." She made her

voice light. "Do you ever have breakfast at Vie de France in the Columbia Mall?"

"You mean the place with the chocolate croissants?"

"The very same."

There was a wistful note in his voice. "That sounds good. But there's so much to do here."

"Mac, you've just been through a pretty tough twenty-four hours. You're entitled to a break."

He sighed. "I guess you're right. I'd better make sure Marcia doesn't need me for anything urgent."

There was a look of relief on his secretary's face as she practically shooed Mac out of the office.

"Nice day," he observed as he sucked in a hearty draft of air before heading toward his car.

"Uh-huh." Katie followed, a little smile flickering around her lips. The weather wasn't really all that wonderful. In fact, it looked as if it might be going to rain. However rain and clouds probably had little to do with Mac's perspective on life.

Katie smiled again as she settled back into the plush upholstery of Mac's sports car. The comfortable seats weren't the only luxury. The windows were the same kind of dark glass that you saw in limousines—which gave the car a feeling of privacy. Mac fiddled with the radio until he found a rock number with a strong beat. Yesterday he'd been as uptight as a man getting ready to face a firing squad. This was much better.

THE PHONE RANG as Helen Austin-Wright was sitting at the inlaid marble kitchen table of her Georgetown home going over her weekend social calendar.

When she picked up the receiver, a familiar voice began, "Hello, Helen, it's Donna. Is it too early to call?"

"No. It's fine. George and I always get an early start on the day."

"I tried to call last night, but you must have been out. I just *had* to thank you for recommending that I try Genesis. What a wonderful place. My first appointment was yesterday afternoon, and you won't believe how well my hair turned out."

"I can't wait to see it," Helen murmured.

"You will tonight at the Commerce Club."

"Tonight?"

"At the Ides of March party."

Helen glanced across the table at her husband, George, buried behind a copy of the *Wall Street Journal.* She knew Wright Chemicals was fighting off a takeover bid. George had been worried about that for months, but lately he'd stopped talking about it. And now he was staying home from the office in the mornings. Had he given up the fight to save the company? Were things worse than he was letting on?

In the past he'd always put a good face on problems—especially with his colleagues. Surely, as a board member of the prestigious Commerce Club, he ought to be attending the party. But he hadn't mentioned it, had he? A worried look wrinkled her brow as she thought about just how many other things he'd forgotten lately.

"Helen, are you still there?" her friend on the other end of the phone line broke into her thoughts.

"Yes, sorry, Donna. I just need to talk to George before he leaves for work. I'll call you back later."

After replacing the receiver, Helen cleared her throat. "Darling, do you know anything about a do at the Commerce Club tonight?"

"What?"

"The Commerce Club. Did you forget about the Ides of March Party tonight?"

"No!" George flung the paper down on the table, his face contorted with anger. "Stop bugging me. Why are you always bugging me?"

"Darling, I just—"

Slinging the paper down on the table, he glared at her. Then he picked up his cup of coffee and slammed it back down into the saucer, sending brown liquid splashing all over the creamy-white surface of the table.

Helen shrank back, the violent look in his eyes sending a tremble of fear down her spine.

In the next moment, the fury was wiped away, replaced by confusion. George stared at the mess on the table. "Did I do that? I—I'm sorry."

Helen began to mop at the coffee with her napkin. "It's all right. You're just under a lot of stress, that's all."

He reached across the table and squeezed her hand. "Stress. That's right. I have to leave. I've got a meeting. You call the Commerce Club. I'm sure we have a reservation. I'm sorry I forgot to tell you about it."

IT WAS ONLY a fifteen-minute drive to the mall, and Katie directed Mac to the parking lot closest to the *patisserie*. As they drove up and down the lanes of parked cars looking for a space, she noticed a dark blue Ford doing the same thing. Apparently the situation brought out the old competitive streak in Mac that Katie remembered from medical school. As he and the other driver approached an empty spot from different directions, Mac stepped on the gas and zipped into the space.

"Tough luck, buddy," he murmured as the other car pulled away and began to circle again.

"Men," Katie muttered under her breath.

"Just testing my reflexes."

And feeling frisky, Katie added silently. She was smiling as they strolled down the lane to the mall door. But she tensed for a moment at the entrance to the restaurant when she spotted the driver of the blue car heading in their direction, one hand lifted to his mouth. He looked as if he were biting his thumbnail. Somehow the nervous gesture didn't seem to go with the broad shoulders and football player physique. Was he nervous? Was he coming to start a fight? However, he loped on past, and she soon forgot all about him.

Because it was late for breakfast and still early for lunch, there was no one ahead of them in the cafeteria-style line. Once they'd gotten their food, they had their pick of tables in the eating area. Instead of pastry, Katie opted for crab soup and Swiss cheese on French bread. She bit back any comment as she watched Mac pick up his chocolate croissant and a cherry Danish. The man had eaten hardly anything in twenty-four hours, but there was no point in lecturing him on nutrition. In fact, under the circumstances, he was entitled to anything he wanted.

Leaning back in his chair, Mac stretched out his long legs beside the table. "Thanks for suggesting that we get away for a little while like this. Sometimes I wonder if I've forgotten how to relax."

"I know what you mean. That's why I force myself to do something wicked every once in a while—like take the afternoon off for some marathon shopping."

Mac laughed. "Sure. Really wicked." He regarded her fondly. "It's strange to realize you're living right in the same area."

"I grew up in D.C."

"Right. I remember."

Katie found herself wanting to catch up on all the old

news she'd missed. "How's your mother doing? I remember you were worried about her being able to keep the ranch," she asked.

There was an oddly strained look on his face, and Katie prepared herself for bad news. But his answer was positive.

"She's fine now."

"I'm glad."

"I've been able to funnel some of my Medizone profits into building up the herd and repairing the buildings. Chip, my younger brother, is running the spread."

"You never did want to be in charge of a ranch."

"No."

The conversation petered out, and they munched their respective meals in silence for several moments. From under lowered lashes, Katie watched Mac. He didn't look as relaxed anymore. Was there something he was holding back about his family? She remembered some of the things he'd told her about the independent, demanding McQuades who had been disappointed when Mac had announced his choice of career. As the oldest son, he'd been expected to carry on the family tradition. They'd had a hard time adjusting to his leaving the ranch. Probably they'd had trouble adjusting to his handicap as well. Had she made him think about that now? Or was he worrying about something else? As more patrons came into the little restaurant, he kept glancing around, as if he was feeling crowded. Maybe he was.

"I can't stop thinking about that crazy experiment of Tom's," he finally said. "I think he was looking for a cure or a treatment for the virus."

Katie jumped on the new line of conversation. "Then when things didn't work out, he went back to Medizone's AIDS research."

"But he wasn't thinking things through very clearly."

"I want to know if this virus has shown up anywhere else in the country. We should have packed up a sample and sent it right to the CDC," Mac muttered.

"We can do it when we get back."

He set down his coffee cup and cleared his throat. "You probably have your own work to catch up on. You don't have to come back there to the lab with me."

Katie chewed the bite of bread in her mouth, wondering how she was going to swallow it. Mac's offhand remark was an easy way of telling her goodbye. Probably there wasn't any point in protesting. Maybe it was better this way, after all. Hadn't she been warning herself something like this was going to happen?

"I'm afraid I need a ride back—to pick up my car."

"Yeah. Your car." He had the good grace to look embarrassed as he put down the cherry Danish and folded his napkin. "I, uh, haven't really thanked you for your help. And for putting up with me."

"I was glad to help. Besides, you were certainly entitled to be edgy. I was, too. I was worried about you."

"You don't need to be concerned about me."

There was nothing left to lose, no need to censor her reactions now. "Of course not, Mac. You're perfectly capable of taking care of yourself."

The sharp note in her voice made him raise his head.

"By the way," she continued. "What was your mother's reaction to your losing your hand?"

His eyes shifted away from hers, and he appeared to be staring at a spot somewhere over her left shoulder. "My mother is a good woman. Salt of the earth, as they say. When I came home after the accident she told me it wouldn't have happened if I'd stayed where I belong. I think she never did come to terms with my defection. Anyway, being in the same room with me makes her uncomfortable." He held up the stainless steel fist. "She couldn't deal with this. I send her money, but I haven't been out to Montana since right after the accident when I needed a place to recuperate. If she doesn't see me, she doesn't have to think about my disability."

"Oh, Mac, I'm so sorry."

"The last thing I want from anyone is pity."

"I wasn't offering pity. I'm just sorry you and your family don't know how to deal with each other. That's the way it was with me and Val. So I know how sad it is."

He made a noncommittal sound.

"And I don't think of you as disabled."

"Then you should go back to the dictionary and check the definition."

"If it makes you uncomfortable to be with me, that's your fault, not mine."

She saw his Adam's apple bob. "Katie, I'm sorry. It isn't going to work. Not with someone I was close to before."

"Not if you don't give it a chance."

"There's too much old stuff in the way."

"A lot of old stuff. Yes. Or is that just an excuse?"

He fished some change out of his pocket and slapped a tip down on the table. Without waiting to see if she was following, he stalked toward the door.

It flashed through Katie's mind that she could call a cab to take her back to Medizone, and then Mac McQuade wouldn't have to suffer her company for another fifteen minutes. But why should she go to the trouble and expense? she asked herself as she trailed after him toward the exit. And why should she make things easy for him?

While they'd been in the restaurant, the sun had come out from behind a bank of clouds. As she stepped through the door, Katie squinted against the sudden brightness and fumbled in her purse for her sunglasses.

When she glanced up again, Mac was over toward her right, head down as he made for the space where they'd parked the car. Apparently he wasn't paying much attention to his surroundings, because he didn't seem to notice the blue car heading along the circular drive toward the mall entrance. It was the Ford that had passed them several times in the parking lot.

Now that it was closer to lunchtime, half a dozen people were heading for the mall entrance. The driver should be slowing down as he approached the pedestrian walkway, Katie thought. Instead the vehicle was speeding up.

"Mac! Watch out!" Katie shouted as he stepped off the curb. Before the words were out of her mouth, she was already sprinting across the sidewalk.

Everything seemed to happen in slow motion after that. Hearing the warning, Mac stopped and looked up. He saw the car because he took a quick step back. But that wasn't going to keep him from being hit. While Katie watched in horror, the wheels on the right side of the Ford came up on the sidewalk as the vehicle bore down on Mac.

Chapter Eight

Katie crashed into Mac at a forty-five-degree angle, knocking him back and to the side. Her sunglasses went flying as they both lost their balance, hit the sidewalk and skidded against the cement.

The car's engine roared in her ears. When she glanced up, she gasped. She'd tried to knock Mac out of harm's way. But the effort hadn't been good enough.

From her position on the ground, the car bearing down on them looked like a tank trying to crush wounded enemy soldiers. The grinding sound of crumpling metal broke around her. Katie squeezed her eyes shut and braced herself, expecting to feel the wheels crush her body. The impact never came.

Instead of plowing into her and Mac, the speeding car had collided with one of the two-foot-high concrete posts that flanked the entrance to the mall and served as seats for shoppers waiting near the curb.

Dazed, Katie reached desperately for Mac. He was already pushing himself off the sidewalk—lurching toward the blue car. The vehicle gunned its engine, made a hard left and careered away.

She could hear Mac cursing. When he knelt beside her

again, she saw worry gnawing at his features. "Are you hurt?" His voice was low and intense.

She tried to talk and found her jaw was trembling too badly. The trembling spread to her limbs. Somewhere in her peripheral vision she noted that a crowd was forming around them, but the entire focus of her attention was on Mac.

"My God, what did that maniac do to you?" he asked.

Katie struggled to choke out a response. "I'm—I'm all right."

Wrapping an arm around her shoulder, Mac angled her gently toward him. "You're sure?"

She nodded. "What about you?"

"I'll survive."

He helped her to her feet and watched as she flexed her arms and legs. She wanted to make sure of his condition, too, but it had become impossible to block out the commotion around them.

Someone handed Katie her sunglasses, and she jammed them back on her face. She was astonished to realize that her purse was still slung over her shoulder. Probably it had helped cushion her fall.

"That guy was insane," a loud voice from the crowd observed.

There was a chorus of agreement.

"He looked like he was trying to mow you down."

"Did anyone get the license number?" Katie asked, swaying slightly on rubbery legs. Mac steadied her by pulling her tightly against his side.

No one answered her question.

"You sure you're okay, fella?" The man who'd asked the question was staring at Mac's prosthetic hand.

"I'm fine."

"Want me to call the cops or an ambulance?" a denim-clad young man asked excitedly.

"I'll take care of it," Mac told him. He turned to Katie, his face carefully neutral. "Let's get out of here."

"Hey, you can't just leave the scene of an accident," someone objected.

"Why not? The driver didn't stay to exchange insurance information." Mac's arm was still around Katie's shoulder as he led her to the car.

At least none of the crowd followed them. As soon as Mac opened the door, Katie sank into the seat, grateful for the special tinted glass that meant no one could look in on them. They were in the middle of the mall parking lot, but at least they had some privacy. She felt the back of Mac's hand press her cheek and reached up to cover his fingers with hers.

"Pretty stupid of you, dashing into the path of a speeding car." His voice was low and husky.

"I—I saw him bearing down on you, and all I could think about was pushing you out of the way."

"You shouldn't have."

"I wasn't very effective. It was the concrete post that stopped him."

"You were effective, all right. If you hadn't hit me like a linebacker, I would have been on the other side of the post."

She felt his lips brush her forehead, his hand smooth back her hair. Before she could react to the tender gestures, she was wondering if she'd imagined them, because Mac was reaching across her and opening the glove compartment. A moment later, she smelled antiseptic, followed by a wet stinging sensation against her knee. Very carefully so as not to hurt her more than necessary, he began to dab at the raw skin.

"You don't have to do that."

"I want to make sure it's clean." After he finished with the antiseptic, he covered the abrasion with an adhesive bandage.

His next question was asked in a barely audible voice. "How do you think I'd feel if you'd gotten hit?"

"I don't know. How would you feel?"

"Katie—"

She drew in a shaky breath. "Mac, you may want to keep pretending that we don't care a lot about each other. I gave up on that a couple of days ago. If you thought I was just going to let you take me back to my car and then disappear from my life again, you were wrong."

He sighed heavily. "Katie, you don't want to get mixed up with someone like me."

"Why not?"

He thumped his stainless steel fist against the steering wheel. "I'm not the same guy you knew back in medical school. I'm bitter. I'm resentful about your having the career I wanted. I've turned into a loner."

"At least you're being honest."

"I'm no good for you."

"Why don't you let me be the judge of that?"

He bowed his head, and she pressed her forehead against his. There was an ironic quality in his voice when he started to speak again. "You know, this may sound strange, but there are women who are turned on by a guy with a hand like mine. It makes him an interesting novelty."

"I was turned on by you long before you showed up with the trick part."

He kept on talking, as if he hadn't heard her response. "I've never put a relationship to the test. I guess I never wanted to find out whether it was real or not."

"Our relationship was real."

"Maybe once. I don't know how to communicate on a sincere level anymore."

Sadness shuddered through her soul. For all these years he must have been so lonely. So lonely.

Yet somehow at the same time, hope swelled deep inside her. She was sure he'd never confided those feelings to anyone else. If he could trust her enough to confess his failings, maybe he could trust her enough to accept the love she'd buried deep inside her for so many years.

A little shock skittered across her nerve endings as she realized what word she'd silently used.

Love.

There was no use hiding the truth from herself any longer. Not when she'd jumped into the path of a speeding car to push him out of the way. Perhaps later the intensity of her feelings would be scary. At the moment, they gave her a feeling of joy. Mac was here again with her. Maybe she hadn't gotten what she wanted with him the first time because she'd never had the courage to reach out and grab it. Yet what if she tried and failed? Well, at least she'd know she'd done her best.

When she felt Mac shift away from her, she stroked her finger down his cheek. "I'm taking a rain check on the rest of this conversation," she murmured.

"I already said more than I intended."

"Maybe that's a good sign."

"If you say so. But I see mall security heading over this way." He pointed toward a small white truck with a flashing yellow light. "And I don't feel like answering a bunch of questions at the moment."

The bubble of intimacy surrounding them burst. Katie carefully flexed her scraped knee as she watched Mac reach for the ignition key.

"I want to check that license number," he muttered as he pulled out of the parking space.

"I thought you didn't know what it was."

"I didn't say that. It's GXS 734. As a matter of fact, I got it *before* we went into the mall."

"Convenient. I guess Mr. Ford didn't like you beating him out of a parking space."

"Mr. Ford! That's good, Button."

"Thanks." Button. His old nickname for her. For the first time since they'd been together again, it had slipped out of his mouth. It had started when he'd teased her about her buttoned-down image. Then he'd told her she was as cute as a button. Her heart squeezed painfully as all the associations came back to her, but she wasn't allowed to dwell on the moment.

Mac plowed ahead with the business at hand. "Do you really believe that was the reason he came after us? The parking space, I mean."

"I—I don't know."

"I think your Mr. Ford may have had another motive."

"What?"

"I'll tell you after we get back to the office. The first thing to do is pack up that virus sample for the CDC. I want to get them working on the identification as soon as possible."

Looking impatient to set the process in motion, Mac pushed past the speed limit as he headed back to Medizone. His expression changed abruptly when he stepped into the hot lab and peered through the glass wall of the isolation chamber.

"What the hell?"

"Mac, what is it?"

He gestured toward the interior. "It's all gone."

Katie stared through the glass in disbelief. The petri dish

with the virus and the rest of the equipment they'd been using had been cleared away.

Turning on his heels, Mac stormed down the hall to the head of lab services. Behind him, Katie trotted to keep up. "Who authorized the removal of my materials from Hot Lab Three?" he demanded.

"Why, *you* did, sir."

"What?"

"Yes, the messenger company arrived while you were out. They took everything away with them, just the way you specified." The woman began thumbing through pages on a clipboard and then tapped a sheet of paper. "Here's the order right here."

Mac snatched the stack of papers away from her and scanned the form. "It's our regular delivery company. But I didn't initiate the request."

"Let me see." Katie reached for the clipboard. When he handed her the form, she looked for the destination. The material was supposed to be going to a hospital lab in downtown Baltimore. "That place doesn't do anything more than standard blood work for doctors' offices," she pointed out.

She and Mac exchanged worried glances, and she could see he was about to voice a comment. Before he could, she shook her head almost imperceptibly. The less they said about this in front of anyone else, the better. Yet they did need some information.

Apparently Mac had gotten the message. When he turned back to the lab supervisor, his voice was more controlled.

"Was it the regular driver?" he asked.

The woman was beginning to look upset. "Why, no, Mr. McQuade. It was an oriental fellow. He said you wanted the materials to go out immediately. I'm terribly sorry if I did something wrong."

"No. It's probably just a mix up. Dr. Martin and I will take care of it."

They went back to Mac's office and closed the door. A quick call to the delivery company confirmed their suspicion that the driver hadn't been from their organization.

"You're right, we shouldn't be talking about this in front of anyone else," Mac acknowledged. "It looks as if somebody went to a rather big risk to get the virus sample. What if we'd been here?"

"But we weren't." Katie struggled to keep the timbre of her voice even. "While they were cleaning this place out, Mr. Ford was trying to run us down at the Columbia Mall."

"Yeah."

"What did you mean when you said he might have another motive besides revenge for taking his parking space?" she demanded.

"It wasn't anything I could prove. But I was wondering if we'd been followed to the mall from here. While we were having breakfast, I kept feeling as if someone were watching us."

"Is that why you were looking around?"

"Uh-huh."

"Well, they didn't get *us*. But all the material is gone."

"No, they didn't get us. And we're going to duplicate the material."

"We can't. We don't have any of Tom's blood."

"Yes we do. I froze the other tube that was in the refrigerator. If it hasn't vanished, too, we're in business." He paused. "However, we're not going to do the work at Medizone. In fact, we're not going to stay in the building any longer than we have to."

Katie felt tiny goose bumps pepper her arms as the implications of the morning's activities sunk in. Someone wanted to eliminate them and all traces of their virus research. And whoever it was, was probably going to come back when they found out the accident in the mall parking lot had failed.

Mac reached for her cold hand. "Come on. The way I figure it, we've got a little window of time to get out of here before Mr. Ford reports back to headquarters. We're splitting as soon as we pack that frozen blood in dry ice and I tell Marcia she's going to have to handle things here—because she's not going to be able to get in touch with me."

Ten minutes later they climbed into Tom's car.

"Your Marcia's worried," Katie murmured as they pulled out of the parking lot and headed north. "Maybe she even thinks you've cracked under the pressure."

"I know. But the less information she's got the better it is for us—and her."

"Who are we up against?" Katie wondered aloud.

"We're going to find out. Too bad I'm not into covert operations," Mac muttered as he checked the rearview mirror to make sure they weren't being followed again.

"I am."

His eyes swung toward her momentarily. "What are you talking about?"

"At least I have the right connections. I've got a friend named Jo O'Malley who's a private detective. Last fall, she helped another friend of mine go underground for a few days."

"Is needing to hide out a regular occurrence in your circle of friends?"

Katie's laugh helped dissipate a little of the tension. "I

hope not. But Jo's a good woman to have in your corner when you're in trouble.''

"So are you.''

"Thanks.'' She shot Mac a surprised glance, but his eyes were firmly on the road ahead of him.

Katie called Jo from the car phone and briefly explained what had happened to her and Mac in the past hour.

"You'd better not come down to 43 Light Street or go home, either,'' the detective advised. "If they came looking for Mac at Medizone, they may very well have your office staked out, too.'' Jo was silent for a moment. Then her voice came back across the speaker. "There's a Marriott Courtyard out near the airport. Why don't I meet you there? Register as Mr. and Mrs. Lam.''

"As in 'on the lam'?'' Katie asked.

"You got it. Your first names are Lisa and John.''

As they drove toward Baltimore-Washington International Airport, Katie risked a glance at the man beside her. His expression was tightly controlled. This time she was glad he kept his eyes on the road, because she was positive her own face mirrored her inner turmoil. Someone had tried to kill them and had stolen incriminating material from the lab. Hiding out made sense, and it was stupid to be worrying about their personal relationship. Yet just the thought of her and Mac spending the night together in a small motel room flooded her system like a brook after a torrential downpour. Yesterday she might have tried to hide her feelings. Now she cleared her throat.

"I'm nervous about sharing a motel room with you, too.''

"I'm not nervous!''

"But I think we can handle the situation.''

"Of course.''

Nevertheless, when they arrived at the motel, Katie was

glad it was safest for her to check in alone while Mac waited in the car. That way she didn't have to confer with him when she told the clerk Mr. and Mrs. Lam wanted two double beds instead of one queen.

As she started to pull out a credit card, she realized that wasn't a good idea—for several reasons. She could explain that they'd just gotten married and she hadn't changed her name. Yet that left them open to being traced through the transaction. Paying for one night took most of her cash, and she wasn't sure how they were going to get more.

Just as they stepped into Room 105, Jo phoned from the desk.

"In a jam, are you?" she asked as she breezed through the door a few minutes later.

Seeing her friend, who had dropped everything and come running to their assistance, brought a lump to Katie's throat. Because she couldn't trust herself to speak, she nodded tightly.

Jo gave her a quick, reassuring hug, then inclined her head toward Mac. "Is it this guy's fault?"

"Now wait a minute!" he objected, his posture immediately defensive.

"No," Katie assured her quickly. "Our being in trouble has just as much to do with my sister as his friend Tom." She wasn't absolutely sure the assessment was true, but she was sure that she and Mac were in this together.

Jo continued to stare appraisingly at her friend's companion. "You've got a reputation for causing trouble, you know, McQuade."

"Is that so? With whom? Or are you going to make me play twenty questions?"

"I'm not going to play games with you. Not when Katie is in danger. Remember that cooperative artificial-limb project a couple of years ago? The one where various scientific outfits around the country were donating their services and shared technologies. *You're* the one who held up approval of the design for six months and added thousands of dollars to the cost."

Mac raised the left hand that had been angled away from Jo. "I did a personal evaluation of the upper extremity model. It needed work. And how do you know anything about it?"

Jo's eyes focused on Mac's stainless steel hand, but she didn't miss a beat. "My husband, Cameron Randolph, had a lot to do with the miniaturized electronics."

"*You're* married to Cameron Randolph?"

"Uh-huh. I've been sharing his house full of inventions for the past year."

Mac shook his head and grinned at her. "Well, I'll be damned. I've been wanting to meet the son of a gun since we exchanged that flurry of E-mail. After he reworked the design, that hand was the best I'd ever tried. In fact, I was using it until a few weeks ago, until Medizone came up with this one." He snapped the fingers, and they responded with a satisfying metallic click.

Jo grinned back at him. "Wait till I tell Cam about this. Better yet, I'll arrange an introduction after we figure out what to do about the mess you're in now."

Katie let out the breath she'd been holding. Both Jo and Mac had strong personalities, and for a while there, she'd been afraid that the two of them were going to grate on each other. Now it looked like things were going to work out rather well.

"I want to hear the whole story of how you got yourselves in this fix," Jo prompted. "Every detail. Then we'll try to sort out what's important."

The two women sat down on one of the double beds. Mac took the chair. For the next hour, he and Katie filled

Jo in on exactly what had happened since she had visited her sister, leaving out the personal details they'd both decided weren't relevant.

"So you suspect both Val and Tom were infected with a virus that's transmitted by intimate contact," Jo mused. "And you think someone is desperate to keep that information from getting out. Why?"

"At first we thought it might have been imported accidentally from abroad—by insect larva or animal hosts." Katie turned to Mac. "Did Tom meet with personnel from other area labs?"

"Yes."

"Well, the government farms out all kinds of secret research. What if some laboratory in the area is involved in a covert germ-warfare experiment that's gotten out of control?" Katie asked. "That would certainly be worth suppressing."

"By robbery and murder?" Mac countered.

"If the stakes are high enough. What if they've blown a multimillion-dollar contract?"

"Maybe it's not the government. Maybe it's some sort of terrorist group," Jo suggested. "How long did you say Tom was exhibiting symptoms—while he was still partially functional?"

"A couple of months at least," Mac told her. "Which doesn't sound like the virus would have a military or terrorist application. They'd want something that struck down victims quickly."

"What if it was going to be used for covert assassinations? And you didn't want anyone to know the person was a target?" Katie suggested.

"Then you sure wouldn't want his wife to get it," Jo offered.

"I suppose we could be dealing with terrorists. But as

far as I know, assassination isn't a policy of the U.S. government," Katie murmured.

"Okay, forget that," Jo agreed. "Let's go back to the germ-warfare theory. Maybe the virus isn't stable. Maybe it's just in the early experimental stages."

"We can speculate until doomsday and not get anywhere," Mac interrupted. "But there might be another way to find out who wants the information suppressed." He wrote down a series of letters and numbers on the notepad beside the phone and handed it to Jo. "This is the license of the car that tried to run us down. Do you think you could find out our Mr. Ford's real name?"

"Was it a Maryland or D.C. license?"

"D.C."

"I have better contacts in Maryland, but I'll see what I can do."

"Meanwhile, we need to grow another sample of the virus," Mac went on. "It's important to send it to the Centers for Disease Control in Atlanta—to see if they've got data on any outbreaks."

"I thought all your materials disappeared," Jo pointed out.

"I still have a frozen blood sample from Tom." Mac gestured toward the thermos container on the floor beside his chair. "Which should be taken to a lab in the next few hours. Then we can duplicate the work."

"I've been thinking about that," Katie interjected. "We don't have to do that part ourselves. I mean, as long as adequate precautions are taken, we can contract out the labor. There are a couple of labs in the area that could handle it—and keep the information confidential."

"How are we going to know they're not the one with a secret government contract?" Mac asked in a level voice.

Katie looked chagrined. "I wasn't even thinking about that."

"Harvey Cohen can tell us," Jo suggested. "I've worked with him before."

"You've worked with Harvey Cohen, too?" Mac asked. "Who don't you know?"

"Who is he?" Katie asked.

"The author of *The Electronic Warfare Game.* Now he's got a watchdog think tank a couple of miles from here, as it happens. He may not know every outfit that has a secret contract—but he'll know which labs wouldn't touch government work with a ten-foot pole."

After a short conversation with Jo, Harvey Cohen recommended R & E Labs in Elkridge.

"Now we just need to find out how this is tied up with the D.C. police's noninvestigation of Val's death." Katie's voice was gritty as she got ready to leave with Mac.

Jo reached out and gently squeezed her arm. "Why don't I make some calls—starting with the D.C. morgue. We can meet back here later in the afternoon. Wait, before you go—" The detective pulled a couple of credit cards out of her knapsack. They were in the names of Lisa and John Lam. "I've used this account when I needed to establish another identity," she explained. "You can pay me back when you have access to your own accounts."

"Jo, you think of everything," Katie marveled.

"I try. And speaking of that, rent yourselves a car—in case someone gets the bright idea of looking for Tom's."

THE TRIP TO R & E LABS went well. Although the facility wasn't as well equipped as Medizone, the staff was cooperative, and Mac was satisfied that they'd be able to duplicate his and Katie's procedures.

The building wasn't more than fifteen minutes from

Katie's house in Ellicott City, and she wished she could go home and pack a suitcase. But she knew that wasn't safe. As they left the lab and headed back toward the highway, she could see Mac checking the rearview mirror. And she kept looking behind them, too, making sure they weren't being followed by a blue Ford or any other vehicles.

"Mac, I'm going to need some stuff. You know, toilet articles, underwear."

"Yeah."

"We could stop at the K mart at Dobbin Center."

Instead of heading for the motel, Mac went back to Columbia. They split up to do their shopping, but met back at the checkout counter. Katie glanced at him as the cashier picked up the long-sleeved flannel nightshirt she'd bought. He was staring at it but quickly reached into the basket to put some more things on the counter.

If they'd gotten married after medical school, they would have been making shopping trips like this for years, Katie thought. Really, it was all so ordinary. A suburban couple stopping at the store on their way home from work. Yet she knew there was nothing ordinary about the circumstances. Even if they were in danger, she was hoarding every moment of the experience—every moment they spent together—like a pirate filling a treasure chest.

They were both quiet on the drive back to the motel. When they stepped in the door, it was obvious from Jo's expression that she hadn't had a very successful afternoon.

"What is it?" Mac asked.

"For starters, my contact at motor vehicles is on leave. So I can't tell you a thing about that license number, or your Mr. Ford."

"But that's not the only thing wrong," Katie prodded.

Jo pressed her lips together, and Katie wished she hadn't put her friend on the spot. "Right. Honey, I'm really sorry.

The best thing to do is give you the scoop straight out.
You're not going to have a chance to check out that virus
in your sister. The D.C. medical examiner's office is very
apologetic. But they say there was a mixup at the morgue.
Valerie Caldwell's body was accidentally switched with
another woman—a hit-and-run victim named Hannah Ca-
bel. She was sent to Flowers Funeral Home and cremated.''

Chapter Nine

Sudden tears gathered in Katie's eyes, and she felt Mac's arm come up around her shoulder. She leaned into his embrace. "Val always felt like she was so alone. After Mom's funeral, she told me she was glad she was going to be buried there, too."

"You can still bury her ashes next to your mother," Jo murmured.

"It's not the same!" Katie heard the edge of hysteria in her own voice and knew her irrational reaction was as much to the whole situation as to this latest macabre twist.

Mac eased her to the edge of the bed and sat beside her, stroking her shoulder. Jo brought her a glass of water.

Katie took a few sips and set the plastic tumbler down with a thunk on the bedside table, spilling some of the contents. "It wasn't an accident!" she grated. "They don't care who gets hurt. They did it on purpose to keep us from tracking the virus."

"That fits with the rest of it," Mac agreed, getting up and walking toward the window where he pushed the curtains aside and stood looking out. After several moments he turned back to Jo. "You've done an awful lot for us, and I hate to press you for anything."

"Don't be ridiculous! I'm here to help."

"Yeah, well, now that we don't have anything else to work with, we've got to track that license number."

"I know." She thought for a moment. "Listen, why don't I approach it from a different angle. I've got a lot of contacts in the Maryland office. One of them may be willing to query the D.C. system for me."

"I appreciate that. And while you're gone, Katie will have a chance to get some rest."

Katie, who had been tensely watching the conversation, didn't protest the suggestion.

When her friend had left, she turned to Mac, her expression quizzical. "Okay, I've already caught on to the way your mind works. You weren't exactly being straight with Jo."

"We need to trace that car."

"Stop playing games with me, too! What is it you didn't want to say in front of her?" Katie demanded.

He sighed. "I'm trying to keep your friend out of danger. The less she hangs around with us, the better off she'll be." Mac took a step toward her. "I keep trying to think of some way to get us out of this mess, too. The trouble is, every time we turn around, the plot looks bigger."

"You mean like the way the cop who did the initial investigation of Val's death was pulled off the case?"

"Like that," he agreed.

"Either someone in the D.C. police is being paid off to bury the case, or the department is a shambles."

"Or we're back to the government conspiracy theory."

"No matter what, we'd be taking a big chance if we went to the authorities for help. I can believe someone down there is praying we'll come forward—so he can turn us over to the bad guys."

For a moment Katie felt as if she were standing in quicksand. It was pulling at her feet, trying to suck her under.

Were she and Mac going to have to spend the rest of their lives on the run? She sat up straighter. "What if they did an autopsy before they destroyed the body?"

"If they did, *someone* is going to get the information."

"Exactly what I was thinking. Or maybe they're going to get the actual tissue samples."

"Except that those could have disappeared just as easily as the lab samples we had at Medizone. But I won't know until I check."

"What do you mean? What exactly do you have in mind?" Katie demanded.

"Going down to the morgue tonight and doing some private investigating."

"Mac, that could be dangerous."

"I've been in a lot of dangerous situations."

"But you don't know anything about the layout of the morgue. You're going to have to take me along, because I'm the one who had a little tour of the place a few days ago. I have a heck of a lot better chance of figuring out where to look than you do."

Mac considered her reasoning. "I wish you were wrong," he finally admitted. "But you do realize we could be walking right into the clutches of whoever wants us out of the way?" Although the question was spoken quietly, his gaze burned into Katie's.

All at once, it was difficult to swallow around the lump clogging her throat. "Yes" was all she could manage.

"Then we'd both better get some rest." Mac crossed to the window and yanked the drapes closed. Then he pulled back the spread on the other bed and slipped off his shoes. Katie watched him, wishing she could say what she longed to say: *Oh, Mac, put your arms around me. Hold me.* Instead she silently slipped her shoes off, too. Mac gave her a long look before plumping up the pillows. Neither one of them got undressed or climbed under the covers. For the next several hours they lay in the darkened room on their separate beds listening to each other breathe.

THE LAST TIME Katie had been inside the two-story brown brick building that housed the D.C. morgue, she'd been desperate to hold herself together in the face of Val's death. Then she'd been focused on her sister's personal tragedy and her own guilty reaction. Now as Mac drove into the parking lot, she couldn't stop herself from glancing nervously behind them where the walls of the city jail loomed.

Death.

Crime.

It was no accident that the two buildings were so near each other—and both tucked out of the way where ordinary, law-abiding citizens didn't have to see them.

Yet here she and Mac were, coming to the morgue on a moonless night to commit a crime of their own in order to prevent a bigger one. However, the rationale wasn't going to make any difference if they were caught. Now that they had arrived, the plot they'd hatched seemed crazy, their plans flimsy. Still they had to give it a try.

Mac pulled into a parking space and cut the engine. On the way down they'd stopped at R & E for some lab coats. Then Mac had pumped Katie for information about the layout of the building. Now neither one of the them spoke, and she could feel the darkness pressing in around her. It was like a heavy blanket, smothering her, but it concealed her, too.

Katie wasn't sure how long they sat in the deep shadows like two thieves waiting to make their move. Twenty? Thirty agonizing minutes?

Finally the silence was shattered by the wail of an ambulance siren. It was what they had been counting on.

Mac reached for the door handle. "You don't have to come with me, you know. You could stay here."

She reached for his hand and squeezed it. "I was pretty sure you were going to say that. Don't even think about trying this alone."

He didn't stop to argue. Jamming his metal hand into the pocket of his white coat, he strode off toward the red-and-white emergency vehicle. Katie quietly closed the car door and hurried after him. They arrived at the entrance to the building as attendants brought in two gunshot victims.

While the bodies were being checked in, Mac and Katie came in as if they belonged there, too. They faded away down one of the white tiled corridors and slipped into an autopsy room.

Disinfectant, formaldehyde, death. The characteristic reek of the place—and Katie's recent memories—made her throat close. Mac must have felt her shudder. Quietly he laid a steadying hand on her arm.

"Let's do it fast," he whispered.

"I—I've been thinking. We have to make sure the whole thing isn't a lie. About Val's being shipped out of here and cremated, I mean."

"Yes. I was wondering about that, too. She could still be here."

"The room where they keep the bodies is down the hall." Now that they were sneaking around the building, it was impossible for Katie not to imagine eyes drilling into the back of her neck as they tiptoed down the hall. Realizing that her hesitant gait would give them away, she tried to walk more briskly as if they had every right to be in the facility.

She might look collected, but she couldn't control her

physiological reactions. Under her borrowed lab coat, her skin had chilled to ice. When she pulled open the door to the refrigerated chamber, the freezing sensation sank into her bones.

Mac was behind her. Paralyzed, she stared at the rows of body-size drawers with neatly typed labels. She'd thought she could handle this, but the other terrible trip down here a few days ago was too fresh in her mind. It was all too personal.

"Katie, if you can't function, you might as well clear out of here."

Mac's matter-of-fact words were exactly what she needed. Her backbone stiffened, and she took several steps into the storage room. "I'm all right."

Silently she began opening the drawers on her left. Mac took the ones on the right. She opened them all, those with labels and those without. She was a physician, but it had been years since she'd confronted so many rigid bodies and lifeless faces. They seemed to accuse her of being warm and alive while they were cold and dead.

It was a humbling experience. Besides, it served no positive purpose. None of the mortal remains was Val's.

"She's not here," Katie whispered as she pushed the final drawer shut.

"Or here, either. Let's check the tissue storage."

They were just closing the heavy refrigerator door when a sound in the hall made them both come to an abrupt halt.

Discovery. She'd been unconsciously waiting to be unmasked for a sneak thief since the moment she'd walked into the building. A uniformed police officer strode into the room, stopped short and looked them up and down, taking their measure. For a heart-stopping moment, Katie forgot to breathe. Out of the corner of her eye, she could see Mac edging around in back of the man.

"Haven't seen you around here before," the newcomer observed. The silver bar on his shirt identified him as Officer Valenza.

As he paused beside a cluttered desk, Mac moved in a little closer and drew the metal hand out of his pocket.

"We're working on a report for the mayor's office," Katie said quickly, snatching up a clipboard from the table beside her. She was surprised that her voice didn't crack in the middle of the lie.

"Homicides?" Valenza pulled out the desk chair and sat down.

"Yeah," Mac confirmed, his tension visibly easing a notch or two.

The officer snorted. "How many is it this month so far? Twenty-five? You can tell Her Honor we need more officers patrolling the streets and fewer statistics for the newspapers to throw back in our faces."

"Isn't it the truth." Mac had quietly slipped his hand back in his coat, and Katie let the breath she'd been holding trickle from her lungs.

"Come on, Dr. Carter, let's finish up."

Katie followed Mac into the hall, closing the door behind them. As she stood there trying to gather the tattered shreds of her resolve, Mac was already striding down the hall. Running to catch up with him, she grabbed his arm. "What were you planning to do back there? Add assault to attempted robbery?"

He shook off her grasp. "I warned you about coming in here. We can't risk getting caught—and turned over to whoever's in charge of the cover-up."

Nodding tightly, she stepped ahead of him and opened another door on their right. It led to an office. Katie had to open several more doors before she found the tissue storage facility. A stainless steel refrigerator was filled with neatly labeled samples. None had Val's name.

"I guess this was all for nothing. We've struck out," Mac muttered.

"Unless it's not with the regular material."

"This is a big place. Do you have any suggestions?"

"Another lab, maybe. One of the autopsy rooms."

She could see Mac weighing the options. Either they left empty-handed, or they took a few more risks. He nodded, and they began moving down the hall again, checking labs and offices. One factor was in their favor. At this hour in the morning, only a minimal staff was in the building. No one else questioned their presence.

Security wasn't exactly tight. But then who in their right mind would break into the morgue? Still, Katie felt her tension growing. Every time she opened a door, she expected to see someone sitting inside in the dark, waiting for them.

It didn't happen that way.

Mac was behind Katie in one of the labs when she started to open a door. In the hall, a man was just passing, and she had a quick glimpse of the side of his face. As she stopped short, Mac slammed into her.

"What?"

For a moment, Katie couldn't speak. The man. His face was ordinary, yet the sight of him had sent a scurry of prickly fingers over her scalp. As he receded down the hall, she focused on his broad shoulders, his loping strides. Suddenly the context snapped into place. It was the man who had followed them into the Columbia Mall, the man who had tried to run them down in the parking lot. Now he was *here*.

"The driver. Mr. Ford. The one who almost killed us," she whispered.

"Where?"

"He just disappeared around the corner."

"Stay here." Mac started down the hall. Katie was right behind him.

When they rounded the corner, the corridor was empty. Mac swore.

Katie wondered if she was so strung out that she'd started seeing things.

The question was answered in the next second when a door to one of the autopsy rooms swung open, and the man they'd been following stepped back into the corridor.

They'd jokingly called him Mr. Ford. This was no joke.

For a split second he stared at them, obviously unnerved as they. Then with lightning-fast reflexes, he reached into his pocket.

Mac, however, was quicker. His arm shot out, catching the assailant's wrist between metal fingers and giving it a whiplike shake.

Mr. Ford screamed; a gun clattered to the floor. Mac kicked it toward Katie, and she picked it up. It was heavy and alien in her grasp.

What in the name of God were they going to do now? she wondered. In the next moment, the issue took on much greater urgency. Someone else must have heard the scream, because feet were pounding down the hall toward the corner they'd just rounded.

Mac threw Katie an urgent look. Grabbing Mr. Ford by the collar, he yanked him back inside the room from which they'd just stepped.

Katie had only a few seconds to decide what to do. Automatically she stuffed the gun into the waistband of her skirt. At least the white jacket concealed it. Now all she had to do was explain the scream.

As a blue-clad leg rounded the corner, she dropped to the floor and tore one of her shoes from her foot.

"Dr. Carter?"

The policeman who'd startled her and Mac earlier in the evening came to a halt inches from her knees. In the next moment, he was squatting down beside her on the tile floor, his service revolver in his hand.

Looking up at him with dazed confusion that was only partly faked, she pressed a palm against her forehead.

"Dr. Carter," he repeated. "What happened? Are you all right?"

Katie continued to stare at him in consternation, until she remembered that Dr. Carter was the name Mac had given her earlier in the evening. "Sorry to bring you running," she gasped. "Yes. I'm okay. Thanks. The lighting's so bad in here, and there must have been something slippery on the floor," she babbled.

He reholstered his weapon, reached for her wayward shoe, and held it out toward her.

"Thank you," she murmured again as she slipped the pump back on her foot. All the while, her ears strained for some clue about what was going on in the autopsy room where Mac had dragged their assailant.

In the next moment, her rescuer reached down to wedge a hand under her elbow, and she knew his fingers were only inches from the gun under her jacket. For a moment, she couldn't draw air into her lungs.

As he pulled her to her feet, he studied her pinched features. "You must have had quite a fall. Want me to take you over to D.C. General?"

"No. I'm fine. Really."

To her horror, now that she was standing, the heavy gun was starting to slip from its makeshift perch in her waistband. Trying not to draw attention to it, she pressed her arm against her side. "Thanks so much for coming to my assistance."

Valenza nodded and looked around. "Your partner leave without you?"

"He had to go back to the office. I'd better get over there before they send out a search party for me."

"Well, take care of yourself."

Valenza wasn't going to move from the spot on the floor until Katie did. Dutifully she started hobbling off down the hall. After half a minute, she risked a quick glance over her shoulder. The officer had disappeared around the corner.

Cautiously, ears straining for any telltale sound, Katie edged back toward the autopsy room where Mac had pulled Mr. Ford out of sight. What was going on there now? She had the gun. How was Mac controlling his prisoner?

As she quietly opened the door, she slipped the weapon out of her waistband and thrust in through the opening, hoping she was ready for whatever she was going to find. However, there was no way to be prepared for the scene that met her eyes. Under the bright glow of a surgical lamp, Mr. Ford was stretched out on the autopsy table like a turkey on a Thanksgiving platter. Several pairs of surgical gloves gagged his mouth. Adhesive tape bound his wrists and ankles and held him firmly to the polished stainless steel surface. Still, she saw his muscles bulge as he strained against his bonds.

No wonder. Mac stood over him, a scalpel clutched in his alloyed hand. It was poised to sweep across his captive's exposed throat.

Chapter Ten

"Lock the door." The menace in Mac's voice sent a shudder rattling down Katie's spine. How did it affect the man on the table? Her eyes flicked toward their captive. Sweat was trickling off his face like water in a thundershower.

Katie stood rooted to the spot, unsure exactly what Mac had in mind.

"Lock the door," he repeated. Fumbling behind herself, she found the knob and pushed the button.

Satisfied that they wouldn't be disturbed, Mac shifted the scalpel away from his captive's throat. The man twitched. "The driver's license in his wallet says his name is Arnie Beale, and he lives in Hyattsville," Mac said in a conversational tone. He reached down and spread the man's fingers for Katie's inspection. "He's a nervous type. He bites his nails." Mac let go of the man's hand and stood staring down at his prisoner.

Katie's breath came sharp and fast as she approached the table. She'd seen the dead laid out like this, never the living. Behind the two men was a diabolical assortment of equipment. Saws. Probes. Clamps. At the moment, none was more menacing than the simple scalpel Mac held.

"What is he doing here?" Katie whispered, as much to distract herself as for information.

"He's been a very busy man. This time he's not trying to run down pedestrians. He's making a pickup." Mac reached behind him and lifted a knapsack off the table. Inside was an insulated specimen carrier. "It's got Val Caldwell's name on it."

Katie stared at the dull gray box with the hinged lid. Tissue samples from Val. The only mortal remains of her sister. Closing her eyes, she fought back tears. It took several moments before she was sure she had enough control to go on with this.

When she opened her eyes, she saw that Mac was watching her. She knew she had to play the scene out— for him as well as herself.

Stiffening her backbone, she took several more steps toward the table and realized she was still holding the gun. She didn't even know if the safety was off, but she pointed it at Beale.

Their prisoner's terrified gaze flicked between the pistol and the scalpel.

"I believe we're going to find out where our delivery boy was heading," Mac predicted, the hard lines of his face a counterpoint to the matter-of-fact words. "Unless I make some kind of fatal slip with this artificial hand of mine." His carefully calculated actions belied the words. With delicate precision, he began to slice the buttons off the captive's shirt.

He had Arnie's full attention. The man's eyes bulged as he followed the progress of the scalpel. Through his gag, he was desperately trying to say something.

Ignoring his grunts, Mac pulled the ruined shirt open and pressed the razor-sharp blade against a broad chest. "Dr. Carter is going to remove your gag, and if you make any sound that isn't an answer to one of our questions, you're going to find you've made a surprise donation to the D.C. organ bank.''

With fingers that had turned clammy, Katie struggled to untie the knots in the gloves. They were tight and hard to undo. Finally, the gag came free with a little pop.

Mac's eyes burned into Arnie's, and he raised a warning eyebrow.

''Who are you working for?''

''I don't know.'' The words were barely more than a hoarse croak.

''Who?'' Mac pressed the blade against the man's perspiration-slick flesh and drew a tiny drop of blood. Holding the scalpel up, he rotated the knife in front of Arnie's eyes. ''Not so much fun when you're on the receiving end, is it?'' he grated.

The hit man began to blubber. ''Please. Please. I don't know nothin'. I don't talk to no one face-to-face. I get my orders over the phone.''

''You expect me to believe you accept snuff jobs from a voice over the phone?''

''I—yeah. For security.''

Mac snorted. A subtle movement of the artificial hand shifted the scalpel so that it was out of the way. With the point of one metal finger, he drew a delicate line down the man's flesh.

As Katie zeroed in on Mac's rigid features, she shivered. The Mac McQuade she'd known had never been this ruthless, this calculating, this diabolical. Yet he wasn't really hurting their captive, she told herself. He wouldn't really hurt him. Would he?

Arnie, who obviously thought he was feeling the knife, rolled his eyes and began to whimper. ''Don't. For cripe sakes, don't cut no deeper.''

Out in the hall, Katie heard several pairs of footsteps

and the squeak of a rolling cart, and her whole body went rigid with dread. God no. Not now. Should she point the gun at the door? Or should she simply pray?

Mac heard the disturbance, too. With a low, dangerous curse, he pressed the blade against their captive's throat again and leaned over the table. "Don't try anything stupid," he hissed.

For a wild moment Katie thought Arnie might be too crazed by terror to cooperate. But the man didn't move a muscle. Like actors in a tableau, the three of them waited in tense silence for the intruder to pass by—or burst in upon them.

When the footsteps and the squeaking cart finally faded, Katie remembered to breathe again.

Mac eased the knife away from the gray, quivering throat. His voice was steady, but a trickle of perspiration at his hairline betrayed his own frayed nerves. "Listen up, Arnie. We don't have much time, and I'm getting impatient." As he'd done with the man's chest, he jabbed with a metal finger against his windpipe.

Arnie gagged. "No! Don't kill me."

"You're not badly hurt. Just a scratch. You'll recover. If you tell us what we want to know."

"Please. I'm supposed to leave the box at a beauty shop."

"Don't give me that!" Mac grated.

"It's the truth. I'm supposed to wrap it like a present and leave it at the front desk. Someone else is gonna take it from there."

"What beauty shop?"

"Genesis."

Over the head of the man strapped to the table, Katie and Mac stared at each other. On the face of it, Arnie's story was crazy. Who would deliver tissue samples to a beauty parlor? Except that they knew that name. Genesis. The shop where Val had worked.

"What other assignments have you gotten over the phone lately?" Mac growled. "Besides orders to kill us."

"Just to search her apartment."

"Whose apartment?"

"The same lady whose name is on that box. Val Caldwell."

Katie felt the breath in her lungs solidify.

"When?" Mac demanded.

"Wednesday night."

The night they'd been in the apartment. Had he been there before them or after? "What were you looking for?"

"Stuff. Face cream."

She wanted to ask him more about it. But several more sets of footsteps sounded in the hall. The building was waking up.

"We've got to get out of here," Mac mouthed over Arnie's head as he replaced the gag.

They withdrew to a corner for a hasty conference.

"I'm not sure how much more we'd get out of him if we had a couple more hours," he said.

"What do we do with him?"

"Leave him."

"But, Mac, what's it going to look like?"

"Damn peculiar. It'll give whoever's behind this something to think about."

Katie wasn't sure she liked it. When she turned back toward Arnie, she gasped. His eyes were rolled back up in his head, and his jaw was as slack as the gag would allow. Had they killed him? Had he died from fright?

Swiftly she crossed to his side and felt for a pulse in the clammy skin of his neck. It was strong but shallow.

The hit man had fainted.

IT WAS A COUPLE OF DAYS into his temporary assignment in Hawaii, and Cornell Perkins was supposed to be observing police-department procedures. But they'd let him off duty at two in the afternoon again. He'd killed the rest of the day with a nap, a swim and dinner. Now he sat in the outdoor lounge at the Honolulu Mainliner Hotel sipping a piña colada and listening to a Don Ho lookalike croon an Island favorite. The casually dressed crowd was enjoying the balmy eighty-five-degree evening. But Perkins was edgy. And not just because he started to realize this assignment was one of those boondoggles that the *Washington Post* would expose in a flash across the front page of the Metro Section if they got a tip. City Faces Layoffs While Police Detective Has All-Expense-Paid Vacation to Hawaii.

Despite the idyllic weather, the gourmet food and the cordiality of the Honolulu police, he felt rotten.

This morning he'd called one of the guys he trusted back at the precinct and fished for information about who had been assigned the Val Caldwell case and how the follow-up was going. All he'd found out was that the death had been ruled suicide and the file closed. So what was the problem? After his conversation with Dr. Martin, he'd been leaning toward that conclusion himself. Until he'd been yanked off the case and sent out here. In the afternoon as he'd lounged by the pool, he'd been brooding about a neat and nasty little cover-up back in D.C. Somebody was getting something out of hushing up the Caldwell investigation, and maybe he was a fool to be sitting here in the sun letting the action pass him by. What the hell was he supposed to do in three weeks anyway? Come back to work as if nothing had happened?

Perkins finished his drink, went back to his eleventh-floor hotel room, and started to pack.

KATIE REACHED for the door handle. She wanted to suck in a steadying draft of air. At the last moment, the mixture of odors in the room stopped her. The taint of Arnie's fear was mixed with all the other evil vapors now.

Out of the corner of her eye, she saw Mac's teeth clench as he jammed his hand in his pocket. She touched his arm lightly but didn't say anything. Silently they stepped out into the hall again.

The building was beginning to fill up with the day staff. There might even be an autopsy scheduled for early in the morning, Katie realized. Which meant they didn't have much time before Arnie was discovered. What then?

As they retraced their steps, people began to pass them at regular intervals. Katie cast her eyes somewhere between the floor and the middle distance. If anyone looked her directly in the eye, she was sure they'd wonder what was wrong. So she concentrated on remaining anonymous, on blending into the institutional green walls.

Finally the door through which they'd entered was only a few yards away, and Katie was about to let out the breath she'd been holding when she came to an abrupt halt.

Another familiar face. The young policeman who had escorted her down here to identify Val's body was talking to the clerk at the desk. Officer Bryant. She even remembered his name.

Mac, who hadn't recognized the danger, was already a few paces ahead of her, but he stopped when he heard her muffled exclamation. Her eyes flicked to his, trying to telegraph a warning as she began to back away. Mac started to follow. But it was already too late. Bryant looked up and saw her.

In her present state, she expected him to pull out his service revolver and point it at her while issuing a stern warning to raise her hands in the air. Instead he gave her a boyish smile.

"Hi, how you doing?" he asked. As he spoke, a look of uncertainty flashed across his features.

"Fine." It was difficult to make the word come out smoothly around the telltale quiver of her mouth.

Beside her, Mac's body went taut—ready to flee, ready to fight. Either reaction was natural. Either one would spell disaster. As much to reassure him as herself, she reached for his elbow.

Bryant looked mildly embarrassed, and Katie suddenly realized what was probably going on. The police officer recognized her, but he wasn't sure of the circumstances under which they'd met. Most likely, he assumed she worked for the D.C. government, and all they had to do was get out of there before he remembered driving her down here to identify a body.

She gave a little sigh. "It's been a long night. I'm dead on my feet."

"Yeah. I know what it's like to pull the graveyard shift."

"Well, see you around."

"Sure."

Mac started to move again. To her mild surprise, Katie found her legs would also function. Moments later they were standing in the watery morning sunshine. Katie sucked in a draft of the chilly air.

Mac tapped her arm. "Come on."

She followed him back to the rented car. They didn't speak again until they'd climbed inside and Katie had reached to lock the doors.

"Who was that guy back there?"

"The officer who escorted me down here after Val died.

I guess he doesn't remember where he met me. Let's go before he figures it out.''

"Right."

Mac started the engine and swung out of the parking lot onto Massachusetts Avenue.

Katie turned and looked over her shoulder, seeing the grim bulk of the D.C. jail receding in the distance. She felt as if she'd just done ten years at hard labor and finally escaped.

"It's good to be out of there," Mac said.

"Yes. I guess it was worth it. I—I didn't like doing that to Arnie."

"He tried to flatten us in the mall parking lot."

"If we sink to his level, what does that make us?"

Mac was silent for several moments. Out of the corner of her eye, she saw his hands tighten on the wheel. His next words took her completely by surprise.

"What did you think I was going to do, kill him?"

"No."

"Or maybe just cut him up a little? Torture him with the scalpel?"

"You wouldn't have gone that far."

"Did you think I was enjoying myself?"

"Mac, mostly I was frightened. Seeing him strapped down on that table. Seeing you standing over him like— like—I don't know—with your eyes blazing."

"It was a calculated effect. I was trying to scare the living daylights out of him."

"You did."

"You were afraid I'd lose control," he persisted. "Don't you know me better than that?"

She couldn't meet his eyes. Two days ago she'd told herself she was in love with him. Now—"I thought I did. A long time ago."

He sighed. "You're right. I went farther than I had to. I guess I was taking out my anger on him. For days I've felt as if I was up against a faceless enemy, and then I finally had someone to attack." She saw him swallow. "Maybe I don't know myself anymore."

Katie wasn't sure what to say. When she reached out and covered his hand, it stiffened on the wheel. He was doing it again, withdrawing when she tried to make contact. This time she didn't have the emotional energy to push it. After a moment she took her hand away and folded it in her lap.

They were several miles from the morgue before Mac spoke again. On a completely different topic.

"Genesis. That's the place where your sister worked, isn't it?"

"Yes."

"It can't just be a coincidence."

Katie murmured her agreement. "All of a sudden it looks like we've been going at this from the wrong angle."

"Do you think an upscale beauty emporium could be a front for some kind of criminal organization?"

She shrugged. "It sounds crazy. However, if you were trying to hide something illegal, it would be a great cover. Maybe Val stumbled onto something she wasn't supposed to know about. That could be a reason why they'd sent Arnie to look for evidence at her apartment." She stopped abruptly and glanced back in the direction from which they'd come, the hair on the back of her neck bristling. "My God, Mac, maybe he went down there right after I left the first time. Maybe he pushed her off the balcony, and Tom saw what happened."

"I'd like to go back and shake the truth out of him."

"We can't." Katie ground her teeth in aggravation.

"I believe what he said, that he's just a little part of

something bigger. The trouble is, we don't know a damn thing about Genesis. As soon as we drop off the tissue sample, we're going to see what we can find out about the place." Katie nodded, suddenly feeling overwhelmed with fatigue and frustration.

HELEN AUSTIN-WRIGHT opened one eye and peered at the green illuminated numbers of the digital clock. 6:32 a.m.

Early.

What had awakened her? she wondered, her mind drifting in a warm, sleepy sea. Sometimes things were so complicated, and it was hard to cope. But not right now. There was nothing that needed her attention for a couple of hours. The decorator was coming at eleven to talk about redoing the family room, and her Genesis appointment wasn't until two. It was going to be a very pleasant day.

She might have drifted back to sleep, except that something was wrong. The room was silent. Too silent. She couldn't even hear George's ragged snoring. Helen patted the far side of the king-size bed and found it empty.

Sitting up, she snapped on the bedside lamp. "George? *George!* Where are you?"

The only answer was a low moan from the bathroom. Helen's throat constricted as she leapt out of bed and rushed toward the closed door. But when her feet crossed over from carpet to tile, she stopped dead and grabbed the wall for support, hardly able to believe what she was seeing.

Naked, George was bending over the sink, a knife clutched in his hand. Blood streamed down his left arm. As she watched, he dipped the knife toward the other wrist.

"No! George, no!" Lunging forward, she grabbed for the weapon. He slapped her away, and she landed with a thud on the hard floor. Staring up at him, she saw the wild, desperate look in his eyes. Somehow she'd known all along that something terrible was going to happen.

It took a moment to catch her breath. "Please, give me the knife, sweetheart. You don't really want to do this. Things aren't as bad as you think. We'll get you some help. Please listen to me."

The words came out high-pitched and trembly, bouncing around the tiled room like an echo in a cheap stereo system. They drove George to a new level of frenzy.

Picking up a three-hundred-dollar china soap dish, he smashed it against the mirror. As his arm swung, blood flew in an arc toward the glass. The dish shattered and the mirror splintered into a tangle of spiderweb cracks and drops of blood.

The look in his eyes when he turned back to Helen froze the breath in her lungs. Before she could back away, George was slamming her into the wall and bringing the bloody knife to her throat.

FOR THE MOMENT, there wasn't much point in continuing to speculate. Katie closed her eyes, giving in to the weariness that had begun to make her limbs feel dragged down by hundred-pound weights. Yet much as she longed to shut everything out, she couldn't turn off the questions swirling in her brain.

Genesis. Maybe this all went back to Genesis. What had Val told her about the place?

The owner was a lady from Japan. A very beautiful woman. Elegant and refined. Who only hired beauticians of the very finest caliber. Val had made sure Katie had known that.

What was the woman's name? Katie drew a blank. But the information would be easy enough to get.

Val had bragged that their line of cosmetics was com-

pletely exclusive—available nowhere else in the U.S.—
and very expensive. The first salon was in D.C. Soon they
were going to expand to other major U.S. cities.

Were their products manufactured here? Or were they
imported from Japan? Slowly, reluctantly, her mind began
to spiral down a frightening path. What were the sanitation
standards in the plant where the cosmetics were manufactured? What were the inspection procedures for nonfood
imports into the U.S.? What if the moisturizer Val was
using had somehow gotten contaminated with a lethal virus? Arnie had been sent to look for something in Val's
apartment. "Face cream," he'd said. What if the owner
knew the products were contaminated and was trying to
pull in the supply before the authorities found out?

Katie's breath rasped in fast and painfully. "Oh my
God!"

"Button, what?"

"Oh God," she repeated as she started to shiver. Suddenly she had to clamp her teeth together to keep them
from chattering. Too much had happened too quickly. Panic, the ordeal of the autopsy room, exhaustion had all
combined to send her over the edge.

"Honey, what is it?"

She shook her head, unable to tell him. They were on
Connecticut Avenue within a few blocks of Chevy Chase
Circle. Mac pulled off onto a side street lined with solid
old houses and found a parking place under a wide-
spreading oak. After cutting the engine, he reached for
Katie, but she shrank back, her shoulders wedged against
the door.

"Katie! I can't help you unless you tell me what's
wrong. Are you hurt? Sick?"

She started to laugh, then had to stifle a sob. "You
thought you had the virus. That somehow it came from

Medizone. That you'd brought it back from a trip. But that's all wrong. You weren't in danger—except from me."

"Stop it! You're not making sense. Tell me what you're talking about."

He reached for her again. Katie batted his hand away. "Don't!" She didn't know that tears were brimming in her eyes. "Stupid. I was so stupid. I used it."

"What?"

"The face cream. I used the face cream Val had hidden in her closet. I even put some on my sore ribs." Tearing at the tail of her shirt, she pulled it up, exposing the skin over her right ribs. "I don't understand what happened to the bruises," she muttered as she stared at her skin.

"What the hell are you talking about?"

"You were right, Mac. She stole it. That's why she hid it. She wasn't supposed to have it, because it was contaminated, Mac. But she didn't know. She thought it was going to make her younger-looking."

"Katie—"

"Don't you get it? The face cream. That's where the virus came from."

Chapter Eleven

Mac tried to pull Katie into his arms.

"No. Don't. Get—away—from—me."

Tears streamed down her cheeks. Her voice was edged with hysteria. Desperately she flailed at Mac. "No. Leave me alone." Her voice rose in a despairing wail.

Ignoring the blows, the words and her confusion, Mac folded her close, stopping her thrashing with his arms and the weight of his body against the door. Pinned, she continued to struggle, sobs racking her body. But Mac's strength and the force of his resolve were simply too much for her. When she had no more will to resist, she slumped against him.

The tears continued for a few more minutes. Finally the husky, low sound of his voice helped to bring her back some measure of calm. Yet they couldn't entirely drive away the fear waiting to swallow her whole.

When he sensed the change in her, he let go his tight grasp on her shoulder.

She winced, and he swore.

"The damn hand—I'm sorry."

"It's okay. You didn't hurt me. I must have gone a little crazy."

He shifted a few inches away, found a handkerchief in his pocket and passed it to her.

Katie blew her nose, her face averted.

Crazy. Like Val and Tom. Was it already starting?

When she shuddered, he tangled his fingers in her hair and gently tipped her face up to his. "You used the face cream you found in Val's closet."

Katie gulped. "Yes."

"And you think it's contaminated?" he clarified in tones that she knew were under tight control.

"Yes." Somehow his manufactured calm helped her get a grip on herself.

"How much did you use? How many times?"

"Just a little bit. But what does that matter, if it's got the virus?"

"You're not thinking the whole thing through. Suppose some of the cream was contaminated? Suppose there were batches that were okay? Your sister was probably using it for months. You only did it once, from one jar. And you're not sick."

She didn't break the eye contact. "Just acting nuts."

"Stop it! You've been up for the past twenty-four hours. You've been through a couple of hellish ordeals. You're entitled to act a little flaky. And if it comes to that, your theory about the face cream is probably a crock of half-baked speculation. It's highly unlikely that it would be harboring a virus."

She ignored the last observation. "You've been up for twenty-four hours, too. You're not wigged out."

"Maybe not now. But I was back in the autopsy room. Or isn't that what you thought?"

"Let's stick to the point. We're talking about my crazy behavior, not yours."

Neither one of them moved. The atmosphere in the car was charged with tension.

"Mac. I'm sorry," she finally murmured, wondering exactly what she was apologizing for. Being afraid she had the virus? Arguing with him? Or pointing out his deficiencies? It was hard to think clearly. Which brought another surge of fear.

Through the panic, she realized that they'd been in this spot before. Only then everything had been reversed. Mac had been the one afraid that he'd been contaminated. And she had been desperate to deny that it was true. He hadn't been a model of rationality. In fact, none of her contentions had made any real difference. Now she knew exactly how he'd felt. And he was in a damn good position to understand *her* feelings.

"I know you're not in any shape to listen to my arguments," he muttered.

"Are you reading my mind?"

"I wish I could."

He pulled her back into his embrace, his lips skimming her hair, her forehead, her cheeks.

"Don't. You shouldn't." The protest was weak.

"I think I need this as much as you do."

The admission made her throat constrict. Wordlessly she let her head drop to his shoulder. After a moment of hesitation, her face turned to press against his neck. He held her, stroked her, murmured soft reassurances.

Oh God, she thought. *If I'm going to lose my mind, if I'm doing to die, I want one last wish before it happens. I want to finally know what it's like to make love to you, Mac.* Yet even as her mind silently formed the request, she knew it was impossible to grant. Putting him at risk like that was something she'd never do. She'd have herself locked in the psychiatric ward of a hospital before she took that kind of chance.

Katie allowed herself to cling to Mac for a few moments longer. Then she lifted her head. "I want to go back to R & E," she said. "I want that blood test."

"Yeah. We'll both feel a hell of a lot better when we know you don't have it."

"Sure." Then another thought struck her. "Mac, what if there's a window when you can't tell someone is infected?"

"That won't be a problem. We'll be using new procedures developed at Medizone."

There wasn't much to talk about on the ride to Elkridge. Katie sat with her hands clenched in her lap, trying not to think, trying not to focus on the knot tightening in her stomach. Morning sunshine glazed the window. The promise of a new day. It seemed to mock her.

Out of the corner of her eye, she kept glancing at the bloodless knuckles of Mac's hand where he gripped the wheel. "At least there's one good thing about my situation," she said.

"What?"

"I'm not going to have to spend the night biting my nails. We've already produced a new batch of antibodies using that frozen blood of Tom's. All we've got to do is draw some of my blood and test it."

Still, the closer they got to Elkridge, the more she felt like a condemned prisoner being transported the last mile to the scaffold.

Yet she had to know. The moment Mac pulled into a parking space, she hopped out of the car. "I'm going down to hematology."

"Okay. I'll meet you in the hot lab."

When she arrived fifteen minutes later with a tube of

blood, she found Mac had had one of the technicians get everything ready.

"Thanks, but I can take over from here," Katie told the young man.

"Yes. I'd like to have Dr. Martin do these tests," Mac added.

If the technician thought anything about the strained atmosphere between Dr. Martin and Mr. McQuade, he didn't comment. He simply did as he was told.

At least she was going to get the news in privacy, Katie thought. Privacy, except for Mac. At the moment, she didn't really want him there, either. Was this how he'd felt yesterday morning when she'd hovered around him?

She sensed him standing close behind her while she introduced the blood into the isolation chamber. Before she could proceed any further, he took her by the shoulders and turned her toward him. Caught off guard, she froze under the impact of his smoky gray gaze.

"Katie."

The look in the depths of his eyes blurred everything else in the room. When she realized his intention, she gasped and tried to push him away. But he had several tactical advantages over her. Strength. Determination. Surprise.

"No—you—"

The words were cut off by the pressure of his mouth. His lips moved urgently, almost savagely over hers. It wasn't precisely a passionate kiss. But it was possessive and primitive and left her clinging to him, gasping for breath.

Dazed, she could only stare up at him as her heart pounded in her chest. Finally she found her voice again.

"Mac. That wasn't a very smart thing to do."

"Finish the test."

"If I have it, you—"

"Dammit, shut up and finish the test."

Time seemed to have ground to the pace of a slow-motion instant replay. Katie turned back to the isolation chamber. Still her hands were strangely steady as she took the stopper off the tube of blood. Finally the slide was ready, and she placed it on the stage of the microscope. A pulse pounded in her forehead as she closed one eye and adjusted the focus.

"Katie?"

"I—I—don't see—"

He moved her gently aside. Unsure that her knees would hold her erect, she stood slumped against the wall watching Mac bend to the eyepiece.

"Thank heaven," he gasped.

She'd hardly been able to believe her own scrutiny of the slide. Now Mac's exclamation of thanks confirmed her own observation. The terror had ended. She didn't have the antibodies. When her knees buckled, she felt Mac sweeping her up into his arms. For a moment he simply hugged her against his chest. Then he started down the hall. "What are you doing?"

"Taking you back to the motel. You're dead on your feet."

"What about the tissue samples we brought?"

"I've already given orders to have them tested. It's time for you to stop arguing. We're both going to feel a lot better once we get some sleep."

THERE WAS A TAP on the door. "One moment." Jade Nishizaka slipped the photo album back into its hiding place. No one but Akio had ever shared its secret with her.

She clasped her chilly hands together in her lap. Soon her brother would be arriving from Kyoto, and she would be glad to see him. How could she not be glad? He was the center of her life. Yet Akio was such an exacting taskmaster. And he would be angry when he learned that everything was not in perfect order.

With the discipline she had cultivated over the years, Jade schooled her features into a Kabuki mask. "Come in."

Ming entered the room. "I have the acceptance list for the Day of Beauty."

Jade's voice betrayed neither her excitement nor her tension as she held out her hand. "Good." The workshops and make-overs scheduled for this coming Monday were being held as a special program for wives of delegates to the National Economic Symposium. The number who had signed up would spell the success or failure of six years of intensive work.

But she and Akio had learned patience. Long ago there had been no choice. Their very survival had been in question. Yet they had lived and prospered and gotten the education they needed. After that had come the courting of investors and the founding of Nishizaka Pharmaceuticals. It had taken hard work and money—and years of research with the herbal products their mother had developed in her small workshop. But finally they'd been ready to create Genesis. She had made the salon a place of luxury and prestige. And she'd watched its word-of-mouth reputation grow among Washington's elite. Every rich woman who visited the nation's capital wanted to spend a day at Genesis. Soon, hundreds of them from around the country would be in one place at one time.

A thousand moths fluttered in Jade's chest as she scanned the list. As name after important name leaped out at her, she felt the tension replaced by exhilaration. Mrs. Calvin Abingdon. Mrs. Donald Treemore. Mrs. Percy

Worthington. Mrs. Vincent Guccini. They were all signed up. And they would all find the secret of eternal youth—and more.

MAC WAS RIGHT, Katie decided as she toweled herself dry after a quick shower. She felt better, but she was so tired it was hard to rub two coherent thoughts together. She'd grabbed one of the bags from their shopping expedition before coming in here. But it was the wrong one.

Rummaging through the contents, she found that the only thing that might be any use to her was a package of T-shirts Mac had bought. Tearing the plastic wrapper open, she pulled one out and slipped it over her head. It was about five sizes too big, which meant it would make a pretty good nightshirt.

The intimacy of putting on Mac's clothes—even Mac's new clothes—made her glance quickly at the closed door. One moment she felt closer to him than ever before, the next he was worlds away. Maybe Mac had changed too much. He was harder, more primitive, less approachable. Maybe he didn't need anybody else, and maybe she was putting her heart in jeopardy by caring. Yet if *he* hadn't cared about her, why had he kissed her right before she'd tested her blood for the virus?

In her present state, the questions were too much to handle. With a shrug she began to clean her teeth with the blue toothbrush Mac had bought. Then, conceding she was in danger of falling asleep standing up, Katie gathered up the last shreds of her strength and opened the door. Tottering across the rug to the closest bed, she pulled back the covers and slipped underneath.

The drapes were still drawn, so that the room was in semidarkness. Mac was talking in low tones on the phone, his head bent. She sensed rather than saw that he was watching her, but he continued the conversation for several more moments before hanging up.

"I've checked in with Jo. She was worried."

"I should have talked to her." The protest was little more than a mumble from under the covers.

"Later. You're beat."

Katie felt the mattress shift as he sat down beside her. "Roll over."

She flopped to her stomach and felt him start to knead the tense muscles of her shoulders. "Nice," she murmured. Under the tender ministrations of his fingers, she drifted off to sleep.

MAC MCQUADE GLANCED at his reflection in the mirror and grimaced. He'd never before worn undershorts decorated with NFL team logos. But the choice in his size at the discount department store had been rather limited. After pulling on the shorts, he held up his left arm and examined the stump of his wrist. Twenty-four hours was an awful long time to wear a metal hand. Now that he'd taken it off to shower, he knew it would be painful to put it back on until he'd given the wrist at least a couple of hours' rest.

His gaze flicked to the bathroom door, as he imagined Katie sleeping a few yards away. Not many people had seen him without his hand. Or without a long-sleeved shirt buttoned at the cuff, for that matter. None of them had been the women he'd taken to bed. He hadn't felt confident enough to let them see him that naked—to face the indrawn breath when they got a look at his deformity up close and personal. Deep down he had the feeling that Katie was different. And maybe if she wasn't, he wanted to know about it now.

The long-sleeved pajama top he'd bought stayed in the

bag. Instead he pulled on a twin to the T-shirt Katie had donned. In the brief glimpse he'd gotten of her as she'd crossed to the bed, he'd liked it better on her feminine curves.

He needed sleep. He was starting to feel like a zombie. Still he continued to hesitate before opening the door. When he finally did, he stood looking at Katie in the shaft of light from the bathroom. She was sleeping deeply, innocently, lying on her side now with her legs drawn up and her brown hair a tousled contrast to the white pillowcase. One vulnerable, gently cupped hand was extended outside the covers and lay on the pillow beside her face. Seeing her like that made him feel as if a mortar shell had just exploded inside his chest.

God, when she'd told him the face cream was contaminated and that she'd used it, he'd just about flipped out. The only thing that had kept him coherent was knowing that one of them had to stay in control. And he had—until he'd kissed her. Right before she'd bent to look at her blood under the microscope.

He didn't want to scrutinize too closely his wild swings of emotion today. Not with regard to Katie. And not with Arnie Beale, either. Yet a nagging question kept eating at him. Did the way he'd wielded the scalpel over the man mean he'd lost touch with his humanity?

When your life was on the line, were such extreme measures justified? Or had their situation been an excuse to unleash the darkest monsters of his being?

Right now his exhausted mind couldn't grapple with such subtleties. And his tired body was having trouble keeping him on his feet.

About all he could handle at the moment was a mattress and cool sheets. His eyes swung to the empty bed across the room, then back to the one where Katie slept. More than once he'd tried to send her away, and she wouldn't leave him. Now the idea of separation made his throat burn. It was more than a sexual need. It was something even more elemental—like the need to breathe. Without giving himself time to think about the difference between fantasy and reality, he crossed to the bed and slipped under the covers with Katie.

Her warmth overwhelmed him as he moved carefully up behind her, his face barely touching the tender skin at the back of her neck. She felt so soft, so feminine. She smelled of cleanly scented soap and lavender. That was the last thing he remembered before falling asleep.

KATIE WAS DREAMING about Mac. Dreaming that he was making love to her. And he was only a few feet away, in the other bed. A flush spread across her face and neck. Then, she felt the warmth of another body beside her and realized Mac wasn't as far away as she'd thought. Her eyes snapped open, and she saw his hand. He was lying on his side in back of her, his arm draped across her shoulder. She didn't question why he was there. She simply looked down at the relaxed fingers that rested against her forearm, and her heart lunged in her chest like a trapped bird throwing itself against the bars of its cage.

When she'd gone to bed, she'd been wondering how she felt about him. Now as she looked at him, all the emotions she'd choked off came swooshing back like a river at flood time. She loved this man.

If she moved just the tiniest bit, his fingers would be touching her breast. Without giving the matter further consideration, she moved.

And his hand was where she wanted to feel it. The sudden flash of sensation was so exquisite that she had to bite her lip to keep from whimpering. This was what she'd craved. This intimacy.

For a while it was enough simply to enjoy the sweet newness of the contact. The contentment didn't last for very long.

"Mac." His name was a wispy sigh on her lips.

She knew the instant he woke, the instant his fingers moved. Stroking. Pressing. Finding the hard bud of her nipple, making her breast throb. No, not just her breast. Her whole body was throbbing. And it was impossible to hold back the shaky little sound of response that had lodged in her throat.

"Button."

She rolled over to face him, her body warm and pliant only a few inches from his.

There were several pounding heartbeats when his gray eyes questioned hers. She saw longing. Desire. Hesitation. And she knew that even though he had chosen to sleep with her, the decision about where they went from here was still hers.

She answered his question by moving the tiniest bit again, bringing her lips to his. It wasn't like the last time, or like the first time, either, when they'd both been taken by the surprise of discovering each other again.

This was deliberate. The long, deep kiss that she'd been craving. It brought her a kind of hot satisfaction. And a deep need for more, so much more. But as his lips moved more urgently over hers, the need became tinged with worry. Would he stop if he knew how much this meant to her?

She might die if he stopped. Yet she had to find a way to slow the pace to something she could handle.

"Mac." There was a catch in her voice as she spoke his name.

"Um?" He pulled her hips tightly against his and stole several small sipping kisses from her lips.

Heat zinged through her again, making it almost impossible to speak. "Mac, I haven't had very much practice at this sort of thing. I—I don't want to disappoint you."

His gaze snapped into focus, and he stared into her doubtful blue eyes. She was so desirable, so sensual, so obviously happy to have him in her bed that it had simply never crossed his mind that she might not be very experienced sexually. Had some insensitive jerk hurt her, made her cautious with men? Whatever the reason for her sudden hesitation, her whispered confession made his heart swell.

"You won't disappoint me, Button," he said gently, as his lips began to nibble on hers. "Just tell me if I'm going too fast, because I don't want to disappoint you, either."

"You won't," she repeated as she snuggled into his arms, enjoying the tantalizing responses he was bringing to life. As they kissed and touched, she found she was reacquainting herself with the man who had excited her so many years before.

He was an electrifying lover. A skillful lover. A playful lover.

She giggled as he teased her about hiding from him, his hand making little forays through the T-shirt. The laughter choked off as he pulled the thin cotton taut against her breasts and admired the way the knit fabric revealed her shape.

In the next moment, he dragged the garment up and over her head. Then in a universal gesture of male possessiveness, he reached to cup her breasts. The fingers of his right hand closed over her heated flesh. His left wrist collided with her chest under her other breast.

He froze. And she saw stark anguish flash in his eyes. Mac started to pull away. She reached down to cover both the right hand and the left wrist with her own hands, pressing him tightly against herself.

"You shouldn't have to settle for second best," he grated.

"You're not second best. You're exactly what I want. What I need."

She brought his hand to her lips, kissing his fingers. She smiled at him as her tongue and lips and teeth began a sensual exploration. His breath stopped moving in and out of his lungs when she reached for the other arm. Her movements languid, she brought his wrist to her lips, lavishing it with the same tender attention she'd begun with his hand.

Mac could hardly believe what she was doing and hardly believe his own reaction. Since the accident, he'd treated that part of his body as nothing more than a dead end. But the caresses of her lips and tongue felt good. Very good.

The unexpected pleasure and the aroused look in her eyes broke through barriers he hadn't even known were there. He swept her into his arms, desperate to give her everything that was in his power to give, no longer hesitant about touching her in any way and every way that would please them both. Yet, the closer they drew to the ultimate joining, the more he sensed that somehow she was slipping away from him.

"Honey, what is it?"

"Mac, I have to tell you—"

She wanted to let him know about something she liked, something that would make it better for her. Some women had trouble telling a partner about things like that.

He lifted her fingers to his lips the way she'd done with his, nibbling at their tips. "Don't be shy with me, Button."

She swallowed painfully and forced the words out. "Mac, I—I haven't made love with anyone before."

There was no way to hide his stunned reaction.

She gulped. "The way I figure it, if making love really didn't mean anything, there wasn't any point in doing it. Not just to say I'd had the experience."

"And now you—"

"And now I think I'll die if we don't go ahead."

He was overwhelmed by the gift she was offering. Overwhelmed that she was offering it to *him*. Yet he tried to keep his voice light. "We wouldn't want that to happen." He pulled her close again, kissing her, stroking her, murmuring words that broke through her anxiety, making it easier for her to talk.

She smiled at him tentatively. "You don't get through medical school without learning about the mechanics of sexual intercourse. It's just that putting theory into practice is a little daunting the first time."

His eyes were teasing again. "Honey, you always were one of the best students. But don't think of this as a final exam. The important thing is to relax and enjoy it."

"I have been."

"Yeah. So have I. Very much."

"But you're probably getting a little impatient."

"Nope. Getting there is half the fun."

He knew just what to say to ease her tension. Just how to rock her on a sea of sensuality, lifting her higher and higher toward sexual fulfillment as each wave broke.

He stroked her with his hand and then his body, bringing her to climax before he'd fully entered her. Then, as she came down off that high, sun-drenched crest, he breached the last barrier. She was so limp with the joy of her fulfillment that her body easily accepted his. There was hardly any pain, only more pleasure as he began to thrust inside her, the deep powerful strokes bringing her to an even higher peak of ecstasy.

Chapter Twelve

They had slept for only a few hours, but Mac woke up disoriented. A shaft of light from the center of the drapes pierced the artificial darkness. He was in a motel room, and there was a woman's head on the pillow beside his. No, not just any woman.

Katie.

As he absorbed her warmth in the bed beside him, a great sense of serenity stole over him. It had been years since he'd felt this kind of peace. He longed to bask in the glow. Yet even as the temptation began to unfurl, he found the strength to overcome desires he had no right to claim. This was wrong. If not for him, then for sweet, innocent Katie who didn't realize what she was getting into with a misfit like him. He was easing carefully away from her when she opened her eyes.

He could tell that her awakening was different from his. There was no moment of disorientation on her part. She knew at once where she was and with whom. Her blue eyes, as they regarded him gravely, were huge and blue like the clearest mountain lakes, and he felt himself falling helplessly into them. Then she smiled, and it was like the sun coming up over the mountains.

"I used to dream about making love to you. Real life is better."

"Katie, this isn't real life."

"It could be."

Suddenly he was powerless to fight his desires. He didn't want reality. He wanted the fantasy to go on. They might have been enclosed in a time bubble where no one and nothing could reach them. With a groan that was part need, part protest, he pulled her willing body against his.

He smiled against her cheek as he sensed her confidence. This time she had a much better idea of what they were doing and where they were heading. And the rewards were even more spectacular—for both of them.

Afterward, replete, and just a little bit smug, Katie snuggled into the arms of the man she loved. "I feel cheated out of all the time we missed," she murmured.

When she felt Mac's body tense, she knew at once that it hadn't been the right thing to say. Raising up on one elbow, she looked down at him. "What's wrong?"

"Nothing."

"Don't put the barrier back up between us. Not now."

"Katie, I can't help it. I've been putting up barriers between me and the rest of the world for eight years."

"You know now you don't have to do it with me. Our being together is so—" She floundered for words and couldn't come up with anything better than "right."

"You didn't think so when we were down there at the morgue with Arnie Beale."

"That wasn't the real you."

"It's as much the real me as the man who made love to you a little while ago. Katie, you don't understand how much I've changed. I'm too messed up to give you the things you deserve."

"What exactly do you think I deserve?" She assumed

he was going to spout some conventional speech about a reliable husband and a house full of kids. But she hadn't thought of herself in those terms at all. For the past eight years, her life had been her career. And when it had hit a snag, she worked herself into a fine state of trying to get it back on track. Actually it would be hard to shift gears into being a contented homemaker.

The self-knowledge made Mac's words particularly painful. "You're obviously a fine clinician and a gifted research physician. You deserve someone who can be proud of your accomplishments. Not some medical-school washout who would feel threatened every time you got a new grant or got a paper published in a medical journal."

She ran her hand down his chest. "Medizone Labs is one of the most respected research outfits in the country. You did that without the benefit of a medical degree. Not finishing school certainly wasn't your fault. Besides, it doesn't make any difference to me."

"That's fine for you. But it makes a hell of a lot of difference to me. Katie, I'm not stupid. I know that for the past eight years I've been trekking off to every godforsaken place on earth to try and outrun my anger about what happened."

"So now you want to convince me there's no future for us?" she whispered, hardly able to get the words out.

"Finding you again was a shock. I tried to tell myself I didn't want you anymore. Well, we both know that was a lie. But it doesn't mean I've figured out how to cope with my deep-rooted insecurities."

If ever a man had proved his worth, it was Mac Mc-Quade. Yet no amount of argument was going to make him see that. If he couldn't come to the realization himself, there was nothing she could do about it. Except maybe show him how unconditional her love was for him.

He broke into her thoughts. "Right now the two of us are in a hell of a jam. And neither one of us is going to have a future until we find out exactly who wants us out of the way and why."

Mac was right. It was easier to think about the immediate danger than to do any more probing at the layers of scar tissue covering his heart.

"Then I think the next step is to test the other sample of face cream, the one you took back to your house," she said. "Only if it's dangerous to go to my place, it's just as dangerous to go to yours."

"Maybe Jo has some thoughts on that."

"Right." Katie sat up and gathered the covers around her chest. Then she phoned their friend, who'd been waiting for their call.

"I can scan the house and the area to see if anyone's watching," Jo told her. "And if Mac doesn't mind giving me the entry code to his security system, I shouldn't have any problem getting in the house."

Mac didn't mind. "The cream's on the top of the bookcase in the den," he said. "And while you're there, get my laptop computer. It might come in handy. It's on the kitchen table."

When Mac disappeared into the shower, the two women continued the phone conversation. "Jo, be extra careful when you go over there," Katie warned. "And don't touch the jar of cream. Use rubber gloves and put it into a sealed container."

"I'll treat it like a biological warhead on a Scud missile. And if I can't get there in a couple of hours, I'll call."

"We can meet in the coffee shop." As Katie spoke she looked down at the rumpled bedsheets, not quite ready to have Jo walk into the room where she and Mac had just made love.

Yet as the three of them slid into the green plastic booth two hours later, Katie knew that even though Jo hadn't said a thing, she'd detected the change in their relationship.

"Did you have any trouble at my house?" Mac asked.

Jo grinned. "There aren't too many ways to bust into an underground house short of breaking the window."

"It's reinforced glass," Mac told her.

"Thought so. Someone did make a frontal assault on the entrance, but your Randolph Security System kept them out."

"Underground house?" Katie questioned.

"It's pretty spectacular. You'll have to get him to give you a tour when we've got more time." Jo turned back to Mac. "Your face cream is in a beer cooler in the car—along with the computer. You can take it to the lab after you tell me about your adventures at the morgue. And by the way, I do have one more piece of information you may be interested in."

"Yes?" Mac asked.

"Tom Houston's body was claimed by a brother in New Hampshire."

"He didn't have any brothers."

"That's what I figured," Jo said. "Whoever is behind this whole thing isn't leaving any loose ends."

"Except that we've still got Tom's blood and the tissue sample from the morgue," Katie pointed out. "They may know about the tissue samples by now. But they can't know about the blood."

She and Mac spent the next twenty minutes telling her about their early-morning break-in—by mutual consent glossing over the part about Arnie Beale. After listening to their account, the detective pulled out a piece of paper with the name of the company that had leased the car. The

Chrysanthemum Corporation. An odd name, which told them nothing.

"I'll see if I can get a lead on what else the company owns," Jo promised.

"As long as you're looking, you might want to see what you can dig up on the guy who tried to run us over." Mac pushed the hit man's wallet across the table. "But I'm pretty sure he's small potatoes."

Jo slipped the wallet into her purse.

"There's also the woman who owns Genesis," Katie added. "Arnie was supposed to leave the tissue sample there. That's where the face cream came from, too."

The breakfast broke up quickly after that, and Mac and Katie left for R & E. The tissue-sample test, although a bit more complicated than the previous procedures had been completed. There was no surprise in finding that Val tested positive for the virus. Next they introduced the second face-cream jar into the hot lab. This time, the results were the same as before. No virus in the cream.

"I was sure we'd figured it out," Katie muttered.

"Yeah." Mac's expression was thoughtful, as though he were barely listening to her. "Um, why don't you go get us both some coffee while I update my notes." He pulled a small notebook from his pocket and began to write.

Still wrapped in her disappointment, Katie went down the hall to the canteen. When she returned to the lab ten minutes later, she found that Mac had put the notebook down and was leaning over the hot lab. She could see that he was mixing something inside the hood and was having trouble trying to work one-handed.

"What are you doing?" she asked as she set the coffee cups down.

"Trying a little experiment. Come and help me get this sample where I need it, will you?"

What did he want to look at with the electron microscope? Katie wondered. Minutes later the question was answered as an image filled the screen. Katie recognized the same nasty-looking virus structure they'd looked at before. Only now there was something different. The virions appeared to be disintegrating.

They both watched the virus particles.

Katie thought about the limited number of other materials in the sterile environment. "What did you add to it? The face cream?"

"As a matter of fact, yes."

She focused on the screen again, watching the virus protein dissolve. "What in the world made you try that?"

"One of those hunches I get out of the blue sometimes."

Katie looked at him with increased respect. She'd always known Mac McQuade was one of the brightest students in their class at Georgetown. Beyond that, the work he'd been doing over the past few years had sharpened his analytical abilities. What he'd dismissed as a hunch was the kind of intuitive leap that came to truly great medical researchers.

Her hand closed over his, and her voice rose with her excitement. "Not out of the blue. We were both assuming there was some link to the face cream. When it didn't turn out to be the source of the virus, you started thinking in another direction."

His expression was doubtful. "Oh, come on. I was just angry that we'd had Jo break into my house for nothing. And I guess I was remembering you trying to show me your bruises. Only there weren't any."

Katie didn't allow his dismissive words to dampen her

enthusiasm. "No, you're like Pasteur when he decided to experiment instead of throwing out a batch of half-dead anthrax virus. What he came up with was the whole theory of immunization."

He laughed. "I don't think this is exactly the same caliber discovery."

She moved in closer and wrapped her arms around his waist. "Mac, a lot of people may be in danger from this virus. And you've just found something that counteracts it."

For a moment neither one of them moved, and she knew that despite what he'd said to her a few hours ago, a special kind of closeness was growing between them. It was the kind of bond they'd had in medical school—two minds on the same wavelength sharing the excitement of new discoveries.

In the next moment, however, he put his hands on her shoulders and moved her gently away. "Don't get too worked up. All we know so far is that some component of the cream dissolves the virions after they're dead. What we need is a live human sample. And I haven't a clue about where we're going to get that."

Katie turned away, as much to hide her reaction to his dismissal as to give herself a chance to think clearly. Tom and Val were dead. Had either one of them passed the illness on to someone else? "Wait a minute. Val talked about another man she was seeing besides Tom. An instructor at the health club where she kept in shape."

"Do you remember his name?"

"Give me a minute, it'll come to me." She pressed her fist against her teeth and nibbled. "Greg something. He works at Body Electric."

"She was intimate with him, too?"

Katie nodded tightly. "I'm sorry, Mac. She wasn't the kind of woman who stuck to one relationship."

His face went hard for a moment. "Well, if he has the virus, I wonder what the chances are he'll agree to cooperate with us?"

"We're not going to know until I go down there and talk to him," Katie said.

"What do you mean, you?"

"Mac, let's face it. Even in the best of circumstances, you tend to be intimidating. Who do you think is more likely to persuade him to cooperate? Or were you planning to kidnap him?"

He considered the proposal for several moments. "Okay, I don't like it, but I'll go along with you—for now."

"Then we'd better call the club and find out what his hours are."

THE BODY ELECTRIC health club was a block and a half off fashionable Wisconsin Avenue—where the rent wasn't quite so high. The next morning, Katie pulled into the small customer parking lot and sat for a moment wondering what was going to happen when she met Greg. Dealing with Val hadn't been much fun. Was her other boyfriend going to be the same way? Worse? Better? Maybe if he was lucky, he wasn't even sick. Which would tell them something about the level of contagion of the virus. Unless Val had been lying about the relationship.

There was no use sitting here speculating, Katie told herself as she climbed out of the car and headed for the entrance. There were simply too many questions she couldn't answer until she talked with Greg. Pushing open one of the heavy frosted-glass doors with a decisive shove, she went inside. The lobby was deserted, but in a surprisingly large room to her right, she could count a dozen men and women working out on stationary bikes, stair-climbing machines, and rowers. Over the speaker system, a Madonna hit set a lively pace.

Katie was looking around for assistance when a young woman in green leotards and a Body Electric T-shirt, came out of the locker room and moved behind the front desk. Her name tag read Tina. "Platinum or regular card?"

"I'm not a member. But I have a few questions."

"If you're interested in joining, I can get Pete to show you around and explain our packages."

"What about Greg? Is he available?"

Tina grimaced. "Greg Scoggins? I don't know what's with him lately. Yeah, he's free right now, but he's supposed to be doing Nautilus training in fifteen minutes. I think he's in the weight room. Down the hall, the second door on your left."

The weight room was empty except for a short, muscle-bound guy lying on the bench pumping a huge barbell up and down like it was a Tinkertoy.

Katie watched the play of his strong biceps as they flexed and contracted. If you judged a person's health by their physique, he was in great physical shape. But Val had been, too.

"Pardon me. Are you Greg?" she asked.

"Yeah. What can I do for you?" After setting down the barbell, he tipped up a plastic bottle of water for a drink, realized it was empty and threw it down disgustedly.

"I understand you might have been dating my sister, Val Caldwell."

Greg's blond eyebrows knitted together. "I wouldn't call it dating. She worked out at the club, and we got it together in bed a few times, that's all. Nothing heavy. That babe sure had an itch, and I was glad to scratch it." Almost as an afterthought, he added, "Sorry to hear about her accident."

Katie tried to keep the look of repugnance off her face. He was putting his relationship with Val in the crudest of terms. But then her sister hadn't had much control over her tongue, either.

Out of the corner of her vision, Katie saw two men enter the room and start their own workout.

"Is there somewhere private we could talk for a few minutes?"

Greg scratched under his left armpit. "Don't think so. My next appointment's going to be here soon. And I'm booked till closing. Besides, there's really not much I can tell you. Why are you hounding me?" Without waiting for an answer, he walked past her and dug a bottle of chewable vitamins out of his gym bag. Shaking a half dozen into his hand, he began chomping on them loudly.

"Who the hell took my water?" he mumbled under his breath. When he spotted the discarded container under the bench press, he picked it up, tried to drink from it again, and seemed shocked to find it still empty.

Katie watched him, trying to maintain her professional detachment. From her brief observation of his unguarded language and his disorganized behavior, she'd bet that Gary had the virus. Was she going to be able to reason with him?

Katie glanced over her shoulder and then lowered her voice. "Greg, my sister may have had something contagious."

His blond head whipped around, and a frightened look flashed in his light eyes. "Wha'da'ya' mean? AIDS?"

"No, not AIDS. It's a long story. But I've got to talk to you today. You might be at risk."

He seemed to waver indecisively for a few moments. "Okay. There's a sub shop across Wisconsin. Come on."

As they passed the front desk, Tina called out to him about his next appointment, but he ignored her. Pushing Katie toward the door, he followed her outside without even bothering to change into street clothes.

When the frigid air hit his heated body, he shivered. "Cold."

"It's a long way to the sub shop. Why don't we go sit in my car? It'll be more private."

"Yeah. I'm not hungry anyway."

They were halfway across the parking lot when two long shadows fell across their path. Katie glanced up to find the way blocked by a couple of large, Asian men. Sumo wrestlers in three-piece suits. It wasn't just their size but also the dangerous looks on their faces that sent a stab of fear to the pit of her stomach.

She might have turned and run, but one of the goons clamped a hammer-hard hand on her shoulder.

"Greg, do something!"

"Take your mitts off the lady!" Crouching down, the exercise trainer jabbed at one of the assailants. He got in a couple of quick blows, but he left his back unprotected. A chop to his neck crumpled him like a piece of dry toast.

The thug turned his attention back to Katie, muffling the scream that would have torn from her lips. Frantically she tried to twist from his grasp. But she might as well have been a dove fluttering in an eagle's talons.

The other man opened the door of a yellow van advertising a cleaning service. Then he tossed a still-unconscious Greg onto a pile of laundry bags inside.

As her captor pushed Katie toward the gaping door, his grip loosened for a moment. Katie went limp and tried to slide under his body. He only laughed, scooping her up

and dumping her on the laundry bags beside the unconscious Greg. A gun was out of its holster and pointed toward her as his companion started the engine.

The man with the gun jumped in behind her and
slammed the door. As they swayed out of the parking lot,
he slapped strips of adhesive over her mouth and around
her wrists, pulling her arms painfully behind her back
while he trussed her like a lamb on the way to market.

Chapter Thirteen

A half block down the street, Mac watched in grim horror as the kidnap vehicle sped away.

"Oh, God! No!" His stainless steel hand clamped the steering wheel so tightly that the hard plastic started to give. With an exclamation that was half curse, half prayer, he switched on the engine and pulled out after the van. He'd thought Katie would be safe enough if he staked out the gym. But he hadn't been prepared for something like this.

It had all happened so damn fast. In a matter of seconds the two big men had whisked Katie and the jock out of sight.

He'd had to stop himself from leaping out of the car and dashing across the street—because a grandstand play could have gotten Katie shot.

Stomach churning up corrosive acid, Mac followed several car lengths behind the van. If only he had a weapon. Or some reinforcements. His eyes flicked to the portable cellular phone on the passenger seat. He needed help. But whom could he call? Certainly not the police. For all he knew, they might be behind the abduction.

What about Jo O'Malley? No, she'd told him she had to take care of some urgent business of her own north of

Baltimore. Was there a chance she'd changed her plans? When he reached her on her car phone and told her what had happened, she instantly dropped the other project. But that didn't do him any immediate good.

"Mac. It'll take me an hour to get there."

"I can't wait that long."

"Call me as soon as you know where they're taking her."

"If I can."

ONLY A THIN RIBBON of light sneaking in at the top of a window illuminated the back of the van. Fighting not to gag on the damp, musky smell coming from the laundry bags, Katie struggled to a sitting position and looked around. Both thugs were up front now, and neither one of them was paying any attention to her and Greg. They must be certain there was nothing to worry about.

Mac, she thought. *Did you see what happened? Are you out there following us? Or did they know you were there and get you while I was inside?* The terror of that speculation brought a silent scream bubbling up in her throat.

For long moments it was all she could do to keep the fear from swallowing her whole. Then, she pulled together the tattered shreds of her equanimity. With all her strength, she tried to break the tape that bound her wrists. Still the bonds held as effectively as if they were metal cuffs.

No good. Was there some sharp projection she could use to cut herself loose? In the semidarkness she could see almost nothing. Moving awkwardly, she felt along the side walls of the van and encountered only smooth vinyl. Maybe there were bolts where seats had been removed from the floor. She'd have to dig down with her feet through the bags of laundry to find them.

Through his gag, Greg moaned feebly. The physician in

her wanted to find out if he'd been seriously injured. But the realist knew that if she didn't get away, they might both be facing extremely shortened life spans. Besides, with her hands and mouth taped, there really wasn't much she could do for Greg, anyway.

As she continued to dig for a cutting tool, Katie tried to assess the situation. From the stop-and-go traffic, she imagined that they were still on Wisconsin Ave. Where were they headed? And what was waiting for them when they got there?

By the time her mobile prison had come to a halt, Katie's arms and shoulders ached from her struggles and the strained position. One of her captors flung open the door of the van, pulled her out and set her roughly on her feet. It was the one who'd laughed when she tried to get away. He laughed now as her knees gave way, and she slumped against the side of the van.

Greg was still unconscious. The other thug hoisted him over his shoulder as if he were almost weightless.

They were at the loading dock of a warehouse. Before Katie could register any more details, the tape on her ankles was cut. Then she was stumbling inside and down a dimly lighted hallway.

"Why are you doing this?" she tried to mumble through the tape.

The only response she got was a hard twist to her bound wrists that shot a bolt of pain up through her shoulders and brought tears to her eyes.

At the end of a hall, Katie was separated from Greg and ushered through an unmarked door. Inside she was astonished to see a fully equipped doctor's examining room.

With frightening efficiency, her captor cut the tape from her wrists, stripped her down to her bra and panties, and strapped her onto the table.

The room was cold; but that wasn't the only reason goose bumps bloomed on her skin. She had to clamp her teeth together to keep them from chattering. What was her guard thinking now? She turned her head away from his probing dark eyes, praying he wouldn't touch her.

He stood with his hands clasped behind his back until a man in surgical dress—mask, gown and gloves—entered and issued an order in a foreign language, maybe Japanese. After a quick, subservient bow, the thug filed out, leaving Katie alone with the newcomer. Most of his features were hidden beneath the paper mask. But she could see his dark eyes in back of thick lenses. Their sharp interest as he studied her tightened the goose bumps on her arms. Dr. Jekyll.

With sudden terrible insight, Katie knew how Arnie Beale must have felt strapped down on the table in the autopsy room. She squirmed against the bonds that held her to the table but it was impossible to break away.

If her mouth had been free, she might have started pleading with the doctor. In growing horror, her gaze followed him around the room as he made methodical preparations for some procedure. Oh Lord. Was he planning to operate on her? Or something worse—like infect her with the virus? Katie felt a wave of nausea edging up her throat.

Somehow she had to keep her fear from overwhelming her. With deep, steadying breaths through her nose she managed to hold the terror in check.

Dr. Jekyll turned back to her and pressed two fingers against the side of her throat.

"Congratulations, you look very calm under the circumstances, Dr. Martin. However your pulse is one-eleven," he said in heavily accented English.

She swallowed.

Reaching to the table behind him, he held up an empty

syringe in his hand. "I will be taking a blood sample and doing an examination. With your cooperation, the pain will be minimal. Without, I make no guarantees."

Katie closed her eyes and felt a swab of alcohol and the jab of a needle in her arm. No, she'd better watch. Struggling to keep the breath moving in and out of her lungs, she forced her lids open and watched him fill three vials with her blood.

When he was finished, the doctor opened a panel in the wall, set the blood inside and closed the door.

"We have a very quick test for HDV15. The results will be available in a few moments."

There were all sorts of inferences Katie could make from those simple sentences. He was very familiar with the virus. It even had a name, which ended in a rather high number. Had he discovered that many natural variations? Or had there been that many laboratory trials?

The speculations made her skin break out in a cold sweat against the slick plastic of the table. The sensation grew more pronounced as the doctor's skilled fingers began to poke and probe her body.

MAC STUDIED the windowless facade of the Rockville warehouse, his eyes narrowed to slits. The goons had taken Katie and the unconscious Greg in through a metal door beside the loading dock. Every cell in his body urged him to leap out of the car and charge that door. Except that the odds were even worse now. The place could be full of bruisers, for all he knew. Or there might be an alarm system guarding the door. Getting himself killed or captured wasn't going to save Katie.

Stealth, speed and surprise were his only weapons. Time and miscalculation were his enemies. If he didn't act quickly, if he didn't make the right split-second decision, they might—

Shuddering, he cut off the thought. Instead he pulled the car back onto the road, drove down to the next parking lot and took sixty precious seconds to tell Jo his location. Then he jogged back to the warehouse.

Just as he rounded the corner, one of the thugs who'd captured Katie and the jock came out of the building, got back in the van and drove off. Well, that had to improve the odds, but it didn't alter his plan of attack.

Mac's mind and body were reacting with jungle instincts now. He had switched into a sort of super aware state in which physical details seemed to leap out at him and contingency plans were processed at lightning speed.

No external surveillance system, or they would have picked him up already. He circled the warehouse and decided that a series of rungs fixed to the side of the building and leading to the roof offered the only other feasible way of getting in. Since the accident, climbing had become awkward because he couldn't pull himself up with the artificial hand. The encumbrance hardly slowed him now.

Once he gained the flat gravel roof, the hand became an asset instead of a liability. With the twitch of an internal circuit, he produced a cutting tool. It sliced through one of the large aluminum exhaust ducts like a sharp knife through gelatin.

Moments later he had lowered himself inside to the edge of a dusty second-floor catwalk. Crouching low and moving quietly through the shadows, he studied the layout below. Most of the large building was either empty or being used for storage. In the center was a section where suspended ceilings blocked his view. Since he couldn't spot Katie, he assumed she was in there.

Near him were several roughly partitioned rooms. Some

were piled with shipping crates. Thankfully most were empty—of both people and equipment.

He froze as his eyes swept over a canteen with a sink, microwave and tables. One of the goons who'd scooped up Katie was slipping two slices of frozen pizza into the microwave oven.

One-on-one made better odds than Mac had anticipated. Slipping under the balcony rail, he leapt. He would have caught the man squarely in the middle of the back, except that just at the wrong moment, his target turned and saw a body hurtling toward him from above.

KATIE TRIED to close off her mind, tried to endure the examination with cool detachment as if the body tied down on the table belonged to someone else. The ploy was only partially successful.

After Dr. Jekyll was finally finished, he busied himself with some of the equipment in the room. When a buzzer sounded, Katie's body jerked. But the doctor calmly turned and opened the pass-through in the wall again.

She watched him study a computer readout.

"Congratulations again, Dr. Martin. You are in excellent health." Stripping off the mask, cap and gloves, he tossed them into a trash container in the corner.

They were face-to-face now. Hers must be pale and bloodless. His was subtly lined—his nose flat, his lips thin, his eyes darkly intelligent. Under other circumstances she might have called him a good-looking man. Now his most prominent feature was the ice behind his dark eyes. She wanted to turn away; instead she used the opportunity to observe him, her mind memorizing details.

For one thing, he wasn't as calm as he pretended to be. A muscle under his right eye twitched, and she suspected that below the surface of his cool oriental manner, he was holding violent emotions in check. Then there was his age. At first she might have said he was in his late forties. A second glance made her suspect he was older.

"There are some questions I must ask you," he said, his accent becoming more pronounced. With a smooth, sharp motion, he ripped the tape from her mouth.

Katie gasped in pain.

"I've found it's best to get the worst over with first. Wouldn't you agree?"

Katie nodded tightly.

"So let us proceed to the meat of our discussion. You and your sister, the spy."

"What?"

"Val Caldwell. Sent to spy on us. Sent by whom, Dr. Martin? Who is your group working for?"

"Nobody. I—that's crazy."

"Please do not strain my patience. You and Mr. McQuade have been conducting research on HDV15 at Medizone. You've stolen tissue samples from the D.C. morgue. And now you have the good fortune to turn up at the health club when we went to pick up Mr. Scoggins. What else do you know about our plans?"

Katie felt her heart thumping wildly inside her chest. "Nothing."

"Who else knows about the virus?"

She had to protect Jo. Yet telling him nobody else knew would be putting herself and Mac in even more jeopardy. "We've talked to the D.C. police and the Centers for Disease Control in Atlanta."

"Lying to me is taking a great risk," he said sternly. "You and I both know the D.C. police are no problem. And I know you have not made contact with CDC. Besides, you had nothing to send them. We removed all the evidence from Medizone, although I conclude you must be working with the tissue samples from the morgue in another lab. Where?''

The extent of his knowledge and the menace in his voice made her blood turn to ice, yet she looked at him defiantly.

''We don't have another lab.''

He reached out and stroked her cheek in a parody of an affectionate caress, then brought his hand down in a stinging slap that made her eyes water.

''You're either very foolish or very brave to defy me, Dr. Martin. But I must know about this spy ring of yours. You weren't carrying any identification when you came to talk to Mr. Scoggins. Wouldn't you call that suspicious? Are you the brains behind the operations? Is it Mr. McQuade? Or was Mr. Houston in charge?''

''There is no spy ring.'' She prayed her voice didn't betray her fear. She prayed she had more time than she thought.

''Where is your accomplice, Mr. McQuade?''

Katie tried to hide the relief that flooded through her. He'd just told her that they didn't have Mac. Unless he was trying to trick her.

''I don't know.''

He touched her cheek again, and she cringed. This time, he didn't slap her. But the implied threat hung between them in the chilly air.

''Your answers are remarkably monotonous, Dr. Martin. But you're not going to destroy plans that have taken years to come to fruition. I have a way to make you talk. You've seen what HDV15 does to the human brain. I can arrange to have you experience the disorientation and the mental deterioration firsthand. Believe me, once you have the virus, it will only be a matter of time before you start to babble out answers to any questions I put to you. Suppose I give you a little bit of time to think about it?''

THE BIG MAN'S REFLEXES were excellent. The pistol was out of his pocket before Mac hit him. As he lifted his arm to aim and fire, Mac acted with a well-honed sense of self-preservation: His alloyed hand came down with the force of a hammer on the thug's skull, sending him to the floor like a block of concrete sinking in a lake. Kneeling, Mac made a quick examination. The guy wouldn't be getting up soon. Mac picked up the gun and waited tensely to find out if anyone had heard the brief scuffle. Apparently no one else was aware of an intruder in the building.

Cautiously Mac pressed his ear against the door and listened. One down. How many more were there? All he could hear was the throbbing of equipment somewhere. Opening the door, he stepped into the corridor and began making his way toward the area that had been hidden from the balcony.

A guard sat at a battered metal desk where two corridors crossed. Luckily he had his back to Mac, who was able to take care of him with a sharp karate chop to the neck. After binding his hands and feet and gagging him with tape from his own desk drawer, he dragged him into an empty room and closed the door again. Two down. He was leaving a trail of unconscious bodies around the warehouse. Sooner or later they were going to come back to life and haunt him.

"WELL, DR. MARTIN, your time is up, I'm afraid. What is your decision? Would you like to experience the virus that drove your sister and Mr. Houston mad?"

"I'll—I'll trade you information."

His eyes flicked to the straps that held her arms and legs. "You're in no position to bargain."

Katie fought the swell of fear that threatened to choke

off her breath. "At least tell me what's going on. What does the face cream have to do with this?"

"Ah yes, the face cream." He smiled with satisfaction. "One of my more profitable discoveries. It's a big seller at Genesis because it restores youth and beauty by cleansing the cells of destructive elements. Moreover, in the case of someone with the virus, it slows the course of the infection."

"I don't understand. Val was using it. And she was very sick."

"I assume she had to ration her stolen supply sparingly. She didn't have enough to be totally effective."

"Why are you doing all this?"

"To right an old wrong," he snapped, his eyes boring into her. "But we're wasting time, Dr. Martin. It's my turn to ask the questions. How long have you known your sister was infected? Where can we find Mr. McQuade?" He raised the hand with the hypodermic and held it in front of Katie's face.

"Right here, pal." Mac slammed the door open and strode into the room. It took less than a second for him to comprehend the scene and point the gun at the doctor's midsection. "Drop the syringe and back away from her— or you're dead."

Dr. Jekyll's eyes flicked from Mac's grim face to the gun. The hypodermic slipped through his fingers and clattered to the floor.

Katie stared at Mac, trying to absorb the sudden shift in reality. "Katie." His smoky eyes locked with hers, and she saw relief, outrage, anger. Then his gaze swept down her body, taking in her state of undress and the straps around her arms and legs.

"What did that bastard do to you?" He snapped his head toward the doctor cowering in the corner.

She tried to reassure him, but she could feel tears welling up in her eyes. She struggled to hold them back. With her hands bound, there was no chance to wipe them away.

"Hang on. We're getting you out of here."

He was stepping toward her, the gun still pointed at Dr. Jekyll, when she heard the sliding panel to her right open again.

"Mac, watch out. There's someone on the other side of the wall." The only gesture she could make was to swing her head frantically toward the opening to alert him to the danger. A second later, it was all too obvious.

There was an ominous hissing sound from behind the sliding door, as if a cage full of snakes had just awakened. But it wasn't an animal threat. In the next second, a white cloud of choking vapor spurted into the room.

As the mist touched her face, Katie's eyes began to sting, and she started to cough. Mac and the doctor were coughing, too.

Poison gas? Would they kill one of their own people to prevent a captive from escaping?

Katie tried to hold her breath. But it was too late. She'd taken in some already.

The noxious mist filled the little room, obscuring the shapes of people and objects. Katie sensed Mac bending over her, fumbling frantically with the strap that held her right wrist. A blade sliced through the restraint, nicking her flesh, and she gasped, taking in more of the contaminated air.

The indrawn breath set off a coughing fit.

Above her, Mac had also started choking. That was when she realized she was only hearing the two of them in the little room now. "The doctor," she gasped. "Gone."

Mac had been between Dr. Jekyll and the door. Had her

captor somehow slipped past? Or was there a bigger panel in the wall—one that could serve as an emergency exit?

Katie could tell that Mac was trying to work more quickly—without nicking her again. As he reached for the hand that was still bound, he inserted his finger under the strap before he cut.

Both arms were free. Katie tried to bring her hands together so she could rub some circulation into her numb wrists, but her muscles didn't respond to her mental commands.

Her vision was beginning to blur. Above her, Mac's face wavered—a friendly spirit come to watch over her in the poison mist. Like the last grains of sand sliding through the funnel of an hourglass, she could feel her grip on consciousness sliding away. Closing her eyes, she sank back heavily against the padded surface of the examining table.

"Don't conk out on me, Button." Mac's voice was urgent as he moved to the end of the table and began to work on her feet. Dimly she sensed that she was free. Yet there was no way she could lift her leaden limbs now.

Mac hauled her up and tried to set her on her feet. When they hit the ground, her knees gave way.

"Sleep," she murmured.

"Not yet." Coughing as if his lungs would burst, Mac hoisted her over his shoulder and staggered like a drunken sailor into the hall.

"Breathe," he gasped, between his own shaky gulps of air. Swaying, he helped her stand against the wall.

Katie obeyed. Still she felt as if her head were stuffed with mattress ticking. Why didn't Mac just let her sink to the floor so she could sleep? Why didn't he give her a blanket so she wouldn't be so cold?

His hands gripped her bare shoulder, shaking her. One

was flesh, the other cold metal. "Katie, I came in from the roof. You've got to tell me how to get out of here. Quick!"

"Umm…"

A stinging slap to her cheek brought her eyes popping open, and she cringed away. "No, please. Don't do it again."

His features were pinched as they swam into focus above hers. "Come on, Katie. I know you breathed in more of that stuff than I did. But you've got to tell me how to get you out of here," Mac repeated urgently.

The shock treatment worked. Mac's face solidified above hers. Her brain was functioning again, at least on a basic level. Straining to clear the fog from her head, she tried to reverse the route she'd taken earlier. "Right, I think."

They both began to move down the hall. To her surprise, she found that her legs were working fairly well. So was her mind. There was something important they were both forgetting.

"Wait. What about Greg?" she gasped as they approached the juncture in the hall where the two captives had been separated.

"Damn! I wasn't thinking about him. Where in the hell did they put him?"

She pointed. "In there. At least they took him through that door when they separated us."

The door led to a room that could have been transported straight from Georgetown Medical Center—except that there were no windows.

Greg, still wearing his shorts and T-shirt, was just climbing out of a bed with metal rails along the sides. Canvas restraints hung around his wrists like oversize bracelets. He backed away when he saw Mac.

"Hey, man, I was just mindin' my own business talking

to that broad about her sister. First you conk me on the bean. Then you stick me with needles. Why are you doin' me like this?''

Mac jerked his head toward Katie. "I'm with the good guys. I've already sprung the 'broad.' You want to come with us?''

"You betcha.''

A pair of folded pajamas lay across the chair. Mac grabbed the striped top and thrust it toward Katie. As they fled down the hall, she struggled to fit her arms into the sleeves. Mac slowed his pace to hers.

"Are you all right?''

"I will be as soon as we get out of here.''

He put her in front of him, and she knew he was intent on shielding her from whatever danger might be creeping up behind them. Greg brought up the rear. But for some reason he wasn't keeping pace with them.

"Hurry up.'' Mac turned to urge the exercise instructor on.

"Got a cramp, man.'' Greg leaned down to massage his thigh.

Their luck ran out as they reached the exit. Mac was still trying to urge Greg on when the door opened and the other sumo wrestler stepped back into the building. For a split second he goggled at the two escaping prisoners and an armed escort. Then, with a whir of motion, he pulled a gun from a holster under his arm and aimed it at Katie's midsection.

"Drop your weapon and hold it right there or your girl-friend gets it.''

Chapter Fourteen

With a vivid curse, Mac let the pistol slip from his fingers.

"All right. Now move back down the hall," the big man ordered, flicking the gun.

Greg balled his fist and made a growling sound. Katie put a restraining hand on his arm. "We can't do anything now."

"No talking!" the thug bellowed. "We're gonna find out why you're not back where you belong."

Katie had begun to turn around, when a flicker of movement in back of their captor made her heart jump in her chest. Another figure had crept up stealthily behind him. It was Cameron Randolph, Jo's husband.

"Oh, Lord, another one," Greg moaned and pointed.

The man with the gun half turned. There was a dull whoosh, and he crumpled to the ground like a marionette whose strings had suddenly been cut.

Cam stood over him holding a peculiar-looking handgun.

"Thank God! But, Cam, what are you doing here?" Katie exclaimed.

"I met Jo at Security Mall. We got here about ten minutes ago and were evaluating the situation." He gestured toward the man on the floor. "When we saw him come in, I figured I'd better follow."

"Thank God you did," Katie said.

Mac stooped to reclaim his borrowed weapon. "Let's get out of here. No telling how many hornets are left in the nest."

Katie took Greg by the arm. The health instructor wrenched out of her grasp and stampeded forward. Dropping to his knees, he started pounding the unconscious thug with balled fists. "You bastard. You're not so tough without your gun."

Cam and Mac tried to pull him up. Katie had more success with words. "If we don't get out of here, the others may come back and strap you in bed again."

Greg looked at her like a little boy who'd been caught punching out a buddy on the playground. "Strap me in bed again?"

"Come on. It won't happen if we get the hell out of here." Mac grabbed the health instructor's arm and jerked him to his feet.

As they left the building, Cam pulled a small box from his pocket and set it on the floor at the edge of the door.

The motley group that stumbled into the parking lot was met by a tense-looking Jo O'Malley who popped out from behind one of the cars, gun drawn.

"I told you to stay in the car," Cam reminded her.

"You're over my time limit." She turned to take in Katie's scant attire and her deathly white face. "Honey, are you all right?"

"Yes."

"We'll fill you in later. I want to get out of here before somebody else bursts through the door," Mac grated.

"The portable EMP unit I brought along will stop them

for a while," Cam told him, referring to one of the devices he'd invented.

When Mac raised an eyebrow, he continued, "It generates electrical waves that disrupt brain activity. Anybody who gets near it is going to get dizzy and pass out."

"Glad you're on our side," Mac murmured.

Even with that extra measure of safety, the group hurried across the blacktop and around the corner where Jo and Cam had parked. As Cam opened the door, Mac gestured toward Gary. "This is Val's former boyfriend. Greg Scoggins."

"Pleased ta meetja," the jock mumbled, extending a large hand, which was ignored by both Cam and Jo.

"Can you take him with you?" Mac continued. "He needs to go to a medical facility that you can trust," he added in a lowered voice.

Still, Greg picked up the key words. "No! No more doctors." The exercise instructor's eyes bulged, and he cringed away from the open car door.

He had just turned to run when Cam raised his pistol and fired. Like the thug before him, Greg slumped to the ground.

"What is that, a tranquilizer?" Mac asked.

"Same idea. But it's not invasive. It uses electronics." As he spoke, he was already folding the unconscious man into the back of his car.

Katie looked around for Mac's car. "Do we need a ride, too?"

"We're in the next parking lot." Mac pointed down the street.

"What happened in there?" Jo asked, her voice strained as she twisted around in her seat to look at her friend.

Katie knew she had to say something to reassure her. "They have a fully equipped examining room inside," she told her. "A man dressed as a doctor took a blood sample from me and did a physical. He was questioning me when Mac burst in." She got the explanation out all right, but the little speech ended with a shudder.

Mac's arm tightened on her shoulder. "Then someone flooded the exam room with gas," he took up the story. "The doctor got away."

"Let's get out of here," Katie added in a weak voice.

Jo nodded in agreement. "I think I know where we can stash the patient."

"Thanks. We'll get back in touch with you when Katie's rested." Mac looked at Jo. "Wherever you're taking Greg, make sure the staff avoids any communicable contact."

"Got it."

Jo looked as if she wanted to say something more. Instead she squeezed Katie's shoulder before her friend exited the car. "We'll talk later," she said.

When they were alone, Mac pulled Katie into his arms for a quick thankful hug. "Are you really okay?" he asked urgently.

"Yes." She clung to him tightly. "Mac, he was so creepy. He kept insisting Val was some kind of spy, and that you and I were in on it."

"What?"

"I know it's crazy."

Mac started the car, accelerated rapidly, and zoomed down the road in the opposite direction from the warehouse. Once they were out of the industrial park, he slowed to the speed limit, and Katie knew he was trying not to call attention to the car. He didn't speak until they put several miles between themselves and the danger.

"I didn't like slapping you."

"Oh, Mac, I know. But you didn't have any choice. I

was really spacey from that gas." Knowing he needed reassuring, she squeezed his arm hard for a moment, and he seemed to accept the gesture. Yet now that the ordeal was over, she couldn't keep up any sort of front for long. As Mac drove toward the motel, she pressed her shoulders into the seat so she'd feel the connection with something solid. Burying her hands in the oversize pajama sleeves, she closed her eyes and prayed that Mac wouldn't ask her any more questions for a while. She'd always had a pretty good idea of who she was and what she believed in. Dr. Jekyll had called all that into doubt. Maybe now, if she didn't have to talk about what had happened to her, she could hold herself together.

Mac seemed to understand her need for privacy, because he drove in silence. When they pulled up in front of their room, she looked down at the pajama top. "I'm glad I don't have to walk through a lobby."

"Let me unlock the door before you get out."

When Katie stepped into the room, she headed straight for the dresser where she pulled out some underwear and a comfortable cotton shift. "I need to wash that place off."

"Do you want me to bring you something to eat?"

"Not now." Before he could say anything else, she stepped into the bathroom and pulled the door shut behind her.

Mac sat in one of the wooden armchairs by the window, listening to the running water, fighting the impulse to follow Katie into the bathroom, pull her out of the shower and hang on to her—dripping wet and naked. He wanted to be close to her. Physically, if that was the only thing she could give him right now. Or maybe she couldn't even give him that. God, he never should have let her out of his sight. If he'd stayed by her side, none of this would have happened.

And now she was hurting. All the way back in the car, she'd been hiding behind her closed eyelids. And her disappearing act into the shower had just been an extension of her withdrawal.

Metal fingers gouged through the wood of the chair arm. He couldn't let her clam up like this. Not when she needed him. Even if she wasn't willing to admit it.

He tried to get control of his thoughts, but the horror show in the examination room blazed onto the screen of his mind. Katie. Nearly naked and looking terrified. Strapped down on a table with a fiendish doctor hovering over her. Dr. Jekyll, she'd called him. He'd had her in his clutches for almost an hour. What the hell had he been doing all that time? The question sent his imagination into lunar orbit.

Yet, he didn't have the right to make her tell him. Not when he'd walked out on her eight years ago without an explanation. Not when he still couldn't say the things he knew she wanted to hear.

It was then that the irony of the situation hit him. After all these years of shutting people out, the shoe was on the other foot, and he didn't know whether he could cope with the pinching sensation.

When he finally heard Katie's hand touch the doorknob, his whole body jerked. Unclenching his hand from the splintered chair, he struggled to make his expression casual as she opened the door. Despite the hot shower, her face was still pale, and she looked as if she'd shatter if she moved too fast.

"Feeling better?"

"I guess." She walked across to the table under the window and stood fingering the room service menu.

"Hungry now?"

"I—no."

"Katie, for God's sake, stop it!"

"Stop what?"

"You've got to talk to someone about what happened. It might as well be me."

When she didn't reply, he forced himself to continue. "I've got a pretty vivid imagination, you know. You were tied up—in your underwear. And all he did was give you a physical examination?"

"He hit me once when he thought I was lying. Mostly it was just a very impersonal going over," she clipped out. "At least he wasn't interested in my body."

Mac let out the breath he'd been holding.

"The physical part wasn't the worst," she said in a low voice.

Had he detected a tiny chink in the armor Katie had donned? Was it safe to try and pry it wider?

Safe or not, it couldn't possibly be worse than the defeated look on her face now. "Whatever happened, don't shut me out. Let me help you deal with it." Levering himself out of the chair, he crossed to where she stood and folded her into his arms. For just a moment she stiffened. Then, with a tiny sound that was half sigh, half sob, she turned and slumped against him.

"I want to help you. Please. Don't be afraid to need someone."

She pressed her head against his chest, and he could feel the beat of his heart thumping against her cheek. After a while, he lifted her up in his arms and sat down again, pulling her with him into his lap and cradling her protectively. But he didn't push her to talk.

Long moments later she began on her own. "Mac, I was so scared of him."

"Anybody would have been."

"He was a—contradiction. Unpredictable. All cool and

collected on the outside. But underneath, he was like a volcano ready to erupt if I didn't give him what he wanted. That was terrifying.''

''What did he want?''

''Information,'' she said, the word muffled by his shirt.

He felt her suck in a deep breath and let it out in a rush. ''Mac, he was going to inject me with the virus if I didn't talk. He was standing over me with the hypodermic when you came in.'' Her voice broke, and she started to shiver violently.

''That bastard. I should have shot him when I had the chance.'' The words were fierce, but he held her tenderly, rocking her in his arms, kissing her hair and her neck, giving her all the comfort he could.

After a few minutes, she stopped crying, but she kept her face hidden against his chest. ''The whole time I was in the shower wondering how I was going to face you, I kept thinking about *No Exit*—you know, that movie where the man and two women are locked in a hotel room in hell.''

''Yeah. By Sartre. We saw it at an arts festival on campus.''

''Remember the scene where you find out the guy went to hell for betraying his friends, because he was afraid of being tortured?''

''Katie, stop it! You haven't done anything to be ashamed of.''

''I was going to try to lie to Dr. Jekyll, to stall for time. But eventually I would have told him where we were hiding out.''

''So? I wasn't there.''

''I know what the virus did to Val and Tom. I didn't want that injection.''

''Katie, don't beat yourself like this. You were in an

impossible situation. This isn't the Geneva convention where you're only supposed to give your name, rank and serial number. Think about those captured pilots on TV during the Gulf War. They were spouting false confessions to save themselves. That's what you have to do when the other guy isn't playing by the rules. You would have been crazy not to give him what he wanted if that was your only alternative.''

''*You* wouldn't have.''

He lifted his head and stared down at her. ''Who do you think I am, James Bond? The right threat can make anybody talk.''

''I know you, Mac. You would have called his bluff. And if he'd injected you with the virus, you would have kept your mouth shut and hoped you could get away so you could come up with a cure.''

''Oh, come on. I honestly don't know what I would have done. Anyway the important thing is that we got out of there before anything serious happened.''

She nodded against his shirt. This time, he felt an elusive difference in the way her cheek moved against him and the way her body shifted in his arms. When he reached to tip her face toward his, he found she was looking at him expectantly.

''Mac, I need you. Make me feel whole again.''

''Ah, Katie.''

Her hands went to the back of his head, pulling his face down to hers. Then she was taking his mouth with the same hunger and demand he felt.

Between hard, urgent kisses, words tumbled from their lips.

''Mac, it was horrible.''

''I know, honey. I know.''

"I didn't want to talk about it. But you were right. I needed to."

"I couldn't let you do that to yourself. It's my fault he got you in the first place. I never should have let you go into the health club alone."

"No. I wanted to do it. You don't have anything to be sorry for." She stopped his protest with a fervent kiss.

He stood, crossed the few feet to the bed with her in his arms, and followed her down to the yielding surface of the mattress. Even before they were prone, they were locked in stormy passion, kissing wildly, fumbling with each other's clothing, trying to get more of each other, all of each other—everything that a man and a woman could give. And there was no way to know which of them needed the other more.

IT WAS LATER in the afternoon before either one of them wanted to stir.

"Think you could eat now?" Mac asked.

"I have the feeling you're hungry."

"Will you be okay if I go get us something?"

"I'm fine."

While Mac was gone, Katie got dressed and made the bed. Feeling restless, she unfolded the complimentary *Washington Post* the motel had left at the front door. At least she could make sure their visit to the morgue hadn't been reported. There was nothing in the Metro section about stolen brain tissue or a courier found strapped to one of the autopsy tables. However she wasn't able to put the section aside without reading the lead story. It was about George Wright, president of Wright Chemical Corporation, who had murdered both himself and his wife, Helen Austin-Wright, in their Georgetown home. Friends had been shocked to hear about the tragedy, although a number of

Wright's colleagues said that he'd been worried about a buy-out of the company's stock.

So much violence in the world, Katie thought with a shudder. The name Helen Austin-Wright plucked at some string of memory, but she wasn't able to place the woman.

When Mac came in, she piled up the paper and set it on the floor.

"Anything interesting?"

"Nothing about our unauthorized visit to the morgue."

"I didn't think there would be. They'd want to keep it quiet. Whoever *they* are."

Katie murmured her agreement as she watched Mac set their milk shakes, burgers and french fries on the table. A little while ago, they'd both been swept up in a firestorm of desire. Yet what exactly did she say to him now? she wondered. Thank you for being there when I needed you? Does your making love to me with all that passion change anything you said yesterday? Specifically the part about our not having a future together? She wasn't about to ask that kind of question.

"I made yours a gourmet burger—with lettuce and to-mato," Mac said with a grin.

"Don't worry about me, I can live for extended stretches on carryout if I have to."

"I remember, back in the bad old days." Mac ended the sentence abruptly and began unwrapping his cheese-burger.

Katie cast around for a less personal topic. "I was thinking back over the scene with Dr. Jekyll," she murmured.

"Umm?"

As Mac's dark eyes focused on her face, she wished she had kept her mouth full of hamburger. "I'm not going off on another guilt trip."

"Good."

"I was trying to make sense of some things he told me."

"I'm surprised he told you anything."

"I offered to trade him information."

"Uh-huh. So even while he had you at a horrible disadvantage, you were plucky enough to manipulate him."

"I was just—"

"Stop denying your effectiveness and eat your lunch," he said, taking a healthy bite of his own sandwich.

The order coaxed a tentative smile from her lips. But after she'd taken a couple of bites, her expression sobered again. "Maybe he was bluffing, but he sounded as if he has an informant at the CDC."

"What?"

"I wanted him to think we'd been talking with them. But he told me very emphatically that the CDC hadn't gotten anything from us. Which must mean our sample hadn't arrived yet. And when it does, somebody will probably scoop it up."

"Damn! Every time we make a move, we're blocked."

"Do you know anyone down there personally?"

Mac quickly came back with a name. "Perry Greenfield."

"Is he someone you can trust?"

"He used to be at Medizone."

"Maybe if we contact him and explain some of what's going on, he can help."

Mac pulled a notebook out of his pocket. "I think we'd better start making a list."

While he finished scribbling several notes, Katie finished her burger.

"Okay. What else do you have?" he asked.

"Dr. Jekyll told me some interesting things about the

face cream. It restores cells—and in the case of the virus, it slows the course of the disease.''

"That explains what we saw in the lab yesterday, but why didn't it work for your sister?''

"He said she'd stolen her supply, and she didn't have enough to do the trick.''

"I wonder what the critical dosage is. Maybe we have enough left to start treating Greg.''

"But we're going to run out. Then what?'' Katie folded down the end of her plastic straw. "Maybe I could pretend I'm a customer and go buy some from Genesis.''

"Forget it! If those goons who scooped you up at the health club knew what you looked like, so will the staff at the beauty shop. I'm sure as hell not going to risk your getting into their clutches again.''

For several minutes Katie picked at her french fries, and Mac worked on his second burger. When he was finished, he wadded up the wrapper. "Maybe we can't do anything for Greg, anyway. Once a brain cell is dead, you can't bring it back to life. It may be that you can only prevent deterioration—not reverse it.''

"I hope for Greg's sake you're wrong.''

Mac nodded. They were both silent for several minutes.

To keep from thinking about Greg, Katie began going over the facts they'd assembled. She put down her milk shake. "Remember how we thought the face cream might have been accidentally contaminated before it was shipped to the U.S.?''

"Uh-huh.''

"The way Dr. Jekyll was talking makes me think disseminating the virus is a deliberate plot. But who's the target?''

"Well, he admitted there's a connection to the face cream. And that leads back to Genesis.''

"Okay. Then let's get at it from a different angle. Who uses the face cream?"

"Women who go to Genesis. Women who can afford to pay high prices for an exclusive beauty product that will make them look young," Mac answered. "And they don't just run in to the salon for a quick haircut at lunch time, do they?"

"No. Val told me they're likely to spend the day, getting the works."

"So they're having all sorts of treatments. What if while they're there getting beautified and pampered, they also get infected with the virus?" Mac asked. "You wouldn't have to use a hypodermic. Any instrument that broke the skin would do it. It could even look like an accident."

"But why? Why give a bunch of women a deadly disease and then keep them from getting sick?"

He shrugged. "I don't have a clue."

"Dr. Jekyll told me he was avenging an old wrong."

"On a bunch of society women who don't have anything better to do than spend their days getting pampered? Maybe they didn't invite him to their debutante balls."

"Debutante balls! It's got to be more significant than that. He's bought off the D.C. police and someone at the CDC to make sure the plot isn't uncovered. And he's so sure that what he's doing is important that he thinks someone has loosed a team of spies on him." Katie was trying to fit all the known facts into some kind of theory when the phone rang. Mac picked up the receiver.

"Hello?" he asked cautiously. A moment later he was smiling. "It's Jo, she wants to know if we're ready to receive company—and some information."

"Sure. How long will it take her to get here?"

"A couple of seconds. She's in the parking lot."

Katie got up and opened the door just as Jo raised her

hand to knock. The detective stepped inside and gave her friend a brief but comprehensive inspection.

"Do I pass muster?" Katie asked, a bit more sharply than she'd intended.

"You're looking a heck of a lot more chipper than the last time I saw you. How are you feeling?"

"Much better."

Jo set down the briefcase she'd been carrying. "Honey, I have a pretty good idea of what you went through. So if you need someone else to—"

"How could you know what it was like?" Katie demanded.

"Because something pretty similar happened to me. Before I met you, a nut kidnapped me and held me captive for a couple of days. I spent most of that time trying to figure out how to keep him from killing me."

Katie gasped. "Oh, Jo, I didn't know."

"I don't talk about it much. I guess I thought I'd put it behind me. But when Mac told me those goons had you, I started flashing back to it."

"I'm sorry."

"Not your fault."

"A couple of days," Katie murmured. "It must have been horrible. How—how did you get through it?"

"At first I felt so alone and scared, I didn't think I was going to make it. Then I started pretending Cam was there with me, giving me the strength to match wits with the guy."

Katie reached for her hand and squeezed it. "That's how I felt. Isolated. Like I wasn't strong enough to stand up to him when he started asking me questions."

Mac who had quietly been clearing away the remains of their lunch, stopped moving. For a moment there was an awkward silence. Then Katie reached out, grabbed his hand, and stood holding on to him and Jo.

"Thank you both," she said, resting her head against Mac's shoulder for a moment. Then she cleared her throat. "We've got a lot of work to do."

Mac pulled up another chair, and they all sat down.

"How's Greg?" Katie asked.

"Worse."

Mac nodded tightly.

"He's at a very discreet private sanitarium—Tucker Manor, in Clarksville."

"I've heard of the place," Katie said. "You did make sure they know he has a contagious, fatal disease that's causing his dementia?"

"I was very clear about his being infected with a virus," Jo assured her. "And I took a blood sample to R & E. What's going to happen to him?"

"We don't know. We're hoping treatment will make a difference—and that we can start working on a cure for the infection."

"Dr. Jekyll must already have a cure," Katie muttered. "Otherwise it would be too dangerous to have the stuff around."

"Maybe somebody has to go back to that warehouse," Mac suggested.

"They've probably cleared out by now," Jo said. "Still, we might as well drop an anonymous tip to the Montgomery County Police that something illegal's going on there."

Mac nodded toward the briefcase. "What have you got for us?"

"A folder on Jade Nishizaka, the owner of Genesis."

"You found out who it was!" Katie exclaimed.

"Yeah, but I don't have much on her. It looks as if she went to a lot of trouble to cover her tracks." Jo stopped and looked uncomfortable. "I don't like dropping this whole thing in your lap. But I promised Laura Roswell that when Mickey Donaldson got out of jail, I'd be available to protect his wife. He made some nasty threats against her and the baby when she instituted divorce proceedings. Now he's back and acting psycho again, and she doesn't have the money to pay someone else for protection. Are you guys going to feel like I'm abandoning you if I leave the stuff and cut out?"

"Of course not," Katie assured her. "You can't just bow out of something like that."

"I can handle things," Mac assured her.

"You're not going to do anything risky without consulting me," Jo clarified.

"If there's an emergency, we'll call you," Katie assured her.

After the detective had left, Katie picked up the folder.

"What does it say about the Nishizaka woman?" Mac asked.

"Not a lot. She's been in D.C. for about three years. Before that she was the president of a Japanese pharmaceutical company."

"From pharmaceuticals to running an exclusive beauty salon. Isn't that a little unusual?" Mac asked.

"It's not illegal. And her record in the States is absolutely clean. She hasn't even gotten a traffic ticket." Katie scanned the few paragraphs. "Her driver's license listed her date of birth as June 15, 1932. From what Val told me, I expected her to be younger."

"She must be well-preserved. Maybe she uses her own face cream," Mac tossed in.

"Of course! Why not?" Katie went back to the meager information. "She was born in some place called Onodo. But that's about all there is. Her marital status is unknown.

So is her citizenship and her education. She's really covered her tracks, which you might want to do if you were up to something illegal. Or masterminding some sort of revenge scheme.''

Chapter Fifteen

"It still doesn't make a lot of sense," Mac muttered. "We're only talking about getting revenge against a bunch of women who happen to patronize a certain exclusive beauty salon."

"No, Mac," Katie contradicted as a sudden insight struck her. "It's not just a bunch of women."

"What do you mean?"

"You remember when you thought you might have the virus? You were trying to protect me. And when I thought I had it, I wanted to make sure I didn't give it to you."

They both went very still for a moment as they looked into each other's eyes. When Mac didn't speak, Katie continued. "Think about the situation with the Genesis patrons. You give them a deadly disease and prevent them from developing symptoms. But they're all carriers."

Mac was nodding as he followed Katie's logic. "The virus is spread through sexual contact. You wouldn't just be giving it to the women, you'd be passing it on to their husbands, too. But the husbands aren't using the face cream. So they're the ones who get sick. Like Tom and Greg."

"And the husbands can afford to send their wives to a very expensive salon," Katie murmured.

"We don't have any names," Mac pointed out. "But, my God, we've got to assume we're talking about individuals at the very highest levels of government and industry. If men like that started going berserk the way Tom did, it could do all kinds of damage."

Katie felt the top of her scalp prickle. "I think I've just had one of your intuitive leaps." Leaning over, she fished up the Metro section of the *Washington Post* and spread it out across the table. "Maybe we're talking about something like this," she whispered as she pointed to the story about Helen Austin-Wright and her husband.

Mac scanned the text. "Was she a patron of Genesis?"

"When I read the story, her name sounded familiar. I think Val bragged about doing her hair. But I'm not absolutely sure."

"I believe we need a list of Genesis customers," Mac said.

"Is that our top priority? Or is it making sure the CDC gets the sample?"

"Both."

Mac took his laptop computer out of the bottom dresser drawer where he'd stashed it. Over one of the government networks, he sent an urgent message to Perry Greenfield at the CDC, telling him there might be a foreign agent intercepting information at the facility. Next he alerted him to a package arriving from R & E labs, summarized what they knew about the virus, and asked if any other cases had been reported. He also asked if the agency could order autopsy results from George Wright and Helen Wright.

"Well, that's all we can do for the moment on that end." Katie picked up the folder on Jade Nishizaka again and began to scan the information. "Wait a minute, there's something I didn't notice before. Something strange. Val told me Genesis had plans to expand nationwide. Yet according to this, they're not even renewing their lease on the D.C. salon. In fact, it's up next month.''

''Maybe they're moving to a new location.''

''Maybe…'' Katie murmured doubtfully.

''Or maybe they're getting ready to skip town—''

''Because they'll be all done with their revenge business,'' Mac finished.

Katie nodded.

''We've got to find out what they're up to,'' Mac muttered. ''Fast.''

''Wait a minute,'' Katie objected. ''Don't you think it's time to call in the authorities? I know the D.C. police are out. What about the FBI?''

''And tell them what?'' Mac asked. ''We've been running around for days. All we have at this point is a mysterious virus, some allegations we can't prove, and a mass of speculation. I'll bet that if the FBI broke into the warehouse, they'd find every trace of that hospital setup had vanished. Besides there's no proof that the virus is connected with Genesis. We've got to take them something concrete.''

Katie sighed, bowing to the inevitable. ''You're right. I guess that means getting in there tonight when the place is closed.''

''After what's just happened to you—''

''I need to prove to myself that I haven't turned into a quivering mass of gelatin,'' Katie finished the sentence, her fists anchored on her hips.

''You don't have to prove anything. You're a research physician, not a spy.''

''That's a good line, coming from the man who's devoted the past eight years to proving himself.''

He scowled. ''That's different.''

"Not really. And if you can't see why not, there's no use discussing it."

Instead of answering, Mac began to put the computer away.

He hadn't gotten any better at dealing with a direct confrontation between them, Katie decided. Moreover, she was too weary to go another ten rounds with him at the moment. "I need some sleep," she told him. "Set the alarm for nine."

Turning her back on Mac, she pulled off her shoes and dress and slipped under the covers. She was going to roll on her side away from him, but she changed her mind and lay on her back watching him stand in the middle of the room looking from her to the other bed.

She'd reached the point where there was absolutely nothing left to lose with this man. But he was hers for now—if she didn't use his aloof tactics when the going got rough. "If you're thinking of sleeping by yourself, it's too late for that," she murmured. "At least if we can't have a civil conversation, you can hug me. A hug would be good fortification for the evening's activities."

She heard him mutter something she couldn't quite catch. For several moments he continued to hesitate. Then he began to unbutton his shirt.

"Probably you want to rest your wrist before we go out," she said.

He didn't comment. Instead, after he'd stripped down to his underwear, he unfastened the high-tech hand and set it on the dresser. Their eyes held for several heartbeats. Then he sighed and slipped into the bed. At first he lay stiffly beside her. But when she snuggled up to his lean body, he wrapped his arms around her. Pressing her face against his chest, she closed her eyes and tried to absorb the essence of Mac McQuade. After this episode in their lives was all over, it might be all that was left to keep her warm.

EVENING FOUND THEM back in D.C., both dressed in new jeans and casual dark shirts, heading for Genesis. It was in a seven-story structure in a fashionable uptown stretch of Connecticut Avenue. A number of the older buildings along the broad avenue had been torn down in the sixties and seventies to make way for boxy yellow brick apartments. But Genesis was housed in a vintage art-deco structure that had been carefully restored to its former glory. Mac drove around the block, sizing up the possibilities for illegal entry. "The roof worked last time I staged a break-in," he mused. "Why don't we try it again?" Katie squeezed Mac's hand. The last time he'd staged a break-in, he'd been rescuing her. He squeezed back.

"How do we get up there?" Katie asked.

"If we're lucky, from the roof next door."

Katie looked up at the adjoining new appartment. It was taller than its neighbor—eight stories high, to be exact. Clambering across a roof that far above the ground wasn't exactly on her list of ten favorite things to do, but she didn't protest. At least, she consoled herself, since the building housed a Middle Eastern restaurant, they ought to be able to get into the lobby as if they were part of the dinner crowd.

In fact, no one even glanced at them, knapsacks slung casually over their shoulders as they made their way to the elevator. They took the car to the top floor and climbed a flight of stairs to the roof. Mac taped the latch on the door so it wouldn't lock and trap them, in case they had to come back that way.

"Picked up that trick from the Watergate burglars," he quipped.

Katie gave him a weak smile.

Eight stories above Connecticut Avenue, there were no guardrails, and a strong wind was moaning across the darkness. Katie grabbed for Mac's hand as they stepped from the shelter of the stairwell. They couldn't risk flashlights because someone in a nearby building might spot them, so they took a few moments to make sure of their orientation.

Katie craned her neck at the stars. Above the glare of the city, they were spread across the sky like sequins winking on black velvet. But their beauty was far less important than the fact that they gave enough light for two fledgling cat burglars to find their footing.

Crouching low, they made their careful way across the exposed gravel surface. After lowering himself to the next roof, Mac helped Katie down. Neither spoke, but when they were both safely across the barrier, he hugged her tightly, and she returned the strong embrace.

"Okay?"

"I've done worse."

Now they were on the wrong side of a locked door, and Mac had to open it before they could gain entrance to the stairs. Katie didn't ask where he'd acquired either the expertise or the set of master keys. Instead she huddled out of the wind in the shelter of the brick wall while he worked.

Finally the door was opened, and they were able to descend the stairs to the second floor, where Genesis was located. This time, Katie stood guard while Mac studied the lock.

It seemed to be taking forever. Then she heard a string of muttered curses.

"What's wrong?"

"I guess it was stupid to think it was going to be this easy. They have an alarm system. Twenty or thirty seconds after I touch the lock, either there's going to be a bell ringing in the hall or a buzzer going off down at police headquarters.''

Katie thought about the high and windy roofs they'd crossed—for nothing. "Cam would probably know what to do about it,'' she suggested, her voice tentative. She really didn't want to get him involved in a breaking-and-entering charge if something went wrong.

Mac shook his head, agreeing with the tone of her voice, not her words.

''Maybe there's a back entrance, but it's probably wired, too,'' Katie muttered. As she spoke, her eyes scanned the hall and began to take in the details. The building was about the same age as 43 Light Street, only a lot more money had been put into sprucing up the interior. Her eyes fixed on the panels above her head. "Mac, the ceiling's been lowered.''

''And?''

''The building's a lot like the one where I have my office. I'll bet the drop ceiling is covering the old transoms above the doors. If they're still there, maybe we can get in that way.''

''It's sure worth a try.''

Katie tried not to think about how this was going to look if someone happened to come through the hall. Instead she donned the gloves she'd brought along and let Mac boost her up so she could push aside the buff-colored ceiling panel in front of the door. By standing on his shoulders, she was able to pull herself up.

''Well?''

''It's here!'' She heard Mac grunting as she moved around on his shoulders trying to pry the transom open. ''It won't budge,'' she reported after several fruitless minutes.

"Do you think you can give me a quick boost up?" Mac asked.

"I can try."

They reversed their positions, and she made her body into a step stool. Mac had to put his full weight on her shoulders for only a moment. Then he used the edge of the ceiling for support as he pulled himself up and disappeared.

It was worse waiting down here, Katie thought, as she listened to the blood pounding in her ears. When she heard a grinding sound, she tensed. It was followed by a muffled exclamation of triumph from above.

Mac came slithering back through the hole and reached down his gloved hand.

The man was strong. With a steady pulling motion, he brought Katie up and off the floor. As she joined him above the ceiling, she saw that the transom panel was lying beside the door. Mac wiggled backward through the opening he'd made. Before she joined him, Katie replaced the ceiling panel.

A few moments later, they were both breathing hard and standing inside the reception area of the Genesis salon.

Katie's face split into a broad grin. Mac grinned back, and they shook hands.

"Maybe we can get a job with Barnum and Bailey," she quipped.

"The one-armed bandit—"

"—and the brunette pushover."

"I believe you were pulled. And I'm not making a career of this unless it pays better than medical research."

"Speaking of research, let's get our work done and get the heck out of here." Katie opened her knapsack and took out a flashlight.

Mac followed suit.

They'd both been too busy for more than a quick glance at their surroundings. Now they took the time to absorb the plush atmosphere. Most of the lights were out. A few dimmed bulbs provided enough illumination to set off the Italian tile floor, blooming hibiscus and white wicker furniture.

"You could go right from here to Club Med," Mac muttered.

"You're going to have to take a rain check for a shampoo and scalp massage."

They both moved to the front desk. A gold engraved invitation to a "Spectacular Day of Beauty with Genesis" lay on top of the schedule book. Katie moved it aside so they could take a quick look at the customers who'd come in over the past few weeks, in case they couldn't find more detailed information.

Mac pulled out the camera they'd brought along and photographed several dozen pages. Looking over his shoulder, Katie pointed to Helen Austin-Wright's home number. Mac nodded. By itself it wasn't proof of anything. Nevertheless it was a good bet her patronage of Genesis wasn't a coincidence, either.

Katie began to search the contents of one of the hairdressing stations. Unless the virus was in a bottle labeled Setting Lotion or Extra Hold Mousse, it wasn't in evidence. Which meant it must be stored somewhere else, because using a container that anyone could pick up and use by mistake seemed much too dangerous.

Mac moved past her toward a closed door. After easing it open, he gave a low whistle. Katie came over and stopped in her tracks. The rest of the salon was elegant, but this room was in another class altogether.

They stepped onto a priceless Aubusson carpet and crossed to a richly polished Louis XIV desk. The traditional furnishings were set off with exquisite oriental accents like a two-foot-tall terra-cotta figure of a Japanese warlord mounted on a stallion. In the corner was an antique Japanese screen decorated with chrysanthemums.

"Want to bet this is Jade Nishizaka's private office?" Mac asked.

"Unless someone else holds the real power at Genesis."

A book inside the top desk drawer had what they'd been searching for—a list of customers, apparently in order of when they'd had their first appointment. It was annotated with each woman's phone number, address and personal information like hair color and makeup selections. Also included was a wealth of personal data such as number of children, entertainment preferences, favorite foods and social affiliations. There was an additional listing for the woman's husband. If he was in the private sector, his company's Dun & Bradstreet rating was included. If he was with the government, there was an evaluation of his political and policy-making influence.

"Pretty detailed for beauty parlor chitchat," Mac observed.

"I agree."

"Why do you think there's a star next to some of the names?" Mac asked.

"I don't know. But Helen Austin-Wright was one of them."

"We'll figure it out later. Right now I want to make a record of this stuff." Katie continued to skim the information as Mac began to photograph the entries. They were both so intent on the book that neither one of them heard the front door open and quietly close. The first inkling of danger was the dark form that suddenly filled the doorway.

"All right, raise your hands above your heads and back away from the desk," a steely voice ordered.

The command was reinforced by a large automatic pistol.

With a sick feeling in the pit of her stomach, Katie lifted her head. She was no more astonished than the man who held the gun. It was D.C. Police Detective Cornell Perkins.

He let out a surprised breath. "I'll be hog-tied! Dr. Martin, what the hell are *you* doin' here?"

"Are you going to arrest us, Officer Perkins?"

"I don't know. What are you up to?"

"Getting the goods on whoever has hatched a plot to give a virus called HDV15 to half the influential men in Washington," Mac answered.

Perkins whistled through large white teeth. "Say what? I just got back into the game." His eyes flicked to the metal hand. "Better start by telling me who you are and what's HDV15 virus."

Mac recounted the last few days' activities and findings, ending with their frightful theory of the deadly virus.

The detective took several moments to digest the information. "Sounds like you had a busy week. You're talking conspiracy?"

"We hadn't put it in quite those terms," Katie told him. "All we know is that there's some kind of revenge scheme."

Mac looked at the weapon in the detective's large hand. "I function better when someone isn't holding a gun on me."

Perkins studied the unlikely burglars. "This may be the stupidest thing I've ever done." With a sigh, he put the gun on the desk between them.

"So now we're supposed to trust you." The aggressive tone of Mac's voice hadn't changed. "How do we know you're not just interested in having us disappear?" he challenged.

"I was taken off this case to keep me from digging up the facts. Now I'm back—and workin' on my own time."

Katie touched Mac's arm. "He helped me that night at Val's apartment. I think we can trust him." She nodded to Perkins. "How much do you know?"

"I don't know squat. Not the real stuff, anyway. So far I've cottoned on to the autopsy switch and the small-time hood who ended up in a drawer at the morgue without any record of how he was brought in."

"Oh God." Katie shuddered. "That must be Arnie Beale."

"You folks know something about that?"

"The first time we saw him, he tried to run us over at the Columbia Mall. The last we saw him, he was very much alive and strapped to an autopsy table," Mac said. "Which is just more proof that somebody in your department is working like mad to cover this whole thing up."

"How did you end up here?" Katie asked.

"A tip from someone who'd like to blow the cover off this whole thing. He even gave me the access code for the Genesis alarm system. There's a cover-up all right, but somebody's running scared."

Katie felt the hair on the back of her neck bristle. "That could mean this is a trap—for you. And we've walked into it."

Mac's protective gaze swung to Katie. "Then we've got to get out of here. Now."

"Not yet," she objected. "We don't have enough information." She looked at Perkins. "Add a mole at the Atlanta Centers for Disease Control to your list of conspirators. And since you're here, could you make sure there's only one door to this place and then stand guard while we keep searching?"

"The Centers for Disease Control. The D.C. police. A

beauty salon. Doc, I'd feel a heck of a lot more comfortable if I had the whole picture.''

''*We* don't have the whole picture. That's why we're here. We'll tell you everything we know as soon as we finish going over this place. But I'll feel safer if you're watching the door.''

''I'm a trained police officer and you're rookie crooks. Who do you think has a better chance of turnin' this place upside down?''

''Ordinarily, you. Except that what we're looking for is the transmission method for a deadly, mind-destroying virus. If you stumble on it and don't know what you're doing, the consequences could be fatal,'' Mac told him.

''I get your drift,'' Perkins muttered. ''Okay, I'll play watchdog for you.''

Mac picked up the campaign chest sitting on the stand beside Jade's desk. ''Before you go on guard duty, could you try fooling with the lock on this thing? You're probably better at it than I am.''

''In for a penny...''

It took the detective only a moment to open the box.

''A picture album,'' Katie murmured as she took out an old-fashioned leather-bound book and turned to the first page. Inside the front cover was a tattered map of Japan. The place names were in Japanese. Two cities were circled.

Black-and-white photographs yellowed around the edges followed the map. The first few shots were of a smiling Japanese family, the young mother in traditional kimono, holding a baby, the father in a business suit. They were standing in front of a modest Japanese-style cottage. The captions were no more readable than the words on the map.

On the next few pages the photographs chronicled the

family's growth. Sometimes a whole raft of other people were also in the pictures. Uncles? Aunts? Cousins?

The small family appeared again. Now there were two children, a young girl and another baby. Several pictures later it became clear that the second child was a boy.

Katie asked. "Do you think this is Jade Nishizaka's family? I remember she came from some city I never heard of. Onodo. If this is the place, it looks like a small town."

The next pictures must have been from a few years later. The family seemed to have moved to the city, to a larger house with a beautifully landscaped traditional garden. The children were older, and the man had exchanged his suit for a military uniform. With the mother, father and children were an older woman and man, both in traditional dress.

"I think I can finally date these," Mac said. "It looks like the father joined the Imperial Japanese Navy."

"In World War II?" Katie asked.

"Uh-huh. I guess he moved his family to town for the duration."

"I'll bet they were living with the grandparents," Katie suggested.

Katie studied the background and the faces, but her gaze kept coming back to the boy. Something about him seemed familiar.

Expecting to see similar snapshots, Katie turned the page. As the new pictures came into view, everyone in the room gasped. Suddenly they were looking at a ruined city, the buildings flattened almost beyond recognition, the landscape charred. Then there were photos obviously taken in a hospital—of disfigured women and children.

There was more horror. Pages and pages of ghastly photos of victims of some sort of terrible disaster. No one wanted to examine them too closely.

Perkins, who had been leaning over Katie's shoulder, put several feet between himself and the book. "Lordy! It looks like the place was hit by an atomic bomb or something."

Katie felt the words like rocks crashing into a concrete wall. "I think that's exactly what happened," she breathed. Quickly she flipped back to the map in the front. "Two cities circled. Probably Hiroshima and Nagasaki. Jade must have lived in one of them."

Mac nodded. "We were all told that dropping the two atomic bombs saved a lot of American lives because we didn't have to invade Japan."

"From the allies' point of view, the devastation was a necessary evil. But if you'd lived through it, you'd probably have a considerably different opinion," Katie whispered.

"Yeah. Your home gone. People around you killed or dying slowly of burns—or radiation sickness. It could warp your whole personality," Perkins agreed.

Katie felt a wave of cold flow across her body. "To right an old wrong," she repeated Dr. Jekyll's phrase. "Do you think this is what he was talking about?"

Mac put a steadying hand on her shoulder. "It's a logical theory," he agreed. "Revenge on a grand scale. And think of the irony. You take away the customer's inner beauty—and leave a hollow shell."

"What do you mean a grand scale?" Perkins objected. "This place may be posh, but it's just one salon."

"With a very selective clientele," Mac countered. "Except that you're right. It's a slow process. You could only do a few women in one day."

Katie went very still, her face a study in concentration. Then she pushed back the desk chair and lit out of the room. A moment later she was back with the gold engraved card that had been in the reception area. "What about this?" she asked, as she set the cream-colored rectangle carefully on the desk. "It's an invitation for the wives of delegates to the National Economics Conference at the Wardman Park Hotel on Monday. How many women whose husbands are high up in the country's major corporations do you think they'll have access to then?"

"I don't know. Maybe there's a list of invitees," Mac suggested.

They found what they were looking for in one of the side drawers of the desk. Not only was there a list of women who had been invited, there was also a notation of who had accepted. It read like a Who's Who of Mrs. Corporate America.

Perkins whistled through his teeth.

"Two or three months from now, you'll get an effect like a bomb exploding in the brains of high-powered executives all over the country."

"Mac, I told you, we've got to let the FBI in on this," Katie said.

"We've still only got a half-baked theory. We need proof that they're going to infect these women with the virus." He glanced at Perkins for confirmation, and the detective nodded in agreement.

Katie shivered. "I wish we could get out of here."

"You could leave."

"I'll stay until we're finished."

Perkins took up his position at the door. At least it was reassuring having an armed police officer on guard duty. At Mac's request, Perkins also took the scheduling book and began searching for the appointments of women whose names had an asterisk on the master client list. "See if you can find out which treatments they received," Mac requested.

He and Katie began going over the salon. One of the first things they discovered was the environmental room, a chamber about the size of a large sauna where all sorts of natural environments could be simulated. At the moment, it was dark and silent as a tomb, and it hardly seemed a suitable depository for anything that could be damaged by heat, cold or moisture.

A more promising storage facility was near the back of the salon. On the top shelf of a locked metal cabinet they found the supply of face cream.

"Well, back to square one," Mac muttered. "We've still got to find the viral induction agent."

"Let's try the refrigerator." Katie pointed to a large, restaurant-size unit.

Inside were several large boxes labeled Cosmetic Sensitivity Allergy Test Kits.

"Is testing for allergies usual for a beauty salon?" Mac asked.

"I don't think so. Not in the ones I've been to."

He opened a box and took out a kit. It was sealed inside an outer plastic bag and an inner foil pouch, each labeled Handle With Extreme Care. Results Will Be Invalid If Tester Touches Any Surface Besides Customer's Skin.

Using his metal hand, he opened both wrappers. Inside was a small metal device similar to the those used for TB tests—although the grasping handle on the back was longer. The business end was peppered with dozens of quarter-inch metal projections—sharp enough to pierce the skin.

"I think we've found the viral induction agent," Katie said.

"I think you're right," Mac agreed. "But we'll have to do a test." He slipped one of the packets into the protective case inside his knapsack.

Katie looked at the shipping labels on the boxes. "There are at least three hundred of these things here. I'll bet they're for the conference."

"Yes, they're probably going down to the Wardman Park tomorrow."

They both came out of the back room to show Perkins another one of the test kits.

"Do you know if the women whose names are starred got an allergy test?" Katie asked.

The officer ran his finger down the list. "Every one of them," he confirmed. "And another thing, all of them were scheduled for a session in the environmental room—whatever that is."

"We saw it back there," Mac gestured toward the interior of the salon. "It's a place where you simulate various natural conditions," Mac told him. "A rain forest at sunrise. A tropical island in the evening. Stuff like that. It's supposed to be relaxing."

"I hope so." Perkins snorted. "They charge $125 for a half-hour session."

"I think we'd better give it a second look," Mac said.

"I suppose you're going to leave me here at the door while you get the grand tour," Perkins groused.

"Afraid so." He and Katie headed back toward the chamber. Mac studied the sophisticated control panel for several minutes before touching it. He turned on only the lights—to bright.

As he opened the door to step inside, Katie put a restraining hand on his shoulder. "I don't like you going in there. What if it's dangerous?"

"If it was dangerous, the customers would complain. But I'll leave the door open."

Still not entirely reassured, Katie leaned into the room, watching as Mac began to inspect the floor, walls and contour couch. Her full attention was on him, so that she didn't see the shadow loom up behind her. Suddenly the lights in the ceiling blinked off.

She screamed as powerful hands gave her a mighty shove. Then she tumbled into the chamber with Mac, and the heavy door slammed and locked behind them.

Chapter Sixteen

"Katie!" In the dark, Mac scrambled toward her. They collided, winced, caught their balance as they grasped each other's shoulders. Mac pulled Katie to him, holding her with a sure, firm clasp. Around her the room seemed to spin, and he was her only anchor to reality.

"Are you all right? What the hell just happened?"

Reaching behind her, she fumbled for the knob and found that it wouldn't turn. "Somebody killed the lights, pushed me in here and slammed the door. It's locked." She tried to keep her voice steady; it was wobbling by the time it reached the end of the sentence.

The room came to life. The twitter of a forest full of birds materialized around them in the dark, and a faint pink glow rose above their heads, as if it were the beginning of a new day. At the same time, the air was suddenly filled with the scent of a pine forest. Even the shapes of the trees were vaguely visible. "Somebody's putting on a show for us," Mac growled.

In itself, the spectacle wasn't frightening. Under other circumstances, Katie would have enjoyed the magic of the illusion. Yet somehow the scent of the trees and the soft pink glow held an unknown threat.

"I wish I knew what was going to happen next," she whispered.

"Yeah. Somebody's playing with the controls." Holding Katie against his side, Mac moved to the door and banged with the stainless steel hand. "Perkins?" he called. "What the hell is going on? If this is your idea of a joke, we're not amused."

There was no response.

"I'm sorry, Mac. We never should have trusted him."

"It's not your fault."

They clung to each other, trying to cope with the terrible isolation of the chamber. Inside, there was no indication that the outside world even existed. Katie shivered, suddenly unable to shake the apprehension that all the oxygen was being pumped out of the little room. Heart pounding, she began to suck air into her lungs.

When she started to feel light-headed, she realized she was hyperventilating. Cupping her hands around her nose, she dragged some of her own carbon dioxide into her system. It helped.

"You okay?" Mac asked. She could tell he was trying to stay calm, but there was a strained edge to his words.

"I'm not going to give them the satisfaction of falling apart."

"Good."

That was easier said than done. It was hard not to imagine the walls of the little room pressing in around them. Closing her eyes, Katie tried to focus on the logic of their problem. After a few moments, she felt a bit calmer.

"Maybe it's not Perkins out there," she finally murmured. "Maybe they got him first."

"Unless he was a ringer all along, and he was just waiting to find out what we knew," Mac countered.

Katie nodded, but she was listening to the noises in the

air as much as to Mac. The twitter of birds was suddenly replaced by the buzz of insects. It was so real, she could imagine their wings beating. As she listened, they turned into a swarm of hornets, zeroing in on her. She ducked. They were all around her head now. Unable to contain her panic, she screamed, swatting wildly with her arms.

"Easy. Easy," Mac soothed. "They're not there. It's all special effects."

She gulped. "I know—it's just—not knowing what's going to happen next."

As if to confirm her words, the hornets vanished and the sound of waves took their place. At first they were a gentle rolling sound far in the background. Then it was as if she and Mac were rushing toward a rocky shoreline. At the same time, the lights went out again. Katie cringed away from the assault of the unseen, giant breakers. Somewhere deep in her mind, she knew it was all an illusion, yet she clung to Mac, unable to dispel the fear that she was about to be swept away by the crashing surf.

Katie shivered as she felt the wet spray break against her face, felt the waves shake the ground on which she stood. The spray became a choking mist, like the gas that had overwhelmed them in the examination room. Only that had been like breathing essence of rose petals compared to this. She was gagging, gasping as every breath became an agony of stinging pain. It was over. Finished. "Mac— I—love—you—" she managed to get out. Then, as the burning in her lungs became too much to bear, she sank into oblivion.

KATIE CAME BACK to consciousness slowly. Her head felt as if it were a giant, throbbing hollow log on which a native drummer was beating. Her lungs stung, and her body might have been battered by hurricane-force winds.

Perhaps it had. They were just as likely as anything else in here.

Her eyes snapped open. "Mac?"

In the dark, he was beside her instantly. "Right here."

"Are you okay?"

"Yes. But don't talk, and try not to move around. I don't think there's much air getting in here."

She fought off a shudder of panic and tried to make herself comfortable against the rubberized floor. Mac was working at something.

"What are you doing?"

"Trying to short out the control mechanism."

She didn't ask any more questions. Instead she reached out and found his thigh in the darkness. He squeezed her hand. Then he went back to working. Her mind drifted on a sea of thickening air. This was so silly. They were trapped like two bears in their cave because somebody had rolled a giant rock in front of the door.

Katie knew the symptoms of oxygen deprivation. And these were it, she thought with a little giggle. Maybe she could write a paper about it for *The New England Journal of Medicine*. No, they'd be stuffy about her not having taken notes.

She went to pull Mac over so he'd curl up with her. No, he was busy doing something. She couldn't remember what. It was getting harder and harder to make her mind work.

Then she heard a popping noise. A moment later, dim light and cold air flooded into the chamber. Grabbing her under the shoulders, Mac dragged her to the door and pulled her out. For several minutes they both lay gasping on the floor.

Finally Mac sat up and rubbed his hand against his forehead. "That was too damn close."

"I know. How did you get us out of there?"

"I found the service panel and I used my personal mechanical toolbox." He held up the prosthetic hand. "They should have taken it off while we were out cold."

"I'm glad they didn't realize their mistake."

Katie watched Mac push himself up. She wanted to tell him to take it easy, but she knew that they didn't have the luxury of resting for too long.

Mac staggered into the storage room. He was back with a triumphant look on his face. "It's still here."

"The virus?"

"Yeah. We've got to kill it before they cart it down to the Wardman Park."

"You have something in mind?"

"You're damn right I do." He took her hand and pulled her up, watching to see how steady she was on her feet. "Think you can help me move the boxes?"

Her body protested with every step she took, but she didn't turn him down.

Mac opened the box and removed one of the packets. "They took my knapsack. I want another sample for the lab," he explained, as he rummaged on the storage shelves for a carrying case and put the deadly cargo inside.

As they began to transfer the virus, Mac told Katie what he'd thought of while he was trying to get them out of the environmental chamber.

"I like the way your mind works," she approved.

"Let's hope we have enough time to pull it off."

"What if they come back?"

"With all those lives at stake, we've got to take the chance," Mac insisted.

Half an hour later, they finished with the special treatment for the virus and began putting the boxes back.

"You think they'll realize what we've done?" Katie asked.

"I hope not. Everything looks just the way we found it. Now let's split."

"What about the door alarm?" Katie asked as they made their way back to the front of the salon.

"You don't feel like climbing back through the transom?" Mac asked as he stuffed the carrying case with the virus into his pocket.

"I'm not feeling quite as spunky as when we came in."

"I can check the cutoff box. Wait right here."

He went back toward the interior of the salon, and Katie turned to watch his broad shoulders disappear. The click of the door lock behind her made her turn. To her horror she found she was facing Dr. Jekyll. An attractive Asian woman stood slightly behind him. But she couldn't compete for attention with the gun the doctor leveled at Katie's chest.

"Raise your hands and back up, Dr. Martin," he ordered.

Wordlessly Katie obeyed.

The three of them stood in the reception area staring at each other. Katie's eyes went from the man to the woman beside him. She couldn't be anyone else but Jade Nishizaka—and there was a definite family resemblance between her and the doctor. In fact, they were grown-up versions of the children she'd seen in the photographs. Jade and her younger brother.

"How did you get out of the environmental room?" he hissed.

"I—Mac did it. I don't know how."

"Akio, it might have been better to have killed them when we had the chance," the salon owner murmured. There was both deference and apology in her voice.

"Are you questioning my decisions?"

This was a woman with complete power in her own realm. Yet she shook her head and cast her eyes down.

"We must know the extent of the plot against us. This time there will be no interruption to the questioning session." Akio's manner changed as he gestured with the gun. "Back up, Dr. Martin."

Katie obeyed and found her shoulders flattened against the wall. The solid vertical surface gave her a false sense of security.

"Where is Mr. McQuade this time?" Akio demanded. "He wouldn't have left you here."

Katie's mind scrambled for a plausible explanation. "He went to get help from a detective friend of ours. I was guarding the virus induction kits."

"Perhaps." He turned to his sister. "Go make sure they're still there."

Katie held her breath as the woman scurried away. What if Mac were in the storage room? What if she discovered him there? However, Jade returned a few moments later—alone.

"Everything's fine." She held up one of the virus packets. "This time I don't want you to wait. Just give it to her."

Katie's gaze flicked from brother to sister. She had to buy some time—for herself and Mac. "I know why you want to infect the women at the conference," she told the pair.

"You couldn't possibly know," Jade snapped.

"Was your mother killed by the bomb the Americans dropped on Hiroshima?" Katie asked.

The beautiful features contorted with pain. "My mother. My grandmother. My grandfather. My aunts and uncles. My cousins. Some of them died in the blast. Some of them, like my poor mother, lingered on—burned, suffering from radiation sickness. She wasn't one of the *Hibakusha*—the survivors. The worst would have happened to me and Akio, too, but we were in the country for the day, visiting friends.''

''It had to be horrible for you, losing everyone like that. My father died when I was little. I know it must have been so much worse for you,'' Katie murmured, hoping she could communicate with the other woman.

Jade ignored the expression of sympathy. ''Your father! You only lost your father. *My* father was killed at sea when his ship was torpedoed by the Americans. When he died Akio and I were alone. But Akio was strong. And he lent me his strength. He helped me understand what we had to do. Do you know how I scraped together money so I could start producing my mother's cosmetics again? I made myself available to the American soldiers. They were willing to pay for a young, beautiful Japanese girl. Even now when I remember the shame of that, it makes me sick.''

''You did what you had to,'' Katie whispered.

''Yes I did what I had to—to survive and grow strong.'' She glanced worshipfully at her brother. ''I revived my mother's cosmetic business and started our pharmaceutical firm. I paid for Akio's education. And now he is one of the world's great researchers. His discoveries have made it possible for us to avenge our ancestors. If his work had taken a different direction, he would have gotten the Nobel Prize.''

''What was your field?'' Katie addressed herself to the brother.

However, the sister answered. ''The field of revenge. But we are selective in our punishment. The women we give the virus to tomorrow are all married to men whose companies participated in the war effort. Fitting justice, wouldn't you say?''

Katie swallowed. ''But they're innocent. They haven't done anything.''

Jade fixed her with a fierce look. ''My mother was innocent. My grandmother. It didn't save their lives. And you are not innocent. You and your sister must have been conspiring for months to stop us. Tell me, did she break into my campaign chest? Did she look at the pictures? Was that why she wanted to stop us? You must have been the brains of the operation, since she was stupid enough to infect herself.''

''Val didn't know anything about it. I didn't know anything about it until after she died.''

''You can do better than that,'' Akio snapped. ''And you will.'' He looked at his sister. ''I am tired of this farce. Infect her with the virus, then we will proceed.''

Jade opened the protective wrapper on the kit. Carefully she removed the inductor and held it by the handle on the back.

Katie felt every cell in her body tense. ''Please, not that,'' she whimpered. ''Not the virus.''

''It's what you deserve.''

''Please. Anything else. Please.''

There was a look of satisfaction on Akio's face.

It barely registered with Katie. The blood pounded in her ears. Yet she didn't move a muscle. They were counting on her to be paralyzed with fear. It wasn't hard to be convincing. Her eyes were fixed on Jade as the salon owner moved forward. Maybe if she were lucky she could get herself out of this and then find out what had happened to Mac.

Jade had stepped between her and Akio, between her and the gun. Steeling herself, Katie waited until the tiny needles pressed against her flesh. Then she grabbed the woman's wrist and yanked her forward. A moment later she was standing with Jade in front of her like a shield. And ownership of the inductor had changed. Katie was holding the metal needle lightly against Jade's neck.

"Drop the gun or I'll give the virus to your sister," Katie said in a dead-level voice.

Akio looked at the two women in horror.

For a moment there was silence in the room. Then Jade began to say something in Japanese, something that changed her brother's expression to one of uncertainty. He looked pleadingly at his sister, shaking his head no. *"Iie."*

Her insistence was just as emphatic. *"Hai."*

Just then from the back of the salon came a high-pitched screech that made the hairs on the back of Katie's neck stand on end. It was followed by a crash of thunder so loud that the whole building seemed to shake. Another volley followed and then another, the noise crashing around them like the waves in the environmental room.

The truth registered in a millisecond. Mac must have seen Jade and Akio come in. Now he was doing the only thing he could to pull the gunman's attention away from her. He was working the controls of the environmental room, amplifying the effects to inhuman proportions.

Katie pushed Jade forward. As she stumbled against her brother, Katie dashed through the doorway to her right and slammed it behind her.

Two shots tore through the wood. She barely registered the sound above the roaring of the thunder. But she saw the splintered wood and ducked behind one of the nail-polish carts. Did she hear a shout from the outer office? She couldn't tell. Then more shots rang out.

Moments later a uniformed police officer barreled through the doorway, his gun drawn. He didn't see Katie.

Instead he barged right past her, heading for the back of the salon. Oh God, he was working for Perkins and he was going to shoot Mac. Without any regard for her own safety, she picked up a cut-glass vase, dumped the flowers on the floor and dashed after the policeman.

Suddenly the cacophony of the sound system died, casting the area in an eerie silence. Still clutching the vase, Katie moved to the entrance of the door, her eyes searching for Mac.

She found the police officer first. He had leveled the gun at Mac who held up his high-tech hand as if it were a weapon. "McQuade, take it easy. I'm one of the good guys."

"Then why are you pointing a gun on me?"

"So you don't kill me first and ask questions later."

One of the questions was answered by a loud sob from the front of the salon. "Akio, Akio, don't die," Jade wailed.

"Perkins got him," the young officer explained. "He's not gonna die if the ambulance gets here ASAP."

"Perkins! Isn't he working for Genesis?"

"Naw. In the past four hours he's shaken up the whole D.C. police department. He's gonna get a medal for sticking his neck out to blow this conspiracy. The guy who set him up has told us everything he knows—including about the mole at the CDC." The officer grinned. "Now, if I put my gun back in the holster, will you promise not to jump me?"

"Okay," Mac agreed. "But you walk in front of us, just in case."

"Sure thing."

In the reception area, Jade was crouched over her brother, still wailing.

"Let me see what I can do for him," Katie offered.

Jade's eyes snapped toward the physician. "Stay away from him. You have the virus."

"Katie, no!" Mac took her shoulders and turned her toward him, searching her face.

She shook her head. "Mac, she's wrong. I don't have it. She was going to give it to me. But she got the inducer from the dead batch we put back in the refrigerator—after we cooked it to 212 degrees in the environmental chamber."

The breath whooshed out of Mac's lungs as he folded her close. She buried her face against his shirtfront, wanting to stay that way for a long time—just the two of them, holding each other. However they weren't alone.

There was a muffled curse from the floor. As Katie raised her head, she saw that Jade had fixed them with a look of pure hatred. But she didn't have much time to spare for Katie and Mac because two paramedics with a stretcher were just coming through the door. They took the wounded Nishizaka down to the ambulance. A weeping Jade was handcuffed and led to a squad car.

When the brother and sister had departed, Perkins turned to Katie and Mac. "I guess you thought I was lying to you the first time we met up here."

Mac nodded.

"Well, I was the one being messed with. The guy who gave me the combination to the security system set me up. Trouble is, you got caught in the trap."

"How did you get away?" Katie asked.

"Jade had two men planted in the D.C. police department. Lucky for me, one of them had second thoughts. He turned me loose and told me what was supposed to come down. That was enough to get me in to see the chief. I would have been back sooner except that I knew they weren't planning to kill you until after they'd questioned you."

"Thanks," Katie told him.

"The Nishizakas aren't a very nice pair," Perkins observed.

"You can feel sorry for the terrible things that happened to them when they were kids. You can even understand why it warped them," Katie said.

"Warped, yeah," Mac agreed. "Nobody in their right mind hatches a plot like that."

"It was Akio's idea," Katie told him. "He was the one with vision, if you want to call it that. Jade had to go along with him because that was the traditional way in Japan. The men made all the decisions."

"Now we've still got to find out exactly how many people have the virus—and what we can do for them," Mac said. "But I have a hunch there's an antidote. Otherwise a meticulous researcher like Dr. Nishizaka wouldn't feel safe working with the stuff. Not when a lab accident would spell disaster."

"I hope you're right. If some of the effects are created before brain cells die, maybe close to normal function can even be restored. Maybe we can still save Greg. But we're going to have to find someone who reads Japanese to look through Akio's materials."

"When we find out where he moved them."

Perkins interrupted the exchange. "There are plenty of other people who can take care of that now. Probably you folks want to go home and get some rest, and we can continue the discussion tomorrow down at police headquarters."

Katie was suddenly feeling distinctly disoriented. It had seemed like she'd been carrying a boulder around on her shoulders for weeks. Now somebody had just lifted it off.

No, that wasn't quite right. She and Mac had reduced it to rubble. Now a cleanup crew was going to take care of the pieces.

She looked uncertainly at Mac and saw that he had the same bemused expression she assumed was on her own face. "Come on. Let's take the man up on the offer before he changes his mind," she urged.

Perkins laughed.

Mac nodded.

A few minutes later they were climbing into their rental car. It was early morning again. Another night on the graveyard shift, Katie thought. As she watched Mac start the engine, she felt her chest tighten painfully. It was all over except for the shouting. Only there really wasn't going to be any shouting. It would be a nice, civilized ending to a very strange interlude in both their lives. Now Mac was going to take her back to the motel to pick up her stuff, and then he'd drive her home.

But she wasn't going to let it happen that way, with no muss and no fuss. She wasn't going to slip quietly back into Mac McQuade's past. She loved him. And if explaining to a very stubborn man why they'd be crazy to simply walk away from each other was going to cause a shouting match, so be it. Only the car was no place to do it. She wanted Mac McQuade's full attention, and she didn't want him running off the road into a tree when she got it.

Silence seemed to suit Mac just fine as they headed north out of the city. Wishing it was a shorter trip, Katie leaned back and pretended to sleep. When she opened her eyes again, she was surprised to see that they were not heading for the motel. Instead they were on a two-lane road in the Maryland countryside. The scenery changed from woods to newly plowed fields, and then to expensive new houses dotting former farmland. It looked like the area south and west of Columbia.

Mac turned in at a gravel drive between two aging sections of fence. The narrow road wound upward through a stand of oaks and maples. As they cleared the trees, Katie saw the summit of a hill. The sun glinted off Mac's sports car parked at a bend in the road. But there was no other indication that they'd reached any sort of destination except an open field. Maybe he knew they were in for a shouting match, and he was going to make sure that she had all the open space she needed to exercise her lungs.

When he pulled up beside his car and cut the engine, she looked at him inquiringly.

"My house."

"Where?"

"Under the hill."

"Right. I forgot you were the dragon under the hill," Katie murmured.

"What?"

"Nothing."

"I thought this would be a better place to talk than the motel room. Maybe it's not such a good idea."

"No, no. This is fine." Katie followed Mac about fifty feet up the road and around a bend to the front of the house, which featured a broad expanse of glass looking out over a meandering river in the valley below.

"Brighton Dam Reservoir," Mac answered her unspoken question.

"Nice view."

"I like it." Mac turned abruptly to unlock the door.

Katie wasn't sure what she'd expected. Once Mac had closed the door, she noted that the floor-to-ceiling window and a skylight kept the room from being dark. Yet there was a feeling of safety from the protection of the earth around them.

Safety from outside interferences. Now that they weren't going to be interrupted, neither one of them seemed to want to start a serious discussion.

Katie focused on the room's decor. The furniture was pine—more serviceable than showy. It contributed to the solid, homey look of the interior.

"Do you want anything?"

"Not now. I—I should call Jo and let her know we're all right."

"Yes. There's a phone in the kitchen."

Katie assured Jo they were safe and gave her a few details about the Nishizakas. Yet as she hung up, she found herself taking a deep breath before she went to find Mac.

He was standing stiffly by the window, looking down at the lake, and she imagined that he often studied the view while he was thinking. "Everything I said the other day about us was true," he said without turning.

Katie felt her heart plummet to her toes. "And?" she managed.

"But I feel like something inside me is going to shrivel up and die if I have to give you up again."

She didn't want him to see the sudden blooming of hope on her face. It would be too terrible if he were only trying to find a way to tell her that he still couldn't place her in his future. Instead she came up behind him, slipped her arms around his waist and pressed her cheek into his shoulder. "You don't have to give me up. In fact, it's going to be a hell of a lot harder to get rid of me this time."

He laughed. "I kind of sensed that. But this is more than just the happy ending tacked on to the dangerous adventure we've just been through. It's dealing with all the day-to-day things I haven't been able to face since the accident.''

"I think part of the problem is that you've been imagining my life has been something like 'Dr. Martin Makes It Big.' It hasn't been quite that way. In fact, there's something that happened to me a couple of years ago that was pretty hard to take.''

He turned so that he was facing her, draping his arms loosely over her shoulders.

She tipped her face up toward his. "I don't talk about this much. Maybe I should have told you before, but I didn't quite know how to start. Do you remember the big scandal at the Sterling Clinic? Front page in the *Sun Papers* for a couple of weeks?''

"The Sterling Clinic. You mean that place in Mount Washington that had to close because of what a few of the doctors were doing? *You* worked there?''

"Yes. Abby Franklin, a friend of mine, uncovered the plot. Of course, I wasn't involved with what was going on. But like everybody else on the staff, I got covered with the debris when the dirt hit the fan. For six months I couldn't get another job. Even Medizone rejected me for a research position that was advertised. The director of personnel said I was overqualified.'' She shrugged. "Maybe that really was the reason. Who knows?''

"I'm sorry it happened, but I never saw your résumé.''

"Even if you had, you wouldn't have called me in for an interview.''

"Not because of a medical scandal that had nothing to do with you personally.''

"Well, it was only one of a slew of rejections. Having a medical degree isn't the guarantee of success that you've built it into.''

He stroked his hand up her back. "I guess you had a pretty hard time. I'm sorry."

"For a while I was depressed. Abby—she's a psychologist—helped me put things in perspective. She suggested I try getting myself a foundation grant. I wrote a proposal and it was accepted. She even offered me the use of her office while she was out of the country. And I've been pleased with what I've been doing. Now I realize that I'm really happier in research than in clinical practice. I thought everything was going fine, until I bumped into you in that closet and found out what's been missing from my life."

"Ah, Katie. What the hell are we going to do?" He didn't give her a chance to answer the question. His hand tangled in her hair and brought her eager mouth to his. Her tiny, indrawn murmur of approval was swallowed up as his mouth covered hers and he kissed her with all the hunger that she knew he'd been trying to hold in check. His hunger matched hers. So did the tension in his body. When he finally lifted his head, they were both trembling.

"Are you going to show me your bedroom?" she asked in a breathy voice.

"I want to." He shook his head slowly. "When I'm with you, when I hold you in my arms and kiss you, all I want is to make love to you."

"Mac, that's the way I feel, too. That's the way it's supposed to be between a man and a woman who've discovered that they love each other," she said softly.

He gazed down into her glistening eyes and swallowed. "Yeah. I heard you say it. You told me you loved me just before we went under. I could have said it, too. Knowing I love you is the hardest part. I've been alone a long time. I haven't been able to go back and see my family. Hell, I don't know the first thing about being a decent husband. I don't know if I—''

She pressed gentle fingers over his lips. "Hush up and listen to me. Eight years ago, something terrible happened to you. You lost your hand. You lost your career. You lost your sense of self-worth. You felt abandoned by your family. And you told yourself you didn't want the pity of the woman who was closest to you.''

"That's quite an analysis.''

"Let me finish. That was then. This is now. You're different. But that doesn't mean weaker. It means stronger. You've proved you can manage very well without a left hand. In fact, you can do some pretty extraordinary things with the replacement you're wearing. You've shown the world you could succeed at a tough, demanding career. You've found out that the last thing the woman you sent away wants to give you is pity.'' The words had been bold. Now, almost afraid to hear Mac's response, Katie removed her fingers from his lips.

"How long have you been working up to tell me all that?''

"It came to me in bits and pieces—things I knew I had to say to you if the two of us were going to make it. I decided it was easier to get it out in one fell swoop.''

"Well, there was more you could have touched on. Like my anger and resentment. You know, the kind of anger that came out when I had poor Arnie Beale strapped to that autopsy table.''

"Poor Arnie Beale was a hired killer. He tried to run us over, remember? You had plenty of reason to be angry with him. Not only that, you were under a lot of stress. We both were. People act out hostilities when they're stressed. But if you want to take your emotional temperature, I think the way you made love to me is a better indicator.''

He closed his eyes for a moment and she knew he was remembering that first time—just the way she was.

"Or the way you saved my life," she whispered. "Or the way you kissed me when you didn't know whether I had the virus."

They were both silent for several heartbeats. Finally she began to speak again in a low voice. "If the MD after my name still makes a difference and you're worried about competing with me professionally, you could give me a job as medical director of Medizone. Then we won't be competing. We'll both be on the same team. And if I write any papers for medical journals, it will be with you as the coauthor. In addition, I have one other stipulation. Either you find someone else to send on those jungle trips, or you take me along."

A slow grin spread across Mac's face. "You really did think this whole thing out, didn't you?"

"I had to. I knew I had to have a viable proposal ready."

"Are you sure you're not bucking for the job of administrator instead of the medical director?"

"I can help you out, if you're in a bind. But I'm afraid I like research better."

"You're so sure of yourself. What if you're wrong about this jerk named Mac McQuade who left you flat eight years ago?"

She laughed. "Let's put that in the past tense with a lot of other old stuff. Mac, I love you. Nothing has ever seemed more right than the two of us together."

"Oh God, Katie. I don't think I can keep fighting any longer. Not when the idea of giving you up is making every nerve in my body raw."

"Thank the Lord."

"Katie, I love you so much." He traced her lips gently with his finger. "It feels so good to say that."

"It feels good to hear it."

He pulled her tighter against the length of his body. "I guess Tom was right all along."

"Tom?"

"I didn't tell you about going through his files after he died. The reason he got together with Val in the first place was because he wanted to contact you."

"What did he want from me?"

"Tom was the only person I could really open up to. A couple of times I talked to him about you. I guess he figured out I needed you."

"How did you feel when you found that out?" she murmured.

"I was upset. Now I'm grateful."

"Oh, Mac. I wish I'd met him—when he was all right."

"I wish you had, too."

They stood holding each other for several moments. "So many terrible things have happened," Katie whispered.

"Then let's make sure something very good comes out of it."

She tipped her head up and gave him a radiant smile. "That proposition, McQuade, deserves some in-depth research."

TRIAL BY FIRE

Prologue

Preparation was everything. Preparation and a heightened awareness of the dark currents that ebbed and flowed through the affairs of men. Currents you could use to your advantage, if you knew the ancient formulas. Currents that could sweep you into oblivion if you made the wrong move.

"Grant the success of this venture." Murmuring an incantation, the Servant of Darkness stepped through the door of the hidden chamber.

Black curtains were the backdrop of power here. They hung from floor to ceiling around the elongated room, shrouding walls and windows and even the door—shutting out what others called reality. Making a cocoon of solitude, and a nexus of power. For there was only one person who entered this secret place and came out alive.

There were no electric lights. Only dozens of long white tapers made in the ancient way from the fat of slaughtered animals and fitted into antique brass candelabra.

A table opposite the door held an open brass bowl. It was full of oil. But the oil was only an inert medium. The important part was the viscous liquid tinged a delicate pink, streaking the contents like the faintest trace of blood.

"For I will see the face of mine enemy." The Servant

of Darkness went down on bended knees before the open bowl and offered a few words in the ancient formula. There were many ceremonies that could be performed in this private refuge. The one tonight was of special, urgent importance.

"And I will smite any who come to challenge my power. From the past and from the present."

There was a moment of silence while the feeling of strength and energy mounted. Then a practiced hand struck a long thin match and touched the flame to the oil. The fuel flared up, and as the mixture ignited, the essence of rotten cherries billowed forth, along with a strong mind-altering drug.

It wasn't a pleasant smell. Yet the occupant of the room leaned over the bowl and breathed deeply, welcoming the momentary sense of dislocation in time and space that the hallucinogen brought. For the unprepared, it could be a terrifying experience. For the initiated, the disorientation would clear away almost at once. Soon it would be replaced by the sure, sharp vision that had served for so many years.

Still on bended knees, the sorcerer approached the inlaid table in the exact center of the chamber. A large square of white silk—the only bit of cloth in the chamber that wasn't black—was mounded in the center.

Knowing fingers caressed the fabric, slick and smooth as a serpent's belly. Then the silk was whisked away to reveal the centerpiece of the room. A perfect sphere of pure crystal. Ten inches across, it rested in a dark metal stand.

"I will see the face of mine enemy," the Servant of Darkness repeated. This time it was a command—a gathering of forces.

The candle flames flickered in the mysterious depth of

the crystal ball, reflected in an endless pattern. Then, among the flames a face appeared.

It was a woman's countenance, hauntingly delicate and framed by a wreath of long red curls. Even the spray of freckles across the nose and cheeks had a winsome appeal.

Sara Campbell. Oh so pure. Oh so innocent.

The sorcerer hunched forward, staring down fixedly at the image shimmering in the crystal, watching the features blur and change subtly. As the face reformed, the skin became clear and translucent. The hazel eyes altered to sea green. The straggly brows were almost tamed.

Different.

Yet the same, for the superficialities were insignificant. More important was the vital spirit of Sara Campbell. The will. The soul within. Sara Campbell might be dead. But her essence had been reborn in a woman living now. In Sabrina Barkley.

"The cycle comes around again. But the master grants a second chance," the cruel voice intoned.

Yes! In this life, things would be different. But first, the two images must be brought together. Merged. Fused. The woman from the past. And the woman of the present. When Sabrina Barkley finally understood the full extent of the horror, she would be destroyed for all time. And the Servant of Darkness would glory in the victory.

Chapter One

In the dim light of the parking garage across from 43 Light Street, Sabrina Barkley folded her hands on the steering wheel and rested her head on her arms for a moment. Although she usually arrived at work full of energy, for the past few days she'd awakened feeling as if she'd spent the night running from an unseen pursuer. The dragging fatigue was accompanied by a sharp sense of anxiety that pressed her shoulder blades taut against the car seat.

Sabrina drew in a deep breath and let it out slowly. She wasn't going to indulge in a case of the jitters now. She had too much to do. Straightening her shoulders, she strode across the street to Sabrina's Fancy, the lobby shop she'd opened on a shoestring a few years ago.

As she walked in the door, her assistant, Erin Morgan, gave her an appraising look. "Hmm. Which is it? Good news or bad?"

Sabrina forced a laugh. "Both. Remember those proposals I've been writing to hotels and restaurants?"

"Of course."

"Well, the hospitality manager at the Harbor Court Hotel called yesterday afternoon. They're featuring local crafts people in some of their promotions, and they've ordered two hundred and fifty of my bath-herb-and-soap baskets to put in their suites for the Mid-Atlantic tourism conference."

"Way to go!"

"Now all I have to do is find the time to make them up."

"You could hire some helpers."

"You're right. I keep forgetting I'm doing well enough for that. But I'd better sit and figure out what extra supplies I'll need."

"I'll take care of things out front."

"Thanks."

As Sabrina crossed to her office, she gave silent thanks once more for Erin Morgan's quiet strength, although she knew her assistant felt just as lucky to be working here as she was to have found her. Erin's husband had been one of the casualties of the Gulf War, and she'd told Sabrina more than once how relieved she was to find a job that allowed her to support her young son and still work on the college degree that was so important to her future plans.

Sabrina closed the office door. A year ago she'd started to decorate the small room but had never really finished. It was dominated by the former school library table she used as a work surface and the antique pigeonhole desk she'd picked up in Fells Point at a going-out-of-business sale. Also squeezed into her private domain were a sofa where she sometimes snatched an afternoon nap and a narrow bookshelf crammed with reference volumes. Well, so much for Victorian elegance. At least the packets of herbs in the storage boxes always smelled good.

Usually Sabrina functioned well in the comfortable clutter, but now that she was alone again, another wave of uneasiness washed over her. Scraping back the desk chair with a jerky motion, she sat and felt her body sag again. After a few moments she made an effort to pull herself together and get to work. She hadn't spent years building up her business so she could fall apart when she got her first big chance to show her stuff.

The seminar on small-business strategies she'd taken last month had suggested that when you were planning a new venture, you should write down all the ideas that came to you, without worrying about details. Kind of like brainstorming with yourself. That was worth a try.

After squaring off at the desk, she picked up a pen and began to scribble on a white pad of paper. Color schemes. Scents. Textures. Herbs. Dried flowers. Unusual? Rosemary. Angelica. Lace. Satin ribbons. Too feminine? Lemon balm. Pastel tissue paper. Excelsior. White lacquer baskets.

At first the thoughts followed each other in rapid succession. Then the inspiration dried up. Sabrina fidgeted restlessly on her chair. All at once it was stuffy in the little office. No—suffocating. Although she dragged several deep breaths into her lungs, it seemed the oxygen didn't help much.

Sabrina tried to focus on what she'd written, but as she bent over the paper, the lines of script blurred. Alarm settled like a lead weight on her chest, pressing the air out of her chest.

The sensation became more acute as the whole room wavered. For an awful moment, currents of heat seemed to ripple through her head, playing over the surface of her brain like static electricity. Frantically her fingers gripped the shaft of the ballpoint pen she was still holding. Then her hand began to move across the page again. But this time the writing instrument took control—as if it were a magic wand and she were under some strange spell. Words and sentences flowed from the tip of the pen. Against her will, they dragged her away with them. Away to another time and another place.

...at the very moment Sara stepped out the door, a screeching raven dived toward the roof of the little cottage.

"No! Get ye gone." Dropping her basket, she rushed at the creature, flapping her apron. But to no avail. The bird circled the chimney before flying off toward the pines at the edge of the clearing.

Heart blocking her windpipe, Sara stood trembling in the little farmyard.

A raven so close to the house. A bad omen.

It was even more terrible if one of the huge black birds went round the chimney. A warning of death.

Gran had been sick this past fortnight. But she wasn't going to die! She couldn't!

"What is it, child?" a weak voice called from within.

Sara poked her head back inside, seeing the old woman covered with rough wool blankets and lying on her bed in the far corner of the cottage. "Just a bee buzzing my face," she fibbed, curling her bare toes in the muddy ground by the door. "Are ye sure naught will trouble ye while I'm gone?"

"Aye. Just get that wintergreen to soothe my old bones, and I'll be bonny. And gather some mountain thyme and coltsfoot. We'll be needing those, as well."

Torn, Sara hesitated.

"Go on, lass."

"Aye." Knuckles white against the dark basket handle, she started toward the craggy mountains. Yet once she was out in the heather with the wind picking up her red hair and the sun warming her lightly freckled face, she acknowledged how sick she was of the dank stone cottage after a week of rain.

First she gathered wintergreen. Then she picked some of the other plants she'd learned to make into healing potions or use to flavor their simple food. She knew all the best places to look, and her basket was quickly full. Then above her on the side of the cliff, she spied a patch of rock speedwell. Gran was partial to the deep blue flowers, each petal with a crimson line at the base.

Setting her basket on a flat slab, Sara began to climb. When she reached the first ledge, she went on to the next. Few of the other village girls would have taken such chances, but timidity had never been one of her virtues. Minutes later, she smiled in satisfaction at her prize, a bouquet that would brighten their humble table. Needing both hands to scramble down, she tucked the flowers in the bodice laces of her wool dress.

She was still twenty yards from the valley floor when she heard hooves pounding across the rocky ground. The animal was dark and magnificent—a destrier, one of the highly trained battle horses. The rider must be a laird from the castle, judging from his rich cloak and fine leather boots. He was having trouble with the mount, yet he might have kept control of the beast if one of Sara's bare feet hadn't slipped on a patch of loose stone.

"Beware," she cried out.

He looked up just as the rocks rained down the side of the mountain toward him.

Too late.

As the missiles struck the horse, the animal screamed and bucked. Horrified, Sara saw the rider tossed into the air, his fall broken by a clump of gorse.

The horse galloped on. The man lay motionless.

Dead.

The omen had been meant for him.

Sara looked around. No one had seen the accident. If

she ran right home, the lairds would never know what she had done. Yet even as the cowardly thought surfaced, she moved toward the still figure.

He lay sprawled on his stomach. Kneeling, she grasped him by the shoulders and rolled him over. His eyes were closed, and gold-tipped lashes lay softly against his tanned cheeks. When she touched his face to brush away the dirt, she sensed the first hint of the man's beard that hadn't fully grown in. His age couldn't be much more than her own fifteen years.

As her fingers touched his skin, he groaned.

He was alive!

With the skills Gran had taught her, she began to assess the damage. His white lawn shirt was covered with dirt. Of more concern was the torn leg of his britches. It was soaked with blood above the knee. Her hands were tearing at the fabric when strong fingers locked around her wrist.

"A wood sprite." His eyes were open now—and as blue as the stained glass in the window of the cathedral. With a shaky hand, he reached out and touched her fiery tresses. His fingers dropped to her shoulder and trailed slowly down to the bright flowers she'd tucked into her bodice. When he rustled through the foliage, she felt the pressure against her breasts. No one had ever touched her so familiarly. For a moment the breath froze in her throat as she gazed down at the hand. It was broad and well-formed—a foreteller of toughness and power to come. She couldn't move. Then, summoning her own strength, she brushed the fingers away.

"Be still," she ordered. "You've been hurt."

He moved his head and groaned, then tried to pull away from her. "You threw rocks down on me."

"Nay. It was but an accident. I meant you no harm.

Please. I'm a skilled healer,'' she said, overstating her
abilities a bit. *"Let me help you."*

He closed his eyes and lay back with a sigh while Sara
retrieved her basket. Luckily she'd gathered some verbena.
A poultice would start the healing of his wounds.

At a nearby stream, she tore several strips of cloth from
her petticoat and dipped them in the cold water. Then,
back at the lad's side, she began to clean his thigh.

Although she saw him clench his teeth as she picked
embedded gravel from his flesh, he didn't cry out.

"You're from the castle?" she asked to distract him
from the pain.

"I—"

"SABRINA! SABRINA!" His hand was on her arm. Shaking
her. But he was hurt. Where did he get the strength? She
stared at the hand in utter confusion. Too small. Too feminine.

"Sabrina. What's wrong?" An anxious voice floated toward her from somewhere close by. Her gaze fluttered
from the hand that gripped her arm to a face that was
vaguely familiar, but not a man's. It belonged to a red-
haired lass.

Sabrina fought a rising sense of panic. Her eyes bounced
from the intruder to the room and back again as she tried
desperately to get a fix on reality. The young woman
kneeling beside her. The place. The time. Herself.

It took every ounce of self-control to hold back a
scream. She was trapped here. But who was she? Where
was she? What was she supposed to be doing?

"Hey, are you going to pass out on me or something?"

The familiar voice and the urgent question were like a
lifeline, and she clutched at them with all her strength. Inch
by inch, she pulled herself to firmer ground.

"Jo?" she finally managed, her voice high and reedy as she stared at private detective Jo O'Malley. Her friend. "What are you doing out in the mountain pass?"

"Mountain pass?"

From the expression on Jo's face, Sabrina knew she must have said something outrageous. She looked away, praying for a safe place to rest her gaze. This time the room made more sense.

It belonged to her, Sabrina Barkley. And she was in the little office at the rear of her shop. Profound relief swept over her. Somehow she felt as if she'd just escaped an unspeakable fate, and she didn't even know what it was.

"You looked like you were in a trance."

"No. Really." Sabrina sat up straighter and cleared her throat, even as she wondered exactly what she was going to say. "I was, uh, using a brainstorming technique I picked up at a small-business seminar." To her surprise, she sounded almost coherent. Encouraged, she continued, "I guess I just got carried away."

She was still congratulating herself on her quick recovery when her eyes flicked back to the pen still clutched in her hand and the lines of script slanting across the page in front of her. A woman climbing rocks. A man falling from a horse.

The handwriting was familiar but the words seemed to have sprung from nowhere. Or her subconscious. Her heart started to pound. My God, what had she written? Reflexively she slapped a herb-seed catalog down on top of the pages.

"You don't have to make up a cock-and-bull story about what you're doing. I didn't know you were into writing fiction. But that's pretty good stuff. Lots of nice description."

"Hmm?"

"That historical novel. I guess you were pretty into it, huh?"

With a profound sigh of gratitude, Sabrina let the misconception stand. "I feel kind of silly, getting all wound up in, uh, something I'm writing."

"I know what you mean. Sometimes that happens with the crime fiction I'm working on."

Sabrina had forgotten Jo wrote detective stories. Now she gave her friend a conspiratorial smile. "So don't tell anybody you caught me, okay?"

"Sure. I understand. It's hard to show your work when you're just getting started." Jo pursed her lips, stood, and leaned on the edge of the worktable. "I was going to ask you a favor. I wish I hadn't barged in like this."

"Jo. It's okay. Honestly."

"Well, a friend needs a special favor."

"Dried bouquets?"

"No, he needs to borrow some of your expertise."

"With growing herbs?"

Jo sighed. "I guess there's just no good way to introduce the subject. It's got to do with the Graveyard Murders."

Sabrina couldn't repress an involuntary shudder. The strange murder cases had been headline news in the *Morning Sun* off and on for weeks. When the first article had appeared, she'd read the whole thing with a sort of morbid curiosity. But the story had given her a very spooky feeling that had made her studiously avoid any of the later accounts. "Is one of your clients involved?"

"No, but the assistant district attorney assigned to the case is trying to get a lead on some of the evidence, and I thought you might be able to help him."

Sabrina's fingers curled around the edge of the chair

seat. The trapped feeling she'd thought she had under control had come screaming back.

Murder. The occult. The first newspaper article had given her the sense of something evil growing and thriving in a dark, obscure corner of the city. She'd been thankful it didn't involve her. Now she felt as if it had crept a step closer. But she didn't want to tell that to Jo, not when she'd successfully convinced her friend she was okay. And she didn't want to give in to the sense of dread she felt. Really, it was probably left over from whatever had happened to her with that story she'd been writing.

So she hid her reaction behind a flippant tone. "If this is another one of your attempts to fix me up with an eligible bachelor, forget it. That computer-designer friend of Cam's couldn't talk about anything but chips and parallel processors."

"This is on the up-and-up. You've heard of Dan Cassidy, haven't you?"

Sabrina thought for a moment. "The guy who was leading the fight to take back the streets from the big-time drug dealers last year?"

"Yes."

"I've read about him. He's supposed to be tough. So what exactly does he need from me?"

"Dan's looking for an expert opinion."

"On what? I don't know anything about drugs. Except for some of the herbal compounds. And they aren't going to command big bucks on the street."

"It's better if *he* tells you what he wants," Jo hurried on. "He's springing for lunch at Sabatino's."

"Did you tell him it was my favorite restaurant?"

"Of course."

Jo must have sensed her wavering. "Twelve-thirty," she said.

"Oh, all right. We can walk over together."

"Um, I can't. I'm testifying in one of Laura's child-abduction cases." Laura Roswell was a lawyer who also worked in the building. Married last month, she was finally getting back to a full schedule after a honeymoon on the West Coast.

"It's just you and Dan," Jo continued. "You'll like him."

"I don't have to like him. This is supposed to be business."

"Okay. Forget that part. But you need to know what he looks like so you can find him. He's got blond hair and blue eyes. He told me to tell you he's wearing a gray suit and a blue-and-gray rep tie."

Sabrina looked down at her own jade green caftan woven with gold threads. "We should make a striking couple."

"Sweetie, you can ditch him right after lunch if you want."

Sabrina watched her friend disappear through the open doorway. Then, almost against her will, her eyes were drawn back to the seed catalog she'd slapped on top of the pad of paper on her desk. Getting up, she closed the door very softly. Her heart started to pound again as she moved the catalog and began to scan what she'd written.

"Color schemes…herbs…satin ribbons…"

As she continued to read, a knot of tension grew in her stomach.

"…at the very moment Sara stepped out the door, a screeching raven dived toward the roof of the little cottage."

The knot expanded, pressing against her diaphragm. The story was so vivid. So real. Where had it sprung from? Then a memory came racing back into her mind like a rescue vehicle with sirens blaring. She'd done this same sort of thing a long time ago. As a kid, when she was feeling sad or unhappy or needed to escape, she'd go out behind the woodpile and tell herself little stories about a girl who lived in a cottage in the mountains with her grandmother. That explained what had happened a few minutes ago. She'd been insecure about the big hotel commission, so she'd regressed or something. Instead of buckling down to planning herb baskets, she'd started writing a romantic tale about another woman from a different time and place.

Sabrina pursed her lips, silently admitting that this had been different. As a little girl, she'd sought the solace of the stories when she was unhappy. This time, it was more like some outside force had compelled her to write. In fact, to be perfectly honest, she couldn't actually remember having composed this vignette.

Sabrina grimaced, feeling suddenly as if bony fingers were pressing into her shoulder. She knew no one was there. Still, it was all she could do to keep from looking over her shoulder. Pushing back her chair, she crossed to the bookshelves and stood with her arms folded, facing the room.

She wished she hadn't said yes to Jo. Instead of blowing her valuable time meeting some guy for lunch, she should be focusing on the work she had to do and also finding out if Erin needed any help. As she stepped into the front of the shop, she found her assistant restocking their inventory of culinary herbs. Her rich brown hair hid her face as she bent over the box of plastic packets.

"I hear you're meeting one of Baltimore's VIPs for lunch," she said.

Oh great, Sabrina thought. Now if I cancel, I'll have to explain myself to three people. But what exactly would

she say? She didn't really want to talk about the strange
feeling that had been hovering over her all morning.

THE LOCKUP DOORS slammed shut behind Dan Cassidy.
This time he was on the outside of the grim gray walls
that surrounded the Baltimore City Jail. Pausing, he rolled
his broad shoulders and sucked in a deep draft of the un-
fettered air, letting the breath out slowly. It didn't matter
why you were inside the jail. You always emerged totaling
up your sins and feeling grateful for your freedom.

This morning, he should also be feeling overjoyed that
he had Raul Simmons behind bars with a signed confession to the Graveyard Murders. Everybody else was satisfied with the way things had turned out. After finding
one of the victim's wallets at Simmons's house, the police
had been happy enough to turn the case over to the district
attorney's office. And the mayor was pressing for a quick
conviction before the fall election.

Dan strode across the parking lot to his car. As far as
he was concerned, there were too many things that didn't
add up. Like the witchcraft angle, for example. Every time
he tried to get Simmons to talk about casting spells and
performing rituals, the man just smiled his secret smile. It
might be the ploy of a coy sorcerer. Or the refuge of a
man who didn't know a broomstick from a toad's tongue.

Pausing with his fist on the door handle, Dan considered
another loose end. The Sabrina Barkley connection. A
crumpled gold-foil token with her logo had been found in
a victim's pocket. It had taken a week of digging to tie
the exuberantly stylized double ess to the lobby shop at
43 Light Street. After that, he'd had her checked out. On
the surface, she was an upstanding if slightly eccentric
member of the business community. But he'd always gone
with his hunches, and the more he sifted through the in-

formation he'd accumulated about her, the more he felt as if something didn't add up.

The direct approach—the one he'd always taken in the past—would be to bring her in for questioning. He couldn't explain to himself why he was hesitating. Why he'd asked Jo to set up an appointment with Ms. Barkley. All she was supposed to think was that he wanted to use her for background on the case. Maybe he'd learn something about witchcraft by talking to her. It just wasn't his main agenda.

Realizing he was sitting in the car with the engine idling, Dan shifted into reverse and pulled out of his parking space. Ten minutes later he was back in front of the stately marble elegance of the Clarence Mitchell Courthouse. From the outside, it looked a heck of a lot better than the jail. Inside, it was a crowded rabbit warren. Luckily, as an assistant district attorney, he rated his own office, even if it was barely big enough for a desk, computer, filing cabinets and visitor's chair.

His secretary, Edna Strause, gave him a summary of the crises he'd missed while he'd been interviewing Simmons. However, there was one piece of halfway-good news.

"Ms. Barkley will meet you for lunch," Edna reported.

"Fine." He ignored the speculative look in his secretary's eyes and closed the door to his office.

It was a relief to loosen his tie and shrug out of his suit coat. Still, it wasn't easy to get down to work. On most days, he thrived on his job. He liked the hectic pace, the hard-fought trials, the negotiations, and especially the satisfaction of bringing criminals to justice. But not when the police dumped a half-baked case in his lap and expected him to produce something a judge could swallow.

AFTER ALMOST A WEEK of clouds and showers, sunlight was finally flooding through the fan transom over the entrance to 43 Light Street. A good omen, Sabrina told herself firmly as she pulled open one of the heavy brass-and-glass doors.

She started briskly down the hill toward the inner harbor. However, during the three-quarters of a mile walk to Baltimore's Little Italy—a neighborhood of row houses where almost every corner sported a restaurant, deli or bakery—her pace slowed considerably. In her enthusiasm for the sunshine, she must have misjudged the effects of the heat and the humidity, because by the time she reached the restaurant's black and white tile entry, she was feeling a bit like a wilted amaryllis in a 110-degree greenhouse.

Usually the aroma of onions sautéing in olive oil and chicken simmering in tomato-wine sauce made her mouth water. Today as she followed the maître d' past street scenes of old Baltimore to Dan Cassidy's table, she fought against a slight feeling of queasiness.

As they approached a darkened corner, the maître d' stepped out of the way and gestured toward a man seated at a table. The man's face and shoulders were in shadow. In fact, from where she stood, her best view was of a pair of long legs crossed at the ankles and protruding from under the table. It should have been an easy pose, yet as her eye traveled upward, she noticed that his fingers were tightly gripped around his water glass. When she took a step closer, he leaned forward and looked up.

God, she thought, he looked like Robert Redford in *Legal Eagles*.

Redford had spotted her. He stood, towering over her. Their eyes met, hers uncertain, his appraising.

"Ms. Barkley?"

"Mr. Cassidy."

His hand was extended, and she automatically reached

to grasp his palm. As their flesh touched, a jolt of unexpected sensation went through her. Not something physical, exactly. More like an electrical charge right to her brain. It brought disorientation, a wave of heat across her skin, and something she couldn't name. Something from deep, deep in her subconscious.

Sabrina blinked as she recognized the sensations. They were similar to what had happened this morning, when the stupid list had turned into a scene from a historical novel.

Cassidy must have caught the odd expression on her face. "Are you feeling all right?"

For the second time today, she smiled and lied. "Just reacting to the weather, I guess." She drew herself up straighter. "I understand you need some help on a case."

"Yeah. I need some insights, all right. But maybe we should have some lunch before we discuss murder."

Chapter Two

Well, at least he had a sense of humor. Or maybe it wasn't meant to be a joke.

While Cassidy studied his menu, Sabrina studied him, scanning his face, trying for the quick insights she often gleaned.

Cassidy was too tall to play Redford. And too tough. The left side of his square jaw was marred by a small scar. And there was a ready-for-action way he carried his body that didn't quite go with the conservative suit and tie.

The blue eyes hidden from view as he gazed down at the menu wouldn't soften the effect. Sabrina couldn't say the same for his lashes. They were like gold fringe dipped with dark ink.

The waiter came and took their order. As soon as he'd left, her attention turned back to her companion. With a wry inner laugh, she realized she wasn't tuning into anything more than the very masculine physical package across the table from her. Dan Cassidy might make her feel off balance, but that didn't mean she wasn't attracted to him. Focusing her concentration, she tried to reach for something deeper, and came up against an almost-impenetrable wall. His guard was up. Against her? Or was he always like this with strangers? At the very least, she had the feeling he didn't like asking for advice.

He glanced up suddenly, discovered her watching and gave her a piercing look she felt all the way to the pit of her stomach.

"Jo says you're in the herb business," Dan said.

"Yes. I started growing them and researching old uses."

"So how did you get from herbs to the arcane?"

"I'm not exactly into the arcane. I hope that's not what Jo told you."

"She said you have a lot of talents. And now you have your own business?"

"Yes."

"What do you sell?"

"Herb products. Some jewelry. Dried flowers." She gestured with her hands. "Anything that catches my fancy. That's how the shop got its name. So what makes you think I can help you?"

Dan didn't answer. He was staring at the double gold ess charm dangling from her bracelet. "You sell those?"

"It's my logo. I put a foil one in with each purchase as a personalized touch."

"Why a double ess?"

"I got to playing with my name and liked this design."

"The charms must be expensive."

"Not really. I get thousands at a time."

"So your business must be doing pretty well."

"I can pay the bills."

"How did you get started?"

His rapid-fire questions went beyond casual interest. In fact, they made her feel as if she were on the witness stand, and she had the odd sensation that he already knew most of the answers. Still, it was difficult not to respond.

"When I was a kid, my family lived in a little community on Stony Creek. I had a crazy old aunt who loved the shore. She used to park herself at our house every summer for a couple of weeks. The rest of the family hated her visits because the place was already pretty crowded. But I'd sit there fascinated when she'd read my palm and tell my fortune from my tea leaves. When she died, it turned out that she had a pretty nice nest egg socked away in the bank. She left it to me.''

"Lucky you. So what do you see in my palm?" Cassidy asked unexpectedly.

Sabrina glanced up at him, aware of a challenge in his blue eyes. At the same time, she remembered the jolt when they'd shaken hands. She wanted to brush off the request. Really, this was silly. She only had a passing acquaintance with palmistry, but Cassidy was offering her an opportunity to prove to herself that the previous reaction had been nothing more than the culmination of her own nervous anticipation. She reached for the large hand he'd extended, cupping it between her smaller ones.

At first neither one of them moved—or breathed. The touch of his warm, dry skin had a strangely mind-emptying effect. When she finally remembered what she was supposed to be doing, Sabrina cast her eyes downward toward his palm.

"Will I get a conviction in the murder-one case I'm putting together?" he asked.

The edge of mockery in his voice brought her back. All at once she thought she understood where he was coming from—why he'd asked so many questions. He wanted to find out whether she was out in left field before he told her about the case. Maybe she'd give him something to think about. "Your life line is very curved and your head line is almost ramrod straight. That's a classic setup for conflict."

"Like what?"

She traced her finger along the crease that made a semi-circle around his thumb. The Mount of Venus at the base was pronounced—a sign of sensuality. She wasn't going to tell him that. Or that he had a strong primitive streak. Not in so many words.

At her touch, his muscles contracted. She wanted to search his face again. Instead she kept her head tipped downward and moved his hand into better light. Now she could see a definite break near where the life line began.

"Did you have a life-altering event in your childhood?"

Sabrina felt his whole body tense and knew that she'd touched a raw nerve. But when her eyes flicked to his face, it was carefully blank. Like a closed door that was marked private.

She swallowed. "Really, we don't have to keep on with this."

The tense look softened into a knowing smile. With his other hand, he took her thumb and pressed it against the pad of skin below his index finger. "Aren't you going to tell me about my Mount of Jupiter?"

Any speculations about his early life were swept away by prickles of sensation that started where he held her thumb against his flesh. She'd felt nervous since she'd met the man, and she fought to deny the response. "Yours denotes assertiveness. Competitiveness. A respect for hard facts. A tendency to scoff at what you don't understand. Am I getting warm?"

She looked up, ignoring the way his blue eyes bored into her. "Why didn't you tell me you'd done this before?"

To her surprise, he laughed, but he didn't let go of her hand. In fact, neither one of them moved.

"We had a palm reader up on a grand-larceny charge

six months ago. She kept trying to convince me that my destiny would work out for the better if I reduced the charge to petty theft."

"And?"

"I guess if she could really predict the future, she'd have stayed a step ahead of the police."

Sabrina raised her chin. "We both know making predictions about specific happenings in the future from looking at a person's palm is about as scientific as running the presidency based on astrological predictions, but each person's hand is still unique. And lines etched there reflect not only physical attributes, but character and personality." She pointed to the fourth finger of his left hand. "There's a very faint mark at the base here. Either you got tired of your class ring, or you took off a wedding band a couple of years ago."

He didn't move a muscle. "Divorced."

They became aware that they were still holding hands and that the waiter had arrived with their food.

Dan took his hand back. She folded hers in her lap.

Halfway through the meal, Cassidy cleared his throat. "Sorry. You're right. I wasn't being fair. This case is putting a lot of pressure on me, but I shouldn't have taken my frustration out on you."

"Want to tell me something about it?"

"Yes. Do the names Ian Alastair or Bette Kronstat mean anything to you?"

Sabrina thought hard. Ian? Did she know an Ian?

She looked up to find Cassidy watching her closely. "No. I don't think so."

"They're the two victims of the Graveyard Murders. We didn't know their names initially, because neither one was found with any identification." He looked around the room. Most of the lunch crowd had cleared out, and the nearby tables were now unoccupied. "I'm sure you've read something about it. Kronstat was found first. Then Alastair. In different graveyards."

Sabrina's fingers wadded the napkin in her lap. "Wasn't there supposed to be a ritual aspect to the murders?"

"Yes. And we've got a confession from a guy who says he did it. The problem is, I'm not sure I believe him." Reaching down beside his chair, he brought out a glossy photograph. "Would you mind taking a look at this?"

In the dim light, Sabrina couldn't see any details. "It's not a body or anything, is it?"

"No. Just a strange symbol."

The assurance didn't make her feel any less apprehensive as he handed the picture across the table. Looking down at the photograph, Sabrina found herself staring at a crude drawing carved into a charred wooden board. It was a wide open, unblinking eye. The sight of it wiped out everything else she'd been feeling. It seemed to be focused on her with a malice that she could feel all the way to the marrow of her bones.

"The evil eye," she breathed.

"What?"

"The evil eye," Sabrina repeated. "It's an almost universal symbol. Every culture has it. The idea is that certain men and women have the power to kill or make you sick or give you bad luck just by looking at you."

"That's ridiculous!"

"Of course. We know that today. But centuries ago when somebody who was perfectly well suddenly fell deathly ill, it was an explanation that people could understand."

"And when they decided whose evil eye had caused the malady, what happened?"

Sabrina grimaced. "The person—usually a woman—

was likely to be accused of witchcraft. In some countries she was hanged. In others, she was burned.'' As Sabrina said the last words, she could hear the horror in her own voice.

Dan gave her a sharp look. ''What does that have to do with a murder in Baltimore at the end of the twentieth century?''

''There are plenty of superstitious people who believe in hexes and curses. In the Middle East, you can still buy amulets to ward off the evil eye. For that matter, there have always been a few people who thought they could get ahead in life by tapping the power of…of…the dark forces. Even in this country, there are modern witches and devil worshipers.''

''So you think, rightly or wrongly, the murder victims were tried and convicted of witchcraft and executed by some vigilante group?''

''I don't know.''

''I'd like to take you over and show you where the most recent body was found and where this eye was in relationship to it.''

''You mean if I don't have anything more pressing this afternoon, you'd like to take me to visit a cemetery where someone didn't bother to bury the latest corpse?'' she inquired.

''You could put it that way.''

A simple yes or no would do, she thought. Yet under the table, Sabrina clutched the wadded napkin as she tried to grapple with conflicting emotions.

Cassidy had raised her curiosity. It wasn't as strong as the fear that if she helped him, she'd be getting herself into something that, for want of a better word, she might label evil.

The assistant district attorney was waiting for an answer.

"I'm sorry," she heard herself say. "I just don't think I want to get any more involved."

Disappointment flashed on his face, then a polite mask dropped into place. "You're perfectly free to decline, of course." Reaching in his pocket, he fished out a small leather case. "Here's my card. If you change your mind, give me a call."

"I will." But she knew she wouldn't.

His expression was unreadable as he watched her hurry away from the table.

DAN CASSIDY'S FACE was still impassive as he headed for the side street where he'd parked his car. A public prosecutor who didn't have a poker face was like an investment planner without a tax shelter. It was only when he'd climbed into his car that the mask slipped.

Back to square one. Or almost. He wasn't sure what to think about Sabrina Barkley. So maybe Ian Alastair had made an innocent purchase at Sabrina's Fancy. Or maybe someone had given him a bar of her bath soap. But there'd been a slight hesitation before Ms. Barkley denied knowing him. And that wasn't all. She'd been nervous all during lunch. Why, if she didn't have anything to hide?

Still, she'd given him something to think about.

The execution of a witch. Had Simmons gone after someone who'd frightened him? Or was he taking the fall for a group? Or was Ms. Barkley deliberately trying to throw him off the scent? Trusting her insights might raise more questions than it answered.

Dan sighed. As he glanced down at his hands on the steering wheel, his eyes went to the place where the gold band had circled his flesh. The line was practically invisible. Ms. Barkley had sharp eyes.

But her personal insights had been the more disturbing

part of the palm reading. Perhaps his own reactions were coloring his judgment. Sabrina wasn't the only one who'd been off balance during lunch. He hadn't just been thinking about the murder investigation. He'd been reacting to the fiery autumn hair, the clear green eyes, the sexual awareness that he could feel zinging back and forth between them when she'd been holding his hand.

As he recalled the pressure of her warm flesh against his, he acknowledged the sensations hadn't all been sexual. There'd been something more. Something that had made him edgy. Her picture hadn't been included in the packet of information he'd collected on her, but he kept feeling as if he should recognize her, anyway. Had she been called to jury duty? Had her name come up in connection with one of his previous investigations? Had he seen her in the crowd at the Crab's Claw Pub down in Fells Point?

None of those sounded right. Because he wouldn't have forgotten her if he'd met her before.

His mind went back to the palm reading, and he grimaced. There weren't half a dozen people who knew about the tragic event that had changed his life. Yet one glance at his hand and she'd seen something he'd thought was invisible. Would she have mentioned it if she'd been worried that he was suspicious of her?

It didn't make sense. But he could certainly understand her turning him down. Well, if she thought this was the last she was going to hear from him, she better take another look at her tea leaves.

SABRINA WAS MAKING some real headway on the Harbor Court Hotel plans when there was a knock on the door. Erin leaned into her office and asked in a low voice, "Is it all right to tell Hilda and Gwynn you're here?"

"Of course. I'll be right out."

Hilda Ahern had been a customer of Sabrina's since she'd sold homemade vinegars and jellies at her Howard County house, and she'd introduced her friend Gwynn Frontenac to the joys of herb teas and exotic spices.

The two ladies were both wealthy widows in their sixties who filled their days with volunteer work, long lunches at the Women's Industrial Exchange, and a never-ending stream of harmless enthusiasms.

Sabrina greeted the two customers with a smile. Hilda was short and thin and wore sporty junior clothing. From twenty feet away, the outfits looked appropriate. But when you saw her up close, you realized that even a couple of face-lifts and nightly application of expensive estrogen cream couldn't rejuvenate skin that had been overexposed to the sun.

Gwynn was tall and gave the impression of a steamship plowing through choppy waters. While some women her size dressed in dark colors, she was partial to large splashy prints, primary hues and broad-brimmed picture hats.

"I stopped in for some of your tarragon vinegar and that divine lavender soap," Hilda began.

"Of course."

"By the way, what herbs would you recommend for the heart? I've been having some palpitations at night," Gwynn inquired.

Sabrina paused with her hand on the vinegar bottle. "You really should ask your doctor about that," she murmured.

"Oh, *doctors*, what do they know? My internist's just going to attach a bunch of electrodes to my chest, give me another one of those beastly stress tests and charge me five hundred dollars for the torture. And he's not going to find anything."

"Perhaps you should try Dr. Davenport. He's much

more sympathetic to sensibilities of refined women like us,'' Hilda put in. ''I've got some free tickets for his lecture tomorrow.'' The smaller woman shuffled through her fanny pack and brought out two bright pink cards, one of which she handed to Sabrina. ''You should come too, hon. He's so knowledgeable about the mind-body connection. I know you'd pick up some pointers.''

''How thoughtful of you, Hilda,'' Sabrina said. ''I've heard interesting things about him. I will try to make it.''

Before they left, Gwynn leaned toward Sabrina. ''It's a long ride back to Ruxton. Can I borrow your little girls' room while you ring up the sale?'' she asked, laying her credit card on the antique oak counter.

''Of course. And be sure to try the new hand cream I've put out.'' She didn't have to tell Gwynn the facilities were through her office, since it was a standard request.

Sabrina and Hilda were chatting when the other woman returned, rubbing rosemary-scented cream into her hands. ''This is quite nice. Can I get a bottle?''

Sabrina added it to the sixty dollars' worth of purchases already on the slip. After the door had closed, she glanced at Erin and found her assistant looking uncomfortable.

''What's wrong?''

''I don't like to repeat gossip.''

''I'm not going to spread it,'' Sabrina assured her.

''You're not really going to get mixed up with Luther Davenport, are you?''

''Why not? What have you heard about him?''

''My mother told me one of her friends went to a free lecture and ended up giving a donation she couldn't afford to his Andromeda Institute.''

''A lot of my customers are excited about him, and I'm curious.''

''Well, leave your checkbook home.''

"I can take care of myself." Yet even as she spoke the reassurance, she silently admitted that she hadn't been doing a very good job of it today.

Bustling back to her office, she got out several boxes of herbs to see how much she'd need to purchase for the Harbor Court project. But now that she was alone, with the pungent smell of thyme, lavender and lemon balm filling the room, her thoughts drifted back to the encounter with Dan Cassidy at lunch. Once again she felt the disturbing prickles of sensation dancing on her skin.

Sabrina dropped the sprigs of thyme on the desk, unaware that she was scattering the tiny leaves. Images flickered in her head. The horseman. The mountain. Dan Cassidy's face. Good grief. Somehow meeting him was getting mixed up with the story she'd been writing.

Struggling to wrench her mind back to the task at hand, Sabrina looked down at the herb sprigs forgotten on the surface of her desk.

She gasped. A malevolent eye stared back at her.

Reason told her it was just an arrangement of twigs and stems, but the illusion was too strong to shake. With a jerky brush of her hand, Sabrina swept everything onto the floor and then sat looking down at the mess she'd made. The eye was gone, scattered at her feet. But the feeling of disquiet persisted.

With a sigh, she went to get the broom. But as she passed the bookshelves, her steps halted in front of the collection of reference books she'd purchased over the years.

Something. Something tugged at her memory. Did it have to do with the story she'd been writing? Or with what she and Dan had talked about at lunch? Or the pattern she'd just seen?

Running her finger along the spines of the books, she

paused at one called *The Secret Tradition*. It was a history of the black arts, written in the eighteenth century. The author, one Silas Purves, had evidently been a believer, and Sabrina had been surprised at some of the nonsense presented as doctrine. She felt a little shiver on the back of her neck as her finger rested on the volume.

Not her preferred sort of reading. But it had been part of a box of books she'd bought at an estate sale.

Sabrina wanted to turn away, but some outside force kept her rooted to the spot in front of the bookcase. The same force seemed to guide her arm as she reached up and pulled down the musty tome. It fell open in her hand, and she found herself staring at a wood carving that was remarkably similar to the photograph Cassidy had shown her. And the eye that had just materialized out of dried herbs on her worktable.

Sabrina's chest tightened in a painful spasm. Somehow she stopped herself from dropping the book on top of the pile of dried greenery. Instead her fingers curled around the worn binding.

After several erratic heartbeats, she was able to bring her gaze back to the crude picture. This time a block of wood with the eye was propped up against a tree. In front of it was a dead man laid out on the ground with his arms folded across his chest. But his face was contorted, his tongue sticking out as if he'd died of some terrible agony.

Sabrina turned her head away to shut out the horrible sight. Was she going to see this disturbing image everywhere she turned?

Perhaps the text would give her some clue about what was going on. Covering the picture with one flattened hand, she began to skim the accompanying passage.

Witches often project their powers by the use of symbols. A representation of the evil eye can be just as deadly as the look itself—for it extends a witch's evil sphere of influence beyond her person.

A body found in the vicinity of such a symbol should be presumed to be the victim of a witch's malice.

Sabrina stared at the passage with distaste. Silas Purves wrote with the strength of conviction. Probably he was sorry he'd been born too late to be a member of the witch-trial court. Sabrina sniffed derisively. Why would the witch be stupid enough to leave such an obvious calling card? You'd only do that if you were darn sure of your power. The sniff turned into a little shudder.

She started to shove the book back and stopped. In good conscience she couldn't pretend she'd never seen the pages. Based on their brief conversation, Cassidy had wondered if the individuals he'd found dead in the cemetery had been tried and convicted of witchcraft. This passage seemed to be saying just the opposite. Which meant that he might be wasting time pursuing false leads.

Maybe she should tell his secretary so he could have someone come over and pick the book up. That would discharge her obligation, and she wouldn't have to actually talk to the man.

Sorting through the clutter that always seemed to multiply in her purse, she dug out the card and dialed the number.

ERIN HAD ALREADY LEFT for the day when the bell over the shop door jingled. Sabrina looked up from behind the counter to find herself swallowed up by Dan Cassidy's disturbing blue gaze.

Neither one of them moved. Then he seemed to realize

he'd been staring and began to look around the shop, his eyes cataloging natural cosmetics, potpourri and handmade jewelry.

"So this is Sabrina's Fancy."

"Yes."

He picked up a stylized foil ess from beside the cash register and held it against the charm that dangled from her bracelet. Instead of putting the foil letter back, he slipped it into his pocket and cleared his throat. "I was surprised you called."

"I didn't expect you to show up in person."

"I was all out of herb tea."

"You don't drink herb tea."

"Maybe I'll take it up," he countered.

"I'll make sure you leave with a starter kit."

"Can I see the book?"

Sabrina bent, pulled the dusty volume from the shelf under the counter and opened it to the place she'd marked.

Instead of going right to the passage, Dan picked up the tome, looked at the gold lettering on the spine and flipped to the title page. "*The Secret Tradition.* Do you do a lot of witchcraft research?"

"No. I don't like the subject. This is really the only book I have. There's actually some useful information on herbs buried in the text."

Dan turned to the marked section, studied the picture carefully and then began to read. When he finished, he closed the book and laid it back on Sabrina's desk. "Perhaps I've been making the wrong assumptions in the murder investigation."

Sabrina shrugged. "At least this is something else to consider."

"Like maybe a modern witch in Baltimore is trying to

extend her evil sphere of influence. Do you know any practicing witches in the area?''

"If I do, they haven't confided in me about their midnight activities. But I told you, there are people all over the country who call themselves witches. Men and women. Most of them say they're connected with an ancient tradition of natural practices. White magic. Or good magic, if you want to call it that. There might be somebody around here who dabbles in the black arts.''

"But we both know magic is a big con." He was baiting her again.

"Is it? Then why does a person who knows he's under a *hungan*'s hex curl up and die?''

"What's a *hungan*?''

"A voodoo priest.''

"It's fear of the curse that kills.''

"So in a sense, the magic did work. It's just like a doctor who gives a hypochondriac a placebo and tells him it will make him feel better. If the patient wants it to work, it just might do the trick.''

The assistant district attorney looked perplexed. "You keep coming up with logical arguments for the illogical.''

Sabrina laughed. Cassidy might be skeptical, but he was sharp. "I guess I like to play devil's advocate.''

"An interesting choice of words, under the circumstances." He cleared his throat. "I don't want to keep pushing you on this. But it's obvious you know a heck of a lot more about witchcraft than I do.''

"The subject makes you uncomfortable," she shot back.

"Yeah.''

"You think it's all a bunch of mumbo jumbo.''

"Yeah." His eyes continued to meet hers.

"You don't like working with someone you consider a nut.''

He flushed slightly. "Opinions can change."

Sabrina lifted her chin. "All right, I'll go to the cemetery with you."

FROM THE PASSENGER SEAT of Dan's car, Sabrina watched him loosen the knot of his tie, slide it from around his neck and toss it into the back seat. "You don't mind if I get out of uniform, do you?"

"Of course not."

His suit jacket followed the tie, folded rather than tossed. Suddenly he looked less civilized, as if the nine-to-five trappings had actually been some kind of disguise. When he leaned over to adjust the temperature control, a gold chain with a primitive-looking medallion swung free. In the center was a blazing sun.

He straightened, and it settled back against the golden hairs curling at his neck.

Sabrina's fingers were drawn to the charm. They closed around the gold disk and held it so that she could see it better.

"That's very old, isn't it? Where did you get it?"

"Family heirloom. Do you know what it's supposed to be?"

Sabrina smoothed her thumb over the design. "In ancient times it was widely believed that man prayed from his heart, the center of his emotional life. That's probably a good-luck charm symbolizing the link between the heart and the sun."

"Interesting."

When she realized the heel of her hand was resting against the front of Dan's shirt and that the gesture was much too familiar for such a short acquaintance, she dropped the ornament.

"It was my grandfather's. He brought it along when the family emigrated from Scotland."

"Scotland?"

"You've been there?"

"I—no."

"Me neither." There was a wistful look in Dan's eyes. "When I was a kid, I used to have a great time at grandpa's place in the country. He left the charm to me, and I started wearing it." He seemed a little embarrassed by the explanation. Or maybe it was the liberty she'd taken.

They both turned away from the intimacy. Sabrina busied herself with the lap belt. Dan started the engine.

Before they reached the city line, he turned off Frederick Road into an area of small red-brick town houses that looked as if they'd been there since the early fifties. It was all very uniform and very middle class until they came to a forbidding stone wall topped by a wrought-iron fence. The road crested a small hill, and Sabrina peered over the wall, staring at old trees and rows of gravestones. Many were elaborate monuments obviously erected in the last century. But the obelisks, angels and crosses were blackened by years of exposure to the elements, and there was a certain run-down look about the place.

Sabrina studied the houses on the other side of the wall. She definitely wouldn't want to live there. It might be all right during the day. At night she'd imagine all sorts of flickering shapes in the shadows under the trees and behind the tall monuments. She'd always half believed in ghosts. Her friend Laura Roswell's adventure at Ravenwood last year had reinforced her conviction that a restless spirit might reach out from the grave and try to affect the affairs of the living.

She was about to wrench her gaze away from the ramshackle city of the dead when a flicker of movement that was both furtive and swift caught her eye. She didn't know she'd gasped until Dan Cassidy slammed on the brakes.

Chapter Three

"What's wrong?" Dan asked sharply.

"I thought I saw someone sneaking around down there."

"Where?"

Sabrina pointed toward an area thick with gravestones. They both stared silently and intently, but nothing else stirred.

"Maybe it was a shadow," Sabrina murmured, wishing she hadn't gasped and given her nervousness away.

Dan nodded and started the car again. But Sabrina kept her eyes trained on the graveyard until the road dipped too low for her to peer over the wall. Perhaps she really had only seen the shadow of a tree branch animated by a sudden puff of wind. But try as she might, she couldn't shake the notion that something more sinister was waiting on the other side of the wall.

"Ever been here before?" Dan asked as he pulled up at the gate. He was scrutinizing her again in that intense way she'd come to dislike.

"No! Why are you staring at me?"

"I'm wondering why you're so nervous."

"I don't like this place. Okay?"

"It's kind of run-down, isn't it?" He nosed the car into

the stone arch that guarded the entrance. Further progress was blocked by a locked gate.

Sabrina wished she was somewhere else. But it was much too late to back out now.

"I'll only be a minute." Dan got out of the car and headed toward the nearby caretaker's cottage. The stone building looked like something out of Grimms' Fairy Tales. Irrationally Sabrina's palms grew moist as Dan disappeared inside. She kept her eyes on the door until he reappeared, followed by a bent old gentleman carrying an iron key that must have weighed a couple of pounds.

"Honk loud when you get ready to leave," he instructed. "If you don't want to get locked in, remember I'm not gonna be around tonight after eight. Got a meetin' down at the church."

Locked in! Sabrina's eyes darted to her watch. When she saw it was just a little after six, she sighed with relief. They should have plenty of time to finish their business and get out again.

"You haven't had any more trouble, I assume," Dan asked as he stood beside the car.

"I haven't heard a peep out of the residents, but then my ears ain't too good no more. Didn't hear a thing when that guy got dragged in here and laid out like the main event in a satanic ritual."

The casual remark set Sabrina's teeth on edge. It also gave a focus to her disquiet. She and Dan had come here because of a murder, and she'd wondered whether dark forces were involved. Well, the residue of evil lingered in the air like something palpable. She glanced at Dan. Didn't he feel it?

"The police will continue to patrol the area," he told the caretaker as he climbed back into the car. "But be sure to call the precinct if there's even a hint of anything suspicious.''

When the gate clanked behind them, Sabrina felt as if she'd just been shut into a coffin. The narrow road winding between the rows of graves contributed to the claustrophobic effect. It had probably been built in horse-and-buggy days, which meant getting a hearse in here must be like shoehorning sardines back into the can, she mused as they rounded a tight curve flanked by a small mausoleum and a praying angel.

"Let's circle around the back of the site," Dan suggested. "That way we won't have to back up to get out."

Poised for a quick getaway, she thought. "Fine," was all she said.

"If we leave the windows open, it won't get so hot in here."

"Okay."

When Dan opened his door, Sabrina remained seated. She didn't usually wait for someone else to escort her out. Now she was in no hurry. As Dan helped her from the car and she stepped onto the dried grass, she felt a wave of heat and humidity wrap around her like a suffocating blanket, making her feel as if the air were too heavy to drag into her lungs. Yet she really didn't want to breathe this atmosphere at all. Not when an ancient, wicked aura seemed to reach out toward her like poison gas drifting through a battlefield. It touched every molecule of flesh on her skin and somehow seeped below the surface, too.

As if she could block out the disturbing sensation, Sabrina clamped her teeth together and wrapped her arms around her shoulders. "Do you feel it?" she asked, hearing her voice rise at the end of the question.

Dan glanced down at his shirtfront, which was already starting to stick to his chest. "The heat? Yeah."

Not just the heat, she almost screamed, her gaze bouncing off the grave markers and crosses and coming back to Dan. He was openly studying her.

"You look so pale. What's wrong?"

"Something. I don't know." She looked around again, this time more slowly, her eyes probing the long shadows blurring the edges of every gravestone and every tree, afraid she was going to spot whatever had been sneaking around before. Only this time it would be much closer.

"I think the graveyard's just got you spooked."

"If that's what you want to call it."

"Are you afraid of ghosts?"

Unwilling to answer, she shrugged, breathing shallowly.

"The site's over there." He pointed down the hill.

If Dan hadn't held her firmly by the arm, she would have hung back as they started down the slope toward the murder scene. She felt as if she were being towed along under water, every movement slow and heavy.

He drew to a stop in front of a large granite slab that was badly weathered. The base had shifted so that the stone listed to one side at a seventy-degree angle. Weeds ringed the area. In the center, instead of a mound was a rectangular depression.

"I guess they didn't pay for perpetual care," Sabrina muttered. Now that they were at the actual site, every one of her nerve endings was at screaming alertness. This spot was dangerous. Very dangerous.

"It's one of the oldest grave sites in the cemetery."

Trying to come up with a rational explanation for the way she was feeling, Sabrina peered at the time-worn surface of the marker. Carved across the front, the name Ridley was barely visible. And the date. 1820? 1828?

"The victim was lying in the depression, with his head facing in the direction of the stone. His arms were folded across his chest," Dan told her. "The carving was propped against the headstone."

Sabrina felt the skin of her belly crawl as she pictured the body lying in the depression. "He was oriented like the man in the illustration," she murmured. "With the headstone taking the place of the tree."

"I wondered if you'd pick up on that." Dan reached toward her. Despite the heat and humidity, she moved closer to him. Her breath was even more shallow and irregular now, and the part of her mind that was still functioning knew it was in danger of shutting down.

"Bad vibrations?"

Sabrina was far beyond putting up any kind of front. "Yes." Unconsciously she took several steps back. As she did, the heel of her shoe came down on something hard nestled in the grass. A bolt of electricity seemed to shoot through her. She felt it all the way to her fingertips. All the way to the tips of her red hair, which stood on end around her face.

"What the hell—" Dan grabbed Sabrina's arm before she toppled over and eased her down to the ground.

She sat there in the weeds, looking around in a daze. The breath that hissed in and out of her lungs burned.

"Are you all right?"

"...hurts..."

"What?"

"My chest...hurts to breathe."

Dan was on his knees beside her, watching her face. The worry in his eyes made her struggle to relax her contorted features. After a moment, she could speak more easily. "It's getting better."

"Thank God." He stroked her arms and shoulders, smoothing down the strands of hair that floated around her face. Her eyes drifted closed, and her head flopped forward against his chest.

"What happened? Did you step on a live wire or something?"

"I don't know," she murmured into his shirtfront.

For several heartbeats he cradled her against himself, stroking her gently. When his thumb skimmed across her lips, her lids fluttered open, and she stared up into his blue eyes. They were as full of surprise and doubt as she imagined her own to be.

"It's my fault that happened to you," he muttered.

"No."

"I practically forced you to come here." His voice was gritty.

"I wouldn't have come if I hadn't wanted to help you."

An unreadable look crossed his face. "Are you sure you're okay?" he asked.

"I think so," Sabrina whispered.

"I want to find out what you stepped on."

Fear leaped inside her chest, and she grabbed his arm. "Be careful!"

"Don't worry."

Her pounding heart added to the pain in her chest as she watched him searching in the grass around the area where she'd been standing. He poked cautiously at the ground.

"Don't."

"It's okay." When he turned back to her he was holding a perfectly rounded white stone. It was smooth, except for the faint image of a star scratched into the top surface.

He peered at it doubtfully. "Maybe it had some kind of electrical charge. It's gone now."

Sabrina looked at the oval nestled innocently in Dan's hand.

Teeth clenched, she reached out and lightly touched a

finger to the star. All that was left was a faint buzzing sensation like insect wings vibrating against a windowpane.

"You don't feel anything?" she whispered.

"What?"

"Tingling."

He shook his head, then looked from her to the stone.

"I'm not making the whole thing up."

"Of course not. I saw your hair standing on end like you'd stuck your finger into an electric socket, and I saw the way it hurt you to breathe." Dan turned the orb in his hand, looking at it from all angles.

Sabrina shuddered. "Put it down."

"What is it?"

"Something bad. Something that's been cursed."

"Cursed? How do you know? Are you saying a spell gave you that shock?"

Put that way, it sounded silly. She shrugged and struggled to her feet. When she swayed slightly, he reached out a hand to steady her. All she wanted was to get out of this place before anything else happened.

"Maybe there's another one." After making sure she wasn't going to topple over, Dan moved off through the weeds, his eyes focused on the ground. Seeing him hunker down, Sabrina hurried to his side. Another white shape nested in the grass.

"Don't touch it."

"Okay. I'll call the lab and tell them to use protective measures when they pick it up." She saw him hesitate. "I'll take you back to the car. Then I want to see if there are any more."

Sabrina had felt as if she were balancing on a razor's edge ever since they'd arrived at the graveyard. The idea of going to the car and waiting there by herself made her throat clog. "No, I'll help," she murmured.

"You feel well enough?"

"Yes." At first the assurance was a lie. Then as she began to walk around the site in the opposite direction from Dan, she did start to feel better.

It took half an hour to find seven more stones laid out in a pattern around and across the grave. The whole configuration was about twelve feet wide and twenty feet long.

"Nobody spotted any of these before?" Sabrina asked doubtfully.

"Most of them are pretty far from the grave, and they just look like stones in the weeds, unless you step on one and it zaps you. Do you think they're like land mines or something? I mean, are they supposed to interfere with a search of the site?"

Sabrina drew in a deep breath and let it out slowly. Dan had been giving her odd looks and making pointed remarks since they'd met. Perhaps the best way to deal with him was to get his doubts out into the open. "Maybe the stones don't affect most people the way they affected me."

He turned to face her squarely. "What do you mean?"

"It probably sounds like a new-age cliché to you, but sometimes I pick up vibrations from people—or things. Like for example, the minute we drove through the gates of this place I started feeling as if something evil was waiting to—I don't know—grab me."

"I guess on some level, I did, too," Dan muttered. "But I was damned if I was going to admit it."

"I appreciate your telling me that."

"I don't like to give in to that sort of feeling."

"Neither do I," Sabrina agreed. "But something bad— or evil if you want to call it that—happened here. A ritual murder, to be specific. And the murderer is almost certainly the one who put those stones around the grave in a certain pattern.''

Dan nodded.

''I was already sensitized by the aura of this place. Then I stepped on the stone and it was like a direct connection to what had happened.'' As she spoke, the hairs on her scalp stirred. ''Does that make any sense to you?''

''Sort of. I think I can understand.''

She'd been braced to have him laugh at her. Now she let out a long sigh.

''A pattern, yeah. So what do you think it means?'' Dan asked.

''I'm not sure. Let's see what it looks like,'' Sabrina answered, glad the conversation was no longer directed at her. Searching through her purse, she found the notebook she always carried and began to sketch the configuration.

Dan watched her work. ''Well, I still don't know what it is,'' he muttered when she'd finished the rough drawing. It appeared vaguely like an irregular rectangle, compressed in the middle. ''Some kind of ancient coffin symbol?'' he asked.

''I don't think so. Each stone has a star scratched into the top. And the one in the upper right-hand corner is slightly bigger than the rest,'' Sabrina pointed out.

''So?''

''I think it's the constellation Orion.''

Dan looked again. ''Damn. I didn't see it at all, but I guess you're right. It's one of the few I learned when I was a kid, but I never could figure out why it was supposed to be a hunter. It looks more like an hourglass to me. As far as I'm concerned, the only constellation that's shaped like what it's supposed to be is the Big Dipper.'' He shrugged. ''But you can look up in the sky and get any image you want just by connecting the dots in different ways.''

''That's a logical way of approaching it. But the ancient Greeks didn't see the stars the way we do. They felt various influences from different parts of the sky and made up stories and images to go with them.''

''How does that explain why someone laid out these stones around the body?''

Sabrina was a lot more comfortable talking about Greek mythology than what had happened to her when she'd stepped on the first star stone. ''Let me tell you a little bit about Orion. He was a giant hunter who kept bragging he could kill any living animal. Finally the gods got tired of his boasts, so they sent a huge scorpion to sting him to death. But Diana the huntress asked that he be placed in the sky. Naturally he was put directly opposite Scorpius, the scorpion, so he would never forget his fateful boast.''

''So he was killed by the gods,'' Dan mused. ''The murderer is looking less and less like the guy cooling his heels in the city jail.''

''Why?''

''He's just an unemployed steelworker named Raul Simmons, as far as I can tell. I think he found Bette Kronstat's wallet after she was killed. I'm willing to bet he claimed responsibility for the murders because he's mentally unbalanced.''

Sabrina nodded, but she was still focusing more on the present clues than the man who'd confessed to the crimes. ''How did the murder victim die?''

''Poisonous injection.''

Sabrina felt a crawly sensation on her skin. ''That fits, too. Like being stung to death.''

''Well, we know the witch is into symbolism. What else about the mythology do you think is relevant?''

"When the ancients gazed at Orion, they felt his aggression and his human pride."

"How do you know so darn much?"

Sabrina flushed. "Do I?"

"Yes."

"I guess I read a lot."

"Lucky for me."

Before Sabrina could demur, Dan stroked his jaw thoughtfully. "Okay, so the victim could be someone who thought he could go up against the witch. Only she got him first."

"And laid him out in the middle of the Orion configuration to make a point."

Dan pocketed the original stone Sabrina had stepped on.

"You keep saying 'she,'" Sabrina observed. "A witch doesn't have to be a woman."

His eyes flicked away from hers. "I keep thinking of her that way."

"Do you picture her with a pointed hat and a broomstick?"

He laughed. "Sometimes."

"If it's not Raul Simmons, it could be anybody. Somebody sitting in front of a computer terminal right now. Or selling plates in the china department of Hecht's. Which reminds me. Did you check out the name Ridley?"

"Yes. The family died out."

By mutual agreement, they had started back in the direction of the car. As they climbed the hill and left the immediate area of the grave, Sabrina felt a profound sense of relief. She glanced at Dan, and he smiled.

She smiled back.

When they came abreast of the car, she stopped and wrinkled her nose. "Do you smell something funny?"

"Rotting flowers?"

"No, cherries, I think." The odor was quite unpleasant.

Dan nodded. "Maybe there's a tree around here, and nobody picked the fruit."

"That could be it," Sabrina answered doubtfully.

Dan turned on the ignition and closed the windows. The air-conditioning whooshed as it sprang to life. It should have cleared out the smell, but after several moments, Sabrina realized that the aroma was even stronger and somehow very compelling. And something strange was happening to her head.

"It's in here, not out there." For some reason, the observation ended with a bouncing little laugh.

"The cherries? So?"

"It's making me dizzy."

"Lighten up. You worry about stuff too much," Dan tossed off.

Sabrina gave him a slow smile. The fruity aroma didn't smell so bad after all. In fact, it seeped into her head like liquor soaking into a sponge cake. Now there was a seductive richness to the scent. A richness that made her breathe deeply.

"Nice," she murmured.

"Yeah."

Dan sounded close, but when Sabrina glanced at him, she found she was viewing him from far away, as if the driver's seat had suddenly migrated to the end of a long tunnel.

Somehow that was terribly funny, and she started to giggle uncontrollably.

"What?"

"Come back here." She reached for him. But her arms weren't long enough.

It was hard to think in a straight line. Hard to put one tiny little thought in front of the other.

Dan gunned the engine. With a jerk, the car shot forward.

Some dim part of Sabrina's brain knew she should be alarmed, but she was having too much fun!

The road was narrow and twisting. As the vehicle picked up speed, Dan spun the wheel wildly, somehow keeping the car on the blacktop.

Then a tree seemed to jump in front of them.

"Watch out!" Sabrina shouted.

This time Dan couldn't move fast enough. The car slammed into the obstacle and came to rest with a jarring thunk. They both pitched forward. Sabrina's head hit the mirror. She cried out in pain. Then she was being snapped back by the seat belt.

A loud blaring noise filled the car. The horn. It wouldn't stop.

Dan swore.

Sabrina looked up. The scene around them blurred and then bounced into focus. She sucked in a terrified breath. The car was surrounded by a wall of flames.

Chapter Four

"Fire!" she screamed above the blaring noise. "Fire!"

"What?"

"Fire, don't you see the fire?" Sabrina shouted, pointing wildly toward the inferno closing in on the car.

Dan looked alarmed and craned his neck in all directions. "Where?"

Her hand swung in an arc.

When he didn't respond, Sabrina shrank down, pulling at the seat belt, trying to fold her body under the dashboard. Ever since she could remember, she'd been terrified of being burned. Now she and Dan were surrounded by a flickering red-and-orange barrier, and there was no way through. She didn't even consider that she might have conjured it up from her imagination. It was too real, too daunting.

A scream tore from her throat as the tongues of flame lapped at the windows, enveloping the car. Soon the heat would turn her skin to ash. She was in hell. In hell where she would burn forever. And there was only the terror, the consuming flames and the cloying, sweet smell of the cherries.

Then the focus changed like a telephoto lens finding its range, and the scene was overlaid with a different hallucination. The grave markers around them were a crowd of people in old-fashioned costumes. Their faces were contorted in anger. The blaring horn was the yelling and jeering of the throng as strong arms reached to drag her toward the red-and-yellow blaze.

No. Get away. Before they tied her to the stake.

Unhooking the seat belt, Sabrina reached for the door handle and bolted from the car.

The evil-smelling flames licked at her hair, seared her skin, whooshed after her. They gained on her as she ran in a zigzag line; she wove unsteadily across the grass, the sound of the crowd speeding her legs.

Footsteps echoed behind her.

"Sabrina. Damn you. Wait!"

"No! Duncan. Save me. Save me."

Then, magically, as if her deep need had conjured up a savior, he was there, swinging her up into his arms.

He turned around, and all at once she knew that he didn't mean to rescue her at all. "No! No! Not the fire. Don't take me back to the fire." With a scream of terror that ended in a spasm of choking, she began to fight him as if all the demons of hell were dragging her into the inferno.

He was trying to hold her arms, trying to restrain her without hurting her. Still she fought against him, her mind spinning, caught between one illusion and the next, unable to find any reality besides the man who held her. She could hear him gasping in lungfuls of air, feel his fingers digging into her ribs, her shoulders, her hips.

"Stop. I won't hurt you, Sara. Never."

Yet even as they struggled, as their bodies brushed and collided in opposition, another stronger, more elemental force came into play.

Male and female—searching, seeking. And all the usual

inhibitions had been stripped away by the drugging vapor that still enveloped them—still held them in its grasp.

The contact of man to woman generated sparks like flint striking steel. All at once the fire was no longer around Sabrina. It was in her.

Dan must have felt the change. "That's it. Don't fight me." His voice was thick. His grasp shifted from force to persuasion. Fingers pressed, kneaded, and began to roam in wide circles across her back and shoulders. Moments— or was it centuries—ago, he'd been trying to carry her to safety. Or into the flames.

Sabrina felt light-headed. Then she looked up at him, focused on the blue of his eyes, and gave a little sob of joy. She was in his arms again, after so many lonely years.

Still, the confusion lingered. For wild heartbeats she thought she might drown in the mysterious depths of his eyes. No, it was more like falling helplessly through layers of cloud cover toward the earth far below.

She heard the ragged edge of his breathing. It matched the painful movement of air in and out of her own lungs. Dan stared down at her, transfixed as if he were seeing her, really seeing her, for the first time. "So beautiful. So very beautiful." One hand winnowed through her wild red hair, slanting her mouth at an angle under his. The other arm pulled her tightly against him into a lover's embrace.

She felt the heat radiating from his big body, the taut muscles of his stomach, the pressure of his broad hands, holding her, trapping her.

Her fear was as great as before. Some part of her sensed terrible danger as though her very soul might flee her being if her lips met his. "No, please."

"You want this as much as I do."

"Yes," she sobbed.

She had to stop. Some small, frightened part of her tried

desperately to pull away while there was still time. It was an impossible attempt. There was no way to resist her own desires. No way to resist the overwhelming rightness of being with him like this again. With a little moan, she twined her arms around his neck and pulled his lips down to hers. She'd ached for him. Pined for him. And it had been so long. So long. An eternity.

Familiar yet strange.

Shattering yet healing.

Overwhelming yet completely natural.

She felt him groan low in his chest. With that deep animal sound of half pain, half pleasure she knew it was the same for him as it was for her.

Her lips opened under his, inviting him to meld with her, to merge, to share his essence.

Joy leaped in her heart as he accepted the invitation. Then they were devouring each other hungrily. Kissing. Touching. Pressing aroused body against aroused body. He shifted her in his arms, pulling her to him as if he couldn't bring her close enough.

His hips moved urgently against hers, and she answered the shifting pressure, thrust for thrust. Her hands slid down his back even as she raised up on tiptoes, seeking to equalize their heights. Then she was trying to tug him down, toward the waiting bed of grass that spread out all around them.

Sabrina had forgotten the blaring of the horn. Until she and Dan were suddenly surrounded by bone-jarring silence.

"Where the hell is everybody?" a voice called into the sudden void.

She felt as if a large, rough hand had grabbed her by the back of the neck and yanked. She tried to shake herself away from its clutches, tried to cling to the rich, sensual dream.

But illusion had vanished.

With a little cry of loss, Sabrina's eyes snapped open. She swayed, grabbed for something solid, and found herself clinging to muscular forearms.

It took several seconds for her to realize she was holding on to Dan.

His face was flushed. His chest rose and fell as if he'd been running hard.

"What?" The question tumbled from her lips. She wasn't even sure what to ask.

"Sa-Sabrina? I—"

She leaned forward, desperate to hear what he was going to say. Instead the same gruff voice intruded again, tearing and ripping at her mind like a saw ripping through silk. "There you are."

Dan looked up, his face mirroring the pain in her head.

A moment later an old man came dodging and puffing through the forest of grave markers.

The caretaker. From the graveyard. What was he doing here?

His eyes were wide. "Lord 'a mercy. In all my born days. Heard the horn. Thought you wanted me. Bad like. Then I saw the car plowed into a tree."

Dan shook his head. With fingers that weren't quite steady, he reached up and touched Sabrina's forehead. She winced.

"You hit your head," he mumbled.

He helped her sit, and she leaned back against a stone marker. Her thoughts were still spinning. When she closed her eyes, she saw flames dancing behind her closed lids.

Heart pounding, she opened her eyes again, and the fire disappeared.

"What happened?" she moaned.

Dan didn't answer. Instead he looked uncertainly back at the car.

So did Sabrina. "The rotten cherry smell..."

"When I started the engine."

"Then everything went fuzzy," she said uncertainly.

"Some kind of gas, do you think?"

It was hard to make sense of what he was saying.

"*Something* knocked us silly," Dan continued.

Sabrina nodded slowly, remembering the unpleasant odor and how spacy she'd started feeling right after she'd first smelled it.

"I'd like to know who the hell cherry-bombed an official government vehicle." He started to laugh and sat weakly beside her. "Damn. My head hurts," he muttered after a few minutes. Then he looked at the caretaker. "Better call the police. And an ambulance."

"Already did."

Sabrina avoided Dan's eyes, trying to remember the sequence of events. Dan had started the engine, and everything had gotten weird and funny, until he'd wrecked the car. And after that. She didn't want to think about after that.

The caretaker was a merciful interruption.

"You still in one piece, missy?"

Sabrina kept her head bent away from the old man. "I've felt better." The words were punctuated by the wail of a siren. In a matter of moments Dan's car was surrounded by emergency vehicles and personnel.

He got to his feet. "Let's hope they don't ask me to walk a straight line."

"You haven't been drinking. I can vouch for that."

He laughed again sharply. "Sure, we'll be each other's alibis."

Sabrina watched him move off toward the lead police car. He still wasn't quite steady on his feet. But he was tucking in his shirt as he walked. Then he combed his fingers through his hair.

Going up to one of the ambulance attendants, he gestured toward Sabrina. Then he took one of the uniformed officers over to his car.

She wanted to watch Dan, but a young man in a white coat trotted toward her. Squatting down, he began to assess her condition.

"Do you remember the accident?"

"Yes."

"How do you feel?"

"Okay. Except for a little bump on the head."

"Cassidy says you were both gassed with something." Sabrina nodded.

"I should take you in for evaluation."

The last thing she wanted was to suffer through the rest of the evening being poked and prodded.

"No, really. I'm fine."

"Let's have a look in your eyes."

She waited while he got an ophthalmoscope and went through the standard routine for concussion.

"Guess you're okay," he said.

Sabrina sank her fingers into the dry grass. A few minutes ago, she'd wanted to keep Dan in view. Now she wanted to disappear before he came back and met her eyes. "I see Mr. Cassidy's busy. Is, uh, there any chance of getting a ride back to my car?" she asked as he turned to leave.

"I'll check."

Sabrina wasn't quite sure how she'd been holding herself together. However, as soon as the man left, she started to shake. Leaning back against the granite headstone, she tried to stave off the nausea that threatened to sweep over her. A cold sweat bloomed on her skin. Grimly, she strove to concentrate on some of the relaxation techniques she'd learned. The effort was only partially successful. Behind her closed lids, images of flames danced and flickered, making her shudder.

When she felt a light touch on her arm she jumped and gasped. Eyes snapping open, she found herself staring stupidly at Dan.

He hunkered down beside her and trailed his fingers gently to the cold skin of her forehead. "The medic said you were okay. You're not."

"I'm fine."

"Can you walk?"

"Of course." At least he wasn't bringing up what had happened between them. But why should he? Probably he was as embarrassed as she.

Sabrina struggled to her feet and found she was swaying on rubbery legs.

Taking her arm, Dan waited until she was steadier. "Are you sure?"

"Yes," she snapped.

He didn't reply as he led her toward a police car parked at the bend in the narrow road. "They need a statement from you, too. You don't want to go to the station house, do you?"

"Not if I can avoid it."

When he helped her into the back seat, she found her purse sitting on the vinyl upholstery. Until then, she'd forgotten all about it. Wrapping her arms around the white straw satchel, she hugged it to her chest.

"What exactly did you tell them?"

"That as near as I can figure out, some sort of gas was released in the car. It made me crash into a tree."

Sabrina nodded. That sounded pretty accurate. He must be used to coming up with coherent observations under stress.

"That's all they have to know," he continued. "Although, they'll probably want to try and dredge up some details of how it made you feel."

Some of the tension seeped out of her shoulders.

Dan stared at the purse still clutched in her arms. "I'm sorry. If I hadn't been so damned determined to drag you here, none of this would have happened."

"You couldn't know," she mumbled.

Further discussion was cut off by the arrival of a uniformed officer. Ritz, his name tag said.

Dan glanced questioningly at Sabrina. "Want to go to your house?"

"All right," she murmured and then gave the officer the address. After Ritz started the engine, she sank back against the hard seat and tried to pull together her scattered thoughts. Her relief was almost tangible as they drove through the cemetery gates.

Beside her, Dan was also silent. She slid him a sideways glance, sensing he was far from relaxed. In the dim light from the passing businesses along Route 40, his chiseled profile was silhouetted against the window of the squad car. On the ride out to the cemetery, they'd been casual acquaintances, but the cherry-flavored vapor had changed that irrevocably. All at once she wanted to get away from him so she could think. Probably he was having a similar reaction. Yet he must have a strong sense of obligation, because he was still sitting beside her in the police car.

They turned off the highway, and Sabrina had to give directions, since the city policeman wasn't familiar with the unlighted back roads of Howard County.

The old farmhouse she'd bought in Ilchester was situated on twenty acres, some of which were wooded. Sabrina had turned the fallow meadows near the house into lush fields full of fragrant herbs. But it wasn't garden-club pretty, and she was glad the darkness hid the somewhat straggly effect.

The impact of the accident was catching up with her. She felt sore and bruised, and stifled a wince as she climbed the steps to the porch. Dan was beside her quickly, taking her arm.

"What hurts?"

"What doesn't? How about you?"

He flexed his own leg and grimaced.

The critters inside must have heard the additional footsteps on the porch. Through the glass panel she saw two pusillanimous cats leap for the safety of the basement. At the same time her shelty, Robbie, came running toward the door, barking as if he were prepared to tear any invader limb from limb.

Ritz took a quick step back when Sabrina reached for the knob. She bit back a secret grin. He'd find out Robbie's character defects soon enough.

A woman living alone in the country might want a dog for protection. Robbie was probably about as much good as those recorded barking tapes she'd heard New Yorkers used. Her sense of security came more from the cats. If they rushed out to be fed when she opened the door, she was okay. If they were already hiding in the basement rafters, there might be an interloper in the house.

When Robbie saw her, he changed his tune and began to leap around excitedly, wagging his tail and sniffing the visitors. Dan stooped to scratch him behind the ears and admire his sleek good looks.

After opening some windows and turning on a couple of lights, Sabrina ushered the men into the sitting room and switched on the ceiling fan. It was one of her few extravagances. Most of the profits she'd made over the past few years had been plowed back into the business. There were whole sections of the rambling house that were little more than storerooms. The furnished parts sported a collection of hand-me-downs and thrift-shop purchases that she'd decorated with bright fabrics, dried flowers and whimsical pillows. But she suspected that the haphazard charm was lost on both Dan and Officer Ritz.

Dan surprised her as he looked around at the high ceilings and wood plank floors. "What a great old place. It's got a lot of potential."

"I think the biggest stumbling blocks are time and money, but I'm working on it."

Robbie hopped upon the sofa and looked at her expectantly. Ritz had lowered himself into a mission oak chair with shocking pink and green plaid cushions.

The dog could only hold Sabrina's attention for so long. Finally her gaze swung back to Dan. "Uh, could I get either one of you something cold to drink?"

"You need to rest. I can get something."

"There's a pitcher of herb tea in the refrigerator."

Well, they could still have a normal conversation, Sabrina thought after she'd told him where to find the glasses and he headed off toward the kitchen.

When he'd left, she sat next to the dog. Ritz opened his notebook. "I'd like you to tell me what happened—in your own words." Sabrina felt her palms grow clammy. It was comforting to stroke the shelty's long fur while she gave a brief account of the gas attack.

"Did you see anybody approach Mr. Cassidy's car while you were at the cemetery?" Ritz asked.

"No. But I wasn't looking that way."

"Nobody else was in the vicinity? People visiting graves or anything like that?"

Sabrina hesitated. "Earlier, I thought maybe I saw something in the shadows. Then the caretaker came running when he realized what was going on," Sabrina recounted, vaguely surprised that she sounded so coherent.

"When did the effects of the gas commence?"

Sabrina thought back. "Pretty soon after Mr. Cassidy started the engine."

"What happened?"

"At first everything seemed funny, and distorted. It looked as if the driver's seat had moved far away from me. Then the car started going fast."

"Is there anything else you think is relevant?" Ritz asked just as Dan appeared in the doorway carrying a tray with three glasses of iced tea, some of the flower-print napkins Sabrina had made from fabric remnants, and a tin of the chocolate-chip cookies she liked to pick up at the bakery in Ellicott City.

Robbie got down off the couch and trotted hopefully toward the man with the food.

Sabrina reached for a pillow tassel and ran the silky strands between her fingers. "The rotten-cherry smell, I guess. That was the first thing I noticed."

"You smelled it, too?" Ritz asked Dan.

"Yes. I assume it was the smell of the chemical. What about the trigger mechanism? Was it the starter?"

"Yes. It was wired like a bomb."

"A bomb!" Sabrina glanced from Dan to Ritz. They both looked impassive.

"Whoever it was didn't want to blow up the car," Dan said. "Maybe they were hoping I'd make it to the highway."

Sabrina went rigid, suddenly understanding the implications. If Dan had been going any faster, they might have both been killed.

"You think we can get this wrapped up?" Dan said.

"Just a few more questions." The officer turned back to Sabrina. "How long did the experience last?"

The tightness in Dan's voice had made Sabrina's pulse start to pound. She tried to focus on the question. "I guess not more than fifteen minutes."

"Short-term effect," Ritz remarked as he wrote, "Besides the laughing, what else happened to you?"

Sabrina swallowed and glanced quickly at Dan. "A couple of different things. After the car hit the tree, I thought we were surrounded by fire. Then for a few minutes I hallucinated. I felt as if I were somebody else, in a different place."

"Somebody else?" Dan asked, his expression odd as he studied her face.

"In the Middle Ages or something. There was a crowd around us, jeering and shouting. They wanted me dead." She looked pleadingly at Dan. "I was confused. I wasn't sure whether you were there to save me or—"

"Or what?"

She shrugged. "Well, it was just, you know, a fantasy. I was feeling as if I were a peasant girl and you were the lord of the manor."

Ritz was taking it all down; Dan had stopped eating the cookie he'd been holding.

"Is there anything else you can tell me about the effects? Anything physiological?" the officer asked.

Sabrina could feel tension zinging around the room like an electric hum. Ritz didn't seem to notice. Dan's gaze shot to Sabrina and then back to the officer. "Like what?" he demanded.

Ritz shrugged. "Rapid heartbeat. Distorted judgment. Visual or auditory disturbances."

"All of those," Dan clipped out.

"When we find out what the substance was, we'll let you know. And if you have any flashback, or anything like that, you should notify the department—and you may want to be checked out by your family physician."

"Yes. Thanks."

Ritz took a long pull on the glass of tea and made a face. "I'd better be going," he said as he picked up two of the cookies.

Dan followed the police officer to the door and onto the porch.

Sabrina sighed with relief and slid down against the sofa cushions, feeling her skirt ride up her legs. It didn't matter what she looked like. It was finally over. Scooping up a couple of ice cubes out of her glass, she wrapped them in one of the napkins and pressed the makeshift pack against her forehead. The cold felt soothing, and she closed her eyes.

But her mind wouldn't shut down. Rotten cherries. Impaired judgment. Visual and auditory disturbances. Yes, she'd experienced all that and more.

Her eyes snapped open again when Robbie jumped up and began to bark.

Chapter Five

"I didn't mean to activate your watchdog," Dan said from the doorway.

Robbie had already stopped playing guard dog, woofing softly and wagging his tail. Dan stooped to pet him.

Sensing he had a cooperative human, the dog rolled over, exposing his tummy for a good scratching.

Dan's hand moved across the white fur in long strokes, but his eyes were focused on Sabrina's thigh. From the floor, he had an excellent view. Quickly she pulled her skirt back down.

"I thought you'd left with Officer Ritz. What are you still doing here?"

"They're sending a car back for me." He didn't move from the doorway. "I wanted to make sure you were all right."

"You could have asked on the way out."

"I'm not going to attack you again if that's what you're worried about." His voice was gritty.

She felt her face color and wished she'd stop reacting that way. There was nothing more unattractive than a redhead whose face was on fire. "It wasn't an attack. And I'm not."

"I wanted to apologize. For dragging you there. For

almost getting you killed. For grabbing you like a maniac.'' He looked as if he might be about to say something more; instead his lips pressed into a thin line.

When he'd gotten up to leave, she'd breathed a sigh of relief that they'd escaped the topic of the torrid little scene that had played itself out down the hill from the car. She'd thought it was all her fault. Now he was telling her the sensual madness had been mutual. Pushing herself to a sitting position, she clutched her fingers against the ice. ''It wasn't something *you* did. It seems to be something that happened to both of us. And about the accident. If I'd been driving, the results would have been the same. When you started speeding up, I thought it was hilarious.''

He nodded tightly.

''Whatever that stuff was, it had us both flying pretty high,'' she said.

''Yeah.'' He got to his feet, and she saw him grimace.

''You're worried about tomorrow's headlines?''

''The police department will keep the story under wraps for the time being.''

''What else is bothering you?'' she asked suddenly.

''What do you mean?''

''I can tell there's something you want to say.''

''The experience brought back some bad memories.''

''Oh?''

''Let's leave it that tonight wasn't my kind of scene at all,'' he said.

''Well, don't assume it was my kind of scene, either. What do you think I am, some flower child left over from the sixties?''

''I didn't mean to imply—'' he swallowed audibly ''—that you were into drugs.''

''Maybe my life-style looks weird by your conservative standards,'' she interrupted him. ''Maybe I've even tried stuff you'd rank on the lunatic fringe. But that doesn't include getting high. Because I was never comfortable with—with—polluting my body." Probably that sounded self-righteous. At this point she didn't care.

He held up his palms. "Okay, so we're both virgins. When it comes to controlled substances, anyway."

They laughed uneasily, still wary of each other. "If you say so," she murmured.

He sat down in the chair that Ritz had vacated, and steepled his hands. "What do you mean by my conservative standards?" he demanded.

She pursed her lips. "I don't know. Law and order. The establishment."

"Guilty, I guess," he admitted. "And how do you define lunatic fringe?"

"Tarot cards. Palm reading. Herbal remedies. Harnessing psychic energy. We don't have a lot in common."

"We both like dogs."

He took things so seriously, which she supposed was why she responded so strongly when he let his guard down. Her eyes flicked to Robbie, who was sitting on the floor beside the chair, not the sofa. She felt her lips tugging up in a smile. So did Dan's. Then he caught himself the way he always did.

"Let's stop fencing with each other and get to the point," he said. "I don't particularly want to talk about what happened, but I've got to understand it—for this investigation, if nothing else. We're two adults and we're alone. Anything we say right now is strictly between the two of us."

"You really want to pursue this?"

"No. But we can't just let it go. How about starting with the murder case?"

"Someone tried to kill *you*," Sabrina whispered.

"Or scare me off. Or maybe they didn't know it was me. They could have been after whoever came out to have another look at the murder site."

"Do you believe that?"

"Let's say, I'll watch my back from now on."

Sabrina shivered.

Dan leaned forward. "I want to understand what happened after we hit the tree."

She felt heat creep into her face again.

"You thought we were surrounded by fire," he prompted.

"Yes," she whispered.

"Where do you think the image came from?"

Sabrina shrugged.

"Were you badly burned when you were a child?"

"I don't think so. It's just something that's always terrified me. We lived down by the shore when I was a kid. They'd have bonfires on the beach at night, and everybody would roast hot dogs and marshmallows. Everybody except me."

"You must have gotten burned when you were a baby, and only your subconscious remembers. Did you ever ask your mother about it?"

"She had six other kids to worry about. It wasn't the kind of thing we took time for. Or maybe she didn't know."

"What do you mean?"

"I was the second from the youngest, and I got left with my older brothers and sisters a lot. If one of them was careless and I got hurt, they might not have told anybody."

"You're kidding."

"Not getting in trouble was a big goal in my family."

Before he could ask her any more questions about her

background, she changed the subject. "Neither one of us was hurt."

"But we're still dancing around what took place." He stood up and turned toward the window. The two cats, who had crept up the basement stairs, scattered again. Sabrina was feeling just as skittish.

Without looking at Dan, she cleared her throat. "We don't know each other very well. That's part of what makes this so difficult."

"Okay. I'll start. First it was kind of a joyride. Then you thought you were surrounded by fire. Then I got the turn-on of my life."

She tried to control the betraying quiver of her lips. "Why do we have to talk about it?"

"I need to know how it affected you."

"My God, couldn't you tell? I was turned on, too."

She heard him let out the breath he'd been holding. "So I didn't force you into something..."

"You didn't force me into anything."

His gaze wouldn't cut her loose. "Are you still feeling it now?"

"Are you?" she whispered, her pulse surging.

He turned back toward her, and she could see honesty and discretion fighting it out on his face. "Yes."

"Maybe we're still under the influence," she whispered.

"Is that what you think?"

"It could be."

"I'd like to know."

She didn't answer, and he sat down on the couch. His nearness made her pulse race even faster. Slowly he leaned toward her, giving her a chance to pull away. She didn't.

His lips hovered questioningly over hers. She tensed, wondering whether she was afraid of him or herself. Or was it the memory of being out of control? She was still frightened by that. Yet she yearned to know how much had been from the drug and how much had been from the man himself.

His lips touched hers.

This time was very different. A man and a woman who were attracted to each other. A man and a woman agreeing that they wanted to get to know each other better and not in a hurry to force the issue.

This kiss was slow, delicious. Impossible to resist. Not what she would have expected from Dan Cassidy.

He didn't rush her, but when she slid her hands around his waist, she felt him smile. Then slowly, very slowly, he deepened the kiss. His tongue skimmed over the sensitive tissue of her mouth, creating new sensations—sensations they controlled, not ones that controlled them.

There was a thrill of discovery, and for long moments they both enjoyed the exploration. Yet the longer it continued the more she realized that the deeper awareness hadn't gone away. On some subliminal level, the pleasure was tinged with danger. If things went much farther, they'd be back at the primitive level of need they'd both felt before.

Did they both sense it? Was that why it had to stop?

Dan lifted his head. Bemused, Sabrina stared up at him.

"I guess that answers the question," he murmured.

Which question? That they were attracted? Or that they had the situation under control? She wasn't about to demand clarification.

His fingers played with her unruly curls. Then he smoothed them back from her face.

"I'm confused," she whispered.

"Are you?"

She flushed.

"I think we're both embarrassed about getting all tangled up together a couple of hours ago. Under normal circumstances, we'd have been governed by the civilized standards of behavior that keep people from acting on their impulses when it's not appropriate. Like now."

She nodded.

"The trouble was, when the cherry bomb hit us, we skipped over the niceties."

"You put that very well."

"Legal training." His fingers moved from her hair to stroke down the side of her face. "We can't pretend it didn't happen."

"We could if we never see each other again."

"Is that what you want?" There was a new tension in his voice.

That would be the safer course, Sabrina thought, but it wasn't what she said. "What do you want?" She held her breath.

He laughed. "To spend the night with you."

A man could admit that. A woman couldn't—shouldn't.

"But I'll settle for dinner tomorrow," he added.

"I can't."

"Oh?"

"I promised two ladies I know that I'd go to a lecture with them."

"Is that what you usually do for excitement?"

"No. But it will probably be an interesting experience. Besides they'll be disappointed if I don't show up."

He looked as if he wasn't sure she was being straight with him. "You could tell me about it at lunch on Thursday."

"All right."

Before he could respond, Robbie jumped up and started barking again.

Sabrina's head swung apprehensively toward the door.

"That's probably my ride." Dan stood quickly and went to the door. Over his shoulder, Sabrina could see another uniformed officer on the porch.

Dan came back to the living room. "I hate leaving you."

Any reserves Sabrina possessed had drained away, and she was past being able to judge the undercurrents of the conversation. Was he referring to his earlier remark about spending the night? Or was he worried that she was going to freak out again?

He must have seen the mixture of emotions that flashed across her face.

"I just want to be sure you're okay."

"I will be," she responded automatically, determined that it was going to be true.

SABRINA SANK BACK into the sofa cushions, grateful that she didn't have to engage in any more sparring—verbal or otherwise—with Dan Cassidy. She was emotionally and physically wrung out, and she might have simply fallen asleep right where she was. But within five minutes after the coast was clear, the two cats came sidling into the living room. Elspeth, a calico with a black-white-and-orange face, settled down on the sofa and began to wash. Malcolm, a ginger tom, initiated a series of piercing wails he knew from experience would propel his mistress toward the pantry.

Sighing, Sabrina pushed herself to her feet and dragged her aching body into the kitchen. When the animals' food and water dishes were full, she stumbled upstairs toward the bedroom. By the time she'd showered and slipped into a light cotton gown, three warm bodies were already waiting for her.

The hot water had revived her somewhat, and she smiled

as she thought about Dan's admission that he wanted to spend the night. Probably he wouldn't have liked the crowded conditions in her bed.

Twenty minutes ago, she'd been on the verge of unconsciousness. Now sleep evaded her. Probably she should have taken something for the headache that had begun to develop.

However, it wasn't just pain that was keeping her awake. She shouldn't have pictured Dan Cassidy up here in her bedroom—even as a joke. Because her nerve endings had begun to prickle as she remembered the kiss. Not the one in the living room a little while ago, which had been relatively safe, but the one in the cemetery when they'd devoured each other like long-separated lovers who were finally back in each other's arms.

But they weren't long-lost lovers. They'd only met at lunch at Sabatino's in Little Italy this afternoon.

By a tremendous effort of will she managed to avoid thinking about the images her mind had served up when she'd been under the influence of the drug. But she couldn't turn off the feelings that had flamed between herself and Dan. They were too powerful to handle.

In her twenty-eight years, she'd never felt so wildly out of control in a man's arms before. Never even close to it. Her relationships with the opposite sex were better described as pleasant. She'd hoped that eventually she'd meet someone to settle down with and raise the children she'd like to have. But she'd long since decided that whatever poets romanticized and women's magazines analyzed to death wasn't going to happen to her.

Until she'd found herself twisting against Dan Cassidy, trying desperately to get closer to his hard body.

Her cheeks heated, and every place that wasn't bruised or bumped tingled pleasurably. With a snort of disgust, she sat up and snapped on the light. The cats and dog looked up inquiringly.

"Go back to sleep," she muttered.

A cold shower didn't sound very appealing. But there were other approaches. She'd been putting off making a grocery list. That ought to sober her up.

There was a pad and pencil on the bedside table. After plumping up the pillows, she leaned back and began to write.

carrots
celery
cauliflower
milk
cheese
lentils
tomato sauce...

The familiar room swam and wavered like a scene underwater. Deep underwater where the pressure squeezed the air from her lungs. Sabrina clutched desperately at reality, struggling to breathe even as she passed more easily through the fear and the barrier her mind tried to erect. Once she reached the other side of the divide, she felt a profound sense of homecoming.

...of a powerful horse brought her to the door of the little cottage. She had wrapped a shawl around her shoulders against the chill wind and stood wiping her hands on her apron as the rider dismounted.

He took off his hat. "Mistress Campbell?"

Sara looked up into startling blue eyes, and the breath whooshed out of her lungs.

"It's the wood sprite," he breathed.

She flushed. "I'm just ordinary Sara Campbell. Who are you?"

"Duncan McReynolds."

They stared at each other. It was two years since the accident out in the mountains. His horse had been nearby. After she'd tended to his wound, he'd climbed back into the saddle and ridden off. Until this moment, she'd never known his name or what had happened to him. But that had not stopped her dreaming about him.

Now here he was, a man grown, standing in front of her. The look in his eyes told her he hadn't forgotten her, either.

Trying hard not to be too obvious, Sara took his measure. His hair was rich and tawny. The promise of power and strength had been fulfilled in wide shoulders that could have moved a mountain, and a stubborn jaw capable of winning an argument with a jut.

"So you survived, did ye?"

"The injury didna kill me, but my sire almost had my hide for laming the destrier." He grinned, bringing a devilish glint to his remarkable blue eyes. Then he seemed to remember what he was doing there.

"I've come to fetch the healer, Elspeth Campbell."

Sara's chest tightened painfully. "My gran."

"Can she ride to the castle?"

"I wish she could." Sara couldn't keep the bitterness out of her voice. "But she's dead and buried since just before the harvest."

"I'm sorry. For ye." His voice took on a more somber note. "And Ian McReynolds."

"Ian McReynolds?"

"Aye. He's bad off. And the physician canna cure him. Then himself remembered the old woman from the village who saved the Lady Tanya when she came down with childbed fever."

Sara saw the look of despair on Duncan's face. "My gran taught me well."

"Would ye come then?"

"Tell me what ails him."

"His lungs."

"They're weak?"

"Nay, they were strong. Until he went through the ice and into the pond. A few days later, he started coughing."

"And shaking? Chills? Headache?" she asked.

"Aye."

"And it came on sudden like?"

"Aye."

So it probably wasn't consumption. But peripneumonia was bad enough. Were her skills up to the challenge?

"What did ye do for him?" Sara asked.

"Fergus McGraw bled him and flushed the poison out of his system with a physic."

And made him weaker, Sara thought, her anger rising. Gran had tried to tell the physician a sick body needed blood to fight off illness. As for making him bring up his supper, that was useless unless he'd been poisoned. "I'll come," she said. "Just let me get my supplies."

Duncan tied up his horse and came in out of the cold while she packed a few things for herself and put her medical supplies into a leather pouch. Now that she was actually getting ready, her hands began to shake. She'd learned a lot from Gran, but she hadn't been the one making the decisions. What if she made a fatal mistake now? And there was another worry. No matter what she did, she might fail to cure the patient. Even with the best of treatment, peripneumonia could go either way.

"I'll bank the fire," Duncan said.

When she turned quickly back a few minutes later, she almost bumped into him.

"Steady, lass." His large hands cupped her shoulders. For a moment they stood by the hearth. *"I never thanked ye for taking care of my leg."*

"It was my fault in the first place."

"Nay. I should never have been out on that horse."

She looked up into his blue eyes, longing to admit her qualms and yet reluctant at the same time. Her only way of making a living was through her healing abilities. If the patient died, Fergus McGraw would warn everyone away from her.

"We'd better hurry. Before it's too late and there's naught I can do."

Outside, mist was pouring over the edge of the mountain and down through the pass.

Duncan took a plaid from his saddlebag and wrapped it around Sara's shoulders. Then he hoisted her into the saddle and climbed up behind her. His strong arms held her fast as he urged the horse forward. Bravely she settled back into his embrace, barely feeling the cold. She was glad he made a wide circle around the Devil's Gorge—a slash across the land where it was said the evil one's tail had touched down when he was flying to a witches' conclave.

Finally she could see the castle in the distance.

The gray stone walls rose tall and forbidding against the winter sky. A refuge or a prison? Sara wondered, as they passed the armed guards at the entrance and plunged into the dark passageway leading to the keep.

Sara felt a tap against her arm and tried to shake the annoyance away. It persisted.

DUNCAN'S ARMS were around her. Why was he hitting her arm? Sabrina looked down in confusion at the orange-and-black paw tapping against her flesh.

It belonged to a cat. Not a man.

Elspeth, who knew she'd finally gotten her mistress's attention, meowed.

Sabrina blinked, her gaze shifting from the cat to the lines of script she'd been writing. As she stared at the paper, a shiver swept over her skin, rippling in waves of fear through her body and her mind. Unable to stop herself from shaking, she sank under the covers, pulling them up around her chin. It had happened again. Like in her office when she'd been brainstorming designs for the baskets. Only this time it was scarier.

Sabrina closed her eyes and forced herself to breathe slowly and evenly as her mind scrambled for solid ground. "The drug attack at the cemetery. That's why you feel so bad now. Some of that stuff is still in your system. You should have been more careful." She chanted the reassuring words over and over. After a while, they had the desired effect.

Sitting up, she looked at what she'd been writing. It started with the grocery list, but after that the narrow sheet of paper was covered with lines of script.

She'd calmed herself. But the fear came zinging back. For long moments, she sat with her shoulders pressed into the pillows and her pulse pounding. Yet even without seeing the words, she knew what story she'd been writing.

It was the tale of Sara again. But she'd known it would be. Now the young woman had a last name. Sara Campbell. And her grandmother was Elspeth. With a deep sigh, she began to read what else she'd scrawled.

When she was finished, Sabrina sat stroking the cat, willing herself back to calm. Elspeth. Well, she knew where she'd gotten that name. All the same, it was weird how the story had just come back again as soon as she'd started writing.

Perhaps the fictional account was a reaction to stress. Was it going to turn into an obsession? She'd even dredged it up when the cherry bomb had hit her. Sabrina's body went rigid. She hadn't wanted to think about the time and place she'd conjured up out of the cherry vapor, but now it was unavoidable. It was the same setting. Except that under the influence of the drug, it had been suffused with danger.

Maybe that was just the way the hallucinogen was supposed to work. Maybe it was supposed to terrify you.

Sabrina grabbed that explanation and held on to it for dear life. Slowly a measure of calm returned. As it did, she went back over the details of the story.

The part about the raven being a bad omen. That was an old European superstition. The craggy mountains, the mist and rain could be in any northern country. But the words were more specific. *Laird. Lass. Dinna* instead of *didn't*. They sounded Scottish. And what had that battle horse been called—a destrier? That would be easy enough to check if she wanted more evidence.

It gave her a strange sense of satisfaction to have pinpointed the locale. Then her eyes narrowed. She was the one making up the story. She could set it anywhere she wanted. But she'd picked Scotland and come up with an awful lot of very specific details.

Well, some of the fine points were things she knew well. Like herbs. Sara's familiarity with the old herbal remedies came straight out of the books she'd read. The Scottish part made some sort of sense, too. She'd always been interested in that country. She'd read a lot about the history and the customs. Back when she'd been a teenager, she'd devoured a slew of historical romances set there. She'd even named her dog Robbie and her cats Elspeth and Malcolm. Good Scottish names.

Sabrina glanced at the clock. Two-thirty. She should finish the grocery list and get some sleep. But she felt a strange reluctance to pick up the pen again while she was alone. Part of her was fascinated with the story. She wanted to find out how Duncan and Ian McReynolds were related. Did Sara cure Ian? Did the obvious attraction between Sara and Duncan develop into anything? And what happened when Sara confronted the doctor? What was his name? Fergus McGraw.

There was a moment of sheer, black fright as she pictured the evil old man. His pinched features were as vivid as if she'd met him on the street in downtown Baltimore. Just as she'd sensed the evil in the cemetery, she knew he was dangerous. Very dangerous. Fergus McGraw wanted to do her harm. If she had any sense, she'd stay as far away from him as possible.

Except that he wasn't real. So there was no way he could hurt her...was there?

Chapter Six

Dan Cassidy wished he'd had the sense to get someone to take his car home. Instead, as the young officer who'd given him a ride downtown pulled up beside the burgundy Olds in the courthouse parking lot, he hesitated. "You okay to drive, sir?"

"I'm not planning to crash into any more trees. And I want to see the report on whatever gassed me and Ms. Barkley as soon as the department has anything."

"Yes, sir."

He didn't linger to chat. In fact, he roared away with a screech of gravel that made it look like the assistant district attorney still had a buzz on. But he didn't care. He was trying to outdistance his conscience. It was bad enough playing mind games with Sabrina instead of explaining about the gold-foil seal in Ian Alastair's pocket. That was only the tip of the iceberg.

In the silence of the car, Dan heard himself swallow. Maybe he couldn't help what had happened in the cemetery, but he shouldn't have kissed her before he'd left her house. Hell, he shouldn't have compounded the infraction by asking her for a date.

He tried to relax his painfully tight muscles. But too many disturbing things had happened this evening. Until

Sabrina had given Ritz her version of the experience, he'd thought he'd understood the effects of the hallucinogen. The drug had sent his mind spinning off into a very strange fantasy.

It hadn't been a good experience for either one of them. Sabrina had been terrified of flames. For a few startled seconds, he'd seen them, too. And he'd assumed her wild cries of fear had suggested the image to him. But what about the other part? She'd said she'd felt as if there were a crowd of people around them jeering and shouting for blood.

He'd sensed the onlookers, too, just at the edge of his vision. Somehow he'd known they weren't after him. They wanted Sabrina, and he was the only one who could save her.

Dan's fingers gripped the wheel more tightly. Again, he felt the terrible urgency to rescue Sabrina. The same urgency that had driven him headlong across the dry grass after her.

His foot pressed down on the accelerator. When he realized suddenly that he was going seventy-five miles an hour, he eased up on the pedal. Behind him, a horn blared just before another car shot past.

Dan vented some of his frustration with a verbal assault that the other driver couldn't hear. It didn't make him feel a damn bit better. Sabrina had said she was a peasant girl, and he was the lord of the manor. Bizarrely enough, that had been part of it for him, too.

How in the world could they have shared that particular fantasy? As he pulled into the garage under his Camden town house, his lawyer's mind tried to come up with an explanation that made sense. He and Sabrina couldn't be replaying anything they'd done together. Perhaps it was a replay of a different type. Could a horror movie or TV program they'd both seen have triggered the fire image? That was certainly easier to buy than some psychic mumbo jumbo. Except that he didn't go to horror movies or remember seeing any scenes like the one he'd lived through tonight. Sabrina might have some clue. If he could bring himself to ask her about it.

He sat without moving in the darkened garage. He'd never been content to let events sweep him along. But how did you take action when you felt as if every step carried you farther and farther onto unstable ground? Which way did you turn when you thought you might crash through the fabric of reality and tumble headlong into—

He didn't dare put a name to what he was feeling. It was too far beyond anything he'd ever experienced—too far from what he considered normal.

All at once, the fear he'd been struggling to suppress boiled over into anger. Someone like Sabrina Barkley had no right to come in and tear his life apart. No, not *someone*. Sabrina.

There was something unnerving about his feelings for Ms. Barkley. Before he'd even met her, he'd felt a compulsion to find out as much as he could about her without letting her know that he was doing it. Then she'd walked into the restaurant and turned toward him. And ever since he'd been fighting a disturbing sensation that her innocent green eyes were going to swallow him up—or that running his hands through her fiery hair would set him on fire. The red-headed witch might as well have cast a spell over him.

Was that why everything was happening so damn fast and making his head spin? Was that why he wanted to protect her and save her so badly? And make love to her until the flames of passion consumed them both?

Dammit, he barely knew the woman. Why did she have such a hold on him? He grimaced, recognizing that he was dangerously close to careering out of control for the second time that evening. And without drugs. For all he still knew, Sabrina Barkley could be the chief sorceress in a diabolical murder ring.

No. That wasn't fair. He had no proof of anything like that. Just a crumpled charm in a dead man's pocket.

SABRINA WAS TENSE all morning. Probably because she was waiting for Dan to call and suspected that it wasn't going to happen. By noon, she'd convinced herself it was for the best. Getting mixed up with each other was all wrong. More, it was dangerous. Instead of hanging around the shop, she drove out to a craft supplier in Towson and picked up two hundred small baskets, plastic bags and ribbons, negotiating a very good price on the bulk order.

Two or three times during the day, she almost decided to call Hilda to say she wasn't feeling well and couldn't attend the lecture after all. But each time she changed her mind. Somehow the prospect of going home to her dog and cats was too depressing.

At seven, Sabrina drove to the Andromeda Institute, a renovated house not far from the Johns Hopkins campus. After stepping through the entrance, she stood looking around at the well-dressed crowd, feeling a bit apprehensive and out of place. Either the faithful were gathered to worship, or a lot of people were curious about Dr. Davenport.

She could see that her presence was being noted. Some of the patrons were her own customers and former customers. Many greeted her with a smile. But a number seemed embarrassed. One, a Mrs. Garrison, who'd been a pretty regular patron until a couple of months ago, wouldn't quite meet Sabrina's eye. Had she done something to alienate her? Or was the lady feeling guilty about not shopping at Sabrina's Fancy?

Well, she wasn't in direct competition with Dr. Davenport, Sabrina assured herself. Or was that the general perception?

The unspoken question did nothing to lessen the tension she'd been feeling since arriving. Nevertheless, when Hilda came rushing over to greet her, she responded with as much enthusiasm as she could muster.

Hilda tugged on Sabrina's arm. "I want to look at the product displays before the lecture. Afterward, the tables are always so crowded."

Others had the same idea. She and Hilda were more or less carried along by the surge of bodies up the stairs into a reception area decorated in what Sabrina could only describe as bastard Greek with Ionic columns and faux marble walls.

Gwynn Frontenac was talking with a slender, tweedy-looking man near an alabaster fountain with a pair of spouting dolphins. A good six inches taller than her companion, she leaned down to catch what he was saying.

Spotting the newcomers, Gwynn waved and gestured. "Sabrina Barkley," she called across the room, "come over here this minute."

As scores of heads turned in Sabrina's direction, she kept a smile plastered on her face. But she wished she hadn't become the center of attention.

"Professor Ashford is very anxious to meet you," Gwynn explained as Sabrina joined the twosome.

She inclined her head toward the man.

"I'm doing an article on alternative medicine, and Gwynn has been telling me about your shop. Perhaps we could get together for an interview," he suggested.

Sabrina glanced quickly at Gwynn, trying not to show

her annoyance. She didn't need someone making false advertising claims for her. "I'm not really treating illnesses or anything like that," she said in a low but firm voice.

"But you do stock herbal cures, don't you?"

"Only the ones that have been in general use for centuries. And that's not really my focus. Really, I'm more into soaps, dried wreaths and food products."

"Hmm. Well, perhaps I'll have more luck with Dr. Davenport," the professor allowed.

"I was just trying to get you some free publicity," Gwynn said when the man had departed.

"Thanks for thinking of me. But it's better if you don't give the impression I'm any kind of healer."

Gwynn reddened slightly. Sabrina spent five minutes making her feel better and then excused herself. Really, she had come here to see what Davenport was up to. And she'd better get on with it, even though what she really wanted to do was turn and flee. Instead she moved quietly about the room taking note of both the people and the displays. One man in particular caught her eye because he was wearing Western boots, a cowboy shirt and a string tie held in place by an ornate silver clasp. The outfit might have cut it in Santa Fe. In Baltimore, it was odd. But his clothing wasn't the only distinctive thing about him. His skin was flushed, and his eyes were very bright. Was he sick? Or terribly excited about the lecture?

When he caught her staring, Sabrina dropped her gaze to a table piled with relaxation and self-motivation tapes. Surprisingly they were free. Well, that was an expensive advertising approach. Were the cassettes simply disguised promotional material? Or were they genuinely helpful? Sabrina tucked two different ones into her purse for future study. Of course, right beside them were the high-priced pamphlets, all written by the good doctor on topics like curing constipation and insomnia, and fighting cancer.

Sabrina was looking over some expensive protein supplements guaranteed for rapid weight loss when she heard her name spoken again.

"Ah, Ms. Barkley."

Turning, she found herself staring into dark, deep-set eyes, the most remarkable feature in a face that would have stood out in any crowd. The man's swept-back hair was silver. His cheekbones were high and broad. And his nose was an eagle's beak.

Sabrina recognized him from the portrait in the lower lobby but wondered how he'd identified her. "Dr. Davenport."

"My good friend Mrs. Ahern pointed you out to me," he said, clearing up the mystery at once.

She was going to be almost as well known as the good doctor by the end of the evening. And on his turf; he couldn't possibly appreciate that.

"I hope you enjoy the lecture."

"Well, I've been curious about you," Sabrina said, hoping he'd take the statement as a compliment.

He smiled. "We do our best to ease the pain and suffering of the world."

A middle-aged woman wearing a turban and a long black dress hurried toward them. "Oh, Doctor, I was hoping to have a word with you in private," she gurgled.

Davenport nodded to Sabrina. "If you'll excuse me." Then he draped an arm over the woman's shoulder. "I always have time for you, my dear. But it will have to be a quick minute. We're almost ready to start."

Sabrina took a seat near the middle of the auditorium. No one was talking. Rather, they were sitting in expectant silence, as if the light classical music playing in the background had put them under some kind of spell. Sabrina felt the tension easing out of her body as she listened to the soothing strains.

The peaceful feeling was dispelled when the man in the cowboy outfit plopped into the aisle chair in front of her. As he turned his head, Sabrina saw his skin had gone from flushed to pale. However, her scrutiny was cut off as the lights dimmed and a swell of music heightened the feeling of expectation. As the last notes faded away, an elegantly dressed older woman stepped under the spotlight at the front of the room like a model about to display a stylish outfit. Instead she delivered a brief, laudatory introduction before Luther Davenport materialized onstage. With the lights gleaming off his silver hair, he looked even more impressive than close up as he paused to acknowledge the enthusiastic applause.

After a few inspirational anecdotes, he segued into a description of his philosophy, which seemed to be based on communion with the natural way, whatever that was.

"Friends, I have gone to the source of wisdom. Once a week I leave civilization behind and commune with nature. In the woods. In the mountains. In the hidden cave only I have ever entered.

"There, I listen to the pulses of the earth—the original teacher of mankind. And I feel their rhythms throb within me. The experience brings me back to the laboratory and the consultation room renewed and recharged, free to turn my energies to the innovative diagnostic techniques and specially prepared treatments that have set many a gravely ill patient on the way to recovery."

That sounded nice. Then Sabrina gave herself a little mental shake and sat up straighter. Nice? More like hogwash.

It was almost a relief when Sabrina was distracted by

an abrupt movement in front of her, until she realized that the man in Western garb had doubled over and was sitting with his head cradled in his hands.

"Hoarding wisdom is as unconscionable as hoarding money," Davenport was saying. "Anyone who can help mankind has a responsibility to share. Through classes, through private sessions, and through booklets published by the Andromeda Institute, I—"

His words were interrupted by a sharp groan. As Sabrina watched in horror, the cowboy pitched forward, hit the floor and lay sprawled in the aisle—white-faced and unmoving.

Several things happened simultaneously. The woman in front of Sabrina scrambled up, knocking over her chair as she backed away. Someone else began to shout for help. Dr. Davenport's voice ceased in the middle of a sentence. And the house lights came up.

"What's happened?"

"What is it?"

Sabrina knelt beside the prostrate figure. The man was shaking violently and struggling for breath. As she leaned toward him, his face contorted as if he were in terrible pain. She grasped the man's hand. "What is it? What's wrong?"

His eyes focused on her. Something in their murky depths made her shudder. Then his jaw clenched, and his body convulsed. With a final shudder, he went perfectly still.

His eyes were closed, his skin had turned gray blue, and he had the look of death about him. Still, Sabrina's fingers went to his neck, searching for a pulse. She couldn't find one, and his chest had ceased to rise and fall. Pressing her ear against it, she tried to find a heartbeat. As far as she could tell, there wasn't any.

"Get an ambulance," she shouted. "Hurry."

Sabrina had no idea whether anyone responded. She was too busy trying to remember the CPR techniques she'd learned a year ago. But performing on a human—one whose life was in her hands—threatened to overwhelm her.

"Can anybody help?" she begged as she flung aside the heavy silver clasp of the man's string tie.

When no one came forward, she began the procedure, counting as she forced air into his lungs and then expelled it. She was dimly aware of the curious faces watching, but she blocked them out and concentrated on the victim until large hands gripped her by the shoulders.

"Thank you, Ms. Barkley. I'll take over."

It was Dr. Davenport. Sabrina stared up at him, awfully glad he was going to assume the burden. Still on her knees, she moved aside and watched as he leaned over the unconscious man. Instead of continuing the standard rescue procedure, Davenport lifted a lid and looked into a dilated pupil. Then he stroked his hands across the clammy skin of the slack jaw.

"What—what are you doing?"

Ignoring Sabrina, Davenport picked up the man's fingers and began to examine the blue-tinged nails with great interest.

"Please. He needs CPR until the rescue squad—"

"I think I can judge the situation better than you," the doctor murmured.

They had been joined by the woman who'd made the introductions. He barked at her, "Quickly. Get me—"

Sabrina didn't hear the last part of the sentence, because it was spoken into the assistant's ear.

The woman rushed away. Sabrina was left staring across

a lifeless body into Davenport's deep-set eyes. They were challenging and commanding at the same time. She felt as if she'd been thrust into some kind of contest. And the loser was going to be the man on the floor.

Chapter Seven

Sabrina could hear a buzz of voices around her, but nobody interfered.

Of course not. Who else was going to defy the director of the Andromeda Institute?

Precious seconds were ticking away. Without blood and oxygen, the cowboy's brain cells would start to die. Bending down again, Sabrina flexed the rigid neck back and started the CPR procedure again. At least Davenport didn't try to stop her.

All her attention was focused on the unconscious man. She didn't see two large men materialize on either side of her. However, in the middle of a breath, she was rudely lifted out of the way by two sets of very strong arms.

"Wait. No."

The gentlemen ignored her. Although dressed in conservative suits, they could have been bouncers in a nightclub. With a firm hold on her elbows, they moved her several feet from the lifeless man.

"No, please..." Sabrina repeated frantically. "Don't you understand? He's not breathing. His heart..."

"Let the doctor do his stuff," someone growled.

A hush had fallen over the room. With a flourish that managed to be both calm and theatrical, Davenport pulled the stopper from a small glass vial. Prying the cowboy's lifeless jaw open, he poured a white, grainy powder into his slack mouth.

Sabrina could feel her own heart thumping like a kettledrum. At the same time, she realized she was holding her breath. For several seconds nothing happened. Then the prostrate figure began to cough.

The breath hissed out of her own lungs. She heard the same sigh repeated many times around her.

The coughing on the floor became louder. The cowboy's jaw muscles twitched. His eyes fluttered open, and he looked around, as if wondering where he was and what had happened.

"The light...the shining light," he whispered.

"My God. Would you look at that," somebody marveled.

There were murmurs of agreement, followed by a babble of excited voices. Sabrina was no less astounded as she stared at the man on the floor who was now struggling to sit up.

Davenport restrained him gently. "Just relax, my friend," he said. "You've been through quite an ordeal. But we've brought you back."

Sabrina couldn't take her eyes off the cowboy. An ordeal, indeed. She'd been sure his heart had stopped. And she knew for certain he hadn't been breathing on his own. What in the world had Davenport given him to revive him like that?

"How do you feel?" the doctor asked.

"D-dizzy...head hurts."

"That's to be expected. Can you tell me your name, my dear fellow?"

"Ed-Edward."

Once again the doctor checked eyes, face and fingernails, this time with a satisfied smile. Then he looked up and appealed to the crowd. "Edward needs air. And privacy. Please move back."

Some of the onlookers obeyed. Others hesitated as if they were afraid they'd miss something.

"What did you give him?" one man asked.

"A special herbal preparation that I keep here at the institute for emergencies," Davenport explained.

"By gosh, I'd like some of that stuff," someone else muttered.

"It can only be used in conjunction with carefully acquired knowledge," Davenport replied smoothly.

"I want to get up," Edward's voice cut into the exchange.

"I wouldn't advise—" Davenport began. But the cowboy was already struggling to his feet. As he tried to right himself, he grabbed on to the front of the director's suit jacket.

A look of distaste formed and was quickly erased from Davenport's face. He glanced meaningfully at the two men who were still silently restraining Sabrina. They dropped her arms, came quickly forward and took hold of the cowboy. A string of curses accompanied his attempts to fight them off. However, in a matter of seconds the bouncers were supporting his weight while hauling him away from the doctor.

"Perhaps we should take him to one of the treatment rooms," Davenport suggested, beginning to move toward the side of the auditorium.

"Wait, Doc," a man in the crowd called out.

"Later. I'll be back later to answer any questions you might have," the director replied. "I believe this man still needs my attention."

People milled around, still talking excitedly about the

unexpected drama. Now that Sabrina was no longer wedged between two burly men, she knelt to pick up her purse. Beside it on the floor was a small circle of rubber about a quarter inch across and half an inch deep. Coarse white grains clung to one flat surface.

Sabrina tensed as she realized she was looking at the stopper to the vial Davenport had been holding. It must have gone flying when the cowboy had clawed at the front of the director's coat.

Pretending to check through her purse, she pulled out a tissue and dropped it on the floor over the stopper. Then she quickly folded the prize into the tissue and tucked it into her bag.

She was straightening up again when Hilda appeared at her side. Tensely she waited for her to ask what she'd been doing. She didn't.

Instead Hilda patted Sabrina's shoulder consolingly. "I'm sure you did your best to help that man. You just don't have access to the same kind of knowledge as Dr. Davenport."

"I guess not," Sabrina muttered. There was no point in trying to defend herself. Probably the best course was to fade into the walls before anything else happened.

"He talked about a light. It's a sure sign of a near-death experience."

"Umm." Sabrina tried to keep her attention focused on Hilda, but out of the corner of her eye she could see people staring at them. Was she imagining the looks of malice on their faces? Did they all hate her? What had she done that was so terrible?

Then, in her mind, it wasn't just looks, it was shouting. Far away and then closer, she heard a crowd jeering, calling for her blood. It was happening again; they were coming after her. Like the hostile crowd she'd conjured up in the cemetery. The crowd long ago.

"Dear? Are you all right, dear?"

Sabrina had been about to cut and run. With an effort, she brought her attention back to Hilda. "What?"

"You look so pale. Are you all right?"

Still too shaken to respond, Sabrina backed toward the stairs.

"I'm sure the doctor will be with us as soon as he makes sure that poor man is comfortable," Hilda said. "Aren't you going to stay for the rest of his talk?"

"No," Sabrina managed.

Turning quickly, she dashed down to the first floor and through the lobby.

Outside, she stood for several moments sucking humid air into her lungs. It didn't help her feel any better. It was hard to shake the illusion that the crowd had been closing in on her, intent on making her pay for her mistake. But she hadn't done anything wrong. Somehow, that was the worst part.

Shoulders hunched, she headed for her car. She was pretty sure what had just happened. She'd been upset and it had all gotten tangled up with the drug experience in the cemetery. That's where the frightening images had come from.

Yet reasoning it out logically didn't help much. All she wanted to do was get away from this place. With a jab of her foot on the gas pedal, she roared out of the parking lot. It wasn't until she reached Roland Avenue that she slowed down. Fingers clutching the steering wheel, she headed for home.

Half an hour later, she turned into the long driveway that led to her house. When she rounded the last curve, her foot lifted with a jerk from the accelerator. Another car was occupying her usual parking space beside the porch.

Sabrina stared at the vehicle. It was almost 10:00 p.m., and she certainly wasn't expecting anyone.

As she debated whether to get out of her car, a figure came around the side of the house from the direction of Robbie's fenced yard.

The dog started to bark, sounding more disappointed than aggressive.

When the visitor stepped into the glare of her headlights, Sabrina saw it was Dan Cassidy, dressed casually in jeans and a striped pullover. He stood with his hands thrust into his pockets, and she couldn't help wondering if she'd conjured up his image.

Then he called out to her, and she knew it was no illusion. "I wasn't expecting company," she tossed out as she exited the car.

Dan would have given a lot to have seen her face. Last night and most of today, he'd been feeling guilty about Ms. Barkley—as much for making her the focus of his misplaced resentment as for anything he'd done. He'd been trying to figure out how he could come clean with her and not drive her away. Then tonight she'd turned up in the middle of another one of his investigations. Ever since the phone had rung an hour ago, he'd been vacillating between astonishment and renewed anger that perhaps the redheaded little witch really had pulled the wool over his eyes. Maybe her nervous act at the cemetery the other night had been part of her plan to confuse him, to throw him off the track. And there were other things that were still hard to explain. Like the hallucination they seemed to have shared. But he chose not to focus on them. It wasn't the important point now. If she'd been making a fool of him all along with her innocent green eyes and her logical explanations, she was going to be damn sorry.

Was she working for Luther Davenport? And did tonight's melodramatic incident somehow tie the two cases together? Or had she simply been in the wrong place at the wrong time once again?

Hating his own confusion, Dan willed his jaw to unclench. It might still be true that Sabrina had been flummoxed by Davenport along with the rest of the crowd. If that was the case, she was undoubtedly feeling pretty bad. But he couldn't keep the other side of the argument from stabbing through his brain like a hot poker. If she'd just earned a tidy performance fee, she was surely cursing her bad luck at finding the assistant district attorney on her doorstep.

Dan's features betrayed none of the turmoil churning in his stomach. The only thing he knew for sure was that since he'd first laid eyes on Sabrina, his judgment had been impaired, his reactions to her had been out of whack, and he hated the accompanying feeling of weakness.

"What are you doing here?" Sabrina demanded in a tone that wasn't exactly friendly.

He turned his hands palm up. Whatever he was struggling with, he'd have to act as if she'd just been through a very traumatic experience. At the same time, he was going to have to be prepared for the consequences of tipping his hand to Davenport if he screwed up. Although maybe things were far enough along that it didn't matter what the old reprobate of a doctor found out. "I thought you might want someone around," he said, taking several steps toward her.

"Why?"

"After what happened this evening."

"You mean at the Institute?"

He nodded.

"Are they broadcasting it on the radio or something?" Sabrina snapped.

"No. Of course not."

"Then what's it got to do with you?"

Dan hesitated. "If I tell you how I found out, you've got to treat it as strictly confidential."

"Yes?"

"Someone at the lecture tonight is under investigation. I had a man in the audience. He called me from his car phone right after the excitement was over."

"Who are you investigating?"

"As I said, it's confidential."

"So the assistant district attorney's not going to tell me anything except that he knows Ms. Barkley made a very public—" she stopped and fumbled for a word "—fool of herself."

Dan closed the space between them and slipped his arm around Sabrina's shoulder. At first she held herself stiffly. Then he felt some of the tension go out of her body. "I know you're upset," he murmured. "I would be, too. But the way I heard it, you did CPR on the guy. That's hardly making a fool of yourself."

Sabrina sniffed. "Explain that to everyone else who saw the miraculous recovery after Dr. Davenport came to the rescue."

Dan turned Sabrina toward him and folded his arms around her. "It's okay," he soothed.

She stirred in his embrace, her face coming up to search his. For the space of several heartbeats as she gazed up at him, he was sure she was going to tell him something she thought was important.

"What?"

"Nothing. Just thanks for being here," she whispered,

the words barely audible. The gratitude was a painful squeeze to his chest. She made a little murmuring sound like birds' wings beating the air and closed her eyes. As she relaxed more fully against him, he began to stroke her back and shoulders.

Moments stretched, and neither one of them moved. "Dan, after everything that happened yesterday, I was kind of assuming you wouldn't call me."

"Why?"

"Because…" She sighed. "I told you. Because the two of us together don't make sense."

"No?" He looked down at her full, sensual lips, trying and failing to come to grips with his own confusion. "I almost went down to 43 Light Street to make sure you weren't going out on a date this evening."

"I wouldn't have lied to you."

He couldn't repress a low, gritty laugh. "In my business, I've learned that people who are afraid often lie their heads off."

"I try not to."

He felt a shiver ripple through her body. Because she was caught in the middle of something illegal and was doing her damnedest to talk her way out of it? Or was it more personal? Did she feel it, too? The invisible force that had wrapped itself around the two of them?

She could have stepped out of his embrace, but she didn't move. He should have thrust her away. Instead he held her tighter.

"Dan…"

He wanted to keep holding her. He wanted to shift her body so that he could claim her lips, feel their incredible softness, finish what they'd started when they'd been wild and out of control. The hot need was still there, even when he'd come back to her house with suspicion uppermost in his mind. She was looking up at him, waiting. Almost desperately, he distanced himself. "I need to find out why you've turned up in the middle of one of my investigations," he clipped out.

"Oh."

The look of betrayal that flashed briefly across her face made his throat ache. He had to remind himself that she kept turning up like a bad penny. "I need some information from you," he repeated.

"Is this how you usually start an interrogation?"

"It isn't an interrogation."

"What is it?"

Several moments passed before he answered. "If I sounded cold a moment ago, it's because I'm having trouble keeping my cool around you."

"Why?"

His eyes locked with hers. "Don't you know?"

She swallowed. "Yes. It's not exactly easy for me, either."

He wanted to ask her exactly what she meant, what she was feeling. Overwhelming physical attraction? Or something deeper? He didn't dare, because he didn't know if she would tell him the truth. Or if he could handle the truth, whatever it was. "I promise I'll behave myself if you invite me in to talk," he said instead.

"Will you?"

"Do you have any herb tea with saltpeter?"

She laughed. "I don't know. I've never gotten that kind of request before. It's usually the other way around."

He waited while she climbed the steps to the porch.

Robbie had gone back inside through his own door and was in the front hall. He started jumping and whining the moment they stepped across the threshold.

"Down," Sabrina ordered.

The dog gave her a wounded look and moved quietly beside Dan.

Sabrina and Dan stood uncertainly by the door. "You relax. I'll get you a cup of tea," Dan offered. Good cop, bad cop, he thought. Only he was taking both parts.

"You're going to know your way around my kitchen better than I do."

"Yeah, but I've about reached the limit of my culinary skills."

Sabrina headed for the living room, Dan for the kitchen. The dog hesitated for a moment before jumping up on the sofa.

When Dan came back, Robbie was cuddled against his mistress, eyes closed and head lolling as she stroked his silky fur. And one of the cats was bravely peering out from behind the easy chair.

Dan stood gazing down at Sabrina for a moment before putting the tray with the tea on the table and taking the easy chair. She wasn't as relaxed as she looked.

"So what kind of doctor is Luther Davenport?" she asked suddenly. "Does he have a medical degree?"

Dan's brows drew together. "What makes you think I know?"

"I think he's the one you're investigating."

"And how would you feel about that?"

"Good."

"Why?"

"I think he's dangerous."

"Why?" Dan continued to probe.

Sabrina looked back at him, struggling to sum up her feelings. "He seems to have power over people. He's like a guru or something. And I've heard he gets big contributions out of the faithful." She told him a little bit about the reaction of the assemblage to the doctor, both before he'd started to speak and after the lecture had begun.

As she described the evening, Dan's posture became less closed. "He has a Ph.D. from a place in California where you can more or less buy credentials."

"Is that why you're after him?"

"I really shouldn't talk about it. But I appreciate your insights." He sighed.

Sabrina hesitated for a moment, thinking about the stopper of the bottle she'd picked up off the floor. It might provide some more insights. But she wasn't absolutely sure she wanted to share them with Dan—yet.

For a few moments they sipped their tea, but they were each keeping an eye on the other. Sabrina could feel several forces at war in the room. Dan wanted information, but didn't want to compromise himself by telling her anything. She wanted to feel comfortable with him but found it impossible to manage that, under the circumstances.

After a while, Dan set down his mug. "Can I ask you some questions about what happened after Davenport took over with Edward?"

"All right."

"Do you think the performance was staged?" Dan asked.

"Staged? As in faked?"

Dan nodded.

"I'm not a doctor. But as far as I could tell, that guy wasn't breathing and his heart wasn't beating."

"And Davenport had a convenient witness to confirm those facts for the audience. You."

Sabrina sucked in a startled breath. She hadn't thought about her role in those terms, but Dan was right. If the whole thing had been a put-up job and Davenport had needed someone to affirm the gravity of the situation, she'd filled the bill pretty well.

"If that's true, the cowboy was playing a risky game," she whispered.

"Maybe he didn't know he was playing."

"What?"

"There are drugs that can stop the heart that can be administered without the victim knowing what's happening. You know, poisons with no immediate symptoms. And some of them have antidotes."

"Perhaps that was it." Sabrina's fingers played with the dog's silky hair as she debated whether to say anything else. If only she could connect with Dan on a more personal level. Or was it better to keep her mouth shut? The only thing she was sure of was that she didn't want him to leave yet.

"Aren't you going to tell me if anything's developed on the other case?" she asked.

He looked surprised, as if he'd forgotten all about the original reason why they'd gotten together.

"There's nothing new on that front," he said.

"Well, then—"

Just as he stood up, the phone rang.

Dan's gaze shot to the old-fashioned oak clock on the wall. It was almost twelve. "Expecting someone?" he asked sharply.

Sabrina shook her head. There was an odd feeling in her chest as she crossed to the side table and picked up the phone. It came as much from Dan's wary expression as her own puzzlement over the late call.

After one more ring, she lifted the receiver. "Hello?"

"Ms. Barkley?" The voice was low and whispery and obviously disguised. "I was beginning to think you weren't home."

"Who is this?"

There was no answer. If she'd been alone, she would have hung up.

Dan had come over and put his hand on her shoulder.

"Who is this?" she repeated.

"A friend." There was a familiar quality to the speech pattern, but it was nothing Sabrina could identify.

"What do you want?"

"I saw you tonight at the lecture."

Sabrina felt the hair on the top of her scalp prickle. She'd recognized dozens of acquaintances there. But which one matched the low-pitched voice? Her eyes shot to Dan.

He gestured and she lifted the receiver slightly away from her head. Bending, he brought his ear close so that he could listen in on the conversation.

"You saw what happened at the Institute?" Sabrina asked.

"With the man. Yes." There was a long pause on the other end of the line.

"Are you still there?"

"I'm not calling about that. I'm calling because you're in danger," the voice whispered.

The prickles traveled from Sabrina's scalp down her spine all the way to her toes. "How?"

"Don't you realize how you figure into all this?"

Sabrina's anxious gaze shot to Dan. "No!"

"Somebody's trying to put you out of business—for good."

Beside her, Dan was standing rigidly, his hand covering hers as she clutched the receiver. She felt cold all over. "Wh-who? Dr. Davenport?"

There was an indrawn breath on the other end of the line. "It's dangerous to talk on the phone."

"Then why are you calling?"

"I couldn't just stand by and let it happen."

"Will you meet me?" Dan mouthed.

"Will you meet me?" Sabrina asked.

There was another hesitation on the other end of the wire.

"Please. You can't just tell me I'm in danger. You have to give me more information," Sabrina pleaded.

After several agonizing seconds, she could hear a breath being expelled. "All right. I shouldn't. But I'll meet you at Penn Station. Downstairs where the trains come in."

"When?"

"In an hour."

Dan shook his head vigorously.

"I can't get there that fast. I'm not dressed. And, uh, my hair's wet. Give me an hour and a half," Sabrina said.

"All right. But you have to come alone, or I won't talk to you."

Sabrina swallowed. "How will I—"

"Don't worry. I'll find *you*."

The line went dead.

Chapter Eight

It was Dan who replaced the receiver firmly in the cradle. Sabrina's fingers were so tightly clenched around it that he had to pry them loose.

"My God," she breathed.

He wrapped his arms around her, holding her trembling body against his. "I'm glad I didn't leave five minutes ago."

"Not as glad as I am," she admitted, sinking against his warmth.

"Has anything like this ever happened to you before?" he asked.

"No. Nothing. Do—do—you think it's a crank?"

"I don't know. Let's try to figure it out. Any idea whether it was a man or woman?"

She shrugged. The voice had been high, and whoever it was had been striving for distortion. Yet there was that odd feeling of recognition. "Something...sounded... familiar, but I can't quite place it."

Dan looked thoughtful. She could almost picture wheels turning in his mind. "They mentioned the lecture. Did you spot anyone you recognized?"

Sabrina laughed and then fought for control. "Plenty of people. The woman who gave me the ticket. Her friend.

A lot of my customers and former customers.'' The last observation gave her pause. "There were a number of people who used to drop by my shop. Regulars who haven't been around in three or four months." Then she remembered the way the doctor had come up to her, pretending to act friendly. "Do you think Davenport has got it in for me?"

"I don't know." She could see he was struggling with a decision, weighing evidence, making rapid judgments. "All right, I'd better put you in the picture."

"Later, are you going to act like I forced you into it?"

His eyes drilled into hers. "What makes you think I'd do that?"

"The way you've been acting all along."

"Stop dissecting my motives," he snapped.

"Stop dissecting mine."

"It's my job."

She lifted her chin. "So let's get on with it. What were you about to tell me?"

"It's Davenport we're investigating."

"I was pretty sure of that. Why are you after him?"

"According to our preliminary information, his name's been linked to a few scams and a suspicious death in Georgia." As he spoke, he watched her face carefully. "But he's been clever enough to keep his hands from getting too dirty. Maybe whoever called you will have something more damaging."

"Yes. What about his assistant? The woman who introduced him tonight. Could it be her?"

"Not unless she's changed her loyalties. She's been with him since Atlanta, at least."

"Well, now you—"

Dan cut her off with a wave of his hand. "Later. I've got to set things up at the station." He reached for the receiver again and dialed. When the call was answered, he began to speak rapidly, explaining the situation. "This is Assistant District Attorney Cassidy. I want a man in place on the lower level of Penn Station before 12:45. And alert Amtrak that we'll be on the premises." He continued the clipped series of orders.

As soon as Dan hung up, he turned back to Sabrina. "You just sit tight. If we get lucky, we'll bring you down to headquarters for the identification."

Sabrina licked her lips. She'd had more than enough difficult situations to cope with in the past couple of days, and she should feel relief that Dan wasn't dragging her directly into this one. But she'd heard the urgency in the caller's voice. First she'd been frightened. Perhaps it was a defense mechanism, but now her fear had transformed itself into anger that someone would be trying to wreck her business. A business she'd poured years of her life into making a success. She couldn't just sit on the sidelines and watch it happen. "I'm going with you."

"No, you're not. This could be dangerous."

She turned to face Dan, her expression urgent. "You heard the call. Didn't it sound to you like this person wants to help me? Maybe he's going to warn me about Davenport. Maybe it's something different, but there's no guarantee you can pick him out of a crowd of travelers. If I don't show up, we might never get another chance to find out what it's all about."

A flicker of doubt crossed Dan's stern features. "Okay. You may be right," he allowed. "But I don't like it. What if it's a nut with a gun, for instance?"

His words made Sabrina shudder, but she pressed her lips together to smother the reaction. Her business. Her life. She had to know. "You're working with the police department. What can they do to protect me?"

"You're really sure you want to go through with this?"

Sabrina took a deep breath. "Yes."

Dan didn't waste any more time arguing. Instead he hurried Sabrina out the door and into his car. When they reached the main road, he turned to her. "Would you have phoned me if you'd been alone when you got that call?"

"I was scared. I would have phoned someone. You or Jo."

"She's a good choice," he said, his expression tightening, "but I'm better."

As a public transportation facility, Penn Station was open twenty-four hours a day. But after midnight there were few trains arriving, few cars in the parking lot and few people about.

A charming place to get shot, Sabrina mused as she stepped through the front door of the massive cast-iron-and-granite structure that had been erected during the glory days of train travel. She felt dwarfed by the two-story lobby with its marble walls and domed skylights.

Dan and several officers had arrived earlier. Sabrina didn't know where they were. She wasn't supposed to know. Her eyes flicked past the bronze candelabra and mahogany benches to the more Spartan room beyond the ticket counter. At the far end were the public stairways leading down to the arrival and departure area, situated two flights below the main waiting room. She checked her watch. Twelve-forty. Time to descend the right-hand flight and wait near the center of the platform.

Was the mysterious caller already on the lower level, lurking in the shadows? Would he use the public access? Or did he know about some other entrance?

"I'm going down now," she whispered, hoping the transmitter she was wearing really worked.

Sabrina's shoes echoed on the metal stairs. When she reached the tracks, she stopped and looked nervously around. In contrast to the splendor above, the arrival area was done in early Edgar Allen Poe. The floor was grimy, the lighting was dim and the air was heavy with the essence of engine oil and sweat.

A handful of sleepy-looking passengers with luggage waited by the side of the tracks for the southbound 12:55 train. Nearby, a janitor swept the platform with a long-handled broom. His efforts didn't seem to have much effect.

Probably the man or woman she'd come here to meet wouldn't want to join the travelers, so Sabrina moved slowly down the pavement in the other direction. Watching. Listening. Waiting for someone to jump out of the shadows and clamp clammy hands to her body.

She had left the main area and was approaching the boundary of the walkway. Maybe she was at the wrong end. As she turned to go back, she thought she saw a flicker of movement near the next to the last support column.

"Who's there?" Sabrina called out.

There was no answer, but her nerve endings tingled, and she was sure she felt eyes following her. Hesitantly she took a step closer. "I can't see you. Come out of the shadows."

"No. I see you. That's good enough." The voice was low and whispery, like the one over the phone earlier that evening. Now it was also shaky, as if the person were unnerved by this face-to-face encounter.

Sabrina's next step drew a sharp warning. "Don't come any closer!" The voice congealed with dread.

"All right. Anything you want. Why did you contact me?" Sabrina asked.

"The Servant of Darkness is hurting too many people."

Sabrina drew in a quick breath. All at once, she felt the way she had in the cemetery—as if an evil presence were hovering in the shadows, ready to spring out at her. It was all she could do to keep from shifting her position so that her back was pressed against one of the grimy walls. "The Servant of Darkness? What do you mean?"

"Evil. Years of evil."

The hair on the back of her neck stood and prickled. Yes. Evil. Desperately she grasped at an explanation she could understand. "Davenport. Are you talking about Dr. Davenport?"

The only answer was a wheezing cough that echoed hollowly through the underground station. Sabrina cast a quick look over her shoulder. None of the passengers appeared to be paying the conversation any attention, but the janitor was pushing his broom slowly in her direction.

"The evil. What does it have to do with me?" Sabrina forced the question through numb lips.

"The Servant is afraid of…you…" The cough had turned to a frantic choking gasp.

"Are you all right?"

"Stay back. Don't come any closer." Fear mingled with labored breathing.

"Why is this servant afraid of me?" Sabrina pressed.

"You don't know? You really don't know?" The speaker gave a strange imitation of mirth before stopping abruptly and gasping for breath. The raspy, labored sound raised goose bumps on Sabrina's arms.

"No. Please. Tell me."

"You fool. Don't…you…remember what happened…all those years ago? In the fire?"

"What fire?"

"The Burning." The voice gasped with pain, and Sabrina saw a figure slump to the floor, a figure wearing an oversize raincoat and a hat pulled low over the face. She rushed forward to help.

"Are you sick?"

"What's happening to me? Ahhh..."

"Let me help you."

"Oh, Satan! Oh, Saraaa...," The exclamation ended in a groan of pain and terror.

"Help. I need help," Sabrina cried out, but she didn't need to shout to get action.

Seconds later she heard footsteps pounding down the platform. Then Dan was beside her, his face pale and strained in the dim light.

She stared up at him in confusion as two other men rushed past. He slung a protective arm over her shoulder.

"Get an ambulance," one of the policemen ordered into his walkie-talkie. He bent over the person on the floor to check for a pulse. When Sabrina tried to help, Dan pulled her back and prevented her from joining the rescue efforts. "They'll take care of it," he said, turning her toward him.

She held on to his arm for support, and for just a moment she had the odd sensation that he needed bracing as much as she did.

"Are you all right?" he asked.

"I...I guess." She couldn't tell him what she was feeling. It took a great deal of effort to keep her teeth from chattering. "You heard all that?"

"The Servant of Darkness stuff. The evil. Yeah."

"Do you have any idea what it means?"

"No. But it's all on tape, for what it's worth."

Their whispered discussion was interrupted by the sound of feet thumping down the stairs. Two attendants arrived with a stretcher and other equipment.

"How did they get here so fast?" Sabrina asked.

"They were on standby. In case..." The explanation trailed off.

Sabrina was vaguely aware that a couple of uniformed policemen were holding the small crowd of curious passengers back at the end of the platform, but her attention was focused closer by. The rescue team had started CPR, fighting for a life that was inexorably slipping away. As Sabrina watched the tense drama, she lost the battle to stay calm. When she shook, Dan's arm tightened around her, holding her steady.

"That's what I was doing at the Institute," she managed, her eyes glued to the trio on the grimy concrete.

"Yeah. I didn't think of that."

Sabrina was thankful it wasn't her responsibility. A pair of trained paramedics were doing the job. And there was another important variation, as well. It wasn't a man lying still as death on the ground. Sabrina sucked in a shaky breath as she got her first good look at the person under the raincoat and hat. The ill-fitted clothing hid a woman.

Sabrina focused on the contorted face. Again she couldn't hold back an exclamation.

"You know her?" Dan asked urgently.

"Yes. She used to be a customer of mine." Sabrina struggled to keep her voice steady. "She was embarrassed this evening when she saw me at the lecture. At least that's why I assumed she turned away when she spotted me."

"Her name?"

"Mrs. Garrison." Sabrina's numb brain scrambled to come up with the rest of it. "June Garrison."

The ambulance attendants had brought one of those portable electric units used to restart the heart. After ripping away the bodice of the woman's dress, one of them pressed the paddles against her skin.

"Clear," he shouted. Current surged through the wires, and the woman's body jerked.

The other medic had his eyes fixed on the controls. "Nothing."

"Again. Clear."

Once more the body jerked, but the heart didn't start.

"I think we've lost her."

The other medic nodded.

Sabrina felt her heart sink.

A train whistle shattered the air. The 12:55, right on time. In the space of fifteen minutes a woman had tried to warn her and died in the attempt. Whatever information June Garrison had wanted to tell her would be buried with her.

The paramedics transferred the body to the stretcher and covered it with a sheet. One of the detectives picked up a small black purse lying on the floor. Since Sabrina hadn't spotted it earlier, she guessed it must have been tucked under the raincoat.

The detective turned to Dan. "I'll arrange for an autopsy first thing in the morning." Then he nodded to Sabrina. "You did a wonderful job, Miss."

"Thanks," she managed.

Dan introduced them. The plainclothesman was Brian Lowell, who had been in charge of the operation.

Dan kept his arm around Sabrina's sagging shoulders as they climbed back up to the lobby. When they stepped out of the muggy lower level into the air conditioning, she started to shiver again.

Dan's fingers gently rubbed her arms, bringing a warmth that felt like a heat lamp on a January evening. "It's over now. All over. She can't hurt you," he soothed as he led her to one of the wooden benches.

Gratefully Sabrina slid down onto the firm surface. She could feel herself drawing inward, her mind shutting down.

Lowell's voice brought her back. "I've had a quick look at the personal effects. There's not much there. June L. Garrison. Age forty-five. Five feet six inches tall," he read from a driver's license. "She's got the usual credit cards."

"Can I see the purse?" Dan asked.

Lowell handed him the black leather bag, and he began to riffle through the inside pockets. Moments later he pulled out a folded pink slip. "Looks like she withdrew ten thousand dollars from New Court Savings and Loan just this afternoon."

"Ten thousand dollars?" Sabrina repeated. "How much did she have in her wallet?"

"Ten dollars and change," Lowell answered. "Wonder what she did with all that cash."

"She was at the Andromeda Institute earlier in the evening. My...my assistant said that people sometimes make sizable donations to Dr. Davenport."

"I was wondering about that myself," Dan said. "Is there anything else you can tell us about her?"

"When she used to come into my shop, she was friendly but on the quiet side. She was always looking for something to ease her rheumatism. Maybe Davenport was helping her." Sabrina gulped. "And now she's dead."

"A chronic illness would make her an easy mark for a con man like Davenport," Dan pointed out.

"The Servant of Darkness. Do you know what that means?" Lowell broke in.

"Sounds like someone who serves the devil," she guessed.

"Well, if she was ill and on strong medication, she could have dreamed up some sort of conspiracy." The officer's voice didn't hold a lot of conviction.

Sabrina sat on the hard wooden bench, feeling as if a hand had closed around her throat. Through a screen of lashes, she looked up at Dan, wishing he could take her in his arms and hold her the way he had when he'd come to her house earlier this evening. But they weren't supposed to be involved. They were only working together on a case.

"I don't like leaving you. But I have to turn in a report," he muttered.

"I understand."

"A few hours ago I asked if you were going to be all right. How about now?"

That was back when she'd only been worried about making a fool of herself. The plot had thickened considerably.

Sabrina pulled herself up straighter. "I'll survive," she said in a voice that surprised her with its strength.

Dan escorted her to a police car, opened the back door and gave her hand a squeeze. She clung to him for several heartbeats. As she slid onto the seat, he looked as if he was going to say something. Instead he turned away and gave some instructions to the driver. Then she was on her way home.

In the darkness, she leaned back against the vinyl cushions, vaguely glad they were more comfortable than the benches in the station. She didn't want to think about what had just happened. She just wanted to go back to her own house and relax. But when June's words began to echo in her head, she was too tired to fight them off.

The Servant of Darkness. The Burning. Satan. Saraaa.

Sabrina jerked erect as her mind echoed that last urgent syllable. In the exigency of the moment, when she'd been worried about so many other things, it had simply been a strangled sound trickling from the lips of a dying woman. In the silence of the police car, it took on meaning.

It wasn't just a sound. It was a name. Sara. The name of the woman in her story.

A bead of perspiration formed at Sabrina's hairline and slid down the back of her neck.

Was she really getting this right? Or had her mind conjured up the connection?

Her story. Reality. She'd convinced herself they were like two sets of train tracks running beside each other. But she could feel them converging. Her story. The fire she'd imagined at the cemetery. The Servant of Darkness. June Garrison. In some mysterious way, they were connected.

More droplets of moisture trickled down the back of her neck, and she reached to wipe them aside. Her palm came away slick and clammy.

Chapter Nine

For the remainder of the ride home, Sabrina sat tensely in the back seat of the police car. Then she waited with her heart thumping against her ribs while her escort walked around checking the house and making sure the doors and windows were locked.

He gave her an appraising look as he rejoined her in the living room.

"It's all right. The house is secure."

"Yes. Thanks," Sabrina managed, hanging on to the appearance of normalcy as she ushered him out. Let him assume she was worried about the house. Better to have him put that in his report than what was really making her feel as if a coil of barbed wire were twisting in her stomach. She watched to make sure he was actually leaving. When she saw his headlights cutting through the darkness down the driveway, she rushed into the little room she used as an office and snatched up a pen and pad of paper.

The story she was writing. It was her only clue to what was going on. She had to go back to it. Tonight. Before it was too late.

Still, when she settled herself on the sofa and took the pen in her hand, she felt a surge of panic as if someone had just dropped a dark, suffocating shroud over her head and started to secure the covering with heavy ropes.

She fought the feeling of claustrophobia. Was she crazy? Or possessed? Was some strange outside power exerting an influence over her?

Shuddering, she tried to loosen her grip on the pen. But her fingers were locked in a death grip.

Her eyes squeezed closed. Then she saw an image. Sara. So like herself. Yet different. Standing on the battlement of a castle, the wind blowing her wild red hair.

She beckoned. And suddenly it was all right. Swiftly and surely, the pen began to move across the page.

Thin morning sunlight slanted in through the narrow windows in the stone wall of the castle. Sara was half dozing in the chair when a flicker of movement made her jerk to wakefulness. She hadn't heard anyone come in, but Duncan was leaning over the bed, looking down into the patient's face.

"He seems much better."

"Aye. I think he's going to be all right." She laid a hand against the sleeping man's cheek. The fever had broken several hours earlier, and his skin was dry and cool.

"Ye must be exhausted, lass," Duncan said.

She stretched and winced slightly.

"You do yourself ill spending the night in a chair like that."

"The serving girl was weary. She'd been with me for hours, so I sent her away."

"How long has it been since you've left this room?"

Sara didn't answer. Days, she thought. But she'd felt a kind of safety in here—after the terrible confrontation with Fergus McGraw. He'd been furious that someone else had been brought to tend his patient, and he'd predicted dire consequences for the man who lay coughing on the bed.

Sara had turned away to tend him. Duncan and several other men had removed the physician forcibly from the room.

Duncan must have seen the expression that crossed her face as she remembered the scene. "You're brave—as well as skilled."

"Not so brave. Is Dr. McGraw still about?"

"He's gone."

"Thank the Lord. I dinna want to face that fierce stare of his again."

"He won't harm ye. I'll see to that." Duncan came around to stand in back of Sara. She felt him behind her, heard the breath stirring in his lungs. There was a long moment of anticipation when she imagined she felt his hands hovering above her. Then he lifted her hair from her neck.

"What are ye doing?"

"You've given so much to Ian. Let me ease the stiffness in your shoulders." His large hands began to knead her tired muscles. It wasn't proper for a man to touch a woman like that, but when she opened her mouth to protest, no words came out. Instead she closed her eyes and sighed. The massage felt good.

"What did ye do for him?" he murmured.

Sara had been drifting with the physical sensations. It took a moment for her mind to focus on the question. "There wasn't so much I could do. Force him to take fluids, keep him quiet, bind his chest, give him something for the pain."

"That sounds like quite a bit, to me. Your gran taught you all that?"

"Aye."

They were silent again. The hands on her shoulders moved to her neck and then into her hair.

"Don't. You shouldn't."

"Your locks are like fire. I've been wanting to touch them," he murmured.

There was a knock at the door. Duncan quickly moved back and dropped his hands.

"Come in," Sara called out, her voice a bit shaky.

The maid she'd sent away after Ian's fever had broken came in. "I'll take over. Go on. Get up for a stretch," she said.

Sara checked the patient's breathing and tucked the covers up around him. "If he wakes, give him some water. And if he's in pain, come and fetch me," she said.

"Aye."

She'd been sitting for so long that she was unsteady on her feet. Duncan grasped her elbow, and for just a moment she sagged against him. Then she straightened. But he kept hold of her as he ushered her down the hallway and out onto the parapet that circled the castle. After the close quarters of the sickroom, the cool morning air felt wonderful, and Sara drank in a long draft as she looked out over the countryside. The valley below them was hidden in the mist, creating the fancy that the rest of the world had gone away, leaving only this high mountain stronghold.

The cold began to make her shiver. Duncan was behind her again. This time, his arms circled her waist. She should move away. Instead she eased back against him, enjoying the warmth and the supple strength of his body. Neither one of them spoke.

"Some wanted to call in Lillias."

Sara had heard dark whisperings about the old woman

who lived on the other side of the mountain from the village. "They say she's a witch."

"Aye. But Calder and some of the others were for it. I argued against her."

"Ye did?"

"Aye. I dinna want her working her spells on Ian. Now I'm doubly glad."

Did she feel his lips in her hair, or was that her imagination?

Nay, not imagination.

She moved her head and felt him sigh as he pulled her closer. Now she was inviting his attentions like a wanton woman.

"Duncan." *Knowing she'd made a mistake, she tried to draw away, but he held her in place.*

"Shhh. I mean ye no harm. I haven't been able to get ye out of my mind all this time, lass. When I saw you at the door of the cottage, it was like a bolt of lightning shooting through me." *His mouth moved over her hair. His hands slid up and down her arms, stroking her, drawing her back into his heat. She closed her eyes, unable to resist the seductive pull. Pleasurable sensations curled through her body.*

When he turned her in his arms, she could only stare up at him, her eyes heavy-lidded. Then reason stabbed at her sharply like a knife in her breast.

This was wrong. It could lead nowhere. Not between a girl from the village and a laird.

"Duncan. Nay."

He ignored her plea as his lips descended to hers. Her hands pushed against his chest. Her body tried to twist out of his arms. But he held her tight—tight. And there was only one place she could escape.

SABRINA GASPED air into her lungs with the desperation of a drowning swimmer who finally breaks the surface of the water. The room had no reality. It was too warm. Too comfortable. Too modern.

The wrong place. In the wrong time.

Then, as if a burlap sack had been roughly turned inside out to reveal a quilted lining, reality reversed itself.

Sabrina's breath was coming in little puffs, and her whole body was drenched in sweat. With a trembling hand, she picked up the hem of her dress and wiped it across her face. She was sitting on the sofa in the living room with a clipboard and a pad of lined paper in her lap.

Robbie slept on a nearby cushion. But across the room, a frightened cat peered at her from behind a chair.

"You probably think I'm going nuts," she said.

As if answering the question, the cat bounded away, and Sabrina was left with nothing but her own doubts. At first she'd felt a warm surge of relief as if she were coming home to Duncan's welcoming arms. But in the end, it had been no refuge. She'd felt a terrible, driving need to escape from the story. From Duncan. From the sweetness of his kiss. Because it had been wrong. And dangerous.

Sabrina pressed her palms against her forehead, feeling as if she were wandering in a cruel maze where every path led to disaster. Was there nowhere she could find refuge from danger? She'd taken up pen and paper to find out what June Garrison had been trying to tell her when she'd died. Fleeing to her Scottish story hadn't given her any answers. Just more questions.

Feeling a pulse pound in her temple, she looked around her cheery living room. In the train station she'd felt a terrifying presence hovering in the shadows. Just like at the cemetery, she acknowledged with a shudder. It had followed her home, and it was hiding in the dark corners where she never dusted, waiting to pounce. If she didn't somehow outdistance the unseen menace, it was going to spring like a hungry tiger and tear her to bits.

THE CLARENCE MITCHELL Courthouse was empty, save for the few clerks who worked the night shift. The assistant district attorney's office was dark, except for the old-fashioned brass lamp, which cast a pool of yellow illumination on the desk blotter. A tape recorder hummed in the center of the lighted circle. As the last words faded from the minicassette, Dan reached out and pressed the stop button. Then he rewound the tape.

He felt the hairs on the top of his scalp prickle as June Garr:son's dying words seemed to echo in the small room. The Servant of Darkness. The Burning. Satan. Saraaa. It might have been the long, drawn-out gasp of a woman in pain. When you listened to the tape, you could interpret it that way.

But as soon as he'd heard it, he'd known it was a name. Sara. And he couldn't explain why it had come from June Garrison's lips.

He'd lain awake at night, hearing that name in his head. It was the same name he'd spoken in the graveyard when he'd gone racing after Sabrina. When she'd been terrified and he'd been trying to save her. At least, that was what his drugged mind had thought he was doing.

Tonight, at the station, he'd felt the same desperate need to shield her from danger. When that apparition in the raincoat had popped out of the shadows and lurched toward her, he'd almost gone rushing down the platform to save her again. Somehow, he'd forced himself to hold back until the drama had played itself out.

Cupping his face in his hands, he pressed his palms hard against his eyelids. It didn't help. In his mind he saw a woman's countenance, hauntingly delicate and framed by a wreath of long red curls. Oddly, he seemed to see it surrounded by a crystal sphere. It was Sara.

As he stared at her, the features blurred and changed subtly. When the face reformed, the skin became clear and translucent. The hazel eyes altered to sea green. The straggly brows were almost tamed.

Now it was Sabrina.

Dan's eyes snapped open, and he jumped up from the chair as if the seat had suddenly become red hot.

Then he went dead still. Sara. Sabrina. Terrified of the fire.

Panic gnawed at his vitals. By an act of will, he brought the fear down to a level he could manage. He knew what was happening to him. What had to be happening. Because there was no other explanation he could accept. He was having a flashback from the cherry bomb.

He let out the aching breath he'd been holding in his lungs. A flashback. Yeah. That was it. He'd never thought he'd be glad someone had drugged him. Now he clasped it to himself. Because if he didn't believe that theory, he'd have to believe...

He stopped, unable to complete the thought.

SABRINA OPENED sleepy eyes and glanced at the clock. She was shocked to find that it was almost eight-thirty. That was very late by her standards. But at least she'd gotten a good night's sleep.

For long moments she lay in bed staring at the crack that jagged like a lightning bolt across the middle of the ceiling, trying to figure out how she felt. In the morning sunlight, it was difficult to recapture the dread and the crazy speculations of the night before. Thank goodness.

After a quick cup of tea and a cookie, she took a shower.

While she was washing her hair, she remembered something that had completely slipped her mind with everything else that was going on. She still had the stopper from the bottle that Davenport had used to revive Edward.

Quickly she washed away the shampoo and dried off. In her bathrobe, she ran downstairs, fished the prize out of her pocketbook and clenched it in her fist. It wasn't out of a story or part of a whispered warning over the phone. It was solid and concrete. And maybe it would yield its secrets.

She could turn it over to Dan. Then she thought about explaining to the police lab how she'd acquired it. Was it stolen property? Maybe they couldn't even accept something like that. Instead of calling the assistant district attorney's office, she got out her phone book and looked up the number for Medizone Labs, where Dr. Katie Martin McQuade had recently assumed the position of director of research.

"Can I hire you to analyze a magic elixir I picked up last night?" she asked when she was put through to her friend.

"Sounds interesting. What does it do?"

Sabrina fingered the plastic bag that now held the tissue-wrapped stopper. "It appears to bring the dead back to life."

"Sounds even more interesting. Bring it right over."

Before Sabrina left, she made a quick call to the shop to tell Erin she'd be late.

"Not to worry," her assistant told her. "I'm just getting out some new stock. And you had a call. From Mr. Cassidy. He wants to take you to lunch again. I said it would be fine."

"Maybe you should have checked with me first."

"Don't you want to go?"

Sabrina reconsidered her response. "Yes. I'm sorry. I'm just kind of uptight."

"After last night, you're entitled."

Sabrina gulped. "You know about last night?"

"Well, Hilda called with a report."

"About the man at the Institute?"

"Yes. She told me to look after you," Erin continued.

"Sweet of her," Sabrina murmured, wondering who else her wacky customer had called. Still, it could be worse. The Institute was bad enough. What she really dreaded was getting into a discussion about the train station. "Do me a favor. When I come in, pretend this is just a normal day."

She could hear Erin take in a breath and let it out. "Sabrina, everybody comes to you with their troubles. You're always there for us. You ought to know it's all right to ask for help with—with problems."

"If I thought it would do any good, I'd take you up on it."

"Well, I'm here to listen, if you need me."

"Thanks."

After hanging up, Sabrina reached down to stroke the cat that had plopped into her lap. She was pretty sure that talking about her present problems wouldn't help. No, that wasn't exactly true. There had always been a part of herself that she didn't feel comfortable sharing. If she started talking about witches and spells and evil eyes, she was going to feel too exposed and vulnerable.

Twenty minutes later, Sabrina pulled into one of the spaces reserved for visitors in the crowded Medizone parking lot. Marcia, the executive secretary, knew Sabrina was expected and ushered her right into Katie's spacious office. Katie's husband, Mac, was leaning against the desk, a mug of coffee gripped casually in his left hand—the one made of stainless steel. The metal fingers had saved his and Katie's life when they'd been in a tight situation six months earlier.

Perhaps Mac hadn't entirely come to terms with the prosthesis. But it was apparent marriage to Katie had changed him. Once he'd avoided people. Now he was comfortable meeting the public. Still, Sabrina was flattered that the company president had taken time off his busy schedule for her.

"Katie told me about your find. I'm always interested in turning up wonder drugs," he explained.

Sabrina knew that before he and Katie had gotten back together, he'd spent his life traveling around the world looking for exotic antitoxins.

"Maybe you don't have to go any farther than Baltimore." Sabrina took out the plastic bag and set it on the desk. Along with it, she gave her friends a capsule summary of the amazing revival and a warning that the analysis of the white powder clinging to the stopper might have impact on a police investigation.

"Can you be more specific?" Mac asked.

"If you don't want to get involved, I und—"

Mac cut her off. "We'll do it. I just want to make sure you're not into something you can't handle."

"I'm just on the fringes," Sabrina assured him, still anxious not to open herself up for a discussion. Besides, going into detail would only worry her friends.

But Katie had been watching the nervous twists Sabrina gave to the silver ring on her right hand. "I know what it's like to be sitting on information you're afraid to trust to the authorities. If you need us for more than lab work, we're here," she said.

"I appreciate that."

Katie took out a notebook. "Even if you don't want to

say more about the case, I do need some information about exactly what happened. Are you sure the victim wasn't breathing when the doctor gave him the stuff?''

''I took a pretty complete first-aid course last year. I couldn't detect either breath or heartbeat.''

''Tell me everything you can about his symptoms.''

Sabrina complied. When she finished, she saw Katie give her husband a quick, pointed look. He nodded almost imperceptibly and picked up the plastic bag. ''I'll take this down to the lab. We'll have to run a number of different kinds of tests, so I'm not sure how long before we get the results. Check back with us this afternoon.''

When he'd departed, Katie put down her pen. ''Sabrina, you're more upset than you're letting on. Are you sure there isn't something you want to tell me?''

''You didn't have to get rid of Mac. I'm worried about business stuff.''

Katie looked dubious. ''You're sure?''

Sabrina forced a smile. ''Everything will work out.''

However, as she drove downtown, she felt her thoughts and her stomach starting to churn again. After pulling into the parking garage, she sat gripping the steering wheel with white-knuckled hands.

She'd sat like this in the car the morning it had all started. Then she'd just had a vague sense that something bad was going to happen. This morning she was smack in the middle of it.

She'd thought it was all tied in with the account she was writing of Sara and Duncan. When she'd gotten home from the terrible scene at the train station, she'd hoped she could get some answers from the story. Now that seemed like grasping at straws. This wasn't about fiction. It was about the here and now.

If somebody wanted to hurt her, all they had to do was

wait until she got out of the car and walked across the street. They could come roaring around the corner and mow her down. Except that wasn't the way anything had happened so far. Moisture beaded on her upper lip as she pictured a witch leaning over a boiling caldron, chanting sinister incantations against her.

Deep down, she'd always wondered if she really believed in the power of evil spells. Was that what had killed June Garrison? And what about the star stone at the cemetery? Even when she'd told Dan it was cursed, she hadn't quite believed it. That was before so many other things had happened.

An echo of the painful shock she'd felt when she'd held that innocent-looking oval in her hand reverberated through her body. It left her breathing shallowly and feeling as if fire ants were crawling on her skin. Scrambling out of the car, she began to run her hands up and down her arms. A man who'd just gotten out of his own vehicle gave her an odd look, and she turned away, embarrassed.

Reaching across the front seat she snatched up her purse and slammed the door with a loud thunk. She remembered what she'd told Dan about magic and witches' curses. If you thought they were going to make you sick or kill you, they probably would. Undoubtedly that was what had happened to her at the cemetery. She'd started worrying that something bad was going to happen even before Dan had driven through the gates. So it had.

Quickly she crossed the street. After entering the building, she stood looking across at her shop. She'd worked hard to make Sabrina's Fancy a success. And she wasn't going to toss it all away. Maybe that was the real threat. Someone was trying to frighten her into self-destructing. But why? She'd been worried that Davenport was out to ruin her, but that didn't exactly make sense. Not when her yearly profit was peanuts compared to what he must be taking in at the Institute. Was he so greedy that he wanted to be the only one selling herb products in Baltimore? Or was the threat from somewhere else?

Had she inadvertently done something to hurt someone? She couldn't think of anything. Certainly nothing deliberate.

"Planning a new window display?" a soft voice asked.

Sabrina whirled toward the door.

"Sorry. I didn't mean to sneak up on you," Noel Emery, the paralegal who worked for Laura Roswell, apologized as she came into the lobby carrying a heavy briefcase.

"That's okay. I was just thinking about something," Sabrina said. "What do you think about featuring some of that silver jewelry I've been getting from the Eastern Shore?" she improvised.

"Good idea." Noel tipped her head consideringly. "I used to help my uncle in his jewelry shop so I know a good buy when I see it. I've had my eye on a pair of your earrings for a couple of weeks. Maybe I should buy them before I lose out."

After they'd chatted for a few minutes, Noel walked to the elevator. Sabrina crossed to the shop. Although the door was open, Erin was nowhere in sight. Then she heard her assistant bustling around in the back room.

Sabrina checked the cash register to make sure there was enough change, but she was still thinking about threats. Davenport was the only one she could identify. If he saw her as a business rival and wanted to discredit her, he'd gotten a wonderful start last night. However, to be prepared, he would have had to know she was going to show up at the lecture. Had he been the one who'd urged Hilda to invite her?

Sabrina pulled a phone book from under the counter and found the number. When she picked up the receiver, she realized Erin was on the phone, talking to someone in a low voice.

"Oh, sorry."

"Sabrina? I'll be off in a jiffy."

Her assistant came out of the back room a few minutes later carrying a box full of decorative metal tea canisters. Sabrina tried Hilda again. But there was no answer. Maybe she was out having a tennis lesson, or was it golf? She'd have to try later.

Sabrina was conscious that Erin was hovering around her. "Are you sure you don't want to sit down for a cup of tea and a chat?" her assistant finally asked.

"No. I need to work. Why don't we change the window display. Let's use those canisters, and some of our silver jewelry, too."

"Yes. Maybe that's what we both need," Erin agreed.

At twelve-thirty, Dan found Sabrina in the lobby staring at the shop window. Her hair stood out in a red cloud around her face, a smudge of dirt tinged her cheek, and a satisfied smile quirked her lips.

Turning to Dan, she felt a rush of pleasure. He gazed back at her expectantly, yet there was a tension around his eyes. She'd seen that look before in her customers—when there was some personal problem they wanted to discuss but didn't know how to bring up. The mixed signals made her heart start to beat faster.

"Hi" was all she said.

"Hi, yourself."

She'd thought he'd be dressed for the office. Instead he was wearing jeans and a turquoise knit top that was wonderful with his blond hair and tanned complexion.

"Where are we going?" she blurted.

"I'm planning to kidnap you."

"Isn't that a federal offense?"

A small smile played around his lips. "I think I'm immune from prosecution."

He reached out to lay his hand lightly on her arm, and both of them stood very still, gazing at each other. For a moment, she felt something very warm and open between them. Then the guarded look was back behind his eyes.

"What is it?"

There was a five-second pause. "Not that I care, but probably you want to wash your face and comb your hair."

Sabrina had forgotten Erin was in the doorway. Now she turned accusingly to her friend. "Why didn't you warn me I was a mess?"

"I think he's telling the truth. He doesn't care," Erin seconded the observation.

Nevertheless, Sabrina made a quick trip to the bathroom to put herself back together. After washing her face and brushing her hair, she snatched up a green-and-yellow scarf from the new stock she'd gotten in recently and slipped it around her neck.

But once she and Dan were alone, neither one of them seemed to be able to dredge up any casual conversation. As Sabrina buckled her seat belt, she slid Dan a quick glance. His expression was grim.

"You didn't have to take me to lunch."

"I wanted to."

"Are you going to tell me what's making you so uptight?" she asked.

He didn't answer.

"Is it about the case? Has something happened that I should know about?"

"It's my problem, not yours," he said cryptically as he started the car.

Dan kept his eyes glued to the noontime traffic. He had a lot to worry about. Unaccountably he was thinking about something that should be at the bottom of the list. His ridiculously out-of-proportion reaction to the June Garrison tape last night.

Maybe it had really been from a drug flashback. On the other hand, now that he was thinking more clearly, he'd decided it was just as likely that he was feeling the effects of extreme stress. He'd seen it happen to other guys. When you were under a lot of pressure and not getting any sleep, your mind played all kinds of stupid tricks. Either you had to find a way to cope, or you quit the department and went in for something tamer, like commodities trading.

He wasn't ready to bail out. But unfortunately none of his problems had vaporized during the night. They'd only gotten worse. After a couple of hours of restless sleep, he'd come back to the office to confront a whole set of unpleasant realities. Starting with the June Garrison preliminary autopsy report and how it affected the Graveyard Murder case.

The chief of police had had something to say about that one, and it hadn't been a very enjoyable conversation. Dan had been angry and frustrated, and he hadn't even been able to say, "I told you so."

He'd come away from the meeting needing to feel that there was *something* effective he could do. Getting Sabrina out of the city had been the most constructive alternative he could conjure up. He hadn't even let himself think about how much he simply wanted to be with her.

So he'd called up her assistant and made the arrangements. Then, instead of sitting behind his desk stewing over the ineffectiveness of the system, he'd played hooky and spent the rest of the morning getting ready. But as soon as he'd seen Sabrina standing there with that mixture of innocence and mystery he found so appealing, he'd realized it would have been smarter to let Brian Lowell handle this particular part of the job.

Which made him a coward. And an underhanded coward, at that. Even if he didn't plan to talk about the weird feeling he'd gotten while he was listening to the tape last night, he owed it to Sabrina to share the information he'd acquired from the police department.

His jaw clenched, and the cords of his neck tightened. He didn't want to start a conversation about the police report on June Garrison. Or about the way he'd brought Sabrina into the Graveyard Murder case in the first place. From a personal point of view, that was the worst part of all.

However, sooner or later he'd have to come clean with her. On all counts. But please, God, not yet.

Chapter Ten

Sabrina pretended to watch the crowds of office workers
and tourists enjoying the summer weather, but from the
corner of her eye she continued to study Dan's tense features. You didn't have to be a psychic to read his clenched
jaw and evasive eyes. Whatever he was worried about
might be his problem, but she'd bet the next month's re-
ceipts from her shop that it involved her.

Last night when she'd wanted to be in on the action at
Penn Station, she'd made it clear that she wouldn't take
no for an answer, even when he'd warned her she might
be walking into danger. Today she didn't feel on such solid
ground. And as she sat with one hand wedged under her
leg, she started to worry about something else. She was
concealing a piece of information she was pretty sure Dan
would be interested in. It hadn't started off as concealment.
But Dan might think that's what it had turned into. She
didn't know how to bring it up, because when she did,
he'd assume she hadn't completely trusted him.

Sabrina saw Dan sigh. "Sorry. I'm being selfish. I just
want to enjoy a couple of hours with you before I have to
start thinking about business again."

Relieved, Sabrina grabbed on to that. In a very funda-
mental way, it was what she wanted, too. "Okay."

His tension went down several levels, and she was glad she hadn't pushed.

Dan headed toward the Science Center, and Sabrina guessed they were going to eat at the Rusty Scupper, several blocks farther on. Instead he pulled up at the entrance to the marina directly across the harbor from the World Trade Center. After cutting the engine, he got out and unlocked the trunk. Inside was a plastic cooler, a shopping bag and a wicker hamper.

"What's all that?"

"Lunch. If you take the hamper, I'll take the rest."

She tested the weight of the basket. "You must have an enormous appetite."

"Yeah." He led her toward one of the small piers. She followed him to a tidy cabin cruiser named *Legal Eagles*.

The name brought a smile to her lips. She'd thought of the Redford movie as soon as she'd met him.

"Yours?" she asked, eyeing the well-cared-for craft.

"Four of us down at the office pitched in and bought her at one of those sales the police department holds twice a year. She belonged to a drug dealer who stretched his luck too thin. Craig uses her the most. But the rest of us get in enough weekends to make the investment worthwhile."

Dan climbed aboard and set the cooler on the deck. When he turned to help Sabrina across the gunwale, he found her already standing on the varnished planking.

"I told you I grew up at the shore. Some of my friends' parents had boats, so you don't have to worry about my going overboard or anything like that."

"Good."

It seemed they'd both made a silent agreement to act like two people out for a day of sun and fun.

"Listen, I was thinking, let's head down to the bay before we eat," Dan said when he returned from stowing the gear.

"All the way?"

"I can do it in forty minutes."

Why not? She'd decided to drop her problems until after lunch. It was even more effective to leave them far behind in Baltimore. Or cast them upon the water, as it were. "Okay. Can I do anything to help?"

"You can untie the ropes."

"Will do."

While Dan climbed up to the the pilot's seat, Sabrina attended to the lines. Then she opened one of the low folding beach chairs and tried to relax as Dan maneuvered the boat out of the marina. But she was too restless to sit still for long.

They cruised past Fort McHenry where Francis Scott Key had watched the bombs bursting in air during the War of 1812, then past Sparrows Point and Gibson Island, the posh enclave at the mouth of the Patapsco River.

As the boat reached open water, the green-and-yellow scarf Sabrina was wearing began to blow around her face. Taking it off, she wound it around the handle of the wicker hamper. Then, curious about what Dan had brought, she began poking through the contents of the ice chest. He had obviously gone overboard at the Harborplace food stalls. Among other things, she found spiced shrimp, crab-claw cocktail, potato salad, marinated vegetables, hot peppers, "buffalo" wings, cheese bread, blueberry cheesecake, cola and raspberry soda.

"I repeat, this is *lunch?*" she asked as she set out containers on the square table in the cockpit.

Dan anchored the boat and sat down in one of the low chairs. "I was working off nervous energy shopping."

"Oh?"

Looking a bit sheepish, he began filling his plate. "Did I get some things you like?" he asked.

Sabrina nodded and dipped a peeled crab claw into the cocktail sauce. "This will do for starters."

Dan leaned back in his seat, looking like a man trying to loaf, but his muscles were too tightly coiled for that.

Sabrina nibbled on a cheese cube, but she pushed more food around her plate than she conveyed to her mouth as she watched Dan watching her. Even if they both wanted to act as if this were a normal outing, it wasn't working. They weren't being honest with each other. She'd tried to get him to tell her what was wrong. He was being evasive. On the other hand, so was she. She hadn't wanted to talk to anyone about what was worrying her. But here she was sitting with the one person who didn't need a two-hour briefing to understand why she was uptight. Perhaps if she took the risk of making the fist move, he'd be candid with her.

Sabrina took a sip of soda to wet her throat. "I'd feel more comfortable if I told you something," she said before she lost her nerve.

"Oh?"

"It has to do with what happened last night at the Institute."

Dan put the chicken wing he was holding back on his plate. "About Davenport? Something you've remembered?"

"It's about the stuff Davenport gave Edward. He had it in a little bottle. And when Edward lurched against him, the stopper must have gone flying. It landed on the floor beside my purse. I found it and picked it up."

"That's withholding evidence. You had an obligation to turn it over to me. Why the hell didn't you?" The question exploded out of him, belying the relaxed pose he'd been cultivating.

Sabrina shrank back. "Did I? You didn't even want to tell me you were investigating him, remember?"

"It could be important. If we can get an analysis."

Sabrina knit her fingers together in her lap.

Dan stared at her. Then he climbed out of his seat and came over beside her, reaching for her. She held herself stiffly as she felt his hands on her shoulders. "Sabrina, I'm sorry," he muttered. "You didn't deserve that."

She didn't, couldn't respond.

His hands tightened on her shoulders. Then they dropped to his sides, and he returned to his chair. "I've been trying to keep my problems to myself. Maybe that was a stupid idea," he said in a gritty voice.

"I think that's true for both of us."

"You know, I've had a man in custody for the Grave-yard Murders. Raul Simmons. I never thought the case against him was very strong. It was blown to hell in a hand bucket this morning."

"Why is that?"

"Because the graveyard victims died of exactly the same poison that killed June Garrison."

Sabrina felt a wave of cold sweep across her body. "Murder? Another murder?"

"That's the one conclusive report I do have on my desk. It's definitely a homicide, unless Ms. Garrison injected herself with a lethal dose of poison before she went to meet with you at the station."

Sabrina wrapped her hands around the chair arms.

Dan plowed on. "The only difference is that the other two were killed quickly. However, as I told you, I don't put much faith in coincidences. The poison isn't something you can go buy at the drugstore. You have to grow it."

"A herbal extract?"

"Yes."

Sabrina studied the tense planes of Dan's face.

"I was wondering this morning if Edward had been given the same thing," he said tightly. "Only in a lesser dose. Enough to stop the heart unless an antidote was given. If I had an analysis of the drug Davenport gave him, I might be able to tell."

Sabrina understood what he'd been thinking and why he'd reacted so strongly. "That would tie Davenport to the murders," she breathed.

"The stopper should go to the police lab."

"I already gave it to a friend who's in the medical research business. She's doing an analysis for me."

He looked as if he were mentally counting to ten. "You're sure you can trust her?"

"Of course. She's very reliable. And she knows how to keep things confidential."

Dan seemed somewhat mollified. "When are you supposed to get the results?"

"Later today."

"I hope you're planning to share them with me."

"At this point, it would be stupid not to. Not telling you in the first place was probably stupid."

"You didn't have any reason to trust *me*," he said in a low voice.

She reached out and covered his hand with hers. "I do now. And...and...there's something else I have from the Institute."

"What?"

Sabrina pulled her purse over, retrieved the two cassettes and handed them to Dan. He read the titles. "'Tapping Every One of Your Inner Resources' and 'The Uses of

Imagination.' You bought these? What's he asking for them, ten dollars apiece?''

"No. That's the funny part. Everything else is for sale at inflated prices. These are free."

"It sounds as if he wants people to take them home. Do you think it's an advertising pitch?''

"I don't know. Let me tell you how I was feeling— before the lecture and while the good doctor was talking. A lot of people I know are wildly enthusiastic about Davenport. It's like he has some magic secret for inspiring confidence. Well, rave notices like that make me skeptical. So I was in a questioning frame of mind when I went to the Institute."

Sabrina was gratified to see that Dan was listening intently. "I didn't like the place. In fact, I was on edge the whole time I was there, until I sat in the auditorium and started listening to the soft music. It had a strangely calming effect on me. And on everybody else who was listening. Then Davenport began the lecture, and it was almost as if Moses had come down from Mount Sinai. After a while, I don't know, I started being in a, uh, receptive mood, ready to give him more than the benefit of the doubt. By the time he was halfway through his lecture, I was beginning to agree with what he was saying. I had to give myself a mental shake to remind myself it was hogwash.''

Dan's eyes narrowed. "You're suggesting there was some factor—some hidden factor, that helped influence you and everybody else favorably toward him?''

"Uh-huh.''

He looked thoughtful. "On-the-spot motivation. Like subliminal persuasion, maybe? I've heard about grocery and department stores doing that kind of thing.''

"Maybe that's why he wants people to take his tapes

home. Suppose when you do, you can get a hidden message along with the free lecture.''

''It's an interesting theory.''

Sabrina gestured toward the tapes. ''Maybe you should send *those* to the police lab.''

He turned the boxes over in his hand. ''One's got a little silver dot in the corner. I wonder what that means.''

Sabrina shrugged.

Dan stood up. ''Maybe only the ones with the markings have the hidden messages. Since you brought it along, I'd like to have a listen.''

''You've got a recorder on the boat?''

''In the cabin.''

''I wish you had a phone so I could call my friend and see if she's got that lab report,'' Sabrina mused.

''Actually, I do. A portable. It and the recorder are both stored where the salt air won't ruin the electronics.'' Dan descended the short flight of steps to the boat's interior. Sabrina followed.

''You'll probably get better reception up on the deck,'' Dan said as he set the recorder and the phone on the table.

''Before I call, could I ask what you found out about June Garrison?''

Dan sighed. ''I was trying to stay away from that.''

''I noticed. Why?''

''There's hardly anything else of consequence to tell, but I can bring you up to speed on Brian Lowell's investigation. Garrison was in the process of getting a divorce. Her ex-husband moved out of town, and the department hasn't been able to get in touch with him. The people in the neighborhood where she lived say she was a conventional sort of housewife. She liked to garden. She took an exercise class at a health club on Liberty Road. Her taste in furnishings ran to Early American rock maple.''

"You're right," Sabrina murmured, the disappointment apparent in her voice. "There's really nothing that gives us a clue about what she wanted to tell me."

"I wish there was more. I've brought you a summary of the report. You can look over it later and see if anything strikes you."

Dan searched through one of the bags he'd brought and handed Sabrina several sheets of paper, which she folded and tucked into her purse.

He slipped his arm across her shoulders. "I know you were hoping we'd figure out how she fit in to all this. It's going to take some more digging."

"So I'm supposed to go back to my herbs and teas and pretend that everything is just peachy?"

"The police will find out more."

"But I'm just small potatoes. What do they care about weird, unsubstantiated threats?"

"I care." Dan's hand shot out and covered hers. "And I can't take any more of this."

"Any more of what?" she whispered.

"Pretending this conversation is only business."

"You're saying it isn't?"

"It would be, if you were simply another witness who had stumbled into a police investigation."

"What am I?" Sabrina whispered.

He still couldn't spell it out any clearer in words. Sabrina had half turned, ready to take the phone up on deck. He pulled her against him, her back to his front. His hands went to her shoulders, kneading and stroking as if he were starving for the contact. And he was. Greedily his fingers tangled in her hair. When he lifted the heavy tresses to stroke her neck, he felt a shiver go through her body. "Duncan did that to Sara," she murmured.

"Who the hell is Duncan? And Sara?" Even as he said

the names, he felt a dangerous ripple of sensation sweep over his body. Then he turned her to face him, searching her eyes as if they held the answers to all the questions he didn't want to ask. The mixture of confusion and certainty in their depth knocked the breath from his lungs. Later, she was going to hate him. He couldn't tell her that. But he had this moment with her. Now. And he wanted her to remember how it had felt to be in his arms.

"I'm not going to let you go," he muttered. Then he pulled her tightly into his embrace, unable to hold back the surge of primitive emotion that swept over him.

Dan could feel her surprise, and then her panic as his lips moved urgently, potently over hers, demanding a response. He sensed that she was clinging to safety like an overturned white-water rafter clinging to an outcropping of rock.

He deepened the kiss with deliberate ruthlessness, holding nothing of himself back. He knew the instant that she surrendered. Relief and triumph took him as he felt a shudder sweep over her.

"Hold on to me," he growled against her mouth.

Her hands climbed his arms, anchored to his shoulders and stayed put.

"Yes," he grated as his mouth took deeper, fuller possession of hers.

His fingers stroked up and down her arms, then found the sides of her breasts. The tiny moan of surrender was like a shock wave zinging through him.

Deep inside, Sabrina knew she'd been waiting for something like this since he'd walked through the door of her shop this morning. No, since their eyes had locked that first time at lunch.

She was his. Her body tuned itself to the wordless vibration rumbling deep in Dan's throat, a vibration that resonated to the core of her soul.

One of his muscular hands tangled urgently in her hair, angling her head so that he could plunder her mouth from a new angle. The other hand slid to the swell of her breast, kneading and stroking. When his fingers found the hard point of her nipple, pleasure shot downward through her body.

She knew he felt her response as he shifted her in his arms, pulling her more tightly into his heat and hardness.

Her body had never answered a man's with such passion. No. Perhaps it had—once. Long, long ago. Blood rushed hotly through her veins. Desire uncurled deep in the pit of her stomach.

He held her close, close for several moments longer. Then he eased his body away from hers.

She heard him cursing softly. "I had to do that," he murmured. "I'm sorry.

She'd been lost in a world where only two of them existed. Her eyes blinked open. Light-headed, she tried to get a grip on reality.

"I'm taking advantage of you again," he confessed.

"Are you?"

"You may think so later."

"Dan?"

"Go make that call," he said thickly. "Before I forget we *do* have business to take care of."

He'd started it. And stopped. And made it very clear he wasn't going to discuss his reasons. Confused, Sabrina picked up the phone and climbed the stairs to the deck.

Behind her she could hear Luther Davenport introducing himself again. Dan was playing the tape. Maybe it would mellow him out.

At the gunwale, she stood for a moment looking out at

the water and taking in large drafts of the salt air. The wind had risen slightly, and waves rocked the boat, so that she had to steady herself with a knee braced against the wooden bench that ran around the side of the deck.

Dan had held her against him the same way Duncan had held Sara. It had felt so right. And so scary. The way it had a long, long time ago.

She didn't understand it. And there was no way to get in touch with something so outlandish. The easier course was to focus on the phone in her hand. After a moment's hesitation, she began to dial. The Medizone switchboard put her right through to Katie.

"I've got the information you want," the physician informed her.

"Great."

Downstairs in the cabin, Sabrina thought she heard Dan make some kind of exclamation above the sound of Davenport's voice. Glancing in his direction, she saw his back was turned to her, making it impossible to catch his eye.

"I'm sorry we took so long," Katie said. "We were looking for something beyond the obvious. But as far as we can tell, there's nothing very startling about this sample. It's a very common stimulant." She named a compound that Sabrina had heard of.

"Um."

"Is that what you expected?"

"I don't know. So it's not a specific antidote for any poison," Sabrina mused, feeling a stab of disappointment. Probably they'd hit another dead end. She looked at Dan again. He stood up quickly and walked toward the counter in the galley area. Was he getting something to eat while he listened to the tape?

"Is the use of a stimulant consistent with the kind of dramatic revival I described?" she asked Katie.

"It could be. Depending on what caused the man's problem in the first place."

"Which we don't know." Sabrina's mind was only half on the conversation now. A wisp of odor drifted toward her. Fruit.

"I've got a written analysis for you," Katie said. "Should I mail it?"

"Umm...hold it at the lab, and I'll pick it up later."

"Will do. And keep me posted on how the case is going," Katie said.

"Yes. And thanks." Sabrina was barely paying attention to her friend as she replaced the receiver. With a strange sense of urgency, she set the phone down on the padded bench along the gunwale. As she started toward the stairway to the cabin, the fruity aroma she'd noticed a few moments ago became stronger, and she realized what she was smelling.

The frighteningly familiar odor of rotten cherries.

Chapter Eleven

Oh God, the drug that had hit them in the car. Somehow, here it was on the boat.

Pulse pounding, Sabrina peered into the cabin. Dan was still standing with his back toward her at the galley counter. She heard him curse, saw him bang his fist against the table. The epithet was followed by a low moan that sent tremors rocketing up and down her spine.

"Dan?"

He didn't answer, didn't react as if he'd heard her at all.

As wisps of cherry vapor snaked toward Sabrina, she coughed, swayed and backed up until her legs bumped against the bench that hugged the gunwale. She knew she was catching the faint scent of the hallucinogen. Even outside, in the fresh air, with the wind blowing, the poison was making her slightly dizzy. She sat down heavily on the bench, feeling fear gather in the pit of her stomach. The terror expanded, oozing through every pore of her body, turning her skin to ice.

For a moment, it held her in its grip. Then she turned her head into the wind and forced herself to breathe deeply, dragging in lungfuls of the salt air. She didn't realize how tightly her hands were clenched until she felt the stabs of pain where her nails dug into her palms.

Her eyes darted to the cabin. Dan was leaning over the tape recorder, breathing raggedly. Her eyes went from his rapt face to the machine on the table and back again. In the background, she could still hear Davenport's voice.

The only conclusion she could draw was that the drug was coming from the cassette. But why? How? She couldn't answer the questions. She only knew the tape had been in her pocketbook. *She* had brought it here. And given it to Dan.

Panic, sickness, guilt rose in her throat. Dan was still leaning over the machine, dragging in deep breaths. When he lifted his head again, he was smiling dreamily.

God, no. It really had him. Now he was courting the effect.

Dan wove toward the counter in the galley again and cradled his head in his hands. When he started to cough, Sabrina felt the painful spasms in her own chest. Then she thought she heard a metallic noise as he rummaged in one of the drawers.

She wanted to rush into the cabin and pull him out of the drugging vapor. What if she held her breath? Would that work?

No. He might struggle. Or more likely, grab on to her and hold her down. If she had to take a breath, she'd be in the same fix. The boat gave a little pitching motion, and Sabrina reached to steady herself against the gunwale. Her frantic gaze darted around the deck and lighted on the phone she'd put down a few moments earlier. If she called the Shock Trauma Unit in Baltimore they could have a helicopter here in minutes. But then what? The copter couldn't land on the deck. And what about the loud whir of the blades overhead? Sabrina shuddered as she remembered her own terror when she'd been under the spell of the drug. What would Dan's mind do with the frightening noise overhead?

Her speculation was cut off as she saw Dan turn toward the stairway and squint into the brighter light outside. "You're out there, aren't you?" He growled in a voice that scraped along her nerve endings like fingernails being drawn across a blackboard.

"Dan?"

On unsteady feet, he moved toward the short flight of stairs that led to the deck. His hand was pressed against his side, concealing something. His expression was cruel and crafty. Instinctively Sabrina took a step back.

Dan reached the top of the stairs and stood swaying with the motion of the boat. Sabrina started toward him. She was stopped by the scent of rotten cherries wafting from the interior—and by the harsh look on his face. For a terrible moment she thought he would pitch backward into the cabin again. Then his right hand wrapped itself around the railing, and he shook his head as if trying to clear away the drugging mist.

"Dan?" Sabrina called again.

He took a very deliberate step toward her and then another. The spark of madness gleamed in the blue depths of his eyes as he advanced, breathing heavily. But at least he was taking in fresh air now. The effects of the drug hadn't lasted too long when they'd gotten out of the car. How many minutes before it wore off now?

She shuddered. Or were the effects cumulative?

"Old witch. What have ye done, old witch?" Dan cried out.

"What?"

"Witch!"

He was advancing purposefully on her now, his right hand raised. Something metallic glinted in the afternoon sunlight, and she saw an eight-inch-long knife that must have come from the galley.

"Dan, what are you doing? It's me, Sabrina."

"No more of your tricks!"

His face a mask of hatred, he kept advancing on her, still swaying slightly so that she alternated between fear of what he might do to her and fear that he would be the one to get hurt.

"Dan," she tried again, her voice rising unsteadily. "I'm not the witch. I'm Sabrina"

"Ye lie," he shouted as he lunged toward her. The knife swung down in an arc. Sabrina dodged aside, her foot thumping against the wicker hamper.

Cursing, Dan came at her again. Snatching up one of the cushions from the bench, she held it up like a shield. The blade slashed through the plastic and into the cotton batting. Dan cursed.

Sabrina dropped the cushion, leaving it skewered on the knife. Dan was forced to grab it with his free hand in order to try and work the weapon free.

He succeeded all too quickly.

"Dan. It's Sabrina. Dan!" she shouted again, praying that the drug was wearing off, praying that she could get through to him.

Thoughts came to her in disjointed snatches. In desperation, she looked around at the sky and the water. Nothing had changed. There was no coast-guard launch speeding miraculously toward her. She was still on her own with a man who was totally out of control.

She was trying to snatch up the phone when Dan whirled on her again. As he turned, she dodged aside. There was nowhere to run except toward the poison gas wafting from the interior. When she reached the stairs, the vapor hit her—along with a wave of dizziness.

Coughing, she dropped the phone. It landed with a splash in the water as she wrapped her fingers around a rung of the ladder that led to the flying bridge.

Behind her Dan was panting, taking in more salt air. Soon he'd be okay. He had to be okay. Because all communication was cut off, and the only thing she could do was keep away from Dan until he came to his senses.

Lips set in a grim line, Sabrina began to scramble up the ladder. The knife slashed at her skirt, ripping through the fabric. With a little sob, she climbed faster.

He hurled a curse, and his fingers scrabbled for her foot, caught her heel. Grimly she wrenched away and the shoe came off in his hand.

"Ye won't get far," he shouted after her. "I'll get ye. For Sara."

Sabrina reached the top of the ladder and scrambled across the flying bridge. Then she was sliding down the windshield at the front of the boat. With only one shoe, she landed unevenly on the foredeck, twisting the ankle of the foot that was still shod. On a grunt of pain, she kicked the shoe off and began to hobble out of range.

Dan leaped to the deck right behind her. As she tried to dodge away, he caught her legs and brought her down in a flying tackle that knocked the breath out of her chest in a painful blow.

Half gasping, half sobbing, she fought to wriggle out of Dan's clutches. They rolled together on the deck, both breathing heavily.

Sabrina tried to pull away. When that didn't work, she beat at him with her fists. But she might as well have been pounding at Mount Rushmore. He was far stronger than she under ordinary circumstances, and the fury of drug-induced madness fueled his vitality.

He pinned her to the deck, straddling her body and

clamping her arms against her sides with his knees. She could see the knife sticking in his belt. The terrible look on his face turned her blood to ice. She was frozen, unable to move. Unable to save herself.

The motion of his hand as he reached for the knife released her. She began shouting and kicking wildly with her legs, making him work to subdue her again.

"Dan, no. Please, Dan."

The struggle to get away scooted her a few inches toward the edge of the boat so that her head and shoulders jutted over the deck, and she was half hanging above the water. But she couldn't move any farther.

The look of satisfaction on his face made the breath trickle from her lungs. Now he held on to her with one hand while he bent to retrieve the knife from his belt.

Staring down at Sabrina, he raised the weapon above his head. The blade was pointed at her throat.

"Dan! No!"

For the first time since the nightmare had begun, he paused. Uncertainty warred with fury in the depths of his eyes.

"Dan. Please. It's Sabrina."

"Tricks! You've made yourself look like her."

Yet despite the fierce words, the hesitancy lengthened, and his grip on her body loosened.

It was now or never. Sabrina wrenched herself away and felt her dress rip as Dan made another grab for her.

His fingers grazed her leg as she plunged over the side of the rub rail.

She heard a string of expletives above her as she hit the water. Then she was below the surface. Swimming underwater, she didn't come up until she was half a dozen yards from her original position.

Dan was peering over the side, but his back was toward

her. Making for the side of the craft, she shook the wet hair out of her face.

Dan turned, spotted her and shouted—part order to halt, part curse. She ducked under the water again, coming up on the other side of the bow.

"Gotta get a gun. That's it. Get a gun and shoot her. I'll shoot the old witch," he muttered.

His heavy footfalls clumped off along the narrow side deck.

Sabrina held her breath, half expecting him to slip and plunge over the side. She didn't want to think about what might happen if he went into the water in his present condition.

Somehow he kept his footing and disappeared into the cabin, where she could hear him rummaging around in the storage boxes. Did he really have a gun? Or was that part of the illusion his drugged brain had conjured up? Afraid to stay where she was and find out, Sabrina swam toward the stern. But her ruined dress hampered her movements. Struggling out of the garment, she tossed it away and watched it fan out across the top of the water like a woman with her arms spread wide.

A noise from the deck brought her attention back to Dan. She could see him again. He was on the catwalk, heading toward the front of the boat.

She froze when she saw that he was indeed clutching a flare gun in his right hand. Oh God, what if he spotted her? She was about to duck under the surface again when a loud report made her body jerk in reaction. Twisting around, she saw a flaming hole open in the middle of the dress where it floated about thirty feet from the boat.

"Got ya! I finally got ya," Dan shouted, his voice a mixture of rage and triumph. "For Sara."

Heart slamming against her ribs, Sabrina hugged the

side of the craft, trying to make herself invisible as the flames quickly sputtered out. Dan thought the dress was the witch, and he'd shot it with the flare gun. What would happen if he saw her?

In the next moment, she heard a moan of agony from the deck.

All sorts of terrible images flashed into her head. He'd hurt himself. He was sick. Unless it was a trick to get her back on board. No. He thought the witch was dead.

Grabbing the mooring rope where it was attached to one of the metal holders, she began to haul herself up the side of the boat, bracing her feet against the transom for leverage.

"I killed her. Oh, God, I killed her."

A moment ago that had been the man's primary goal. Had the shots startled him to partial sanity?

With a surge of strength, Sabrina pulled herself toward the gunwale. Her body was shivering, and she had to clamp her teeth together to keep them from chattering. From where she huddled below the level of the deck, she couldn't see Dan. But she could hear him.

"Sabrina. Oh, please. No. Sabrina. I did it all over again, didn't I?"

There was another groan of agony. Dan was still hidden from view, but she saw the gun as it went sailing through the air into the cabin, where it crashed against the bulkhead.

"Oh, God, Sabrina."

Suddenly she understood the source of Dan's torment. He'd shot a hole through the middle of the dress. But he thought he'd killed her. Not the witch. *Her.* Sabrina.

Panting from the exertion, Sabrina pulled herself high enough to peer into the boat. As she craned her neck over the gunwale, she saw Dan. He was on his knees a few yards from her, swaying almost imperceptibly back and forth, his face cupped in his hands. "I couldn't even play it straight with her, and now she's dead," he moaned.

The words made no more sense than anything else he'd been saying. In fact, anything could still happen. But Sabrina was willing to bet her life that some measure of sanity had returned. Throwing herself into the boat, she landed in a wet heap on the bench. There were no cushions to soften her fall. They'd been scattered in the struggle across the deck when she'd been trying to fend off the knife.

Dan's head snapped up. Dull blue eyes blinked and finally focused. For a moment Sabrina saw hope bloom. Then he shook his head, and his shoulders sagged as if he wasn't able to credit what he was seeing. But then why should he? He thought she was dead. He knew he still might not be in possession of his faculties—that reality and illusion might be cruelly twisted.

"Dan, it's me. It's Sabrina," she said, clambering toward him. He didn't move. He didn't breathe.

"See? I'm all right." As she spoke, she took him in her arms, holding him, rocking him, marveling at the warmth of his body against her wet skin. "Oh, Dan. I'm so sorry," she whispered.

"Sorry?"

"The tape—"

"Why are you so cold?"

"I'm all right," she repeated.

He ran trembling hands over her shoulders and water-slick back. "It's really you. It's not a dream."

"It's really me." His large frame began to shake, and it was several moments before he got back some measure of control. "Where are your clothes?" he asked.

A flush bloomed on her skin as she focused on the state of her undress. "In the water. Don't worry about that."

His hand skimmed over her warming skin and winnowed her dripping hair. "You're alive. You're really alive. I didn't shoot you."

"No."

"Thank the Lord."

His touch became more possessive, more urgent as if the contact were the only way to assure himself that she was really unhurt, that she wasn't one more illusion conjured up by the cherry mist that had filled the cabin. His lips moved over her face, coming back again and again to her mouth. His hands found her breasts, playing over the hardened nipples through her bra.

A little moan escaped from her lips and she clung to him. They were both kneeling on the deck, swaying slightly with the motion of the waves, their bodies molded together by arousal.

Then his grip on her shoulders changed, tightened painfully. All at once his fingers were digging into her flesh.

When he groaned, the sound was harsh and tinged with pain. Sabrina's eyes fluttered open, and she struggled to focus. Dan's face was deathly pale and slick with a fine sheen of perspiration.

"Dan. What's wrong?"

He slumped backward against the wooden bench and sprawled there, breathing heavily.

"Dan?"

"I'm okay."

She knew he wasn't. She glanced at the cabin, wanting to help him inside to one of the bunks. But it wasn't safe to go in there yet. Instead she collected the cushions where they'd been scattered around the deck and arranged them as best she could. Then she eased him down until he was supine.

He lay with his eyes closed and his arm across his forehead. His breathing was labored. When a large wave rocked the boat, he gritted his teeth.

"Does your head hurt?" she asked.

"Yeah."

Sabrina sat down on the deck and reached for his wrist.

"What are you doing?" He tried to jerk away, but she held him.

"Taking your pulse."

It was rapid but steady. Even as she counted the beats, she felt the rate slowing. And some of the color had come back to his ashen face.

"The drug. Like in the car," Dan finally whispered.

"Yes."

"How?"

Sabrina's features contorted. "The tape I gave you," she said in a low voice. "Somehow the cassette must have been fixed to give off the vapor when it was played."

She felt his fingers close around her wrist. "It's not your fault."

She swallowed.

"Davenport," Dan muttered, his eyes still closed.

"It's hard to believe he'd go that far to affect people's minds. I mean, do you think there was some kind of mistake? An experiment that wasn't supposed to be distributed?"

His eyes blinked open. "How come it didn't get you?"

"I was up on deck calling my friend, remember?"

"So this time I'm the only one who wigged out," he said in a deadly dull voice.

"It's strong stuff. I started to feel it, too. Even up here in the fresh air. But I could get away. You couldn't."

"Lucky you." His voice was still thick. He started to push himself up and winced.

Sabrina laid a gentle hand on his shoulder, unnerved by how easy it was to hold him in place.

"Now I remember." He spoke slowly and deliberately. "You went outside to make the phone call, and I wanted to play the cassette and see if it had the effect you talked about. Then everything went out of focus." A look of horror took over his face. "I...I tried to kill the witch. With the knife. We were fighting."

His eyes bored into her, and she was suddenly very conscious that she was wearing nothing more than a soaked bra and panties.

"It wasn't the witch. It was you."

"Dan, you're not responsible for what happened. It was the drug. You couldn't help yourself. You didn't know what you were doing."

His rough curse made her grip his shoulder more tightly.

"As if the rest of it isn't bad enough, I end up trying to murder you." His voice was raw now.

The rest of it? She wasn't sure what he was talking about. But it didn't matter. All she wanted was to give him whatever warmth and comfort she could. "Oh, Dan." Bending down beside him, she folded him into her embrace.

He buried his face against her neck as his arms came up to circle her shoulders. He clung tightly for several seconds. Then he eased away. "I brought some extra clothes. In the bag. Put something on."

Sabrina got up and crossed to the tote he'd set on the deck. Inside she found a yellow knit shirt. After dragging it over her head, she pulled her wet hair out of the collar. The tails covered her thighs. Technically she was decent.

When she turned back to Dan, she saw that his state of mind hadn't improved. If anything, he looked more upset.

"The drug. Right. I couldn't help myself when I tried to kill you." His voice dripped with sarcasm. "I was under the influence. That's what they always say."

Sabrina sat back down beside him, stroking her hand against his forehead. "In this case, it's true."

She felt the tension radiating through his body. "Why is it," he said in a voice barely above a whisper, "that so many of the best things and the worst things that have ever happened to me all involve you?"

"The best?"

Pushing himself to a sitting position, he brought his lips to hers and kissed her very gently. It was warm and sweet, but it had a flavor that sent a tremor of fear through her body. "Sabrina, you're a very giving, very caring person. But you've got to take care of yourself, too," he murmured. "Do you know how to pilot this launch?"

"Yes."

"Good. Because the best thing for you to do right now is to take this boat back to Baltimore so you can get off and walk away from me."

It took a moment for Sabrina to realize what she was hearing. "Dan, don't you understand? What happened a few minutes ago isn't your fault."

He leaned back against the bench glaring at her. "Stop patronizing me. It's taken a couple minutes to clear my head. But I sure as hell remember what I was doing down in that cabin after you left. I was leaning over that tape recorder sucking as much of that stuff as I could get into my lungs. *Trying* to get higher."

"I know you're upset. That's natural," Sabrina soothed. "But you really aren't thinking clearly. The drug had you under its influence. It was making you want more."

Sabrina was riveted by the look of mixed disgust and dread on his face. "Dan, what's wrong? Did you ever—" She fumbled for the right words. "Are drugs a problem for you?"

He laughed mirthlessly. "Not the way you think. It wasn't me. It was my best friend in middle school. He was into LSD." The sentences came out in jerky bursts. "We were roommates on a trip to Ocean City. He jumped off the roof of the hotel."

"Oh, Dan, no."

"That was enough to scare me off dope for good. And somewhere along the line, I turned into a self-righteous bastard when it came to drugs." He winced. "In college, if someone was smoking pot at a party, I got up and left. I was never going to get near anything mind-altering— because until Jerry got mixed up with acid he was a perfectly normal kid, just like me. And if it could happen to him…"

"So that was behind your war on drugs?"

"Yeah."

"And I'll bet you already have a report on—" she gestured toward the cabin "—that stuff. What is it?"

He sighed. "I called the lab this morning. They couldn't tell me much. The drug is a hallucinogen, which we already know. It's designed to be inhaled. The effects are potent but relatively short-term."

As he spoke, his voice had gotten stronger. Undoubtedly it was far easier for him to focus on lab reports than on himself. "Designed?" she questioned.

"Right. There's nothing with a similar chemical makeup on the street, as far as we know. This was produced in a private lab. Somebody tailor-made the stuff."

An idea suddenly hit Sabrina. "Dan, Davenport is selling medical advice. Suppose people who use the tapes have a crazy, terrifying experience they can't explain? Wouldn't that and the hidden message send them running to him for treatment?''

Dan looked doubtful. ''It sounds pretty risky. And I'm not going to use it as an excuse for myself.''

Sabrina tried another approach. ''Why are you so angry with yourself? This is my fault. *I'm* the one who brought the drug on board.''

''It doesn't matter how it got here. The important point is what it did to me just now.'' His face turned hard and bleak. ''Do you want to know what I was feeling? Fury. It took me over. I went berserk. Everything was swept away except raw violence. I had to strike out against anyone who was nearby. And you were it.''

She saw the horror on his face as he tried to come to grips with what had happened to him.

''How do I know I'm not going to do it again?'' he asked in a low voice.

''Dan, if you were thinking clearly, you'd stop doing this to yourself. You told me the hallucinogen is very powerful. Everyone has a violent component. The drug blew it out of proportion, that's all.''

He gave her a considering look. As the silence stretched, she felt her nerves grow taut.

''All right, so getting involved with a guy who should have been in the locked ward at Springfield State Hospital doesn't scare you away. What if I tell you I've been lying to you since you walked into our luncheon appointment?''

''What are you talking about?''

''I didn't ask to meet you because I wanted your help. I asked because I thought you might be a murderer.''

Chapter Twelve

Unable to move, Sabrina stared at Dan.

"What? What are you talking about?" she finally managed.

He swallowed sharply. "The police found one of the gold-foil charms from your shop in Alastair's pocket. The ones you put in with packages. That's why I was interested in them and your bracelet."

Sabrina could literally feel the blood draining from her face as she pushed herself away and stared into Dan's piercing blue eyes.

"You're making this up," she gasped. But even as she cried out the denial, there was a strange ringing in her ears, and for a moment the scene around them wavered and flickered as if it might slip out of existence and replace itself with something that had happened a long time ago. Yet the past was too dangerous a place for her to flee.

"I'm not making it up. It's the truth." His voice was flat and dead. Dan's face was as pale as hers. "I didn't know how you fit in. You could have been the technical adviser, supplying the witchcraft know-how. You proved to me you had a pretty good background in the subject."

Bits and pieces of the previous few days came flying back at her, each one as sharp and piercing as a broken shard of glass. Finally the one that stuck painfully in her psyche was the evening she'd come home from the Andromeda Institute and seen Dan spotlighted in the headlights of her car. "That night, after Davenport suckered me into trying to help Edward... My God, you weren't at my house waiting to comfort me. You were there to pump me for information."

"Yes."

"No wonder you didn't want to tell me who was under investigation." She gave a harsh little laugh. "You thought I was working for Davenport. Didn't you?"

"Yes. That night I did. Until you got that phone call from June Garrison. Then—"

He didn't finish the sentence. But it didn't matter. Sickness swept over Sabrina. When she felt her hands begin to shake, she tucked them under her legs and pressed them against the deck. She had to hold on to something. She'd been so dumb, letting herself care about Dan, letting herself lean on his strength. And he'd just been playing with her. Unwilling to let him see the tears gathering in her eyes, she swung her body away.

They sat in frozen silence as Sabrina listened to her heart pound. Finally she was able to push herself off the deck. Then, with lurching steps, she started for the front of the boat. At first all she wanted to do was get as far away from him as she could. As she raised the anchor and climbed the steps to the pilot's station, she tried to concentrate on what she had to do to get out of here. That was better than letting the pain swallow her up.

Savagely she twisted the key in the ignition. The engine sprang to life. Dan hadn't taken the boat very far from the mouth of the Patapsco. It wasn't going to be all that difficult to get back to Baltimore. The minute her feet touched the pier, she could walk away from everything she'd dared to hope for with him and never look back.

At first Sabrina kept her attention glued to the shoreline. She shouldn't give a damn about Dan Cassidy's welfare, yet she couldn't stop herself from worrying about the effects of the drug. Dan had gotten another heavy dose just a couple of days after the first one. This time there had been more physical effects, like the headache. Was he really okay? For several minutes Sabrina succeeded in keeping herself from glancing back at the place where he'd been sitting on the deck. Then she couldn't stop herself from looking.

Dan sat immobile, staring into space, his arms clasped around his knees. The wind was blowing, and the scarf Sabrina had been wearing when she'd come on board had worked its way off the handle of the hamper. With a fluttering motion, it started to blow across the deck. The sudden movement caught Dan's attention. Scrambling up, he reached out and snagged the length of fabric before it could flap over the side of the boat and into the water.

Then, as if the exertion had been too much for him, he sat down heavily again. As Sabrina silently watched, he wrapped the long rectangle of silk around one large fist. After staring at it for several seconds, he closed his eyes and pressed it against his mouth, moving the soft material back and forth across his lips. Long moments passed before he carefully tucked the scarf into her purse.

The breath had stopped moving in and out of Sabrina's lungs as she'd peered down from the pilot's station at Dan. While she watched, he swiped at the corners of his eyes with his hand.

But he'd told her—

She'd assumed—

Sabrina stopped short. What *exactly* had he said? Nothing at all about his feelings for her. In fact, now that she thought about it, she realized that he'd focused on the one thing that he knew would cut her to the very soul. His duplicity. He knew it was the only thing that would drive her away. And the technique had worked quite well.

Why? To protect her? Sabrina closed her eyes, trying to come to grips with what she'd been feeling for days. Since the moment she and Dan Cassidy had set eyes on each other in Sabatino's dining room, there'd been something strange going on below the surface of reality. The feeling of disorientation. The feeling that she knew him well. The feeling that her destiny was wound up with his. She couldn't explain any of that, and she'd been afraid to probe too deeply.

Yet, ignoring the sensations hadn't made them go away. She'd been on edge for days. And it wasn't just because of the Graveyard Murders, or Dr. Davenport, or June Garrison. The wariness tingling at the ends of her nerves had as much to do with her reaction to Dan and the strange story she'd been writing as anything else.

Dan and Sara.

Duncan and Sabrina.

She made a strangled exclamation when she realized she'd mixed up the names of the couples.

With a silent stab of shame, she admitted that a few minutes ago her anger and hurt had been tinged with relief that she wouldn't have to dig any further into the conundrum of how past and present intersected.

Did she have the guts to toss away the safety line Dan had offered her?

She had to. For her peace of mind, if nothing else.

Moving with deliberate swiftness, Sabrina cut the engine. As the motor sputtered and then stopped, Dan's head jerked up, and he stared at her.

"What are you doing?"

Without answering, she descended the ladder, walked to the anchor and sent it splashing into the water. For several seconds, she stood with her back to Dan, gathering her courage together.

Then she turned. "All right, Cassidy, I was going to run away just like you wanted. But I've changed my mind. I think you owe me the truth."

"I've told you the truth."

"Part of it. The part you wanted me to know. But you've left something out. *Why* did you tell me you arranged our first meeting because you thought I was involved in the murders?"

"Isn't it obvious? I felt guilty."

"I saw you holding my scarf."

He looked away, and Sabrina realized she wasn't ready to tackle that part yet. "Okay, let's talk about something else."

"What?" His voice was angry.

She didn't mince any words. "About the fantasy you conjured up when you were under the influence of the cherry stuff a little while ago. About your violent reaction to it."

A muscle twitched in his cheek and his jaw clenched.

"You said the violence was directed at me because I was convenient. But that isn't true. You were trying to kill the witch. Is it because of the Graveyard Murders?"

"No."

"Then what?"

His expression was closed.

"All right, don't tell me about the witch. Tell me about Sara. Who is she?"

"I don't know. It's just a name I picked up at the station. From June Garrison."

She could see from his face that he was lying. It had meant something to him. "I don't think that's all you know about her."

He sat with his lips pressed together.

"Dan, tell me."

"The rest is just my imagination. Can't we drop it?"

"No."

He slapped a fist against the deck and winced. "Dammit. All right. She…she looks something like you. But that's not so surprising. She lives in a little cottage near the mountains. She cures people with her herbs. The doctor doesn't like it. Neither does the witch. It's not too hard to figure out where I got any of that, either."

The hair on the back of Sabrina's neck felt as if someone had touched them with an electric cattle prod. "And Ian? Is he in the story, too?"

"Sure. Why not?"

"You know a lot of details about this fantasy of yours, don't you? A lot for a quick drug trip."

He shrugged.

"What did the witch do to Sara?"

"There was a trial. The old woman tried to save herself by giving evidence against Sabrina—" He stopped abruptly. "I mean Sara. She told the judges that Sara was in league with the devil."

Sabrina sucked in a piercing breath. So that was where the story was leading. Crossing to her purse, which still lay on the deck, she opened the bag and pulled out several sheets of folded paper. "Maybe you'd better read this," she said.

Reluctantly Dan took the offered pages. Sabrina submitted no explanation. So, after one more questioning glance, he began to read.

Sabrina wasn't able to wrench her gaze away from his

face. She was completely absorbed by the changing panorama of emotions as his eyes moved down the page.

"Where in the hell did you get this?" he asked, his voice gritty.

"At first I thought I made it up. I used to tell myself tales about another time and another place when I was a kid. But this experience is different." Sabrina gestured toward the pages. "I started writing the story in my office when I was supposed to be working on a plan for some bath-herb-and-soap baskets for the Harbor Court Hotel. You can't get much farther from the Harbor Court Hotel than that."

She continued with her explanation, deliberately including all the details she'd been afraid to confide to anyone else. "The really scary part is that it's not anything I knew I was going to put on paper. Every time I'm alone and I pick up a pen to write a grocery list or make notes on something to do with my business, I sort of go into a trance. Then when I snap out of it, there's more of the narrative down in black and white.

"At first it skipped big chunks of time. Sara met Duncan when she was out gathering herbs a couple of years before that episode you have there. Then he came to get her grandmother to cure Ian of peripneumonia. But the grandmother was dead, so he took Sara back to the castle. He keeps coming on to her, but she's afraid of getting sexually involved. She knows someone of his class can't marry a girl from a cottage in the mountains."

With a dark look, Dan crumpled the pages in his fist. Afraid he was going to toss the balled-up mass into the water, Sabrina scrambled up, rushed across the deck and pried his fingers open. "I'd like to keep the evidence, if you don't mind."

"What evidence? I don't know what you think this

proves. Under the influence of drugs, sometimes two people share an experience.''

''How can they, unless they plan it first, or agree beforehand to communicate the images of whatever it is they're experiencing?''

Dan shrugged again, his expression closed.

''Besides, I started writing this before either one of us got cherry-bombed. Before we'd even met, for that matter.''

''So what conclusions do you draw?'' He didn't sound as if he particularly wanted to hear the answer.

Sabrina laced her fingers together. ''I've been too... scared to draw any conclusions. I know you think I'm into weird stuff. But nothing like this has ever happened to me before. If it had, I might be coping better.''

Dan nodded tightly.

''Are you going to tell me you haven't sensed something strange between us?'' Her hands gestured helplessly. ''Some feeling that we already knew each other before I walked into Sabatino's? That if we just open our minds, we'll discover something extraordinary?''

''This is crazy.''

''Is it?'' Sabrina clenched her fists to help steady herself before plunging ahead with the thoughts that had been worming their way around the barriers she'd tried to erect in her mind. ''I suppose you've never entertained the idea of reincarnation.''

''That's bunk.''

''A man and a woman with unfinished business between them. So they come back to work things out.''

''Oh, come on. Have you ever heard of anything like that? I mean, besides in the movies?''

''People have written about their experiences. You know, like Shirley MacLaine.''

"And you believe it?"

"I wasn't ever sure." Sabrina laid her hand lightly over Dan's, feeling his muscles jump at the contact. "Okay, we don't have to talk about reincarnation. We don't have to try and explain why you and I are independently coming up with pieces of what looks like the same historical story."

"The same fantasy, for all we know," Dan interrupted, but his voice didn't hold the ring of conviction.

"Where is it set?" Sabrina asked suddenly.

He shrugged. "Middle Earth?"

"How about Scotland? Does that sound right?"

"If you say so."

"I can see that my bringing up the subject hasn't exactly elevated your opinion of me."

"Sabrina, I'm sorry. I admit something odd is going on. But I'm just too conventional for an off-the-wall explanation like that."

She sighed. "It's pretty clear I don't have anything left to lose with you, so I might as well keep digging myself in deeper. A while ago when you tried to make sure you were getting rid of me, one of the things I felt was relieved. Dan, since I met you, I've felt as if I were—" she flapped her arms helplessly as if trying to get her balance "—standing on unstable ground. And it's slipping away from under my feet."

Sabrina saw the sharp look that disappeared almost as soon as it flashed across his face. "Isn't that how you felt, too?" she asked. "Wasn't part of your confession motivated by fear of getting involved with me—because you couldn't deal with what was happening between us? Is that part of why you'd like to think of me as a nut?"

"No! Dammit." The blue of Dan's irises had deepened to something resembling the sea at twilight. "You want the truth? I'll give you the truth. The first time I started breathing that drug, it made me want you the way I've never wanted any other woman. This time, it opened up the top of my head like the lid being peeled back from a can.''

The image made Sabrina shudder.

Dan's gaze was riveted to her face. ''My brain was all tender and exposed, and I felt as if icy cold air was pouring over the tissues, seeping down into my skull and through my body. And what I knew when the lid snapped back into place was that if I kept on trying to get close to you, I was going to hurt you. I don't mean I was going to break your heart or anything. Nothing quite so relatable. I mean I knew that I was bad for you, that getting close to me was the worst, the very worst thing that could happen to you. This time I was trying to kill the witch. The next time—''

Sabrina cut him off before he could finish. ''Oh, Dan. No. You wouldn't hurt me.'' When she reached for him, his arms came up stiffly to prevent her from getting any closer.

''You say there's unfinished business between us. Your tale about Duncan and Sara? How does it turn out?'' he demanded.

''I don't know.''

''Well, since you're assuming it's the same story, I seem to have supplied some critical details. The old hag clinched Sara's witchcraft conviction. I'll bet her boyfriend Duncan didn't save her from burning.''

Sabrina shuddered, remembering the flames she'd imagined engulfing the car. Then she lifted her chin. ''Dan, you can't argue it both ways. First you tell me that even though we're both independently coming up with details of Sara and Duncan's lives, they have nothing to do with you and me. Then you turn around and try to use the same facts as an argument for why you're going to hurt me.''

He slapped his fist against his hand. "Okay, you've got your feelings, and I've got mine. But I'm used to dealing with facts. Evidence. Unfortunately there's nothing here that either one of us can prove.''

Sabrina moistened her lips. "There's something we can try.''

"What?''

"What if you could talk to Sara, ask her some questions?''

"Oh, come on.''

"Dan, when I start writing the story, I...I sort of turn into her. I mean when I come out of it, I feel like her.''

His arms were folded tightly across his chest, and his shoulders were hunched. "I've never been to a séance. I'm not going to let you drag me into something equally ridiculous.''

Sabrina raised her eyes to his. "Dan, the—the violence you were so worried about was directed at the witch. Don't you think it's worth trying something a little bizarre to find out why you hate her so much? If it doesn't work, all you've lost is a few minutes of your time.''

Dan looked away from her, staring out at the rise and swell of the waves. The sun was low in the west, painting the hills and troughs with shifting splashes of pink and orange. The shifting colors flickered in his vision like flames.

He closed his eyes, but that didn't dispel the image—or dissipate the raw tension gathering in his body. In his life, there'd been plenty of times when he'd been afraid. Nothing came close to what he was feeling now. He could picture himself diving into the water and striking out toward shore. He was a strong swimmer. Probably the boat was close enough so he could make it.

Except that he wasn't going to bail out now. Deep down, he'd already been playing with some of the crazy theories she'd been spouting just now. But he'd been afraid to face them, so he'd lied to Sabrina about his reasons for getting together with her. He'd also used her for bait at the train station. He'd almost killed her this afternoon. The only way to get back a little of his self-respect was to do what she'd asked.

"If you want to try the experiment, I guess I owe you that much," he said in a low voice.

"Not just me. Yourself. And *us,*" she added in a whisper. But he heard.

HE GAVE HER a little time to get started. As he peered down into the cabin, he could see her sitting at the table writing. She didn't look up when he came inside, nor did the pen pause in its trip along the paper.

"Sabrina?" he whispered.

She didn't answer.

"Sara?" The name trembled on his lips.

His heart was thumping as he came up behind her and bent to read what she'd been writing. As his eyes skimmed the words, his hand moved to her shoulder, pressing, establishing a physical connection that had suddenly become as necessary as breathing.

The morning air was cool and crisp with the promise of an early fall. Sara knew that she had only a few more weeks to gather enough plants to see her through the winter. Basket in hand, she made her way to the cliffs where many of the healing herbs grew. Her feet knew the path, leaving her mind free to wander.

So much had happened in the past year. Ian McReynolds had recovered fully from the bout of peripneumonia, and news of her healing had spread across the glen. Now even clansmen from beyond the mountains sought out her little cottage to buy potions for coughs and rashes. She liked helping people. She also liked the tidy nest egg in silver coins hidden under the floor of the cottage—and the chickens and sheep she'd collected for her services.

But the more success she had, the more malicious the physician Fergus McGraw grew. Aye, she was sure he'd been behind the rumors she'd heard floating around the village. Mistress Campbell was associating with Lillias, the witch. Next they'd have her dancing naked in the moonlight. Or worse.

So far, people still sought her out. But she'd detected a number of speculating glances, and her customers seemed much more interested in making their purchases than in chatting with her. Maybe Duncan could do something to squelch the gossip.

Duncan. Just thinking about him made her heart skip to a sprightly highland tune. She reached down and picked a handful of wintergreen and brought the fragrant leaves to her nose. There was something about the fresh minty scent that reminded her of Duncan. He'd been away for over a fortnight on business for his father, and she'd missed him with an ache that told her she cared too deeply. He'd come to her almost a dozen times since she'd returned from the castle last winter, all on the pretense of buying remedies for members of his family. After the purchases were made, he always lingered, wanting to talk and touch, and bring a blush of rose to her cheeks with his stirring kisses.

Sara sighed. She knew where things were leading, and

it wasn't to the church. Duncan, Duncan, what am I gonna do with ye, lad?

She rounded the path to the mountain pass where she'd first met him. As if by some magic summons, there he was riding through the clearing on a spirited black horse. Sara blinked, sure she'd conjured up the image. But it was really him. She knew she should hold herself back. Instead she waved joyfully as she ran to meet him.

He dismounted and gathered her into his large embrace. "Sara! I was on my way to see ye when I thought I spied a red-haired wood sprite climbing down from the crag."

"So you came up to investigate, dinna ye? I think you're a wee disappointed to find a lass instead of the sprite," she teased, giving him a little hug back. It felt so good to be in his arms again.

The corners of his lips twitched in a roguish grin. "And I think the lass is searching for a compliment."

"Nay. It's not your fine words I'm looking for."

"A kiss then?"

"Nay. Not that either," Sara tossed back, thrilling to the light bantering between them and the way Duncan's eyes had turned a deep-water blue.

"Oh, the lass is in a bartering mood then, is she?"

"It depends on what ye have to barter."

Duncan swung her around and sat her on a flat rock. He removed a pouch from his horse and pulled a fine gold necklace from its depths.

"A trinket for a kiss." He opened her hand and placed the gift in her palm.

"Oh, Duncan. It's beautiful." Sara's fingers brushed over the intricate sunburst design on the gold medallion. "It's the prettiest thing I've ever had."

"Then wear it next to your heart and think kindly of the lad who brought it, will ye?"

"Aye."

*Duncan took the necklace from her hands and slipped
it over Sara's curly red hair. Then he pulled her to her
feet. With a feather-soft touch, he traced over the necklace,
stroking where the gold nestled between her breasts.
Through the fabric of her dress, she felt his touch like a
brand and trembled. Why was she so weak to want a man
she could never wed? But when she was with him, that
argument had no more weight than lamb's fleece.*

*His hands left her neck to comb through her thick hair,
and her own arms anchored around his waist. Then his
blond head was bending to hers, and she was letting him
take the kiss she'd earlier denied. It was sweet, sweet. And
arousing.*

*And soon she was letting him do more. Letting his hands
mold and shape her breasts. Letting his fingers pull open
the laces that held her bodice.*

HE DIDN'T KNOW when he'd stopped reading. Or when
she'd stopping writing. When it had simply started happening. To both of them.

"Duncan. Dan. Don't stop. Not this time. Oh, please,
don't stop."

The frantic entreaty came from the woman he held in
his arms. The woman whose body moved and twisted
against his with the same urgency he felt.

Chapter Thirteen

Present and past merged, wavered, tried to stabilize, and finally came to an uneasy accord.

But time and place were of little importance now. Not when this man and woman were finally in each other's arms, bound together by ties stronger than the forces that would tear them apart.

She had been born for him. Reborn for him.

A muffled sound of craving came from her throat. He drank it in like a man who'd somehow survived a long, parched season of need. In that instant, the terrible years of waiting were swept away. Banished.

"Duncan. Dan."

At the words she'd spoken, her eyes blinked open, colliding with his, held and locked. There was a new light— a new understanding—shining in their blue depths.

"Sara. I lost you once," he rasped. "I won't lose you again, Sabrina."

"You didn't believe me."

"Shh—I can't explain it. I only know I can't let you go." His voice was deep, urgent, persuasive.

The confusion of place and time persisted, tantalized, made them both dizzy. All the more reason to cling to the one solid reference point in the universe—each other.

Slowly the confusion gave way to abiding certainty as hands touched and lips brushed, giving and taking pleasure. Time was precious. And they had squandered far too much of it already.

Suddenly, by silent, mutual consent, they both tossed aside all restraint. Sabrina tugged at the oversize shirt she wore, pulling it over her head. Dan's shirt joined it on the floor. Then her hands were sliding across his chest, glorying in the sight of his magnificent physique and the feel of his hard muscles and crisp hair. Her fingers found the gold chain around his neck, drawing her eyes to the medallion.

She gasped and stared at the golden circle. "The sunburst. It's the same one."

"We can talk about it later." As he pulled her back into his arms, the chain slipped from her fingers. For a moment, she was vividly aware of the burnished medallion pressed tightly between their flushed bodies, the metal heating and sizzling from their desire. Yet almost immediately the mystery of the necklace was eclipsed by the sensations of Dan's lips moving questingly over hers.

A sigh of pleasure flowed from him even as his fingers went to her back, unfastening the clasp of her bra, sending it quickly to join the unwanted shirts. His hands moved over her breasts, inflaming her. When his thumbs and fingers found her hardened nipples, liquid heat shot through her body to her very core. One of his hands followed the hot trail downward, flattened against the soft skin of her abdomen, teased the margin of her navel, glided even lower to slip inside the waistband of her panties and drag them down her hips.

When Sabrina was naked, Dan's hand slid back up her thigh to tangle in the springy curls at the juncture of her legs.

On a little sob, she arched into the caress, inviting more, melting as he found her most sensitive flesh.

Sabrina was so weak with pleasure that her knees gave way, and for breathless moments she clung to Dan. Then he swung her into his arms and carried her toward the tiny bedroom cabin. He laid her gently on the bunk and stood gazing down at her, his face suffused with passion.

"So beautiful." The deepened texture of his voice was like a caress.

"So are you. What I can see."

His eyes locked with hers, he reached for the snap of his jeans, shedding the remainder of his clothes in one quick motion.

She was torn between wanting to admire him and needing to feel his naked skin against hers. Need won, and she held out her arms imploringly. He came down beside her on the bunk, and she knew by the way he clasped her body against his that their need had been the same.

He let out a long sigh of relief, and Sabrina turned toward him, stroking his cheek. "I've wanted this for so long." It might have been a strange thing for a woman to say to a man she'd only met a few days before. Yet the look in his dark eyes told her he understood perfectly. It had been an eternity since they'd held each other intimately.

Dan nodded gravely, reaching up to press her fingers. "When I...when he made love to her, he didn't take her virginity. He didn't think that was right."

"I know."

"This is the first time. The first real time."

"Yes."

Their lips brushed, nibbled, held, opened for a long, deep kiss of affirmation.

Sabrina had known the instant she'd wakened from her

trance and found herself in Dan's arms that something amazing and splendid was happening. It was still happening, moment by moment—to both of them. Strong forces had worked to keep them apart. But they were together. The wonder of it made the breath trickle from her lungs. Later, they could puzzle it out. Later.

They lay on their sides, facing each other on the narrow bunk. Touching. Kissing. Stroking. Exploring. Loving.

Neither one of them wanted to hurry. They drew out the pleasure, letting the power of their feelings build slowly, beautifully, until it was impossible to postpone the joining a moment longer.

He was inside her, then. Hard and deep and throbbing.

She looked up into his face, touched his cheek, murmured wordless syllables that both welcomed him and proclaimed her pleasure at their joining.

The slow pace was over almost as soon as he began to move, and her hips answered his. Now it was all blinding heat and urgency. A man and a woman giving and taking everything, seeking and finding mutual joy.

Climax took her, spreading out from the point of greatest pleasure in a series of shock waves that brought a cry of ecstasy to her lips. Then she felt him follow her into euphoria and her own rapture was complete.

It had begun slowly. It ended slowly. With kisses and murmurs and sighs.

"Perfect. That was so perfect."

"Yes."

Sabrina snuggled closer, wishing that nothing would intrude. But now that her body was returning to normal, her mind struggled to make sense of what had happened. "The witch tried to keep it from happening. This time, we won." Sabrina didn't know she'd spoken aloud until she felt

Dan's body stiffen. Raising her head, she saw the shock of recognition in his eyes.

He nodded slowly, as though trying to deal with a totally alien concept that had come to hold the ring of undeniable truth.

"Dan, what's going on?"

"I don't know."

"But you believe me? That it was us, all those years ago? That we've come back to finish something?" she asked, holding her breath as she waited for his answer.

"Making love with you was like the fulfillment of a promise someone made a long time ago."

"Yes," she breathed.

"But when I try to think about us, I still have trouble with the logic of it."

She could feel her mouth drawing down.

He touched his fingers to her lips, pushing at the corners as if he could turn them upward. "It's hard for someone like me to cope with the paranormal."

"The paranormal," she repeated.

He looked surprised that he'd even said the word. "I've always taken things at face value. Something like this isn't *supposed* to happen. If you can't trust the version of reality you've always thought you knew, what can you trust?"

Sympathy welled inside her. Yes, for someone like him all of this must be terrifying. It was bad enough for her. "We both fought against it. We couldn't fight the truth. Or wanting to make love with each other. I think that's why in the car the drug had that effect on us. As soon as our minds were...freed from normal constraints, we wanted this."

He pressed her face into his chest, kissed her fiery hair. When she heard him laughing softly, she raised her head inquiringly.

"At least it wasn't yohimbine bark," he said.

"What's that?"

"A drug with aphrodisiac qualities. Some members of the counterculture experimented with it in the sixties. The users got about an hour of heavy-duty fun out of it. Then they were violently sick for hours afterward."

Sabrina made a face. "Why would anybody want to take something like that?"

"I guess they thought the pleasure was worth the pain."

"How do you know about it?"

"I've read a heck of a lot about drugs—the common garden variety as well as the exotic. That one struck me as plenty odd."

"And in all your reading, you never came across anything like the cherry-bomb stuff?"

"No. Nothing."

She rested her head against his chest again, feeling his heart thump against her cheek and knowing his tension hadn't gone away. "What are you thinking about?"

His fingers stroked through her wavy tresses, as if that could dissipate his anxiety. "God, I love your hair."

"I'd feel better if you'd be open with me," she murmured.

He sighed. "I owe you that, don't I? After what I've already done."

She tried to make herself breathe normally and couldn't manage the effort.

"Unfortunately what I told you out on the deck is still true," he said with deadly calm. "Sabrina, getting mixed up with me is dangerous for you. Like getting involved with Duncan was dangerous for Sara. When he took her to the castle, that started the rivalry between her and the doctor, maybe between her and the witch, too."

Sabrina swallowed. "You could be right about Sara and Duncan, but how do you know about us?".

"I can't give you any facts. I just *know*. In my bones. And the hell of it is I know we're going to find out."

"Dan, why is this happening? Who are we, really?" she asked in a small, frightened voice.

"A man and a woman who've loved each other for a long time."

She drew in a startled breath, hardly able to believe he'd said what was in her heart.

"There is that," she whispered, turning to brush her lips against his. "Somehow we've got a second chance to make it come out right."

When he stroked her cheek, there was a touch of regret in the gesture. "If we can."

"Dan—"

"Even without the paranormal, there's enough going on now to make me plenty nervous. The Graveyard Murders. Edward. June Garrison. After what she told you, I was worried about making sure you stayed safe. I brought you out here where I could keep an eye on you while—"

"While what?"

"When you get back to the city, there will be a number of protective mechanisms in place."

"Like what?"

"Like a surveillance team assigned to Davenport so we'll know if he makes a move on you. Like somebody keeping an eye on 43 Light Street."

"Is that why you called the shop to find out my plans this morning?"

"Yes. And I checked back with Erin."

So that's who her assistant had been talking to when she'd been so nervous on the phone.

"I didn't want you to start worrying—before we got a chance to talk," Dan continued.

"And now it's all right."

"You know what I mean." He held her close, and they lay silently in each other's arms.

"I tried to tell myself June was just talking about someone who wanted to put me out of business. But I couldn't stop thinking about witches and spells and evil eyes." She shuddered. "You can't protect me against something like that."

"You think the supernatural could hurt you?"

"I wish I didn't. But that's the problem. If I think so, maybe it could."

Dan looked as if he wished she hadn't brought the subject up. "I'd give a lot to know how this all fits together," he grated.

"Maybe we can figure it out."

When Sabrina started to sit up, Dan's eyes went to her breasts, and she felt her nipples tighten.

"Maybe it would be less distracting if we got dressed before we talked," he said thickly. "Because what I want to do instead of talking is pull you back down on the bed again."

"Yes."

Their eyes locked and held for wild heartbeats.

"Making love to you isn't going to keep you safe," Dan said as he got up and opened the drawers under the bunk. After digging through the clothes inside, he handed Sabrina another shirt and a pair of shorts. When they'd both gotten dressed, he pointed toward the ice chest and hamper they'd stowed in the galley. "I can offer you dinner, though."

She nodded, remembering the quantity of food he'd brought. "Was dinner part of your plans?"

"I guess it was in the back of my mind."

It was almost dark when they came back up on deck. Dan turned on the running lights, and they pulled their chairs close to each other, getting out food and drinks in the semidarkness. Sabrina wasn't very hungry, but there was something comforting about the normality of the shared activity.

After a few minutes, it became obvious that Dan's appetite wasn't much better than hers. He reached for her hand. "Tell me about your story. The parts I haven't read."

Sabrina began to fill in details, knitting her fingers through his as she spoke. There'd been no one she thought would understand. It was a wonderful relief to simply let the tale pour out.

When there was nothing more to tell, they sat in silence, hands clasped.

"The thing I'm thinking," she whispered, "is that it's not just us who came back."

"You're talking about the other two major characters—the doctor and the witch?"

"Do you think that's crazy?"

"It's spooky. But once your mind admits the possibility of reincarnation, then you have to start asking yourself why. It's pretty self-centered to think it's for our personal gratification."

"I like the gratification part," Sabrina whispered.

Dan squeezed her hand. "So do I."

"Do you think it's arrogant to wonder if we came back to stop some evil that's survived the centuries?"

"The witch's evil," Dan muttered.

"I wish…I wish we could just live our lives in peace, but it's not that simple."

"You've convinced me," Dan sighed.

"I keep trying to figure out how the past and present are related. This time, some things are different. I'm interested in herbs, but I don't claim to be any kind of healer."

Dan nodded.

"And then there are the other players. In the twentieth-century version of the story, it looks as if the doctor and the sorcerer are the same person," Sabrina continued. "Is there any evidence to link Davenport to witchcraft?"

"I told you we were investigating him because of fraudulent medical practices in Georgia. I haven't run across any specific witchcraft allegations."

"June obviously knew more than we do," Sabrina said slowly. "I mean, about how the past and the present are connected."

"Damn. That makes sense. But where did she get her information?"

"Maybe she was Davenport's confidante."

"Why would he tell anyone what was going on?"

Sabrina shook her head. "Maybe she worked for him and they had a falling out."

"That could be." Dan cleared his throat. "What about the sample you took to the lab? I, uh, didn't get to hear the report."

"The white powder wasn't any kind of antidote. More like a general-purpose stimulant—which means we have no idea what Davenport gave Edward in the first place."

"Mmm."

"Let's try to tie it into the old story. You...you said the witch framed Sara."

"The way Davenport left one of your foil seals in Ian Alastair's pocket," Dan grated, his countenance darkening and his hand jerking away from hers. "And I fell for it."

Sabrina went very still, remembering vividly how she'd

felt when he'd told her he'd suspected she was involved in the murders. "You were *supposed* to think I did it," she murmured, finding his hand again.

His fingers remained rigid, and Sabrina went on speaking almost desperately, hardly aware of what she was saying. "It wasn't your fault. You were trapped in this situation, the same way I was. Davenport has a big advantage over the two of us. He manipulated you, just the way he got me to help him show everybody who came to the lecture the other night that he can work miracles. He *knows* how we'll react. Don't you get it? We're working in the dark, but somehow he's figured out the whole story." She stopped, breathless, realizing what she had said.

Dan's gaze was riveted to her face. "Why are we floundering around like this if *he* has inside information?"

"Maybe he has access to old records. Maybe he—" she gestured helplessly "—has some supernatural advantage. Maybe the story came back to him, the way it did to me. Only earlier."

"The more we find out, the less I like it."

Sabrina sat forward in her seat. "But we have to know more. Would you mind...what about if I try writing it again?"

"So you can find out if Duncan betrayed Sara?"

Sabrina took her bottom lip between her teeth. "If he did, we need that information," she said in a voice that was barely above a whisper.

"Yeah."

"Dan, I'm sorry. I don't know what else to do. Maybe we'll find that Duncan saved Sara."

"I wouldn't count on it," Dan grated. "But if you're going to do it, I'm going to stay with you."

"Maybe it won't work if you're looking over my shoulder."

"I think it will. Now." Unconsciously they drew closer together. "If it doesn't, I'll leave while you get started."

Sabrina was afraid of what she might find out. But even if it was bad, she wanted Dan there with her, in the worst way.

Neither one of them spoke as they stored the food and went back into the cabin. Trying to look purposeful, Sabrina set the pad of paper and the pen on the table. She was about to sit when she felt Dan's hands on her shoulders.

"Not yet." Turning her quickly, he brought her body tightly against his. "It was getting cold in Scotland the last time you were there. I want you to take something with you to keep you warm."

His lips molded themselves to hers. His fingers combed through wild red hair.

Her wordless little murmurs were lost in his kiss as her hands slid up and down his strong arms.

When he finally lifted his head, they were both trembling.

"I'd better start," Sabrina whispered.

Dan's hands dropped away from her body, and it was all she could do to keep from pulling them back. Instead she sat down. This had been her idea. Why did she dread it so much?

She looked up at Dan uncertainly, and he slid onto the bench beside her. She didn't have to do this, she told herself frantically. She could just forget about going back.

He said nothing. She picked up the pen. For a moment it felt alien in her fingers. "This will work," she said as she began to write, feeling Dan watching over her shoulder. "Because we need to know what happened to Sara and Duncan...."

*...Bam. Bam. Bam! The pounding on the door was loud
enough to wake the dead. But it was more fear than aggravation that captured Sara Campbell as she moved away
from the warmth of the fire and went to answer the urgent
call. She'd had the feeling all day that something bad was
going to happen. And she'd thought about fleeing to the
secret cave in the mountains she'd discovered on one of
her herb-gathering expeditions. She and Duncan had lain
there in each other's arms more than once. If she left a
slip of paper with an ax head on the table, he'd know
where to find her, because the way to the cave was marked
with a stone resembling that shape.*

"Who is it and what do ye want?"

"Murray Frye to see the healer."

*She opened the door a bit and held the candle up to
illuminate Frye's face. He was a tall, bulky lad of perhaps
twenty.*

*"Mistress Campbell. The lass Megan has taken a turn
for the worse. We dinna think she'll make it through till
morning. I've come to fetch you to town."*

*Sara looked at the anxious countenance of the lad on
her doorstep. Was he only worried about Megan? Or was
it also the rumors he'd heard.*

*The whispers behind her back had frightened Sara right
enough. And she had half a mind not to go with him, even
though she knew him to be a cousin of the young girl she'd
treated over a fortnight ago. "Megan seemed to be much
improved when last I saw her."*

*"Aye, she was. But this afternoon, she collapsed again,"
Frye explained, not quite meeting her eyes. "You'll
come?"*

*Sara thought of the wee lass and found it impossible to
refuse. "Let me get my medicine."*

Frye stepped into the cottage. When Sabrina turned back

from getting her supplies, she found him hunched near her bed. He straightened quickly.

"Let's go."

The ride into town was cold and dark and nothing like the time she'd been cradled in Duncan's strong arms. But she hadn't seen Duncan in over a fortnight. When he'd told her he was being sent south to settle some of the laird's business, she'd begged him not to leave. He'd told her he didn't have a choice. But he'd done what he could to quiet the wagging tongues before he left.

Frye's touch was rougher than Duncan's. Perhaps that was the way he treated all women. But she couldn't shake the feeling that something more than Megan's illness was troubling him.

The family's greeting was tense as they ushered her into their small stone abode on the outskirts of the village. A crackling fire burned in the hearth. Not far away, Megan lay tossing and moaning in her cot.

Sara dropped to her side and laid a hand on her forehead. The child's skin was cold and clammy. Her pupils were dilated, and from her tortured utterings, a wild dream must be haunting her sleep. "I dinna think she has the fever. She's too cool to the touch. It must be something else. Help me loosen her dress."

The light wool slid from the girl's shoulders, revealing a series of ugly red patches. Behind her, family members gasped in horror.

"The mark of a witch!" *Murray exclaimed.*

"No. No. The work of poison, I think," *Sara said as she straightened and turned toward the family.* "We need to get a strong emetic down her immediately. I've something in my bag. But we need to steep it in boiling water."

No one moved to the kettle. Instead the elder Frye stepped forward. "Then Fergus McGraw was right. You're *a witch just like Lillias, and you've doomed the lass with your evil potions.''*

"That's poppycock and you well know it," Sara responded, struggling to keep her voice from quavering. But the glowering look in their eyes brought a wave of panic to her own. She had to get out of here. Now.

Sara took a step toward the door. But she wasn't quick enough. In an instant, she was grabbed from behind and held tightly between the two large men.

"Your daughter's certain to die if you don't wash the poison out of her system. Let me help her."

"I'll not have a witch touching me bairn again," Mrs. Frye declared, taking a protective step toward the cot. "Or in my house as bold as brass."

Sara's own palms were clammy cold as the men pushed her outside into the bitter cold. After her hands were securely tied with coarse rope, they left her under Murray's guard. "Please let me go. I'll do you no harm."

"Too late for that now. I was at the castle today and heard there will be a reward out for your capture by tomorrow morning. I've got you now, and I'm meaning to collect the gold," the young man sneered.

"Reward? I've done nothing wrong. There must be some mistake. Duncan McReynolds will vouch for me."

"He's not here to vouch for you, my girl. You'll have to tell it to the judges at your trial, now won't you? But when they find the evil-eye symbol under your bed, that will clinch it."

Sara stared at him in horror. "But I don't—"

"Oh, no? I think ye lie, lass."

Sara struggled to break free, but his burly grasp held her prisoner. Tears stung her eyes as he pulled her down the street like a common thief. Someone had put a price

on her head. But it was all a terrible mistake. Would any-
one believe her?

SHE WAS COLD, so cold. As if icy fingers had wrapped
themselves around her very bones. She tried to speak. All
she could manage was a shaky exclamation.

"Sabrina. Come back. It's all right. You're here. With
me."

"Dan. Oh, Dan." All she wanted to do was cling to his
strength, burrow into his warmth. He held her, rocked her,
murmured reassuring words.

"It's like...at the Institute," Sabrina groped for words.
"She was tricked into treating someone...."

"It was the other way around at the Institute," Dan said,
the grating sound of his voice telling her how much he'd
just been shaken.

Sabrina tipped her face toward his. "It's all right. It's
going to be all right."

"I don't think so. I didn't keep you warm, did I? He
wasn't there to help her when she needed him, either."

"Dan, you don't know. Maybe Duncan came back."

"I wouldn't count on it."

"What happened to you when I started writing?" she
asked, determined to change the subject.

Sabrina felt him shudder. "It was strange. First I was
reading over your shoulder, seeing the words you were
writing. Then it changed, and I was—" he stopped and
looked perplexed "—seeing it in some kind of old-
fashioned print. In an old book or something."

"You kept reading?"

"For a while. Then it was like I was there somehow.
With you. Watching from the shadows. I kept shouting at
you. I mean Sara...."

She squeezed his arm, telling him she understood the confusion.

"…trying to warn you to get away. I—I saw him drop the evil-eye symbol under your bed. But you couldn't hear me. There was nothing I could do to save you."

"Oh, Dan. It must have been terrible. Frustrating. I'm sorry."

"I think it was worse for you." He didn't seem to want to talk about it. Instead he tugged on her hand, and she followed him up on deck. The cool breeze blowing off the water helped clear her head.

"The book you saw. Maybe it exists. Maybe there's a record of what happened."

"Yeah."

"We should go back to Baltimore and try to find it."

"I wish…we could just stay here. Or take this boat down the coast where no one can find *us*."

Sabrina pressed her lips together, sensing what he hadn't put into words. Out here on the water they were isolated in a little world of their own. A safe little world. Back in the city lay uncertainty and danger.

"We've got enough food for days. I guess that's what I was really thinking," Dan admitted.

"I wish it was that simple. Running away, I mean. But we've got to go back and face whatever is going to happen."

Dan slipped a protective arm around her shoulder. "You don't have to sleep at your house."

"I have to feed the animals."

"We could do that first."

"The cats don't mind being alone so much. They've got each other. But Robbie…"

"Then we can both stay at your place, unless you're trying to get rid of me."

"I wouldn't do that."

Dan gave Sabrina a quick, fierce hug before they climbed up to the pilot's station together. She didn't want to talk about the case on the way back to the city.

"It's so strange to feel you've known someone for a long time, but you don't know much about their life now," she said.

"Yes. I was wondering, did you have any, uh, special affinity for Scotland?"

"I read historical novels about it all the time, and I used to get all wrapped up in the locale and the characters. And I told you about the stories I wrote. They must have been set there."

"Did you write about Sara?"

"I think so. At least, a girl and her grandmother who lived in a cottage. What about you? Did you have any special interest in Scotland?"

"Not really." He stopped. "I only had the medallion. *It* was from Scotland." In the darkness, Sabrina heard him draw in a deep breath and let it out slowly. "But the minute your name came up in connection with the case, I felt as if I had to get close to you. And I was afraid you'd slip through my fingers if I just went about a straightforward investigation. You were a compulsion, and I couldn't understand why I was making decisions that were so out of character."

"That day at lunch. I was afraid of you. And drawn to you at the same time."

"Afraid. Yes. That's what I'm worried about."

"We'll handle it," she said, wishing her voice conveyed more conviction. She reached up to touch the gold charm that still hung around his neck.

"It's yours, I think," Dan said in a husky voice, taking it off and slipping the chain quickly over her head. "I guess my family's been keeping it for you all these years. I guess that can't be a coincidence.''

Sabrina looked down at the gold circle. "I shouldn't take it. It's too valuable."

"I want you to have it." She might have protested. Yet it felt so right hanging around her neck that she couldn't give it back.

They rode in silence for several moments. "Why did you get divorced?" Sabrina asked suddenly, and then was shocked she'd blurted such a blatant question.

"I blamed my wife for a lot of things. Maybe the real problem was that I didn't care enough. Maybe I couldn't care about anyone but you."

"Oh, Dan." Sabrina pressed her shoulder against his, hardly able to believe he was being so open. "That's how it's always been for me," she agreed. "I wanted to get married. Have a family. But I just couldn't picture myself spending the rest of my life with any of the guys I met."

"I'm selfish enough to be glad."

Sabrina let her head drop to Dan's shoulder. She was consumed with the need to know this man. To know all about him. Raising her head again, she gently reached up and touched the scar on his chin. "Where did you get this?"

"In a fight in high school. When a bunch of tough guys called me a chicken for not trying pot."

"Oh, Dan."

"I came out of it a bit worse for wear. But I guess I did enough damage so they didn't mess with me again."

The lights of the city twinkled in the distance, beckoning them closer. It should have been beautiful sailing into the harbor. Yet Sabrina felt her stomach tightening more and more the closer they got to the dock.

It seemed as if they'd been gone for years. But it was

only a little after ten when Dan cut the engine and maneuvered the launch toward the slip.

For a summer evening, the pier area looked strangely deserted, Sabrina thought as she climbed out and began to secure the mooring line. As soon as she'd finished, she was surrounded by several men who had come rushing out of the shadows. Two wore business suits. Two were uniformed police officers.

Dan had told her he'd arranged for protection. But this sudden flurry of activity wasn't what she'd been expecting. Something must have happened.

Sabrina took a step back.

"Don't move. Raise your hands above your head," one of the men shouted.

It was then Sabrina saw they all had guns drawn. And they were all pointed at her.

She couldn't have moved if her life had depended on it. All at once she realized the speaker was Brian Lowell, the man who had directed the operation at the train station.

"Ms. Sabrina Barkley?"

"Yes. Of course. We…we…know each other."

"I said raise your hands above your head."

"Wh-what?" Sabrina stammered through her confusion, making an effort to comply.

Behind her she heard a curse, just before Dan's feet hit the deck.

"Stay where you are, Cassidy," Lowell called out.

"What the hell's going on?" Dan demanded, his chin raised in anger toward the man in charge. Both detectives boarded the boat.

"Ms. Barkley is under arrest for the murder of Luther Davenport."

Chapter Fourteen

"Luther Davenport?" Sabrina gasped.

"Yes."

"I don't understand." She stared at Lowell, struggling to take in what he was saying. The police were supposed to be protecting her from Davenport. And now—

With a tremendous effort, she forced herself to abandon every painfully arrived-at conclusion she and Dan had recently made.

"On what evidence?" she asked.

"I can't discuss that here. You have the right to remain silent…" Lowell began the phrase Sabrina had heard in countless movies and TV programs.

Sabrina swung back to Dan, who was having a whispered conversation with the other detective. He glanced at her, but his face was as blank as it had been that first day at lunch when she'd told him she wouldn't go to the cemetery.

"Dan…"

"I'm sorry. You've got to go with Lowell."

"Aren't you coming with me?"

His fists were clenched at his sides as he shook his head.

The detective moved Sabrina toward the cabin. "Face the wall."

Sabrina complied and cringed as she felt the man's hands moving over her body, searching for weapons. She was all too conscious she was wearing nothing besides her sandals and the borrowed shirt and shorts. God, what if he went inside the cabin to search for weapons or other evidence? Her wet underwear was down there, and the bunk where she and Dan...

She turned to Dan one more time as Lowell cuffed her hands. He wasn't looking at her now.

Pride kept her from calling out to him again. It was almost a relief when the detective hustled her away. Almost, except that she felt utterly alone and betrayed as she collapsed against the plastic seat in the back of the police car and tried to keep her body from shaking. At the station she held herself stiffly while she was photographed and fingerprinted, trying to distance herself from the abrupt orders and clipped demands for basic information.

Finally she was allowed to make a phone call. It was to Laura Roswell, the only lawyer Sabrina knew. Laura and her assistant, Noel Emery, arrived at the station in less than half an hour. Noel came right in to see Sabrina. Laura went to find out what she could about the case.

Sabrina and Noel stared at each other across the dank, dirty little room set aside for interviews. That morning they'd been laughing and talking about jewelry and show-window displays. How could everything have changed so quickly?

"Oh, honey, I'm sorry you're in this mess," the paralegal sympathized as she gave Sabrina a supportive hug.

"Me, too." For several moments Sabrina clung to her friend. She'd put up a good front since Lowell had taken her off the boat. Inside, she'd felt so afraid and alone.

Half an hour later, Laura joined them around the scarred metal table. When Sabrina saw the look on the lawyer's face, a ball of tension formed in the pit of her stomach. Laura squeezed her hand. "It's going to be okay."

Sabrina clung to the reassurance as Laura extracted a slim file from her briefcase. Noel pulled out a steno pad.

"Is there anything you want to tell me?" Laura asked gently.

Sabrina tried to gather her thoughts. "I—I—thought Davenport was trying to kill me. Now I don't understand what's going on." To her chagrin, she found that tears had gathered in her eyes and begun to slide down her cheeks. Noel silently handed her a tissue and gave her time to collect herself.

"I was able to find out some things upstairs," Laura told her. "Davenport died very early Friday morning. But since he was supposed to be off on a trip, his assistant didn't find him until just before lunch. A ten-thousand-dollar donation from June Garrison is also reported missing."

"But how could they think I was responsible for any of that?" Sabrina asked.

"There's a lot of circumstantial evidence. Last night at the Andromeda Institute, several witnesses saw Davenport humiliate you during the medical emergency."

Sabrina felt the ball of tension in her stomach start to grow. "I felt like he did it on purpose. But surely that's not a motive for murder and robbery."

"They also found another one of your gold charms in Davenport's office."

"And they think I'm stupid enough to commit a bunch of murders and leave such an obvious calling card?" Sabrina asked through gritted teeth. "Are they charging me with the Graveyard Murders, too?"

"For the time being, it's just this one." Laura pressed

her hand again. "I know how hard this is for you," she murmured. "It happened to me, remember?"

Sabrina nodded. A year ago Laura had been accused of murder. But she'd proved her innocence. It gave Sabrina a glimmer of hope.

"You've got to hear the rest of it before we can start to put together your case," Laura said.

Sabrina braced for more bad news. "Okay. What else do they have?"

"The police got a search warrant for your house."

"But they couldn't possibly find anything there," she exclaimed in disbelief.

Noel nodded sympathetically.

"They did. Ten thousand dollars in cash in June Garrison's original bank envelope stuffed into the back of your desk drawer."

"But I don't know anything about the money."

"Someone obviously planted it there," Noel put in. "I guess it was whoever really killed Davenport."

"Is there anything else?" Sabrina asked.

Laura sighed. "After they found the money, they went tramping around your property and discovered a stand of lily of the valley growing out back."

"Since when is it against the law to grow them?" Sabrina asked.

"The preliminary results are in from Davenport's autopsy. Lily of the valley poisoning was the cause of death."

Sabrina leaned her elbows on the table and cupped her head in her hands.

"I know you feel like a ton of bricks has fallen on you," Laura murmured. "Whoever did this to you *wants* you to feel that way."

Sabrina raised her head.

"So they've won the first round. Now, is there anything we can start building your defense on?" Laura asked.

"I—it's all going to sound so crazy. It already does."

"If Noel and I are going to help you, we've got to have some facts."

Sabrina pressed her lips together. "Facts? Are you going to believe I'm the reincarnation of a woman who lived in Scotland two or three hundred years ago and that a witch living at the same time is also back and trying to do me in? Are you going to believe Dan Cassidy was there, too? Or are you going to try to get me off by reason of insanity?"

"Tell us about it," Laura encouraged.

At first it was difficult for Sabrina to keep her voice steady. But as she went through the sequence of events, it became easier and easier to talk.

When she finished, she anxiously scanned her friends' faces.

"You're right. The authorities are going to have trouble dealing with it," the lawyer predicted.

"What about you?" Sabrina whispered.

"You're talking to a woman who had a run-in with a ghost not that long ago."

Sabrina nodded.

"Unfortunately I don't think we can count on a judge to be as open to the paranormal."

"If it helps, I do have all the Scotland episodes I wrote down."

"They don't really prove anything. They could be something you made up."

Dan had said that, too. Before…he let them take her away. Sabrina clamped off that line of thought. "I swear, I didn't make it up."

"I just want you to know what the opposition will say."

Laura put the folder back in her briefcase. "Do you think the assistant district attorney will corroborate your story?"

"I don't know," Sabrina answered honestly.

"Well, I'll try to contact him immediately. And as soon as I can arrange your bail hearing, I'll let you know when it's scheduled."

"Is there anything else you can think of?" Noel asked. "Anything that would help you?"

"Ask the police to check the free tapes Davenport was giving out. It can't hurt if they find the subliminal messages or the ones that are drugged."

They talked about a number of other details and parted with another heartfelt round of hugs. But once Sabrina had been taken back to her cell, she felt worse than before Laura and Noel had come. Now that she was alone, she couldn't imagine how she was going to get out of this trap someone had lured her into and sprung so neatly. The case against her was simply too hopeless. And she wasn't sure which was worse—her arrest or the feeling of hurt and betrayal that surged over her every time she thought about Dan Cassidy. He'd as much as told her he was going to turn on her when it came to crunch time. She felt something inside her shrivel and die. She hadn't believed he would let her down. Not when she'd come out of the story and found him holding her so tightly. Not when they'd been making love.

She should have listened to him when he'd told her to take the boat back to Baltimore and walk away.

WITH A SENSE of unreality, Sabrina tried to pull herself together for the bail hearing Monday morning. Noel had brought one of her most conservative dresses, she noticed, as she changed out of the jailhouse coveralls she'd been issued.

As the guards led her to the hearing room, Sabrina scanned the faces of the crowd in the hall. It was almost a shock to see how many of her friends from 43 Light Street had come down to support her. But the one face she wanted most desperately to see wasn't there. Of course not. Dan had thrown her to the wolves.

"As soon as you get some rest, we're going to start working on the case," Laura said after Sabrina had been released on five-hundred-thousand-dollar bond guaranteed by Jo O'Malley's husband, Cameron Randolph, CEO of Randolph Electronics. "I have a friend who's a very sought-after criminal lawyer who has agreed to be part of the defense team."

"Yes. Thanks. Have you found out anything we can use? What about Davenport's tapes?"

"The police lab has checked several of them. They do have subliminal messages. But none of them is drugged."

Sabrina had hoped for more.

"I also talked to Dan Cassidy's office."

Sabrina flinched.

"He's been ordered off the case. And ordered to stay away from you. Apparently the department is furious about the way he handled things."

"Too bad for him," Sabrina muttered.

Jo, who had been standing a little to the side, came up and joined the conversation. "I guess I got you into this, by asking you to go to lunch with Cassidy," she said in a low voice.

"It's not your fault," Sabrina told her. "He could have used anyone for the contact."

Jo looked a bit relieved. "But I should have figured out that you weren't just writing a story that day when I came in, shouldn't I?"

Sabrina shook her head. "I didn't *want* you to know. I put on a pretty good act, if I do say so myself."

Noel had parked her car where she could avoid the reporters out front. Half an hour later, she walked into her own house, closed the door behind her, and stood leaning thankfully against it. Katie had been stopping by to take care of the animals. But the warm greeting Sabrina received from her dog and cats made her eyes mist.

After washing off the jailhouse stench under an almost scalding hot shower, Sabrina came back downstairs. Physically she felt better. But she was still all torn up inside. When she thought about Dan, tears gathered in her eyes. But she had to stop thinking about him. That was over. Now she had to figure out how to save herself.

As she sat at the table, she felt as if the kitchen walls were closing in around her. It was all coming together again. She'd assumed that this time around Davenport and the witch were one and the same. Now the only conclusion she could come to was that the witch was alive and well and had set her up again. She had no idea how she was going to confront the overwhelming evidence in the present case. But she still had another avenue of attack. She could try to find out what had happened before.

Hope leaped in her breast as she ran to get a pad of paper from her desk. She didn't know how the story ended. Maybe Duncan had come back in time to save Sara. Maybe that meant Dan was...was...

Sabrina closed her eyes for a moment, willing herself not to hope for anything from Dan. It was better not to think about the man and his motives.

Taking a pad of paper from her desk, she grabbed a pen and sat at the kitchen table.

Each time it got easier.

Elspeth meowed plaintively.

"I'll be back in a little while," Sabrina told her. Then she began to write.

"Please, let me find another clue to what's going on. Something that will help me..."

It had been weeks since she'd bathed. Weeks since she'd changed her clothes or had a decent meal. Weeks since she'd felt the wind on her face.

Sara raised her eyes to the tiny slit of light that came in through the window high up in the wall of the cell where she was being held. Sometimes she could catch a glimpse of blue sky. More often, there had been nothing to see but dull gray.

In the days before her trial she'd undergone the humiliation of being stripped and examined by several clergymen for a witch's mark. The brown mole she'd had on her bottom since she was born was judged to be conclusive. Even after that terrible experience, she'd clung to the hope that Duncan would come back and pluck her from the mess she was in.

But the committee of judges had been selected, and she'd been brought before them to answer to a dozen charges of witchcraft. People she'd treated and ones she'd never even met came forward to testify against her. The most damning words came from the physician Fergus McGraw, who blamed her for the death of three children. Her words of denial fell on deaf ears.

Lillias Weir was in the prisoner's dock, too. Sara had stared in disbelief as she'd begun to defend herself by heaping all the blame on Mistress Campbell.

But there'd been witnesses against Lillias, too, with plenty of ghastly tales to tell. In the end, Sara suspected, nothing she nor Lillias said or did would have made any difference. After less than an hour of deliberation, the court had found them both guilty and sentenced them to a public burning in seven days.

"No," Sara shouted. "I dinna do the devil's work."

"Be silent, girl," the chief judge warned. "Or it will go worse with ye. Be glad we don't have to get a confession from ye before we burn ye."

Sara shuddered, remembering the instruments of torture she'd been shown. But she hadn't confessed, and mercifully she was not tortured.

With a silent scream, she was dragged away and thrown back in her cell where she huddled shivering on the pile of dirty straw they'd allowed her for a bed. For the first few evenings, she couldn't eat the crusts of bread they brought her for dinner, and the rats carried the food away. Then her mind slipped into a desperate fantasy. Duncan would come. He'd find some new evidence that would save her. Or he'd storm the jail and rescue her, and the two of them would ride away on the destrier. They could go to the cave in the mountains that she'd showed him. That was safe. He could hunt with his sling and throwing stone the way she'd seen him bring down rabbits. And when the search for them was over, they could leave the country and go somewhere else where no one would pursue them. But in her moments of despair, she knew it would never happen. Then she wished she had a leaf of monkshood to swallow. It would provide a quicker, less painful death than the one she knew awaited her.

At noon on the seventh day, they came for her. As she was hustled toward the town square, flanked by guards on either side, she held her head up high. She had done nothing wrong. Let them remember later that she'd gone to her death with dignity.

The crowd was large and jeering. Their cruel shouts echoed in her ears as the burly men led her to the stake.

Then Lillias was brought forward. This was the first time Sara had seen her since the trial. The woman appeared to have aged ten years. Lines were etched in her face, and her eyes shone with a hatred so strong that even the guards cowered.

Coarse hemp bit into Sara's wrists as she was pulled against the stake and tightly bound. Then her tormenters stepped away, leaving her back-to-back with the older woman. At the edge of her vision, she saw men standing with torches and cringed, forcing herself not to look at them.

"I see your fine lover from the castle dinna come and rescue ye," the witch hissed.

Sara closed her eyes for a moment. "Why do ye hate me so much?"

"You've brought this on us both by challenging Mc-Graw."

"Aye, it may be I brought it on myself. Your own mischief damned you."

The bailiff was reading the decree.

"...for consorting with the devil, they will be consumed by the fires of hell forever. Let it be done."

Sara couldn't hold back a frightened cry as the men with the torches came forward and the acrid smoke drifted toward her. The evil smell grew worse as they touched the burning tips to the tinder-dry straw. For heart-stopping moments, the red flames danced playfully along the edges of the straw. Then they suddenly leaped up and raced toward her.

She screamed in terror and then in pain, twisting against her bonds, trying with all her strength to get away from the flames licking at her clothes and her skin. The smoke scorched her lungs. The terrible crackling sound surrounded her. Closing in tighter and tighter.

Then the only thing she could hear above the roar of the fire was Lillias's shrill voice. It seemed to build in power. Like the flames.

"I curse the lot of ye in this foul town. And I fix an entail on the spirits of Sara Campbell and Fergus McGraw. Ye will not escape me. This is not the end. It is but a pause. The circle will not be complete until the Servant of Darkness prevails."

SABRINA WAS CHOKING, gasping for breath, huddling down with her hands flung over her head as if that could protect her from the flames. With a frightened cry, she staggered to the living room, and sank onto the sofa cushions. For long moments she simply lay there shaking.

She'd be writing no more stories of Sara Campbell. Sara was dead. Burned at the stake. Sabrina was too stunned to do more than drag in shaky breaths of air.

She tried to block out the scene. But she could still see the flames racing toward her and then shooting up around her so that every avenue of escape was blocked. Now she knew for certain where her fear of fire had come from.

The terror threatened to envelop her again, the way it had at the cemetery. But she fought against the hideous vision, gradually bringing it down to manageable proportions. As she did, she grasped one stunning fact she hadn't known before. The witch had gone to the stake with Sara. The witch had died, too. Sara had lost everything. But so had Lillias. Or it seemed that way until she'd evoked some sort of curse.

Had it worked? Had she given herself a second chance?

Sabrina sat with her chin in her hands, trying to puzzle it out. The witch had only called back Sara, the doctor and herself. What about Duncan? What was he doing here?

She clenched her fists, feeling her nails dig into her

palms. What did it matter? Duncan had abandoned Sara to her fate. Dan had done the same thing. On orders from the district attorney's office. Perhaps Duncan had been following orders from the laird.

Tears were threatening her again, and she pulled her purse off the floor to get a tissue. As she dug through the contents, her fingers encountered several folded sheets of paper—and a circle of metal. She pulled them both out.

The metal was the medallion Dan had given her. The police had taken it away, along with her other personal possessions when she'd been processed. But they'd given it back when she'd been released on bail. As she stared at the sun carved into the surface, the tears began to roll down her cheeks. Tears for what she'd felt when Dan had placed it around her neck. Tears for what might have been.

Acting on an impulse she couldn't justify in any logical way, Sabrina slipped the chain around her neck and tucked the medallion out of sight inside her blouse. The weight of the emblem against her chest was somehow very reassuring.

But she should certainly give it back to its owner. Sabrina reached to remove the chain again and stopped, fighting the feeling of dread that swept over her when she thought about taking off the medallion. All at once she remembered when Laura had come into her shop last fall with a charm she'd wanted put on a chain. She'd worn it around her neck when she'd been in danger, and it had saved her life.

Sabrina sat with her eyes closed for several minutes, her hand pressed against the metal that had warmed to the temperature of her own skin. She couldn't explain why, but it made her feel safer. And she needed all the reassurance she could get. Perhaps it was only a tangible link to the past. Perhaps it did hold some protective qualities, although it hadn't saved Sara. Still, she wanted to wear it for the time being.

Finally her hand dropped to her lap, rustling the papers that she'd forgotten about.

What were they? Sabrina spread the forms open and stared at them. They were the report on June Garrison that Dan had given her.

So far, June was the one person she'd encountered who admitted she knew something about all this. But it was pretty unlikely that the witch had simply told her the story. So where had she gotten her information?

Sabrina's eyes zeroed in on the address. The police had searched her house, but perhaps they hadn't known what they were looking for. Certainly they wouldn't have been after anything that would help *her*. What if she could get in there and have a look for herself?

The idea was compelling. Now all she needed was an expert at breaking and entering.

"YOU *LIKE* DOING THIS," Sabrina accused as she and Jo O'Malley slowly drove around the block off Cold Spring Lane where the modest Garrison house was located.

"Don't tell my husband."

"Cam probably knows."

Sabrina was feeling better than she had in a long time. For days she'd been swept along by events out of her control. Finally she was doing something on her own behalf.

Jo made short work of the basement lock. Then they were hurrying through the silent house. On the way over, they'd discussed strategy. It would have been quicker to split up and each investigate different floors. But Sabrina felt she was the only one who really knew what they were looking for. So Jo had given her a crash course in search procedures. She and the detective moved through the rooms together in an orderly pattern, carefully checking drawers and cabinets, under sofa cushions and rugs, and behind heating vents. At first it was a disappointing effort. Then, in the master bedroom, Sabrina happened to glance at the books piled on the window seat.

One was an old volume with a torn leather binding. She felt her throat close as she read the title *History of the Scottish Inquisition.* She'd wondered if the facts were written down in a book somewhere.

With trembling fingers, Sabrina extracted the volume from the pile, skimmed the table of contents and thumbed through the pages. It became apparent very quickly that the book was a documented account of witchcraft persecution in Scotland.

"Scotland is surpassed only by Germany in the zealousness of its witch trials. Secular courts shared prosecution duties with the clergy who acted the part of inquisitors."

Following was a partial record of Scottish trials beginning with a man named John Fian in 1590 and ending in 1704 with a group called the Pittenweem witches.

When Sabrina got three-fourths of the way down the list, she felt chills run up her spine.

In 1682, in the village of Killearn, two women, Sara Campbell and Lillias Weir, were tried and burned as witches. Sara Campbell had been brought up on a dozen charges, including killing three children by witchcraft. The most damaging accusations came from a physician named Fergus McGraw.

Sabrina didn't realize she'd made a strangled sound until she found Jo standing anxiously beside her.

"What have you got?" Jo asked, staring at the open page.

"It's all here," she croaked. "The names. The charges. The trial. Just like I've been writing about." She thrust the book at her friend, stabbing her finger at the page and feeling a surge of triumph.

UNFORTUNATELY Harry Rosenberg, the attorney who'd agreed to help with Sabrina's case, didn't think the book was going to be much help. And his defense strategy seemed to revolve around finding who had framed Sabrina.

Good luck, she thought as Erin drove her home from his office. Tired and dispirited by the four-hour meeting, she flaked out on the couch. Since there was hardly anything to eat in the refrigerator, Erin volunteered to go out and get some groceries.

A while later, Sabrina's eyes blinked open. She'd hardly slept the night before, but under the circumstances, she hadn't expected to fall asleep.

"Feeling better?" Erin asked in a voice that sounded artificially chipper as she set down several plastic bags on the kitchen counter.

"A little." Sabrina glanced at her watch. Had Erin really been gone almost two hours? It couldn't have taken that long to get the groceries.

Sabrina sat up and stretched. "I guess you thought I needed a rest."

"And some food. Let me fix some sandwiches. Is sliced turkey okay?"

"Yes," Sabrina murmured, wondering if she could force a sandwich down.

Erin was putting the milk in the refrigerator when the phone rang. "I'll get it."

"Who is it?" Sabrina asked as she came into the kitchen.

Erin jumped. "Oh, I didn't know you were standing there. "It's...it's Gwynn Frontenac."

"Gwynn?" The woman could be so trying. She didn't have the energy to cope with her now. Shaking her head, she whispered to Erin, "Tell her I'm asleep."

"She says it's important."

Sabrina sighed and reached for the phone. Erin handed her the receiver and then busied herself with putting groceries away. "Yes?"

"Oh, Sabrina, I read about you in the papers. I want to tell you how sorry I was to hear that you'd been falsely accused."

"Yes, well, thanks..." Since the story had hit the news, customers had been calling to express similar sentiments. Each time, Sabrina felt her chest squeeze. Now the deep, booming quality of Gwynn's voice made the pressure worse.

"My dear, I know you must be trying to marshal your defenses," Gwynn intoned.

"Yes."

There was a pause during which Sabrina felt her fingers tighten painfully on the receiver.

"I think I might have some information that would be helpful."

"About what?"

"The Servant of Darkness."

Chapter Fifteen

The sky was overcast, and a few raindrops were just starting to sprinkle across Sabrina's windshield as she turned onto the long, tree-lined drive that led to Gwynn Frontenac's house. The three-story stone mansion was set far back from the street and hidden by a screen of pines. Ancient rhododendrons clustered around it, obscuring the gray walls, as if hiding secrets.

Sabrina, who had never been there before, stared in fascination at the structure. It was one of those monstrosities the newly rich sometimes built in order to make a statement. Was this Gwynn's taste? Or her late husband's? As Sabrina peered up at the long, thin windows, round tower and crenellated roofline, she decided the residence looked like a cross between a fortress and a castle. If she went inside, would she ever come out?

She drew in a deep breath and released it slowly, pretty sure her own melancholy mood was responsible for the out-of-proportion reaction. Although the house was ugly, that didn't make it sinister. Still, she was glad she wasn't going in there alone. While she'd gotten ready, Erin had called Noel, who had agreed to meet her. But she hadn't shown up yet. Sabrina tapped her fingers nervously on the steering wheel as she waited for her friend. A curtain stirred at one of the windows. Was Gwynn looking out, wondering why she was sitting in her car? Sighing, Sabrina got out and rang the bell. Gwynn, who opened the door herself, was dressed in a bright orange-and-green silk dress accented with heavy gold jewelry. As always, the effect maximized her height and her girth.

A mixture of relief and anticipation flashed across her features. "Sabrina, I'm so glad you could make it."

"I'm anxious to hear whatever you know that might help my case."

"Yes. I'm sure you are. Come inside and we'll have a nice cup of your herb tea while I tell you all about it."

"Noel Emery is supposed to be meeting me here," Sabrina said uncertainly as she turned and looked back down the driveway.

"Yes. She just phoned. She's running a bit late and said for us to go ahead and get started. Come make yourself comfortable."

With a grimace, Sabrina stepped across the threshold.

Gwynn locked the door and pocketed the key before leading the way down a hall into a formal living room.

Sabrina shivered as a cold draft of air hit her face. The place looked uncomfortably like a museum, filled with heavy Tudor furniture and decorated with paintings in dark colors and themes. Wishing Noel would arrive, Sabrina perched on the edge of an overstuffed brocade love seat. Gwynn took the chair opposite her and began to pour from an antique silver teapot.

"Sugar and milk?"

"Just sugar. You—uh—you said you know something about the Servant of Darkness?"

Gwynn passed her a cup. "I need to give you some background first. You know Hilda was the one who got me interested in Dr. Davenport."

"Yes." Sabrina took a sip from her cup. The blend was familiar, yet it had a slightly odd, heavy taste.

Gwynn looked uncomfortable. "I don't want to tell tales about a friend. But I think she was somehow emotionally involved with the man."

Earlier, the chill of the house had enfolded Sabrina. As she sipped her tea, she realized she was starting to feel warm and a little light-headed. She loosened the button at her neck.

"Are you okay?" Gwynn asked.

"Yes. I think so. What do you mean by 'emotionally involved'?"

"I'm afraid Hilda might have developed a romantic interest in the doctor. She hung on to everything he said, wrote him letters, even asked my opinion about some of the notes he sent her."

"He wrote her letters?"

Gwynn nodded. "But I could tell he was leading her on. I suspect he was only interested in getting her to make a big contribution to the Andromeda Institute. Perhaps she found out."

"You're not trying to say you think she killed him, are you?"

"Well, he may have been playing this game with other women, too. But when you finish your tea you ought to take a look at some of the letters she sent him. They're upstairs in my workroom."

"Why do you have them?"

"They're copies. Hilda often asked my opinion about phrasing and grammar and such."

Sabrina drained the hot drink and tried to concentrate on Gwynn's words. Her mind was starting to fog up. "It's hard to believe that Hilda could do something like that."

"You remember how excited she was about his lecture.

She was the one who convinced you to attend. I also saw her taking a handful of your pretty gold esses one time when we were in your shop.''

Her words seemed to echo softly around the room, making it hard to catch on to them. Sabrina leaned forward trying to get closer to the source. Suddenly the large woman was beside her, laying a hand on her arm. "I know all this must be making you feel confused."

"Yes, confused." Sabrina tried to shake the haziness that was stealing over her. "What does this have to do with—" She stopped abruptly wondering what she had been going to say.

"You will rely on my advice, won't you?"

"I—"

"Let's go upstairs. I think you'll get a better understanding of what's really happening."

Sabrina let herself be guided to the stairs and began to climb with Gwynn at her elbow. Her legs felt heavy as if she were wearing lead boots. Something didn't make sense. Why would Hilda leave her love letters with Gwynn? But she didn't have the mental energy to pursue the thought. They gained the second floor and walked down another hall. It was dark with a slight sickly-sweet smell.

Gwynn's fingers dug into her arm.

They rounded a corner and came face-to-face with an old picture in a gilt frame. It was a print of Hieronymus Bosch's *Garden of Earthly Delights* depicting the wild, out-of-control cavorting of naked men and women—many in very nasty poses.

Repelled, Sabrina drew back.

"Bosch is so good at depicting the pleasures of the flesh, don't you think?" Gwynn murmured. "But his devils are a bit off-putting."

Sabrina wasn't sure how to respond.

"The letters are in here," her guide said, stepping aside so that Sabrina could precede her into a room a little farther down the hall.

It was a workroom, the source of the sickly-sweet odor in the hall. As Sabrina stepped inside, she could see the walls were lined with shelves of glass jars. Some contained familiar leaves. Others held molds and fungi and things she didn't want to examine too closely.

"I think you'll find the design on my floor quite interesting," Gwynn whispered, giving Sabrina a little push into the room.

She looked down, seeing a familiar pattern of stars painted on the polished boards. They were like an hourglass. But it was the hunter, Orion, the giant whose boasting had offended the ancient gods. And she was standing right in the middle of the pattern.

Sabrina felt a web of power stronger than any mortal hands grip her, hold her.

"There are a lot of advantages to being a rich widow," Gwynn murmured. "I'm not an ignorant country bumpkin this time. So I have more weapons at my disposal to defeat those who defy me. Now, turn around and submit to me."

In slow motion, every movement a terrible effort as her muscles fought the command, Sabrina turned to face the large woman.

Gwynn looked completely transformed. The slightly dotty widow had vanished. In her place was someone who knew she wielded power. She was holding up a wide velvet cord emblazoned with the evil-eye symbol. The malevolent image seared into Sabrina's brain, branding through flesh and bone.

"Don't move. I have you now. Soon we will be going

upstairs to complete the ceremony,'' Gwynn ordered, her voice high and piercing.

Fear welled up from deep in Sabrina's soul. *Run. Get away. You, you're the one,* her mind screamed. *You're the witch. It was you all along. And I never suspected.*

Gwynn smiled as if she knew very well what was going through Sabrina's mind.

The witch began to advance toward her, holding up the cord. Sabrina cowered back, unable to break the hypnotic spell holding her immobile.

Then a loud thumping noise from above made her body jerk. In that one desperate moment, Sabrina wrenched her gaze away from the eye.

''Obey me,'' Gwynn shrieked.

Summoning every ounce of strength she could muster, Sabrina staggered toward the side of the room. When she stepped outside the pattern of stars, it was as if a terrible crushing weight had been lifted from her body.

''No. Stay there,'' Gwynn railed.

Sabrina's hip hit the workbench. Her hand groped behind her for a weapon, found only a glass bottle and hurled it with all her strength.

It hit Gwynn in the chest. Air groaned out of the large woman's lungs. Her knees crumpled, and she screamed as she fell forward into the middle of the Orion pattern.

''It will hold you,'' Sabrina found herself calling out. ''The way it held me. You forfeit the power to me.''

She didn't know if that was true. But maybe if Gwynn believed—

Sabrina darted past her attacker and out of the room.

Whatever was in the tea had fogged her brain, making it difficult to reason, difficult to make her limbs work.

Somehow Sabrina kept herself focused as she staggered down the hall. All the doors were locked.

Fighting a wave of dizziness, she struggled to think. She should go down. Out of the house. She couldn't drive, but she could run for help.

At the stairs, she hesitated. Every fiber of her being urged her to flee, but somehow she knew there was something upstairs she had to get first. Something that would free her once and for all.

Instead of going down, Sabrina began to climb. On the third floor, she began to try doors again. Finally she found one that was unlocked.

Certain the thing she needed was inside, she entered the room. It took a moment for her to remember that she'd have to secure the lock so that Gwynn couldn't follow. When she turned back to face the room, she tried to stifle a gasp of shock. Under ordinary circumstances, the place would have been frightening. It was an elongated chamber that could have been the set for a Dracula movie or something equally sinister. In Sabrina's present state, it was like a black hole ready to swallow her.

The walls were completely shrouded by midnight curtains, except for the strange symbols that broke the surface on either side of the door. The only illumination came from the candelabra fitted with tall white tapers placed at intervals around the room.

But more disturbing than the physical setting was the sense of ancient evil that permeated the place. There'd been echoes of it in the graveyard when she and Dan had come to look at the murder site. Downstairs in the workroom it had grown stronger. Here the malevolence hung heavy in the air as if it had soaked into the very fabric of the black curtains, which now gave it back in waves.

Sabrina wanted to back out of the door. She'd made a terrible mistake, but now there was no place else to go.

She pressed her shoulders against the stout wood as she waited for her eyes to adjust to the eerie, flickering light.

She had run up here and trapped herself. This was what Gwynn had wanted all along.

The sudden knowledge that she wasn't alone was an icy breeze blowing across Sabrina's skin. Her eyes probed the flickering shadows, searching for danger—and searching for another way out. She moaned low in her chest and shrank back as the curtains at the far end of the room stirred and parted slightly. Paralyzed, unable to breathe, she watched as a figure shouldered itself partway out of the concealing drapery and stood in stark relief against the black background.

Her confused mind struggled to process what she was seeing.

Gwynn. Somehow the witch had gotten in here. Through another entrance.

Sabrina fumbled for the lock.

But the tall masculine figure wasn't Gwynn in her blaze of bright silk. Instead Sabrina found she was staring at a disheveled Dan Cassidy. His white shirt hung open where buttons had been pulled off. His blond hair dangled in his face. And as he tried to thrust farther forward, Sabrina saw that his hands were pulled in back of him and fastened to a stout wooden post.

He seemed to realize who had come into the room at the very moment she comprehended it was him. As his eyes sought hers out, his face went from agony to anger and back to agony. While she stared into their depths, he pulled himself up straighter, thrusting his face toward her, and she realized with a start that a flesh-colored gag prevented him from calling out to her.

Since she'd drunk the tea, she'd felt woozy. But in that

blazing instant when her eyes locked with Dan's, her thoughts snapped into focus.

She hadn't seen Dan since Lowell had taken her off the boat and hustled her away to jail. In her hurt and pain, she vowed to forget Cassidy. Now a muffled, urgent sound welled up in his throat.

When she took a step toward him, he began to shake his head and twist his body furiously against the post. But there was no hesitation on Sabrina's part. He needed her, and she went to him. The anguished look on his face as he stared helplessly at her almost knocked the breath from her lungs. Then she saw the ugly red gash partially hidden by the hair that had fallen across his forehead.

"Dan. My God, Dan." With fingers that felt insensitive as metal prongs, she clawed at the beige scarf that served as a gag. It seemed to take forever. Finally she dragged it down so that it fell around his neck.

"Get out of here," he rasped as soon as he could speak.

"What?"

"Sabrina, it's a setup. The witch tricked me. Get out of the house while you can."

She blinked, trying to take the words in. "I'm not leaving you here." She dropped to her knees and began to inspect the coarse hemp that bound his wrists. It was wound securely around the wooden post. The way she'd been tied to the stake before they'd burned her. A long time ago.

As she worked at his bonds, Dan talked to her in a low, urgent voice. "Sabrina, she told me a lot of stuff after she tied me up. She's Lillias come back. She's got a whole group of people so frightened and captive to her persuasive techniques that they'll do anything she says. Sign over their insurance to her. Steal from their employers. If you try to cross her, you end up dead. Like the graveyard victims. She killed them as a warning.''

''And June Garrison?''

''She was working for her. She figured out some of what was going on and tried to get Gwynn to take her on as an equal partner. Gwynn drugged her and used her to spy on you and Davenport—and to set you up for his murder. She's absolutely ruthless. She's already killed four times that we know of and maybe a lot more. Now get out of here. Save yourself.''

Sabrina ignored the advice. If Gwynn had told Dan that much, she didn't expect that he was going to be able to pass the information on. But why had he fallen into her trap? ''How did she get you?'' she panted without pausing in her task.

''She said she had information that would save you.'' His voice was raw.

Sabrina's eyes shot to Dan's. They locked and held as her fingers gripped his.

The door rattled. Sabrina's heart leaped into her throat. Dan swore vehemently. The clatter continued as Sabrina's fingers began to work more frantically at his bonds. In her desperation, she tore off several nails below the quick. But she didn't stop unknotting the cords.

Somewhere in her mind it registered that the rattling had stopped, but it didn't affect her labor.

Dan strained against the bonds, making her task more difficult. ''Don't!'' she protested. ''Stay still.''

She felt the tension gathering in his body as he forced himself to stand perfectly quiet when every instinct urged him to pull away. Then he must have felt a loosening at the left wrist. He gave a mighty jerk, and the left hand came away with the rope dangling.

''Sabrina.'' He pulled her into his arms, clamping her

tightly against him so that the medallion was squeezed between them. Then he lifted his hand to her chest, touching the sunburst through the fabric of her blouse. "You're wearing it. I thought you wouldn't." His voice was thick.

"I had to."

For a burning moment, neither one of them moved. Then Dan tore his eyes away from Sabrina's face. "We've got to get out of here," he grated. "Before it's too late." Turning to the wall opposite the door, he began to pull the curtains aside, searching for a window. White woodwork appeared behind one panel. But the opening was completely blocked by plywood nailed firmly in place.

Dan picked up one of the heavy candelabra, blew out the tapers, and bashed the metal base against the wood. It barely dented the surface. He swung again and again. Given time, he might batter his way through.

If they had the time. But they didn't. All at once, a sickeningly familiar smell drifting toward them.

Rotten cherries. Lord, no.

Holding her breath, Sabrina dashed toward the door and tried to twist the lock. To her horror she found that it no longer turned. She'd thought Gwynn was trying to get in. Instead she'd locked the door from the outside.

Dan redoubled his efforts. But the plywood held. Sabrina shrank away toward the far end of the room. When she felt as if her lungs would burst, she was forced to take a breath. As soon as she did, she felt her chest burn and her head fill with mist.

Dan raised the candlestick like a club.

"Drop it," Gwynn ordered, stepping into view. "Or I'll shoot your girlfriend." She must have come in through a door that was hidden by the draperies.

Sabrina caught the flicker of candlelight on the dull metal surface of the gun the witch held in her hand.

With an angry growl, Dan dropped his own weapon.

Sabrina stared from him to the tall woman. There was nothing she or Dan could do except watch in horror as the vapor filled the room.

Dan's face contorted. Finally he gasped in a draft of the drugging stuff.

There was no escape. It was only a matter of time until Lillias could do anything she wanted with them. Make them think anything she wanted.

Sabrina shook her head, trying to clear away the confusion. Not Lillias. Gwynn.

As she looked toward the end of the room where the hallucinogen was pouring in, she saw their captor standing still as a statue watching them.

"Erin didn't call anyone except me. I have control of her mind."

"H-how?" Sabrina choked out, clinging by her fingernails to sanity.

"Subliminal messages on the music tapes I gave her. A little trick I picked up from my late friend Dr. Davenport. Isn't it wonderful how many more tools there are nowadays?"

Sabrina flinched, knowing this was a woman sure of her power, sure of her control. Or had the drug garbled understanding? Erin? Had Erin really been helping the witch?

Gwynn laughed. "Your assistant was very helpful. She switched the cassettes in your pocketbook—for ones I'd drugged."

Speechless, Sabrina stared at her.

"And now I must insist you stay for the excitement of the ceremony. It just wouldn't be the same without the two of you." Gwynn turned to Dan. "You couldn't leave well enough alone. I didn't summon you, but you came back, anyway. You thought you could kill me. You were wrong.

You should have died when I booby-trapped your car. Now I think you'll wish you hadn't joined the party.'' Gwynn's terrible laugh cut through Sabrina's flesh, scourging all the way to her bones. The room slipped in and out of focus. Tumbled thoughts careened around Sabrina's mind.

Gwynn's revenge.

Lillias had planned. For so long. Her and Dan together. No, not Dan. He was a wild card. But now she'd kill them both.

Kill them both.

Probably by poison. Or would she burn them? Sabrina cringed. No, not in the house. She couldn't do that in the house.

The room was filling up with the cherry vapor. It swirled around Sabrina, a rough blanket smothering her body. Thoughts slithered away like bugs skittering from the light.

They had to get away. She looked wildly around. Nowhere to turn. Nowhere to hide. Except perhaps one place. If they could get there.

''Sara,'' she called. ''Sara, help me. Don't let it happen again.''

''Stop! No!'' the witch commanded. ''Yield to my power over your mind.''

Sabrina ignored the command. ''Sara. Please, Sara. Come to me.''

The air seemed to tremble. In the flickering light, the focus shifted. Back, back to another time. Before the scene could slip past, she reached out and clutched on to it, the way she'd clutched the pen when the writing had carried her back.

''No! Stop!'' the witch cried out.

Sara ignored her. ''Duncan, I need you, Duncan,'' she called. For an agonizing moment, she thought he wasn't going to come to her. Then he was beside her, grasping her shoulder. "Sara. It's not too late then, lass?"

"I won't let it be too late."

"Damn ye, Sara Campbell," the witch shrieked, her voice rising in a desperate wail. "Yield to me. Stop."

Duncan grasped her hand. With an urgent tug, he pulled her down behind the heavy table in the center of the room.

A crack of thunder sounded just as something hot and dangerous shot past Sara's head. Swearing, Duncan thrust her closer to the floor. "Give me the medal ye wear," he grated. "Be quick."

Thunder boomed again as Sara reached around her neck and pulled the medallion free. When she gave it to Duncan, he pressed her hand. Then he moved away from her so that he could swing the large medal pendant in a circle around his head the way he'd swung his sling and rocks when he'd taken her hunting. The disk whined as it flashed through the air. Standing, he gave a bloodcurdling shout and let the missile fly, just as the thunder cracked again.

The metal disk crashed into one of the candelabra, tipping the brass fixture on its side. The candles hit the curtains, and the dry black fabric instantly blazed up.

"No. Duncan. What have ye done? What have ye done?" Sara cried out.

The witch shrieked.

Terrified, Sara shrank away from the fire. Then there was only the cloying, sweet smell of the cherries, the shouts of the villagers calling for her blood, and horror of the crackling flames as they raced out to meet her.

Chapter Sixteen

With a terrible scream, the witch dashed to the spot where the curtains had caught fire. Cursing, she beat like a madwoman at the flames, using the coils of heavy rope that had held Duncan to the post. But the frantic effort was wasted.

Heat billowed up as the red-and-yellow tongues lapped greedily at the hangings. While the witch rushed first in one direction and then in the other, the fire moved relentlessly around the room, forming a flickering circle that lighted the secret chamber in all its lurid detail.

It was like a scene from hell. And Sara had been cast into the inferno once before. Speechless with horror, she tried to crawl under the table.

"No. We've got to get out of here." Duncan grabbed her, pulling her to her feet.

"Please. Not the stake," she choked out, coughing on the thick smoke that billowed around them. "Not the stake."

She tried to wrench out of his grasp, but he held her fast.

"Sara, stop. Don't fight me. You've got to trust me if I'm going to save you."

The urgency, the pain and the fear in his voice made

her head jerk up. Her eyes locked with his, seeing both his anguish and the reflection of the flames flickering in their blue depths. There was no time for thought, no time to reason it out. Once and for all, she had to choose.

"Sara, please."

In the moment of decision, she gave him her trust. Her life. She reached for his hand. It might have been the only solid thing in the flickering red and yellow universe. Holding on to Duncan with all her strength, Sara stumbled after him, gasping on cherry vapor and smoke.

The fire surged at Lillias. With a curse, she jumped back, dropping the rope. Then, crying out her anger at the top of her lungs, she whirled and fixed Sara and Duncan with a terrible look.

"You haven't won. You'll die here. Together," she promised, as the thunder sounded one more time. "I'll send you to hell before I let you get away."

Hot pain sliced across Sara's arm. She cried out and stumbled.

With a shout of raw anger, Duncan lunged at the witch, knocking savagely at her hand. But she was almost his equal in size, and she was strong. In the flickering, diabolical light, the two figures struggled, coughing and wheezing. Then something heavy clunked to the floor. Somehow, Sara knew that Duncan had knocked a terrible weapon from the witch's grasp. In the next moment, he caught the large woman by the shoulders. With the victory cry of a Scottish warlord, he spun her around and sent her hurtling toward the burning draperies.

She shrieked as the flames caught her dress, then her hair. Crying out in pain and terror, she beat at her clothing.

Sara was transfixed in horror. Wasting no time, Duncan caught her up in his arms and began to stumble toward the door Gwynn had used. A line of fire raced from the wall and tried to snare them. He leaped out of its path and stumbled toward the door.

They were both choking and gasping in the smoky haze, and Sara pressed her face into his shoulders and squeezed her eyes shut.

He surged across the threshold into blessedly cool air, and they both dragged oxygen into their burning lungs.

Duncan started toward the stairs. Sara gripped his shoulder. "Wait."

He looked at her questioningly.

Twisting back toward the burning room, Sara raised her head and began to speak in low, measured tones. "I call on the powers of good in the universe to put a final end to the Servant of Darkness. Lillias will not return to this earth. Her second chance is spent. She is vanquished, now and for all eternity."

A terrible scream of defeat and pain came from within the burning chamber. Then the flames were leaping from the doorway, and a thundering crash shook the floor. That was the last Sara saw before the world went black.

SABRINA'S EYES blinked open. She lay on the grass under the shelter of a tree, a coat blanketing her. For a frightened moment, she tried to remember where she was and how she'd gotten there. Then her gaze took in the ugly stone castle several hundred yards away. Flames flickered behind the windows and shot through the roof, sending a column of black smoke into the air.

All at once she remembered being in the middle of the fire. And the witch. She cringed in horror, until she felt a gentle hand on her shoulder.

"Easy, honey. You're safe. You just fainted, that's all."

"Duncan?"

"It's Dan."

Sabrina stared up at him. Duncan had come to her when she called him. Dan was here now. When she saw his face and shirt were streaked with soot, and the arm of his shirt was singed, her chest squeezed painfully. She tried to reach toward him. Only it hurt to move her left arm, and she winced.

He came closer to her, hunkering down beside her on the grass, stroking the hair softly back from her forehead. "You need to lie still," he murmured. "She winged you. It's not bad, just a flesh wound, but it probably hurts like hell."

Sabrina looked down in confusion at the white gauze circling her arm.

"It's from the first-aid kit in my car," Dan explained.

Sabrina nodded and sank back against the makeshift pillow he'd made.

"It's all over." His voice was edged with relief—and regret.

Sabrina's heart leaped into her throat. "What's all over?" she croaked.

"The horror. The murder case against you. Gwynn didn't plan on my leaving that room alive. So she told me a hell of a lot before you got there. About how she'd set up the Graveyard Murders so I'd suspect you," he grated. "And how she trumped up the Davenport case against you. I could have sent her to the electric chair—if she wasn't dead already." Dan's face had gone tight with strain. "I want you to know you're safe. From the witch. And from the district attorney's office."

"Yes. Thank you."

"If you'd rather not have anything more to do with me, I'll understand."

Suddenly it was almost impossible to draw air into her

lungs. "Do—do you want me to have anything more to do with you?"

He swallowed hard. "Yes."

She reached out toward him. It was all the invitation he needed. Leaning down, he gently pulled Sabrina into his embrace. Her good arm came up to circle his back. Her face pressed into his shoulder as she absorbed his scent, his strength, his essence. They clung to each other tightly.

"Oh, Dan, I was so scared. The fire. I'm so afraid of fire." She lifted her gaze from his face and stared at the burning building.

Dan found her hand and held it tightly. "I'm sorry. It was all I—Duncan—" He stopped and shook his head in confusion. "What happened in there is damn hard to describe."

"I know. I think we were all there. You and Duncan and me and Sara. At least that's the way it was for me. Sara was in control. But I was there, too."

Dan nodded. "Yeah, Duncan and me. I was pretty sure the witch wouldn't be able to handle fire, either."

Sabrina swallowed painfully. "You did the right thing. But I couldn't have gotten out of there on my own. You—you saved my life."

He drew back so he could look down into her face. "Well, I think you saved mine twice. Once on the boat when I was too crazy to know what I was doing. And then when you got me loose."

Sabrina fumbled for his hand and locked her fingers with his. "I'm not keeping score."

Far across the lawn, a terrible roar drowned out the conversation. Sabrina blinked and gasped as she saw the building caving in on itself. Massive stones showered down; sparks and fire shot up into the air. Dan sheltered Sabrina's body with his own. But they were far enough away to be out of danger. Awestruck, they listened to the structure's groan of agony and watched it crumble until only one of the side walls was left standing.

"She built herself a castle," Sabrina whispered. "Now it's gone."

"She's gone. For good. You made sure of that."

"I did, didn't I?" There was a note of wonder in Sabrina's voice. "No, I think it was Sara who thought of it."

They stared at the wreckage of the house, the visible symbol of Lillias's final demise. When Dan finally spoke, his voice was gritty. "What happened to you this time is all my fault."

"No."

"At the graveyard, in the train station, the name Sara woke half-formed memories that terrified me. I should have trusted what was happening between us. But I couldn't cope with feeling solid ground shifting away from under my feet—feeling as if I were losing control."

"Dan, it was frightening. Even for someone like me. But you're so down-to-earth. You just couldn't handle it."

"Don't make excuses for me."

"All right, I won't. If you promise what happened in the past won't taint the future."

"*You're* saying that to *me?*"

"Yes. I need someone like you. Someone who's solid and down-to-earth and sensible. Someone who's all the things I'm not."

He gripped her hand tightly, but his face was still etched with pain. "Sabrina, I've got to tell you the rest or I'll never have any peace. I've been in hell. After Lowell took you away, I had to act as if I'd abandoned you again."

She took her lower lip between her teeth. "Laura told me they ordered you not to contact me."

"I didn't have any choice if I wanted to keep my job and stay where I could do you some good."

She held him tightly. "I know that now."

"I've been going over the evidence and every other damn aspect of the case practically twenty-four hours a day trying to find a way to clear you. Then Gwynn Frontenac called and told me she had what I needed, and I was stupid enough to go rushing over here."

"Not any stupider than I am. I fell into the same trap," Sabrina told him.

"When she had me tied up in that chamber, I thought I'd failed again." Dan's voice was raw. "I thought there was no way I could save you. That was the worst part. Failing after I'd been given a second chance." His mouth hardened. "The first time around Duncan should have married Sara and taken her away before it was too late."

"He couldn't do that."

"He'd decided to. He thought maybe they could make a life together in America or something."

Sabrina's eyes widened. "How—how do you know that?"

"I dreamed it. Very vividly. Just like when you were writing your story."

She looked at him questioningly.

"It happened when I finally fell asleep at my desk, the night after you were arrested." Dan's eyes were flushed with anger. "Duncan's father didn't want him mixed up with Sara. That's why he sent him away. When he heard about the trial, he came rushing back, but he was a few hours too late. They'd already burned her. But he went to the pyre at dawn and got the medallion."

Sabrina put her arms around him again. "You didn't hear Lillias's dying curse. She called herself and Sara and the doctor back. She didn't include Duncan. He included himself in. And this time he saved her. You were the factor she hadn't counted on.'' She stroked his cheek. ''And I think that's where the violence came from. You're not really that way. But you were angry about what the witch had done to Sara. And angry that you couldn't punish her all those years ago.''

''I thought of that,'' he admitted. ''After the dream. I could have torn her to pieces with my bare hands—if I could have gotten them on her.''

''Well, you have a primitive streak, but you mostly keep it under control.'' She gave a little laugh. ''I knew that when you asked me to read your palm.''

''Why didn't you tell me?''

''I did. In a kind of oblique way. When I was, uh, talking about conflict.''

''Sabrina, don't ever be afraid to be honest with me.''

''I won't. Not anymore.''

''Do you remember on the boat when you asked me who we were?''

''Yes. You said a man and a woman who loved each other,'' she breathed. ''Oh, Dan, I thought you couldn't really have meant it.''

''I mean it, all right. I love you. I have for a long, long time.'' He traced his fingers over her lips and stared down at her as if he hardly believed his good fortune. He kissed her tenderly, lovingly, and then with more passion. And she returned the passion, murmuring her love for him against his lips.

When he finally drew back, they were both breathing raggedly. ''I think I'd better restrain myself until after I get you to a doctor.''

She tipped her head, listening to the sound of a siren wailing in the distance. ''I'd argue the point, but I think we're going to be interrupted by the fire department.''

"Yeah."

Sabrina touched Dan's lips. "There's something else I want to do. Besides make love to you."

"Get married?"

"Are you proposing?" she asked, a smile dancing on her lips.

"It's about time, don't you think?"

She giggled, then turned serious again. "I want to go back to Scotland with you. To Killearn. That's where they lived."

"It won't bring back bad memories?"

"Some. But I can cope with them now. They're not going to interfere with the good stuff." She caressed his cheek with her palm. "I'd like to see if we can find the place where they met. And where Sara lived with her gran."

"If that's what you want."

"Only if you're with me."

He pulled her into his arms, arms that had finally led her to safety, to love. "Sabrina, I'll always be with you."

magazine

♥——————————————— **quizzes**

Is he the one? What kind of lover are you? Visit the **Quizzes** area to find out!

♥——————————————— **recipes for romance**

Get scrumptious meal ideas with our **Recipes for Romance**.

♥——————————————— **romantic movies**

Peek at the **Romantic Movies** area to find Top 10 Flicks about First Love, ten Supersexy Movies, and more.

♥——————————————— **royal romance**

Get the latest scoop on your favorite royals in **Royal Romance**.

♥——————————————— **games**

Check out the **Games** pages to find a ton of interactive romantic fun!

♥——————————————— **romantic travel**

In need of a romantic rendezvous? Visit the **Romantic Travel** section for articles and guides.

♥——————————————— **lovescopes**

Are you two compatible? Click your way to the **Lovescopes** area to find out now!